Restored

Books 1-3

Restored

Books 1 - 3

Ocean of Regret

Sea of Rescue

Bay of Refuge

Mary E Hanks

www.maryehanks.com

Suzanne D. Williams Cover Design:

www.feelgoodromance.com

Cover photo: oliveromg @ Shutterstock

Visit Mary's website:

www.maryehanks.com

You can write Mary at

maryhanks@maryehanks.com.

Restored

Ocean of Regret (Part 1)

A prodigal is coming home. Three years ago, Paisley left her husband, her father, and the seaside town where she grew up. Now, she's coming back to start over ... alone. Judah told himself whenever his wife came home, he'd do everything in his power to win back her love. *That's exactly what he intends to do.*

Sea of Rescue (Part 2)

Paisley Grant must overcome her worst fears in the aftermath of a hurricane that nearly destroyed her small hometown. She came home to make amends, only to find her life in upheaval and filled with challenges to cope and survive. And now that she's alone in a devastated town, will she have to depend on ... *the one person she never wants to see again?*

Bay of Refuge (Part 3)

Judah wants to be the one Paisley turns to, the one she clings to— *not the one she runs away from.* Paisley has a propensity for running from trouble. Will Judah's kindness and grace be the stick-to-itiveness she needs to make her stay?

Basalt Bay Residents

Paisley Grant – Daughter of Paul and Penny Cedars

Judah Grant – Son of Edward and Bess Grant

Paige Cedars – Paisley's younger sister/mom to Piper

Peter Cedars – Paisley' older brother/fishing in Alaska

Paul Cedars – Paisley's dad/widower

Edward Grant – Mayor of Basalt Bay/Judah's dad

Bess Grant – Judah's mom/Edward's wife

Aunt Callie – Paisley's aunt/Paul's sister

Maggie Thomas – owner of Beachside Inn

Bert Jensen – owner of Bert's Fish Shack

Mia Till – receptionist at C-MER

Craig Masters – Judah's supervisor at C-MER

Mike Linfield – Judah's boss at C-MER

Lucy Carmichael – Paisley's high school friend

Brian Corbin – Sheriff's deputy

Kathleen Baker – newcomer to Basalt Bay

Bill Sagle – pastor

Geoffrey Carnegie – postmaster/local historian

Casey Clemons – floral shop owner

Patty Lawton – hardware store owner

Brad Keifer – fisherman/school chum of Peter's

James Weston – Paul's neighbor

Sal Donovan – souvenir shop owner

Sue Taylor – City Council member

Penny Cedars – Paisley's mom/deceased

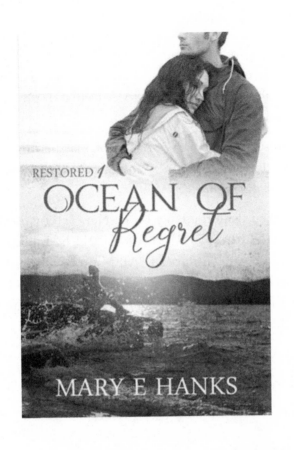

Ocean of Regret

Restored 1

Mary E. Hanks

Suzanne D. Williams Cover Design:

www.feelgoodromance.com

Cover photos: micromonkey @ Fotolia, satamedia @ iStock

Visit Mary's website:

www.maryehanks.com

You can write Mary at

maryhanks@maryehanks.com.

For Brice,
A sweet brother, a man of God, and one of the good guys.

For Jason,
Always for you. My hero.

Author's note:

I've taken many creative liberties in this story—all I can say is, "That's the way it happened in Basalt Bay!"

Restore me, and I will return,

because you are the Lord my God.

Jeremiah 31:18

One

Paisley Grant steered her Honda Accord back into the right lane after passing a white pickup on Highway 12 that looked oddly familiar. Wait. Was that Judah's truck? She stared hard into the rearview mirror, focusing on the male driver in the vehicle behind her. No, the guy with the beard was probably in his fifties, not thirty-three and clean-shaven like Judah. What a relief. Besides, at this time of day he'd be working in Basalt Bay, Oregon. Right?

Her rapid heartbeat settled down, but the idea of spotting her ex-husband in the middle of Washington State, on the same day she was passing through, sent her brain into a tizzy. Especially considering three years ago, she wrote Judah a Dear John letter, then left town. In all these years she hadn't contacted him, either—that was selfish, she realized now. He didn't deserve such treatment. Neither did Dad.

She felt the weight of her mistakes all the way down to her toes. But at the time, fleeing from Basalt Bay was the only way to break free from her crushing grief. Other reasons too. But they all boiled down to one thing—her feelings for Judah Grant had turned stone cold.

After four years of marriage, the passion of love, dreams, and even conflicts, withered and dried up like kelp stranded on the beach after high tide. What good was fighting with her husband when nothing mattered? When she didn't care? And in not caring, in her empty dissatisfied existence, she sought out something—*anything*— to make her feel again.

She made her share of mistakes. Swore never to return to Basalt Bay, located twenty miles north of Florence, on the Oregon Coast. Yet, here she was driving toward the Pacific Ocean. Another blunder? Maybe. If only she'd had a clue that going back someday would be as painful as leaving in the first place, she might not have fled. Then again, she may have run away sooner.

On the fateful night of her exodus, nothing could have stopped her. No sage advice anchored her to a town of gossips who despised her, or to a husband who didn't understand her. No light in the window coaxed her to return to the house where the evidence of too many mistakes lined the walls. Oh, if walls could talk, they'd have a tale to tell.

The things she said and did in her haste to make her callous heart beat as it once had were irreversible. However, maybe, just maybe, in the days ahead she might be able to make amends with those she hurt—even if it killed her. And she thought it might.

She inhaled deeply, longing for the first scent of sea air she took for granted for twenty-five years and craved since leaving the ocean. Still a hundred miles inland, she didn't smell anything yet, but she would soon.

She'd already been on the road for four days—minus gas stops, a few daytime naps at rest areas, and three nights of less-than-satisfactory sleep at the cheapest motels—since emptying her studio apartment in Chicago and heading west. Three years ago, she chose the Windy City because it was far from home, and big enough for a woman on the run to get lost in. However, four days ago, she didn't feel the least bit sad leaving the 300-square-foot shoebox she lived in, or driving away from the place where, to make ends meet, she worked as a stocker in a grocery store by day and a server in a diner by night. She mostly kept to herself. Because if anyone asked questions or pried into her past, then she would have been forced to face things she didn't want to think about.

Like now, and for most of her solitary drive across seven states, especially the bazillion miles of flatland traversing Montana, her thoughts were as tumultuous as the breakers along Oregon's coastline. The closer she got to Basalt Bay, and its 1,150 residents, the more anxiety she felt. The more questions churned in her mind.

After all this time, how can I face Judah?

What will Dad say?

What have the town gossips concocted about me in my absence?

Will Paige even speak to me?

With each question her heart pounded harder in her chest, reminding her she *was* more alive now, no longer dead to her emotions like before she left Basalt. Still, passing milepost after milepost, she fought a primal instinct to turn her car around. To disappear again. To forget the past, with its truths and its lies, that ate at her conscience like a relentless seagull—even though she tried hard to bury it beneath two thousand miles, two jobs, and no one knowing where she was for three years.

Good thing she ditched her cell phone when she moved east. Her family hadn't been able to call and tell her they were ashamed of her. Or demand that she come home, grow up, and face her responsibilities. Which she wouldn't have done. Not for Dad. Nor for meddlesome Aunt Callie. And not for Judah—her ex in every sense of the word other than by law.

As her purple car gobbled up miles along Highway 12, the difficulties she fled from in Basalt weighed upon her. She had to remind herself not to dwell on past mistakes. Those thoughts were dangerous. Toxic. So she stuffed guilt and regret deep inside where all her other mistakes were stored.

Blasting country music on the radio, she sang along loudly, then recited the Pledge of Allegiance, the Twenty-Third Psalm, her wedding vows—more hazardous thoughts—to keep her mind occupied. Still, internal pictures of those she failed, and devastated, wouldn't stop flashing an endless slideshow.

If only she could start over. Do something differently. But

what? Never marry? Follow her brother Peter to Alaska? Try harder to get along with Mom? Too late for any of that.

The image of two graves—one large, one small—twisted something tight in her chest. Stole the air right out of the car. Uh-oh. Why did she allow her thoughts to run amuck? Her breathing felt devoid of oxygen. Her hands shook. *Not now. Please!* She sucked in dry, unsatisfying air and hit the steering wheel, hating the precursors to an attack.

She scratched at the strangling sensation in her throat. Yanked at her t-shirt neckband, trying to make it bigger. She lowered the window and inhaled. A breeze scented with pines brushed her cheeks but didn't cool the rising temperature of her skin.

Apprehension roiled inside her, but she was determined to keep driving. If she focused on the road and clung to the steering wheel, this incident would pass the same way others had.

Then, like a victim stuck in a whirlpool, thrashing around in water to save her life, negative thoughts and fears dragged her down to a dark place where exercising normal respiration became almost impossible. Where her heart thundered in her temples. When this awful feeling came over her in Chicago, she couldn't look anyone in the eye—as if every stranger on the Red Line "L" knew things about her she didn't want anyone to know.

Hadn't she left Basalt to find privacy? To grieve alone? That, and a million other reasons, repressed her breathing now, made her feel like someone held a pillow over her mouth.

A familiar pile of bricks pressed down on her chest, constricting her lungs, and muddying her thoughts.

Ungrateful daughter—the last words her mother said to her.

You were a terrible wife—what she often told herself.

Even your unborn child knew you wouldn't be a good mother—that worst assessment of all came from her father-in-law. *Horrible, horrible man.*

"I would have been a great mom!" She shouted at the rearview mirror as if it were the man's face. Then she sobbed, and a cry wrenched itself from her heart.

Why was she going back to Basalt? To a place where people believed Mayor Grant's lies? Where locals held grudges that ran canyon deep? She should have stayed in Illinois.

She slammed on the brakes, bringing the car to a stop in the middle of her empty lane. She stared at her moist dark eyes in the mirror. Saw a foggy daze in her irises. She struggled to catch her breath and bring her emotions under control. When a car approached from behind, she engaged the gas pedal again. She'd pull over in a minute if this black cloud didn't pass.

After driving two thousand miles west, returning to Chicago wasn't an option. She couldn't stop here in the mountains. But did she want to face the people back home?

She shuddered. Her hands shook where she held them against the steering wheel. The muscles in her esophagus tightened, threatening to cut off her oxygen. "Oh, God, h-help me." She didn't pray much in the last four years, held onto a few grudges of her own, but lately she talked to Him a little. Especially when her throat clenched, making her think she might die. Although she didn't know if He listened to her desperate prayers.

The instant relief she wished for didn't come. Her heart hammered double-time against her ribs. Her breathing turned shallow and hoarse. Would she pass out like she did a couple of times before?

"One." *Inhale.* "T-two." *Exhale.* "Th-three." Sometimes counting helped sidetrack her long enough to catch a breath. Not happening this time.

She banked the vehicle right, almost oversteering into the ditch. Her car came to a thudding stop on the shoulder. Slumping against the door on the driver's side, she sought a momentary respite. Who would come to her rescue along this mountainous stretch of highway? She drew in a puny amount of air. Hot tears filled her eyes. Her heart throbbed in her ears. She clutched her chest. Was she having a heart attack? At twenty-eight years old?

Would she die alone? Without making things right with Dad? Or Judah? Her body trembled with cold, then burned with an internal fire.

Breathe.

I can't!

Why did she choose this inland route? Highway 84 along the Columbia River would have been faster. Emergency vehicles could reach her quicker—if she had a cell phone to use. She probably should have gotten a new one in Chicago, but she didn't want anyone to find her.

A truck blasted by. Had she even turned on her flashers? Her fingers fumbled to find the button that would turn on the hazard lights.

She took in short breaths. Coughed.

Someone might assume she was having an asthma attack, but the doctor at the last hospital said she wasn't. He labeled it a panic attack, probably due to a crisis or something she hadn't faced—a *lame* diagnosis. What did he know about her life, or whether she needed to face something?

What she needed now was to flag down a vehicle. Someone who'd call 911 for her. But for several long minutes no cars passed. Where were the trucks blasting exhaust when she needed one?

Then she remembered something she brought, just in case. She stretched out her hand toward the backseat and flailed around under some blankets. Her fingers clutched a folded lunch bag. She pulled the paper to her mouth, forcing herself to breathe into the balloon-shaped bag. With each in and out breath, the paper made a crinkling sound.

She shut her eyes, then opened them slowly.

Find five things of beauty—one of the tricks she practiced during other attacks. Five things seemed like too many items to list when she couldn't breathe. Maybe that was the point.

Inhaling and exhaling into the squashed bag, she peered out the windshield.

Ponderosa Pines.

Mt. Rainier.

Beautiful blue sky.

Inhale. Exhale.

An RV with a painting of a smiling cougar sped past her in the left lane—didn't stop.

Did she hear a bird calling?

There. Five things.

Her chest didn't burn as it did before. Cool air seeped back into her lungs, reminding her of a waterfall pouring into a dried-up creek bed. The terror lessened.

Sighing with relief and exhaustion, she tossed the bag into the back—near enough to grab again, if necessary. She switched off the hazard lights and stared at her blotchy face in the rearview mirror. Wiped mascara smudges from her cheeks.

That was close. Way too close.

For the last year, panic was the scary monster under her bed. The unconquerable thing no matter how many beautiful items she acknowledged. The psychologist she finally agreed to see last month said there were reasons for her episodes. *Obviously.* But contemplating unhappy details caused more attacks which made her more fearful. So pondering her past—Paige, Peter, Mom, Dad, Judah, Aunt Callie, and others in Basalt—was off-limits.

Right. Her self-imposed rule didn't help. The episodes got worse, forcing her decision to head home.

Yet, how could she talk to family members and townspeople, or heaven forbid, confront them, without experiencing the granddaddy of all panic attacks? She'd end up in the hospital in Florence, south of Basalt. Or dead. Although, the doctor assured her that wouldn't happen. A lot he knew about how she felt during a panic attack.

She took a deep breath, then exhaled. To reach her hometown by dusk, when the tourist shops were closed and the beach empty, and still be able to see the ocean, she had to get back on the road. If all went well, she'd slip into town without any locals seeing her.

She steered her Accord onto the highway and lectured herself. For the next two hundred fifty miles, en route to the ocean and then down the Oregon Coast Highway, she was going to focus on driving. *No* dwelling on the past. *No* thinking of awkward conversations to come.

Instead, she would imagine her favorite place in all the world— Basalt Bay Peninsula. As soon as she arrived, she was going to jog out to the farthest point of land protruding into the Pacific, drop down on the boulder jutting into the water, and listen to the crashing waves. Feel the sea spray cascading over her. Breathe in all the damp salty air her lungs needed.

She'd be home.

Maybe that would be healing enough.

If only.

Two

Judah Grant clutched the steering wheel of the company's sixteen-foot open-air skiff as he maneuvered through hammering rain and robust currents off Basalt Bay. He could almost follow this route blindfolded—although his supervisor, Craig Masters, and their boss, Mike Linfield, wouldn't condone such unsafe practices. During his eleven years at Coastal Management and Emergency Responders, commonly called C-MER, he'd driven a skiff along the coastline hundreds of times. Although, today's boat ride was choppier than usual. At least his rain jacket and bib overalls beneath his life vest kept him dry.

Due to the current poor visibility, he was on the lookout for chunks of driftwood or one of the more peculiar items—ice chests, patio furniture, bicycle tires—he'd seen floating in the surf during other high winds. However, he couldn't worry about floating debris too much; he had an important job to perform.

For the last month, ever since hurricane winds barreled up the coastline from the waters of southern Mexico all the way to Portland, Oregon, shocking meteorologists and scientific agencies with its unprecedented strike on the western seaboard, Judah was tasked with measuring high and low tides and monitoring coastal erosion in the Basalt Bay vicinity. The violent storm known as "Hurricane Addy" slammed the seaside town with eight-foot tidal surges, combined with a super tide and heavy rains, and took out a house-sized chunk of land next to the public beach. Since then, C-MER was gathering information and watching for warnings of any other potential storms.

Even now, C-MER employees were paying close attention to a tropical storm developing in the same region that Addy did, just in case it made its way north. Hopefully, it would fizzle and disappear into the sea the same as a plethora of storms had in the past.

Judah's mission to keep the residents of Basalt Bay safe usually helped him stay focused on the job. Today, with the three-year anniversary of Paisley leaving him and the four-year anniversary of the birth of their stillborn daughter approaching, he might have a harder time keeping personal thoughts at bay.

Still, he forced himself to concentrate on last month's storm that caused substantial damage to some of the beachfront buildings. During the apex of Addy, beached logs floated with the high tide and, propelled by strong waves, rammed into shops built on pilings, broke through windows, crashed down doors, even walls. Hundreds of thousands of dollars in damages were reported in the touristy section near the waterfront. Casey Clemons's Floral, Basalt Bay's only flower shop, was forced to close.

Paige's Art Gallery and Coffee Shop, his wife's sister's business, sustained the worst damage of all the buildings that were victims of the storm. Almost irreparable. Such a shame. Paige had high hopes for restoring her investment, but at some point it wouldn't be worth her throwing more money into it. Not that he'd say that to her.

Although, he would be surprised if Callie Cedars, Paisley's aunt on her father Paul's side, hadn't already spoken to Paige about it. Callie, with her short-cropped salt-and-pepper hair and rotund physique, was known around town for dishing out unsolicited advice. Woe to the person who got in her headlights of criticism. Judah grimaced as he thought of a few of his own encounters with the woman's "words of wisdom."

He steered the skiff around a nearly submerged log, and his thoughts returned to his sister-in-law's plight. Paige was a strong, determined woman. Her mother's death, Paisley's desertion, and an unexpected pregnancy hadn't knocked her down. He doubted the aftermath of Addy would keep her down, either. But if rumors were true—although he tried not to listen to the gossipmongers at Bert's Fish Shack—Paige lost her financial battle thanks to the bank refusing to loan her the money she needed.

He hoped his father, Mayor Edward Grant, an investor in the locally-owned bank, didn't have anything to do with such a decision. Maybe he'd ask Dad. Not that the two of them were on chatty terms—not since Judah married Paisley Cedars against his father's wishes. Old history that still irked him.

Mercy and grace, he reminded himself. *Lord, help me.*

If Judah had the resources, he'd fund Paige's project himself. The town needed the art gallery for local artisans to display their work. Unfortunately, his beachfront cottage on the south side of town was also damaged during the storm, although not to the same degree as his sister-in-law's building. But still, at his slower-than-a-slug repair rate, he'd be remodeling for the next year. Unless he sold it "as is."

A knot twisted in his gut.

A wave surged up the shore on the portside of the skiff, then swirled back toward him as if eating up every shell and pebble on the narrow stretch of beach—similar to how discouragement had eaten him up lately. He groaned.

A child playing alone near the surf on the next small stretch of beach caught his attention. He slowed down the skiff's speed and scanned the area. A woman stepped out of a red car in the parking lot and yelled at the kid, motioning the boy toward her. Good. The currents were too unpredictable here for any child to play unattended.

Judah resumed his charted course paralleling the shoreline, his thoughts returning to his damaged home. Maybe he needed a fresh start. Ever since last month's powerful storm, he'd pondered selling the two-bedroom sea-level cottage. Without Paisley, he didn't have the heart to put the effort into rebuilding their dream house. But selling? Wouldn't that be driving the final nail in the coffin of their marriage?

He groaned again.

Hadn't his wife leaving him three years ago done just that?

No one in Basalt Bay would blame him for selling. Not after Paisley left him a Dear John letter and then never contacted him again. Terrible way to leave a man.

He wiped rain water, maybe a few tears, from his face. He knew better than to regurgitate past problems during work hours. Especially when he was in a skiff in lousy weather. He stared forward, focusing on the sea swells in front of him.

A couple of seconds passed before he realized in his mind's eye he was seeing that crumpled-up note at the bottom of his bedside drawer. *I don't love you. There's someone else. Always has been. You should get on with your life . . . without me. Paisley*

Lies. A man knew whether a woman loved him or not. His wife *had* loved him, at least in the beginning. Yeah, things soured. But he figured she said that garbage about another guy to keep Judah from following her.

It worked too. For a while. Until he got his head back on straight.

Before he married Paisley, he was certain he couldn't live without her. That they *had* to be together, no matter the cost to them or their families. Without parental support or approval, they disregarded the traditional route and eloped. Happy and free, they thought. And, man oh man, when she was finally his wife, to have and to hold, talk about heaven. Bittersweet memories.

The last three years proved his theory false. He was surviving without her—although a lonely existence.

He steered clear of Beachhead Point, a protrusion of boulders surrounded by wooden pilings to keep boats from ramming into the mass. As he passed the orange flag marking the farthest point of the bulk submerged beneath the water, for some reason he recalled Paisley's accusation that he had a cold shoulder toward her, that he didn't care about her—something he denied. But after much inner contemplation, and considering how things turned out, there was a chance she might have been right. He probably inherited from his father the character flaw of drawing into himself and shutting out the world. Not that he wanted to compare himself to his dad.

However, that same withdrawing into himself may have given him the strength to face life without Paisley. To cope on some level other than feeling sorry for himself and being angry with her all the time. Even so, after a thousand days to ponder all they went through, he'd do things differently, given the chance.

Even if the gossips' tales swirling around town were true?

Agitation gripped his gut every time he thought of the rumors. Of the possibility that Paisley left town with another man. Combined with her note, the stories caused him a lot of sleepless nights. He prayed harder than ever. Cried his share of tears.

But when folks accused her of criminal activity—starting a fire in the mayor's office, trashing the library, and stealing from Miss Patty's Hardware—he had enough. Paisley wouldn't do those things. And if she didn't commit those crimes, she probably didn't leave with a stranger, either. He even stood up for her during an ugly town meeting—which probably made his mayoral father resent him even more.

As Judah approached the peninsula jutting into the waves ahead, he slowed down the engine. Thoughts of the childish term Paisley had called the mostly-basalt, rocky outcropping—Peter's Land, after her brother—came to mind. What would Judah's father think of such a pseudonym for a segment of the town's defining coastline? Edward Grant didn't approve of topics he deemed foolish. Or of a son who didn't live up to his expectations.

Judah's sigh felt dredged from beneath his ribs. Enough thoughts of Dad. And Paisley. He had work to do.

As he rounded the tip of Basalt Bay Peninsula, a sputtering from the engine surprised him. Did he run over something? He listened to the hum of the motor. Steadier now. He peered around the exterior of the boat. Didn't see anything afloat. Must have been a fluke.

He grabbed his binoculars with his left hand, still steering with the fingers of his right hand curled around the steering wheel and peered through the lenses toward the shoreline. After Addy hit, he noted some deterioration of the soil on the north side of the peninsula. After that, he labeled five of the largest boulders on the outcropping of land—Sample A, Sample B, etc., starting on the ocean side—so he could keep accurate notations.

Wait a sec. He fixed his gaze upon the high rocks midway back from the point. Something was different. Had the five-foot boulder he labeled Sample D shifted? It couldn't have. Yet, today, it appeared angled in a northerly direction. Odd. Was movement of such a giant boulder possible? Due to the storm? Or because winds from the south had increased significantly this fall?

Maybe his eyes were playing tricks on him. He squeezed his eyelids shut, then opened them and peered through the binoculars. Same result. Sample D had moved! A possible danger. A disaster if the sand beneath the boulder was undercut and gave way. What if a kid climbed the rock—as he did many times as a child—and the stone shifted? Tragedy might follow.

Not on his watch. He'd go ashore after his rounds. If nothing else, he'd wrap yellow warning tape around the rock until a work crew from C-MER inspected it. He shifted gears to forward and made a lazy turn, then aligned the boat parallel with the shoreline, his gaze at attention with the possibility of seeing anything else amiss.

Up ahead, he saw Baker's Point, where the gazebo was smashed to pieces during Addy. For decades, that picnic area was a local favorite for marriage proposals, birth announcements, and other celebrations. Folks in Bert's Fish Shack were already bombarding him with questions about when the structure might be rebuilt, as if he had any say in the matter. Maybe they thought he had connections with the mayor. Fat chance.

He steered into the next wave, veering the skiff away from his favorite landmark—Mountain Peak Rock, a gigantic basalt monolith only accessible at low tide. For a moment, he pictured Paisley and him exploring the giant rock, holding hands, telling each other their dreams and secrets. Stealing kisses. Man, he'd missed the closeness and camaraderie with her for so long now. Ached with longing for it.

The skiff's engine sputtered. Then died.

Judah groaned and turned the key for the starter. Nothing but silence, except for the sounds of the wind and the waves smacking against the skiff.

Without power, the boat jarred into the next wave, rattling his teeth. He tensed as another swell crashed into the starboard side, rocking him crazily. A second wave hit the skiff broadside, sending water spraying over the helm and drenching him. *Oh, man.*

Standing, rocking, trying to remain centered and balanced, he grabbed the top edge of the seat so he wouldn't be knocked into the sea as he made his way to the outboard engine at the stern.

The next incoming wave plunged the skiff toward shore, sending sea-foam arcing over him. He spit out a mouthful of salty water. His heart racing triple-time, he tried anticipating the next wave strike. He hadn't been in a stalled skiff in years. As the rolling waves rushed out to sea, dragging the skiff with it, the boat careened straight toward Mountain Peak Rock. Dangerously close. Next time, he could be crushed against the massive monolith.

He yanked on the manual pull cord protruding from the engine cover. Nothing happened except an empty clattering of parts as he pulled, but no ignition. The engine couldn't be out of gas—he checked before leaving the dock.

Rain fell harder. Water pelted his face and rushed down his coat and rain pants. An incoming wave rammed the side of the skiff, almost lifting it out of the ocean, throwing him to the side.

"God, h-help." He coughed out the words that came to his mind.

He grabbed the oars. Powerful waves beat against the boat, pointing the bow east, then north. All it would take was one giant wave to sink him. He was a good swimmer, but fighting a raging current? That was another thing altogether. He wouldn't lose the boat if saving it were an option. He plunked the oars into the oarlocks as a three-foot wave sloshed over the side, partially filling the small craft.

Judah grabbed a plastic container attached to the bench with a cord and bailed water fast. His efforts seemed futile. Water was coming in faster than going out. Another wave. He didn't have time to brace for it. After it left him facing the wrong direction, he dropped the bucket, grabbed hold of the wet oars that were hard to hold onto, and rowed against the tidal force. Straining his muscles, he propelled the partially-filled skiff toward land, praying his efforts would get him to shore.

Just ahead, he had to find a way around Deadman's Reef—aptly named for dangers others faced when they got too close—but he was having a hard time seeing through the rain. Where was the safest route around the reef?

His hood had blown off, and his hair dripped water down into his eyes. No time to brush the moisture away.

A hundred yards south, he saw a sloping sandy place where picnickers sometimes spread blankets and ate meals—a good place to beach the boat.

Pull. Groan. Pull. Groan.

His shoulders ached. He growled with the effort to get the skiff past the reef and then the breakers. *God help me.*

With a final lunge, he plowed the boat through turbulent foaming white waves. But then, the front of the keel rammed into an underwater sandbar, and stuck. The abrupt stop nearly knocked him off his seat. When he saw how badly the stern plowed back and forth in the waves, almost like a pirate ship's mizzenmast caught in a hurricane, fear raced up his spine. What if the boat jerked free and flipped? If that happened, he didn't want to be in the craft.

He'd have to do the thing he never imagined doing in such rough seas, although he trained for it. He made sure his life jacket was secured, then he stepped onto the backseat of the skiff. Closing his eyes and plugging his nose with his hand, he leapt outward, tucking his legs like a cannonball jump, and landed hard in the roiling ocean. Water and sea-foam plowed over his head, submerging him, sucking him down to the ocean floor, maybe eight-feet deep. He kicked and came up sputtering and spitting.

The next wave smashed over his head and pressed his shoulders against the bobbing skiff. Part of him wanted to climb back into the boat for safety. But ignoring the cold water and the momentary terror of being thrown about by the sea, he gripped the left gunwale and kicked his boots hard in the water. With waves rolling up to his chin, he fought to stay upright and propel the skiff toward shore. Still determined to save it, he used the incoming wave's momentum and shoved with all his might.

The boat gave way and his head went under again. He came back up, spitting saltwater and kicking. Finally, his boots thudded against something solid. He pushed his soles off bottom soil, then tripped over a rock. Exhausted, and still fighting the gravitational pull of the sea toward open waters, he flailed his hands in the direction of the towrope. He missed the first time. Tried again. He grabbed hold of the rope, using his waning energy to drag the skiff toward shore. The heaving waves propelled the boat forward, but the pounding waves against his back and legs nearly took him down.

When he couldn't nudge the boat forward another inch, he struggled against the cement-like muck gluing his boots to the sea floor. Weary, and drenched beneath his raingear, he made it to shore and wrapped the towrope around a drift log. His double bowline knot would have to be sufficient. The stern bobbed back and forth in the bubbling surf. If the tide got much higher, despite his efforts, the craft might break free and be lost. Nothing more could be done now, other than calling for backup.

He unclipped his life jacket and tossed it in the skiff. His teeth chattered as water poured down his t-shirt. A blast of wind hit him, sending shivers racing over his shoulders and along his spine. He could use a blanket and a bucketful of hot coffee to fend off hypothermia.

He had to keep moving, stomping his feet, but walking in water-logged boots was miserable. Should he hike toward town? Or head for his house in the opposite direction where he could change clothes? He should try calling the office first.

With stiff fingers he patted his coat, relieved to find his cell phone still in his pocket. Gingerly, he pulled it out and tapped the black screen with his index finger. Nothing. He pushed the fingerprint button. No blip, light, or anything.

Lord? A little help would be appreciated. He groaned at his impatience. He was alive. Thank God for that! And the boat wasn't lost—something else to be grateful for.

He'd noted his time and destination on the clipboard back at C-MER, so his coworkers knew where he went. But he wasn't expected back for another hour. He couldn't stand here, freezing, and wait for someone to come looking for him.

He gazed down the rocky beach toward the south. Mostly seasonal homes in that direction. And he didn't have a landline at his place. He'd do almost anything to get out of these wet boots, but he had a duty to perform. Two, actually. First, see to the company skiff. Then, post a warning on the rock at the peninsula.

Judah shuffled through slimy mud and wide tide pools en route to Bert's Fish Shack, the closest business from his location. His chilled legs felt like stilts. He gritted his teeth as he leaned forward, bracing into the wind and rain. At least, Bert's had coffee—a small consolation. Maybe the business owner would lend him dry clothes. He pictured Bert Jensen's response: "Playing in the water, Sonny?" Bert called him Sonny ever since Judah was a kid. It used to make his father furious. Maybe that's why Bert continued the habit. Judah almost snickered, but he was too cold.

When the peninsula came into view, he automatically perused the rocky protrusion of land and checked the unstable rock's position. *Wait.* Was someone—a woman?—sitting at the tip of the peninsula with waves splashing up on her? In such strong winds? "You've got to be kidding me."

Despite his fatigue, Judah veered away from Bert's, his boots bogging down in wet sand. If a tidal surge hit the foolish woman seated on the tip of the peninsula, he'd have to perform a rescue. "Tourists," he muttered.

The next time he glanced up, the woman's hands were extended toward the water, palms out as if welcoming the waves to hit her. He froze. Déjà vu. Only one person he knew would sit so close to the edge of Basalt Bay Peninsula in torrential rains—like she had no fear of the untamed current. As if she greeted the ocean like her dearest friend.

Paisley.

A chill that had absolutely nothing to do with his wretched condition sprinted up his spine.

Three

For about twenty minutes, Paisley had been sitting at the edge of *Peter's Land* with its swirling, foaming, crashing waves catapulting over the rocks and over her. Icy water shot up her shins, knees, and even as high as her thighs. She gasped at the shocking sensation of cold waves hitting her, but then as white spray exploded all about her, she laughed like she did as a child sitting in this exact spot.

Bigger waves imploded, and she didn't retreat. Wasn't afraid. The sea's dance mesmerized her. She tasted salt on her lips and licked it. When a more powerful wave splashed up to her stomach, she drew in a sharp breath, but didn't shuffle backwards. How had she stayed away from *her* ocean for three years?

But then, a memory from when she was young and played on the peninsula for too long crept into her thoughts. She could almost hear Mom yelling at her to get in the pantry, a dark scary place, and think about her rebellious behavior. Paisley begged Mom not to shut the door—that pondering her mistakes with the door open worked just as fine. Mom didn't listen.

Paisley shook herself. She was home now. Loved the sea. *Focus on that.*

Another wave crashed against the boulder, soaking her. She braced her feet against the basalt as water splattered up her chest and face. This time she didn't laugh. Her past was here like a living, breathing organism. Every beach and inlet held memories.

She and Judah had spent hundreds of hours walking hand in hand along these rocks, dreaming of a future together. She loved coming here with him, sharing their love of the sea. They often walked to the edge of the peninsula and kissed. Made promises. Some she'd broken.

Don't go there.

The pinched feeling twisted in her throat. Despite her icy wet condition, heat prickled up her neck. Her heart rate increased. No, no. She would not have another panic attack. She was home at Basalt Bay. She should feel amazing peace by the sea.

Except, didn't she sit on this same rock the day after her graduation debacle? Then, after the light went out of her life forever, didn't Judah find her here weeping inconsolably? She remembered how he lifted her tenderly in his arms and carried her to their car. Then, a year later, after being humiliated by her father-in-law, she sat here with guilt choking her. She thought it would be easier to disappear than to have to see the hateful man ever again, or to explain what happened to Judah. That night she wrote him the note and then drove out of town.

The good, the bad, and the ugly had been contemplated on this boulder. How could she ever let go of the past?

Four years ago, she sat here six months pregnant, whispering to her unborn daughter about the fun they were going to have running on the beach. After two previous miscarriages, Paisley prayed her third child would be born healthy and love the sea the same way her mommy and daddy and grandpa and Uncle Peter did. But Misty Gale's heart stopped beating in Paisley's womb.

Then her own heart broke like a clam shell dropped on stone. She couldn't fathom how a loving God allowed so many bad things to happen to her. That's when she stopped talking to Him. And drew into herself.

"The babe is in a better place," Aunt Callie told her.

What better place for a baby to be than in her mother's arms?

"It was God's will," Maggie Thomas, local innkeeper and Paisley's thorn in the flesh, said with a self-righteous sniff.

Why people said such ridiculous things to grieving mothers, she would never understand. Each time her heart hardened a little more.

Mom didn't say a word about Paisley's loss. She didn't express any grief over the death of her own grandchild. Paisley never understood that, either.

The waves rolled in and out, a perpetual motion, the sea and her past mixing together.

Her neck felt itchy. She didn't taste salt on her lips anymore. Her heart thudded an irregular beat.

Find five things of beauty.

I don't see beauty. I should leave.

She fought to breathe and swallow normally. But she stayed in the water's spray until she barely felt the cold. She gazed outward, searching for something. Anything.

A jack salmon leapt into the air, its sides glimmering in a ray of sunlight.

Whitecaps bobbed like sailboats in a tornado.

In the distance, a fishing boat.

A thin rainbow.

Mica glistened near her shoes.

She inhaled and exhaled. A wind gust blasted against her back, pressing her forward almost into the waves. She clenched her stomach muscles and planted her feet against the wet rock, resisting the pull.

She remembered how Mom wouldn't step foot in saltwater. How she said she didn't trust the currents or the creatures beneath. What did Mom think was under the water's surface? A Pacific Ocean Loch Ness Monster? How silly. Paisley and Peter didn't pay any attention to her fears, however, their sister Paige took her warnings seriously.

While Paisley and Peter spent their time running up and down the rocky beaches of Basalt Bay and swimming in the ocean every chance they got, Paige was content to sit at home and draw and paint with Mom. Paisley and Peter were the adventurous ones like Dad. Maybe that's why Peter and Mom argued so much, especially when he decided to head north to fish with Uncle Henry in Alaska, instead of going to college.

Peter didn't attend Mom's funeral, either; although, no one faulted him for his decision.

More grievances.

Another strong wind blasted against Paisley and she turned away, glanced toward the public beach. That's when she saw him—a man stomping across the sand, waving his arms. Was he yelling at her? She swept her wild-flying hair out of her eyes to see him better.

The man wore a dark green slicker drooped to his nose, and his rain pants shimmered with moisture. He kept trudging toward her. His heavy step made her think his boots must be filled with water. Had he been in a boating accident?

She stood, her legs trembling. A wave hit her at knee level, almost knocking her over. Her heart pounded as if it knew something she didn't.

The guy shoved his hood back, and startling blues pierced her gaze.

Judah.

A hitch caught in her throat.

He grimaced and waved his arms again. Yelled something.

How did he find out she was in Basalt? She didn't want to see him today. She needed to get her bearings first. Then figure out how to explain. Could she outrun him to her car?

Although, one glimpse of his sapphire eyes set her heart on fire with something she hadn't felt in four years. Not love . . . but something.

"*I promise to love you 'til the end of time*"—her wedding vow rushed through her thoughts.

Suddenly, she was desperate for air. She sucked in a long draw of unsatisfying oxygen. A searing pain burned up her chest. "I c-can't bre—" Judah turned blurry. The sea disappeared. From raspy breaths to no air in five seconds, this attack hit her swift and hard.

She dropped to her knees on the ocean-drenched rocks, clutching two stone protrusions as waves slammed against her, nearly forcing her into the water. She fought for her next breath. For life, it seemed.

"He—" She tried to say, "Help!" She reached out her hand toward Judah. Did he see she was in distress? Needed him?

Concern crisscrossed his face. Then he was running. Climbing rocks. Clutching hand over hand to get up the boulder pile. Did that warmth in his gaze mean he still cared for her? That he might forgive her?

She floundered to suck in air.

The beautiful eyes she adored in the past seemed to be speaking to her. Telling her that he'd save her. Before the water swallowed her whole?

"Paisley?" His voice. Had he called her *my love*?

A fog. Then blackness.

Four

Judah charged up the rocks, with water-filled boots and little regard for his own safety. When Paisley met his gaze even for that split second, it felt like an electric shock to his heart. Joy. Astonishment. Fear. A flood of emotions barreled through him. But then she fell, unconscious, dangerously close to churning water.

"Paisley!" He yelled, but his voice got drowned out by the roar of crashing waves. He had to reach her before she slid into the ocean. From this distance, it appeared the current tugged on her shoes. If a big wave hit—

God, save her!

Inwardly he pleaded with her to wake up and move back. He kept calling her name as he climbed the mound of basalt he clambered over a hundred times as a kid. He knew every indent for his boots to best maneuver the rocks. Even so, his foot slipped. Lousy boots. He dressed for riding in the skiff, not rock climbing. He had to hurry. Paisley needed him. Seeing her limp form, an emotional power surge hit him, fueling him with strength to climb the rest of the massive rock formation.

One powerful gust could topple her into the fomenting sea. If that happened, perish the thought, he'd do whatever he had to do to rescue her, including jumping in himself. *Hold on. I'm coming.* Then prayer again. *Lord, help me save her.*

Once he made it to the top of the rocks, he scuttled down the trail to the tip of the peninsula, some thirty feet from where he climbed up. As soon as he reached Paisley, he dropped to his knees and pulled her limp body into his arms. "Oh, sweetheart." Such a powerful need to protect her overcame him. He tried to be gentle with her in case she sustained injuries in her fall, but he still held her to him. "Come on, Paisley, wake up." He turned her cheek toward his chest, offering her his warmth, even though he didn't have much to give.

He pressed two icy fingers against her neck. A pulse. *Thank God.* He leaned his ear toward her lips, checking for air. A brush of warmth touched his cheek. Relieved, he rocked her. "Paisley? My love."

A wave splashed forcefully against them, snatching one of her loafers. He watched it churn in a circle, then disappear into the vortex. That could have been her. What if he'd gone home instead of heading for Bert's? What if he hadn't been close enough to see her or help her? God must have been directing his plans today. *Thank You!*

He nudged Paisley's legs away from the rocky ledge, farther from the water still breaking over them. What was she thinking, sitting here with waves bursting over her? Didn't she realize the danger?

He groaned. That was the Paisley he'd known for twelve years. Always doing chancy things. Exciting things. Wasn't that one of her charms?

He stroked her cheek. "What were you doing out here in the rain, so close to deep water?" He knew this was her special place. He leaned his body over hers, sheltering her from the rain and incoming waves. "I've missed you so much, Pais." He didn't think she heard him.

Long eyelashes flickered. A glimmer of dark chocolaty eyes peeked out from nearly closed eyelids. A low moan. "J-Judah?"

"It's me, babe. I've got you." Relief spiked through him. His wife had finally come home. He'd do anything to keep her from wanting to run away again.

Paisley rotated her right shoulder and groaned. Why had she fainted? Was she sick? He wanted answers, but he wouldn't bombard her with questions, yet. Other than, "You okay?"

Her dark eyes opened to half-mast. She squinted at him, then glanced away. Was she uncomfortable with him being so close? Too bad. He wouldn't ease his hold on her until he knew she was all right. Maybe he'd carry her to the parking lot, unless he called for an ambulance first. Oh, right, his cell wasn't working.

"You scared me when you fell. How are you feeling?" He wanted to tell her how wonderful she looked to him. How her sparkling eyes made him long to kiss her like a man desperately in love with his wife. If he were so bold, would that scare her off?

Slow down, Grant. Give her space.

"I . . . couldn't . . . breathe."

His thoughts returned to the crisis. "And now?" He brushed wet hair off her forehead. He gazed into her eyes, checking to see if her pupils were dilated. Maybe he should scoop her up and transport her to the hospital in Florence. She might need medical attention.

"I'm b-better." She didn't sound better. Her inhalation seemed frantic. "I need to stand up." She pushed her right hand against his chest.

"Okay. Let me help." He stood and nudged his hand under her elbow, and with his other hand at her back he helped her stand. "You want to get checked at the ER?"

"No, I'm fine."

"But you passed out."

"I know." She drew in a long breath.

Another wave hit them. More water sloshed into his boots. He ignored the cold but couldn't stop his teeth from chattering.

"Thank you for rescuing me."

"Of course."

Waves continued breaking over the boulders, sending sea-foam bursting into the air. For a moment, they just stood there staring at each other. As if seeing each other for the first time. Or memorizing one another after their three-year separation. Either way, he loved gazing into her eyes and knowing she was finally home—that, maybe, she'd come back to him. Although, he saw a certain caution, or a desire to keep distance between them, in the way her gaze didn't quite hold his.

"I'm so glad you came back." Hadn't he prayed this morning for the chance to be a better husband to her? He dared to touch her cool cheek.

She stepped back. "It was time."

For him it was time thirty-six months ago, but he didn't say so.

When she swayed slightly, he put his arm around her and led her from the edge, focusing on getting her to safety. He avoided the path beside the boulder that might be in jeopardy. "If you walk out here again, beware of that rock." He pointed at Sample D. "It may have shuffled down the slope a bit."

"How?" Her eyes widened.

"Wind, probably."

"What's with the boarded-up buildings in town?" She limped without her right shoe.

"Hurricane Addy hit a month ago." He helped her step down from a large flat stone, wondering if she still felt weak.

"Really? Like the night—"

"Worse." He guessed what she was about to say. After they lost Misty Gale, he was out in the skiff in a tempest. Just released from the hospital, Paisley drove straight to the peninsula. He found her huddled on the edge, soaking wet, trembling, weeping. That night he took her in his arms also.

"Were you out there when it happened?" She nodded toward the sea.

He linked her hand in the crook of his arm and walked her slowly toward the parking lot. "I was." His skiff nearly capsized— no need to tell her that. "The house took a hit."

"That's sad. I know how much you love it."

She said, "how much *you* love it"—not how much she loved it. Something for him to ponder later.

"Where are you staying?" Thinking better of that, he quickly rephrased. "Did you want to stay with m-me?" Now, why was he tongue-tied?

"I don't think so." A blush crossed her wet cheeks. "I mean—" She shook her hair and saltwater droplets splattered his face. "I'm going to stay at the Beachside Inn if Maggie has room."

The Beachside Inn? That she didn't want to stay with him wasn't a surprise. Not after what she said in her letter to him three years ago. Staying at Maggie Thomas's? That shocked him down to his soaking wet socks.

"You could, you know"—he took a risk—"stay with me. In the guest room, not in our room. I wouldn't expect, I mean—"

"Things have changed between us, Judah."

"I know that." Of course, he did. Still, he hadn't given up hope that their love could be restored, even though three years had passed. "You can come home whenever you want." He kept his voice soft. "The cottage is yours too."

She inhaled what seemed like a fifteen-second breath. "I need time to figure stuff out."

After all these months, she *still* needed time to think? Inwardly, he groaned. Then he remembered about her fainting and determined to focus on her needs. "Are you sick, Pais?" A knot formed in his middle at her possible response.

"You could say that."

"Oh, no. What's wrong?" Cancer? Her mom died from that disease.

"I'm not sick in the way you might think." She touched his arm as if offering him comfort.

She was sick, but not in the way he thought? Confusing. And cryptic.

Her footfall increased in speed, creating space between them. Obviously, she didn't want to talk about whatever illness she had. He subdued his need to press for answers. Getting her to her car and out of the rain was the most important thing right now.

He trudged closer, reducing the space between them. "Are you here to stay, Pais?" He needed to at least know that.

"Can we talk about it later?"

"Sure." For her benefit, not his own peace of mind, he changed the topic as they approached her Accord. "How's the car running?"

"Good." She patted the wet hood. "Other than two flats. Can you believe it? Two."

"God was watching out for you." *And me.*

She withdrew a key and unlocked the car. "Thanks for helping me, Judah."

"You're welcome." He blocked her entry into the driver's seat. "You probably shouldn't drive." He held out his hand as a request for the key.

"I'm fine." She nudged his arm away. "Really."

Her coloring seemed more normal now, so he stepped back. "If you need anything, call." He thought better of that. "Actually, my cell phone's dead. Got soaked."

She slipped into the front seat and wiped strands of wet hair off her cheeks. Shivering, she nodded toward him. "You must be as miserable as I feel."

"It's a long story." He thought about his need to call the office. "You don't have a cell phone, do you?" He should have thought to ask her before, but he'd been preoccupied.

"No."

He stared at her for several moments. When she first left him, he tried calling her cell a hundred times. Left dozens of messages. Eventually, he deduced she must have gotten rid of it. Didn't want him contacting her. A tough thing for a husband to accept that his wife severed all communication with him.

"I haven't had one since I left."

Just like he thought.

So, she stayed in that rundown apartment building, riding the "L" to work, wandering around the south side of Chicago alone, then traveling cross-country without a cell phone? Who did that in the twenty-first century?

His wife, apparently.

His chest suddenly burned. That Paisley wouldn't appreciate his knowing her whereabouts for the last two of their three years apart made him avoid meeting her gaze. Not that he did anything wrong in searching for her. But what would she say when she discovered that, thanks to modern technology and his hiring a detective, he had photographs of her entering and leaving her dilapidated apartment? At some future time, he'd come clean. Not today.

He coughed. "The engine on my skiff died. I had to jump in the bay. Now, I have to find a phone to call work."

"Oh, wow." She pointed toward her passenger seat piled with packages of snacks and empty wrappers. "Get in. I can drive you to Miss Patty's." She grabbed food containers and tossed them on the floor in front of the backseat.

"Thanks." He dashed around the car and dropped onto the mostly-clean seat, happy to prolong his time with her. "I'm getting your car wet." He shifted on the seat.

"Me too." She brushed off her sleeve and chuckled, the sound reminding him of a perfectly played chord on Mom's piano.

He'd missed her laugh. Her nearness.

He let out a long sigh, realizing for the first time in ages, and even though it might be a temporary high, his world felt righted. As if he was living in a fog for thirty-six painful months and could suddenly see clearly.

She started the engine he tinkered with plenty of times in the past, and out of habit he listened to the hum. He heard a slight rattling. Might need a tune-up. Spark plugs. Oil change. Especially after the extensive drive. But he wouldn't mention anything that might reveal he knew how far she traveled.

As warm air from the heater reached his fingers, a sharp tingling dueled with relief in his nerves. He sat quietly as Paisley drove through town. He didn't even comment on her missing shoe. The silence wasn't as uncomfortable as the shivering taking over his body. His teeth chattered almost uncontrollably.

Paisley giggled, apparently at the sound he made. She held out her hand. It was shaking too. She turned up the lever on the heater.

"We both better get out of these wet clothes." A red flush skittered over her face. "Oh. I. Didn't mean—"

He clamped his lips shut to keep from laughing, but inwardly smiled. Getting out of their wet clothes was an innocent comment for a wife to say to her husband, but she was obviously embarrassed by it.

"Yeah, we're pretty soaked." He wrung out the edge of his shirt sleeve and glanced out the window to avoid her gaze or cause any further awkwardness.

After he called C-MER, would Paisley drive him home? If so, would she come in and talk? Any chance he might convince her to stay?

Five

Maggie Thomas opened and closed her mouth five times before acknowledging Paisley's question. Paisley had never seen the woman speechless before.

"Do you have any rooms available?" She asked again. Her icy fingers gripped the edge of the well-worn counter at the Beachside Inn. She wouldn't have come to Maggie's except it was the only overnight accommodations within the city limits. She shuddered as a chill rustled up her back. If she didn't get out of her damp clothes, she'd be sick by tomorrow.

"No one told me *you* were in town." Maggie sniffed and made a face as if something in the room smelled rotten. "You should have made reservations online."

"So, no rooms?" Fine. Paisley would drive to Florence, or farther south to Coos Bay. Might be better to put some miles between her and Judah anyway. What was he thinking asking her to stay with him like there wasn't a sea of hurts swirling between them? Even though he said she could stay in the guest room at the cottage, how awkward would that be sharing the rest of the house? And the heated way he gazed at her before he exited the car? She hadn't expected that. She didn't think of him as anything other than her *ex*-husband, right? "I'll go somewhere else." She strode toward the door.

"I didn't say there were no vacancies."

Paisley paused and glanced back at the woman she avoided for most of her life. "What then?"

Maggie peered over her maroon reading glasses at Paisley as if checking her for bugs or lice. Did she look that bad? She was dripping water on the floor.

Could she sleep under the roof of this judgmental woman who would probably send out a citywide text about her arrival the instant Paisley walked out the door? Thanks to her past story-swapping with Aunt Callie, another gossip queen in Basalt, Maggie had done her share of harm. A bitter taste filled Paisley's mouth.

"A room?" A sharpness she meant to subdue cut through her words.

Maggie squinted. Then frowned. "This *is* an inn." She pointed at the window. "The vacancy sign is up. Although, I can refuse service to anyone I want."

Of course. "May I have a room?" Paisley forced her voice to a sweeter tone.

"How many days will you be staying?"

"I don't know."

Maggie glared, tapping a rhythm on the countertop with her squared purple nails.

"Three nights." Paisley tossed out a number as she tried not to roll her eyes. By then she'd know whether she could stay in Basalt, or if she needed to find another coastal town to live in. Maybe Yachats, although the smaller neighboring town to the north was probably a little too close.

Mrs. Thomas harrumphed and clicked keys on the keyboard, staring at the computer screen. She quoted a tremendously steep price for it being the off-season.

Paisley cringed, thinking of her limited funds.

"Due in advance." The innkeeper eyed Paisley like she expected her to rip her off. "I take credit cards with proper ID, but I prefer cash."

"No problem." Paisley wouldn't give Maggie the satisfaction of hearing her complain about the cost. She pulled a stack of twenties from her wallet and slid them across the dented counter.

"Hmm." Maggie held up one bill, then another, to the light as if they might be counterfeit. Without glancing at Paisley, the older woman finished the transaction, then dropped an old-fashioned key in her hand. Apparently, Maggie still hadn't modernized the Beachside Inn.

Paisley almost reached the door before Mrs. Thomas cleared her throat loudly.

"I remember what you did."

Paisley stilled. Had Maggie found out she pelted the inn with mud balls when she was a teenager? "What did I do?" She didn't turn around, but she imagined Maggie's squinty gaze aimed at her. If Paisley wasn't desperate for a room and a place to sleep, she'd get back in her car and head south on Highway 101.

"I won't soon forget, either."

Her and half the town, it seemed.

"You must have a good memory." *And a wicked tongue.* Paisley gritted her teeth. Irritation steamed up her pores, heating her core in opposition to her chilled frame. Slowly, she faced the innkeeper. "I don't know what you're implying. You might as well spit it out, Mrs. Thomas, since you seem bursting at the seams to do so."

"I'm talking about the night you crept through my inn." Maggie pulsed a purple fingernail.

"To use your bathroom, that's all." Paisley bristled. What did the woman think she'd done?

"Next morning, my pearls were missing." Maggie's eyelids scrunched to thin slits. "Mama gave me those for my sixteenth birthday. Same ones Gran wore on her wedding day."

"You've got to be kidding." Did every act of thievery and mischief in Basalt fall at Paisley's feet? Would she never outgrow the locals' disdain?

"Everyone knows you're a thief." Maggie's chin lifted.

"Thanks to your lies." Paisley's backpack banged against the doorframe as she exited the office. She pictured herself throwing fistfuls of mud at the windows of the inn, again. However, she was a mature adult now. She paid Maggie for a bed for three nights—in cash. She'd use that room or else curl up against a chunk of driftwood on the beach right in front of the Beachside Inn. Then, what would Maggie Thomas have to say?

Stuffing her anger deep inside, Paisley tromped around the first of three narrow, archaic-looking buildings with cedar shakes flanking the outer walls, then strode down the walkway. Stopping at the red door that matched the number on her key, she paused, her limbs shaking. She'd anticipated the return to her hometown might be fraught with struggles, but to think after all these years, Mrs. Thomas condemned her for stealing some family heirloom Paisley had never even seen. What else might she be blamed for?

Edward Grant's face flashed through her mind. Did he still blame her for ruining his son's life?

She groaned.

Inside the tiny motel room, she removed her wet clothes, dug leggings out of her pack and slid into them, used the facilities, hung the "Do Not Disturb" sign on the outside doorknob, then collapsed onto the double-sized bed, curling up in the blankets. After all the hours she spent on the road, then that exhausting episode at the peninsula, she succumbed to sleep in seconds. However, her last thoughts before drifting off were of her opening her eyes after she fell on the rocks, and finding Judah holding her tenderly. Of his deep blue eyes gazing into hers.

Then long-forgotten love songs filled her dreams, and she slow danced with someone.

Hours later, a loud banging at the door awakened her. When she opened one eye, filtered sunlight glinted through the narrow window.

She pulled the pillow over her head. If she ignored whoever was at the door, would they go away? What time was it anyway? She peeked out from under the pillow and peered around the room. On the wall, an anchor-shaped clock with a set of oars for hands pointed at twelve and three. Three o'clock in the afternoon?

Goodness, she slept a long time. And she was still tired enough to keep sleeping. She closed her eyes.

The banging came again. Didn't they read the sign?

"I don't want the room cleaned!"

After another round of knocking, she hurled a pillow at the door. "Go away!" Had the "Do Not Disturb" sign blown off the door handle? She wouldn't put it past Mrs. Thomas to remove the sign on purpose.

"It's me, Pais." Judah's voice. "I took a chance on this room being yours, since it's the only one with the sign on the door handle."

She didn't want to see him again so soon.

"You okay?"

"I'm still sleeping." She yawned. "Come back tomorrow, okay?"

His chuckle reached her. Why were the walls of the inn so thin? She heard something shuffle against the door.

"I brought food." He must not have heard her comment. "You're probably hungry."

Her stomach growled. Perfect timing. She hadn't eaten in twenty-four hours. "Okay. Just a sec." Grumbling, she stood and pulled on a sweatshirt. She ran her fingers over what had to be messy bed hair in need of a washing. In three steps, she was at the door. Opening it, she saw Judah leaning against the doorframe, smiling at her. She'd always loved his masculine grin. What was that song she was thinking about last night? Something about a man loving a woman. Not what she should be contemplating right now.

"Hey."

"Hi."

He clutched a white bag with a Bert's Fish Shack logo. Just seeing the bag, smelling something wonderful, made her mouth water. Would he hand it over? Or did he expect to come in? If so, she had to set clear boundaries. No admiring his smile. No staring into his shiny blues. Meeting his gaze, that seemed to be staring straight into her heart, was totally unacceptable. And no talking about them getting back together, either.

She was hungry, that's all.

"Bert's best." He held up the bag. "Want to go down to the beach and eat with me?"

No. "Uh, maybe."

"I have an idea I want to run by you." His eyes seemed moist like he might be near tears, and she wondered why. Was her being back in town emotionally difficult for him, too? "What do you say?" His dark hair blew slightly in the wind. "Come eat and chat with me?"

Eating and having a conversation seemed harmless. "Why not? I'll use the bathroom, then be right out." She shut the door before he entered the room or had the chance to say anything else.

Was she making a mistake in thinking they could hang out and talk, as if a mighty storm hadn't wrecked their marriage? What did Judah want to discuss? She said okay about meeting him for lunch. Maybe she could still do that and then draw those lines she already decided on.

After washing up and putting on a thin layer of gloss—due to dry lips, not because she was having a picnic with the man she loved for three years, then despised for four—she pulled on a knitted hat.

Would Judah go along with making their separation more permanent? Surely, he suspected that outcome after three years without communication. But he was so nice to her yesterday on the peninsula, then again on their drive out to the cottage, making her remember some good things about their life together. She had loved him. But then, they fell out of love and away from each other in the aftermath of overwhelming loss.

Time to move on.

Yet, seeing him again sparked something undeniable in her. Something gentle and endearing about him surprised her. After all this time apart, was there possibly a smidgeon of romance, or love, still lingering between them?

Ugh, no.

Hadn't she called it quits the day she left him? And every day since? All that remained was signing papers, right?

Unless her fickle heart discovered he still loved her.

Not even then. She was in Basalt to face her past and then start a new future—independently and alone.

Judah's concern about her passing out was the reason for his kindnesses. As her husband, he'd acted coldhearted. Didn't understand her. She told herself that over and over for a year before she left him. Now, as she stared at herself in the antique mirror, she wondered. Was he indifferent and judgmental toward her, or was that her perception of him based on her own indifference?

She groaned. Too deep of thoughts.

One thing she knew, she couldn't encourage an attraction between them that might linger like fumes, then combust and evaporate. Maybe she should feign illness. Renege on lunch. Although, she *was* famished.

Phooey. She slammed the motel room door behind her on her way out—not caring that Mrs. Thomas probably didn't approve of guests slamming doors—then she trotted toward the beach below the inn.

Judah wanted to talk? Fine. Let him get whatever he needed to say off his chest. Then she was making one thing clear—she no longer planned on being his wife.

Six

Had Judah taken a risk by inviting Paisley to meet him at the beach and then not sticking around to wait for her? She needed time to get ready, right? Besides, if Mrs. Thomas saw him lingering around a woman's room, she might call the cops. Better for him to stay clear of Mrs. Thomas. He had enough trouble with her in the past.

But what if Paisley took off? Distress danced a jig over his heart—a familiar reaction. She wouldn't put him through that again, would she? She drove two thousand miles to get here. She must plan on staying for a while. Longer, if he convinced her to move in.

Slow down, chump. She left you. Period.

Yeah, yeah. Had he ever been able to sweet-talk Paisley into doing anything she didn't want to do? If she came back to him— and he doubted she was ready to do that—it had to be on her terms. Still, he wished for the outcome he daydreamed about for two years.

He sighed.

Earlier at work, he was so distracted. His thoughts kept replaying the moment he saw Paisley fall on the peninsula, his wild trek across the sand, trying to reach her before something worse happened, and then how amazing she felt in his arms again.

In between contemplating yesterday's events, he went with Craig to retrieve the beached skiff. Fortunately, they found it anchored to the log where he tied it. After they bailed it out, they dragged the boat back to the C-MER dock where mechanics could work on it. Then they backtracked to the peninsula to check on Sample D. Scrapings against a companion basalt rock bore chalk-like markings, confirming the rock had moved. Why, was the question. There were no recent earthquakes. No superstorms other than Addy.

After taking pictures with the new cell phone he was issued, he wrapped yellow tape around the rock to warn tourists and hikers of possible danger. Then Craig steered the skiff back to C-MER. The whole way, Judah lined up excuses for taking off a few hours early. Normally, he was committed to his research and duties. Today, thoughts of Paisley held his thoughts captive. Did she go see her dad? Was she feeling okay?

Back at the office, he was useless. After staring at one screen of storm data for an hour without assimilating anything he read, it was time to leave.

He uncurled the top of the bag, snagged a french fry between his fingers, and stuffed it in his mouth. He stared at the waves rolling up the sand.

Maybe he should sprint back to the inn and check on Paisley. Make sure she didn't leave. He groaned at the recurring thought. What if in the future things got rough in their marriage—if they got back together—would she run at the first sign of conflict? When he disagreed with her about something, would he fret she'd be out the door by morning? Man, he had to stifle those relentless, nagging thoughts that ate away at his peace of mind.

He devoured a couple more fries. Sighed.

He chose this chunk of driftwood to sit on, midway between the inn and the ocean, so Paisley could find him. Unfortunately, it was within Maggie's binocular range. Was she watching him now? If he did anything out of line—not that he planned to—the innkeeper would probably chase him with her broom. She did that when he was ten and built a sand castle on her property. That day, she shot out of her office, yelling like the world was on fire, swinging her broom. Nearly hit him, except he was a fast runner.

Mrs. Thomas called his parents too. Dad grabbed Judah by the arm and chewed him out all the way to the Beachside Inn. His father demanded that he apologize to the woman of "upstanding character"—if she was ever an honorable person in the community, Judah hadn't figured out when. All that fuss and embarrassment over a sand castle? A bad memory still.

To make matters worse, after Paisley left three years ago, Maggie showed up at C-MER claiming Paisley stole some priceless necklace. She demanded he reimburse her loss. Without proof, he refused. Ever since, he avoided the cranky innkeeper.

His stomach growled. He hadn't eaten breakfast. Barely slept last night. Around three a.m., he got up and trudged down to the strip of sand below his cottage. Sometimes he walked to the seashore when he woke up worrying about Paisley and their separation. Now she stayed a mile away from him, and he longed to be near her. If only she wanted that too.

A brush of sand pelted his lower back. He swiveled on the aged log to see Paisley, dressed in a long Chicago Mets sweatshirt, navy leggings, and a knitted hat on her head, wearing a slight smile. "I heard there was free food around here." She sniffed the air.

Was she keeping things light? If so, he'd go along with that.

He lifted the bag and pointed at Bert's logo of a salmon with a crown on its head. "Best burgers on the West Coast."

"Can't wait." She dropped down on the log, leaving a defining space between them.

He ignored the distance she created and dug out the wrapped sandwiches. He handed her one.

"Oh, um, about the cheese?" She quirked an eyebrow.

As if he'd forget. "No cheese. I remembered."

"Thanks."

Her sweet smile left his gaze lingering a little too long on her rosy lips. Lips that used to taste of cotton candy on a summer night. Lips he kissed so many times before. Inwardly, he groaned. *Tone it down, Romeo.*

He bit into his burger. At least he could count on a hamburger from Bert's remaining the same.

Next to him, well, not quite next to him, Paisley sighed. "Mmm. I've missed these."

But not him? Man, why did he have to jump to that conclusion? He groaned, then covered it by clearing his throat.

"You okay?" Her voice came softly.

"Yeah, fine." A small mistruth. He chomped into his cheesy bacon burger and focused on the salty flavor of Bert's finest.

"What did you want to talk with me about?" Paisley's wrapper rustled in her hands.

Judah's mind went blank. He just wanted to be near her. He didn't plan on blurting out something that might cause her walls to go up. But he wouldn't tiptoe around her as if he had to avoid Mom's freshly mopped floor, either.

He stuffed a fry into his mouth. After he swallowed, he nodded toward the water. "How does it feel to be back at the beach? You always loved that." So did he.

"I'm glad to be home."

Home? A 220-jolt zinged through him. Home to him? Her dad? The sea?

With effort, he tamped down his internal overreaction to her words. "I'm glad you came home, too."

Her dark eyes turned almost black. One eye squinted at him as if she were trying to figure out something about him.

His hunger abated, he set the remainder of his burger on the wrapper. Time to tell her what he was thinking. "Look, I realize it may seem too soon for me to be saying this, but I'd like you to move back in with me."

Her jaw clenched. She shook her head.

His nerve almost vanished, but he promised himself to tell her the truth if he got the chance. He clasped her smaller hand and noticed her ring wasn't on her finger like his wedding band was still on his left hand. That was a bad sign. He peered into her eyes that had often reminded him of dark chocolate. If only she weren't so aloof now.

"Judah—" Paisley pulled her hand free and stood.

He tugged on the sleeve of her sweatshirt. "Please hear me out? Then you can go, if you want."

She stared toward the ocean as if debating his request. Then she sat down stiffly on the white faded log and nodded once, but didn't look his way.

He needed to clarify something. "What I meant was, I'd like for you to move into the guest room."

Her shoulders lifted and fell. "Still won't work."

"Why? I said the guest room. Not my bed." Man, too much hurt blasted out in those words.

"I'll never sleep in your bed again." She bristled. Arms crossed. Her eyes squinted at him.

"Never, huh?"

"I want a divorce."

Sharp arrows plunged into his heart. Although, he should have known she'd want to end things with him. Hadn't he pictured them getting a divorce in the first year of their separation when he was so angry at her? But then, his heart changed. God was changing him. "Not me. I do *not* want a divorce." He had a right to his opinion, too. "Please, come back to the cottage. Stay until you've seen your family. That will give us time to talk things over."

"There's nothing to discuss." She leaped to her feet and moved a few steps away from him, obviously putting distance between them.

"I doubt you believe that." He stood and walked through the sand to stand beside her. "Three years and a world of hurts, and you think there's nothing to discuss?" He didn't believe her, wouldn't let himself believe her.

"I've m-made my d-decision." She hiccupped or coughed. Her breathing sounded irregular.

"There's two of us in this marriage." He felt determination rush through him. He let her walk away before. He wouldn't make the same mistake again. "There always has been two of us."

"Funny you should say that now." Paisley glanced at him, tears and pain evident in her gaze.

In that second, he saw her as the broken young wife who begged him to stay with her in the hospital after they lost their baby, and his frustration melted into nothingness. He saw her as the wife who he should have held close to him all that night, supporting her through the toughest time of their lives. Instead, after she fell asleep, he went home and returned to work the next day, finding a measure of solace in his job. A sword of regret pierced him. So many mistakes.

He had to say what was on his heart now. "Paisley, I'm so sorry I wasn't there for you like I should have been when we lost Misty Gale."

She drew in a sharp breath.

"You're still my wife." He needed to say this. "And I . . . I still love you."

Even though they hadn't talked things out, God was working in his heart, bringing healing and love, teaching him about forgiveness and grace. He wanted to offer her the same mercy he experienced. Maybe someday she could forgive him too.

She met his gaze, shook her head as if telling him to stop talking.

He wouldn't be the person who reverted into silence during an uncomfortable topic ever again. "We're still a family, you and me."

"No, we're not." She turned away from him. "Not anymore."

Her words felt cruel, but the remembrance of the vulnerability he saw in her gaze moments ago made him want to take her in his arms and hold her. He didn't have that right, but he wished he did.

"Three years ago, you left me. You said you didn't love me anymore." He touched her shoulder gently, wanting her to turn around. When she didn't, he watched her in profile. "Paisley, I've changed. I know I wasn't there for you like you needed me to be. And I'm so, so sorry you felt abandoned. I never wanted you to feel that way."

Her breathing turned loud and raspy. Did she have pneumonia or something? She didn't say anything. Just put her hand on her chest and seemed almost in a trance. Had she even heard him? The only sign that she may have been touched by his apology were a couple of tears dripping down her cheeks. Her face crumpled. Then a sob.

"Oh, sweetheart." He moved closer until he faced her, then pulled her into his arms, and she didn't resist. "If you'll give me another chance, give us another chance, I promise to be a good husband to you." He stroked her back. Felt her shudder. "I want you with me as my wife."

She shoved her hands against his chest and glared at him, although tears still ran down her cheeks. "It's too l-late for that. Don't you s-see?"

"Come stay with me for a few days." He was being persistent, but this was his one and only shot. He had to take it. "It'd be better than staying at Maggie's."

"Anything would be." She wiped her cheeks, then scuffed the toe of her shoe in the sand. "But I can't."

"Can't. Or won't?" Uh, that might have been too pushy.

"What do you want from me?" She asked such a loaded question, but she was still avoiding his gaze.

A couple of answers came to mind. A real marriage. A wife who loved him. Instead, he said, "I want you to come home." The simple truth.

"I left you, Judah."

"I know." Hurt sizzled through every fiber in his body. "But I want you back." If only she could see inside his heart, she'd know he was sincere.

She huffed. "As what?"

"My wife. Friend. Lover." He threw down his cards. Hadn't she asked him to be more open with her three years ago?

"You've got to be kidding me."

"I'm not. I'm asking you to come home. Separate rooms are fine." He'd take what he could get. Having her close enough to talk with, to try to work things out, would be a miracle.

"How can you even ask that?" She inhaled and exhaled loudly, seemingly unable to catch her breath. "H-how can you say 'm-marriage, friend, *lover*' after my being gone for three years? After all I've done? How do you know I haven't been with . . . with someone else?" She kept her head down, and her shoulders sagged.

His litmus test of grace. Acid burned through his gut. He didn't trust himself to say anything for a few seconds. "I don't. But that doesn't change anything." He already battled his decision on his knees and in prayer during his skiff rides.

She faced him then, thrusting out her hands as if exasperated. "We're finished, Judah. I don't love you!"

It was hard to have a comeback for an absence of love.

She trudged through the sand toward the inn, leaving a gaping trail through the tall beach grasses.

His emotions felt wrung out and raw. If he were a drinking man, he'd head for Hardy's Gill and Grill for something to dull his senses. Yet, he couldn't let Paisley go off alone. Even if she didn't love him. Even if she'd been with—

He didn't finish the thought.

He scooped up the trash they left on the log, then he tromped after his wife, stepping into the footprints her rubber boots made in the sand—two footprints becoming one. The old Judah would accept her terms and leave her alone. She wanted a divorce? Fine. He'd been alone longer than he would counsel any friend to hang onto a dream of reconciliation. All these years, he waited faithfully for his absentee wife to return. He was true to her in mind and body. Now she was back and still didn't want him? Why should he push for her to come home?

Other than mercy, grace, and forgiveness, he didn't have an answer. He stomped after her, his footfalls heavy in the sand.

Something didn't add up. Her words didn't ring true. If she went astray like she implied, why did her eyes light up like sparklers when she opened her eyelids to find him holding her on the peninsula yesterday? As if she missed him too.

Paisley kept a steady pace, heading straight toward her motel room. Judah's legs could easily outdistance her, but he stayed about ten feet behind. However, if this was his last chance to speak up, he had to say what was on his mind and heart. What he would have said before she left, if he'd been wiser.

"We need to talk, Paisley." He had to yell over the breeze billowing from the sea.

"Leave me alone!" The wind snatched the words and threw them over her shoulder. "We're done talking."

"I don't think so."

She whirled around and jabbed an index finger toward him. "You are *not* setting the rules!"

His temper ignited, bursting into flame, matching the fire in her gaze. He reduced the space between them in a few steps. "Why not?" He parked one hand on his hip, the other hand clinging to the food bag. "You ran off. Left me to face everyone alone. I'm the one who had to explain your absence to your own family. Why can't I make a few rules?" Paisley flinched, but he kept going, fueled by her previous rejection and the injustices between them. "You've been running the show for three years. Camped out in some low-income studio apartment in South Chicago, while I—" Oh, man, he didn't mean to say that out loud today.

Her mouth dropped open. "What? How do you—?"

"That's right." He gritted his teeth. "I've known where you were for the last two years."

"How . . . how did you—?" Her eyes widened. She breathed loudly.

"Didn't you wonder why your landlord suddenly reduced the rent two years ago?" His voice rose.

"N-no-o." The one syllable word came out as three. She pressed her fingers against her temples.

"How do you think it made me feel to know my wife had to put two thousand miles between us to get far enough away from me? That she hated me so much she wanted to disappear from everything and everyone she ever knew?" He breathed harder now too.

"How did you find me?" The wind blew her long dark hair across her face. She fingered it away, making her look younger, more like the woman he fell in love with. The one who still filled his dreams. And the one who said she didn't love him anymore. "I thought you might follow me. Come looking. But you d-didn't." She inhaled and exhaled noisily.

"You thought—" In an instant, his anger melted into a puddle of wounded pride. She wanted him to come after her? A slug in the stomach wouldn't surprise him nearly as much. "Paisley, I, uh, I didn't know. If I knew you wanted me to find you—"

"It doesn't matter."

Obviously, it did. She sounded defeated, looked defeated, and he didn't feel like the victor. He reached out to her, but she impatiently brushed his hand away.

"I didn't mean to tell you that I knew where you were yet." He ran his hand through his hair, frustrated. "Being without you has been hard on me. Now that you're here, I just want to make things right, to try to fix things, but I don't know how."

"You can't fix it. Or m-me." Her uneven breathing reminded him of someone with asthma he knew in high school. "I have to know. H-how did you f-find me?"

"I hired someone. A detective." He didn't want to explain this now, especially when he could see she was getting more upset.

"So, what? You saw p-pictures of m-my wretched cracker-box apartment? P-pitied me?" She seemed to be breathless, then she ran the rest of the way to her motel room door, hacking all the way.

He followed her, determined to stay right with her until she slammed the door, locking him out. As she shoved her key into the doorknob, he clasped her shoulders and turned her around. "Paisley, what's wrong with you?"

She didn't answer him. Her cheeks were pasty white, her breathing scattered.

What could he do to help her? He dug in the wrinkled food bag and yanked out the leftover iced tea cup that had a bit of liquid left in it. He pulled off the lid and thrust the container into her hands. "Drink this."

She clasped the cup to her mouth and swallowed a couple of gulps. Then she laid her hand over her upper chest, breathing with wheezing sounds. He didn't know what else to do.

When she dropped the empty cup and fell to her knees, drawing in great breaths of air, he sank to the ground beside her. "Should I call 911?" He yanked his new cell phone out of his slicker.

She grabbed his hand. "It w-will p-pass. Just h-hold m-me." She sank into him, wilting like a flower left out in the hot sun too long.

He gladly wrapped his arms around her, holding her against his chest, rocking her, and praying.

After a few moments, she pushed him away and lunged for the bag their lunch came in. Dumping the contents on the sidewalk, she bunched the bag to her mouth. She inhaled and exhaled rapidly as if hyperventilating.

"Breathe slowly. Not so fast." He rubbed her shoulder.

She nodded, her eyes filling with tears. She pointed toward the ocean. Then at something else. She stared straight at him, breathing into the bag, her dark eyes going from fudge color to black then brown again. Finally, she lowered the bag, let out a long sigh. "Panic." She picked up the food wrappers and the cup she dropped on the ground.

Compassion for her gripped him in the center of his chest. "How long has this been happening?"

She shrugged. "A while."

"On the peninsula yesterday, when you fainted, was this why?" He gulped over the hardships she must have endured in the last three years. Had she suffered with these attacks all by herself? "Panic, huh?"

She nodded. "This time . . . about what you said."

"About coming home with me?"

"And your knowing where I've been." She swallowed. "I thought no one did. I made sure no one did—even if I may have secretly wished you would find me."

He'd have to be more careful about what he said. Except, now he wanted to be with her through whatever she was dealing with. Protecting her. Caring for her. Loving her as the husband he still was. "I wish you'd reconsider. Come live with me."

"No." Paisley stood and opened the door. Before she slipped inside, she paused. "But thanks for helping me. That was kind of you." She closed the door.

Kind? An ache started in the pit of his stomach and ended in his brain. What could he do to show her that he loved her with an undying, unconditional love that went far above kindness, no matter what she said about them getting a divorce?

He wouldn't forget the devastated look on her face during the panic attack. What if that happened again? He didn't want her to be alone. Not tonight. Not ever. He'd go home and grab a sleeping bag. Then he was coming back and staying at the foot of her door. He wanted to be close in case she needed him.

The only thing that gave him a moment's pause was the thought of Mrs. Thomas finding him sleeping in front of a guest's door. But even if she beat him with her broom and called the police, he'd willingly face the consequences to protect Paisley. His Paisley. His love. His wife.

Seven

The next morning, Paisley riffled through the remaining bills in her wallet. She already used up a lion's share of her traveling fund. Gas expenses crossing half the continent were more than she planned and spending three nights at the Beachside Inn was highway robbery. She had to figure out what to do next. Stay with Dad? Paige? A heavy weight settled in the pit of her stomach. She couldn't accept Judah's offer.

They needed to settle things, but she didn't even have enough money for a divorce. Maybe looking for a job should be her first step.

Sometime in the night she heard Mrs. Thomas yelling at someone in the walkway between the buildings. Paisley crept to the peephole and tried to see out, but she couldn't tell who Maggie was speaking to in such a demeaning tone. Was a vagrant sleeping near Paisley's room? She shuddered. Maggie threatened to call the police. And she may have even hit the guy with a broom.

When no sirens sounded, Paisley figured Mrs. Thomas was satisfied that the drifter left. Still, she had a hard time getting back to sleep after the ruckus.

Now her mind churned with indecision. Should she talk with Dad this morning? Did he know she was in town? Maggie must have alerted Aunt Callie who would have gone straight to Dad. When did his sister ever keep a secret? In fact, Paisley was surprised Aunt Callie didn't already show up at the Beachside Inn demanding to see her.

Paisley needed to talk with Dad, but the thought of entering the house where she had the last argument with Mom, seeing the closed pantry door, staring into the peculiar eyes of paintings she hated as a kid, shattered something within her. It made her never want to visit her childhood home again. Yet, she'd promised herself she would.

Maybe she should walk down to the peninsula first. Fortify herself before seeing anyone.

The phone rang. Who would be calling her? Judah? Aunt Callie? Warily, she picked up the old-fashioned white receiver. "Hello?"

"Maggie Thomas, here." The woman's voice came through the line clipped. "You tell that ex-husband of yours to stay off my property!"

"Why?" What did he do now?

"The pervert loitered outside your door last night, probably trying to peek through the peephole." Maggie harrumphed.

"What? No way." Judah wouldn't do that. *Ohhh.* Was he the one Mrs. Thomas yelled at? Had she hit him with a broom, again?

"He slept in a sleeping bag right there, in front of your door. Without paying for the privilege." Maggie snorted. "He took off when I threatened to call his dad. I'll have you know Mayor Grant won't put up with such shenanigans. I've called him about the reprobate before."

Reprobate? Judah? What a joke. But then, Paisley had to tamp down the burn of anger her father-in-law's name caused.

"If you plan on spending another night here—"

"I do." Paisley cut into the woman's tirade. "I already paid—"

"Then Judah Grant cannot be on my property, you hear me?" Something about the woman's snippy tone reminded Paisley of her mom yelling at her to leave and never come back.

"Well?" Maggie demanded. "Do you promise to keep the scoundrel away from my inn?"

Her words cranked up Paisley's irritation. "Unless he pays, right?" That probably sounded like the flippant girl she used to be, but she didn't care.

Maggie gasped. "I'll have you know I can refuse service to anyone I wish."

So she told Paisley before. "No wonder no one wants to stay at your rundown inn. Your rooms are archaic. The toilet barely flushes. The shower's cold. Even though it's off-season, your prices are outrageous!" As soon as she uttered the heated review, she wished she hadn't.

"Get out!" Maggie shrieked. "Now. Get off my property!"

"Mrs. Thomas—"

"I don't need your tainted money. I want you off my premises immediately." An object clattered in the background as if something dropped and broke. "Now, you've done it!"

More blame cast at her feet. "Maggie—"

"Mrs. Thomas."

"Mrs. Thomas, I'm"—she forced out the words—"I'm sorry."

"I don't want you in my 'rundown' establishment for another night." Maggie huffed. "Vacate by noon or I'll call the authorities. Brian Corbin is deputy now, you know."

Brian Corbin? High school troublemaker, Paisley's prom date, and a co-conspirator in a few of her mischief-making schemes? She could picture him in jail. Not the one tossing criminals into the slammer.

"I paid for another night." She gritted her teeth, old angst toward this woman steaming up her pipes. She had a few choice words she'd like to say, maybe some mud balls to fling.

"I guess you paid for Judah's stay last night, after all." The woman had no mercy.

"Fine."

"Fine."

The receiver clicked loudly in Paisley's ear.

Fire simmered in her gut. She wanted to march over to the motel office and give Maggie Thomas a piece of her mind, a blaze that had been smoldering for years. Here she planned to make up for past mistakes. Now, she wanted to do something notable on her exodus from the tiny rental—like stuffing the toilet full of beach sand.

She whirled around and grabbed the few items she unpacked and put them into her backpack. She wouldn't stay in this shoebox another minute. She collected her toiletries from the ridiculously small bathroom. How Maggie charged top dollar when the facilities hadn't been updated since the sixties, Paisley would never know. Someone should report her to the Better Business Bureau. Blast her name all over the front page of the Basalt Bay *Journal*.

Settle down. No use going nuts-o on a woman who wasn't worth it. She was better off getting out of this dump.

What did Maggie say? Judah slept by her door in a sleeping bag? That didn't make sense. Surely, he knew such an action would incite the innkeeper's anger toward both of them. Was he worried she'd disappear again? Concerned for her health?

Before she left town, she accused him of being heartless and uncaring. Perhaps he was showing her he had changed, like he said.

Not that it mattered. Only, in some way she didn't quite understand, maybe because she'd been alone for so long, it did matter. The idea of him watching over her, wanting to be close, for whatever reason, pleased her.

She scooped up her backpack, raincoat, and boots, tossed her room key on the TV tray near the door, then left with a firm door slam. Hopefully, Maggie heard that. Staying at this inn was a lousy idea. Didn't something bad always happen when Paisley came within twenty-five feet of the innkeeper?

No doubt, Mrs. Thomas already informed Aunt Callie about kicking Paisley out. Dad would hear about it too.

"Basalt Bay's gossips are back at it," she grumbled.

Before she went to see Dad, if she went to see him today, she had another stop to make. She was going to find out for herself why Judah slept by her door.

Eight

Paisley drove her Honda Accord through town, avoiding eye contact with anyone on the sidewalks along Front Street, and pondering the dilemma of where she should stay. On the north side, she swerved into the parking lot of the C-MER building—Judah's second home. In the past, she came here to bring him lunch or deliver a vanilla latte or to discuss some aspect of their lives. Today, she felt weird crashing into his turf. Not really his wife. Not exactly his ex-wife, although she planned to change that. She stared at the "Visitors Only" sign in front of where she parked. Was visiting him at work okay?

They had things to discuss. Although, she didn't want to move back in with him, right? Too much emotional baggage. But Maggie *had* given her the boot. Paisley could ask Dad about staying in her old room, but she hadn't gotten up the nerve to see him yet. Was she crazy to consider moving in with Judah, even temporarily?

She leaned her forearm against the steering wheel and rested her forehead against her wrist. What was she doing? What woman planning a divorce—who put two thousand miles between her and her husband for thirty-six months—would entertain the idea of sharing the same space with him again?

Perhaps, one whose spouse slept outside her motel room door? Ugh. She had to get the heroic image of him curled up outside, watching over her, out of her mind. And what about him knowing where she was for two years? Even paying a portion of her rent? She still couldn't believe he did that. What about the way he held her when she fainted two days ago? How his sparkling blues shined down on her with something akin to adoration. Hadn't he called her "sweetheart" and "my love"? Kindnesses she was starved to hear. Mercies she couldn't ignore. Although they changed nothing. Or did they change everything?

Talk about confusing.

She got out of the car and strode toward the steps of the main entrance, her shoes scuffing through a layer of sand on the footpath. Around the ocean side, and thanks to strong incessant winds, sand got everywhere and into everything. On the first step of the single-story building, she paused and stomped grit off her sneakers.

What if the possibility of her staying at the cottage made Judah expect something more than she wanted, like romance or getting back together? She turned around and gazed at the parking lot filled with about twenty-five cars.

She could head to one of the other coastal towns. Look for a cheap motel and a serving job. Her wallet was thinner than when she left Chicago, but she had some money. If she ate skimpily, or not at all, she had enough for a couple nights' stay. Sleeping on the beach was a possibility, if it weren't for the threat of unexpected storms.

She sighed. She came this far. Why not at least talk with him?

She stared at a slanted tree growing through a tall mound of sand. Such determination and endurance it demonstrated by having pressed through the resistance. Was that like Judah pushing through every argument she hurled at him against their marriage and them staying under the same roof? She caused him enough grief, why did he even wish to be around her? He said he didn't want a divorce. Why wouldn't he choose that after the way she deserted him and told him she loved someone else? Something twisted inside of her at the lies she piled up.

He was better off without her.

Stiffening her back, Paisley jogged up the steps, then entered the glass entryway of the C-MER building.

A woman dressed in bright pink stood behind the receptionist's desk, gaping at her. Mia Till? How did the young woman advance from being a mailroom assistant to the receptionist of this prestigious company? Shock blared from the short-skirt-wearing woman's owlish eyes. Her hand covered her mouth.

"Mia," Paisley offered first.

"Paisley, is that really you?" As if she didn't know. Mia shook her variegated blond locks.

Discomfort bristled inside Paisley. Maybe she should have changed into something a little more feminine before coming here. "It's me. In the flesh."

Her mind flipped through times in past years when she wondered if something might be going on between Judah and Mia. Even before she left, the young assistant seemed flirty with him at office Christmas parties Paisley attended. Then Aunt Callie caught wind of rumors in town and demanded answers. *Why are you permitting that hussy to fawn over your husband?* Paisley hadn't "permitted" any such thing.

Judah wasn't the only recipient of the woman's flirtations, either. Rumors spread that she'd been friendly with a few of the C-MER men—many of them husbands and fathers whose heads were momentarily turned by the leggy blond coworker.

But considering Paisley's past actions, she didn't have any right to judge the other woman. However, her first instincts toward Mia weren't polite, either.

"Did you just waltz back into town?" Mia smirked.

"Something like that." Paisley ignored the "waltz" bit. "I'm definitely back."

Mia's red lips surrounded glistening white teeth that appeared over whitened. "It's . . . so fab . . . to see you again." Mia cleared her throat awkwardly as if distracting Paisley from her insincere words.

"Yeah, you too." *Cough, cough.* "Is Judah around?"

"Of course."

Paisley turned toward the door at the back where she visited Judah at his cubicle in the past.

Mia dodged in front of her, palms outward, like a security guard keeping a child from a priceless sculpture. "You can't just go in there." Her hands lowered, and she straightened her short skirt.

The woman's apparel didn't seem very professional.

"Why not?" Paisley crossed her arms, her resentment rising. The model-wannabee thought she could stop her from speaking to Judah? She could walk through that doorway any time she wanted.

"There are procedures we follow now." Mia's voice turned crisp.

The company's previous receptionist, Mildred Mackey, always let Paisley go into the work area. No problem. No questions asked.

"Judah is in a meeting." Had Mia whispered his name on purpose? As if she had a claim on him?

I think I'm going to be sick. Paisley didn't plan on stirring up anything with Judah, but she didn't want him dating this makeup junky. He deserved someone good for a second wife. Someone better than Mia Till. *Someone better than me.* Her gut tightened.

"I can wait in his cubicle." She took a couple of steps toward the door again.

"No, you can't." Mia waved her hands in front of her. "Things have changed since you've been gone."

Apparently.

A haughty expression crossed the office worker's face, as if she were peering down on Paisley. Which was accurate since Mia wore four-inch heels. Oh, were those *So Kates*? Paisley stared at the sparkly red shoes while trying not to gawk. Those beauties had to be five hundred bucks! What kind of salary did Mia make?

"If you'll just have a seat—"

"No, thanks." Should she remind the pink-clad foyer police that she was still married to Judah, and therefore had access to him?

But then, didn't she give up her wifely rights when she wrote him that note and disappeared? Not that Mia needed to know their personal information. Or maybe she already did. Had Judah explained their marital status to her? Was he lonely and—?

Ugh. She didn't want to think about that. The mental image of Judah pressing his lips anywhere near this woman's red mouth made Paisley's stomach turn. She should have grabbed a bagel or coffee before charging into such a volatile situation.

"Wait here"—the receptionist pointed toward the lobby—"and I'll call Judah. He may not have time for you today." One of her sleek eyebrows arched.

He might not have time for this surprise visit, but eventually he'd exit that door and head for his truck. When he did, she'd be waiting. For her to leave now would be a point on Mia's scoreboard. Paisley wasn't having any of that.

She strode to the giant window with its southerly view of the dunes and ignored Mia. Did she think Paisley might make a run for the forbidden door? Her impish nature made her want to do that very thing just to see how the other woman might react.

Instead, she feigned disinterest and stared out the window. Outside, the dunes topped with long beach grasses weren't far from the building. If they were open to the public, it would be a fun place to tromp around and explore.

"Paisley."

She turned at Judah's soft voice, in time to catch him smiling at Mia. Gratitude? Or something else?

That twist in Paisley's stomach wrenched tighter.

Mia's toothy grin had a suspiciously more-than-friendship quality.

A growl started somewhere in the pit of Paisley's stomach and emerged from her mouth. She met Judah's surprised gaze. *Mia? Really?*

Maybe he was more eager for things to be finalized in their marriage than he admitted. But if that were the case, why did he sleep outside her door? And tell her he loved her.

Judah's brow furrowed. "You okay?" He stroked his hand down her arm, and she didn't back away from his touch. Not with Mia watching them from behind her desk.

"I'm fine." *Not really.* While things could never go back to how they were between them four years ago, if Judah took up with Mia,

Paisley was getting out of town. "What's going on here?" She bobbed her head toward the receptionist, then glared at him.

A blush she'd rarely seen on him hued his cheeks. "Nothing at all." His Adam's apple bobbed, revealing his discomfort over the question.

She stared at him more fully. His black hair stuck out in a few places like he'd dragged his fingers through the strands in frustration. Dark shadows beneath his eyes made him look fatigued. Probably exhausted after a restless sleep. Which reminded her of Mrs. Thomas's accusation.

"What were you doing sleeping outside my motel room?" Her fists landed on her hips.

A huff came from the other side of the room. Paisley should have lowered her voice. However, Mia hearing that detail might be perfect. The receptionist needed a reminder that Judah had a wife— for now.

"You heard about that, huh?" He sighed.

"I don't have a place to stay, thanks to you. Maggie kicked me out." She stared into his eyes that resembled tide pools on a clear blue-sky day.

"Oh, man." He stroked his hands down both of her arms, something he did in the past when he tried comforting her.

She should have stepped back from his touch, but she didn't. Not for Mia's benefit this time. Although, she didn't want to analyze why.

"I'm sorry, Pais. I didn't mean for that to happen. I just"—he linked their pinkie fingers, something else he used to do—"wanted to be near you. Listening, in case, you know—"

In case of a panic attack? In case she ran? When he drew her to him, for the slightest breath of time, she allowed a hug. She leaned her forehead against his chest, seeking comfort or a bit of human kindness. He laid his palm on the back of her head and kissed the top of her hair. She inhaled deeply of his Old Spice scent, remembering how she used to joke with him about smelling like her dad. He still did.

What happened to us?

She almost got choked up. Until she recalled where they were and who was watching. Besides, she didn't want to be close to Judah physically. Only, in that moment she did. She wanted him to wrap his arms around her and—what? Kiss her? No, no. That's not what she wanted. She stumbled back a couple of steps. Crossed her arms— a protective measure. Yet her traitorous gaze glanced at his lips a couple of times. Bad idea.

"What will you do now? How can I help?" He swayed his hand toward the couch as if to ask her to sit down.

She ignored the gesture. "About your offer." She spoke quietly now, not wanting Mia to hear this part.

He smiled, and there was something lovely and inviting in his expression that gnawed at a tired, lonely place in her spirit. They were such good friends before. Could they find a way back to that, without the complications of marriage and romance?

"You mean it?" His eyes lit up. "You want to come back and live with me?" He spoke loudly. As if he wanted Mia, the only other person in the room, to hear.

That didn't make sense if he'd dated her.

Paisley glanced over her shoulder and saw the receptionist talking on the phone. Mia's gaze darted toward Judah, then Paisley, like she was watching them. Hopefully, she wasn't speaking with Aunt Callie. Did she have connections to Basalt's gossip ring?

"I thought we could talk about it, you know, since I've been kicked out. Unless you meant for that to happen." She peered into his gaze, seeking ulterior motives.

"Of course, I didn't." He huffed. "I never meant for Maggie to see me. You know me better than that."

She knew each of them avoided the woman for their own reasons.

He glanced over his shoulder as if checking on Mia also. "I'm in meetings all day. Do you want to head out to the cottage and get settled before I arrive?"

"Okay." There was something he had to know. "Look, I need a room, and that's it." She lowered her voice. "There's no hope for us. You've got to understand that."

"There's always hope." His eyes flooded with moisture.

She blinked back a tug of emotion that surprised her. "I just need somewhere to hang out while I figure out a job and my life. Your place would only be a temporary stop in the road."

He jerked like she slapped him, and she hated his reaction. But then, as if she didn't say something that might destroy his hopes, a soft smile replaced his momentary grimace. Apparently, whatever bitterness she caused him in the past didn't affect his ability to offer her a genuine smile. She stared at his soft mouth a tad too long.

If she were going to share space with him, she had to remember her own strict rules. No staring at his inviting lips. No gazing into his blue eyes. And stay fifty feet from his bedroom. By then she'd be outside. Maybe sleeping in the hammock on the porch would be safer. For whom? Judah? Or herself?

"The key's still under the crab shell on the porch." He grinned. "I made up the guest bed yesterday, just in case."

Even when she adamantly said she wouldn't stay with him?

"You did? Thanks." Although, the thought of staying at his place again made her feel unsettled, maybe afraid. Like she was embarking on a journey in a rowboat without oars.

"Judah, Mr. Linfield wants you to rejoin them in the conference room." The receptionist held up the phone as if she just took a call.

"Okay. Thanks." He lifted a hand.

Paisley didn't see any guile or attraction toward Mia on his face. In fact, his eyes seemed to be glowing toward Paisley. But that meant she was gazing into his blues again.

"Now?" Mia's nails tapped a steady, annoying rhythm on her desk.

Judah touched Paisley's little finger. "We'll talk later, huh?"

"Sure." Warmth spread through her. "Oh, sorry to have bothered you," she called after him.

"I'm glad you came by. Stop in any time." He winked at her before sauntering back through the door he exited a few minutes ago.

Any time? She bet Mia wouldn't approve of that.

Paisley made a beeline for the main entrance, avoiding further contact with the office help.

"When did you get back, anyway?" Mia sure moved fast in those heels.

With one sneaker out the door, Paisley paused, surprised by Mia following her. "Two days ago."

"Funny your aunt hasn't seen you."

So, Mia *had* talked to her. "How would you know whether I've seen Aunt Callie?"

"Oh, we talk." Mia's laugh tinkled like a windchime. "I met her when I first moved to town. She's the one who introduced me to Judah, and he helped me get my job." She swayed her hands toward her desk.

He did? "Well, uh, I've got to run." Before she said something she'd regret. She rushed down the steps to the path.

"Goodbye, Miss Cedars."

Hearing her maiden name, Paisley didn't turn back to dispute it. She might even reclaim it if she and Judah went their separate ways. Now, why didn't that sound as appealing as it had before?

Nine

Paisley climbed the three broken-down wooden steps at Dad's house, each board creaking with old age. She stood there for at least ten minutes, staring at the glass square in the wooden front door, trying to get up the nerve to knock, debating whether to turn around and go back down the stairs. She didn't see any movement inside, which was good. She needed a few minutes to collect herself.

She scratched at a tightness in her neck. Swallowed.

God, if You're there, please help me breathe normally through this visit.

She quickly searched for five things. There—a child's half-chewed tennis shoe. Mom's rhododendron bush in need of a trimming. A brown dog collar draped over the railing. Four rocks near the screen door. An upside-down empty soup can. She breathed in and out, controlling any overreaction to being here.

The house she pretended was a pirate's ship when she was a kid could almost be called a beach house. If it weren't for the row of houses on the ocean side of the street, she would have had the perfect view of the sea while growing up. However, that didn't stop her and Peter from running through the neighbors' yards to reach their beloved beach and finding treasures left after high tides.

Thinking of Peter, her childhood friend and confidant, had the calming effect she needed. If only he were here. Had Dad or Paige heard from him while she was away?

She lifted her fist to knock on the door, then paused. Would Dad understand why she left three years ago? Why she didn't call? Was he still upset about her not attending Mom's funeral?

Something thumped on the steps behind her. She whirled around.

"Why, if it isn't Paisley Rose." Aunt Callie's voice bellowed like she was hard of hearing.

"Aunt Callie, hello." Paisley subdued her groan, frustrated that her aunt found her before she got to speak privately with Dad.

"I heard . . . you . . . were . . . home." The plump woman huffed up the stairs as if there were fifty steps instead of three. "It's about time you came home and faced the music, Missy." The older woman pressed Paisley into a hug, squashing her against her ample body.

Face the music, indeed! "Nice to see you too, Auntie." She used the endearing term half-heartedly.

The screen door screeched open. By the noise, her dad hadn't oiled the hinges in years.

"What's the r-racket out h-here?" Dad's voice broke, making him sound much older than sixty. His gaze met Paisley's, then flitted away. He didn't extend his arms in a hug. Didn't invite her in.

The muscles in her throat bunched up. *You can do this.* She came back to Basalt to see him, didn't she? "Hi, Dad."

He stared off in the distance. Didn't respond. He looked so tired. Were his eyes bloodshot? Maybe he wasn't sleeping well. Or sick?

"See who's here, Pauly?" Aunt Callie nudged Paisley. "About time she showed up, wouldn't you say?" She stomped her foot on the porch as if demanding Dad's attention. "We don't blame her one bit for leaving that no-good son of Edward Grant, do we?"

At her aunt's harsh assessment, a rock slammed into Paisley's heart. While she didn't think kindly of Mayor Grant—she pretty much despised him for the way he treated her—Judah didn't deserve the same branding. Had Aunt Callie told people around town that her leaving was all his fault? Inwardly, she groaned. She *had* left him to deal with why she left, just like he said.

Dad's reticence in moving toward her made Paisley shuffle back to the cracked post on the porch. She leaned against the wood, taking a casual stance she didn't feel, and forced herself to breathe calmly. "How are you, Dad?" She looked at him even though he didn't return her gaze.

"Oh, so-so." He seemed to be staring at the broken slats on the porch floor. His eyes were more gray than blue now, and liquid flooded his orbs as if he were suppressing tears. Although, she couldn't be sure. His hair was grayer. Thinner. More wrinkles lined his eyes and mouth. A scar of some sort creased his chin. A shaving accident? He still didn't take a step toward her. Should she drop down on one knee and beg for his forgiveness? That seemed overly dramatic, especially with Aunt Callie watching her every move.

"Hamburger's on sale down at Lewis's Super." Aunt Callie chatted, filling in the awkwardness. "Did you see the blockbuster price on chicken, Pauly? My, my, haven't seen such low prices in a decade, have you?" She went on about picnic supplies being useless in late September.

Dad stared at something in the yard, maybe the old apple tree, or else he was trying to glimpse the ocean. Obviously, he was avoiding eye contact with his daughter. Did he wish she hadn't shown up at all?

Paisley forced herself to swallow. To breathe in and out lest she fall apart and make a complete mess of this first visit.

"You just going to stand there like a zombie, Pauly?" Aunt Callie huffed. "I need some sweet tea. Got any?"

"Nah. Haven't made any in a week." Dad ran his fingers through the strands of gray hair sticking up vertically.

"Figures." Aunt Callie snorted. "Guess I have to do everything." The older woman plodded into the house with heavy footsteps. The screen door slammed shut.

Then silence.

Maybe Paisley should go in and help. The icy chill left in her aunt's wake was hard to bear.

Did Aunt Callie depart to give Paisley and Dad some time alone? Strange, considering she usually wanted to hear all the details about everyone in Basalt. Was she standing inside the living room, listening?

Collecting gossip to distribute later? The notion irked Paisley. She didn't appreciate people talking about her.

Inside, the oven drawer squawked open and closed, reminding her of old times. Sounded like Aunt Callie was using the pot they always used to make sweet tea in.

"Where you been all this time?" Dad's unexpected question made Paisley jump.

"Oh." She met his gaze for a moment before he glanced away. "Chicago."

"That far, huh?" He fiddled with his thumbnail.

Had he ever been concerned about her? Missed her? Or with the embarrassment she caused, was her absence a relief?

More silence. Anxiety twisted and turned in her stomach. But what did she expect? So this talk wasn't progressing as she hoped. At least, they were both still standing here. She should say something. "You're right, I went far enough to get away from everything and everyone."

A wounded look crossed Dad's face, which made her feel terrible. He gnawed on his lower lip. "Seems you and Peter had the same idea—run as fast and as far as possible."

"Yeah, I suppose." No use lying to him.

A crash came from inside.

"Lousy pitcher!" Aunt Callie shouted. "Pauly, I've done it. Broke the only decent thing you got in this house to make tea in." She said something derogatory.

"I better see what she's done now." Dad shuffled toward the door.

He didn't ask Paisley to come in, so she didn't follow him. The door scraped against the edge of the doorframe, then clattered shut. Lots of things seemed wrong with the place. Didn't Dad do repair work anymore? Judah could fix the door. Good night, with the right tools she could fix it. Living alone taught her how to do a lot of stuff she never did before.

She leaned against the porch railing—the one she and Peter draped a blanket over and hid behind to throw mud balls at the neighbor's house—and noticed the peeling paint on the porch walls, the gaps in the floorboards, and the broken window by the side of the door held together with duct tape. Had it been damaged in the storm that hit other buildings in town? Or was age and neglect catching up with it? The ancient house had seen better days, that was for sure.

"Can't you buy anything?" Aunt Callie's voice rose from inside. "Penny would be shocked to know you haven't purchased a thing since she's been gone. How am I supposed to make tea?"

"Go home, woman!" Dad shouting? "Make tea at your own place and stop meddling in my affairs."

Even when dealing with Peter's and Paisley's shenanigans, Dad rarely raised his voice. He was more the brooding type. An internalist. His glare spoke buckets more than she ever wanted to hear him say out loud.

Aunt Callie harrumphed, then made a bunch of rattling sounds. Apparently, she was determined not to leave the kitchen without her beverage. She probably didn't want to take off as long as Paisley and Dad hadn't talked things out. She'd hunt for something to make tea in, even a bread pan, just for an excuse to eavesdrop.

"For your information"—Dad's voice got louder and forceful, surprising Paisley even more—"I've bought my own groceries for years. Even before Penny passed on." He cleared his throat as if it wasn't used much. "Paisley isn't the only one who's been gone for a long time." Hurt seeped through every word like blood through a bandage.

Paisley dropped to the edge of the porch, her shoes on the next step down, as an awful silence engulfed the house behind her.

Aunt Callie's voice came softly then. "Your daughter's here now, Pauly." Aunt Callie sticking up for her? Big surprise. "Aren't you going to speak with her?"

Paisley held her breath, waiting.

Dad muttered something about too many burned bridges.

Aunt Callie burst through the doorway, letting the screen door slam, and handed her a chipped glass filled to the brim with tea. A couple of ice cubes clinked against the sides. "Here you go, Paisley Rose."

"Thank you." She sipped the still-warm tea, then swished the ice cubes around. Wasn't Dad coming back out? Now might be a good time to talk about those burned bridges.

Aunt Callie took a long chug of tea, then sighed like it was the best thing she ever tasted. "Nothing like tea to calm the nerves." She dropped onto the rocker that looked ready to topple over or disintegrate in the next windstorm. She scooted her backside deep into the seat as if she planned to spend the night there.

Paisley toyed with condensation on the outside of her glass, feeling insignificant next to her aunt.

"Chicago, huh?" On each back-and-forth motion, the rocker thudded.

"Uh, yes."

"Too far from the ocean for me." The woman made a tsk-tsk sound like no one should live in such a dry climate.

"There's a large lake. Waves and everything." Paisley shrugged. "But not the sea."

"Not by a long shot."

If Dad planned to hunker down and avoid her, Paisley should leave. Give him time to adjust to her being back in town. Maybe he was more shocked than angry. She shouldn't take his reaction personally. But, boy, oh boy, did she. Leaving town became more tempting in this minute of rejection than two days ago when she first arrived. But maybe that's what Dad, and Judah, feared. That she'd run again as soon as she got the chance.

How could she prove them wrong?

"Seen Paige?" Aunt Callie's blackish gaze pierced Paisley's.

"No."

"Going to?"

She hated the grilling. "Eventually." Paige was her sister. Not that they were ever close. Or that Paisley felt she owed her sibling any explanation.

"I heard that no-good husband of yours bedded down in front

of your door at Maggie's." Aunt Callie had to bring that up. "Disgusting, if you ask me. As if you'd stoop to taking him back. Word on the street is—"

Paisley blocked out her aunt's rambling for a moment. Judah may have been foolish to sleep by her door, but his actions were far from disgusting. Honorable and sweet, perhaps. She tuned back in.

"Serves Edward Grant right to have his lowdown son dragged through the mire of a divorce. The mayor is far too pompous." Aunt Callie drained her tea glass in a noisy guzzle. "That you married into that self-righteous family on the cliff riles me to the bone."

Indignation burned through Paisley's veins. "Auntie"—this time she said the word crisply—"I haven't decided if I'm going to divorce Judah." Now, why did she say that? Of course, she'd made up her mind. But she didn't want Aunt Callie going on and on about the Grant family, and Judah as if he were the worst person in Basalt. Besides, Paisley's last name was still Grant. Her aunt should respect that.

"What do y-you mean you h-haven't d-decided?" Aunt Callie coughed like she was choking on her tea. "I thought that's why you left. To get away from the scum of the sea."

"Yes, I had to get away from him"—she came back to Basalt to be honest—"and a few others." She gave her aunt a pointed glare. "However, Judah's a decent guy. He doesn't deserve your scorn."

Aunt Callie scoffed. "He put you, and therefore this family, through a world of hurt." If glares could burn something, Paisley's skin would be on fire. "It's time you end this farce of a marriage and start living like a Cedars." Her lips bunched up in a scowl.

Did Aunt Callie presume that all she had to do was point her finger and Paisley would jump to do her bidding?

"I have to go." She set down her tea glass on the porch railing, then rushed down the stairs. If she said anything else, she'd say too much. Which would mean more apologies.

"Hold on, young lady!" Aunt Callie shouted.

Paisley didn't pause. She got into her car, started the engine, and backed up. Speeding might get her into trouble with Deputy Brian

Corbin—that's all she needed—so she drove slowly away from Aunt Callie who still sat in the rocker on the porch.

It hurt that her father hadn't come back outside. Like he didn't want to speak with her at all. If her own dad didn't want her, who did?

I have loved you with an everlasting love.

Oh. At the beautiful sentiment she hadn't thought of in such a long time, warmth spread through her. Did God still care for her even after the way she'd acted toward Him?

She sighed, not daring to answer that question. However, the inspiring words soothed some of her pain over Dad's cold reaction. But not completely. Not when the man who could have opened his arms wide in forgiveness and welcomed her home didn't.

Ten

Judah knew he'd been in too many meetings when he couldn't stay focused on anything the speakers said. But when Mike Linfield, a man he considered to be a temperamental boss, stood up and shouted at attendees sitting around the conference table as if they purposefully neglected the coastline and left it unprotected, Judah bristled at the lambasting. He and his coworkers were conscientious about their jobs and public safety. Why else would they put in such long hours and contribute so much effort to protecting the citizens of Basalt Bay? However, while part of him wanted to say something contradictory about Mike's accusations, since Paisley came by a couple of hours ago, his mind *had* been preoccupied.

He forced himself to concentrate on Craig's introduction of safety measures for future evacuations. That worked for about a minute. His heart wasn't in today's sessions, no matter how important they were. Especially when a memory of Paisley and how things used to be in their relationship danced through his mind. Then his attention to policy details faded lightning fast as he remembered how she would snuggle up with him on the couch, like she never wanted to be far from him, and they watched a show next to each other, or sat close and talked. He could almost smell her rose-scented perfume, feel her hand clasped in his as if their palms were glued together—at least in the early days of marriage. Was it possible for them to recover those warm emotions and the sweet love they lost?

God could do anything. But what if Paisley didn't want to be his wife anymore? If she pursued a divorce regardless of what he wanted? There was nothing he could do to stop her then. He suppressed a groan that would have given away that he'd again tuned out what Craig was saying.

What about the things Judah previously decided? Hadn't he spent hours and hours praying about what he'd do if Paisley came back? And if she ever cracked open the door to reconciliation, hadn't he determined to do everything in his power to love her like the husband he should have been before?

During the last twenty-four months of knowing her location, so many times, he wrestled with the impulse to go to her apartment and beg her to come home. But, other than the one time he bought the plane ticket, he knew if he flew to Chicago and insisted she return with him, she'd dig her heels in even more. She had to find her way back to him in her own time.

And now she was here. Hallelujah!

Please help her remember our love, before it's too late.

But it was never too late for him to show her forgiveness and grace, right? Hadn't God called him to be a good husband, no matter what? To love Paisley even though she made it clear that a relationship with him was impossible. That the only way she'd move back into the beach cottage was if things remained platonic between them. *Platonic*, seriously? Not his choice, but he agreed.

He covered a disgruntled moan with a cough, then took a sip from his water bottle. Time to listen in to Craig again. A few slides displaying north and south routes out of town flipped through the PowerPoint rotation. Things Judah had seen before. Still, determined to pay attention, he leaned his elbows on the table and faced his supervisor. Craig described the congestion the duo corridor exits encountered during Addy. He expounded on details of damage to the southern arterial during the flooding stage and how the repair work wasn't finished yet.

If another disaster hit, and Judah hoped it never happened, keeping Paisley safe would be his priority. In the next second, Craig's monotone voice got whisked away by thoughts of her. Maybe Judah should tell his wife what he was thinking—that she was the most important person in his life, that he'd do anything for her, including risking his life to save hers. If he told her that, would she realize how much he cared? How much he still loved her? That he'd never again put his job above her?

His thoughts flitted back to when their relationship altered forever. Four years ago, a day after their baby was born without life—even the thought of holding Misty Gale, so tiny and still in his arms, squeezed something tight in his chest, choked him up— Paisley got out of the hospital earlier in the afternoon than he realized. If he knew, he would have been there. But he was on patrol during a threatening storm, and unbeknownst to him, she drove back to town in a deluge of rain and wind, alone. After work, he went straight to the hospital in Florence where he found out she'd been discharged. He drove by the cottage, but she wasn't there. Crazy with worry, he feared she might have had an accident along Highway 101.

But then, he thought about the peninsula, the place she loved most. There, he found her slumped over at the edge of the point, devastated, broken, sobbing her heart out. He felt so helpless. A failure as a husband. He should have stayed at the hospital with her. Skipped work. Shared more in their grief. If he did, they might still be a real couple. Truth was, he didn't know how to deal with such overwhelming heartache, then. Still didn't.

He blinked fast to rid his eyes of moisture. No use falling apart in front of his coworkers about something that happened four years ago. Yet, if the loss still affected him, it had to be tough for Paisley too, especially with the anniversary of their child's death approaching.

"Right, Judah?" Craig's dark eyes stared him down, one eyebrow lifted. Did he know Judah wasn't listening?

"Yep. Absolutely." He nodded. Gulped. What did he just agree to?

It seemed he deserved his superior's wrath for inattentiveness. When Craig continued his presentation, Judah sighed, relieved the speaker hadn't pressed for an answer about whatever topic he wasn't listening to.

What was wrong with him? Usually he was passionate about how storms could harm his community and how C-MER would assist their neighbors during a disaster. In an earlier session about the possibility of ocean plates scraping each other, getting stuck, and then shifting, sending out a powerful wave surge toward Basalt Bay and other cities along the Oregon Coast, he was completely engaged. But then, that was before Paisley showed up, demanding to know why he slept outside her motel door.

Now Craig was speaking about how to safely evacuate all the citizens in town—which seemed an impossibility given the narrow road system and the city only having two junctions with the main highway. "Whether it's a tsunami or a Category 3 hurricane"—he pointed at a photo of a tsunami illuminated on the wall—"residents will be aware of imminent danger faster thanks to our recent purchase of a new early warning system. In the future, evacuations will be more efficient and swifter."

"Here, here," someone in the back affirmed.

Others clapped.

The words about "imminent danger" made Judah shudder. Hopefully, the town would never have to face a storm like Addy again. The men and women seated around the perimeter of the table had to be prepared in case it did happen.

Someone asked Craig a question, and Judah zoned out again. He'd have to warn Dad to keep his big mouth shut about his grievances toward Paisley. His father seemed incapable of silencing his opinions. In his official capacity as mayor, he usually acted civil. However, since Paisley left, Dad took every opportunity to inform Judah of what he thought of the woman his son chose for a wife. He called her names that riled Judah every time, widening the emotional gap between them.

Finally, the training session ended. A few coworkers stuck around to ask questions, but Judah shot through the door, grabbed his jacket from his cubicle, then hustled out to his truck. He was eager to get to the cottage to see if Paisley arrived yet. On the way home, he'd pick up salmon sandwiches at Bert's. Even though they had burgers from there yesterday, he didn't want either of them cooking tonight, giving them plenty of opportunity to talk.

At the beach house, seeing Paisley's car parked in the narrow driveway again gave him a surge of hope. "All things are possible," he reminded himself. As he walked up the path toward the front door, he listened to the gentle roar of the surf coming from below the house. Man, he loved the smells and sounds of the ocean. He opened the unlocked door. "I'm home!" It felt amazing to say that to his wife again. He set the food bag on the counter. "Paisley?"

When she didn't answer, concern slashed through him. What if she collapsed? Ran? No, her car was outside. She loved the sea and was probably at the beach. He'd take their dinner down there. She'd like that.

He threw on his Oregon Ducks sweatshirt and grabbed the food bag on his way out. He didn't have far to go. As soon as he tromped over the slight rise, he spotted her dark hair blowing in the wind. She sat on the sand, her face lifted to the partially sunny sky, and her eyes were closed.

What a beauty. He grinned. Couldn't help himself. His life had meaning again. His wife was home! Now, how could he convince her to stay?

She left you once; she'll leave again. A negative voice that sounded like his dad's whispered in his thoughts.

Not if I can help it.

Judah stopped in the middle of the wind-brushed trail and stared up to the heavens. He took a second to collect his thoughts and pray. God could heal and restore them. His wife was here now, and he'd rejoice in that blessing.

With a lighter step he approached her. "There you are!"

She opened her eyes and waved at him. Her smile made him weak in the knees. Forget butterflies. Being in Paisley Grant's presence caused a tidal wave of emotions to barrel through his core.

"I see you stopped at our favorite diner." She pointed at the bag.

He loved that she used the term "our favorite," as if she still thought of them as a couple with favorite things to share.

"I couldn't resist." He couldn't resist her, either. If he thought she wouldn't mind, he'd plant a doozy of a welcome-home kiss on those rosy lips. Too soon. He'd respect the safe distance she asked for. He dropped onto the sand beside her, the sides of their hands touching. Too imposing?

She scooted her backside about a foot away in the sand, giving him an answer. He wouldn't be discouraged. God was working. Judah was depending on Him.

He checked the contents of the bag. Two fish burgers. Fries. Two plastic containers filled with iced tea. He handed her a cup, a package of fries, and a paper-wrapped sandwich. "House special. Your favorite."

"Salmon burger with avocado?" She sipped her tea and her gaze met his. "Thanks for remembering."

"Of course." *I remember everything about you.* He nudged her arm playfully. "Besides, Bert's special hasn't changed in years."

She unwrapped her sandwich and took a bite. Her quietness made him wonder what she was thinking.

He thanked God silently for the food, then bit into his meal. Suddenly, he felt famished. Sitting through all those meetings gave him an appetite. Or maybe eating a meal with his wife made him feel normal, finally. He inhaled the salty air, felt the wind brush against his face. Life was good. So good.

"Thanks for this." She held up the wheat bun oozing in green guacamole sauce. "And for letting me stay at the cottage."

He swallowed down a fry. "No problem." Didn't she see how happy he was that she sat here with him? Should he say so? No, the look of caution in her eyes kept him still.

"It'll just be for a few days, you know."

A pain searing his throat had nothing to do with the hot sauce Bert added to his sandwich. Time to shed a lifetime of confrontational resistance. "Look, Paisley"—he faced her—"I want you here with me more than anything."

"But—"

"No buts." He took a chance and laid his hand over hers in the sand. "I get it. You were unhappy in our marriage. And you left."

Her eyes widened as if she were shocked to hear him speaking so forthrightly. She pulled her hand out from under his, like he figured she would.

He took a deep breath. "You're here wanting to end things with us. But so we're clear, I don't want that. I never did."

Her mouth opened and closed, but she didn't say anything.

"I've had three years to consider what I'd say to you when I got the chance, so I plan to speak my mind. I want to hear what you have to say also." His heart hammering in his chest, he bit into the sandwich he'd lost his appetite for and set it aside.

Paisley's lip trembled. "If you feel that strongly, maybe I shouldn't stay with you." She crinkled up the sandwich wrapping paper.

The wall that rose swiftly and effortlessly between them blasted away his confidence. If she'd said that to him in the past, he would have taken off for a beach walk by himself. Never again. He told her things would be different. He meant it. If being honest caused embarrassment or made him look foolish in her eyes, so be it. A rotting bandage of hurts and past mistakes needed to be ripped off. Even if yanking off that bandage might tear apart his chance to have her in his house, or in his arms, again. They both needed healing, although their mutual scars might remain.

"Do you remember the day you promised me forever?" He stroked her knuckles, needing some contact between them, and gazed into her eyes. "I do." He kept his voice soft.

She swallowed and pulled her hand away. "It didn't work, Judah."

Her unfinished sandwich was on her lap. Apparently, neither of them were hungry now.

He sighed. "I believe things can still work between us."

"I don't see how."

"We'd have to focus on fixing the things that went wrong before." He wished for a magical phrase or a romantic line that would touch her heart and bridge the chasm. None came. Honesty might be better.

"Pais, I know I messed up. I let you down in a hundred ways. I've relived those last arguments we had before you left until I can't bear to think about them."

"Me too." Her admission surprised him. She cleared her throat. "Not that it changes anything. But since you were being honest—"

"Why can't it change everything?" He was laying his heart on the line.

"Judah—"

"I mean it. I still love you, Pais. I care for you as a person and as my wife." Her silence tore at him. "Is it because . . . you love . . . someone else?" The words wrenched from his mouth, but he had to know if what she said in that note was true. If what the town assumed was true. Not that it changed whether he wanted to stay married to her. Even if she fell for someone else in the past, Judah planned to try winning her back. He promised her forever in his wedding vows. He promised himself too, and God.

"It isn't that."

"Really?" His heart skipped a beat. "I'm so glad." He wanted to throw his arms around her and hug her.

"Don't be."

Dread replaced his relief. "Uh, why not?"

She groaned. "Don't you see? If I were in love with someone else, this would be simpler." *If?* So she *had* lied. "Then you'd accept my reason for divorcing you."

"No, I wouldn't." His heart would be broken again, but he would still try reconciling with her. A commitment was a commitment to the end, no matter how difficult, terrifying, or rocky the journey might be.

"Yes, you would." Her eyes filled with unshed tears. "I know you, Judah."

Something about the way she said she knew him pricked his heart. "You know who I was before we lost Misty Gale. You don't know the man I've become since you've been gone." He picked up a handful of sand and tossed it into a pile.

"Maybe not." She fingered a pebble, picked it up and threw it onto his sand mound.

"Guess you'll have to stick around and find out for yourself." Was he flirting with her so soon after his feelings were pummeled by her threat of divorce? He sighed. "I prefer to think I've matured, but that might be pushing the truth a little." He tossed a few small rocks on the pile, just like old times. "I hope I've become a better man."

A tear trickled down her cheek and she swiped it away. Seeing her even a little emotionally broken sent a fierce protectiveness through him. If only he could wrap his arms around her and hold her against his chest as he did during that panic attack of hers.

"Thing is, while you may have changed, I'm the same ol' me." She sipped her tea. "There's no hope of change for us."

Judah disagreed. God's love could change everything. Of course, so could bitterness. Best not to go there. Instead, he sought a lighter turn in the conversation. "You know when I first fell in love with you? Twelve years ago when I saw you pelting mud balls at the Beachside Inn." He snickered, then flipped a rock on to the pile.

"All this time and you never told Mrs. Thomas?" Her eyes squinted at him.

"Not on your life." He linked their pinkies, knowing she'd probably pull away. She did. "The best part is . . . I still love you."

She snorted like she didn't believe him.

An impish thought came to mind, something that might make her smile. He pointed offshore to where a fishing boat plodded through the surf. Cupping his hands to his mouth, he yelled toward it, "I love Paisley Rose Grant!"

"Stop that!" She sounded indignant and threw a handful of sand at him. "What's gotten into you?"

He laughed, enjoying the more carefree interaction. "I told you I've changed. I said I love you, and you, Mrs. Grant, didn't believe me." He jumped to his feet and, barely containing his laughter, yelled at the top of his voice, "I love my wife!"

She leaped up. "Judah, stop already!" But she was chuckling too.

He'd missed having fun with her, teasing her, spending time together. He gazed into her eyes, stroked a strand of dark hair back over her ear, then he almost did something that would have made her mad. He leaned in and nearly kissed her on the mouth. When he realized how close he came, how much he wanted to touch his lips to hers, he let his mouth briefly caress her forehead instead.

"Want to walk?" He reached out his hand toward her.

She glanced at him but didn't accept his offer of handholding.

"Stubborn. Same as always." He teased.

"I told you I'm the same. I bet at heart you are too." She took off running down the sandy beach toward the dunes.

He left the food where it was, knowing they'd be back to clean up in a while. Then he ran after his wife, hoping her perception of him might change, and for love to find its way back into both of their hearts.

Eleven

Paisley awoke to sunshine splashing across the twin bed in the guest room where she slept, and to the unfortunate clatter of banging pots in the kitchen. Why was Judah making all that racket? She checked the alarm clock on the nightstand. Seven o'clock? Too early for a Saturday morning.

A firm knock sounded on the closed door. "Paisley? I'm making scrambled eggs."

If she didn't answer, would he assume she was still sleeping? Or, maybe, that she escaped through the window? "Yeah. Uh-huh." She grumbled.

"Pleasant this morning, are we?"

She'd show him pleasant by swinging open the door and chucking her pillow at him. But then he might think she was flirting. She didn't want that.

She remembered how she ran down the beach last night with him chasing her. How he yelled that he loved her at a fishing boat going through the bay. What was with him? When did he become so open and honest? And affectionate? Things deteriorated in their relationship long before she left. Why was he flirting with her now? He told her that he'd changed. That God was working in his life over the years they were apart. Maybe she'd ask him about that sometime.

"We can eat on the veranda. It's a lovely morning." His footsteps moved down the hall.

The veranda? So, he didn't forget what they used to call the six-foot by six-foot section of broken cement pavers. They'd planned on redoing the outdoor space, making it large enough to have friends over for dinners, but never got around to it.

She might as well get moving. Judah made enough noise to wake the whole south-side community, except most of the neighbors were summer dwellers who already left for warmer parts.

After she washed up in the bathroom, she shuffled outside into the brisk September ocean-side air. Judah had placed a two-foot circular café-style table with two wrought iron chairs in the middle of the "veranda." He even set a little fall greenery in a vase between two turquoise plates filled with scrambled eggs and canned peaches. He bowed slightly and swayed his right hand toward the spread. Why was he being so charming this morning?

She reached for her coffee cup and dropped onto the chair with a sigh. The sweet steaming brew made waking up early not quite so painful. It was nice of Judah to add a dash of coconut creamer too. She smelled it immediately. One of the chair legs wobbled on the broken paver beneath her. "Oops." Some coffee spilled on her sweatshirt.

"You okay?" Judah eyed her from across the table where he sat down.

"The chair—" She groaned. No use pointing out his flawed patio furniture.

He jiggled his chair. "They both need work." He winked. "Kind of like us."

"Yeah, yeah." She rolled her eyes. If he didn't let up on pushing for a marriage makeover, she'd be out the door before she finished the toast he'd added to the table. She eyed him coolly.

He shrugged and smiled, then seemed to focus on his food.

She slid her fork under a bit of egg and took a cautious bite. Not bad. "When did you learn to cook?" Her grumpy tone came out before she filtered it. Judah had been pleasant to her ever since he found her unconscious on the peninsula. Why not attempt to be polite herself?

"Practice."

She appreciated his honest answer when he could have said something mean—*Otherwise I'd have starved after you left me.*

She sighed, then ate her breakfast in silence, glad Judah seemed to realize she needed quiet. Or maybe he required some time to ponder this situation they were in as much as she did.

After they finished eating and he refilled their cups with coffee and more coconut creamer, Paisley turned in her chair in the direction of the sea. A seagull traipsed across the dune to the left of the trail. A rustling in the trees made her think it might be a squirrel.

"I was hoping you'd help me with something today." Judah smiled at her.

"Like what?"

His blue gaze sparkled with playfulness or mischief.

"What do you have up your sleeve?"

"Other than the sand you threw at me last night?" He chortled. "Hard to get that out of my armpits."

That made her laugh. "Seriously, what's up?" She had her own agenda. People to see. A job to find. Hopefully somewhere else to stay.

One of his eyes squinted, then he gazed toward the ocean. Was he nervous about telling her something? He'd been generous about letting her stay here without strings attached. She could probably help him for a couple of hours, but then she needed to go see Dad again. "Got a window to replace, or something?"

"Sort of."

"Sure, I can help."

He seemed about to say something, then he stood and scooped up their plates, silverware, and glasses. "Meet me at my truck in twenty minutes."

"Wait. I thought you needed help here." She grabbed their cups. "Where are we going?"

"To town. Someone else needs assistance."

"Who?"

Judah stopped mid-step, the plates wobbling precariously. The turquoise pottery shimmered in the morning sun, but he obviously collected too many items. As the plates careened from his grasp, she lunged forward.

"Judah!" She caught the plates, but one crystal water glass—a wedding gift—toppled and smashed into a bazillion pieces against the pavers. "Oh, no."

"I can't believe I did that." He groaned and dropped to his knees, picking up shards of glass. "You okay?" He glanced up, his cheeks aflame with obvious embarrassment.

"I'm fine." She set the cups and plates on the table, then knelt next to him. Did he even know the glass's sentimental value?

"Sorry." He stood and placed chunks of broken crystal on a plate.

"Accidents happen." She stood and did the same with the shards she picked up, feeling a little sad about the glassware. In the years she was away, she never thought of the glass's unique "G" design. However, this one breaking now seemed symbolic. Like everything she ever hoped for about marriage and relationships eventually broke or died.

Sigh.

Judah piled dishes back in his arms.

"Let me help this time." She took the other glass from him, protecting it without saying so.

He gave her a sheepish grin. "I wanted to make you a nice breakfast and clean the dishes on your first morning back."

"You did make a nice breakfast. Thank you." She took a few more items out of his hands. For a second, she experienced déjà vu. Eating together and then cleaning up the kitchen side by side felt so familiar. Hadn't they helped each other with after-meal chores hundreds of times?

Inside the narrow kitchen, she bumped into him on her way to the sink. "Oh, sorry."

He leaned back to open the fridge and ran into her and didn't apologize. His twinkling eyes made her think he might have meant for that to happen.

This housing arrangement was already putting them in an awkward proximity with each other when she was wanting to keep her distance. She still wanted that, right?

"I can finish up here while you get ready." He nodded toward the guest room.

"Oh, sure." She was glad for his offer to do the chores, but why wasn't he telling her who needed their help? Why the secrecy? What about the stuff he said about honesty and speaking his mind? Time to test that theory. She walked to the sink, then gazing up at him— he was four inches taller than her five foot eight—she saw his eyes widen as if he were surprised to see her standing so close. "Who did you say we're going to help?"

He didn't break their gaze, but by the loud gulp he made, his swallowing seemed impaired. Stalling? Finally, he said, "Paige." He set the plate he was holding in soapy water.

She didn't expect that answer. "Why?"

He wiped his hands on a towel. His gaze met hers, as if begging her to understand. "If you could just trust me, Pais. Please come with me and you'll see why."

"Not good enough." Yesterday's meeting with Dad and Aunt Callie was difficult enough. Today she had to go back and try again. She didn't need the stress of talking with Paige too.

"You've seen Addy's destruction around town." He rocked his thumb toward the plywood spanning the living room window.

She shrugged. "Hard to miss."

"Paige's business was—"

"Business? Since when does Paige own something?" News to her. "What kind of business?"

"An art gallery."

That sort of made sense. When they were kids, while Paisley and Peter were out fighting imaginary ocean dragons, Paige was at home, sketching them.

"She put in a coffee shop last year." His shoulders rose, then dropped. "The whole thing was damaged."

"Huh."

Judah frowned, probably at her apathetic tone.

Despite being sisters, she and Paige were never close. "Was it a souvenir shop?" She had a hard time wrapping her mind around Paige being a businesswoman.

"An art consignment shop." He washed a couple of plates. "She provided a spotlight for local artists' work."

"And it's ruined?"

"Pretty much. She needs a helping hand, that's all." He grabbed a few more dishes off the counter and slid them into the soapy water.

"Maybe you can help her while I sort things out with my dad." Paisley smoothed her palms over her face. She needed a shower. Another cup of coffee. "Yesterday's attempt was a bust."

"I'm sorry to hear that." Judah wiped his hands on the dish towel again. "Here's the thing. I know things have been off between you two for a while."

"Try our whole lives." Old frustrations simmered up her breastbone. She glared at him, annoyed that he was trying to fix things in her family.

"Reaching out to her might—"

"I don't need you stirring the pot." She groaned. "Don't you have enough dysfunction in your family without messing with mine?" Time to end this conversation. "I'm going to take a shower."

"Paisley—"

She stomped out of the room, entered the bathroom and slammed the door. Staying with her ex was a bad idea.

Why did he think she'd consider working at Paige's art gallery as if a fortified wall wasn't erected between them as kids? Mom's favorite child versus the worst kid in Basalt. The two sisters were doomed from the beginning.

And since when did Paige want to own an art gallery? Mom was the painter in the family. Although she was no Picasso, anyone who stepped inside the Cedars's house could see the abstract paintings that brought fear and awe into Paisley's girlish heart. Especially when she was locked in the pantry with a ghoulish eye staring at her from a partially finished canvas.

Now, she'd have to face some of those paintings later today—if Dad allowed her inside the house.

Twelve

Judah hesitated outside Paige's gallery, toolbox in hand. Showing up to assist his sister-in-law was the right thing to do. To say he wasn't frustrated with Paisley for leaving without saying anything to him would be a lie. Maybe he had pushed her about meeting up with her sister. But he didn't see any harm in asking her to help out. Might break the ice between the siblings who hadn't spoken in years. If he were blessed with a brother or sister, he wouldn't want an iceberg of hurt feelings caught between them. An image of Dad came to mind. Well, maybe he was a tad hypocritical. He groaned.

Mercy and grace.

Apparently, Paisley felt it wasn't any of his business to meddle. But Paige was her sister, and Paisley was still his wife, which made it sort of his business. Besides, he and Paige had become friends in the last couple of years. Her building sustained serious damage during Addy. Wasn't that reason enough for him to pitch in?

He also hoped Paisley might meet her adorable niece, Piper. He didn't think she even knew about the toddler yet. Something he thought the two sisters should share in person. Now he didn't know when that might happen.

He knocked on the plywood-covered door. It budged open beneath his knuckles. "Hello! Paige? It's Judah."

"We're back here!" A feminine voice that had to be Paige's

called from somewhere in the cavernous building. "Edward and I are trying to open up a window."

Edward? Judah's footstep froze to the swollen laminate beneath his shoe. His dad was here?

"Grab some tools and join us, if you dare."

If you dare? As in, if you dare to face the work? Or, if you dare to face Mayor Grant? His good feelings about helping Paige dissolved.

His gaze fell to the aged metal toolbox he clung to that had belonged to his granddad. His father wasn't a handyman. Did he even own a hammer or a tool box? The always-well-groomed mayor getting his hands scuffed and dirty seemed like an oxymoron. What was Dad doing here? Had he anticipated Paisley might show up? Was he here to cause trouble? A knot twisted tighter in Judah's gut.

Maybe it was a good thing Paisley didn't come with him. Was Paige even aware that her sister was in town? Maybe Dad told her. Was that why he was here? To stir up problems between the two families? As if he hadn't already done enough.

Good grief, his thinking was getting paranoid. Judah should have gone with Paisley to face her dad. She probably needed his moral support. Of course, her leaving without speaking to him was a clue she didn't want him tagging along with her.

His scrambled eggs churned in his belly. If he slipped away now, would Paige be offended?

Just then, with a red bandana wrapped around her dark hair that matched Paisley's, Paige Cedars bolted through the damaged back doorway, a huge smile on her face. "Howdy, brother-in-law. Am I ever glad to see you!" She pranced into his arms and gave him a fierce brotherly hug.

Hard to un-volunteer now. "Hi, yourself." He patted her shoulder. "How's it going?"

"I was afraid you'd take off." Nodding toward the back of the building, she made a face. She guessed right. "Where's that brat sister of mine?" So she had heard. Her eyes sparkled as she gazed past him as if Paisley might be hiding somewhere in the room.

"She didn't join me. Sorry." He hated disappointing her. "Never know, she might show up later." Although, he doubted that.

Paige's sad expression let him know she doubted it, too.

"Oh, well." Her grimace transformed into a smile." "You're here. The world's a better place already."

He chuckled, feeling unworthy of such praise. Especially since he'd been contemplating hightailing it out of here, thanks to his father's presence. Still, Paige's sentiment lightened his mood. "Where's Piper?"

Paige got a proud-mama smile on her face. "She's at a play date with a neighbor."

"Sorry to miss seeing her."

"She'll be sad to miss "Unca Dzuda" too." She nudged his elbow. "Enough stalling. Let's head into the back of the gallery where the worst damage is." She waved for him to follow.

How about if he fixed the front door? Kept a building's length between him and his father? "Sure." He nodded, but his feet scuffed the floor, moving slower than a crab at low tide. He stepped over a pile of damaged boards and dawdled over them.

Paige seemed to understand and waited on the other side of the dark space.

After a minute, he followed her through the chaos that was previously a beautiful foyer and coffee bar to get to the ocean side of the structure where the work of Oregon's artists was no longer on display. As soon as he entered the empty gallery, he smelled the damaged wood. Rot? Mold? Man, he hoped not.

"Nice to see you, Son." Edward Grant's gravelly voice reached Judah before he saw the man. How long had it been since he heard his dad call him "Son"?

"Dad." Judah peered through the semi-lit room that had been boarded up for weeks.

His dad wore a tie and held a pry bar. The tool looked out of place in his smooth hands. "Glad you squeezed in time for a little civic duty." Leave it to Dad to hammer some guilt into Judah.

"I'm glad to help Paige any time I can." He nodded at his sister-in-law who must be feeling awkward in the middle of the father/son barbs. Paisley was right. His family did have its share of dysfunctional quirks. He shouldn't have pointed out hers.

"Thanks, Judah." Paige approached the partially exposed window. "Your help means a lot to me."

Dad chuckled in Judah's direction. "Too bad you didn't marry *her.*"

"Dad!"

"Mr. Grant!" Judah and Paige both spoke at the same time.

"Just teasing." Edward coughed.

Judah glanced in Paige's direction. What did she think of his father's rudeness? She probably understood the dynamics of family difficulties better than most.

"Where do you need my help?" He'd have to jump right in, or Dad's comments would fester under his skin. Dad knew that too. That's probably why he said such irritating things.

"Edward offered to help take down this window covering." She pointed toward a section of the wall where a sheet of plywood let a smidgeon of light in around it. Looked like Dad had it about half off.

Judah grabbed a hammer from his toolbox, then inserted the metal claw under the bowing wood and tugged. The window frame would need repair. The whole thing might have to be redone.

The two of them worked, prying and yanking on the board, without speaking until the plywood came down in a flurry of dust and clambered to the floor. Paige coughed from behind him. Judah covered his mouth in case any of it was moldy.

When the dust settled, Paige groaned. "Looks worse than I imagined."

The window frame was busted. The wall beneath it had caved in.

"Have you had it inspected for mold?" Judah hated to ask.

She frowned, then sighed. "The insurance company did an inspection four weeks ago after Addy."

Something smelled off when he first came in. "You might want to have someone check it again."

"Seriously?"

"He's paranoid, that's all." Edward waved both hands at Judah like he didn't value anything his son said. "A worry wart. Same as his mother."

What? He wasn't a big worrier.

"What you've got to do is get everything uncorked. Let the boards breathe." Edward guzzled water from a plastic bottle. A splash of liquid dripped down his chin and made a streak on his button-up shirt.

"I'd hate to go through mold removal." Paige paced in front of the gaping window overlooking the bay. "I'm still waiting on the insurance settlement."

"But you had good insurance, right?" Dad's voice sounded superior, which irked Judah.

"Yes, of course." She nodded. "The usual. Property, liability, flood."

"That's good." Judah attempted a reassuring smile, hoping she didn't feel thrown under the spotlight by him and Dad. "You've done everything right. I'd just have someone check for mold again, if you can swing it." He knew she didn't have much capital, but ignoring a bad situation might make it worse. "If it turns out to be nothing, that'll be a good thing."

"But expensive."

"I know a guy," Edward offered. "I'll give him a buzz."

"Really?" Paige stepped closer to Dad. "Why would you do that for me?"

Exactly what Judah wondered.

Dad dropped the empty bottle on the floor instead of asking where a trash can or recycling bin was. "What's a mayor for if not to help a fellow citizen in need?" His voice rose dramatically like he was giving a stump speech. "We have to work together in desperate times such as these."

Yada yada. Since when did Dad help citizens in low income conundrums? A political scheme? Desperate for votes? Something didn't add up.

"Thank you so much." Paige rocked her thumb toward the foyer. "I brought chocolate chip cookies, if either of you are hungry."

Judah eyed his dad. What was he up to?

"Thank you. I love chocolate chip cookies." Dad nodded once at Judah, as if to ease his mind, then tromped into the entryway.

Judah didn't follow, although he might have a better clue about his dad's motives if he eavesdropped on Dad's and Paige's conversation. Instead, he continued working on the window frame. It looked like it needed more help than he or Edward—neither of them being carpenters—could give.

He used a planer to scrape ragged edges from the ledge. "Do you have any spare lumber around?" he called toward the foyer. Maybe he could try repairing the broken section.

Paige stuck her head around the corner and rocked her thumb toward the opposite side of the room. "Salvaged wood in that pile."

"Thanks." He trudged over and picked up a couple of decent looking two-by-fours that might work.

Dad made a disgruntled sound from behind him. "You going to tell your old man what's going on?"

Judah turned, board in hand. "Going on? You tell me."

"What's your ex-wife doing back in town?" Dad squinted and bit into a cookie. Chocolate lined the creases of his lips.

Oh, that. Judah kicked his booted toes against a damp board, his miffed level rising. "She's staying at my place, so I'd appreciate it if you didn't call her my 'ex.'" Why did his father always have to push him off the cliff of frustration?

Dad gulped down his cookie. "You're kidding me, right?" He crossed his arms, and Judah figured a lecture was forthcoming. Just what he needed. "You've got to wear the pants, son. Who does Paisley think she is crashing back into town after what she did to you? What she did to all of us?"

"Dad, let it go, will you?" Judah stacked as many boards as would fit in his arms, his rough treatment of the wood inviting a few slivers.

"I won't let it go. You know how much her vandalism cost me?" Dad thundered. "What the town says about her? How can I forget that? How can anyone?"

Judah groaned. Everything came down to money, or appearances, with Edward Grant. "I don't want to talk about it." He let the pile of boards drop to the floor. The clatter echoed in the empty room. He crossed his arms, imitating his dad's stance. "If you're so determined to pry and push your nose in where it doesn't belong, we've got a problem."

Dad took a step closer, his eyes bugged, a look Judah saw numerous times growing up. "Since when is a dad asking his son a question considered prying?"

"Oh, now you're going to pull the dad card?" He didn't want to be disrespectful. He felt a tug inside to settle down. Was that the Holy Spirit cautioning him to not say something he'd regret? If only he listened.

Judah glared at his dad. Dad glared back, fire in his gaze.

Paige rushed to the midpoint between the two men, her hands outstretched. "Whoa. What's going on in here?" Did she think they were about to come to blows?

With the forgiveness Judah was working on almost forgotten, he thought that too. "Nothing." He gritted his teeth. Only one way to end such awkwardness and keep himself from yelling at his father. "Sorry. I have to go."

"But—"

He grabbed his tools. Marched through the foyer. Couldn't get out of there fast enough. "I'll be back another time, Paige."

"Okay, I understand." Her voice sounded small and distant.

That he wasn't keeping his word about helping her today throttled something deep inside him. But while the proverbial smoke billowed from his ears, he couldn't stay in the same room as Dad. He didn't trust himself. And he didn't trust his father to not say something aggravating. How dare Dad discuss Paisley as if Judah wanted her gone as much as he did? Dad knew nothing about how he coped for the last three years. Not once did the man ask how he was doing in the absence of his wife. Instead, he spread his rotten negativity about her around town.

Judah still didn't get why a man of wealth and authority in Basalt Bay would suddenly be interested in Paige's gallery. He stomped in the direction of his truck. He needed coffee and answers. Only one place where he could get both. Bert's Fish Shack usually churned with gossip. It was about time he had a chat with the diner's owner. If anyone knew some dirt on the mayor, it would be a long-time resident of Basalt Bay like him.

Thirteen

Paisley had been sitting on the irregular floorboards of Dad's front porch for over an hour with the wind blowing against her and a light rain falling. Seeing the old rocking chair where she spent countless childhood hours reading and daydreaming, the apple tree she climbed hundreds of times, and the steps she skipped up and down as a kid, made her feel nostalgic. Observing the rundown parts made her sad.

The apple tree in front of the living room window had been here for as long as she was alive, probably for as long as Dad lived here. Now, boards were propped under its bent limbs. How much longer before the whole thing fell over? The grass was overgrown and sickly looking. Weeds were knee-high. Most of the plants Mom had tended were dried up. The whole house needed a paint job. Why wasn't Dad keeping things groomed? Did he need help?

And when did the yard shrink? She remembered how she and Peter and some of the neighbor kids played Annie Over, tossing a ball over the roof of the simple two-story house. Whoever caught it would run around to the other side like a tsunami wave was chasing them and throw the ball at someone. The property didn't seem small then. A matter of perspective, she supposed. As a kid, Oregon felt ginormous, and Basalt was the center of her universe.

Dad's 1968 Volkswagen Beetle finally pulled into the driveway and came to a rattling stop. Dad didn't wave. Didn't acknowledge her. He just sat in his burnt-sienna antique for a long while. Did he wish his eldest daughter would take the hint and leave him alone?

Not this time, Dad.

Although, she wouldn't pressure him, either. Their reunion had to come naturally. Slowly, like a simmering stew that couldn't be rushed. Mom used to yell at them not to taste the stew until she added her secret ingredient, whatever that was. If only Paisley had a secret component to making everything okay between her and Dad again. Was he pondering the years when he didn't hear from her, or the misunderstandings between Mom and him and her, or his disappointment over her marrying Judah on the sly? She groaned at the list of grievances.

When the rusty '68 driver's door creaked open, an eternity seemed to pass before she saw movement inside. Dad sat there not making eye contact. Frowning. Staring forward as if ignoring her long enough would make her go away. Any childlike wish for a happy welcoming from her father crumbled for a second day in a row.

If it came down to one of them outwaiting the other, it would be him. She never won a staring contest or a stand-on-one-leg competition in her life. She was the impatient one. Her personality didn't do well at the waiting game.

Dad still didn't move.

Anxiety rushed up her middle, a brain freeze in her gut. She sat stiffly on the porch, her toes tapping the only part of her that moved.

What if something was physically wrong with him? Or he was having a heart attack?

She stood and tried to see him without staring.

Enough wondering and waiting. She marched to the parked vehicle. Three feet from the open door, she stopped. "You okay?" When he didn't answer, she covered the distance. "Dad?" She leaned down and peered at him.

His hands clutched the steering wheel as if adhered, flesh to torn leather, and he didn't meet her gaze.

"Dad?" She spoke louder.

No smile. No nod. Just a tic in his jaw. The rejection scraped her insides. Watching him in profile, seeing moisture puddling in the eyes of the man she admired for all her childhood, dug a well of pain inside her wider than the Pacific. If there was one person in the world she never wanted to disappoint, it was this man. Her hero. Her protector—until the pantry lockups. She never understood why he didn't intervene on her behalf. Now, he wouldn't look at her? Like she was poisonous. Or repulsive. Was he ashamed of her?

Knots formed in her stomach. A bitter lump in her throat nearly choked her. "C-can't you s-say something?"

Silence, then, "Why are you h-here?" His voice, and his hands on the steering wheel, shook.

"To talk with you." She dug her fists deep inside her coat pockets, chilled from the hour of sitting on the porch. A scattering of leaves hit the car and brushed her legs. "Can we go inside? Looks like a storm is coming." She glanced up at the gray clouds overhead.

"I meant, why are you back in Basalt Bay?"

"It was time to come home. I wanted to see you. And Judah." What else could she say that would bridge the chasm?

"Time." He snorted and wiped the back of his big hand across his lips. "Three and a half years ago, before you snuck off and left town, that's when it was time to come home. Before your mother died."

So that's what his cold shoulder was about? He was bitter toward her about the funeral? "I know. I-I couldn't." Nothing would compensate for such a grave transgression.

"Wouldn't, you mean." He cut her a cross look.

"True. Not then. I'm here now, Dad. We need to talk." Although, this conversation wasn't going well either.

"Too late." He crossed his arms. His chin jutted out, reminding her of Peter.

Too late. Too late. Dad's words repeated in her mind. Did he mean their relationship was over? That he wouldn't ever talk with her about the past? If so, why put herself through standing in this blustery wind, and through the humiliation of begging Dad to forgive her?

She should get in her car, turn the heater on high, and head to the cottage.

She couldn't cave so easily. A strong breeze off the ocean pressed her forward. She stiffened her knees to keep from falling against the VW. "Some coffee would be nice." Was that too much to ask? She rubbed the toe of her shoe against the threshold of the car opening.

Why didn't he get out of the vehicle? He couldn't sit here all day.

"Fine," she grumbled as a possible solution came to mind. She charged around the Volkswagen, then yanked on the passenger door handle. It didn't budge. "Come on." Had he secured the lock to keep her from getting in? "Dad, please open the door."

Silence.

Pulling again on the handle didn't help. She groaned, imagining herself kicking the door until Dad gave in and unlocked it. But a temperamental display would probably remind him of the teenager she'd been, not the woman she was. Although, standing near her father, and him not speaking to her, made her feel like that young, confused girl.

"Okay, so you don't want to talk with me!" Her voice was loud enough for their elderly neighbors, Mr. and Mrs. Anderson, to hear, but she didn't care. "Sitting in the car to avoid me is ridiculous. We're both adults. Yes, I made some terrible life decisions. I admit that." She stomped around to Dad's open door again. "Are you going to stay in the car until I get on my knees and grovel? If that's what you need me to do, I will." He barely blinked. She was out of ideas. "Will you *please* come in the house? I'm freezing. I'll even make the coffee." She tried softening her tone.

No response.

"Oh, for the love of Pete." As soon as she said the phrase, she thought of her brother Peter. Dad sniffed, wiped his nose. Perhaps his thoughts ran in the same direction.

"Every night I pray for you and Peter," he said quietly. "Every night my heart breaks for what I lost."

Tears she didn't want any part of filled her eyes. She tried ignoring the rivulets as they dripped down her cheeks. She knelt on the gravel and overgrown weeds next to Dad's car. Tentatively, taking a chance on another rejection, she laid her hand over his on the steering wheel. "I've missed you, Dad."

Tears streamed down his cheeks too. Shoulders hunched, he sobbed out loud, his body quaking. For a moment, she felt frozen as the man she'd never seen weeping before leaned his forehead over her hand on his, crying like a brokenhearted child.

She did this to him. Guilt pierced her. Was her arrival too great of a shock? Should she leave?

No, she came too far to run now. She was here to make amends where she could. She patted his shoulder. Leaned her cheek against his arm. "I'm so sorry, Dad." She didn't even know if he heard her whispered words.

Then, taking her by surprise, he leaned slightly out of the car and his arms dragged her against his chest. He held her close, her cheek pressed against his soft flannel shirt that smelled of Old Spice and him, rocking her, and they both cried. No words were spoken. None were needed. He patted her back, and she did the same to him. He kissed the top of her head as he did many times throughout her childhood. Then he released her and wiped his face with the palms of both hands.

She wiped tears from her cheeks too, chuckling over the two of them crying and sniffling. It was a healing embrace, one she was thankful for. A fresh start, she hoped. Maybe he'd take her up on that coffee now.

"You should go." He lifted his chin in the direction of the ocean.

She hadn't expected that. "Why?" Didn't they just share a loving father/daughter moment of significance? Why was he sending her away?

He shook his head and bit his lower lip like he couldn't explain.

"Can't we try to talk?" She gazed into his grayish eyes.

"Will talking erase what's happened?"

"No, but—" A lead weight landed in the pit of her stomach. "Not erase exactly."

"Then what?"

Communicating with him was so much harder than she thought it would be. "I want to help you understand why I left." Could he fathom her grief? Or forgive her wrongs? "I want you to tell me what you're feeling too."

"Your mom wanted to see you—at the end." Both of his shoes landed in the weeds. He stood shakily in increments, as if doing so hurt. Was something wrong with him?

"I'm sorry I disappointed you." She swallowed. "And her." Not that she would have done anything differently at the time. Now, with three years of regret built up? Maybe.

Dad shut the car door, then shuffled toward the house, his gait unsteady.

She scooted under his arm, offering support he didn't shrug off. They walked beside each other the way they did when she was a girl and they were on their way to the beach, or to get ice cream at Bert's, only much slower. She glanced up at the apple tree, thinking of times when he let her jump from a limb into his arms. *"I'll catch you,"* he'd said. She trusted him completely then.

When did that perfect trust in another human being cease?

Something squeezed tightly in her chest.

A picture of herself sitting on the pantry floor in the dark, wishing her daddy would rescue her, came to mind. Old thoughts better stuffed away. But if she never took a glance at her past, how could she hope to live at peace in her future?

When they got to the porch, Dad stopped leaning on her and reached for the handrailing. It wobbled beneath his grip—something else that needed mending. He hobbled up the worn steps. The old place was as broken down as Dad appeared to be. He paused at the screen door, his hand on the brown rusty knob.

She held her breath, wishing he would invite her in. She'd convinced herself she didn't want to go inside and see Mom's paintings. But in this moment, her dad inviting her to come home was the greatest hope imaginable.

"Come back tomorrow?" His question was not what she anticipated, but perhaps he was offering her a white flag.

"I will." And the next day. And the next. She'd keep returning, trying to get him to talk, telling him again how sorry she was, until he forgave her and asked her to come inside.

"Paisley?" This time he sounded more like her dad, more like the man who shared her love of the sea. For a second, she wished he'd call her *Paisley-bug*, his nickname for her when she was a kid. Too bad she ordered him to stop calling her that when she turned eleven.

"Don't expect too much from me."

Ice particles re-formed around the perimeter of her heart. Was she expecting too much? Was forgiveness and love from a father to a daughter too lavish a gift?

She blinked fast. *Don't cry. Don't cave in.* "See you t-tomorrow, Dad." She tried her best not to be emotional, but she had only so much tolerance for rejection.

The screen door clattered shut.

Just then, the gray clouds let loose with a heavy rain. Paisley ran to her Accord parked on the narrow street. When she got in and turned the key, the engine hiccupped and rattled. Strange sounds. But when the car went into gear normally, she turned on the windshield wipers and the heater, then accelerated down Front Street. Maybe she'd look for Judah and ask him to check the engine.

Despite her recent emotional turmoil with Dad, when her stomach growled, grabbing some lunch sounded appealing. Maybe some comfort food. Hot coffee with lots of creamer. If she located Judah, maybe they could go to the Fish Shack together. Talk. At least *he* hadn't rejected her. In fact, he had opened his arms and his heart to her, even though she stomped his hopes of reconciliation into the ground.

How could she keep ignoring such a kindhearted man who said he still loved her?

Fourteen

Just as Judah stepped inside Bert's diner, his cell phone chirped a sound that made his heart race. The sharp clang meant one thing— an emergency. He yanked the phone from his back pocket and pressed it to his ear. "Hello." He plugged his other ear with his finger to stifle the café's rumble of voices. "What's happened?"

"That storm we've been watching?" Mia spoke quickly. "It's moving up the coastline fast—like Addy did. Possible hurricane force winds. May strike landfall by midnight, if it continues on its current trajectory."

"Oh, man." A second storm hitting Basalt Bay—unlike any that previously hit their shores with such ferocity in fifty years?

"Craig said get to C-MER pronto." She paused. "Please hurry, Judah."

Adrenaline ignited faster than he could answer. "Ten minutes."

"Make it five." Their connection ended. Mia probably had a slew of workers to call.

Clouds had been rolling in all day, although nothing unusual about that over the ocean. If C-MER thought this storm was a real threat, would they initiate the new early warning system? As far as he knew, it hadn't been tested yet. Bad timing. But did a storm ever hit in good timing?

If the winds lashed the coast like the previous storm, combined with high tides and flooding, they'd have to evacuate everyone.

Daylight hours would be less complicated for initiating exit strategies. At night some citizens might refuse to budge from their homes, he knew this from previous experience.

Since he was already at the diner, should he give Bert a heads-up? The Fish Shack was located next to the old cannery near the end of Front Street where some of the worst damage happened last month. The business owner had been forced to close for ten days while he and a crew rebuilt an entire wall. The outer portion of the building still wasn't finished, and the dock remained upended. Bert wouldn't take news of another storm well, but Judah felt compelled to warn him.

However, he didn't want to start a panic, and he wasn't authorized to make any announcements yet. The winds might still die down or change course. Over the years, he was called into work many times, only to discover the anticipated storm veered away. Hopefully, that would be the case today.

He marched over to the register where Bert was explaining serving etiquette to a teenage boy. In a hurry, Judah rapped his knuckles on the counter. "Can I talk with you for a second?"

Bert stroked his grayish handlebar mustache and squinted. Apparently, he didn't appreciate anyone interrupting him, Judah included. However, he grunted in acquiescence.

Judah waved him toward a window facing south.

"What's up, Sonny?" Bert's thick brows quirked.

Judah rocked his thumb toward the window. "Take a gander at that."

Bert leaned over and squinted in the southerly direction where a bank of clouds was building steam over the ocean. He whistled. "Another doozy?"

"May hit landfall tonight."

Bert thumped his palm against his forehead. "I can't win. The whole weather system is out to get me." A little dramatic, but nothing Judah wouldn't expect from the man who attached a fifteen-foot salmon replica to his roof, then lost it a week later during Addy.

"It might blow over." Judah patted Bert's arm. "I thought you should know. Stay safe, my friend." He opened the door and dashed out into the rain. The exchange cost him three minutes.

"What about the alarm?" Bert yelled after him, his voice almost lost in the winds already blowing in from the ocean.

Judah stopped running, glanced back. "We'll sound the alarm if it comes to that. We don't want a panic."

"Yeah, yeah, thanks." Bert waved, then shut the door to his diner.

Judah sprinted to the parking lot, jumped in his two-door pickup, and gunned it toward the main road leading to the north side of town. As he sped past Basalt Bay Peninsula, the higher than usual sea spray catapulted over the point in explosive white bursts. Good thing Paisley wasn't sitting out there with such rough waves today. Was she at her dad's? When Judah knew more about the weather threat, that stirred up too quickly for his comfort, he'd call Paul's and make sure Paisley was safe. As soon as possible, he was going to buy her a cell phone so they could communicate with each other easier.

Almost to C-MER, he mentally checked off the tasks awaiting him. He'd probably have to go out in the skiff for a pre-storm check of the coastline. During Addy, he nearly didn't make it back to the dock. Talk about an adrenaline rush. Even so, if that's what had to be done, he was one of the most experienced boatmen at C-MER. He was prepared to do his job.

No doubt, his workplace would be a chaotic hub of employees seeking up-to-the-minute weather updates and answering frantic calls from concerned citizens. If the storm worsened, Craig would release a preliminary statement to radio stations and marine outlets. In the case of imminent danger to the town, he'd send out a wireless emergency alert. Once initial warnings were issued, if winds increased to upper hurricane levels, or dunes were found to be deteriorating, or if severe flooding caused road closures out of the city, they'd sound the evacuation sirens.

It might be a long day. And night.

Judah entered the parking lot where sand swirled across the pavement, looking almost like snow flurries. A couple of branches tumbled by. The wind was picking up.

He pulled into a parking space as several other workers exited their vehicles. Some held onto their hats and ran toward the building. Judah turned off the engine, said a prayer for wisdom and safety, secured the hood of his raincoat, then jumped out of his truck. Rain and sand pelted him. He leaned forward and braced into the wind.

Inside the C-MER building, coworkers scurried around, carrying stacks of printed pages from the copy room into their work zone at the back. Others spoke loudly into their cell phones. Shouting came from the conference room. Someone was obviously upset. Several guys hovered over blueprints, not making eye contact. He didn't see Craig.

"Judah!" Mia waved him over with both hands.

"Where's Craig? What's my assignment?"

She flipped through post-it notes on her dry-erase board. "He's in there." She jabbed her thumb in the direction of the conference room. She cringed as several voices rose. Sounded like a shouting match.

Judah nodded toward the ruckus. "What's going on?"

She shook her head as if to say, "*Don't ask.*" "You know Craig's brainchild?" She leaned closer, her voice a whisper. "That amazing state-of-the-art early warning system?"

"The answer to all our problems?" He attended enough lectures about it with Craig leading the charge.

"Right. Doesn't work."

"What?"

"Tech hasn't been able to activate the test. Mike Linfield tore in here a few minutes ago, screaming at everyone." She winced. "He's threatening pink slips."

"Not good." No doubt, Craig's job would be on the chopping block if his crew didn't get the system running, especially with the whole town counting on the alarm. "What am I supposed to do?

Normal storm routine?" Judah knew the drill, but did Craig have any other tasks for him?

Mia sorted through her notes, flinging several of the colorful squares on the floor. "Here it is." She held up a bright orange one. "Judah"—she read—"check the rock on the peninsula and the dunes south of town. Get anyone off the beach who's stupid enough to be taking pictures there."

"Right." There was always someone who wanted to capture a photograph or a video of a tempest despite signage warning them to stay off the beach during a storm. "Will do." He hustled into the locker room.

Knowing he was going into a potentially dangerous situation on the water, he wanted to be prepared. He grabbed a bomber-style float coat with an insulated hood, rain bib overalls, rubber boots, and warm gloves, then headed to the equipment checkout station. Once he located the clipboard and signed out his skiff, leaving a notation of his checkpoints, he exited through the back door.

As he strode down the ramp to the dock, the increasing winds and rain battered him. Nothing like facing strong gusts and curling waves in an open skiff to make him feel alive, and at the same time, cause his insides to quake. He'd done it before and survived. With God's help, he could do it again. The thought of Paisley made him hesitate. Hadn't he promised to put her first? Yet, he didn't even call to check on her. He groaned. No time for that now.

But always time for a short prayer. *Lord, please be with Paisley. Keep her safe at her dad's until we find out how bad this squall will be. Be with me in the bay. In Jesus's name.*

By the time he returned, Craig and his team would surely have the warning system figured out—preferably without anyone losing their job. C-MER was tasked with monitoring the coastal region and alerting towns to potential danger. If they couldn't accomplish their basic mission, they'd have a crisis. No wonder Mike Linfield was outraged.

However, despite the whitecaps bubbling around the docks, Judah felt optimistic the winds might still change direction or die down. Too early to tell. Other than the prediction that hurricane winds were on a possible trajectory of making landfall by midnight.

Please, God, stifle the storm as You've done so many times.

Before untying the sixteen-foot skiff from the dock, Judah made sure he had oars and a bailing bucket. Check, check. He patted his coat pocket; cell phone in place. He sat down in the driver's seat, turned the key to start the engine, then checked the fuel gauge. He had a moment's hesitation as he thought of his boat ride the other day when the engine stalled and he jumped into the waves. He didn't want that happening again today.

Following the no-wake rule, he steered slowly through the docking area, the skiff bobbing and dipping up and down and side to side with the waves. He brought the boat around the protective bar of rocks a C-MER crew built about a decade ago, and then slowly moved into open waters. The sea rolled in swells.

His hood flew off his head and bounced against his back. Good thing it was secured to the coat or he would have lost it. He pulled the covering onto his head and tied the knot beneath his chin. About a hundred yards out, sheets of rain fell like nails, pelting him and the boat. Winds building in velocity forced him to slow down and take the next waves carefully, or he'd be swamped. Following orders, but anticipating possible danger in the waters ahead, he pointed the bow toward the peninsula, repeating his prayer for safety.

Lord, help us all.

Fifteen

As Paisley reached the southern end of Front Street, her car coughed and rattled, nearly stalling. She gunned the gas and kept it running, but the engine's hesitancy alarmed her. She quickly pulled into a parking space next to where she thought Judah was volunteering, then turned off the motor. For a few minutes, she sat there staring at the damaged, sad-looking building on the ocean side of the street where plywood had been nailed over the front windows. So this was Paige's art gallery, huh?

Despite Paisley's reluctance to see her sister, she got out of the car, slammed the door, and dashed through the rain until she reached the alcove near the entrance. The wind billowed against her as if it were trying to stop her from taking shelter under the torn awning. A sign hanging sideways read *Paige's Art Gallery and Coffee Shop*. She brushed raindrops from her coat, then pulled on the door handle. It didn't give. Wasn't there supposed to be a work party here? She tugged on the doorknob again. Nothing. If Judah was finished helping Paige, where did he go?

She banged her knuckles against the plywood in case someone was inside.

"Why, if it isn't Paisley Cedars." The artificially sweetened voice that came from behind her had to be Lucy Carmichael's.

Paisley wanted to disappear into a crack in the sidewalk. She slowly faced the friend-turned-nemesis she antagonistically called "Red" in high school.

"When did *you* get back in town?" Lucy's acidic tone made Paisley's stomach churn.

Old feelings resurfaced like a piece of cork let loose from a sunken ship. She forced herself to breathe normally. Hard to do with her heart hammering against her ribs.

"Hello, Lucy." Paisley plastered on a fake smile that had to be as convincing as the one on Lucy's lips. "So, you still live in Basalt Bay?"

"Always have. Always will." A gust of wind blew off the redhead's knit cap. She chased it down the sidewalk, then jogged back. In a move that surprised Paisley, her old classmate scooted into the alcove beside her, too close for comfort in the confined space.

"Can you believe this weather? You hear about the storm?" Lucy's freckles were less noticeable now than in high school. Apparently, she outgrew her teenage awkwardness and, hopefully, her meanness.

Paisley remembered their last fight on graduation night—a terrible row in the middle of the street over Brian Corbin, who turned out to be unworthy of anyone fighting over him. Paisley had shouted and called Red a "freckled face warthog." Thinking of the unkind words she hadn't thought of in ten years made her cheeks heat up. A heaviness filled her chest and softened her response. "Sure, it looks like the storm is already here." She'd be a fool not to be able to read the signs after living next to the ocean for most of her life, but she didn't say so. She leaned out of the nook where she'd taken refuge, trying to get a glimpse of the sea and distract herself from her guilty thoughts over things she said to Red years ago.

"I wonder what they'll call this one." Lucy shrugged. "Betty? Beatrice?"

"I hope it won't come to that."

"Bet it will." Lucy's eyes glimmered.

Paisley had never been in a storm with strong enough winds to deserve a name. Other than the ones locals dubbed "Storm of the Century" or "Storm of '02" or "Basalt Bay's Fury."

At the end of the street, just beyond the Fish Shack, waves exploded against Bert's broken dock. It would be exciting to get close enough to see farther into the cove during such strong winds. Plus, she would jump at any excuse to get away from the woman who invaded her personal space.

"I'm heading over to City Hall." Lucy rocked her thumb toward the town's governing offices across the street. "You should find somewhere safe to wait out the storm."

Not at City Hall, that was for sure.

"Nice seeing you." Paisley said the obligatory words.

"You too." Lucy nodded toward the building behind them that used to be O'Reilly's Fine Dining when Paisley was young. "Your sister's place took a beating during Addy."

"Yeah, I can see that." Paisley maintained her aloof tone, but in truth she felt badly for Paige's loss now that she saw the extent of damage. Unfortunately, she didn't feel any empathy about it this morning. She'd have to apologize to Judah about that, too.

"You want to get some coffee and see what the mayor has to say about Bertie or Belinda?" Lucy pointed to the two-story town centerpiece.

"Nah, think I'll head down to Bert's and have a look."

"You and your daredevil ways, Paisley Cedars." Lucy scoffed.

"Grant." She corrected even though she previously imagined herself reverting to Cedars.

"Just for now, right?" Lucy's gaze pierced Paisley's. "All of us single girls know Judah Grant's about to become the hottest bachelor in Basalt Bay."

Mia, Red, and how many others waited in line to chase after Judah once he was officially free? Pain arched up Paisley's middle. But why should she feel jealous? Hadn't she relinquished him three years ago? *Yeah, but my ex-friend going after my ex-husband?* The notion riled her.

"Find shelter." Lucy leaned closer and shouted above the howling wind. "I don't want Judah risking his life out there hunting for you." She winked as if she told a joke, then she jogged into the street with the wind whipping her long red hair like a rope.

So Lucy thought she had a chance with Judah? Did they ever go out? Paisley glowered, contemplating Lucy's assessment of Judah being the "hottest bachelor in Basalt Bay." But then, heat crept up her neck. Other than the bachelor bit, she had to concede with Red's sentiment. He *was* handsome. But Lucy and him? *Come on.* Was her taunt more about revenge, since Brian Corbin took Paisley to prom all those years ago? If so, why didn't Lucy pursue the police deputy now that he was more reputable in the community?

Suddenly, rain fell like buckets of water were being poured from the clouds, but the wind seemed to have let up a little. Should she make a run for the peninsula? She imagined the waves pounding the beach, foaming and frothing over the rocks. She'd love to sit on her favorite boulder and experience nature's fury again. Did she dare?

As she stepped out of the alcove, raindrops pelted her raincoat. The sky was dark, the sun obliterated by dense, low-hanging clouds. An eerie feeling overcame her. A rise in barometric pressure, or some premonition of disaster?

Maybe they were in for a storm unlike any she'd experienced. Would it be as destructive as the one that rammed logs through Paige's building and broke the windows at the cottage? Should she heed Lucy's warning to find shelter? She could head over to Bert's and get some coffee, but the Fish Shack seemed even more in line with a storm surge from open waters. Besides, the diner looked dark. No cars in front. Had it already closed?

What if the town's emergency alarm sounded? Judah had probably been called in to work. No help there. What would she do without a reliable vehicle?

Harsh winds shoved her back into the recesses of the building's entrance. Boards above her creaked as if they might give way. Her shelter of sorts didn't feel very safe. Where should she go? Too far to hike to the cottage. Dad's? She hated the thought of him weathering the storm alone. Of course, he lived here his whole life. He'd know what to do.

Another blast of wind careened past her, whirling trash and papers. The storm seemed to be worsening before her eyes. The gallery sign crashed to the cement. Paisley screamed. Another board came loose and fell on top of the sign. Enough of this. She dashed into the rain, cinching the hood of her raincoat until she peeked out of a two-inch circle, the better for no one to recognize her. A powerful gust pressed her against the outer wall of the gallery. She clung to a piece of decorative metal, waiting for the wind surge to cease.

When a lull finally came, she lunged for the next alcove near the entrance to Nautical Sal's Souvenirs. She cupped her hands to the glass and peered inside. The lights were off. The big windows in front were boarded up. Had the owners done that today?

What about Dad? Did he board up any windows? Thinking of the neglect she saw earlier, in the overgrown yard and the house's peeling paint, she doubted he did anything to preserve the old place.

Just then, a howling siren pierced the air with one short blast. Did that mean they had to evacuate? But, wait. Only one tone? Wouldn't a real evacuation siren go on and on, or else have a rhythm of long and short blasts? Something wasn't right. Where could she find out the town's emergency plan?

City Hall.

Ugh.

At that moment, the most overstated building in Basalt was being overrun by citizens charging up the sidewalk and disappearing inside the wide doors. Did she want to join them?

Uh, no.

But if they had to evacuate, she needed to know what to do.

The wind blew her back against the wall of the souvenir shop just as a "No Parking" sign flew at her. She raised her arm to deflect the metal from hitting her face. The sign clattered to the cement, and she leaped onto the sidewalk. She had to find somewhere safer. Bracing into the wind, she faced the structure housing the city departments and a community gathering place. Someone had probably prepared coffee and snacks. She wouldn't mind a giant-sized cup of coffee and a place to get out of the rain.

Running in spurts, then holding on to signs, she made her way across the street. At the last sign—a tsunami warning—the rain fell harder than ever, rolling down her slicker onto her pants, puddling on her shoes. Two inches of rain had accumulated on the street. Too bad she didn't wear rubber boots today.

Everything within her resisted going inside the government building. She remembered the last time she saw Edward—his ugly words and his condemnation of her. But she couldn't stay outside, gripping a sign for dear life.

With her heart pounding like it might pummel through her chest wall, she dashed for the front door. She didn't know what she'd say to Judah's father, if she saw him.

But the odds of her *not* seeing Mayor Grant inside City Hall were highly unlikely.

Sixteen

Judah steered the skiff through a series of jarring waves, eyeing the turbulent seas ahead. He'd rarely seen a sky as pewter colored as this one, except at night. As in every other stormy weather event when he had to check the coastline, his thoughts turned prayerful. *God, be with me. Wherever Paisley is, be with her. Protect the citizens of Basalt Bay.*

He needed to stay focused on the emergency, but his concern over his wife's whereabouts hadn't let up. He pictured her the way he saw her on the peninsula three days ago: limp, unresponsive, and with waves crashing over her. The memory made his heart thunder in his chest. Surely, she wouldn't go back there today. Not in such terrible conditions. Yet, she was exactly the sort of person who'd want to see the effects of the storm on the ocean—he knew that much about her.

Fortunately, he was headed in the direction of the public beach. If she, or anyone else, were on the rocks there, it would be his duty to get them to move to safety.

With his hand on the throttle, ready to increase speed, his phone chirped the emergency alert that ramped up his fight-or-flight response. He snagged his phone out of his coat pocket.

"Judah, here." He adjusted the throttle, keeping the skiff moving slowly.

"Return to base now!" Mia commanded.

He bristled at her tone. "On whose orders?"

"Craig's," she snapped.

He swallowed back a curt response. "He said I was supposed to—"

"Things have changed." She sounded riled. Maybe the alert and all the franticness around the office were taking their toll on her. "The storm is becoming a monster. We just received updated satellite reports. Hurricane winds combined with up to thirty inches of rain, on top of an already high tide, are expected to lash the coast within hours. And the emergency—" Her next words were garbled.

"What was that last part?" The wind's roar and the rumble of the engine made it difficult to hear.

"The preliminary alert failed," she shouted. "A pitiful blast, then nothing. Get back here immediately." She took a breath. "If the tech team can't fix the system in the next few minutes, we'll have to go door to door alerting everyone."

You've got to be kidding me. Texting would work better than knocking on every door in Basalt Bay. Of course, some folks didn't have mobile devices, especially the elderly. "Okay. Thanks, Mia." He ended the call and made a wide one-eighty. Now he wouldn't be able to check the peninsula and make sure Paisley wasn't there. Hopefully, she was at her dad's.

As he steered the skiff back toward C-MER, he recalled his father telling him about a time when the sheriff banged on his parents' door in the middle of the night, warning of flooding conditions. Dad's family escaped to higher ground, despite Grandma not wanting to go. The way Dad told it, Grandpa scooped up his wife and carried her over his shoulder to their car, Grandma kicking at him the whole way. Judah would have enjoyed seeing such fiery passion in his family. It made him wonder what he'd do if Paisley dug in her heels about leaving.

In every storm, there were those who didn't want to leave their homes. But if a life-threatening wave approached, and folks refused to budge at C-MER's urging, law enforcement would step in.

Terrible news about the new warning system's glitch. Mayor Grant would be enraged, along with the city council and dozens of citizens who contributed financially. What a mess.

Back at the berth, Judah took extra precautions securing the skiff. As he walked toward the ramp, a blast of wind knocked him to the other side of the dock, almost to the water's edge. *Whoa.* His arms shot outward, flailing as he fought for balance. He gasped at the near miss, then regaining his footing, leaned his head down and forced his legs to move forward up the ramp. The feeling of helplessness in such strong winds made him remember how he was caught off guard in the storm a month ago. That was one freaky boat ride back to C-MER.

Maybe that's why Mia seemed upset today. She'd probably been out of her mind with worry for the guys caught in boats during Addy. He recalled her hugging him when he returned, saying she was glad he was alive. Nothing personal. It was just how she acted with all the guys, right?

Now, as he entered through the back door at his job site, Mia stood there ready to hand him a plastic sleeve with a stack of papers in it, all businesslike. "Here's your information packet. You've got midtown. Notify every house on your list about a potential evacuation." She rattled off her spiel as if she weren't nervous about the approaching storm, although her voice on the phone a few minutes ago told him otherwise. "Mark off addresses on the sheet. Tell residents to check this phone number for a recording"—she tapped the top of the first page—"or online at this website for emergency updates and shelter information." She patted his arm, her palm lingering on his forearm a tad longer than necessary. "Judah, I'm glad you don't have to be out on the ocean during this one."

"Uh, thanks. Me too." He put two steps between them.

As she walked away, he didn't watch. Had he ever? He didn't think so. Still, Paisley's question about what was going on between him and Mia bothered him. His answer of "nothing" had been true for him. It still was.

Scanning the sixty addresses Mia gave him, he recognized Paul Cedars's place about midway down the list. Good. That meant Judah would have the chance to check on him and make sure Paisley was safe.

If an evacuation happened, they could leave in his truck together. His vehicle would be more efficient in flooding conditions than Paisley's low-riding car.

He made a beeline for Craig's office. Five guys lined the small room, leaving a couple of workers standing outside, their heads bent down as if listening but avoiding eye contact. Judah joined them and watched the interaction between Mike Linfield and Craig through the open door.

"This is an outrage!" Mike's face was tomato red. "We purchased an expensive high-tech system and your knuckleheads can't figure out how to make it work?" Mike jabbed his finger at Craig's chest. "Heads will roll over this mistake!" The manager slapped his palm against the desk and leaned down, glaring around the room, person by person.

Judah gulped. He could almost see fumes blasting out of the room that wasn't much larger than his cubicle.

"Equipment malfunctions, sir, nothing more." Craig's tone sounded edgy, lacking any hint of contriteness. Might not be such a great approach, but he was probably catching all the flak for the problem. "We'll get it fixed, I promise."

"You better. Too many things have 'malfunctioned' on your watch, Masters." Mike's icy tone could have formed crystals on the window.

Judah thought of a few things that went wrong recently: his skiff engine dying, Sample D moving, the busted gazebo at Baker's Point. Not that Craig's work performance had anything to do with those foul-ups.

"Can we get back to the plan? Time is essential." Craig nodded at the circular wall clock.

"Your plan failed." Mike sneered. "If I didn't need you to fix this embarrassment today, I'd fire you on the spot."

Craig's shoulders jerked. Every person in the area probably gasped like Judah did. If Craig could get fired that easily, what about the rest of them?

"Do we have approval to knock on doors and reach out to the community? You know, *attempt* to save lives?" Craig's voice held barely controlled anger—Judah recognized it by all the times he heard him get riled at some of the other employees in the past. "Or shall we continue rehashing this debacle over failed electronics that will soon be fixed and forgotten?"

In the ensuing silence, Judah kept his gaze averted.

"Why are you morons still standing here?" Mike yelled at the cluster of workers. "Get out there and reach as many homes and businesses as you can before five."

Five? Judah checked his watch. Thirty minutes? Not possible. Even so, he scurried from the office door with the others.

"Wait!" Craig's voice bellowed.

Judah's footstep paused mid-stride.

"We don't want a panic." Craig sounded more in control, less volatile. "Use the term 'possible' evacuation. The same warning is being released by text, social media, radio, and TV. Most folks will know what to do. Our main concern is for those who don't." He sounded like an orator encouraging the troops before battle.

"Go!" Mike bellowed and pointed toward the door. "What are you waiting for?"

Judah, still wearing his raingear and boots, sprinted through the building and out to his truck, the same as his coworkers were doing. Hopefully, an evacuation wouldn't be necessary. With any luck, the high winds blasting sand and tree limbs across the parking lot would veer back to sea. If it hit Basalt Bay head-on, his hometown might never be the same again.

He had to find Paisley.

Seventeen

Paisley sneaked into the back of the cramped community room at City Hall, trying to reach the coffee table on the other side of the room without anyone noticing her. She kept her raincoat hood pulled snugly around her face. Maybe Mayor Grant wouldn't see her. *Please, please.*

Right then, Edward seemed preoccupied with questions citizens were hurling at him. Was an evacuation imminent? How would they evacuate the elderly? What about pets? Why did the emergency system blare once, then stop? What was really going on? By the sounds of their voices, the townspeople were blaming him for all problems relating to the storm. *He's more powerful than I imagined,* she thought sarcastically.

The mayor kept repeating his mantra that Basalt Bay's Coastal Management and Emergency Responders were doing their best. He admonished everyone to have patience with the process. "We'll get through this storm in fine shape as we have all the others."

Paisley rolled her eyes.

Several residents groaned like they weren't pleased with his contrived answer, either.

She stole a peek at her father-in-law. He looked grayer than he had three years ago when he yelled at her and told her she wasn't worthy of his son. Considering what he said to her, his caring tone now sounded like hogwash. Under the best of circumstances, he wasn't a thoughtful person. Why should she expect him to be one now?

"That you, Paisley?" Lucy leaned near her face.

Not again.

"Twice in the same day. I can hardly contain my happiness." The redhead spoke in a monotone that exaggerated her displeasure in running into Paisley again.

"Yeah, me too." Paisley was sipping bland coffee from a Styrofoam cup, mostly staring at the floor. How did Lucy spot her so easily?

"Guess you'll be glad *he*"—Lucy jerked her head toward Mayor Grant—"won't be your father-in-law much longer." She had the audacity to grin. "What a pain in the neck, huh?"

Paisley ignored the comment. She wouldn't give the woman who claimed to be in line for Judah's affections any ammo.

"How will we know if we have to leave town?" Someone in the front asked.

Edward ran his right hand through his wavy hair. "We're waiting to hear from C-MER. Hopefully, a full evacuation won't become necessary."

"Why wait? It's obvious their system isn't working," Lucy called out.

Paisley wished she weren't standing by the outspoken woman. What if Mayor Grant glanced this way? She kept her gaze lowered, still sipping the bad tasting coffee.

A rumble of voices erupted.

"People, we haven't received any official word that the system isn't working." The mayor's voice got louder.

"Judah Grant said the town is on high alert." When did Lucy speak with him? "He said everyone should be prepared to evacuate."

Paisley glanced up. At the mention of his son's name, Edward flinched.

The voices of worried homeowners broke out again.

"The second I hear from C-MER, I promise I'll let you know!" Edward shouted, his hands cupped around his mouth. "For now, go home and treat this like any other storm until you hear differently from me or someone in an official capacity." He turned on his heels and stomped down the hallway, probably to call Mike Linfield or Craig Masters.

Paisley cringed at the thought of Craig coming down here. That man wasn't trustworthy. A scum. The unfortunate way she discovered his true personality was another secret stacked against her. Had Craig ever hinted to Judah about what he tried to do? Did Edward tell his son what he observed the night she left? She'd rather Judah didn't hear about that from either of those two losers.

She inhaled deeply, but the air seemed void of oxygen. She coughed. Felt her heart palpitate. She shouldn't have been thinking about Craig. Or Edward. She gulped down another swallow of coffee. Her face turned hot, her neck itchy. She needed more air. She bent over, one hand on her chest, hoping no one saw her distress.

"What's wrong with you?" Lucy leaned down next to her. "You okay? Need a doctor?"

Paisley shook her head, biting back another cough. "I-I'm fine."

"You don't look so good." Lucy peered at her as if seeing through her facade.

Paisley stepped back, uncomfortable with the woman's scrutiny. "I think I'll head out." Outdoors she could get fresh air and move farther from emotional triggers. Maybe then, she could stop contemplating the things she had to tell Judah but didn't want to. Yet if she didn't explain, how would she ever be free of this internal chokehold?

Almost through the crowd and nearing the front doors, she was overcome by dry coughing and the feeling of intense pressure on her chest. *Please don't let me pass out.*

"You okay, dear?" An older woman patted her shoulder, surprising Paisley with her grandmotherly tone. "Heavy atmosphere makes me cough too."

Paisley faced the white-haired woman she didn't recognize— strange, since she knew most everyone in the small town—staring at her with navy-hued eyes.

"I have peppermint oil in my bag. I carry it all the time. Might help you breathe better. Would you like some?" The lady who was dressed in purple outerwear smiled, her face dissolving into a million beautiful lines. It had been ages since anyone, other than Judah, treated Paisley with such kindness. Was she an angel in disguise?

"Okay, thank you." Paisley had used essential oils before. Sometimes they helped. Right now, she'd try anything to not have an attack at City Hall. All she needed was for Edward to see her at her weakest.

"I'm Kathleen Baker, by the way." The white-haired woman dug around in her bag that resembled a beach tote more than a purse. Several items clinked like the kitchen sink might actually be in there. Her hand stilled, then she thrust her clenched fist toward Paisley. "Here you go, dear."

Paisley had always hated it when people in Basalt called her "dear"—like it was a judgmental term. Something about the gentle way Kathleen said the word removed any sting. She opened her palm and a small dark brown bottle lay on its side. She grabbed the jar, untwisted the top, and breathed deeply of the strong scent. Coughed.

"Try again." Kathleen patted Paisley's arm.

She sniffed the peppermint aroma, then coughed again, but her airways felt clearer. She secured the bottle and handed it back to Kathleen. "Thank you so much."

"Keep it." The older woman closed Paisley's hand around the jar. "You need it more than I do."

Normally, she would argue that she was independent and didn't need anyone's help. This time, she slid the jar into her raincoat pocket. "Thanks."

Kathleen moved through the crowd toward the front of the room. Paisley continued toward the exit, a difficult task now that the room's capacity was maxed out.

Just then, Mia Till shoved through the doorway, almost colliding with Paisley. Her eyes were wide, her face wet. She smoothed her hand across her mascara-smeared cheeks and stared at Paisley before barging into the middle of the group, shouting, "Hold up, everyone! I have news."

Shushing sounds spread across the room.

Someone must have notified Mayor Grant. He bolted out of his office and pushed through the sardine-packed room toward Mia. "You have an update for us, Miss Till?"

Apparently, in this tension-filled room, Mia was the official C-MER rep. Why was she here instead of Judah or Craig? Although, Paisley was extremely thankful not to see Craig. Being in the same room with Edward created enough tension.

"Are we evacuating?" Mr. Carnegie, postmaster and local historian, blurted the question that had to be on the forefront of everyone's thoughts.

"Not yet." Mia waved and giggled at someone across the room.

Paisley groaned at the worker's flirtatious ways even in the face of a crisis.

"When will we know?" someone in the back asked. Other questions followed. "Why did the siren sound for ten seconds then stop?" "Is the storm worsening?" "Isn't it safer to leave now than to wait until the last minute?" "What about sandbags?" "Why isn't C-MER answering their phone?"

"Citizens of Basalt Bay!" Mayor Grant shouted above the clatter. He raised his hands. "Please, listen to what Miss Till has to say."

"Thank you, Mayor Grant." Mia gave the man a wide smile before she ran her fingers through her rain-soaked blond tresses. How could she look such a mess, yet still resemble a magazine model? "As you can see, the storm has worsened. The latest news from the C-MER weather station is that wind gusts may *possibly* reach seventy-five miles per hour or more tonight."

Huffs. Groans. A few people pushed toward the door.

"The same as last time!" The feminine voice was Maggie Thomas's.

Paisley put her hand over the opening of her hood to keep the woman from spotting her.

"Yes, it appears to be rushing up the coastline much like Addy." Mia palmed the air as if to quiet everyone down.

A couple near Paisley argued over whether they should leave town immediately.

"Why don't we evacuate now for safety?" Pastor Sagle waved his hand. "We know what happened last month."

"Because the winds may still shift directions like previous storms." Mia smiled confidently, like she was the voice of authority.

"We know what happened all right. The road washed out. Folks were stuck." Mrs. Thomas's voice carried blame. "Wasn't it *your* responsibility to get the roads fixed before another storm, Mayor Grant? That's the reason folks voted for you—so you'd work for them." Her chin rose. "Not me. I never voted for you."

Gasps. A round of applause.

"We didn't expect another storm to hit so soon." Edward cleared his throat. "I'm doing my best, Maggie."

"Your best?" Mrs. Thomas cackled. She rocked her thumb toward the windows. "You got your new windows in. What about our roads?"

"Yeah." "That's right." A clattering of voices. "What about the roads you promised?" "We need a new mayor." The attitude of the crowd became agitated. Angry glints filled the eyes of some closest to Paisley. Three burly fishermen she recognized as the Keifer brothers moved forward, fists clenched, as if to do Edward harm.

Paisley felt emboldened by their action. Not that she wished her father-in-law ill. But she wouldn't mind if some tough weathered-looking guys with snarls on their faces took him to task.

"South Road is still passable." Edward tightened his tie as if that made him look taller or braver. The opposite effect happened.

"Single lane," Mr. Carnegie called out. "It's been difficult for mail delivery all month."

"Maybe that's why the Mayor hasn't called for an evacuation." Maggie shouted. "Because we can't all make it out of town alive."

A thunder of voices blasted off the walls. Some people shoved their way toward the door. Others yelled threats. The three fishermen moved forward like a gang out to claim their turf.

"Wait, you guys!" Mia climbed on top of a receptionist's desk and stomped on the wooden surface with her now soaking wet *So Kates*. Didn't the woman own boots? "Listen to me!"

Some townspeople stopped pressing toward the door, but they didn't give up their floor space.

Mia clapped her hands. "Waiting is hard, but right now, it's just a storm out there like we've experienced time and time again. It's coming in at about forty miles per hour with only the *possibility* of increased speeds and only a chance of it hitting landfall."

"Does it have a name yet?" Lucy's voice.

Mia frowned like she didn't want to answer. Then, "A short time ago, when it reached thirty-nine miles per hour, we started calling it Storm Blaine." She shrugged. "Our team is going door to door giving preliminary warnings. But I repeat, the wind may change directions or die down entirely. You all know that is true."

A mumble of agreement crossed the room.

"And if it doesn't?" Mrs. Thomas's demanding voice rose above other grumblings. "Stay home and twiddle our thumbs until 'Storm Blaine' is too horrific to escape? No, thank you!" She pushed through the crowd, making her own aisleway. "I'm getting out of town."

The mob pressed toward the door in a frenzy of shoving and yelling. It appeared there would be a race for the single-lane South Road exit from the city after all.

"We don't want a panic." Mia stomped her foot. "Please, come back!"

Too late.

Kathleen clasped Paisley's hand. "Why isn't the town alarm working, dear?"

"Good question." She patted the woman's hand, hoping to return some of the comfort Kathleen offered her earlier.

"What about the public warning system?" Paisley yelled toward Mia. "When will it sound?"

The C-MER receptionist glared at Paisley and shook her head as if telling her to be quiet.

What? This gathering didn't deserve the truth? That Mia might be following protocol but not giving them vital information was unacceptable. Lives were at stake. The residents of Basalt Bay trusted C-MER to be the eyes and ears in the weather world. Paisley let go of Kathleen's hand and pushed through the cluster of people. Regardless of her aversion to Mayor Grant, she undid the tie on her hood, exposing her face.

"What aren't you telling us, Mia?" She moved to stand next to the receptionist as Mia descended the desk with Mayor Grant's assistance.

"You." Edward's eyes were as wide as snowballs.

"Yes, it's me." Filled with semi-false bravado, she turned from her father-in-law and addressed Mia again. "What gives? We have the right to know the truth."

"That's right," Kathleen agreed from beside her.

"Yeah, tell us what's going on." Brad Kiefer, one of the fishermen Paisley recognized as a classmate of Peter's from high school, stood on her other side.

Standing between the two of them, she felt momentarily protected.

"Everyone should go home and stay safe for the duration of the storm. We'll be fine as rain come morning." Mia's tight smile said she wasn't saying anything else. She rushed toward the exit as if to escape Paisley's questioning.

"I don't think that saying works in this squall." Paisley followed her. "Look, if C-MER even suspects an evacuation, tell me now. I have to get my father out of town."

"Like I said, you'll have plenty of warning." Mia sashayed into the crowd.

Mayor Grant blocked Paisley's exit. "I'm sorry to see you back in town." His eyes glinted.

"Yeah, me too." She tried sidestepping him.

"Stay away from my son." He hissed in her ear.

She wouldn't give him the satisfaction of knowing he irritated her. "Well, Edward, that's hard to do since I'm staying in his house."

He didn't react or look surprised. Had Judah already told him?

She resumed her stride, putting distance between her and her father-in-law, as she joined the group fleeing City Hall.

Outside, the rain and winds hadn't let up. Would Storm Blaine become Hurricane Blaine tonight? A garbage bag and a lawn ornament blasted across the street in front of her. Walking even two feet in a straight line was difficult. She wouldn't make it to Dad's on foot. She'd have to drive her car.

As she leaned into the wind, her thoughts turned to Judah. Where was he? Hopefully not in his skiff in this wretched weather.

Eighteen

Judah thought he heard a low rumble of thunder as he stomped through several inches of standing water on the street near Paul Cedars's house. That the storm hadn't veered away from land yet worried him. The possibility of another high-powered wind strike kept him sloshing through water to the next house and the next. He'd already knocked on thirty doors, and he was only halfway down his list.

What if the townspeople couldn't evacuate fast enough once an official alert came—if one came? He felt the weight of that possibility as he issued his preliminary warnings. He learned from Addy that Pacific storms moved a bit differently than the simulations they practiced and planned for in their C-MER training. They had to be ready for anything.

Most people were home and acted appreciative that he stopped by with the emergency information. Some had boarded up their windows—something he wished he had time to do to his cottage. Others were packing up their cars, just in case. A few told him a family member was at the public beach stacking sandbags for a levee. He knew the team from C-MER assigned to that task would be grateful for the help.

Preparing for the possibility of a severe storm in an area recently hit by one was difficult. At least, Judah and others from C-MER were doing their due diligence. Everyone's safety was foremost in their minds.

When he strode up the soggy path to Paul's, and Paisley's car wasn't in the driveway, he groaned. She didn't go to their beach house, did she? With its sea-level flood position, that was one of the worst places to be during a high-water storm. The most dangerous of all would be the peninsula. She wouldn't go out there. Of course, she wouldn't. Still, his chest constricted. If Paul said she went to the cove, Judah wouldn't have a choice. He'd do anything to keep her safe. But what about his commitment to helping all the others in Basalt Bay? He would be facing a moral dilemma, but wasn't his first responsibility to his wife?

He reached the Cedars's porch and rapped firmly on the door. "Coastal Management and Emergency Responders!" He beat on the door again.

So far, his flotation coat kept him mostly protected from the elements. However, the rain and wind pummeled his face and hands. Water had been trickling down his neckline, soaking his shirt, and causing discomfort. But, no matter how wet and cold he was, he wouldn't stop until he got through his list—unless he heard that Paisley was at the peninsula.

The door opened slowly. Paul Cedars's eyes widened. "Judah."

"Hello, Paul." He didn't have time for chitchat or to feel nervous in front of the father-in-law he hadn't seen much of in the last three years. "Is Paisley here?"

"Not since earlier." Paul pushed his black-rimmed glasses up the bridge of his nose and peered at Judah. "Everything all right?"

"Do you know where she is?"

Paul shrugged. "Probably where she spent most of her life."

A shudder coursed through Judah. "You mean at the beach?"

Paul nodded and closed the screen, probably to keep the wind out, not to stop Judah from entering.

Despite his apprehension for his wife's safety, he issued the warning he came here to give. "Hurricane winds may possibly hit tonight. And the new warning system isn't running yet." He pulled on the screen handle and passed Paul a damp copy of the printout he'd been distributing over the last hour and a half. Even though the papers were in a protective sleeve, each time he opened it, a little rainwater got inside. "Read this. Check the website or call this number for updates. That way you'll know if you have to evacuate and where to—"

"I'm not leaving." Paul lifted his chin as if anticipating an argument.

"That's not wise, sir. If only you'd—"

"My choice. Nothing you can do about that."

Judah could see where Paisley got her stubbornness.

"Your house isn't beachside, sir, but it sits low. Please reconsider, for Paisley's safety, if not your own." Judah edged toward the steps. He'd used up his time allotment for this property. He had to move on.

"Like I said, she isn't here." Paul shut the door.

"Yeah, but she'll head here as soon as she hears you aren't leaving!" Judah shouted toward the closed door, not knowing whether Paul heard him. Paisley's dad probably wasn't thinking clearly. Ever since his wife died and Paisley left, he didn't act like the man Judah knew him to be in the early days of his acquaintance with the Cedars family.

Judah said a prayer for him, then stomped toward the Andersons next door. His urgency to get through the row of addresses, and find his wife, made him press on, despite the wind and pouring rain. Was Paisley at the beach? If they had to evacuate, would she go with him? Even if her dad refused?

After he checked off twenty more homes from his list, his phone buzzed. His hands were so cold he could hardly move them. However, he answered, thinking it might be Paisley.

"Hello." He swept rainwater off his face.

"How many houses left?" Craig's voice.

"Nine."

"Hurry up and finish." His supervisor spoke tersely.

"I'm trying. Conditions are bad."

"Same as everywhere. Other team members are wrapping up. So should you." Now that Craig's job was on the line, he seemed more uptight than ever.

Judah kept walking. "What's the verdict on the storm?" He charged up another set of stairs to a porch without a light.

"Category 1, if it hits at all." Craig spoke quickly. "We've seen this pattern before. It will probably head out to sea."

Too much guesswork in his assessment for Judah's peace of mind. He rapped on the door knocker. A child opened the door a couple of inches. "Get your mom or dad, please." The kid trotted away, and Judah returned his attention to the call. "Get that warning system running, will you?"

"That's the plan." Craig spit out a word Judah chose not to decipher. "Or else I'll lose my job."

Judah figured.

"You too." Click.

What? Why would he lose his job?

An older man, maybe the child's grandfather, came to the door, stopping Judah from further pondering. He went through his memorized warning, explaining the possible severity of the approaching storm and what to do in case of evacuation.

No one answered at six of the remaining houses. At each of those, Judah curled up the printout and stuck it inside the screen door.

When the last of his assignment was done, he sighed in relief. By then, the rain was blowing sideways. Maybe he should sprint down to the beach and see for himself if Paisley was there. But what if they had to evacuate suddenly? They'd need his four-wheel-drive truck in a washout.

Powerful gusts shoved him as he trudged in the direction of where he left his pickup on the other side of midtown. Had anyone informed Mom about the possible evacuation? With all of Dad's responsibilities concerning the town, had he even thought to update his wife?

Judah kept splashing through the water en route to his truck, but he pulled out his cell phone. He searched the contact list and tapped "Mom."

As soon as she answered, he spoke, "Hey, Mom, you probably know this, but the storm is worsening. Possible evacuation. I wanted to make sure you knew."

"Thank you, Son."

At her endearment, a knot formed in his chest. He felt badly about ignoring her because of his frustrations with his father. Although, it was hard not to do when Mom and Dad lived in the same house.

"What will you do?" she asked.

"If we evacuate, I'll head to a shelter. You?" He spoke as he trudged down the street, slightly out of breath.

"Oh, you know, we live on the hill. Our fortress."

Did that mean she was staying put? "Alone, you mean?"

"Dad will get here when he can." She sighed like it was an old argument she didn't want to discuss.

"Mom—" Maybe he should drive up and get her. She could ride in the truck with him and Paisley. Of course, she had her own four-wheel-drive vehicle for getting up to their cliff-side home.

"I know it's your job to tell everyone to leave"—she chuckled—"but I'll be fine."

"Why don't you drive down and stay at the shelter with me and Paisley?" What would she say about his wife being back in town?

"Oh, Judah. She's back?"

So she didn't know?

"Yeah, she's staying with me."

"That's wonderful news."

"I think so too." Unfortunately, he didn't have time for visiting. "I gotta go. I just knocked on sixty doors, alerting people about the storm."

"My son, the hero." Sounded like she smiled.

"Just doing my job." He coughed.

"A good one, too. Love you, Son."

Her words warmed a chilled part of his heart. "You too, Mom." He ended the call, and his truck came into view. As soon as he got inside, he made his numb fingers start the engine and crank up the heater. He undid his hood and slid it off so he could see better.

His phone buzzed. His hands shook, and he fumbled the phone, almost dropping it.

"Yeah?"

"Mom again." He heard her swallow as if tugging back emotion. "If you . . . and Paisley . . . want to come up higher, you're welcome here, okay?"

He didn't know what to say.

"The view of the ocean is fantastic."

He wouldn't mind waiting out the storm with Mom. But Dad? How would he respond to Paisley's presence? Judah couldn't put his wife through that kind of ordeal, especially since she'd probably feel uncomfortable around his dad. So would he, for that matter. "Thanks, Mom. Nice of you to offer."

"I know you're busy, but I wanted to invite you."

"Okay. Talk to you later." He clicked off, then sighed. Mom meant well. She'd do everything she could to make Paisley feel welcome. But no one, and he meant no one, could stop Edward Grant's verbal attacks once he got started.

Judah drove toward the beach, the truck tires rolling over downed tree limbs and debris on the street. At the beach parking lot, with blowing rain and the wind churning an already high tide, water poured across the pavement. He was surprised to see just how much seawater and rain had accumulated. After the wave receded, he maneuvered the truck through what looked to be about six inches of standing water, maybe more. He stopped at the northwest corner of the lot where he had a clearer view of the peninsula and the beach below.

So far, the sandbag levee the crew built was standing, although it looked kind of narrow for enduring strong waves. Had they rushed the job? He hoped it could hold through the night. At least, no one appeared to be on the beach. That was a relief.

He turned around and drove slowly out of the parking lot. Then he took a pass through downtown, searching for any sign of Paisley's car.

A few people rushed out of City Hall. Of course, citizens would gather there to question his father. Craig probably sent someone to issue current weather updates.

He saw a lady in a mini-skirt—hard not to notice someone dressed up like that in a torrential storm—rushing down the sidewalk. At least she wore a rain jacket, although it looked too short to do much good. Wait. Mia? Craig sent Mia to City Hall to represent C-MER? What was he thinking?

Judah pulled over to the curb and lowered the window. "Mia!" he shouted to his coworker. "Need a ride?"

She scurried toward him in spiked heels. Her feet had to be soaked. "Oh, Judah, you're a lifesaver." Giggling, she climbed into his truck. "Thanks so much. I parked up the street, that way." She pointed toward the west side of town. "Cars were parked all along Front when I arrived."

"Why were so many people here?"

As soon as she buckled her seatbelt, he drove in the direction she pointed.

"Oh, you know, worried locals demanding answers." She thumbed her chest. "Good thing I showed up. Your dad appreciated my knowledge too." She laughed like it was a pay raise.

"Hmm." He didn't appreciate the familiar way she talked about his dad, as if she were on close terms with him. Judah clenched his jaw. Maybe Mia just acted flirty with every man in town. He remembered Paisley commenting in the past about Mia's male-crazed behavior. Not that his wife had ever had anything to worry about in that corner.

"I also stopped by Hardy's Gill and Grill to let people know." She shivered, then giggled.

Inwardly, he groaned. Had she been drinking on the job? "You okay to drive?"

She laughed again. "You're sweet, Judah. I only had coffee."

"Okay." He pulled in next to Mia's red sports car, hoping she was telling him the truth. "Be safe out there."

"You too." She laid her palm over his hand on the steering wheel. He pulled back. She grinned like she didn't notice his cool response. "If you need a place to stay, you know, a safe distance from the water, you can join me. My apartment is on the second floor."

"That right?" Was she just being friendly or offering something more than a safe place?

"We could watch old movies—or something." She winked.

She *was* being flirtatious.

"You should go." He nodded toward the door. He didn't want to be rude, but he didn't want her thinking he was fishing for a romantic interlude.

"I'm serious about a place if you—"

"Thanks, but I'm looking for Paisley. She'd be welcome to join all the people you're providing shelter for, right?" *Good thinking, Grant.*

Mia's mouth closed and opened a few times. "Oh, uh, sure. Why not?"

If the rain wasn't thrashing his truck's roof, he'd laugh at how fast she climbed out. At the last second, she glanced back. "She was there."

"Where?" His heart skipped a beat.

"City Hall."

"Paisley was at City Hall . . . with my father?"

Mia nodded and leaned forward into the truck.

"Did she say anything?" If his dad was impolite—

"She said she needed to get her father out of town. Maybe she left with him." Mia rocked her eyebrows. "Nothing for you to worry about then, huh?"

Even if he didn't plan on doing everything a husband could do to regain his wife's love, he wouldn't take Mia up on her suggestion. Not only was she not his type, he still had strong feelings for Paisley. One second with her in his arms three days ago proved that.

He put the engine in gear. "Thanks, Mia."

Wearing her pouty expression, she slammed the door. Then she wobbled in her heels to her car with gusty wind blowing against her. Once he was sure she made it into her vehicle, he pulled into the street and plowed through the water flowing across the pavement.

There was an eeriness about the steely gray, almost black sky. The silence following the next blast of wind made the hair on his neck stand on end. He heard about pre-wave conditions when the air went graveyard-still just before the worst slammed into a town. Were they almost to that point?

He hoped not. A severe storm with hurricane winds might undercut the fragile sand structure that had been deteriorating around Basalt Bay since Addy. Like Sample D sliding on the peninsula. If that kind of a squall happened tonight, what buildings would suffer damage? What flooded roads would become impassable?

He had difficulty seeing through the downpour, the condensation on the windows, and the rapidly moving windshield wipers. Leaning forward, he gnawed on his lower lip and stared straight ahead. A stress headache pounded between his temples, but he ignored it. He had to find Paisley.

Maybe he should drive back to Paul's and check again. His father-in-law said he wouldn't leave. Paisley might be there by now.

Judah's truck splattered a wave of water over the sidewalk as he zoomed west on Front Street. He came to a fast stop in front of the Cedars's paint-chipped house. Stepping out of the truck, he faced away from the onslaught of rain. No cars were in the driveway. So his wife wasn't here. What about Paul? Had he changed his mind about leaving? None of the windows on the house were boarded up.

Judah tromped over the wet walkway and up the porch steps. He pounded three times on the wooden door, even though he doubted anyone was home. No sounds came from inside. He rapped three more times, just in case.

Before he got back to his truck, the warning system blasted a wail loud and long enough to hurt his eardrums. His boots froze midstream. Another siren sounded three short blasts, then that hair-raising long one again. The muscles in his gut clenched.

Basalt Bay was officially under evacuation.

Nineteen

Before Paisley went to check on Dad, she wanted to drive by the peninsula, just for a minute, so she could store the memory of waves bursting over the point in her mind forever. What if a tidal surge destroyed the coastline and it was never the same again?

At the public beach, seawater rushed across the parking lot—something she'd never seen before. Slowly, she drove through standing water to reach the far side of the lot, then parked as close as she could get to the peninsula. She didn't turn off the engine or her headlights.

On the beach, a long pile of sandbags resembled a short castle wall. White water burst over the entire peninsula in great spurts and explosions. The water receded. Then bam! A wave tumbled over the beach, crashing into the pile of sandbags, and cresting onto the parking lot. Her car jerked and swayed with the water's rush. *Whoa.* Staying here might be too dangerous. She put the car in gear. Time to go to Dad's and get out of this storm.

The engine hiccupped and sputtered. Then died.

"No, no, no." She turned the key and pumped the gas pedal several times. "Come on." When nothing happened, she tried again. Same result. She groaned. Did the car stall because a belt or something got wet? Driving through the water on the pavement was probably a bad idea.

She pulled on the hood lever, hating the thought of stepping into the swirling water that looked about six or seven inches high, strong enough to knock a person over. But she couldn't sit here and do nothing. No one knew where she was. She didn't have a phone to call anyone to come get her.

As soon as she got out of the car, water rushed forcefully against her ankles, chilling her, and nearly knocking her over. To keep herself upright, she ran her hands along the side of the slippery, wet vehicle—not much help, but some—as she waded toward the hood with harsh winds slamming against her.

Something banged into her thigh, and she gritted her teeth. When she glanced down, a beach chair was wedged between her and the car. She shoved it away, and it half floated, half flew, across the parking lot, then was gobbled up by waves. An image flashed through her mind of her being stuck in the Accord and it being swept out to sea just like that chair.

A shudder raced through her.

She was foolish to have come here in such extreme conditions—her impetuous nature was getting her into trouble again. Her desire to see the peninsula didn't seem important now.

Fighting the next blast of wind, she lifted the hood of her car and secured it so she could check inside the engine. She could barely see anything through the darkness. Still, she felt around but didn't find any loose wires. It had gas. Electrical failure? Maybe.

So much for using this car to escape if they were forced to evacuate. She slammed the hood, then made her way back to the door, wading through cold water. When she grabbed hold of the handle, she froze. She didn't want to get inside—not if there was any chance her car might be dragged into the sea with her in it. What should she do?

Out on the peninsula, white water burst against the boulders, then sea spray shot high into the air so beautifully, almost majestically, in its display of power and fury. A breath caught in her throat as she watched. But then, waves crashed up onto the parking lot, ramming against her, nearly taking her down as she clutched the door. She felt trapped, like she was in the middle of a disaster movie, or in a nightmare, and she fought the impulse to scream.

As soon as the wave abated, she ran, splashing through the water on the pavement. The wind buffeted her back, shoving her upper body forward. She almost tripped, caught herself, then kept sloshing toward town. Could she make it the few blocks to Dad's?

Just as she reached Front Street, the public warning system blasted a loud spine-tingling alarm. So they were going to evacuate, after all?

What about Dad? Would he leave his home? If so, maybe she could catch a ride with him. Help him somehow. This could be her chance to make amends. She walked faster.

A truck zipped past, splashing a four-foot wave of water, drenching her. "Hey!" She yelped and wiped wetness off her face. She groaned but kept sludging through the water.

If Dad decided to weather the storm, she'd stay with him. The old house where she grew up wasn't much higher than sea level, but it had a second story. Was it strong enough to withstand a massive wave? She thought of how Paige's business looked battered and broken. How the upended dock at Bert's Fish Shack must have been rammed with a gigantic wave. Was that what would happen to her childhood home tonight? To her hometown? Anxiety rippled through her.

A vehicle stopped beside her, splashing her with more water. She groaned and turned to yell at whoever it was. When she saw Reverend Sagle peering out the window at her, her anger melted.

"Need a lift, Paisley?" His voice sounded kind.

His SUV was already loaded down with household belongings. Where did he expect her to sit?

"That's okay. Thanks for asking." She kept walking, fighting the wind blowing against her.

The pastor drove his vehicle alongside her. "Aren't you leaving town?" His wrinkled face showed concern.

"Maybe." The wind knocked her against a lamp post. She held on for a moment, glad for something stationary. She remembered the day she and Judah asked Pastor Sagle to marry them on the sly. He refused and said he wouldn't perform a wedding without their parents knowing, even though they were both of age. She held a grudge about that ever since.

"Where's your car?"

"Stalled at the beach. I'm on my way to Dad's."

"He's not home." The older man shook his head.

"How do you know?" She wiped more moisture off her face and stared at him.

"I saw him at your sister's." He waved his hand in a westerly direction. "They were loading up her car."

Dad was leaving town with Paige? Disappointment hit her. She wanted to be the one to help him, for him to need her during this storm. However, his escaping with his youngest daughter was probably a good thing. At least, he was safe. They were safe.

Where did that leave Paisley? Would the second floor of Dad's house be high enough and hold together while she waited out the storm—alone? It had an attic, although small and terrifying.

"Let me drive you somewhere. You need to get out of the rain before you catch your death of cold." The pastor smiled in a grand-fatherly way. "Where's Judah?"

"I'm not sure." She took a shallow breath. "Okay, um, would you take me to my dad's?"

"Sure. Sure." He shoved some stuff off the front passenger seat. "Get in."

Paisley rounded the SUV and opened the passenger door, thankful for the pastor's offer. Maybe he hadn't meant any harm in not hearing their wedding vows. Besides, that was seven years ago. Water under the bridge, and all that.

The items he removed from the seat were on the floor now.

"Sorry. Not much room for your feet."

"That's o-okay." Her teeth chattered as she sat down and shuffled her soaked tennies in the limited space. She extended her hands to the warmth blowing from the heater. "I appreciate the ride. Thank you."

"Of course."

The siren sounded again, a weird, horrific wail, reminding her of a dying animal. Three short blasts reached them as Pastor Sagle drove down the watery street, his car creating a wave of its own.

"I could drive you east, if you don't mind close quarters." He nodded toward the backseat piled with stuff. A gust of wind blasted against the vehicle, shoving it slightly sideways. "Whoa." He gripped the steering wheel. "It's getting worse."

She didn't want to consider how bad the storm might get when the idea of staying at Dad's by herself had her rattled. "Why didn't you leave town earlier?"

He clicked the windshield wipers to a higher speed. "I had to make sure some elderly folks were safely on the bus or heading out of town with family."

So he was a considerate, helpful guy, after all. Like Judah. She sighed.

"I hate to think what will happen if the winds increase." Pastor Sagle shook his head.

Her thoughts exactly.

The swish-swish of the blades kept time with her heartbeat. Would she be stuck in this dreadful storm with everyone gone from Basalt but her? Panic as intense as the wind outside clambered through her veins. She pictured herself huddled upstairs in the old house, maybe hiding under her bed. No way would she climb into the attic. She went up there to look for Christmas ornaments, years ago, and felt suffocated in the tiny space.

They rode the rest of the way without speaking. The loaded vehicle came to a stop on the deserted street in front of Dad's. It was weird not seeing a single parked car in the neighborhood. She glanced up at the dark two-story house and wondered how the frail-looking building would manage in hurricane winds. It had weathered decades of storms, hopefully it was tougher than it appeared.

"Thank you for the ride." She nodded at the pastor but didn't attempt to open the door. A minute longer and the wind might settle down enough for her to run to the porch. A cardboard box bounced down the sidewalk, zipping past the vehicle.

Pastor Sagle watched her intently. "I'd feel better if you came with me. I have friends in Eugene where you could stay."

"Thanks, but Judah's probably looking for me." She said it more for the pastor's peace of mind than her own. Had Judah already left town thinking she'd done the same thing? If only she had a cell phone.

"Probably?"

"You know how busy C-MER is during a storm." She thrust open the door.

"He'll be along shortly, then?"

She doubted it. "Thanks for the ride." She stepped into winds strong enough to hurl her down the street like the cardboard box she saw a minute ago. She slammed the door, then bracing her knees, leaned forward into the gusts and trudged through the yard and around the house to where she knew the back door would be unlocked.

The wailing of the sirens came again, sending tingles up her spine. How many times would she have to endure that noise before the storm ended its rampage?

As she pulled open the screen door at the back of Dad's, the porch light shut off—like a "Vacancy" sign turning off. She remembered how Dad didn't invite her inside earlier. How he told her to come back tomorrow. *Well, I'm here now.*

All the neighbors' houses seemed dark too. The whole town must have lost power.

She couldn't see the door handle she was so sure would open, but when she grabbed hold, it didn't budge. When did Dad start locking this door? She shook the doorknob. It didn't give. Had he hidden a key? If so, where? This was never a problem when she was a kid. She came through the unlocked door a million times before.

Had Dad secured the door against looters? Or because he didn't plan on coming back for a while? Both thoughts hit her hard. If burglars showed up, how would she protect herself? And in her father's exodus with Paige, did he even consider his other daughter's safety, or her need for a place to stay?

A blast of wind shoved her against the screen door. She had to find a way inside quickly.

She leaned over the porch railing, peering through the dark for anything that would make a good hiding place for a key. Where Mom's petunia garden used to be, Paisley spotted a pet rock Paige painted ages ago to resemble a salmon. She dashed down the steps, clinging to the loose handrail so the wind wouldn't capsize her. She scooped up the oval-shaped rock and checked underneath. No key. She looked under a couple of other items, but when another wind surge pressed her into a bush, she grabbed the salmon-shaped rock and gripped it firmly.

She stomped back up the steps, fighting the gusts, and yanked open the screen. Then, protecting her face with one arm, she pulled her other hand back, and flung the seven-inch rock like a football through the door window. Glass exploded into tiny pieces all over the porch. Some must have scattered on the floor inside also.

Carefully, she picked glass shards off the window frame and dropped them onto the porch. Her hands were stiff and shaking from cold, so she didn't want to make the mistake of ramming her knuckles against any sharp glass. When the lower edge of the frame seemed clear, she reached her hand in and unlocked the door.

She pulled her arm away just as a loud crash made her jump. Did a tree fall? She couldn't risk going around to the front yard to see. She had to get out of the pounding rain and wind. Grabbing the knob, she pushed the door open, being careful not to step on broken glass. She'd clean up the mess later.

Inside, she shoved the door closed, then rushed up the darkened stairway between the kitchen and the living room in search of a change of clothes. With the electricity off, the furnace wouldn't work, so she had to hunt for something warm to wear.

Teeth chattering, chills skittering across her body, she opened Dad's bedroom door and rushed to his oak dresser. Yanking drawers open, her fingers fumbled around for something thick that might fit.

Dad wasn't a large man, but he was taller than her. She found one of his flannel shirts. Sweatpants? There.

She shed her wet clothes as quickly as she could with numb fingers and pulled on the dry things. She explored in the closet and found a weathered wool coat that smelled of Old Spice. It might be a bit scratchy but should help her get warm. She sniffed as she plunged her arms into the jacket, enjoying the scent as memories of her dad when she was a kid floated through her thoughts. Sadly, no time for a trip down Memory Lane. She had a possible hurricane to prepare for. She dug in the drawer again and clasped a pair of thick boot socks. Perfect. She sighed just thinking of getting her feet toasty.

She grabbed the essential oil bottle out of her pocket that Kathleen gave her earlier and tucked it in Dad's coat pocket. Now to locate supplies, mainly a flashlight and water for drinking.

A loud crash shook the house.

She stood still, afraid to move. Then, knowing she had to face whatever it was, she tread slowly down the steps, her heart pounding in her ears. Through the darkness bathing the living room, she saw the apple tree protruded through the broken front window by about five feet. Its limbs fluttered like ragged flags. *Poor thing.* A blast of wind barreled through the gaping window, knocking several paintings off the walls. Knickknacks dropped from Mom's whatnot shelf, bursting into pieces. What a mess.

How was she going to get the tree out of the window? The wind bombarding the interior might devastate Dad's belongings, but she didn't want to go back out into the rain and yank on the tree. She didn't have the strength to move the heavy trunk, anyway.

If only Judah were here to help her get through this miserable night. But he wasn't. She was alone—like she had been for the last three years. Come what may, she would have to take care of whatever tasks befell her.

Twenty

Judah decided to check the beach one last time in case he and Paisley somehow missed each other earlier. He drove his truck slowly into the parking lot. His headlights cut a beam of light straight across a parked car on the far side. *Oh, no.* Paisley's Accord? Dread slammed through his middle. Had she gone to the point where he found her the other day? The image that played through his mind ever since the moment he found her collapsed on the rocks made him feel sick to his stomach now. What if she lost consciousness and—?

"Oh, God, please no."

He leaped out of his truck and splashed through the water rolling across the parking lot in waves, wading toward his wife's purple car. Seawater poured into his boots, and he grimaced. The wind blasted him with a pounding force, but he leaned into it and kept moving forward. He had to find her. When he reached the vehicle, he held his breath, warring with himself, both wishing he'd find her there, and afraid he would not. He leaned down and shone his cell light on the inside. The car was empty. A wave of thankfulness came over him, then an equal wave of dread and fearful thoughts assaulted his mind. Had she come here to see the waves? What if she was hurt? Where was she?

He tromped through the water, easing his way closer to the peninsula, wishing he brought a spotlight. His truck headlights allowed him to see the ocean water breaking through the levee his crew and city volunteers built. The narrow barricade wasn't holding the avalanche of waves this storm was bringing. But, at least, no one was on the beach or on the peninsula, as far as he could tell. Yet how could he know for certain Paisley wasn't here somewhere?

A wind surge shoved him four feet backwards. He nearly toppled over. *Play it safe, Grant.* But he didn't have time to play it safe. Not when his wife's life might be in danger.

They should have evacuated with the rest of Basalt Bay's citizens by now. They might have thirty minutes or so to get out of town. Any longer and the junction of South Road and Highway 101 could be under water, blocking their escape route.

"Paisley!" He yelled toward the whitecaps breaking over the rocks. Another wave hit the boulders, sending a spray of water twenty feet into the air.

"Oh, my goodness." So much power existed in the sea tonight. He peered into the darkness and called her name in each direction. If she were out in this tempest, maybe hiding in the cleft of a rock somewhere, the shrieking wind and crashing waves would override the sound of his voice. He shouted louder.

Maybe she didn't even walk onto the peninsula. But, if not, why was her car here?

"Paisley!"

A nearly overpowering gust of wind hit him just as a wave pounded his knees and splashed seawater up his thighs. He wouldn't be able to remain standing if the surge got any stronger.

He waded toward his truck. A loud crash made him glance back. A churning, violent-looking geyser of water cascaded over the peninsula. As the wave receded, a gaping hole remained where Sample D used to sit. Whoa. The rock fell into the sea?

Forget seventy-five miles per hour. This wind had to be closer to eighty-five or ninety.

He yanked open his truck door, fighting wind pressure, and climbed in, dripping water all over his seat. He needed a plan. And he had to stay positive or go crazy. Paisley's car was here. Why?

A police siren sounded in the distance. Deputy Brian and other officers were probably helping people in distress. Some who were determined to stay in their homes, despite the storm, may have changed their minds now. Was the entrance to South Road still passable?

Help me know what to do. Judah prayed. *Show me how to find her. Stop the storm if it's Your will, but please keep Paisley safe either way.* Immediately following his plea, he felt a measure of calmness seep into his spirit. A verse came to mind, a gentle reminder of God's continual help. *God is our refuge and strength, an ever-present help in trouble.* He repeated the words twice, needing the comfort. God was with him. *He* was present to help both Judah and Paisley get through the storm.

Feeling more confidence than he had a few minutes ago, he gazed back at Paisley's car being beaten by wind and water. Sometime between when he checked the peninsula earlier and now, she was here. What if she caught a ride with someone? Her dad? Paige? That made sense, until he remembered Paul said he wasn't leaving town. Had he changed his mind?

With a groan, and one last prayer that Paisley wasn't anywhere near the sea, Judah sped out of the parking lot, skidding the truck tires through eight or more inches of water. He drove down the empty, blackened Front Street that went through the middle of town. Most of the businesses were boarded up. He passed by City Hall. No movement there. Dad must have gone home.

A garbage can careened in front of Judah's pickup. He stomped on the brakes. Debris peppered his truck with sounds of metal hitting metal. Soggy newspaper pages clung to the windshield. A clattering noise came from the wiper mechanism. The duo blades skimmed across the windshield with a thud, thud, thud, then quit working.

He groaned, then stopped the truck in the middle of the road. Out of habit, he looked both ways, not that any other cars were on the street. He slid out of the vehicle and made his way to the front with blasts of wind shoving him backward. Pressing himself against the hood, he yanked wet papers off the front window. A few chunks wouldn't budge from the linkage. Hopefully, it wasn't down in the windshield wiper motor. Otherwise, he'd have a hard time driving.

Back in the cab, he found only one windshield wiper worked—on the passenger side. He grumbled and put the truck in gear. His lights made blurry shadows ahead, like someone was walking. But when he lowered his window, hoping to find Paisley, no one was there.

Would he be able to see through the rain well enough to get to Mom's? And what if Paisley was still in Basalt Bay? Had anyone stayed behind? He hadn't heard any more police sirens. The piercing sound of the public alarm was painful enough to send the most resilient people fleeing town. No wonder Craig fought to have the new system installed. Too bad it failed in its preliminary attempts. But the tech team prevailed. Thank God. Lives would be saved because of it.

Paisley must have left with her family. Judah had to believe she was okay. That she found somewhere safe to wait out the storm. He turned onto South Road, heading toward Mom's—until a gnawing question ate at him. How could he leave and find safety for himself without knowing for sure that his wife was okay? He pulled over to the side of the road. He had to think and pray.

"Lord, You know where Paisley is. If she's in any kind of trouble, send help. Rescue her. Let us have a chance for our love to be restored. Your will be done."

The wind slamming against the truck made a howling sound through the slight opening at the top of the passenger-side window that never fully closed. Good thing his truck was a solid vehicle. Lighter automobiles might have been blown over by now.

An image of Paisley's stranded car came to mind. The other day he heard a slight ticking in the engine. His heart beat faster. Was it possible her car stalled? That, maybe, she drove onto the watery parking lot near the peninsula and the timing belt got wet? That would explain—

He put the truck in gear.

If that happened, where was she now?

Paul wasn't home. Paisley and Paige hadn't reconnected. What if she went to the cottage? His blood froze. Their beach house was too close to tonight's turbulent seas. And too far for her to have walked in such strong winds.

He made a quick U-turn. He'd start at her dad's. Then Paige's. And he'd keep looking until he found her.

Twenty-one

Strong gusts barreled through the open living room window, but Paisley tried to push the apple tree out. It wouldn't budge. A chainsaw would solve the problem, if she could find one—and if she knew how to operate one. Finally, she gave up and went in search of something to cover the whole window. In the morning, she'd figure out a better solution.

With the flashlight in hand that she found earlier, she scrounged around in the kitchen drawers until she located a small plastic container with nails. Beneath the sink she unearthed a rusty hammer she used more than a decade ago to build a tree fort. Good thing she knew her way around the place. Next, she hunted for a blanket. In the cupboard above the washing machine, where guest linens were stored when she was a kid, she found a queen-sized quilt someone in the family must have sewn. She and Peter used that same thin blanket for a rainy-day fort, ages ago. Too bad it might get ruined now.

She set the flashlight on the coffee table, propping it toward her work area. After she nailed the green quilt to the left side of the window frame, and with powerful winds still blowing through the open space, she stepped onto the tree trunk with one foot and placed her other foot on the recliner in the corner. Balancing herself, she lifted the edge of the blanket and pulled the fabric taut across the gaping window. The town siren wailed again just as a blast of wind hit her, knocking her off the unsteady perch. Impatiently, she jumped up again.

She lifted the hammer, ready to drive the nail through the blanket and into the wall at the right, when a loud rumble like a truck engine made her pause. She listened closely. Had a car door slammed? Suddenly, someone banged hard on the front door. Paisley dropped the hammer.

"Just a sec—"

She stepped back, her foot in midair and the quilt clutched in her hand, as a man-sized person lunged through the open window and dove into the blanket. She screamed as whoever he was took her down with him, both of them thudding against the tree, groaning, then tumbling onto the carpeted floor.

Paisley shoved against the person and stood. "What do you think you're doing?"

The marauder jumped to his feet and the blanket fell from his face. "It's me, Pais."

Judah?

Shock and relief dueled inside of her. "What are you doing here?"

"Paisley, I'm so glad to see you."

Then she was in his arms, and they were hugging, him clinging to her, or maybe she was clinging desperately to him. Whatever spitting-mad rage she felt toward an intruder moments ago disintegrated into a gut-deep appreciation that Judah was here, and that he'd come looking for her. "I'm so glad to see you, too."

She stepped back a little, but they still held onto each other's arms. The wind raged all about them, yet the fierce conditions didn't seem as scary now.

"Oh, Pais. I'm s-so"—he seemed choked up—"happy you're alive."

"Well, me too." She pointed at the floor, then rubbed her hip. "Did you have to do that?"

"I did." He grabbed the flashlight off the table and pulled her across the living room toward the staircase. "C'mon. Hurry."

"Wait. What are you doing?" Fear scrambled up her chest. "I have to cover the window. The tree's—"

"Too late for that." He kept pulling her up the stairs.

"Why? What's going on? Judah, wait."

"I think a tidal surge is coming." He didn't let go of her.

"Now?" She followed him up the stairs, past the pictures of her and her siblings that remained on the staircase wall, with dread filling her. "How big?"

"Big enough. Water's pouring across the street as we speak."

"Oh, no." What should they do? Grab food? Water? She jerked her hand free and turned back.

"Paisley, no!"

"I have to get something." She ran back down the stairs, and rushing to the fridge, flung open the door. Dad had some water bottles. She grabbed several.

Judah was right behind her and scooped up a foil-covered bowl out of the fridge. "Get upstairs. Now!"

Outside, either the booming of thunder or the sounds of heavy objects crashing and falling made her pause. "Judah, listen. What is it?"

By his shocked expression, he heard the loud roar too. "Ruuuuun!" He pushed her with his free hand toward the stairway. "Don't stop for anything."

They sprinted up the steps, Judah fast on her heels, as something smashed against the house. The whole place thudded like a semitruck rammed into it. Judah shoved her into her old bedroom and slammed the door. He breathed hard, his eyes wide.

"Will the house hold?" Shivers raced over her skin as she stared at him leaning against the door as if his sheer strength might keep out the storm. "Otherwise, what are we doing in here?"

"Where else can we go?" He met her gaze with such tenderness, she didn't want to look away.

"There's an attic," she whispered. She wouldn't go up there alone, but with him, maybe. She set the water bottles on the end table next to her old twin bed.

He shook his head. "Just stay here by me. And keep away from the window." Finally, he seemed to relax a little—even though the howling winds still sounded threatening—and stepped away from the door. He set the bowl and the flashlight next to the water bottles. With a rusty-sounding sigh, he dropped onto the bed, then tugged on his rubber boots. He pulled hard like they were stuck. After a few attempts, he managed to get them off, then slid out of his coat and rain pants and wet socks. The pile of outerwear made a water stain on the wooden floor. Not that she cared.

Something screeched loudly across the floor downstairs. She dropped down beside Judah on the bed, closer than she would have if it didn't feel like the world was crashing down around them. When he laid his arm over her shoulder and tugged her against his side, she didn't pull away. She might have even leaned into his chest a tad, and wrapped her arms around his waist, just for comfort.

"It'll be okay." He was trying to reassure her, she could tell, but he couldn't know for sure they'd be safe. He ran his palm over her arm. "God is with us."

She wanted to believe that, but when the house shuddered again, she held her breath, waiting for something horrible to happen. The flashlight created weird shadows on the steep ceiling overhead that exaggerated the eeriness of them hiding out in her childhood bedroom while a tempest raged. She scooted back a little to see his eyes. "Why didn't you leave town with the others? I mean, I'm glad you're here"—if only he knew how glad she was to not be alone—"but why didn't you go?"

"I couldn't." His face puckered like he was about to cry, but she knew better. The Judah Grant she knew before didn't cry. "I, um, found your car down by the peninsula, and I thought—" He winced.

"Oh. You thought I was sitting on the point?" That's what he meant earlier about being glad to find her alive.

"Yeah." His blue eyes filled with some undefinable emotion.

She couldn't break free of the warmth in his gaze. Had a wretched storm not been threatening them, she probably wouldn't have done it, but when a tree or something large scraped the window like it might bust through at any moment, she clasped his hands and held on tightly. He clutched her hands, too.

The rain fell hard, then, as if rocks pounded the roof above them. Listening, yet trying not to listen, she resisted the urge to fall into Judah's arms for more of his comforting assurances. Because, if she did, that would be unfair to him, since she didn't mean anything by it, right? Still, she didn't move away. Although, when the pounding overhead let up, she released his fingers, embarrassed by her clinginess.

Thankfully, he didn't mention her reaction. "I almost went out on the peninsula to look for you."

"That would have been terrible." A picture of him being swept into the sea while hunting for her flashed through her imagination. She shivered. That he nearly risked his life to find her made her want to scoot closer to him again. "What happened?"

"I couldn't get out there." He bit his lower lip. "The whole thing was covered in water. I didn't want to think of the possibility you might be hurt . . . or lost."

Like she'd just been thinking about him.

He stood and walked to the window facing the backyard—the one where Paisley sat on the windowsill daydreaming of their wedding seven years ago. He peeled back the faded blue calico curtains. A flash of lightning lit up the window. "The wind and waves almost took me out."

She drew in a sharp breath. "Then I would have hated myself worse than I already do." And another person might have passed away without her having the chance to make things right.

He scrunched the thin curtains together, then swiveled around quickly, his eyes wide. What did he see that caused such a startled expression? "Don't ever hate yourself, Pais. God made you beautiful, inside and out. You're full of adventure and life and goodness. I love those qualities about you."

Goodness? No one ever said that about her before.

"God loves you. And so do I. We're going to be okay."

Where did so much confidence in him come from? Especially in the middle of a storm that was shaking her family's house, and her, to the core?

He grabbed an afghan off the end of the bed and wrapped it around her shoulders. He rubbed his hands over her arms as if to warm her, when he had to be freezing too.

"Thanks, but you need this m-more than m-me." Teeth chattering, she clutched the blanket her mother crocheted a lifetime ago.

"Don't worry. I'll find another." After he grabbed the flashlight, he opened the closet door and pulled out an extra blanket and pillow. "These will come in handy." He tossed them on the foot of the bed.

The window rattled. Paisley jumped, her nerves on edge. Something clattered on the roof, then scraped down the side of the house.

"Loose shingles." Judah opened a drawer where her socks used to be kept. "The storm's bound to get worse before it gets better. In my experience, most do." Was he talking about the weather outside or about them? "Since we're situated beneath the steepest point of the roof, we should be fine right where we are."

She swallowed, wishing she had his positive outlook.

He pulled off his soaking wet shirt, his shimmering chest glowing in the flashlight's beam. She closed her eyes, not wanting to be caught staring at his bare, sleek upper body. Good thing he didn't know what she was thinking—that she loved the way he used to hold her close in his arms, like he thought she was precious. Ugh. Too much time, and too many hurts, had passed since those days. They cared about each other as friends now, just waiting out a storm in the same room. That's all.

Then why did her heart pound so hard?

She glanced up. He put a throw around his shoulders. Good. She sighed.

When he sat down on the bed next to her, a little too close, she stood, anxiety twisting her nerves. "What do we do now?" She took a step toward the window, but he clasped her hand and drew her back.

"Stay away from the window."

"Why?" She wanted to see whatever he had. How bad was it out there? Wind and rain pelted the glass, a duo assault on the old panes.

"The glass might give any second."

She stepped back. "Think the wave made it this far?"

"Sounded like it." He cleared his throat. "And looked like it." He let out a sigh. "Why don't you try to rest. It'll be a long night, and all we can do is wait it out."

"What if the roof collapses?" She sat down next to the head of the bed and shivered as she glanced up at the arched, white painted ceiling illuminated by the flashlight.

"I'm praying it doesn't."

That he was praying and trusting God, even though he lost so much, too, was inspiring. Maybe God was listening to Judah's prayers. In fact, maybe He listened to hers by sending Judah here. She was thankful she wasn't alone right now, hiding under the bed and scared out of her wits.

"Hungry?" Judah grabbed the bowl off the dresser.

"Kind of." Mostly, she needed a distraction. She snuggled into the afghan surrounding her shoulders. If the elements outside weren't throwing such a tantrum, sitting next to Judah and chatting as if nothing was wrong between them would have been like a dream.

"Let's see what we have." He pulled the foil off the bowl, then pointed the light at the pottery dish. "Ah, mystery meat."

His lighthearted comment eased some of the tension in the room.

She chuckled at the memory of how they used to call the meat in fast foods and casseroles "mystery meat." "Sloppy Joe sauce, perhaps?"

He stuck his index finger in the red sauce and lifted it to his tongue. "You're right."

"Cold tomato sauce *and* no silverware?" Didn't sound appealing.

A loud, booming crash made her clutch Judah's arm.

"The stairs, I think." He leaned his head against hers for a moment.

"Gone?" She whispered.

He nodded tensely, but then seemed to visibly relax, maybe for her benefit. "So, we'll have to be creative without a fork." He shuffled back to the closet. A trail of wetness followed him across the floor. His jeans had to be soaked.

"Your pants are dripping."

"Sorry."

"I didn't mean that. You should just take them off." Heat blazed up her neck. "Oh, I didn't mean anything—" Ugh. That was the second verbal blunder she made about removing their clothing in the last couple of days.

Judah leaned out of the closet and looked at her with a raised eyebrow. Then he smiled. "I know what you mean, Pais. Thanks for being concerned about me." He ducked back into the closet, nearly out of sight.

She heard some shuffling. Then he tossed his jeans out onto the floor with the other wet clothes.

What was he going to wear now? He wouldn't find anything that fit him in her old closet. A moment later, he shuffled out with the throw that was previously around his shoulders wrapped snugly around his waist like a skirt—which meant his chest was bare again.

She averted her gaze. "I can take the flashlight into Dad's room and see what he has that might fit you."

"Your dad's shorter than me."

"I know."

"See what I found?" He waved something in the air as he sat down beside her.

"What is it?"

"A ruler." He wiped it across the blanket. Then he handed her the grade-school measuring tool and the bowl. "You first."

"A ruler for a fork?"

"Uh-huh. Use what's at hand, that's my motto." He grinned.

"Yeah, since when?"

"Since I've been caught in a few storms." He picked up the other blanket off the bed and wrapped it around his shoulders like a shawl.

She remembered what he told her the day she arrived back in town about his jumping into the ocean and fighting the current to get his skiff to shore. He was resourceful. Maybe, with his ingenuity and her gritty determination, they'd be okay waiting out the storm in her old room. "After we eat, I'm finding you some dry clothes." It would be a relief for her when he covered his skin that smelled too spicy for her senses with them sitting so close.

"Fine." His eyes twinkled in the dim light. Did he sense her discomfort? "These, um, batteries might not last long."

"I put in new ones this afternoon." She shrugged. "But who knows how long they've been in Dad's drawer?"

As if in answer, the light flickered. What would they do if it went out? For now she needed to see the mystery meat. She grabbed the flashlight and aimed it into the bowl.

"How about if I hold it while you eat?" He took the flashlight and redirected the light.

She ate a bite. "Not bad." Although, his watching her was disconcerting. She let the meat roll over her tongue. "Turkey burger. Mystery solved." She ate a few bites then handed him the bowl. "Your turn."

He passed her the flashlight. Their fingers touched, and a familiar zing raced up her spine. Why was she feeling butterflies around a man she lived with for four years and avoided for three? No excuse, but some part of her was tempted to lean in to his strong arms again.

The storm was at fault. It forced them into a situation of closeness she wouldn't have chosen or thought she wanted a week ago. Not that anything would happen romantically. Goodness, no. And yet, what if it did? What if deep inside she still harbored feelings for Judah?

Maybe . . . even . . . loved him.

Ugh. She scooted against the creaky headboard, putting space between them. Love and marriage weren't in her plans anymore.

She kept the light shining on the bowl but saw his beautiful blue eyes in the peripheral beam. With a certain intrigue, she watched him eating. Every time the ruler grazed his moist lips, she swallowed. A slight glob of red sauce was stuck in the crease of his lips, but she rejected the impulse to bring attention to his mouth. His soft lips that she—

Enough! She leapt off the bed and yanked open the door. "Um. I'll be right back." She needed a room's length to keep herself from doing something foolish—like touching his lips or, heaven forbid, kissing him! Her wayward thinking was due to fatigue and fear over their possible imminent death because of the storm. Nothing else. Still, even with that reasoning, she trembled from her reaction to him. She was romance starved, that had to be it.

In Dad's room, she scrounged through his drawers, then tossed a flannel shirt and some pajama bottoms that would probably fit Judah into a pile on the bed. The window panes rattled and crackled and seemed on the verge of breaking. She didn't want to be in here if that happened.

Just then, a huge crash rocked the house. She fell against the dresser. Groaned.

A cry or a loud moan came from her old bedroom.

"Judah? What's wrong?" She ran out of her dad's room and down the hall.

Twenty-two

Something crashed against the window, and an explosion of glass shrapnel hurtled across the bedroom. Judah yanked the blanket over his head and dove under the pillows near the headboard. A searing pain shot up his leg. He tried to muffle the cry that tore from his mouth. Every muscle in his body tensed. He gritted his teeth as the blast pummeled the room with tiny fragments. Objects fell from shelves to the floor. Pictures dropped from the walls, and the wind continued its rampage in the small space. Holding his breath, he waited for the surge to abate, praying for the house to hold and begging God to keep Paisley safe. He tried to ignore the agony in his calf.

"Judah!" Paisley burst through the bedroom door.

He jerked upright. Grimaced. "Don't come in here! Stay back."

Her light beam swept across the floor which was strewn with tree branches and glass fragments and childhood memorabilia, ending at the gaping window and darkness beyond. The whole room looked devastated.

"Oh, no." She stepped toward him.

"Stay back, Paisley. I mean it. There's glass everywhere. We have to get out of here." Although, he wouldn't be able to step on the floor in bare feet. The boots he dropped earlier were probably filled with glass. How could he get off the bed without slicing his foot?

Paisley gasped. "Judah! Don't move."

"Why not?" Adrenaline shot through him.

She pointed the flashlight at the bed. "L-look." She whimpered.

His gaze followed the light. A crimson stain spread across the quilt. Then he saw why. A three-inch jagged glass shard was embedded in the outer, lower portion of his left calf. "Oh, man." He moved his leg slightly, then clenched his jaw to hide the pain. Inwardly, he groaned. If he'd kept his wet jeans on, this might not have happened. Or not as badly. What should he do?

The light shifted as Paisley came closer. "What can I get? Tell me what you need. Does it hurt? Of course, it hurts." Her face crumpled like she was about to cry.

"I'll be okay. I, um, need a clean cloth to wrap around my shin." He held out his palm to her. "Stay back, though."

She fidgeted like she didn't want to do what he said.

With the wind still blasting things off the shelves, one of them could get hit with something else. For both of their protection, they had to get out of this room. With the glass impaled in his leg, he would be useless. If Paisley needed him, he wouldn't be able to do anything. So despite his C-MER first aid training that it was better not to remove an embedded item, he was going to have to do just that. He grabbed the edge of the blanket to use like a glove, then he clutched the three-inch piece of glass between his index finger and thumb. He gritted his teeth, wishing for something to bite down on.

"What are you doing?" She shrieked.

He met her gaze—she shook her head as if begging him not to do it, but her gaze never left his. He stayed focused on her. The woman he loved. The woman he wanted to protect. Then he pulled out the impalement in one anguish-filled movement. He moaned loudly. Blood squirted. He fought the urge to yell again. Then he pressed his fingers hard against the wound, his teeth chattering. *God, help me.*

"Oh, Judah." Paisley was crying now.

He grabbed another dry edge of the blanket and held it against the cut, sopping blood, fighting dizziness. "I-I need something to wrap my l-leg. Maybe s-some scissors to c-cut up this blanket."

"Wait." She clomped out of sight, taking the light with her. The door crashed closed.

He needed a second to collect himself, anyway. Leaning back in the darkness, he heard loud crashing and rushing water outdoors, maybe downstairs. He groaned, then his thoughts turned to prayer. *Lord, please keep us through the night. Help this roof to hold.*

In a few seconds, the room lit up again. Paisley tossed him a thin but long towel. "It's clean."

Stopping the blood flow was his main concern, especially since he didn't know how soon he could get to a medical facility. He wrapped the towel snugly around his calf, cinching it, knowing it probably wouldn't do the job effectively. He'd need stitches, come morning. Once the oversized bandage was secured, he carefully stood. He yanked the bloodstained blanket from the bed and tossed it over the glass on the floor. He grabbed a water bottle, then gingerly limped into the hallway, grimacing with every step. The wind slammed the door shut behind them.

Paisley got under the crook of his arm, supporting him. A moment later, lightheadedness hit him. He sank against the wall, bumping a picture of Paisley as a kid to the floor. All they needed was more glass beneath their feet.

"Don't worry. I never cared for that picture." She wrapped her arms around his waist.

He liked her being close, and the way she was trying to take care of him was comforting, but he wouldn't play on her sympathy. He was supposed to be the one protecting her.

"You okay?" She glanced up at him. "I can't believe you pulled the glass out yourself."

"I had to." Still in a lot of pain, his thoughts seemed muddled. "Um." He cleared his throat. "Which room?"

"You need to clean the wound, right?" Her gaze met his over the light coming from the flashlight. He read fear in her eyes.

"Not right now." He wanted to reassure her somehow. "We're going to be okay, Pais."

She nodded but looked doubtful.

He loved how soft she felt, her arms around him, and how caring she was being. Maybe she did still love him. He swayed slightly, clenching his jaw at the burning sensation in his leg. "Does your dad have a first aid kit?"

"I don't know." She let go of him. "I'll go look."

"No." Pain shot up his calf, and he didn't hide his facial reaction quick enough.

"You're hurting. I'm so sorry, Judah." She gripped his hand. "C'mon. Let's get you settled in Dad's room. Then I'll hunt for a kit or some bandages."

"I don't want you wandering around the house. Stay close to me, okay?" As soon as they entered the bedroom, he saw the bank of large windows was being battered by wind gusts and hammering rain. "These windows might break too. Any windowless rooms?"

"Not up here." She shook her head. "Even the bathroom has a small one."

He sat on the bed, unsure what to do next.

Paisley grabbed the water bottle, undid the lid, and handed it back to him. He took a sip, then she set the bottle on the dresser.

"Let me help you get this shirt on." She directed his arms into a flannel shirt, then did up the buttons for him. "Here's some pajama bottoms, but I don't know how to get them on over your injured leg." She held up black checkered pjs.

"I'm okay for now." He'd put them on later, when his injury felt more stable. He still had the blanket wrapped around his waist.

Paisley fluffed a couple of pillows behind his back. Maybe he'd close his eyes for a minute. "I don't want to bleed on your dad's blankets."

"Don't worry about it." She grabbed a smaller pillow and gently propped it under his leg.

He moaned but stifled it with a yawn.

She smoothed her hand down his arm. Stroked his forehead. Her being his nurse wasn't so bad. Although, he wished the injury hadn't happened. He sighed.

"You okay until I get back?"

He'd rather she stayed by him, but he probably needed a better bandage. He linked their fingers and drew her closer to him. "Sure. You be careful." He looked up at her, saw her shining dark eyes gazing back at him sweetly. Her soft expression made him want to span the distance between them. Just one brief kiss. Would she allow them a moment of tender affection in the middle of this terrible storm?

They stared at each other for a good thirty seconds, their faces, maybe, a foot apart. She blinked slowly, her gaze meshed with his. He gulped, his heart kicking up a rapid beat. He licked his lips, anticipating what their first kiss might be like after their three-year absence.

She glanced at his mouth, then her gaze skittered back to his, then she was glancing at his mouth again. *Oh, Paisley.* He let go of her hand and stroked the backs of his fingers down the side of her cheek, felt the softness of her skin. She closed her eyes and sighed. Was she looking forward to something romantic happening between them as much as he was? Sure, he needed a distraction from the pain in his leg. But kissing her? Them breaching the harrowing gulf that existed in their marriage for so long had to mean more than a mere distraction in the middle of a hurricane. It had to mean she wanted the same thing, that she wanted them to still be together—husband and wife—like he did. Did she?

A moment later, she opened her eyes and gazed at him, and that warm, amazingly gentle look he couldn't resist was still there. An invitation, it seemed. Even if she wasn't in the same place as him emotionally, he wanted to draw her closer and feel her in his arms. He smiled at her, hoping she could see he was giving her an invitation too. She smiled back, with an almost shy look.

Then, somehow, the distance between them was gone. Her lips were pressing against his, soft, pliable, caressing, needy, yet gentle, and oh, so sweet. He kissed her with all the love he'd stored up in his heart. He pulled her to him, his arms going around her back. Her feet stayed on the floor, like she was bracing herself so as not to lean against his leg, but she was kissing him too. Or maybe, she was the one who kissed him first.

Several unbelievable moments later, she drew back and gazed at him beneath lowered eyelids that seemed filled with deep emotion. She smiled, and he grinned back at her.

"That was one amazing first kiss." He met her lips again.

"Mmhmm." She stroked her hand down the side of his face this time, gazing into his eyes. He leaned his mouth into her palm and kissed her skin.

He sighed and closed his eyes, wondering if he possibly imagined the whole thing. But then, he must have dozed off. Or lost track of time. Surely, only a second passed. The next thing he knew, the house rumbled and groaned as if it were in the throes of collapse. What was happening?

From somewhere, Paisley screamed.

Judah shot off the bed faster than he would have thought possible, given the condition of his leg. "Paisley?" He limped down the hallway in the dark, wishing for his cell phone light. "Where are you?"

The structural shudder came again. A thundering crash. Then he froze, waiting for the ceiling to cave in on him. "God, help us. You are our strength in time of trouble. Nothing can happen to us that You don't know about. I'm trusting You for favor and safety and peace." He continued limping through the darkness. Where had he left his phone? "Paisley?"

"Judah!" She banged on a door down the hall. "Judah!"

"I'm coming." Letting his fingers trail along the wall, he followed the indents and doorways until he got to the bathroom. Light from her flashlight splayed beneath the door. "You okay, Pais?"

"Oh, Judah, you're here." She whimpered. "I'm so s-sorry." She seemed to be talking through the crack.

"I'm here, sweetheart. What's wrong?" He rapped softly on the wood. "Open the door."

"I can't. It's s-stuck." She shook the knob again. "I h-hate it in h-here. I don't w-want to be l-locked in this t-tiny space." She sounded panicky.

He had to get her out of there. He knew about her claustrophobia, although he didn't know why she suffered from it. "Stand back. Let me try shoving against it."

"No, I don't w-want you h-hurting yourself even more." She sniffled.

"I'm okay." He wanted to reassure her, although he cringed at the pain to come. "I'm going to shove against the door."

"D-didn't you hear that crash?" She banged against the door like she was ramming into it.

"Hold up, in there. Yeah, I heard. Did something happen?" He positioned his shoulder against the door.

"I think a tree crashed onto the roof." Her answer sounded tinny and distant.

"Oh, man." He automatically looked up but didn't see anything in the dark. Was the roof unstable? Near collapsing? It sounded that way a few minutes ago. "Are you safe where you are?" He'd break down the door if he could, but might that be worse for the structure if a tree was on the roof above them?

"The r-roof caved in. That's why the d-door's jammed." She shook the handle. "The window broke too. And—" A moaning sound made his heart rate accelerate.

"And what?" He shoved his shoulder firmly against the door. Nothing gave. He'd have to back up and ram his weight against it.

"There's a lot of w-water out there, Judah."

So, she saw what he had earlier—the whole area was flooded. "It'll be okay." He remembered her panic attack on the peninsula, then again outside the Beachside Inn. He didn't want that happening to her while she was alone. "I'm going to try to get you out of there."

"Okay."

"Stand in the tub." He knew the tub was the farthest spot from the door.

"Too much glass in it."

He hadn't thought about that. "Stand wherever you feel safest."

He heard her shuffling back.

"How's your leg?" Her concern for him in the middle of her own nightmare was endearing.

"I'll be fine." For now, he had to ignore the discomfort. He stepped back about five feet—hard to tell in the dark.

"Judah?"

"Yeah?"

"Thank you for coming here. For finding me." She was quiet for a moment. "I would have been terrified going through this alone."

"You're welcome." Tears filled his eyes. He came so close to going to Mom's. What if he left without searching for Paisley? Thank God, he hadn't.

For a second, he imagined himself back in his high school glory days playing football, then he shoulder-rammed the door powerfully at close range. Intense pain tore through his injured leg. He groaned and fell backward.

"Judah?" Paisley's flashlight danced light around the door's edges.

"Yeah." He gritted his teeth. "I think you're right. The roof caved in. The door's stuck." He smoothed his hands over the door-frame, searching for whatever might be hindering it from opening. He found a bulge at the top. What if he got the door open, but the roof fell on them? *Lord, help us.*

He slid to the floor, adjusting the blanket around his legs, and tapped on the edge of the bathroom tiling beneath the door. "Paisley?"

"Uh-huh?" Her voice came softly. The light shone on the floor. He heard her drop down on the other side of the door.

"I can't get you out tonight. I'm so sorry. We'll have to wait until morning." He tried to keep his voice calmer than he felt.

A few moments passed. "Thanks for trying." It sounded like she slumped against the door and groaned.

He wished he'd done more to keep them safe. "Are you all right in there?"

"Kind of freaked out." Something rustled on the other side of the door. She was probably clearing glass away from where she sat. "How's your cut?"

"Hurts." Understatement. "At least, I can't see it." He touched the makeshift bandage and found it damp. Not a good sign.

"Why don't you go back into my dad's room, or use Peter's old room across the hall, and rest. I'll be okay." He could tell she was anything but okay, yet trying to be brave.

All he wanted to do was protect her and hold her. "I'm not leaving you, Pais." Now or ever.

He felt her little finger brush against his hand beneath the door. Adjusting his position, he leaned against the doorframe and moved his finger to touch hers. He sighed and closed his eyes.

"Think it'll get w-worse?" The worry in her tone was obvious.

"Hard to say. Hopefully, the worst has passed."

"And the tree over me?" A shuffling noise sounded like she curled up on the floor. "Think the house will hold?"

He stretched out on the linoleum, grimacing as he propped his throbbing leg on his other ankle. Their little fingers still touched.

"I hope so. Think you c-can sleep like this?" He heard the groggy sound in his voice. He shivered—from cold or possible shock. He tried to suppress his teeth from chattering, so Paisley wouldn't hear and be even more concerned.

They lost contact for a moment. Then she was back. "Can you talk to me for a few minutes?"

"Sure." He blinked to stay awake. "What do you want to talk about?" Did she mean talk about deeper things? Like why she left? About hurts in their past? Or something light?

"Tell me what you've been up to for the last few years." She sighed.

Ah, platonic things. But then he remembered their kiss—he didn't only imagine that, right? Because there wasn't anything platonic about that romantic moment that was engrained in his thoughts forever. Even if it was caused by charged emotions after his injury, Paisley's tenderness toward him made him think she still had warm feelings for him. That made him smile, despite his pain and the uncomfortable position he was laying in.

Then, with their pinkies touching, he talked to her about things he'd seen on his skiff rides with C-MER—gray whales, leaping salmon, and overly-curious sea lions. He told her about his ideas for restoring their beach house, including making the veranda bigger. He wanted to share about that first year she was gone. About how angry he was until God finally got ahold of his heart. He wished he could confess about the day he bought a plane ticket to Chicago on the spur of the moment. But the soft sound of her snoring reached him, so he'd wait for another time to share that story.

He closed his eyes and thanked God for Paisley being close to him. A small miracle. If only that door weren't stuck, him on one side and her on the other. But then his thoughts skimmed through other things that stood between them—the past, the secrets, the rumors—and that door seemed to represent a whole lot of things he didn't want to contemplate right now.

Maybe he'd spend a few minutes praying. He winced as he moved his leg, trying to get comfortable. Before long, he felt himself relaxing too.

The last thought as he drifted to sleep was of Paisley's and his kiss.

Twenty-three

Paisley stretched, and her feet bumped into something. The toilet? What was she doing on the bathroom floor? She peeled her eyelids open and stared at the cracked, bulging ceiling above her. The storm's madness came rushing back to her, followed by thoughts of Judah's injury, and then the . . . kiss. *Oh, my.* She bolted upright and took a deep breath.

Through the broken window, she saw early morning haze hung low in the sky.

They'd survived.

The flashlight still rested in the same place where she set it on the floor last night, but without any light coming from it. She clicked the off switch, although the battery was obviously dead.

She glanced beneath the door. Judah's pinkie still rested slightly on her side. Had they slept close enough to touch each other's fingertips all night? Sweet, sweet man. *Sigh.*

A warmth spread through her at the remembrance of that moment in Dad's room when she leaned down and touched her lips to Judah's. How she acted every bit the wife she told herself she wasn't, so many times. Yet in that crazy instant of fearing for their lives, something within her longed to be his wife, his sweetheart. He'd been in so much pain, and she thought they might die. And when he kissed her back, *deep blue sea in the morning,* everything she ever loved about Judah Grant came rushing back to her.

Now, glancing up at the damaged ceiling hanging low and tilted, an image flashed through her mind of what could have happened if the tree crashed through the roof. She could have been crushed—both of them badly injured. Perhaps God protected them through the night. *If that was You, God, thank You. I mean it. I really am thankful.*

She heard rustling on the other side of the door. A groan. Judah's finger disappeared.

"Judah?" She got on her hands and knees. "You awake?"

"Uh-huh."

"How are you?"

"Hurting all over." He groaned again.

"I'm sorry. Just move slowly, okay?" It was strange how comfortable she felt talking with him, when just a couple of days ago she thought she never wanted to see him again, let alone sleep next to him. Now she'd give anything to be on the other side of this door, helping him, being close to him—at least until they got through the aftermath of the storm. Her stomach growled loudly. "I'm hungry. How about you?"

He chuckled, then moaned.

"I hate that you're hurting, and we can't do anything about it." She leaned her back against the door. Even though she couldn't see him, knowing he stayed in Basalt to be with her comforted her and made her feel calmer than she had in a long time. She pictured herself curling up next to him without the door between them—his arm around her, her cheek resting against his chest—if only he didn't have the injury. "How's the leg?"

"I'll live." She heard movement. "I'm going to take a look around, find my phone, and try to put on those pajamas."

"Judah?" Her voice sounded too needy, so she cleared her throat to hide it.

"Yeah, Pais?"

The soft way he said his nickname for her made her sigh. "Don't go far, okay?"

A pause. "I won't." His bare feet shuffled away.

"You might find some shoes in Dad's closet." Oh, right, her dad's shoe size was smaller than his. "Uh, never mind." She shoved her back against the door, wishing it would spontaneously open.

Judah's footfall got fainter, like he went in the direction of the stairs. What if he fell or hurt himself and she couldn't get to him?

Ugh. No dwelling on negative what-ifs.

She stood and tiptoed around a pile of glass. Then, leaning over the edge of the tub, she peeked out the broken window. Water was still everywhere. Junk floated inside the backyard fence. The dilapidated shed that was in the corner of the property her whole life now lay on its side. The spruce tree she'd loved to climb when she needed solitude straddled the corner of the house—apparently overhead. Were all the shingles from the roof floating in the backyard? Such devastation! How long would it take for the water level to go down?

Judah tapped on the door.

"Yeah?" She scuttled back to her spot on the floor.

"The stairs are gone, as I suspected."

"Oh, no."

"Water must have come in through the living room window and beneath the door."

Her father's home was terribly damaged. Was it even fixable? Had any of Mom's paintings survived? Not that she cared. However, Dad might mourn their loss.

"I called Craig."

"What?" Her heart rate ramped up to hyperdrive. "Craig Masters? Why would you do that?" She never wanted to see that cad again.

"We need help getting you out of there." His calm and steady voice made her think he didn't know anything about Craig's offenses.

She'd rather tie washcloths together like a rope and risk climbing out the bathroom window than to ask the man who caused so much trouble between her and her father-in-law three years ago for help. "Can't you c-contact the p-police or someone else?" Her voice cracked, and she didn't attempt to hide her reaction.

"Police are preoccupied. Craig said he'll try to get here in an hour." He bumped the door as he sat down on the floor. "What's wrong with Craig helping us?"

Now wasn't the time to explain. Things were still tentative and unsettled between her and Judah, even with that kiss. Or maybe, more complicated because of it. She didn't know what the next step for them would be. But discussing Craig's wrongdoings this morning? No, thanks. "I'd prefer it was someone else, that's all." She swallowed hard, hoping he didn't read too much into her hesitancy.

After a pause he asked, "Did something happen between you and him?"

Why was he pursuing this subject? She didn't want to talk about that. Whenever she had to tell Judah about her deepest struggles, she'd rather be gazing into his shining blues, seeing his understanding, maybe even his compassion. Not sitting like this with a door between them.

Although, was it possible that a solid wooden door blocking her from seeing the disappointment in his eyes might be for the best?

She groaned.

"Pais, you can tell me."

If she did, would the tenderness in his tone disappear? Would he hate her? She grabbed a washcloth off the edge of the sink and twisted it in her hands, wringing out some of her fear and frustration. She could refuse to explain. But he deserved to hear the truth from her. They had an hour. She glanced at the door, imaging him sitting on the other side.

She took a deep breath. If only she could talk to him *and* keep herself from having a panic attack. "Okay, there's something I need to tell you about the night I left."

Twenty-four

Judah adjusted his pajama-covered leg, waiting for Paisley to continue. Apprehension crept up his spine. Whatever she was going to tell him might threaten the tenuous ties between them as devastatingly as the storm endangered this house last night. Why did she react so strongly to Craig's name? What if the rumors about Paisley and a guy were true? Were the two connected? His wife and his friend? Talk about a brutal betrayal.

But there he was jumping to conclusions. Hadn't he determined that no matter what transpired in the past, he was going to offer her forgiveness and grace like Jesus offered him? Like Hosea in the Old Testament did with his bride? Although, right now, Judah didn't want to contemplate any similarities between Hosea and himself. Just the thought of the story, or of something going on between Paisley and Craig, made his insides quake. Her continued silence added to his suspicions.

Mercy and grace. But sometimes, mercy and grace were easier in theory than in action. *Lord, help me.*

"Pais?" He forced his tone to sound calm, contrary to his inner turmoil. He tapped the floor under the door with his little finger, silently inviting her to come closer.

A few moments passed before her little finger touched his. He sighed and thanked God. He was grateful for how close he felt with Paisley during the storm. He wouldn't let that go easily.

"You can tell me anything." He needed to hear his wife's heart regardless of the pain in his chest over any possible unfaithfulness. "About Craig . . ." he coaxed her.

"He, um, he was the one who . . ." Her voice trailed off.

Tension tightened every muscle in his shoulders. "The one who what?"

"H-he did s-something he shouldn't h-have." Her voice shook.

Oh, man. If his supervisor hurt her in any way, he'd— What? Punch his lights out? Have him fired? That might already be happening. It would be difficult not to want revenge. "What did he do?" He ground out the words.

"Well, uh." She blew out a long breath. "The night before I left, I got really angry with you."

"I know." He relived their argument many times. "We both said things we shouldn't have." He knew he had.

"Afterward, I went out drinking."

He figured that was the case, since she went out on her own more often after they lost the baby.

"I had too much to drink, and at the bar I said some things I didn't mean. I may have been flirtatious with a few of the guys around me." She drew in a raspy breath. "C-Craig was there, drinking too."

Judah clenched his other hand, knowing she couldn't see his reaction.

"We were at Hardy's Gill and Grill. Not together, of course."

"No?"

"No." She huffed. "He happened to be there when I was there. However, I was probably making a fool of myself." She took a breath. "When I left, he did too. Then he, uh, offered to take me home."

"He knew who you were, right?"

"That I was married to you?" She cleared her throat. "Yes."

Judah muffled a groan as his irritation escalated. Still, he kept his pinkie next to hers. "Then what happened?" The Lord had to be helping him stay calmer on the outside than he felt on the inside.

"I didn't think I should drive, so I accepted. I thought he was just being nice." A pause. "But when we got to his car—" She stopped talking and it drove Judah crazy.

"Please, just say it. I need to know what happened." He felt his arms shaking with suppressed tension.

"It'll make you m-mad." She gulped like she was subduing a sob.

"Maybe, but I want you to tell me so I can understand." Even though frustration raced through him, he had to find a way to reassure her that whatever she said, he was here for her. That he loved her unconditionally. "Take your time, Paisley. It's okay. I'm not mad." Well, not mad at her.

"O-okay." She groaned. "It's just hard to tell you this stuff."

"I know." He waited, although it was a test of his patience. He needed to hear everything—he'd waited three years for this conversation—but it wasn't easy to listen and do nothing.

"He, um, he grabbed my shoulders roughly"—she inhaled loudly—"and pressed me back against his c-car."

Rage sizzled through Judah.

"Then he kissed me h-hard. H-he acted as if he were going to—" She pulled her hand away from his. A moan or a subdued cry came from the other side of the door.

That his supposed friend dared to push himself on Judah's wife, against her wishes, was more than he could handle. He slapped his other hand against the floor.

"Ju-u-dah?" He heard her fear. The regret.

Oh, man. "Sorry, Pais." He clenched his fist against his front teeth, trying to control his anger. He sighed. "Go ahead. I want to hear it all, really I do." *Grace and mercy. Grace and mercy.*

"Okay." She paused. "So, um, thanks to the quantity of liquor I consumed, I wasn't in my right mind. He probably wasn't either, although there's no excuse for his a-actions." Her voice shook. "Or maybe, I don't know, I may have kissed him back at first. Or gave him the wrong idea."

So hard to hear. "No, whatever he did was not your fault. He can be an overbearing clod." Judah thought of the callous way Craig told him he'd probably be out of job and the rough way he spoke to some of the other employees at work. Besides, the guy should have treated Paisley honorably, no matter what.

"I didn't want anything to happen with him, so, so I pushed him and tried to get away." She sobbed. "I told him 'no!' He wouldn't listen."

Judah growled, then tried to cover it with a cough. He was struggling to stay calm and not overreact.

"I kicked him in the shins. Slapped his face." Her voice rose. "Oh, Judah, you have to believe me."

"Of course, I do." Although, rage pummeled through him toward the man who dared to act aggressively toward his wife. Even so, he made sure his pinkie was under the door for when she was ready to let their fingers touch again. "Did he, did he hurt you?" The moment of truth.

She groaned. "H-he would have."

He expelled his breath, but any relief was short-lived. All this time Judah considered Craig his friend. Yet, in three years, that man never had the guts or the decency to come clean about what he attempted. Judah's anger intensified. He had to know the whole story. "What stopped him?"

She let out a tremulous sigh. "Your dad."

"My dad?" Judah sat up straighter.

She inhaled and exhaled loudly. Then coughed.

"Pais, it's okay." He slowly released his clenched fist and kept his voice gentle. "I'm so sorry for whatever happened that night. Just tell me, okay? How was my dad involved?"

"I will explain, promise, b-but I don't want to have a p-panic attack."

Her breathing sounded even more ragged. His heart filled with compassion for her. "I don't want that either. Just take your time. Relax for a minute." He pushed his little finger under the door. "Sweetheart, you can stop talking for a while if it will help." If he could knock down this door, he'd sit beside her, hold her, and try to comfort her.

He heard a noise, then he thought he smelled peppermint candy.

She breathed deeply. Coughed.

"You okay? What is that scent?"

"Peppermint oil. Someone gave it to me." She cleared her throat and the sound came from below the edge of the door. Was she laying down now?

He stretched out, wincing as he adjusted his leg. He craned his neck until he could see under the door with his right eye. She was there, as if trying to be closer to talk with him. Unless resting like that helped her breathe easier.

"I love you." He needed to say the words. "Whatever happened between you and Craig, I want you to know I love you. I still want you to be my wife." He determined months ago to tell her that. But right now, he knew every word was true. "That kiss we shared last night? It meant everything to me."

Her one eye that he could see filled with unshed tears. She nodded. "That n-night, other than what Craig tried to do at first, n-nothing else happened between him and me."

"Really?"

"But your d-dad—" She made a wheezing sound.

He waited, wishing he could do something to help her. Some, but not all, of the mystery of that night was clearer now. He and Paisley argued, then she left and didn't come home until sometime after he went to bed. The next morning he found the note saying she was leaving and that she loved someone else.

"Your dad came around the corner. Saw us. Craig and me." Her little finger moved next to his. "By then, I was fighting and scratching and kicking mad."

He tried to picture the scene, her struggling against Craig's advances, and Dad observing the attack. "Dad never said a word about that to me." Why didn't he explain what he witnessed? Why would he allow his son to suffer in silence for three years?

"I'm not surprised." She stared at him through the crack under the door. "He hates me. Always has."

While that frustrated him to no end, he didn't disagree. His judgmental father had said too many negative things about Paisley. Judah gritted his teeth as a powerful surge of anger over past issues with his dad meshed with his current fury. "So what did Dad do?"

"He grabbed Craig by the shirt collar, shook him hard, then threw him to the sidewalk." Her eye blinked. "I didn't know Edward had that in him."

"Me, neither." His estimation of his father went up a notch.

She shifted on the floor. "He *kicked* Craig and told him he better not touch me again or he'd call the cops."

"Wow. Good for Dad." Yet, why didn't he tell Judah the truth?

"But then, he turned on me." She made a low growl.

"Turned on you how?" Surely, his dad hadn't harmed her.

A long silence.

"Pais?" Anxiety rippled up his neck.

"He grabbed my arm and yanked me down the street. Called me a"—she gulped—"a prostitute."

Judah groaned. Hadn't his father said similar things about her to him? Every time Judah shut him down, but the man was so spiteful.

"He said I wasn't worthy of a man like you. Never had been. Never would be." She drew in a stuttered breath. "J-Judah, he was r-right."

"No, he wasn't. I'm sorry he said such terrible things to you." His heart broke for her and what she'd been through without him. "I wish I'd been there."

"What would you have done?" Her voice softened.

"Slugged Craig to Timbuktu. Chewed out my dad." He inwardly groaned. "I would have brought you home. Loved you like the husband I wish I'd been."

"Oh, Judah." She sighed. "I never deserved you."

"Of course, you did." He tapped her little finger. "We were in love."

"Past tense."

"Present, for me." Then it was his turn to sigh as he wondered what that earth-shaking kiss meant to her. And he had another question. "When you left, did you go because of me? Or Craig? Or Dad?"

"Not Craig. But there were problems between you and me. Between me and this town." She moved farther away from him, their fingers losing connection.

"Did that have something to do with my dad?" He still tried to see her beneath the inch-and-a-quarter space under the door.

She groaned like she didn't want to say anything else. She was sitting up now, her legs crossed.

"You might as well tell me. I'll find out." He'd confront his dad. If he asked about that night, would Dad tell him the truth?

"He told me to leave and never come back." She paused. "Or he'd smear my name and our relationship by telling everyone he caught me having an affair . . . until you'd gladly leave me."

"You're kidding." That's how the rumor spread? By his own father? Acid churned in his gut.

"I-I'm not kidding." She inhaled loudly, sounding asthmatic. "But I was looking for an escape. So many bad things happened. The miscarriages. Misty Gale. Mom. Our . . . difficulties."

"I know." Sadness replaced his angst.

"Edward drove me home that night and said awful things to me." She sniffed. "Then he handed me a wad of money. And I . . . I did his bidding. I left you." She sounded wounded. "I've regretted that decision for a long time."

He couldn't believe the extent of pain his dad caused them. He tapped the floor with his finger. "C'mere, Pais."

After a minute, she leaned down beside him as she had before. He heard her huff a little like she was tired. Same as him. But tired or not, this was his moment to share something vital with her.

"I still want to be your husband." How could he make her see into his heart? "I'm in this marriage for the long haul. Isn't that what I promised you on our wedding day? You and me forever. I meant it that day. I still do." He felt so much vulnerability in those words. He held his breath, waiting to hear what she'd say.

"How can you still want that?"

"I do, that's all that matters." He stroked her finger. "Please, give *us* a second chance."

"I don't know if there even is an us."

How could she say that after their kiss? "Oh, Pais, there's definitely an us."

She sighed. "I haven't told you all the things I've done."

"Well, I haven't told you all the things I've done, either." He smiled at his own drama, although there were things he needed to tell her. "Whatever we have to say to each other, I want you, Paisley Rose Grant, to be my wife . . . from this day forward. To have and to *hold*." He emphasized the last word and hoped she got his message. "We're going to be okay, you and me."

"How can you be so sure?" She watched him too, both of them gazing at each other beneath the door.

"We're surviving this storm, aren't we?"

"I hope so. But I don't like being in this tiny space."

"I wish I was in there with you." He prayed she saw the sincerity in his gaze.

She blinked a couple of times. "Me too."

Her answer encouraged him, but would she still feel the same way after their rescuer arrived?

Twenty-five

A vehicle door slammed outside. Craig, no doubt. Paisley cringed. How would Judah deal with seeing his coworker now that he knew the truth about the scoundrel? And even if Judah's response to her telling him all that stuff hadn't been as terrible as she feared, the thought of interacting with Craig made her stomach churn.

"He's here." Judah tapped the floor. "I just got his text."

"I know." She hated that she needed Craig's help at all.

"Pais? I'm right here."

She appreciated the kindness she still detected in his voice. Not that his being on the other side of the door remedied the tightening in her chest when a ladder scraped the house below the broken bathroom window. The top rung swayed just beyond the gaping glass, and a bitter taste filled her mouth.

Breathe.

Craig was here to help her get out of the second story, then she never had to see him again. Although, this was a small town, and it was hard not to run into someone.

"Hey!" Craig's voice. "I'm coming up."

She didn't answer.

"It'll be okay," Judah said softly. How he managed to remain positive in the face of everything she told him, and what happened, she had no idea.

Suddenly, the villainous face in her nightmares filled the window. Craig nodded and smiled at her, a greasy look. She kept one arm crossed over her ribs like a shield. Didn't say anything. She wouldn't speak to him at all, if she could help it.

"Judah asked me to come get you." He broke a couple of chunks of glass out of the window frame.

She still didn't move from where her finger touched Judah's.

"Hey, Masters!" Judah yelled, and his voice had a steely quality she never heard before.

"Yeah?" One of Craig's eyebrows quirked at Paisley. Could he tell by Judah's tone that she told him about his behavior that night?

"Help my wife out, then come around to the other side of the house for me." His vocal intensity didn't soften.

She was surprised he didn't add some warning about Craig keeping his dirty hands off her. But then, he wouldn't want to risk her safety by riling their rescuer.

"Be around in a minute. Water's about a foot high. Worse at the crossing." Craig glared at her. "Are you coming out, or not?"

If there was a second option, she'd take it.

"Pais?" Judah spoke quietly, probably so Craig wouldn't hear.

She leaned down. "Yeah?"

"If he even touches you once, he'll answer to me."

She smoothed her index finger along his pinkie. Then she stood but didn't clasp Craig's outstretched hand. She wouldn't have contact with him, physical or otherwise, if there was any way to avoid it.

"I can do this myself." She stared into his dark eyes she once found attractive. Too bad she ever entertained such fickle notions. Judah's blue eyes were more beautiful, and truer.

"You sure?"

"Positive—about a lot of things." It felt good to return the glare he gave her a moment ago.

Craig scowled. "Fine by me." He disappeared from the window, grumbling. "Too bad I came all this way, at my own peril. A lot of thanks I get."

She wasn't thankful to him at all, other than Judah getting the medical help he needed.

When she was certain enough time passed for Craig to be off the ladder, she leaned out the window. "I'm going now." She wanted Judah to know what was going on, even though she was sure he heard her exchange with Craig.

"I'll have my arms around you in a minute, sweetheart." Judah's voice sounded husky.

She smiled. Then she double-checked for glass on the window frame before climbing out. The ladder wobbled, and her gaze darted to Craig's. He stood at the bottom of the ladder, in shin-deep gray water, smirking. Had he let the ladder sway on purpose? *Rat!* She didn't want him here. Didn't want to step off the ladder and have him standing too close, but she required his holding the ladder steady.

When she reached the last rung, which was submerged in brackish water, Craig had already stepped back. At least he had the courtesy to do that.

She put her stockinged feet into the cool water, then waded carefully over uneven ground, not wanting to misstep and fall on her face in front of him. She shuffled toward the front of the house, easing around floating trash and roofing shingles, leaving Judah's coworker to retrieve the ladder. When she rounded the corner, the damage around the flooded neighborhood shocked her. Downed trees. Branches. Garbage everywhere. Across the street, the Weston's camping trailer was on its side. Judah's truck had butted up to the porch where the steps used to be. The scene was surreal. Weird.

She tried to glimpse the ocean between two of the neighbors' houses across from her, but it was hidden by low fog. With all this water, how much damage happened in town? Had Dad found sanctuary somewhere? He'd be discouraged to see his family home and land now.

Craig waded around the house, his boots swirling the water. The ladder clattered in his arms and scraped the corner of the house. No use telling him to be careful with all the other damage. "Which window?"

She glanced up to the second floor.

"Over here." Judah lifted his hand from Dad's open bedroom window. At least those panes didn't break last night like she feared they might.

Craig made a muffled sound of agreement.

"Did you see your truck?" She gazed up at Judah.

"Can't believe it moved that far."

"Must have been some wave." Craig settled the ladder against the house. "Come on down when you're ready."

Craig glanced at her, and she averted her gaze.

But, a moment later, Judah groaned, and she glanced up. He clutched the top rung, his pajama-clad injured leg dangling free. Did he almost fall?

"Judah, you okay?"

He stayed still for a few seconds, gripping the sides of the ladder. Then slowly he lowered his foot covered in one of Dad's wool socks onto the rung. "Give me a minute. I'll get there."

"No hurry, man." Craig gazed upward, his face contorted. Was he worried for Judah after seeing the bloodstained cloth on his leg? Or anxious to get out of the flood zone?

Paisley shuffled through the water to grab Judah's arm and help him reach the ground. Craig got under the other arm, and together they led Judah away from the ladder and toward Craig's monster truck. Good thing he drove a tall vehicle to get through all this standing water.

"Guess we got the wave we didn't think would hit, after all." Craig nodded his dark hair in the direction of the ocean. "What possessed you to disobey orders and stay in town? You could have been killed."

"I had my reasons." Judah glanced at her and winked.

She smiled back at him. Her hero.

"Why don't you sit in my truck? I'll have a look at your leg." Craig opened the truck door.

After Judah pulled himself up onto the seat, Paisley stepped back and watched as Craig retrieved a first aid kit from the backseat.

He seemed to know what he was doing as he rolled up the pajama fabric and untied the bloodstained faux bandage from Judah's leg. Judah groaned, and Paisley wished she were close enough to hold his hand. He looked pale. It seemed he'd lost a lot of blood.

"It's inflamed." Did the C-MER employee have medical training? Was that why Judah called him?

Paisley cringed at how red the gash was.

Craig washed the injury with antiseptic, and Judah groaned again.

"You need stitches," Craig said gruffly.

"Yeah, yeah." Judah gritted his teeth.

"I mean it." Craig secured a square gauze over the cut with white tape. "An antibiotic, probably."

"But he'll be okay, right?" That was all that mattered.

"Sure, he will." Craig nodded.

Could she trust anything he said?

As soon as Craig finished taping the wound, Judah slid down from the truck, landing back in the water.

"Hey, that cut needs to stay dry." Craig pulsed his thumb toward the interior of the truck. "Get back in there. I'm taking you to the ER in Florence."

"No, that's all right." Judah shook his head. "Thanks for rescuing us, though."

Why was he refusing to see a doctor? Because of her? His flushed cheeks made her think he might have a fever. Was the cut infected?

"Craig's right." She nudged Judah's arm. "You should go get stitches." Even if that meant she'd be alone, he required medical attention. "And you probably need that medicine."

"Come with me?" His warm blues met her gaze.

Before she could answer, he pulled her against his chest, holding her close. She rested her cheek near his heart and sighed, thankful to be standing next to him without a door in the way.

"I told you I'd be doing this in a few minutes," he whispered near her ear. He ran his palm down the back of her hair.

She breathed in the masculine scent of him. If home was where the heart was, she was home in his arms. But what if this feeling of closeness with him was due to the storm and the harrowing experiences they went through together? When the crisis was over, would she feel the same way toward him as she did right now? She glanced up and met his gaze. Sighed.

Craig cleared his throat like he felt awkward standing there watching them, which was fine with her. Let him feel uncomfortable all day long.

But then, Judah eased his hold on her. He ran both of his palms up and down her upper arms. "You okay?"

"I am. You?"

"I'll live." He smiled, and the way he gazed into her eyes, even though her villain was nearby, spoke volumes to her heart.

Judah was a kind and trustworthy man, she knew that now more than ever. He said he still wanted her for his wife, and that they'd work together on the things they hadn't done so well at before. Did she want him for her husband? Could they, perhaps, try again and see what happened?

She clasped his hands, her gaze still fixed on his.

Was she willing to trade all her preconceived ideas for a chance at happiness, maybe love? And if so, how could she let him know her heart was changing without saying so in front of Craig? She leaned up on tiptoe and kissed Judah's rough, unshaven cheek.

His eyes lit up.

She grinned, feeling a little amazed by her new, tender feelings toward him, even if she had some doubts. "What now?"

"Marriage?" He laughed.

"I didn't mean—"

"You coming or not?" Craig asked gruffly and climbed into his truck.

Judah watched her intently. "You too. I won't go without you."

"I'm sorry, but I can't." No matter how her heart felt stirred toward Judah, she wouldn't ride in Craig's truck. "You go." She unclasped their hands. "I'll stay and work. The water should start going down soon, right?"

"Might not for a few days. Come with me, Pais. We'll spend time talking." He kissed her cheek, his lips lingering close to her mouth. If she moved her lips half an inch . . . but no, Craig was watching. "Please?"

Her heart kicked up a beat. Judah's gaze held so many promises.

"I'll be here when you get back." After what she told him, he had to understand she didn't want to be in close proximity to Craig. "Besides, I want to clean up before Dad sees any of this."

"But—" Then he sighed as if accepting his inability to convince her otherwise. "I need to tell you something." He rubbed his forehead like it hurt. "I should have mentioned it last night, but I didn't want you worrying even more."

"What is it?"

"Judah!" Craig barked from the truck. "I gotta go, man."

"Hang on a sec." Judah frowned at Craig, then turned back to Paisley. "Your dad told me he wasn't leaving Basalt Bay."

"When was that?"

"When I first stopped by his house to give the pre-alert." He clasped her hand. "Sorry. I should have said something."

"I would have gone looking for him if I thought he might be alone."

"I know."

She recalled what the minister told her last night. "Pastor Sagle saw Dad loading Paige's car. Most likely, he left with her."

"Well, then, that's good."

"Yeah, but he'll be sad when he sees all this damage."

"It'll need a restoration." He stroked a few strands of hair away from her cheek. "Like us."

This time she didn't get angry over his marriage-makeover talk. He was right, if they were even going to consider starting over, they'd need a complete redo. But first his leg needed stitches.

"Go and get fixed up." She tugged on his hand. "That gash looks bad."

"I can't stand the thought of leaving you." He glanced in the direction of the house. "Only work outside, okay? The place is unstable."

"I will. I just have to go in for—"

"No." He grabbed her arms and pulled her against him again. "Promise me you won't go in the house until I get back. And stay away from power lines."

"Okay. Promise."

Craig blasted his horn.

Judah pulled his cell phone out of his pocket. "Here. Keep this."

"But you need it."

He clasped his hands around hers and gave her the phone. "I'll use Craig's, or I'll call you from the hospital."

"All right. Thanks. Hurry back."

"I will." He touched her cheek, and she thought by the gentle look in his gaze he might kiss her. Instead, he limped a few steps, then glanced back. "You know I have to talk with him, right?"

"Please, don't make waves." Tears stuck in her throat. "I needed you to understand, that's all."

"And I do." Did that mean he wouldn't talk with Craig? "Stay safe."

"You too."

He stepped up into the vehicle and closed the door. The monster truck pulled into the flooded street, and Paisley lifted her hand, wondering how long she might be here by herself. Had any neighbors weathered the storm too? Or would she be the only person left in Basalt?

As the truck rumbled down Front Street, Craig stared back at her through the side-view mirror with a dark glint in his eyes. What did such a brooding expression mean?

Twenty-six

The ride back to Highway 101 was one of the worst overland trips Judah ever endured. With each bump and jarring motion of the giant truck, he clenched his teeth and fought the urge to bellow out in pain. The junction of South Road and the highway was completely flooded and impassable. Large chunks of pavement had broken off the road due to water damage and soil erosion, and some pieces had fallen down the cliff. But thanks to Craig's ability to maneuver an off-road four-wheel-drive vehicle, they kept moving.

So far, Judah hadn't confronted Craig with Paisley's accusation. He was praying about it. How would God have him address the grievance? Paisley's unwillingness to ride in Craig's truck showed him just how much she was still affected by his supervisor's misdeeds. He couldn't keep silent much longer. While he was thankful Craig rescued them, part of him wondered why. Because of their friendship? Or his guilty conscience?

After they traveled several miles down the coastal highway, the ride became smoother, and Judah, not able to keep his eyes open, nodded off to sleep. But each time the truck hit a pothole or drove over a branch, he awakened with a start, grimacing at his leg burning like it was on fire. Then his thoughts roiled with snippets of Paisley's confession and his fists clenched. He imagined himself planting them in the driver's face—the opposite of offering grace, he knew.

And not only was he dealing with his anger toward Craig, he was furious at Dad also.

And yet, what if Dad hadn't intervened that night? The story could have ended far worse. Had God sent him there to protect Paisley? It was hard for Judah to imagine his father listening to any heavenly direction. He groaned, not caring if Craig heard.

"Hurting?" Craig glanced his way.

"Hmm." He didn't trust himself to say more than that.

"Want me to call your parents?"

"Why?" Judah felt instantly defensive. "Since when are you chummy with my parents?"

Craig's mouth dropped open, he squinted at Judah, then faced the front windshield again. "I wouldn't say 'chummy.'"

"Enemies, perhaps?" Judah muttered under his breath.

The truck nearly leaped over a tree limb. Judah grabbed hold of the door bar to steady himself.

"Your folks are probably worried with your staying in Basalt Bay during a hurricane, that's all." Craig made a "tsk" sound. "I still say it was a stupid move."

Judah didn't have to explain anything outside of work to him. When the vehicle swayed again, he moaned. "Can't you drive straighter?"

Craig smirked. "There's your fighting spirit."

"Oh, I've got plenty of fight left." Judah glared at Craig. He didn't have any reason to show respect to the other man, now that he knew he didn't deserve admiration. However, he was failing at the attitude of grace he was striving for.

"What's gotten into you?" Craig's eyebrow quirked. "Delirious with pain, or something?"

Judah gnawed on the inside of his cheek, irritation knotting up in his chest until he couldn't remain quiet another second. "If I am delirious, it's with rage," he spit out. "Truth is, I'm furious over something I heard—about you." Forgiveness would have to come later. Right now, standing up for his wife burned in his gut like a wildfire.

"What did I do?" Craig shrugged and acted guiltless.

"As if you don't know." Judah clenched his fists.

Craig coughed. "If Paisley told you some garbage about me, don't believe a word, man. We've been pals for too long."

So, he automatically assumed it was Paisley who told him? *Guilty!*

"Pals?" Judah almost yelled. "Were you my 'pal' when you kissed my wife? When you tried forcing her to do something she didn't want to do?"

"Is that what she told you?" Craig smacked the steering wheel with his right palm. "Look, she's been gone all this time, and now she comes back, spouting half-packed bologna? Get real, man. Would I kiss your woman?"

"I would never have thought it of you." Judah glared at him again, looking for culpability.

"See there."

"So, you deny making an advance on her?" Even if he denied it, Judah wouldn't believe him.

"Advance? C'mon. You're out of your mind, Grant." Craig turned on the blinkers for his approach to Peace Harbor Medical Center in Florence. The parking lot was already packed with vehicles. "Since I've never been alone with her, how could I have kissed her?"

Something didn't add up. Pain and lack of sleep might be making Judah's thinking fuzzy, but Paisley wouldn't concoct that kind of story. Last night she cried when she explained Craig's aggressive actions toward her. She was broken up about it, even after all this time. Was Craig bald-faced lying to cover his tracks? Or, since he'd been intoxicated, was it possible he didn't remember what happened?

When the truck came to a stop, Judah opened the door and slid out before his coworker ran around the vehicle. He winced at the ripping sensation in his calf, but he kept limping forward, aggravation churning in him. At the front of the truck, he pointed his index finger at Craig. "Look, Paisley is my wife, and I believe what she told me. Stay away from her. You hear me?"

"Yeah, sure. Of course." Craig shrugged again, like it was a non-issue.

Judah gritted his teeth, doubting he could work with this guy again. Unless he forgave him. But that might take time, especially if Craig continued denying the offense.

As he moved toward the ER entrance, an idea came to mind. "All I have to do is call my dad."

"About what?"

"About that night." Judah held out his palm to stop Craig. "He was there. He can tell me what he saw."

"Ask him then." A tic twitched in his supervisor's jaw. Maybe he was more nervous about Mayor Grant becoming involved than he let on.

Judah wasn't going to get into a scuffle in the hospital parking lot, and besides, he still needed Craig to drive him back to Paisley. So, this matter would have to be tabled. He switched topics, but he couldn't turn off his annoyance with Craig as easily. "Why did you say I might lose my job?"

"Positions are in jeopardy over the system malfunction." Craig scowled. "Mike Linfield wants to blame someone."

"I didn't have anything to do with the alarm." That wasn't part of his job description.

"No?" One of Craig's bushy black eyebrows rose.

"No."

"The mayor pushed for the upgrade, didn't he?" Craig rubbed his hands like he was cold, or else plotting something. "Even the town helped back the investment."

"So?"

"So"—Craig snorted—"didn't you discuss the new technology with Daddy?"

Judah could almost smell the blame being thrown at him. "Years ago, maybe." He and his dad hadn't been on friendly terms in seven years.

"Mike wants a scapegoat. So will the mayor." Craig nodded his head toward Judah as if the answer were obvious.

He was tempted to knock the sneer off Craig's face, even though they were standing in the hospital parking lot. "It's not going to be me, I can tell you that." Wanting to put distance between them, Judah resumed his limp toward the entrance where others were already lined up outside the ER. Two offenses were piled up like a broken levee against his previous friend—how he treated Paisley and his lies. What Judah did about them remained to be seen.

"You could make a deal." Craig caught up to him. "Get the mayor to pull some strings." He swayed his thumb back and forth. "For both of us."

"You've got to be kidding." A sinking feeling twisted in Judah's gut. "What do you have to do with my dad?"

"Nothing," Craig said quickly. "You're implicated because of his involvement."

"And you."

Craig scoffed. "No idea what you're talking about."

Your dad came around the corner. Saw us. Craig and me. By then, I was fighting and scratching and kicking mad. Paisley's description of that night pulsed through Judah's thoughts.

He was going to speak to Dad, all right. Then he'd find Craig and tell him just what he thought of him—even if it got him fired.

But first he needed stitches. And a ride back to Basalt Bay.

Twenty-seven

For the last four hours, Paisley had been working outside, sloshing through shin-deep water, gathering and stacking tree limbs, broken boards, and shingles into a huge pile in the front yard. She collected sopping wet garbage and more boards from the backyard too. Her most difficult task was making herself follow Judah's instructions to stay out of the house. Once, she ignored his warning and climbed over the apple tree and went through the front window to get inside so she could unlock and open the door. Thirty seconds, that's all—long enough to be saddened by the standing water covering the floors of the home she grew up in. What a cleaning job this was going to be.

If Judah didn't return soon, she wouldn't have a choice about going inside. She had to find somewhere to dry off and get warm. She'd already been working in the cold, wet conditions for too long. What if he didn't make it back before nightfall? She shivered at the thought of staying in the swamped, dark house alone. It was weird enough working outside in silence without seeing anyone else in the neighborhood. A ghost town, for sure.

Fortunately, there was fresh drinking water—for now. Thanks to the spigot on the side of the house still working, and after making sure the liquid ran clear, she guzzled enough to satisfy her several times. But she was ravenously hungry. Another reason to go inside.

Was anyone else left in Basalt? Front Street was flooded. She could wade a few blocks, shouting out greetings to see if anyone answered. However, Judah warned her to stay away from downed power lines. To get around safely, she needed a rowboat, which Dad didn't have.

Judah's phone buzzed in her back pocket. She yanked it out, her cold fingers fumbling with the screen. "Hello?" She hadn't checked caller ID.

"Who's this?" A woman's voice.

"Paisley. Who's this?"

Click.

Wait. Who was that? She climbed up on a pile of wood to get out of the water, although the large boots she found floating in the backyard earlier were filled with liquid anyway. She thumbed through the menu to recent calls. Mia's name came up last. A work-related call? Or personal? Why did she disconnect? Paisley groaned. Then pressed redial.

"Yes?" Mia's voice again.

"Why'd you hang up?" No pleasantries were needed.

"Just checking on Judah." Mia sounded defensive. "I'm calling all the workers."

And hanging up if a female answered the phone, hmm? Paisley swallowed back her spiteful assessment. "He isn't here."

"He's required to have his work phone with him at all times." Mia's bossy tone irked Paisley more than her hanging up did.

Not wanting Judah to get in trouble because he lent her his phone, she had to explain. "There was an emergency. Craig drove Judah to the hospital. He gave me his cell."

"Oh, no. Judah's hurt?"

Mia's gushing tone grated on Paisley's nerves. Still, they were in a disaster, so the truth seemed necessary. "Yes, he was. We stayed at my dad's house last night."

"In Basalt Bay?" Mia screeched.

"Uh-huh."

"You could have been killed!"

One, two, three. "You think I don't know that?" Paisley suppressed a groan. "At least, we're alive."

"Thank God."

"Yes." *Thank You, Lord, for letting us live*—she sincerely meant that. However, two seconds of humility didn't absolve her frustration. "Was there something you wanted? I have work to do."

"You say Craig took Judah to the hospital?"

"Yeah. In Florence." Maybe she shouldn't have given her those details.

"Thanks, Pais." Mia ended the call abruptly.

Paisley groaned. She didn't allow anyone to call her "Pais" other than Judah.

Her stomach growled. She craved comfort food, especially after that phone call. Maybe a frosting-covered donut and a twenty-ounce cup of heavily creamed coffee from a barista. Impossibilities today.

To get her mind off her hunger pains, and her angst toward Mia, she returned to her work. An hour later, she had to figure out how to climb inside the kitchen safely. The large spruce still leaned against the roof. Hopefully, it wouldn't cave in the structure any more. Peering around the watery backyard, she spotted a lawn chair that might work to support her while she peeked in the kitchen window.

She waded through the flooded yard and grabbed the patio furniture. One leg wobbled in her hand. Would it hold her weight? Near the back porch, she leaned the chair against the wall. She stepped up on the seat, then propping her right foot on the top edge, heaved herself upward. Grabbing the framework around the window, she held on and peered inside.

From this angle, she saw all the way into the living room, with the apple tree its uninvited centerpiece. The water may have gone down a little since she pried open the front door earlier. Everything that previously decorated the walls, including Mom's garish paintings, were floating in the water, some face down. She should have felt relieved. Never again would she have to stare at the distorted images and wonder what Mom had been thinking when she painted them.

But for some reason, she didn't feel relief. A deep sadness filled her chest. Maybe because they were Mom's, and she was gone, and Paisley didn't have any chance of making amends with her now.

Sigh.

She made herself refocus on the scene before her. The couch cushion on the kitchen table was evidence of how high the water had been or how strong the winds blew through the open window. The chairs by the table were knocked over, and whatever kitchenware had rested on the countertop was gone, swept away by the watery intruder.

The frame around the back door, beneath the bathroom she slept in, was crushed. She wouldn't be able to open that door. When the stairs fell, they apparently exploded. Broken wood was piled up in front of the back door and the washer and dryer like a beaver made a dam there. Maybe she could break out the kitchen window and climb in. Judah's warning to not go inside rang through her mind. But he wasn't here and might not make it back until tomorrow. Terrible thought.

The phone buzzed. *Judah?* She leaned back to retrieve the device from her pocket, and the chair wobbled precariously. Then she was falling backwards, gasping as she landed with a splash. Water cascaded over her head and shoulders, but somehow, she managed to keep the phone extended in the air.

She stood quickly, dripping as if she'd been swimming in the ocean. She tapped the screen. "Hello."

"Paisley?"

Hearing his voice, she almost cried. She took a breath. "Hey, Judah."

"You okay?"

"Mmhmm. You?" She shivered, clenching her teeth to keep them from chattering. She had to find dry clothes soon.

"I'm all s-stitched up." He sounded groggy. "P-pain meds m-made me a l-little woozy."

"I can imagine. Glad you're feeling better." She rubbed a sore place on her hip from the fall. "How soon can Craig drive you back?"

A gulp, then silence. "Thing is, he, uh, left."

"What?"

"He isn't answering his phone. I don't know w-what to d-do. Or how to get b-back to you." He groaned, and she wondered about his slurred speech. "Everything's k-kind of f-fuzzy right now. I'm sitting in the hospital l-lobby, using the public phone." He laughed oddly.

Did that mean he wouldn't be coming back tonight? Even though he had a genuine medical emergency, the thought of her solitary evening ahead, in the dark, incited instant fear in her. "Did you, um, talk with Craig about what I told you?" Was that why he abandoned Judah?

"Maybe. Can't r-remember." He cleared his throat. "I'll find s-someone who can drive m-me back."

He probably meant that, but he was in pain and dependent on others. Not many would chance driving in such flooded conditions. Florence was on the coast, too, and had probably been hit as badly as Basalt. Travel between the two towns would be almost impossible. Maybe she should have endured Craig's presence long enough to ride to the hospital with Judah. At least, then, they would be together. She wouldn't be here alone.

Too late for second thoughts.

"I'm going to break into the kitchen to get some food." She might as well confess her plan to him since he'd hear about it later. Besides, he wouldn't expect her to sleep outside.

He made a disgruntled sound. "I didn't want you going in the house by yourself. I remember that."

"I know, but I have to sleep somewhere." Without electricity. With gaping windows and howling winds rushing through the house.

"I'll g-get to you some—" Then, deep, nasally breathing. Did he just fall asleep?

"Judah?"

"Oh, what?" He snorted. Yawned loudly.

"Are you okay?"

"Uh, yeah, sure. D-drowsy. C-can't—"

"Judah! There you are." A feminine voice in the background sounded familiar. "I've looked everywhere for you."

"Mia?" Judah sounded surprised.

Mia was at the hospital? *Oh, no.*

"I'm so glad you're here and alive." Her tone was all sugar and honey.

A muffled sound like Judah's hand shuffling over the hospital phone reached Paisley. Or else Mia hugged him.

That wasn't an image Paisley wanted in her thoughts.

"Mia's here," he explained as if she didn't hear the woman's voice. "I think I've found my ride back to Basalt Bay." He suddenly sounded stronger. Why was that?

"I don't think that's such a good idea." What kind of car did Mia own? Was it high enough off the ground to drive through flooded waters? Paisley bit her lip and shook her head to keep back what she wanted to say—*stay away from Mia.* Instead, she whispered, "Be safe, Judah."

"I will." He let out a soft breath. "Pais?"

"Yeah?" She wished he were here now, linking pinkies, saying he loved her. Instead, she felt like she was the only person left on the planet.

"I'll be w-with you s-soon." His garbled words were barely understandable.

"Judah, come with me. You need rest. Let me help you." Mia's wooing tone was the last thing Paisley heard before the connection ended.

Judah didn't even say goodbye.

Paisley stared at the cell phone, feeling abandoned. All too aware of her soaking wet, miserable condition.

So Mia was saving the day for Judah? How did the town flirt plan to help him find rest? And what about Craig? Had he and Judah exchanged words?

Paisley gazed around her dad's property that looked more like a shallow lake in the waning afternoon light than the yard she and her brother and sister used to play in. Dark gray clouds overhead appeared ominous. Another storm? That's all she needed.

She trembled, dreading the night ahead, and wished for morning to come quickly.

Twenty-eight

Instead of climbing in the kitchen window, Paisley waded around to the front of the house. She pulled herself up to the porch, using Judah's truck for leverage. Once she was inside the living room, every creak and crackle of the ceiling above made her skittish as she treaded through six inches of water on her way to the kitchen. Feeling numb and barely aware of the chilly wetness on her skin, she yanked open cupboards, ready to eat anything in sight. She nearly burst into tears of joy when she discovered peanut butter, strawberry jam, and bread that wasn't stale.

She grabbed a knife out of the drawer where they always stored silverware and made two sandwiches. She tried opening the refrigerator, but it wouldn't budge. Too much water remained in front.

She took her sandwiches out to the porch and dropped onto the rocker Aunt Callie sat in the other day. She propped her boots on the railing, and water poured out from them. While working, she adjusted to being wet and miserable, but with night coming, cooler temperatures were settling in and chills raced through her body. She needed a hot bath. Or an electric blanket. Dry clothes and a warm bed would do. But all the clothes were upstairs. And where would she sleep? The second story was off limits. Everything in the living room was drenched.

As she gobbled up her first sandwich, the one room in the house she hadn't looked in yet came to mind. The pantry. The dark, dreadful place. She remembered its long shelves where she might be able to climb up and get out of the water. No, she wouldn't sleep in there. Even if she was exhausted and in need of warmth.

What would she use for a light after dusk? She had Judah's cell phone, but the battery power was nearly gone. She needed to get settled before nightfall.

I can't sleep in the pantry.

She rocked back and forth in the rocker, water splashing with each movement, munching her food. Maybe she'd grab a blanket and sleep right here.

The unexpected rumble of a loud engine made her jump to her feet. She swallowed down the last chunk of peanut butter bread as a black truck barreled around a downed tree in the road and then skidded, plowing through water in the yard and shooting a ten-foot spray over the porch. Cold water hit Paisley, and she cried out.

Whoever was driving so recklessly needed to learn some manners. She didn't recognize the mud-speckled truck with its darkened glass. It looked like a high-end model. The window lowered slowly. She stared inside, curious to see if someone brought Judah back. As soon as she recognized the driver, panic as powerful as the wave that hit Basalt assailed her.

"Get in." Edward Grant rocked his thumb toward the other door.

Did the mayor think she'd go anywhere with him on command? She stepped backwards, but her oversized boot caught on an uneven floorboard and she tripped, nearly falling into the water on the porch. What a sight that would have made in front of her overbearing father-in-law. "Why should I go with you?" She made herself stand still, her chin up. She had her pride.

Edward smirked. "If it were up to me, I'd leave you here." He messed with his phone like he was checking for texts.

"I'm fine here, anyway." Would she honestly prefer to stay in a dank, cold, and lightless house—even in the pantry—over going with Edward and spending the night in her in-law's luxurious mansion on the cliff? If that meant riding in the same vehicle and staying in the same house with the coldhearted man who paid her to leave Judah, then yes, a million times over.

He stared at her wet clothing. "Uh-huh. I see how fine you are." His eyes glinted, but he didn't make the slightest move to get out of his truck. Probably didn't want his expensive shoes getting wet. "Well, I don't want all that water and mud on my truck seat."

"No worries, then, since I'm not going with you." She lifted her hand in mock civility. "Thanks for checking on me." In all her thoughts about making amends, Judah's dad never crossed her mind as a recipient. Today wouldn't be an exception. Still, she asked, "How did you know I was here?"

He chewed on something black, maybe licorice, before answering. "Judah called. Asked his mom for someone to retrieve you. I drew the short straw."

So Judah was still looking out for her. "Is he okay?"

Edward's eyebrows lifted. "Like you care."

"I do, believe it or not. Where is he?" Concern for Judah's well-being was the only thing that made her risk asking Edward anything. The night Mayor Grant chased off Craig, the repulsive things he said to her, and her exodus from town raced through her thoughts now. No, she wouldn't get in his truck, even if he were her last good option.

"He's injured, but you know that." He bit off a chunk of black licorice—she was right about that—and chewed before continuing. "Overnighting in Florence with that sweet tart, what's her name? Mia Till." His eyes glistened like he enjoyed delivering the news.

Her heart hardened a notch.

"Get in, or I'm leaving without you." His voice turned gruff. "Bess wants you up at the house, so I'll bring you there. Once you've cleaned up, I'll drive you to the airport. Anywhere you want to go, I'll pay. As long as it's far away from my son."

Those were about the vilest words he could say to her—other than what he told her three years ago about her unborn child knowing she wouldn't be a good mother. Her gut clenched. She forced herself to turn her back to him and walk through the front door. Then, out of spite, or maybe because she was determined to stick to her guns and make amends with Judah, she leaned against the doorframe as if she didn't have a care in the world. "No, thanks, Eddie"—she knew he hated that nickname. "I think I'll stay. Basalt Bay is my home."

Edward made a guttural sound, spit a wad of chewed black candy in her direction, then gunned the truck. A wave of water and brown muck splattered her, covering the places that weren't already wet and muddy. She flicked grit off her face.

In the lonely silence, a question gnawed at her insides. Was Judah really staying with Mia?

Twenty-nine

Judah sat on the cot he was assigned to at the emergency shelter in Florence, his knees supporting his elbows, and his fists propping his pounding forehead. Over one hundred fifty cots were arranged around the high school gym, and the rumble of voices was nonstop. He needed quiet and a good night's sleep. He doubted he'd get either. At least the strong pain meds the nurse gave him were wearing off. He seemed to be thinking clearer now. And he was thankful for the large-sized jeans that fit loosely over his injured leg a volunteer distributing emergency clothing had given him.

He recognized quite a few people from Basalt Bay here. For most, it was their second night away from home. Judah was fortunate to find an empty bed at all. Although, Mia's proximity concerned him. She sat on the cot next to him wearing a pouty expression. The couple who slept in their spots last night found a room in a motel in Eugene, otherwise this shelter wouldn't have beds for Judah and Mia.

"I don't see why we came to this sardine-packed hostel." She groaned like it was the worst place in the county. Apparently, thankfulness wasn't in her mindset. "Why didn't we check into a hotel?"

"They're all full, you know that." Besides, he would never have gone to one with her. He glanced around the populated room. In one corner kids were playing games. Adults sat on cots looking fatigued and discouraged—probably due to the update they received that they couldn't return to their homes yet, and might not be able to for a week. Bad news indeed. "I'm thankful for a place to sleep." Although he wished Mia had a bed on the opposite side of the room. Her whiny, demanding attitude was grating on his nerves. One thing kept his irritation manageable—she had a cell phone.

"Could I use your cell again?"

She didn't meet his gaze. "I don't know. I have to conserve battery power."

"It'll be a quick call. I need to check on Paisley." He extended his palm, hoping she'd set her phone on it.

"You sent the mayor after her." She huffed. "You've done your ex-husbandly duty."

He subdued his spike in irritation and clasped his hands together. "I'm not her *ex*-husband."

"Yet." She rolled her eyes. "Why you keep chasing a woman who doesn't want you when there are so many waiting for you to pull the marital plug, I have no idea." She plunged her hand into her bag, then pulled out a tube of lipstick and spread a thick red film over her lips.

He bit his tongue to hold back a rude response, then settled on an honest one. "She's my wife and the fact that I love her are reasons enough."

Mia's fingers clutching the tube of gloss came to a standstill. She met his gaze with a look of absurdity. "After all she's done to you?"

"For better or for worse." He held out his hand toward her again. "May I use your cell, or should I go ask one of my more compassionate neighbors?"

"Fine. Make it fast." Glaring, she tossed him her zebra-striped phone.

He caught it, then punched in his phone number. He turned away from Mia's gaze.

"Hello," Paisley answered.

"Hey." He closed his eyes, trying to shut out the noisy gym, and savoring the sound of her voice. "You okay?"

"Yeah." She spoke quietly. Was the connection bad?

"Did my dad find you?"

"He did." She sniffed.

Then silence.

Oh, man. What did Dad say to her? "Did he, um, explain that I can't get back tonight?"

"Uh-huh."

Her cryptic responses let him know something was wrong. "I'm sorry I can't make it back. The road's busted up and washed out. Craig had a terrible time getting through to take me to the hospital." His excuses sounded lame. Craig should have brought him back to Basalt Bay. Instead, he left without even telling Judah. "I'm sorry for sending my dad. I know you probably didn't want to go to his house, but I'm staying overnight at a storm shelter in Florence and can't get to you. I wanted you to be somewhere safe." She still hadn't said anything about going to his parents' place. Was she mad at him for calling Dad? Were things weird at their house? He imagined Dad asking Paisley all kinds of embarrassing questions, although Judah begged him to be polite. "My mom loves you. You know that, right?"

Still, silence.

"She'd do anything for you." He swallowed hard. "Maybe you can stay in one of the rooms in the loft, farther away from Dad. Just until morning, okay?"

A sigh, then, "I didn't go with him."

"What?" That may have come out harsher than he meant, but what she said shocked him. "Paisley, why not? What happened?"

Mia leaned in. "What's wrong?"

He shook his head at her, wishing she hadn't said anything. If Paisley heard her, she might jump to the wrong conclusion.

"I couldn't, that's all." Her breath came in a huff. "Was that Mia Till? Your dad said you were staying with her."

A sharp pain seared up his chest like a bad case of heartburn. "I never told my dad that." How did his father find out he was with Mia? He glanced at the C-MER receptionist. Did she call his dad?

Paisley cleared her throat. "So that wasn't Mia, then?"

"No, it was. But—"

"I've got to go." She sounded frustrated. "I have to find some-where dry to sleep. Everything's wet. The water went down a couple of inches, but not much."

"Wait, Paisley, don't hang up." He stood and winced as pain splintered up his leg. "Craig left, and I couldn't find someone else to drive me back. The underside of Mia's car sits too low." He hated to tell her the next part, especially now that she was staying at her dad's alone. "Word is the National Guard is at both the South Road and North Road junctions, keeping residents from reentering Basalt Bay." He heard her gulp. "They're telling us those roads have to be fixed for public safety before they allow anyone to return. I'm so sorry you're there by yourself."

"Me too."

A lump filled his throat. "Are you inside the house now?"

"It's almost dark out, so I came in." She drew in a raspy-sounding breath. "No lights."

He felt helpless, and so far away from her. "I'm sorry I left you."

"Don't be. This isn't your fault." She paused. Sighed. "Your leg was in a bad way. You had to go."

Her words made him feel a little better.

"Are you in less pain now?"

"I am." He wished he was with her. "Please, be careful tonight."

She made a sound like she was shoving something. "Wish I could get this tree out, then I'd cover up the window."

He groaned. "I'm going to find a way to come to you tomorrow, even if I have to walk in. I promise." He didn't know how he'd get there—gimpy and limping, most likely—but he would find a way.

"The battery, Judah." Mia waved her hand in front of his face, making it hard to ignore her. "You think this is a fast phone call?"

"Wait a sec, is she sleeping next to you?" Paisley's tone turned sharp.

He wouldn't lie, even to ease her worry or his discomfort. "Yeah, that's how it worked out. I'm sorry. We didn't have any choice."

"I think there's always a choice. I—" Paisley exhaled. "Look, Judah, no judgment, okay? Just, um, sleep well."

"You too." He couldn't let their conversation end in frustration or suspicion. "Pais?"

"Yeah?"

He wished he were holding her safely in his arms, kissing away her worries, and staying close enough to comfort her through any panic attacks she might have. Instead, he was twenty miles away from her in an overcrowded gym, sitting on a cot next to Mia. "I'm praying for you."

"Thanks."

As soon as the call ended, Mia snatched the phone from his hand. She stared hard at the screen. "Battery's shot. Thanks a lot." She threw the device into her bag.

He never knew her to be so crabby and self-centered before. "Sorry." It seemed he was saying that a lot. He laid down on the cot and flung his arm over his eyes. If only he could shut out the noise in the gym as easily—and the haunting image of Paisley spending the night alone in a flooded house without electricity.

He should be with her. But what else could he have done? The medical team said his cut was infected. That it was a good thing he came in when he did. Twenty stitches proved his need for medical intervention. Still, he felt responsible for Paisley being on her own in Basalt Bay. He should have insisted she come with him. He thought of his grandfather hefting his grandmother over his shoulder. Maybe Judah should have tried that. He released a long sigh.

Mia laid down on her cot, less aggressively, it seemed. "It'll be okay, Judah." Her fingers brushed the bare part of his wrist.

He jerked his arm out of her reach, sat up. Paisley's words replayed in his mind. *Always a choice.* Even now, he had a choice to do the honorable thing. He stood on his bum leg, then snatched up the coat the volunteer gave him earlier.

"What are you doing?" Mia clasped his wrist.

He peeled her fingers from his skin, none too gently. "I'm going to find somewhere to sleep on the other side of the room."

"Why?" She made a flirty face. "Oh. Are you worried about us being so close?" She ran her index finger along the blanket on the cot he deserted.

"Not in the least."

She crossed her arms. "Then what?"

"I'm concerned with what my wife, the woman I love and want to spend the rest of my life with, might think of this arrangement, nothing more." He pushed his arms into the coat.

She harrumphed. "I don't see what the big deal is."

"Obviously, you don't." He walked away without a backward glance. Even if he sat on the floor all night, this was his decision. He'd spend the time praying for Paisley's health and safety, and for their reconciliation.

In the morning, he was going to find a way back to Basalt Bay and his wife, no matter what the officials guarding the road had to say about his plan.

Thirty

The apple tree wouldn't budge, so Paisley gave up trying to move it. The blanket she used to partially cover the window last night was sopping wet, which meant she couldn't secure the opening, either. One more night would pass with cold air filling the house. Fortunately, another storm didn't hit.

Earlier, she corralled wooden chunks from the collapsed stairs leading to the second story into a pile in front of the dryer. Broken boards, nails, handrails, and other debris still littered the kitchen and laundry area, but it had gotten too dark to continue working. By ten p.m., a little more floodwater drained from the house—something to be thankful for.

Throughout the evening, she used Judah's cell phone for light as needed, but its weak luminosity meant battery power was fading fast.

She'd put off the inevitable long enough. She had to find somewhere to sleep, or at least, to wait out the night. Everything in the living room was soaked, including the couch. Stretching out on the kitchen counter was a possibility, if she cleaned it first, except the wind blowing through the front window all night would be freaky. Even wild creatures could come in. She shivered and went in search of bedding.

In the cupboard above the washing machine, she found a twin-sized comforter and a beach towel. Then grumbling at her predicament, and the fact her arrival at Basalt Bay coincided so closely with hurricane winds, she trudged through the kitchen. At the closed pantry door, she stood there for about two minutes, staring through the darkness at the closet-sized entrance. She gulped and tugged on the knob. Now or never.

She stepped inside the narrow room and tapped the cell phone light—it flickered. The air that hit her smelled stagnant and musty, and not just because of the few inches of water on the floor. The small space seemed unused, and mostly empty. Hadn't Dad stored anything in this room since Mom died?

A harrowing picture of herself as a kid, huddled on the floor, skinny arms around knobby knees, waiting for her sentencing of an hour to think over her mistakes to end, pulsed through her thoughts. A couple of times, an hour turned into two because Mom forgot about her. Once when that happened, Paisley hurled two soup cans through the window, making enough space for her to squeeze through. Mom had been livid. After that, the escape route was boarded up, the way it appeared now. A shudder overtook her. How could she sleep in here?

Judah said he was praying for her. Did he sense she needed peace tonight?

The light flickered again. She aimed the dwindling glow on the three skinny shelves that resembled a miniature bunk bed. She pointed it at the wet floors. No moving creatures. A few boxes rested on the lower shelf, probably Mom's unfinished paintings. Mason jars and old canning equipment lined the upper shelf. The middle ledge appeared the most feasible for a makeshift bed.

I can do this. I'm an adult now.

Then why did she feel every insecurity she ever experienced rushing through her like a time bomb ready to implode? Her heart throbbed hard in her chest. Her arms shook.

The cell light shut off. Instant darkness engulfed her. She clenched her jaw and grabbed hold of the shelf in front of her. She counted to ten. Then taking a deep breath, she visualized the ocean, *her ocean*, the way she loved it when she sat on the peninsula and let

sea-foam arc over her head. In her mind's eye, she felt the spray
cascading over her hair and caressing her cheeks. Then she thought
of Judah's blue eyes staring into hers so sweetly—and that moment
last night when their lips touched, and he held her close. She'd never
forget how bonded she felt with him through the storm.

She inhaled and exhaled. Panic averted.

Sigh.

At least this room had a door that closed and would keep the
wind out, unlike sleeping on the kitchen counter or on the washer
and dryer. The shelves were dry. She ran her hand over the middle
board to get rid of any dust or dead spiders, even though she couldn't
see what she was doing. She spread out the towel and blanket, her
faux sheet and comforter, going through the motions of preparing
for bed even though she doubted she could sleep.

Her clothes had to come off to dry. She hung Dad's sweatpants
and socks on some wall pegs. Shivering, teeth chattering, she climbed
up and huddled under the blanket in the dark, wishing for the warmth
of a sleeping bag or two thick quilts. The shelf moaned but held.

She squeezed her eyes shut, blocking out shadows of yesterdays.
She'd lay here and wait for morning, then before long, Judah would
be here. No thinking of Mom's unfinished art pieces stored in this
room. No contemplating the half-painted purple irises of a blurry
child resembling Paige. Or the brightly-colored round face that might
have been a portrait of Aunt Callie. Or the one Mom said was of
Paisley falling off the rocks and into the ocean—was that her greatest
fear? Although, Paisley had never recognized herself in the distorted
paint-splotched canvas.

The house's creaking intensified. Every noise caused by the wind
coming in the windows made her shrink into herself, her arms
clutched about her ribs. Even though she couldn't see the board
above her, it felt too close. Her whole body curled into a fetal
position shook with cold. And fear.

She hated the pitch dark. Even when she and Judah were married,
she kept a night-light on in the hallway. Something about blackest
darkness made the air seem unbreathable. Poisonous.

Ohhh.

In her tiny Chicago apartment, where the panic attacks started, did she feel stifled and trapped? Unable to breathe in enough air?

Something crashed upstairs.

Paisley sat up, bumping her head on the upper shelf. She groaned. Something probably fell over, that's all. Even if a wild animal came inside, the pantry door was closed. Nothing could reach her. She blew out a breath and laid back down, listening, on edge.

If Judah were here beside her, his arm around her shoulders, she wouldn't be afraid. What a kindhearted man he'd become. Or was he always like that and she just didn't notice? No, something was different. Perhaps, his relationship with God? Judah mentioned Him more, as if he relied on Him in ways he hadn't before. She appreciated his promise to be praying for her.

She replayed their kiss in her mind again. Passion was obviously still there between them. What about marriage and commitment? Did she want to be married to him?

Last night, when she was locked in the bathroom, their fingers touching beneath the door, she imagined a life with them starting over as a married couple. Of course, that was before Edward taunted her with the news Judah was spending the night next to Mia.

She groaned, then stared into the dark at what she knew to be the solid shelf above her. Another time, she hid here when the three siblings were playing a game of hide-and-seek. Paige opened the door, took a quick look inside, then yelled that Paisley wasn't in the pantry. Afterward, Paisley gloated at having tricked her sister so easily. She won the game because Paige was too afraid to hunt for her in the creepy room—yet she'd never been locked inside. Unless she had, and Paisley never knew. *Oh.* She closed her eyes, pondering that.

Then she thought of their cottage. Had the storm destroyed the beach house they loved from the moment they saw it? She remembered how much she'd looked forward to bringing Misty Gale home. *Sweet baby, I miss you so much.* Tears filled her eyes. And her heart—was that possible? Yet her breathing didn't turn raspy. She actually thought of her daughter, even about missing her, without having an attack.

Thank God. Was the Lord healing her? Was He, perhaps, with her now in the scariest place of all? Last night, with Judah's and her pinkies touching, it seemed a layer of callousness broke free from her heart. And today she felt more alive. Not whole. But better.

She breathed in and out, relaxing. Maybe she could fall asleep, after all.

An engine roared to a stop outside.

Paisley sat up fast and slammed her head into the shelf again. She moaned, then froze. Who would be here after ten o'clock at night? Who was in Basalt besides her?

Looters? Edward again?

She tried to listen over the thundering of her heart.

The engine motor revved a few times. A warning?

The phone buzzed next to her. She silenced it. "Hello," she whispered. What if whoever was outside was calling her?

"Pais?"

"Judah." His name came out in a rush.

"I had to call you one more time." He spoke fast. "James Weston let me use his cell phone."

James was Dad's neighbor across the street, but she was only half listening. The rest of her was cued in to the sound of the truck shutting off outside. Then the silence.

"Pais, I wanted you to know, I moved to the opposite side of the gym, away from Mia."

"O-kay." She spoke softly, not wanting whoever was out there to hear her.

"I'll find a way to get to you as soon as—"

"Someone's here." She cut into his words.

"What? Who?"

"I . . . don't . . . know," she whispered.

A clatter at the front of the house jarred her insides. Fear prickled up her skin. She held her breath.

"Someone's there? Outside?" His voice rose.

"Yes." She had to get back into her wet clothes. She climbed down from the shelf.

"Do you have a stick or a tool to use if you have to?"

"For a weapon?"

"Yes."

If she could hurl Mason jars like mud balls, she'd be fine. "I have to go." How could she hit anyone with a glass jar? What if it was a National Guardsman? Or a FEMA worker? But why would they come so late?

"Paisley, wait. I'm praying for you." His caring words spoke to a need deep inside her.

"You're a wonderful man." Static came over the connection. The battery had to be nearly dead. "I'm sorry for hurting you."

When his voice came back talking about something else, she didn't think he heard her apology. "You should pray too, Pais. Trust God to keep you safe. He's with you. I'm going to keep praying and believing until the second you call me back."

She almost tapped the end button. His voice stopped her.

"I love you."

Then silence. The connection was lost.

She set the cell phone down on the shelf, then grabbed the soaked pants and forced her feet into the legs, struggling to put on the cold, wet fabric. She shoved her icy toes into the big boots. Forget socks.

As silently as possible, she crept to the door and opened it an inch. From previous experiences, she knew how to pull up on the handle so it wouldn't squeak.

A light that had to be coming from a flashlight splashed around the kitchen walls. Someone *was* looking for her.

Her heart pounded frantically. *Lord, help me. Protect me.* She didn't like desperate prayers, but she said the words internally anyway.

She closed the door, then returned to the shelf and picked up the phone. She shook it hard, hoping to coax the flashlight on even for a second. She pointed the faint glow toward the boxes, then she dug through them quietly, searching for something solid.

One box contained old broken picture frames. She grabbed two skinny boards. They wouldn't do any real damage, but she could hold them up and make a fierce expression, like she might be aggressive.

What if the other person had a weapon?

The cell light shut off again.

God, please protect me. Stop whoever this is from doing harm. In the darkness, she thought of the way she shunned Him for the last several years. *I'm sorry for being angry at You and holding a grudge.*

She opened the door again and peered out with one eye.

"Paisley?" A deep male voice she recognized turned the blood in her veins to ice.

She shut the door and pressed her back against it. She needed more than a couple of chunks of wood to protect herself. Maybe she should get on her knees and beg God for mercy. No time. Instead, she opted for the words in her heart. *I know You've taken good care of my baby, Misty Gale. I've heard You're a good Father. Please rescue me. I would like the chance to make peace with my family.*

Heavy footsteps thudded through the house. "Paisley?" His gruff voice drew closer.

She didn't move. What if the cell worked and Judah called, giving away her hiding place?

A splash of light illuminated the watery space near her boots. She held her breath, her heart throbbing in her throat. She clutched the sticks. The Mason jars were within reach.

Instead of opening the pantry door, as she anticipated he might do, the man trudged toward the other side of the house. Did he think this room was a closet she couldn't fit into? An easy mistake, considering the narrow door. Or did God, somehow, make the handle invisible? She'd heard of miracles like that, although she never experienced one. With bated breath, she listened to the man's footfall as he scrounged through the lower floor, calling her name.

She had to act quickly. She tapped the cell phone screen. The slight flicker of light let her know she didn't have a chance of placing a call. She'd send a text.

She wanted Judah to know two things. Her fingers flew over the alphabet keypad.

I love you too.

She wished she could see his face when he read those words. Hadn't she been in love with him since the day he gazed into her eyes and called her beautiful over seven years ago?

She took a deep breath, trying to calm her frantic heartbeat. Then she tapped in words that would make her husband feel crazy since he couldn't reach her until tomorrow.

Craig's here.

I hope you enjoyed *Ocean of Regret* and are rooting for Judah and Paisley's journey together. Please take a minute and write a review wherever you purchased this book. They say reviews are the lifeblood for authors, and I would consider it a personal favor if you wrote one. Even one line telling what you thought about the book is helpful. Thank you!

About Basalt Bay

I took many creative liberties with my imaginary coastal town and its stormy weather and C-MER—and I loved doing it! To all those who live on the Oregon Coast, please forgive my embellishments. I enjoy the Pacific Ocean and the Oregon Coast so much that I wanted to create my own little world there.

For readers with a scientific inclination, if my meteorology or oceanography facts appear skewed, all I can say is, "That's the way it happened in Basalt Bay!"

If you would like to be one of the first to hear about Mary's new releases and upcoming projects, sign up for her newsletter—and receive the free pdf "Rekindle Your Romance! 50+ Date Night Ideas for Married Couples"—at www.maryehanks.com/gift.

A Special Thanks to all who helped make this book happen!

Paula McGrew . . . You have been such a blessing in my life. Thank you for tweaking my work, helping me dig deeper into my characters, and for cheering me on with affirming words. I hope we can meet in person someday!

Jason Hanks . . . Thanks for letting me ramble about my writing projects on our many walks. And thanks for being my go-to guy about car parts and boat operations. Love you forever!

Suzanne Williams . . . I love your cover designs! Thank you for another beautiful one. Your talent is a gifting, and I love the emotion and beauty in your artwork.

Michelle Storm, Mary Acuff, Kellie Wanke, Melissa Hammerstrom, and Jason Hanks . . . Thank you for being wonderful beta readers. Every story needs a testing audience, and I thank you so much for being willing to weather the storms in Basalt Bay with me. Thanks for your critique and your encouragement. I appreciate you all!

Daniel, Philip, Deborah, Shem, Traci, and the special people in their lives who smile and act interested when I *just have* to show them my latest cover before anyone else has seen it. Thanks for the cheers. I love you guys.

Papa God . . . I'm so thankful for the chance to write a story of redemption and reconciliation again. Thank *You* for putting these stories in my heart.

www.maryehanks.com

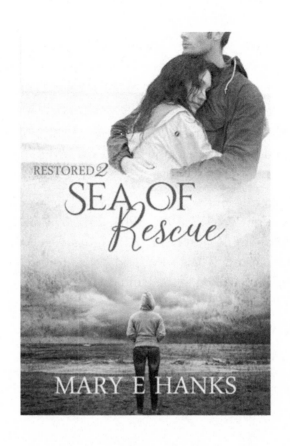

Sea of Rescue

Restored 2

Mary E. Hanks

Suzanne D. Williams Cover Design

www.feelgoodromance.com/

Cover photos: micromonkey @ iStock; narcisopa @ Shutterstock

Visit Mary's website:

www.maryehanks.com

You can write Mary at

maryhanks@maryehanks.com.

For Mike,

My sweet brother who led me to Jesus many years ago.

For Jason,

The guy whose green eyes still make my heart flip-flop.

Author's note:

I've taken many creative liberties in this story—all I can say is, "That's the way it happened in Basalt Bay!"

When anxiety was great within me,

your consolation brought joy to my soul.

Psalm 94:19

One

Ice-cold adrenaline raced through Paisley Grant's veins as she leaned against the pantry door, an empty quart-sized Mason jar clutched in her right hand. She ignored her shaky breaths, her throbbing heartbeat, and the heat rising in her flushed cheeks, because her nemesis, Craig Masters, was out there, somewhere, maybe just a few feet away.

Was he waiting to hurt her? Terrorize her? She couldn't put her finger on any other motive for his late-night arrival.

Swallowing past the bitter taste in the back of her mouth threatening to choke her, she clamped her mouth shut lest she make a sound and give away her hiding place. She gripped the jar tighter, mentally and physically preparing herself to hit the intruder, if it came to that. *Please, God, don't let it come to that.* In her left hand, she held two long skinny wooden frame pieces from Mom's old busted canvases. It was an odd collection of weapons, but she'd do what she had to do to survive.

She pressed her ear against the crack of the door, listening for the next sound that might alert her to Craig's location. Was he in the kitchen? Farther away in the living room? She didn't shuffle an inch, afraid her boots might make a ripple in the standing ankle-high water left by the flood following Hurricane Blaine. How long could she stand statue-still like this without him finding her?

A shiver raced along her nerves, imploding in her brain, or so it felt, as she thought of another time when Craig caused a terrible fear to rise in her. Her hand clutching the jar shook. Her heart hammered double-time against her ribs. Lightheaded, she blew out a breath. Had she locked her knees? She flexed her leg muscles. Inhaled silently.

Why was the man who worked with her husband, Judah, at C-MER, Basalt Bay's Coastal Management and Emergency Responders, being so quiet now? Moments ago, he yelled her name over and over. White fear had spasmed up her breastbone, leaving a spark of pain in her chest. Now, waiting in the pitch dark, with nothing but silence and her wild imagination, was nearly as terrifying.

If she could figure out how to run through the flooded house and escape without him seeing her, she would. But charging through the swamped kitchen, and dashing through the living room where Mom's paintings still floated in seawater, without Craig catching her? Impossible.

She swallowed hard. Kept the jar clutched to her chest.

Even if she could elude him, what then? It was late. Dark outside. The whole town was without power. No streetlights. And thanks to overcast skies, no moonlight. The neighbors had covered their windows with sheets of plywood, and probably locked their doors, before fleeing town prior to the hurricane. She'd have a hard time breaking into any houses.

Her thoughts rushed back to Craig and how she could get away from him. He was a solid man. Muscular. A football player in his high school days. Still, she was gritty and wily. She'd kick, swing her elbows, flail at him with her Mason jar and the broken frame. Then run like crazy. What if she couldn't get away? If he grabbed her wrist. Forced her—

No! She'd stay alert. Watch for her chance. Her previous altercation with him flashed through her mind. That time she fought him, kicking and scratching—a losing battle. He overpowered her, even drunk as he was, until Mayor Grant came along. That her father-in-law wound up being a hero *and* a scum revolted her still.

A door squeaked open, then thudded closed. The front door? Had Craig been outside looking for her?

The muscles in her fingers contracted around the Mason jar's neck. She could do this. Protect herself. God was on her side—if Judah knew what he was talking about. *Please, please.*

The man's boots made a thwump-thwump rhythm as he strode across the kitchen where the floor wasn't carpeted, coming toward her. She pressed her weight against the door. Lifted the glass weaponry. How hard would she have to hit the man to knock him out?

As a kid she was a pro at throwing mud balls. Had a good aim. If she hurled this jar at Craig—to protect herself—she was going to make it count. He'd probably need stitches. A visit to the ER in Florence.

"*Paishley?*"

Why did he slur her name like that? Her heart skipped a couple of beats.

"I been *lookin'foryou.*" His gruff voice ran the words together. "You think you can hide from the *mashter* of search and *reshcue?*" He made a snarky laugh. Something thudded as if he ran into the wall. He said a foul curse word. Was he drunk?

Something crashed. She jerked, then wished she hadn't. Did he see water swirling on the other side of the door?

What if his broken speech and bumping into things were an act? A lure to get her to come out of hiding. She had to be careful. Cautious of his tricks.

"I foun' your ole man's *shtash.*" He sounded like he was pickled.

What stash? What was he talking about?

"Daddy's an alcoholic, hmmm?" He crashed against the wall right next to her hiding place.

I don't want to hurt him. But if he comes in here, I'll do whatever it takes to stop him.

"Women drive men to drink. That what happened to your dad?"

Her dad wasn't an alcoholic. An image of him barely able to walk up the front steps yesterday pinged in her thoughts. She never knew him to be a drinker. He used to say he hated beer. Was he drinking to bury his grief over Mom's death?

Then again, maybe Craig was hoping for her lapse in attention. Her distraction. She stiffened, leaned firmly against the door.

"*Paishley* Grant!" He rattled the doorknob.

She gripped the jar. This was it.

"Funny how *thingsh* work out." His tone changed. He sang a couple of muddled lyrics from a country love song.

Why didn't he just open the door?

"*Paishley?*" His loud voice came through the crack between the door and the doorframe. A flashlight beam blasted through the narrow space, creating stripes of light across her clothes.

She froze.

"Peek-a-boo! I *shee* you."

Two

Ever since the phone connection with Paisley went dead, Judah Grant had been tromping around the perimeter of the parking lot of the storm shelter in Florence, Oregon, praying one second, ranting the next. He needed peace. Paisley needed a miracle. Despite the darkness and the late hour, he hobbled past the cars outside the high school gym, rehashing their phone conversation.

"Someone's here."

That made him crazy. *"What? Who?"*

"I . . . don't . . . know."

The staticky exchange left him with haunting questions. How could she not know who was there? A stranger? Looters?

He asked her about a weapon. Told her he'd be praying. Did she hear the worry in his tone? Sense his love for her in his voice?

God, please protect her. Rescue her even though I can't be there.

His thoughts leapfrogged over the events of the last thirty hours. His notifying Basalt Bay residents of the approaching storm. His search for Paisley. Violent winds. The window exploding. The glass impalement in his calf. His and Paisley's separation. Tonight, they were only twenty miles apart, but that distance seemed more like a hundred miles.

What if looters were in his hometown? Judah hated that a few lowlifes might take advantage of people in distress, invading homes, stealing, causing havoc. If that happened with Paisley there by herself—

His heart throbbed so hard it felt like it could burst out of his chest.

What if it was Craig? Hadn't the man driven Judah to the ER, then disappeared? What if his coworker—

No! He could not think the worst, or the terrorizing thoughts tumbling about like circus acrobats in his brain would drive him mad. He had to have faith, building up his confidence that God was working in their lives. Yet, Judah couldn't control every troubling imagination that pulsed through his mind over what might be happening. He should be there with his wife, his arms around her, protecting her. He should be the one fighting off an intruder. Not her.

His footsteps pounded the damp, uneven pavement, and his newly stitched calf caused an odd rhythm as he walked. Each step made him grimace, but he kept going, wouldn't stop.

A little while ago, he tried calling Paisley back with James Weston's—a neighbor who lived across the street from Paisley's father—phone. No answer. Went straight to voicemail. Useless. Frustrating.

As he plodded along, passing vehicles he recognized—the bakery delivery truck, Mia Till's sports car, another coworker's SUV—he begged God to save his wife, to protect her against evil, including looters, Craig, or Dad. Although, now that he knew the truth about Craig's past behavior with Paisley, he considered his father the lesser of the three evils. He even hoped it might be him coming to her aid. Not causing her grief the way he had last time.

Oh, God, be with my Paisley. Keep her safe.

What if she experienced another panic attack? Alone. Around some stranger. Judah walked faster. His leg burned with intense pain, so he slowed down. Kept praying. Waiting out the night. Questioning God's will. Then praying for more faith.

A war battled within him. Trust versus anxiety. Doubt versus faith. A double set of arch enemies. What-ifs resounded in his mind. What if Dad lured Paisley away with money again? What if Craig pressured her to do something against her will like he did before? What if it were strangers, looters, too numerous for her to fight off? What if they—

"No!" He would pray and believe that God was greater than his worst fears. Come morning light, he'd find a way back to Basalt Bay, even if he had to walk the whole way. With his limp? Yeah, right.

He trudged around a low spot in the pavement that was still flooded with water. He passed the entrance to the gym that had been built since he went to high school here. The toe of his shoe tripped over a surface crack. He caught himself, grimacing at the tug in his calf. If he couldn't take one lap around this parking lot without stumbling, without being in pain, how could he walk all the way to Basalt Bay, twenty miles away? He groaned.

The displaced residents were told they might have to stay here for a week, or longer, until the roads leading into town were fixed and utilities restored. Surely it wouldn't take that long. He had to find a way back. Someone would drive him. James Weston. Or one of his coworkers. If none of his friends could help, he'd rent a car or hire a driver.

He gritted his teeth and kept trudging forward. He didn't care how late it got. Didn't care if anyone heard him calling out to God. "You tell us in Your Word to love our enemies." He glanced up at the dark sky. "The thought of an enemy hurting my wife is more than I can bear. Please, protect her. Help me too. I don't want this awful fear boiling in my spirit. I care for Paisley so much, and I know You love her too."

Inwardly he quoted Scriptures. *Even though I walk through the valley of the shadow*— Wait! No reciting verses about the Valley of the Shadow of Death. *I will sing of your strength, in the morning I will sing of your love; for you are my fortress, my refuge in times of trouble*. He quoted the verse from Psalms again. That was better. Comforting. *You are my refuge, God.*

He wanted to trust the Lord to be with Paisley, just like he believed for two of the three years she'd been away from him that God would bring her back. Finally, hallelujah, she returned. Then the mega-storm hit. His world turned upside down with his injury, her confession about Craig, and her refusal to get into that man's truck. Their separation—again. Now, this dreadful waiting and wondering. The doubting.

Lord, I'm sorry for my doubts. You are a good Father. With good plans for us.

"Judah?"

Mia? *Ugh*. He'd rather keep a football field's length between him and the flirtatious receptionist from work.

The click of her high heels crossing the pavement in an otherwise silent night preceded her. "There you are, Judah."

His name on her lips sounded soft, sultry. Made him want to run like Joseph ran from Potiphar's wife.

"What's wrong? I can see something is bothering you."

Her intruding on his quiet time bothered him. "It's nothing that I want to talk about. You should go back inside the gym."

"Has something happened?" Her voice sounded more caring instead of coy, this time. "Did you get bad news from Paisley?"

"I'm not discussing it." He was being abrupt, but someone might see them out here, alone at night, and misinterpret what they were seeing, draw the wrong conclusion. Basalt Bay's rumor mill was a force to be reckoned with, especially when it came to Paisley and him.

Mia wrapped her arms tightly around her middle. "It's cold out here. How can you stand it?" She shivered dramatically, her teeth chattering.

Was she fishing for him to find a way to help her get warm? Maybe offer her his coat? He wouldn't do anything that she might interpret as romantic. "I didn't notice. You should go back inside where it's warmer."

Not many hours ago, he put a gym's length between them. He'd wanted to reassure Paisley that he was doing the honorable thing as her husband, but he was also frustrated with Mia.

The receptionist didn't heed his advice about going back into the shelter. She stood in front of him with her shining doe eyes peering up at him. She might not mean to come across so flirtatiously, but she seemed schooled in the art. Her soft tone of voice, her being here with him in the middle of the night, felt suspicious.

"What have you been doing out here all this time?" She glanced over her shoulder as if checking to see if someone else might be out there too.

"Walking and praying. Waiting for morning."

"So, something is wrong. Are you okay? I'm here for you, Judah." She put both of her hands on his arm, gazing up at him.

He stepped back, disengaging her fingers from touching him.

"If you want to talk or need someone just to be with you . . ."

Her words put him on edge the way fingernails scraping across a chalkboard would.

"If you'll excuse me, I'm going to continue walking." He resumed his limping stride, hoping she'd take the hint and leave him alone.

Her high heels clicking behind him let him know she didn't. He stopped suddenly to speak to her again. She bumped into him.

"Oh, sorry." She giggled. Another scraping sound on that mental chalkboard.

"Why don't you head back inside? You've got to be freezing."

"You're sweet to be worried about me." Mia leaned into him, shivered, as if drawing from his warmth. "Judah, you must know that I care about you."

Whoa. "What do you mean?"

"You've got to know how I feel." She reached her hands toward his chest.

He backed up several steps. "I don't know what you're implying."

"We care for each other as friends, right?"

"Okay, yeah."

"Colleagues, and maybe more?" She grinned as if she expected him to agree.

Oh, good grief. "Friends and colleagues, yes. There's no 'more' to it. Return to the gym, Mia. And stay there." He hobbled away from her. Would have run if he could.

Her little confession meant her previous flirtations weren't just his imagination. Or Paisley's. That knowledge slammed into his chest like a rock. A warning.

Mia's heels clicked faster, closing the gap between them. "What's wrong with you, Judah? You can talk to me."

He didn't want to talk to her. He'd all but commanded her to go into the storm shelter, and she acted as if his words were an invitation for her to keep walking with him. Where was the disconnect? What else could he do? He trudged forward.

"Is something wrong with Paisley? Is she sick?"

"No."

"Injured?"

"Just leave it alone, will you? Leave me alone." His voice rose and he didn't try to hide his exasperation with her.

"I'm sorry about earlier when I touched your cot." She sighed. "I was confused. Getting mixed signals. You know?"

He stumbled over an uneven chunk of pavement. Came to a complete stop. "Mixed signals? Are you kidding me?"

"I thought you were interested in me. Really, I was flattered." She gave him a wide smile. "I knew you and Paisley weren't together anymore."

Her words were a dagger twisting in his gut. "You're wrong. Paisley and I are still married."

She squinted like she didn't believe him.

"When did I ever act as anything other than a friend and coworker to you?" He'd never flirted with her. Never would while he wore his wedding ring. That silver band was a constant reminder of his faithfulness to his wife.

"I just thought that you were handsome. Friendly. A nice guy. Sweet smile. Lonely, maybe."

Her giggle made him feel dirty. Like he really should run.

"I assumed you felt the same way about me." She splayed her fingers through her blond locks.

"Look. I'm a married man, Mia. I'm sorry you thought that I returned your feelings. You were wrong. I have no interest in you as a"—he didn't even know what to say—"as anything other than a coworker. If you can't see me as a friend, and only as a friend, we cannot even talk." He pivoted sharply and marched through the center of two rows of cars, limping toward the front door of the gymnasium. Once he got there, he counted vehicles to alleviate his annoyance with her.

Finally, the sound of her heels alerted him to her presence.

Twenty-nine. Thirty. Thirty-one.

"If you ever change your mind, or, you know, things don't work out between you and Paisley"—she drew in a breath—"I really like you, Judah."

"Don't ever say that to me again."

"But—"

"Go inside." He yanked open the front door. How could she think he cared for her in that way?

"I'll always be here for you, Judah Grant." As if she didn't hear one word of his denial, her fingers trailed along his hand on the door before she slipped inside the building.

He couldn't pull back his hand fast enough. He plodded around the parking lot again, working off his frustration. How many more minutes until daylight? How many more laps around this parking lot until he could find a way back to Basalt Bay and the one woman he couldn't bear to be away from any longer?

Three

"You know how I know where you been hiding, Little Red Riding Hood?" Craig kicked the pantry door.

Water swirled near Paisley's feet. *Little Red Riding Hood?* Did that mean he thought he was the Big Bad Wolf? Her heart pounded like a bass drum beneath her breastbone. Her breathing became tight and shallow.

Don't panic. You're going to be okay.

Would she be okay? How long did Craig know her hiding place? Was he toying with her fear? Manipulating her? Her hands clenched the protective items a little tighter. She needed something to focus on, something to ground her. She concentrated on the cool glass held in her sweaty palm, the curve of the round jar against her fingers.

"Here's a fact for you"—he snorted—"our extinguished mayor knows everything." He didn't correct his improper English. "He's watching you. Big Bad Daddy-in-law *shees* you."

Craig was out of his mind, on alcohol or drugs. How could Edward know anything about her, let alone see where she was hiding? Yet, standing here in the dark with shards of light crisscrossing her clothing, shivers raced over her skin. Even if her father-in-law knew something about her, why would he inform Craig? The two were hardly buddies.

Craig rammed into the door. If he kept doing that, he'd dislodge the old hinges from the frame. She wouldn't be able to hold the door against his weight.

"Judah's with Mia Till." He belched. "Can't call out to him for help. Mayor Grant, n-neither."

Like she would ask Edward for anything. She could take care of herself. And Judah wasn't with Mia. He called Paisley earlier to inform her that he moved away from the wanton flirt. She trusted him more than she trusted anything Craig said. Besides, Judah was praying for her right this minute. Hadn't he said he'd keep praying until she called him back?

She heard a strange noise. Heavy breathing. Or snoring. *Wait.* Did Craig fall asleep standing up? Probably faking. Yet, for several minutes she listened to his deep, nasally inhaling and exhaling. If he had conked out leaning against the door, this was her chance to escape. But he blocked the exit.

Earlier, when Judah's cell phone light still worked, she noticed the wooden slats nailed to the outside of the small window frame. Could she kick them out and slip through? She didn't have a hammer. And if she made too much noise, Craig would hear it.

Feeling more confident that he might actually be asleep, she stepped away from the door. She crept to the shelves in the dark, then set down the wooden boards. With the Mason jar still secure in her right hand, she shuffled to the window, keeping water movement to a minimum.

With her left palm, she reached into the window area until her hand brushed against rough wood. Applying pressure to the boards, she tested them. One edge felt loose. She set the jar by her feet, close enough to grab quickly. She shoved her shoulder against the wood. Nothing gave. She pushed again, clenching her teeth.

A rustling came from the other side of the door. *Oh, no.*

She whirled around, flailing her hand near the floor, searching for the jar. *Where is it?* Her fingers clutched the top just as the door burst open. Blinding light from Craig's flashlight blasted her. She stood and pulled the jar back over her shoulder, her heart pounding in her ears. If he took one step closer, she'd let him have it. Then she'd grab the other jars and hurl those at him like mud balls.

"*Shurprishe!*" He stumbled forward. "About time you and I had a little dish—" He paused as if to think. "Talk." He swung the flashlight's beam back and forth in the small space. "What d'ya say, Paisley-bug?"

How did he know her dad's pet name for her? She hated hearing the endearment on the skunk's lips. She glowered at him even though she couldn't see his face in the bright light.

"You gonna throw that or what?" The light bobbed toward the jar, then back at Paisley's face.

"I will if you don't back up." A twist of her wrist, that's all it would take, and he'd have a lump on his head the size of Mt. Hood.

"I don't mean any harm."

Right. All this fear churning in her middle that he'd caused, and he didn't mean any harm?

He wobbled as if he might fall over, the light bobbing with his drunken movements. "I mean, I didn't come here to hurt you. Or cause you any trouble." The last phrase sounded like a whimper.

She didn't, wouldn't, believe anything he said.

The flashlight's glow pulsed toward her makeshift bunk. "You been *shleepin'* here?"

She wasn't going to talk with him about sleeping arrangements. Should she throw the jar then try to get past him?

"Don't look at me like that. I'm not a *monshter.*" For a second, the light flashed on his face. His goofy smile was an oxymoron to the man she knew him to be. "I'm a nice guy."

"Stay back."

"I'm not the enemy." He lifted his other hand, palm out. He filled the narrow doorway. No escape. "Aren't you gonna ask why I came here?"

She knew what men like him were after. Cad. Rattlesnake.

"Don't believe me? I'll show you. You can go to *shleep.*" His hand lowered to the doorknob. "*Notgonnado* anything you don't want me to do. Never would."

He had a short memory. Unless he meant "never again."

Slowly, the door closed until total darkness surrounded her. A breath caught in her throat.

Was he really going to leave her alone? Then why did he sneak through the house after dark like a criminal returning to the scene of a crime to finish the job? Maybe he was stalking her just to make her fearful. Why do all of this and then walk away?

The sound of his footsteps got quieter, more distant.

She blew out her breath but kept her arm raised, the jar ready. Terrorized, yet conflicted, she shuffled through the few inches of water, stopping at the closed door. She lowered the jar slowly, then leaned against the wood as before, listening.

Somewhere out there, he crooned another country tune, slurring the words. He belched. Guffawed. *Disgusting man.* Cupboard doors slammed. Several thuds made her think he might be throwing wood chunks to the floor, probably off the washer and dryer, or the kitchen counter—places she contemplated sleeping earlier.

"G'night, *Paishley.* We have more in common than you think. *Shweet* dreams."

Yeah, right. She wouldn't close her eyes tonight. And they had nothing in common. She lowered the jar to her side. What now? Stand here until morning?

How could Craig even go to sleep? He had to be soaking wet. Freezing. Although, the alcohol he must have consumed might keep him warm, for now. When that wore off, what then?

This whole go-to-sleep routine might be a subterfuge. Or, if he was wasted, he might sleep soundly. React slowly.

A few minutes later, the sounds of throaty snoring reached her.

Was this her chance to escape?

Heart galloping beneath her ribs, she clung to the Mason jar. With her other hand, she reached out into the dark and grabbed hold of the comforter she used earlier. She'd need it to survive the cold night. In cautious movements, she pulled up on the door handle and inched it open. She froze. Waited a few seconds. Craig still snored. If he was faking, he was a good faker. If he made an aggressive move, she'd stick to her previous plan of throwing the jar at him.

The house was pitch dark as she shuffled through standing liquid, hoping she wouldn't bump into any floating objects. Even though she couldn't see, she knew the way. How many times had she crept into the kitchen late at night to grab a snack when she was young? Although, there'd never been seawater on the floor before.

She heard water rustling around her boots, felt the wind blowing through the window. Craig's rhythmic snoring propelled her forward.

Being careful not to fall over the branches of the apple tree that crashed through the window during the storm, she half crawled, half lunged through the gaping hole, trying to soften her landing on the porch.

"*Paishley*?" A loud thud. A groan. Had he fallen off the counter? She didn't wait to find out.

She slid off the porch, into the darkness beside Judah's white pickup. She sneaked across her dad's watery front lawn. Glancing back once, she didn't see any movement on the porch, or in the window. Carefully, she waded across the street, pausing only to crawl over a downed tree.

Since it was too dark to go far, she strode across James Weston's yard, stepping around debris and the travel trailer laying on its side. Then she crept up onto his porch, ducked down, and waited tensely for several minutes that felt like an hour. Finally, when Craig didn't follow her, and she didn't hear any suspicious sounds coming from the other side of the street, she sighed.

Thank You, God.

She shuffled over to the bench that leaned against the front of James's house, sat down, and wrapped the comforter around her shoulders. Her insides shook. Her teeth chattered.

But she was safe, for now.

Four

After stumbling in the dark too many times, Judah trudged inside the gym, plopped down on the floor in the corner where he was before, and fell asleep sitting up. Although he'd determined to keep his all-night vigil, the spiritual and emotional wrestling matches, and the aching in his calf, took their toll.

Now, with his forehead propped against his folded arms, which were braced against his bent knees, he awoke to an awful neck kink. He leaned back against the wall, wincing as he stretched out his leg, and turned his neck slowly back and forth. He sighed, and the murmur of early risers huddled around the coffee table reached him.

"How long can they force us to stay here?"

"As long as they want."

"I think it's a conspiracy to keep us away from our homes."

"Maybe they want looters to get our stuff!"

"I'm finding a way back today."

That idea snagged Judah's interest. He stood, moving in increments, feeling the effects of not only having slept on the floor, but having walked around the parking lot too many times on his injured leg last night. Maybe that had been a mistake. But he couldn't regret the time he spent praying for Paisley. For their marriage. He glanced at his watch, clicked the digital display. Six a.m. Time for coffee.

And another pain pill. But if he took one, he might be too groggy to be of much good. He wanted to stay alert, hoping for a chance to return to his wife.

How was Paisley doing this morning? What was she doing? His thoughts raced to prayer. *Lord, be with her, keep her safe.* How many times would he pray those words before he saw her again? What if something bad happened to her last night? A rush of worry hit him. But he reminded himself that trusting in God's faithfulness was the only way he could stay in the right frame of mind. Yet he kept struggling with that. *Lord, help me. Bless Paisley. Keep her safe. Please, let me find a way to get back to her today.*

He trudged toward the table loaded down with two large coffee-pots, a dozen stacks of Styrofoam cups, various creamers, and a bowl full of sugar packets. He gave the platters piled high with donuts a once-over. Another unhealthy breakfast. His stomach roiled as he imagined the grease-laden pastry. Even so, he grabbed an apple fritter and downed it in four bites. The first chance he got to eat a real meal he'd take it.

He filled a disposable cup with steaming coffee. Forget creamer. He needed the pungent bite of full-strength caffeine.

James Weston stepped up beside him and reached for a cup. "Morning." His white hair stuck up in random tufts. His face appeared even more wrinkled than yesterday. Didn't look like he slept well last night, either.

Judah swallowed a gulp of the strong brew. "Good morning. Thanks for letting me use your phone last night. I appreciate it."

"No problem." The older man sipped his drink. "Everything turn out okay?"

"Not sure." Judah lifted his cup to his lips, wishing he had more information. "You didn't get any calls from Paisley, did you?"

"Nope."

Judah doubted the cell he gave her had battery power left, any-how. If only he made different choices yesterday. Not going to the ER with Craig. Staying with Paisley. Too late for regrets. He needed to face facts and act quickly. Take every opportunity. "Oh, uh, James."

"Yes?" The man lifted his shaggy uneven eyebrows.

"Any chance you could drive me as close as you could get to South Road?"

"You heard the police report." James's mouth turned downward. "No one can go back 'til the road's fixed. Sorry excuse, if you ask me. Nothing to be done about it, though."

"I thought if I could get near enough, I'd hike overland across the dunes, then follow the beach. The Guardsmen would be none the wiser." Judah didn't want to cause trouble for James, but his wife's safety was more important to him than following the local emergency rules and regulations.

"Highway's impassable, they say."

"Impassable?"

"Mudslides are the topic of the morning." James nodded in the direction of a group of men huddled near the entryway, coffee cups in hand. "All of us are in the same boat, chomping at the bit to get home." He made a tsk-tsk sound. "Hate this waiting." He shuffled over to the group.

Judah had to find someone willing to drive him to the dunes. He grabbed a maple bar and stuffed a couple of bites in his mouth. The frosting soured in his stomach. Or maybe his reaction had more to do with his anxiety level. If he had his truck, returning to Basalt Bay wouldn't be a problem. He'd park south of town and hike in, the way he explained to James. Who else could he ask for a lift?

A couple of coworkers approached the coffee table. As soon as they made their selections, Judah stepped forward and questioned them about the possibility of catching a ride. Both said they wouldn't be going back to Basalt until the evacuation ended. A couple of other guys seemed interested in off-roading. However, none were willing to risk getting in trouble with the law. Apparently, Deputy Brian wielded a long arm of fear in the community.

Judah understood people's reluctance to get involved. They'd fled from a second, unprecedented hurricane strike on the western seaboard. Were temporarily outcast. At the mercy of strangers' kindnesses. Unsettled over what damages may have happened to their houses and businesses. But where did that leave him? He couldn't hike twenty miles. Not with his injury. Why couldn't things work out easier? He rubbed his free hand over his whiskered chin and groaned. Then downed his cool coffee.

"Something wrong?" Mia's unexpected voice so near him made the hair stand up on the back of his neck. "Anything I can do to help?"

"Uh, no." He automatically stepped away from her. Why did she think something was wrong? Was she eavesdropping on their conversation? "Thanks, but there's nothing you can do."

She winked. "You'd be surprised how resourceful I can be."

Ugh. Her early morning flirtation made him want to growl out a rebuke. Would she never stop?

"Need a lift somewhere?" She reached for a cup. "Because if you wanted me to drive you somewhere, I would."

You've got to be kidding me. The only person willing to help him get back to town was Mia? Why would she even offer after what he said to her last night? After he rebuffed her flirtations. Maybe she felt badly. Or was this just another ploy?

"You want to go back to Basalt, right?"

"I do."

"Well, then." She filled her cup with dark coffee. Smelled it, grimaced. "I'm your girl Friday." She giggled as she poured in creamer, then more creamer, stirring rapidly with a plastic stick.

How would he explain this twist in his plans to Paisley? And what if Maggie Thomas, Basalt Bay's gossip queen, found out that Mia called herself his "girl Friday?" He'd be the talk of the town. Accepting Mia's offer would solve his immediate problem but might create a whole slew of other ones.

He thought of an excuse. "Your car might not be able to get back to Basalt Bay."

"Why not?"

"It sits low. Heavy rainfall during and after the hurricane caused mudslides." A blessing in disguise? He'd ask to use her phone to call about a car rental, but he knew her cell was out of battery power.

"What else am I going to do today? Sit around here doing nothing?" She shook her long blond hair off her shoulders. "They'll probably have the roads cleared by the time we get up there, anyway, don't you think?"

"Hard to say."

"The Guardsmen might not let you through, but I'll drive you as far as I can." She smiled. "I can talk my way out of most anything if we get stopped."

He didn't doubt that.

"Your call." She seemed to be trying to help, and not acting overly friendly. Maybe she took his words to heart last night. "I'll keep my hands to myself. Promise." She winked.

Inwardly, he groaned. How could he even consider taking her up on her offer?

"I'm going to finish this coffee, then I'll meet you at my car." Her gaze danced toward the front of the gym. "A drive will be a perfect way to spend a few hours, don't you think?"

"Oh, sure." If he could endure the twenty miles with her. Hopefully, he wouldn't regret it.

"Good." She grinned and pumped the air with her fist.

Now, why was she so enthusiastic about driving him north? Maybe he should tell her he was having second thoughts. Third thoughts. But he wanted to get back to Paisley as soon as possible.

He strode to the restroom to wash up. When he returned, Mia stood by the door, her fingers rapidly tapping the screen of her zebra-striped phone. Last night she got angry with him when he used up the remaining battery power. Had she found a way to recharge her phone?

"Ready?" Mia dropped the device into her purse. "I'm heading out." She curled her index finger for him to follow.

Like a puppy on a leash, Judah trailed behind her through the rain. Warnings shrieked through his brain—*Walk away. She's untrustworthy. Wait for someone else.* Yet, he didn't listen. This was an opportunity to get back to Paisley quickly. Even if he rented a car, the process would take time. Time he could be spending back in Basalt Bay with his wife.

In a second the sports car engine purred to life. He opened the passenger door and climbed in. When he shut it, the seatbelt automatically locked into place. The tug against his chest reminded him of a dungeon door closing, keeping him a prisoner. *Lord, help.*

Twenty miles, that's all. He'd direct their dialogue to work-related topics. Or to the weather. Maybe listen to music.

But as the car zoomed out of the parking lot, the windshield wipers going fast, Mia kept up a steady drone of conversation, filling in the awkward silence with prattle and giggles. "I can't believe how Hurricane Blaine destroyed the area. Can you? How could you stay in Basalt during such high winds? It's a good thing that more than your leg wasn't hurt." She nudged his arm.

He pulled his elbow in toward his side.

"I would have been scared out of my wits. Out of my mind. Not you. Oh, Judah, you're too good, too kind, to leave poor Paisley behind. How sweet and admirable of you. You're my kind of hero." She patted his wrist—reached over the center console to do so— then returned her palm to the steering wheel. "Sorry. I forgot." Her playful expression didn't contain any remorse.

His discomfort increased. "I'm not a hero. I wanted to be with Paisley during the storm. Still want to be with her. She's my wife." He placed his left hand with the silver wedding ring on his finger on top of his other hand, in an obvious position where she might notice.

"Oh, right." She rolled her eyes. "Your wife." She muttered something about an absentee spouse not being good wife material.

Annoying woman. At least she stayed quiet for a couple of miles. In a few minutes, he'd tell her where to drop him off, maybe a half mile before the cutoff into the bay. He'd hike through the brush, make his way over the dunes, and finally get to see Paisley. A tug in his calf reminded him that walking over the mountainous sand piles wouldn't be an easy task. Still, he'd do whatever it took to be with her before nightfall.

"You okay?" Mia must have seen his grimace.

"Mmhmm." Shifting, he adjusted his legs in the small confines of the front seat area. He'd much rather be riding in his truck than in this knee-cruncher. But each mile brought him closer to the woman he loved. Soon their separation would be over. *Thank You, God.*

"Those stitches must hurt something fierce." Mia reached over as if to pat his thigh.

He lifted his hand, intercepting her fingers before she could touch his leg. He glared at her.

"Habit." She made a pouty face.

"Just stop, will you?" Habit? *Come on.* Hadn't he told her that he didn't reciprocate her feelings? Why did she keep pushing herself on him?

"Okay, okay. Don't bite my head off."

He probably was testy after his short sleep, responding sharper than he would have on the job. But they weren't at work. And if she treated him romantically at C-MER, he would tell her to stop, also. Now that he knew how she felt about him, he wouldn't tolerate her flirtations even a little.

He had never led her on, never meant to. Although, he was an idiot for not noticing her interest sooner.

"Uh-oh." Her tone deepened.

"What?" He'd been staring out the side window.

"Trouble ahead." She muttered an unladylike word.

He squinted through the rain-splattered windshield. Just before the next curve in the road, a traffic control flagger held up a stop sign, waved it. "That doesn't look good."

"What now?" Mia brought her car to a slow stop.

The fluorescent-yellow vest the worker had on nearly glowed over his dark green raincoat. He approached Mia's side of the vehicle.

She lowered the window and gave him her typical wide smile. "Hi, there. Aren't you cute in that flashy gear?" She giggled.

Oh, brother.

"What's happening up ahead?"

"Washout. You can't go through. No one can pass until repairs are finished." The flagger nodded in a northerly direction. "Could be days."

"You're kidding, right?" A total closure of Highway 101? Judah couldn't believe it. Was the whole universe against him and Paisley getting back together? Of him coming to her rescue.

"Pavement's busted up badly too." The guy pointed toward the west. "Not to mention, another storm's on its way."

Judah groaned. Just what the area didn't need. More rain. More flooding.

"Thanks for the info." Mia passed the flagger something and laughed. What did she give him? A business card? To a stranger?

"Thanks." The guy stuffed the card in his raincoat pocket and grinned.

She closed the window. Waved at him for an awkward amount of time. "What should we do now?"

Judah would have commented on her unscrupulous behavior, but he already felt so frazzled, he just shook his head. "I don't know." He pinched the bridge of his nose. This morning's donuts glugged in his stomach.

Lord, some wisdom would be greatly appreciated.

One thing after another had gone wrong, barely giving him time to catch his breath. With no way of contacting Paisley and explaining the delays, what was he supposed to do? What would she think if he didn't come back today? A horrible sensation of being a failure as a husband, again, scraped through his insides. He'd determined to put her needs before his own, to be there for her in ways that he hadn't been before she left him, but how could he do those things when he couldn't even make his way back to her?

Mia did an abrupt U-turn. "Sorry it didn't work out." She touched the screen on the front console. Classical music filtered into the air. "I have an idea. Let's badmouth all the problems the hurricane has caused."

What good would that do?

"Stupid storm. Ruined everything. Left us homeless. Terrible food at the shelter. And the coffee? Don't even get me started. A national disaster right there!"

She was acting lighthearted, obviously trying to cheer him up. Instead, his thoughts raced down a dark avenue. *Paisley. Craig. Looters.*

Paisley. Dad. Craig. Was his wife okay? Safe? How could he get to her despite the road closure? Even a rental car wouldn't help him now.

He groaned. Why had so many bad things happened?

A verse squeezed into the middle of his frustrations. *Trust in the Lord with all your heart and lean not on your own understanding.* He appreciated the reminder. He still wanted to trust God and believe for the best. *Have faith, Grant.* He sighed.

But if Craig or someone else was causing trouble for Paisley, Judah had to do everything in his power to get there. He couldn't just return to Florence and sit around in the storm shelter, eating donuts and drinking bitter coffee.

Lord, I promised Paisley I'd come back this morning. I want to keep that promise.

"Would you be interested in a homestyle breakfast? We could stop at a diner on the way back." Mia glanced at him without her usual frivolous gleam. "A real meal would help you feel better."

He had told himself he'd jump at the chance for a hot meal, but he didn't want to put himself in a compromising situation. Especially one where someone from Basalt Bay might see him with Mia and spread gossip. And he wasn't in the mood for chatting just to fill the time. His sigh came out more like a rumble.

"That does it." Mia smacked the steering wheel with her palm. "We're getting some honest-to-goodness food in you. Then the world won't seem like such a horrible place."

He didn't know about that, but he was hungry. After he ate something, he had to come up with a new plan for getting back home.

Five

Paisley opened her eyelids and squinted against the early morning light streaking across the sky. Where was she? She blinked a few times. Oh, right. Last night, she hid in the pantry. Escaped from Craig. Slept on James Weston's porch. Where was Craig now? She braced her right elbow against the wooden bench and peered over the railing, surveying Dad's house and yard that rested in shadows across the street. No sign of the intruder, other than his monster truck parked crookedly in the front yard. He must be either sleeping off his hangover or wandering the neighborhood looking for her.

She ducked back down. Had to stay hidden.

She ran her hands over her eyes, down her cheeks. Her nose felt frozen. Her muscles were stiff from her neck to her hips. But she was alive. Cold, but alive.

Would Judah make it back this morning? Or later in the day? How could she avoid his troublesome coworker until he arrived?

One thing was for certain, staying here on this porch in broad daylight wasn't an option. If she could figure out how to get inside James's house, she'd take care of her immediate needs. Use the facilities. Scrounge for food and water. But the windows were boarded up; the door had to be locked.

Too bad Dad didn't take similar precautions with his house. If he had, Judah wouldn't have gotten injured. Craig wouldn't have broken into the house. And she wouldn't have gone through those hours of terror alone.

But Judah *did* get hurt. Craig *did* invade her space. She *was* alone. Running for her life. Or hiding for her life. Even if Craig said he wouldn't hurt her, she doubted his intentions, his integrity.

If he was still sleeping, now was her chance to put distance between them. She had to find somewhere safe to stay until Judah returned. She might be able to hide inside her sister's art gallery. Or break into City Hall. But in this small town, if Craig was determined to find her, he probably would, right?

Not if she could help it!

She wadded up the blanket and shoved it to the end of the bench. Then, standing but hunched over, her nose barely above the handrail, she crept across the porch. She dashed down the steps, then waded over to a bushy tree in James's yard and hid behind it.

Everything seemed quiet. Too quiet, perhaps.

She shuffled through the water, her boots making a swishing sound that seemed exaggerated in the otherwise silent neighborhood. She noticed a watermark on the side of the next house that showed the water level had gone down a couple of inches since yesterday. A relief. But how long would it take for the receding water to make its way out to sea?

When she heard an odd sound, she dodged behind another tree. Was Craig following her? She peered around the trunk. A multi-colored beachball bobbed across the surface of the flooded street. It scraped against a dead-looking bush, skipped over some sticks and floating debris. She blew out a long breath and trudged forward, moving cautiously in the slightly downhill section where the frothy water reached her knees.

The hurricane's destructive force had affected most of the houses and yards in the neighborhood. Downed trees, outdoor furniture, tires, toys, trash, and shingles peppered lawns, driveways, and flooded streets. A canoe rested cockeyed on one porch. A motorcycle lay on its side on top of a flipped skiff. Porches were ripped off and separated from houses. Some sections of roofs were on the ground. A picnic table leaned through a broken window.

Seeing the damage to her childhood neighborhood tugged on Paisley's heart, made her feel sad for the people who would soon be coming home to the terrible mess and all the hardships. It also reminded her of the struggles in her own life. The losses that had squeezed the joy right out of her, and a few times even stole the breath from her body. This town needed a restoration. A healing. But so did she.

As her legs trudged through the water, heading toward town, the unnerving silence started to get to her. The sense of being the only person left on the planet was like an oppressive weight pushing down on her, making her more nervous with each step. Of course, Craig was in the ghost town, also, but that was far from comforting.

She kept her gaze on the water in front of her lest she trip over something unseen. The next time she glanced up, she saw a power pole leaning over at an odd angle, its wires dangling precariously close to the surface of the water. For a second, she froze. Judah warned her to watch out for downed power lines. She'd have to find a safer route.

Veering away from the danger, she shuffled to the curb, then stepped up using the lower edge of her boot to guide her footing so she didn't trip in the water. She skirted around a few houses, cutting across backyards and alleys, and ended up behind City Hall. Her legs ached from the effort of walking against the flow of seawater, and she hadn't even gone that far.

Compared to the other buildings in town, City Hall appeared to be in perfect condition. Boards tidily covered the windows and front door. Some trash floated in the parking lot, but nothing was broken or smashed in around the structure.

Should she try to get inside? There might be supplies. Water. Even, food. The mayor was still up at his house on the cliff, right? She didn't want him to catch her prying off a board from one of his precious windows. Although, she was still his daughter-in-law. He might understand her need to break in to find food.

She groaned. *What am I thinking?* If she caused any damage here, Mayor Grant would despise her even more. Just thinking of the man who had never approved of her caused her blood pressure to rise. And the things Edward said in the past about her not being good enough for his son, about her not being a good mother to her unborn daughter, and the way he paid her to leave Judah three years ago, burned in her thoughts. Each of those offenses still had the power to wound her heart and to create a greater schism between her and Judah. No, she didn't want anything to do with the horrible man or his place of business.

She couldn't get away from City Hall fast enough, although the floodwaters impeded her progress. Her boots felt like fifty-pound weights as she shuffled through the current, searching for someplace to get out of the muddy water.

On both sides of the city street, she observed more damages. Awnings dangled by threads. Signs were busted. Roofs gone. A sailboat had crashed into the front of Bert's Fish Shack, its stern the only part remaining outside. How would the quirky, but sometimes temperamental, owner react to that?

Across from her, the roof from Nautical Sal's Souvenirs lay broken and piled up like a beaver's dam. The heavy rains had surely ruined everything in his shop. Such a shame. She imagined Sal, one of the kindest, jolliest business owners in Basalt, stepping out of his store when she was a kid to tell her about an agate he found in a tidal pool. Would he be able to put his business back together after all this destruction?

Suddenly, she realized she'd been standing out in the open for too long. She was supposed to be hunting for a hiding place. Glancing over her shoulder, she perused the flooded street behind her. Didn't see anyone. She peered at the doorway of Paige's art gallery where she ducked under the awning before the hurricane hit. Beyond a pile of debris, the door appeared to be open, perhaps caved in. She wouldn't even have to break in. She hurried toward it.

What if Craig was in the gallery? Left the door open. She stopped. Apprehension twisted knots in her middle, but she couldn't remain out in the open on the street like this. And there might be food inside her sister's building. It had been a coffee shop, too, right? Besides, Craig was probably still back at her dad's, sleeping off his stupor.

Taking a deep breath, she tentatively entered the building. She paused until her eyes adjusted to the darker room, listening. She didn't hear anything other than the roar of the surf coming from beyond a glassless window. Fortunately, the room had an open layout, not lending itself to corners and easy hiding places.

A cone of light coming through the back of the building drew her forward. Uh-oh. A chunk of the roof was gone. She saw clouds through the hole. Several shingles dropped down and clattered to the floor, barely missing her. She leaped back. Was the building unstable? Was she safe here?

She strode away from the corner, keeping her distance from it. She waded through a couple of inches of water on the floor to reach the open window. The wind coming off the ocean blew hard against her, but she welcomed the powerful rush of sea air against her cheeks and hair. She breathed in deeply of the tangy, musty aroma. Sighed. Below her, gray turbulent waves charged over the sand, crashing against pilings, sending sea spray bursting into the air.

After the next wave abated, she studied the shoreline. Sandbags that C-MER employees and residents had piled up in the last minutes before the storm were torn up and scattered by the waves. Too bad those didn't hold.

Leaning farther out the window, her hands against the lower frame, she perused the parking lot on the far side of the beach where she'd left her purple Accord. It was gone! Had the sea swallowed it up during the storm surge? What else could have happened to it? The loss—yet, another loss—gripped her emotionally. Sure, it was only a car. But it seemed like more, like it had been a protective friend, her only friend, on her long journey home. She sighed.

Her stomach growled, reminding her that she needed to find food. Turning from the window, she crossed the room toward the coffee bar. Behind the counter, she yanked open several cupboard doors. Dishes. Serving utensils. Coffee supplies. She pulled open a couple of drawers. Snacks! She'd never been so happy to see packaged food. Breakfast bars. Granola bars. Cookies. She tore the wrapping off one, stuffing the contents into her mouth without checking the flavor. Chocolate mocha. *Delicious.* The next one was vanilla. *Mmm.* She tore into another package. Banana cream pie. She would have eaten them even if they tasted like cardboard, but this was much better. She found water bottles, opened one, and guzzled it.

Hunger and thirst abated, she peeked inside a narrow cabinet that resembled a locker and found several articles of clothing hanging on hooks. She grabbed a sweatshirt. Paige's? She slipped out of Dad's damp flannel shirt, tossed it on the counter, then tugged on the sweatshirt. Next, she fingered a long blue artist's shirt. She put that on over the sweatshirt—anything to help her stay warm. Finding pants would have been fantastic but wishful thinking in a place like this.

She felt around on the shelf above the hooks. Touching some fabric, she pulled it down. A kid-sized blanket? Maybe an employee of Paige's had a child. Paisley draped the square around her shoulders like a shawl. Sighed.

Now, she needed to find a hiding place in case Craig showed up. She stepped over chunks of wood and shells and piles of kelp as she walked the perimeter of the room. She opened a door and found a small bathroom with a lock on the doorknob. Perfect.

She came full circle, ending up at the window. She took in the spectacular view of the beach all the way to *Peter's Land*, her childhood name for the peninsula she'd dubbed after her brother. Seeing the gaping holes where giant boulders used to sit, she nearly cried at the changes to the landscape. For decades, the rocky barrier protected the town from fierce storms. Unfortunately, Addy and Blaine, nearly back-to-back hurricanes, had taken their toll on the city's fortress. The rest of the peninsula must be in Davy Jones's Locker, the resting place for sunken ships in some of her favorite pirate stories when she was a kid.

Part of her wanted to hike right out to the edge of the rocky outcropping, to sit on the point with sea spray dancing and exploding about her, to forget the difficulties and her fears of the last few days, but if Craig came skulking around, he'd see her. No, this gallery was the safest place, as long as she stayed away from the hole in the ceiling. She had food and water. A bathroom. She'd wait here until Judah arrived.

Or else, Craig found her.

Please, hurry, Judah.

Six

Judah stood in a line at an outdoor tent the National Guard and FEMA had set up for displaced residents to discuss problems and ask questions. Some folks ahead of him were complaining about a lack of food supplies. Others demanded to know when they could return home. A few even accused the Guardsmen of purposefully keeping them from their properties.

As an emergency worker himself, he felt sorry for the two uniformed men in the tent who were probably tired of the repeated questions, the demands for them to speed up the process, and having to deal with the frustrated evacuees in the long line. Judah also agreed with some of the disgruntled people. The authorities should do more to help, and yes, speed up the process. Wasn't that why he stood in line? Hoping someone would have mercy on his situation and help him get back to his wife? He heard the frustration building in the voices around him, and he doubted anyone in charge would have compassion on him, either. How could they assist him and deny others?

"Excuse me. Excuse me." Was that Mia again?

Judah turned to find her pushing past several people in line. She clutched two cups of coffee. Was one of those for him? If so, his annoyance at finding her still following him lessened a little.

"Sorry." She laughed and smiled as she squeezed past folks in line. Her grin seemed to disarm the grumpiest among them.

"No worries." "Come on by." "That's all right," some called out.

She stopped beside him. "Here you go." She handed him a to-go cup with a lid on it. "Vanilla latte, just how you like it."

"Uh, thanks." How did she know his coffee preference? He never talked about it with her. And they didn't have any specialty coffees at work. As soon as he sipped the brew, he closed his eyes. Sighed. He'd missed this.

"Have a plan?" Mia bumped his arm with her elbow. "Are you going to beg someone with a tank to get you around the closed road and into Basalt? Good luck with that."

"No plan. But I have to try something." He took another swig of the sweetened drink. "Can't sit around twiddling my thumbs."

"Well, you could." She chuckled. "I'm sure Paisley understands that you're injured."

Maybe. What he didn't understand was why Mia was here. They ate big breakfasts at a packed-out diner. Said goodbyes. She left to go shopping. "You don't have to wait here. Drive back to the shelter. Shop, whatever. I'll catch a ride with someone. Or walk." Besides, if a ride north didn't materialize, he wanted to check out a jewelry store, alone.

"No worries." She kept in step with him. "Want to take a drive after you're finished here?"

"A drive?" He wasn't leaving town other than to head to Basalt Bay.

"Maybe to Newport. Coos Bay." She shrugged.

"Why would I want to go farther south, farther away from my wife?"

Mia didn't meet his gaze. "Any place is better than waiting around the shelter. Besides"—she grinned—"I need a shopping trip." She slid her free hand down her slacks. At least she wasn't wearing that mini-skirt getup she wore during the storm. "I need warmer things. Jeans and a sweater."

He wasn't going anywhere else with her. "You should go do that. Thanks for trying to help me get home." No reason he couldn't be civil. They'd enjoyed a decent conversation about workplace policies over eggs and pancakes. Although, he noticed a few raised eyebrows from folks he recognized.

"No problem. I'd do anything for you, Judah. Help in any way I can." She sipped her coffee, her gaze dancing toward him.

Not liking her easy transition into flirty behavior, he changed the topic. "Have you spoken with Craig lately?"

"What? Oh, you mean, since the hurricane?" She turned, waved at a guy.

"Have you?" He shuffled forward in the line.

"I spoke with him yesterday." She stepped forward too. "He called to see how you were doing."

"When?"

"Beats me."

He could tell her to check her phone for details, but they weren't working. He didn't have authority to push for answers. However, the topic reminded him of another question that had been bothering him. "What about my father?" He kept his voice quiet so others in line wouldn't hear. She didn't know Dad personally, did she?

Her smile disappeared. "What about him?"

"Did you call him yesterday, too?"

She coughed. "Look, you were injured. Of course, I called him. What's the big deal?"

"Stay out of my family stuff. And stay away from my dad. I mean it." He gave her a stern glare. His father could probably be swayed by a younger woman's laughter and attention. Recently, Mia had said some things about the mayor that sounded suspicious. Things that made Judah question his dad's faithfulness to his mom. But it was probably nothing. Mia was just a flirtatious person.

For a few minutes, she acted hyper-focused on her drink. Each time Judah took a step forward, she did too. She didn't take a hint very well.

Judah was third in line now, and he recognized the man at the head of the group.

Brad Keifer, a local fisherman, gesticulated furiously. "I need to get back to my house tonight. How can we make that happen without a bunch of red tape garbage?"

"That won't be possible." The officer's voice sounded tense. Weary, most likely. "No one, and I repeat, no one is returning to Basalt Bay for a few more days, possibly a week." The guy behind the desk wore a crew cut and appeared to be in his mid-forties. His stiff upper lip and squinting eyes declared he wouldn't budge from his position. "Our men have the road barricaded. Anyone caught crossing the divide will face stiff penalties. The roads must be repaired for public safety. Utilities have to be restored."

"Oh, come on! That's the same malarkey we've been told for two days." Brad removed his rainhat, dashed his fingers through his dirty-blond hair, then slapped his hat back on. "I have to get my gear. Head out to sea. I've wasted enough time with this Blaine mess."

"That's unfortunate for you. Nevertheless, you'll have to wait patiently like all the others." The man in uniform gave him a brisk nod. "If that's all, sir—"

"No, that's not all." Brad punched the air with his index finger. "I've stood in this stupid line for over an hour. I demand answers!"

"Hothead." Mia smirked.

Judah felt empathy for Brad's exasperation. He wanted answers too.

"I've given you the only response possible." The man in green apparel crossed his arms. "Now, if you'll step aside, I'll talk to the next person in line."

Brad said something sarcastic and downright rude.

The Guardsman clicked his fingers toward a wide-shouldered security guy who immediately stepped forward.

"Yes, sir?"

"Escort this man—"

"No need." Brad growled and stomped away. "What a waste of time. I'll find my own way back."

How did the fisherman plan on circumventing the guards and getting into Basalt Bay? Judah had to find out. He strode from the line, following Brad's angst-filled footsteps the best he could.

"Judah, what are you doing?" Mia screeched after him. "After all this time waiting, you're walking away? It's almost your turn!"

He paused. "Goodbye, Mia. Go back to the shelter." Hopefully, she wouldn't follow him again.

Seven

As Paisley stood in the center of the art gallery, she smelled something, sniffed a couple of times. Craig's aftershave? She tensed. Made a 360-degree pivot, checking the room. No one else was here. Maybe the familiar scent was just her imagination.

She strode to the open window, watching the surf pounding the seashore. *Wait.* A man was on the beach! Craig? No, this guy didn't have that man's broad shoulders. He wore a raincoat and trudged through the sand, stumbled, seemed to be having difficulty walking. His back was to her; she didn't recognize him. But this meant someone else had stayed in Basalt!

It couldn't be Dad, right? He left with Paige the night of the storm. And yet—

The man tripped. Caught himself. Walked an unsteady gait across the soggy sand. She still couldn't see his face. He staggered, nearly fell.

What if that was Dad?

She dropped the blanket she was using as a shawl and charged across the gallery floor. She shoved the door open wider, scrambled over the trash pile in front of the building, and ran down the sidewalk, not caring what might happen if Craig came after her. If Dad had weathered the storm, and she didn't know if that was him, she had to rush down to the beach and talk to him. Why would he be staggering? Was he injured? And if it wasn't her father, someone else might be in distress and need help.

She raced around Sal's shop, leaping over driftwood and trash and seaweed. She reached the boulders she climbed up and down hundreds of times as a youth. Today they were wet and slippery, with water cascading down from the street above. Debris and chunks of wood were peppered between the rocks. Still, she instinctively knew where to place her next footfall.

Due to the nearly high tide, she didn't have much room to walk along the flat part of the beach. As the next wave receded, she ran forward across the wet shifting sand, staying closer to the big rocks than she normally would to keep from getting splashed.

Just ahead, the man tripped on a sandbag that had been washed away from the others. He flung his arms into the air and yelled as if talking to someone in the heavens. Paisley stopped and watched him. Couldn't make out his words. Still couldn't see his face. Then, he bent over, hands on his knees, and threw up on the beach. Poor guy. He stood upright, hacked a couple of times, turned slightly. With his face in profile, *his* nose, *his* thick black glasses, Paisley knew it was Dad.

"Dad! Dad! It's me, Paisley." She ran hard, her boots skidding in the sand.

He turned toward her, a scowl lining his face. He blinked as if he had no idea who she was. He rubbed the back of his hand over his mouth. "It's you." His voice sounded gravelly. Dry.

"It's me, Dad." She rushed right up to him. Threw her arms around him, hugging him tightly. "It's so good to see you." He didn't return her embrace. Seemed lifeless. Of course, he'd just been sick. Might be weak. She took a step back. "Are you okay? Why are you in Basalt? I thought you left with Paige."

His eyes flooded with moisture. "I thought you—" He flung his hand toward the sea. "I saw your car."

"You did? Where was it?"

"Submerged. Lost."

She gazed out toward the breakers.

"The purple roof. Waves rolling over it. I thought. I thought you might be in it. Gone too."

"Oh, Dad." She hugged him again. He patted her shoulder awkwardly. She stepped back far enough to get a good look at him.

His face was greenish. Probably due to his being sick. Scraggly whiskers covered the lower part of his face. He must not have shaved in days. His eyes looked bloodshot. Weary. His clothes were dirty and wet. Maybe smelly. Craig's words about having found her dad's stash of alcohol came to mind. Was that why he looked so unkept? So sickly?

"Where did you stay during the storm?" If she knew he remained in town, she would have searched for him.

He stared at the water with a dazed look, didn't answer. His teeth chattered. A dark cloud moved overhead, creating a shadow over his face.

"During the hurricane, where did you stay?" She asked again, but the wind seemed to grab her words and whisk them away. She linked her arm with his. "Come on. Let's find somewhere to get you warm. You need to dry out."

"Everyone left." He stared at her. "Where is she?"

"Who?"

"Paige."

"I don't know. I haven't seen her. Don't you know where she is?"

He shook his head, sighed, seemed confused. Was he in shock? Hungover?

"Come on." She led him to the parking lot. The only place she knew to go was back to his house, but what if Craig was there? "Where did you wait out the storm?" The pastor's words about Dad loading up Paige's car had reinforced the idea that he left town. Obviously, Pastor Sagle was wrong about that.

Dad's gray gaze met hers. "At your sister's."

"Is Paige here too?" If so, Paisley wouldn't have to worry about Craig pestering her. Safety in numbers and all that. "Is she at her house?"

Dad mumbled, acted as if he didn't know what she was talking about. "I want to go home." He pulled away from her grasp, trudged east, toward his house.

She ran after him. Stopped in front of him, holding out her hands. "Dad, wait. Let's go to Paige's, okay? Where does she live? Is her house around here?" The farther they got from Dad's, the better.

He turned in the opposite direction, scratched his head. He seemed to be trying to figure out which direction to go. In a small town there weren't a lot of options. He pointed south, then north. Why didn't he know where Paige's house was? "That way, I think." He pointed yet another direction. Was something wrong with his memory?

She recalled Pastor Sagle pointing toward the west side of town when he said Dad was loading up her sister's car. "Show me where Paige lives, okay?" She tugged on his arm.

"She's not there." He pulled down on his knit hat, covering his ears. "Is she?"

"Probably not." Otherwise Dad wouldn't be wandering the beach alone in the rain, when he was sick, right? "Let's find Paige's house and get you inside." This time he moved in the same direction she did. Although, she didn't have any idea where they were going. She'd have to watch for his burnt-sienna Volkswagen.

"Piper isn't home, either."

"Who?"

Dad pointed east. "That's the way to my house."

"I know." Did he think she forgot the way to the house she grew up in? She kept leading him west, hoping he'd recognize the way to Paige's.

As if in doubt, he glanced back over his shoulder several times.

They passed the ice cream shop where he used to bring her when she was young. She spent many happy summer evenings chatting with him, there, about the sea, or showing him treasures she found on the seashore. Dad never seemed to tire of hearing her talk. Now, he barely seemed to know her.

He coughed hard, leaning over like he might be sick again. His lips looked dry and cracked. He groaned.

"You okay?"

He yanked his arm away from her grasp. "Where are you taking me?" He stumbled. His eyes had a foggy haze to them. He squinted at her. "Who are you?"

A sickening thud landed in her spirit. "It's me, Paisley." What happened to her father? Was he ill? Did he have dementia? She felt terrible that this might have happened to him while he was alone, when she was away for those years. More guilt for her to bear.

His breathing sounded noisy. He was agitated, almost combative. "I don't want to go anywhere with you."

"We're going to Paige's, remember?" She tried to keep her voice sweet.

He stilled. "Do you know the way?"

"No. But you do, right? Where does Paige live?"

He shrugged, shook his head, then shuffled across the road toward Pastor Sagle's church. She kept in step with him, close enough to grab his arm if he stumbled. They walked a couple of blocks, wading through more water. They trudged past Aunt Callie's boarded-up house.

"Do you know where Aunt Callie is?" She was curious whether he remembered who his sister was.

"Gone. Same as everyone else." At least he knew that much.

"She's probably safe in a storm shelter somewhere."

He didn't agree or say anything else as they walked two more blocks, heading toward C-MER. There, on the right. She spotted his antique Volkswagen parked sideways in the driveway of a blue single-story house. Did the storm surge put it there? Or were Dad's driving skills that bad?

The windows on the house were all boarded up. Dad's doing? Maybe that's why he hadn't taken care of the windows at his own place. He probably assisted Paige, then it got too late. A tree lay on its side in the soggy front yard. Branches and garbage were scattered across the grass like everywhere else in town. Dad stuffed his hands in his coat pockets. "This is it."

"Okay." Paisley imagined her dad huddled inside the bungalow during the hurricane. "Is this where you stayed during the storm?"

The image of how she'd been stuck in the upstairs bathroom at his house flashed through her thoughts. At that point, it would have been too dangerous, impossible, for her to go out and hunt for him.

He seemed troubled, like he couldn't remember. Couldn't stay focused. Maybe Craig was right. Maybe Dad's stupor was alcohol related.

"Let's get you inside and find some dry things." She tugged on his arm again. "Is there any food here?"

"No electricity."

"I know." If he was plastered, shouldn't she smell liquor on him? She leaned closer, sniffed. He smelled of the sea. Maybe of the vomit staining his boots. He needed a change of clothes.

He shuffled up the driveway. Then walked through the carport, toward the back of the house.

In the small subdivision backyard, a swing set with a built-in fort lay on its side, leaning against a back fence. The previous owner must have had kids. Maybe Paisley and Dad could get rid of the broken structure, clean up the yard, talk. She'd ask him what was wrong. Would he even know how to answer?

What happened to the dad she knew and loved? Did her three-year absence have anything to do with how he was acting now?

Eight

Paisley followed Dad into the back door of the house, trying to imagine this place as Paige's home. The blue walls of the kitchen were mostly covered with artistic sketches and paintings. Geese and duck knickknacks lined the countertop, along with a small pile of smashed, empty soda cans. A sippy cup lay on its side in the sink. Why was a kid's cup in Paige's house?

Dad strode into the dark living room and grabbed a flashlight off the coffee table where a pile of empty snack and candy wrappers were spread out. He flicked on the switch, creating a circle of light, then dropped onto the couch with a long weary-sounding sigh.

The beige carpet was wet, stained, and Paisley felt the squishiness beneath her boots. While seawater had found its way inside, thanks to someone's forethought in boarding up the windows, there wasn't standing water here like at Dad's place.

The presence of a rocking horse in the corner surprised her. As did the bundle of toys crammed into the TV cabinet. Was Paige babysitting? Paisley thought of the child-size blanket she found at the gallery. Perhaps her sister was watching a coworker's kid.

Dad closed his eyes, muttering something about being old and tired. Needing sleep.

"First, you need to change your damp clothes. Take off those boots. Did you bring any extra things to wear?" After not being present in his life for over three years, it felt weird to boss him around.

He gave her a dull look as if he were looking straight through her, not even seeing her. He closed his eyes again.

She sighed. "How about if I scrounge up something to eat while you go change?"

"Not hungry." He opened his eyelids and stared at the blank TV screen. "Wish ESPN worked."

Is that how he spent his days? Eyes glazed over, staring at the television. That would explain his house being in disrepair. Didn't he work at Miss Patty's Hardware anymore? He used to be everyone's handyman. The guy people came to for advice on how to fix things. This man, this apathetic person, she didn't even recognize.

"I'm thirsty. Soda's gone."

She pictured the pile of smashed cans on the counter. "I'll see what's here." She strode into the kitchen. Water would be better for him. She tried the faucet. It spit and sputtered. The town's water source must have been shut off. She opened the fridge and got hit with a blast of warm air. And something smelly. A couple of water bottles were on the shelf. She grabbed one, carried it back to Dad. Even though she opened the lid and handed it to him, he didn't acknowledge her or drink much. She secured the lid, then set the bottle on the coffee table within easy reach.

Maybe she could find him a blanket. Taking a couple of steps toward the hallway, she glanced back. A childhood feeling of love for him came over her, along with a wave of regret that so much time had passed without her having tried to make amends. But she was here now. "I'm so glad you survived the storm, Dad."

He didn't return the sentiment. Didn't meet her gaze. His cheeks seemed flushed. Did he have a fever? He got sick on the beach. Maybe he had the flu. "Why didn't you leave town with Paige?"

"Why didn't you?"

His gruff comeback surprised her.

"My car stalled on the beach."

He muttered something indistinguishable.

She noticed the flashlight's glow shining toward the opposite wall across from Dad, lighting up an electric fireplace with picture frames displayed on the mantle. Curious, she snatched up the flashlight and strode to the hearth. She aimed the light at the first image. Dad and Mom, ages ago when they looked happy. She splashed light on the next one. Paige, Peter, and Paisley as kids. Then Dad, Paige, and a—a baby? Paisley shone the light directly on the infant. A dark-haired newborn. In Paige's arms. Why did Paige have a picture of a baby with her and Dad? The next one was of a toddler with blond hair. Did the baby's hair lighten? Then one of a child playing on that swing set out back. Another of a Christmas tree with the girl, Paige, and Dad.

Paisley's heart beat a war dance in her chest. "Who's the kid in the photos?"

Dad didn't answer. She swung around. He stared at her blankly.

"Dad, who's the little girl?"

"Piper." The same name he mentioned earlier.

"And she's—?"

"My granddaughter."

A tug in her spirit turned over a rock wedged inside of her ever since she lost her own baby. Paige had a daughter? One who lived. *Breathe in. Exhale.* She blinked fast. This wasn't the time to get sucked into a tempest of emotion. It took a few minutes for her heart rate to settle. For her breathing to normalize. Inwardly, she buried the feelings alongside the pile already there. One of these days she'd have to face those things.

She glanced at the photos again, taking in the new information. Paige was a mom. Which meant Paisley was an aunt. In her three years away, she missed out on this too. On seeing her sister pregnant. Her sister delivering a beautiful baby girl. Piper's toddlerhood.

"Is Paige married?" She hadn't noticed a man in the photos.

"No."

So her sister was a single mom. That took grit and bravery. Her estimation of Paige went up a notch. Maybe Paisley wasn't the only Cedars girl the town gossips told stories about now. Not a kind thought, but one that gave her a measure of relief. A sense of camaraderie with her sister. "I didn't know she had a baby." She hadn't made any attempt to see Paige since she came back. Two days ago, when Judah tried to get her to help him at the art gallery, was this why? So she'd find out about Piper. Why didn't he just tell her?

The child in the photos was a mini-Paige with blond hair and a sweet smile.

Paisley swallowed that lump in her throat. *Don't cry.*

"Too bad you never called." Thick blame bled through Dad's tone.

Guilt settled beneath her breastbone. "I'm sorry about that." How many times would she have to apologize before he believed her? "I wish I had called." Him. Judah. Paige.

Setting the flashlight on the coffee table, she sighed and dropped down on the couch next to Dad. Not close. He did nothing to span the distance or to reassure her that he still loved her, even if she had disappointed him. It seemed he didn't have any emotion. Except, maybe for Piper. At least he was willing to talk about his granddaughter.

"Can you tell me about her?"

"Who?"

"Piper." She wanted to ask him if Paige was still with the father. And why they didn't get married. Instead, she asked a question he might be able to answer. "How old is she?"

"Two. Or three." He sighed as if the conversation were difficult.

"I still can't believe Paige is a mother." Paige, who never seemed interested in the sea, or swimming, or treasure hunting the way Paisley and Peter did, was a parent. Paige, the little sister who always stayed close to home, close to Mom, had grown up. A businesswoman and a mommy. Although, her gallery was in terrible condition, perhaps irreparable.

"She's a good mom too." Dad gave her a stern look, like he expected her to disagree.

She would have commented, but he was shivering almost violently. "You're freezing. How long were you on the beach?" Not waiting for an answer, she jumped up and ran down the hall, searching for a bedroom, a blanket. She came to a room decorated in rosy pinks. Must be Paige's. Paisley hunted for a suitcase that might be Dad's. Not seeing any, she yanked a floral comforter off the bed. She ran back into the living room, covered Dad, tucking the edges around his shoulders. She kneeled on the wet carpet and yanked off his hiking boots and damp socks. He leaned into the corner of the couch, and she propped a pillow behind his shoulders.

"Don't need help." He still shivered. He clutched the blanket to his chin, his teeth chattering.

"You need to get warm, or you'll catch pneumonia."

"Just leave me alone."

She wanted to ask, *Why are you drinking? Why aren't you taking care of yourself?* Maybe she'd look for some food and give him a minute to cool down. "I'm going to hunt for sandwich makings."

"I told you I'm not hungry." He sounded belligerent. "You don't listen. Never did."

"I'm sorry." There, she said it again. "I am hungry. I think you should eat something too, but that's your choice." Two days ago— was it less than forty-eight hours since she heard that harrowing emergency alarm?—she was disappointed that Dad didn't need her help. Now he did, whether he'd admit that or not.

She strode into the kitchen, then scrounged around in the warm refrigerator. All the stuff in here probably needed to be thrown out. She hunted in the cupboards. Everywhere were signs of a child's presence. Sippy cups. Cartoon characters on plates. Child-proofing devices on the drawers. Fish crackers. Small packages of cereal treats. At least, Paige kept a supply of bread, peanut butter, and jam— Paisley's diet of late. She quickly made two sandwiches. Brought one to Dad.

He stared glumly at the food. He covered his nose and mouth with his hand. Did the strong smell of peanut butter sicken him after his throwing up on the beach?

"Sorry, there weren't many options." She set his portion on the coffee table before she dropped back onto the couch. She devoured her sandwich in a couple of bites. All she'd eaten for the last two days was PB and J, those breakfast bars at the gallery, and that sloppy joe sauce she shared with Judah.

"I n-need—"

She shuffled on the cushion to better see him. "Do you want to go back to the bedroom and rest? Get out of those clothes? I can hang them up in the bathroom to dry." Although, considering how cold the house was, they wouldn't dry quickly.

Suddenly, his eyes rolled back into their sockets. He jerked like he was having a spasm. Or a seizure.

That freaked her out. "Dad! Are you okay?" She shook his arm.

After several seconds, he coughed. "Where . . . am I?" He gazed at her dully.

Something must be terribly wrong with him, with his health. And she was alone. Without a cell phone or any way to contact emergency help.

"We're at Paige's, remember? Are you tired? Feeling sick again?" She snuggled the comforter around him where it fell from his shoulders. He must have gotten too cold down on the beach. "Do you have any spare clothes here?"

"I need my—"

"Clothes?"

His eyes watered. "Med-di—" He swallowed hard as if getting the word past his lips was painful, or too difficult. Was he choking? "Meds." He huffed out the word.

"Meds?" Something *was* wrong! His heart? "Where is your medicine? I'll get it for you." She jumped up. If he'd gone without a prescription that he needed, maybe that's why his thinking was fuzzy. Why he seemed grumpy and agitated. "Dad, where are the drugs you're taking? What are they for?"

His face scrunched up like he was trying hard to find the answer.

"Just tell me where they are, and I'll get them."

"H-home." He exhaled.

"Your medicine is . . . at your house?" At the same place where Craig was probably waiting for her?

Dad nodded. Let out a long shaky sigh.

"Where in the house? I'll, um, run over and get them and come right back." Not getting what her dad needed wasn't an option. A tenderness filled her as she stared at her childhood hero. "What's wrong with you, Daddy?"

He shuffled his shoulders back and forth as if seeking a comfortable position. "D-don't want . . . meds." He stared at something across the room. Or at nothing.

"How long since you took them?"

He licked his dry-looking lips. Shrugged.

She opened the water bottle again, held it out to him. "Was it before the storm? What kind of meds?" He clamped his mouth shut, so she set the water bottle back on the table.

"Don't—" He slumped over.

"Dad!" Was he asleep? *Please don't be unconscious.* "Dad! Wake up!" She shook his arm. "Can you hear me? Talk to me. Say something."

He mumbled incoherently. At least he was conscious.

"Dad, you okay?" She didn't want anything bad happening to him. She already lost her mom. She needed him. Wanted their relationship to be mended and restored. But first he needed to get well. For that to happen, he had to have his medicine.

Did she dare leave him alone, even to go after what he needed? And at her own peril? She would never choose to go back to the house where Craig might be. This was an emergency. No other choice.

"Where did you leave the meds?"

"F-fridge," he whispered hoarsely. "Maybe."

Maybe? "Okay. I'll be right back. You stay here. Don't leave." She didn't want him wandering down to the beach. With tidal changes, it could be dangerous. Deadly. She kissed his rough cheek. "I love you, Dad."

In a couple of minutes he snored softly, so she crept out the back door. This time, when she saw the swing set on its side, an affectionate feeling came over her. Her niece played here. Paige pushed her little girl in the swing the way Paisley had imagined doing with her own child. Sadness and joy mixed together within her, but she couldn't dwell on that. *Focus on Dad. On what he needs.*

Was Craig still lurking around her father's place? What were her chances of getting in, grabbing the medicine, and getting out without him noticing?

Nine

Paisley tread through her swamped childhood neighborhood, watching for any movement that might signal Craig's presence. In several low-lying places, she trudged around deeper water to keep the cold liquid from filling her boots. As she got closer to Dad's, she slowed down, peering around trees, stepping over debris, ready to bolt if she even saw Craig's shadow. Was he still nursing his hangover? Or searching for her?

At the corner of Front Street and Second, she paused to listen. Thud, thud, thud. A hammer? Who was in Basalt besides her and Dad? Or was Craig working on something in Dad's backyard?

She dashed behind the Shelton's gnarled spruce tree that was close to her father's property line. She got a glimpse of the front yard. Didn't see anyone.

If Craig was preoccupied behind the house, maybe she could sneak inside, grab the medicine, and slip out again. The possibility of him finding her, grabbing her, made her heart pound faster. But what else could she do? What other choice did she have?

Hunched over, she crept across the yard, her boots sloshing through the brackish water. If she could just reach the porch—

Craig rounded the corner of the house, a snarl on his face, muttering to himself. Was he still drunk?

She froze, startled to see him even though she knew this was a possibility. What now?

He stared straight at her, his eyes wide.

A pulse of white fear raced up her spine.

"Paisley." His arms were full of chunks of wood. At least, he couldn't grab her without dropping them. "You're back. Finally."

When he tossed the stack of wood onto the pile, adrenaline shot through her. She spun on her heels, charged around the Shelton's house, her boots flinging water and mud in her attempt to escape.

"Paisley!" He yelled from behind her. "Wait."

Not a chance. Determined to put distance between them, she barreled through the neighbors' backyards. Her old stomping ground. She knew the best places to hide. She ducked behind the tool shed next to Lucy Carmichael's parents' house. She pressed her body against the rough wooden wall, waited. Listening. Where was he?

"Paisley!" He sounded close.

She didn't move, wouldn't give herself away, despite her throbbing heartbeat and the air burning in her lungs. But wasn't she putting off the inevitable? Dad needed her to hurry.

She felt a tickle in her throat like she just got a whiff of black pepper. Terrible timing. She held her breath, resisting the urge to sneeze.

"Paisley, I want to help." Was he on the other side of the shed? "I'm not here to hurt you. You have to believe me."

She didn't believe anything he said. She hunted for a chunk of wood, anything to grab for protection. There. A couple of branches. If she made a run for it, she could scoop up one to use if she had to.

"Why do you think I came all this way? Stayed with you all this time?"

Stayed with me? Stalked her, more like. The tickle in her throat increased in intensity. The sneeze expelled from her mouth before she could stifle it.

Craig stepped into view, his palms out. "Just stay calm."

Calm? Paisley glowered at him, then sprinted past him, not pausing to grab the branch. Mud flew off her boots, splattering her arms and face, as she dodged back the way she came. She leaped over a downed tree. Ran around the corner, heading for Dad's front porch.

Craig's boots clomped right behind her. "What's wrong with you?"

She went straight for Judah's pickup, and using the hood for leverage, heaved herself up onto the porch. Craig climbed up too. Got between her and the door.

She grabbed the old wooden rocker, keeping it between them. She'd have one chance to shove it at him, hopefully to knock him off the porch. Then she would dash for the fridge and grab the medicine. How she'd get past him on the way out, she didn't know. Unless she hit him hard enough to knock him unconscious. She shoved the chair toward him like a lion trainer.

"Settle down, Paisley." Craig spread out his hands toward her. His eyes looked tired, bloodshot. "We're the only two people left in Basalt. We need to help each other. Work to survive this ordeal. I didn't mean to scare you last night."

Sure, he didn't. "I don't need your help." And they weren't the only ones left in Basalt. "I want you to leave my dad's property. Now!"

"Or what?" A challenge leapt into his gaze.

There was the look of the man who forced her to kiss him once before. And she recalled his "Little Red Riding Hood" comment. Wouldn't forget that, either. "You don't want to know 'or what.'" She'd do whatever she had to do to help her father—and get away from Craig again.

"I've been cleaning up for you and Paul." He pointed toward the garbage pile. "I'm helping out the family. You can trust me."

Trust him? Like she trusted a rattler. She held the chair taut. How did he know Dad's name, anyway? Oh, right, small town. Everyone knew everyone.

"Let's work together, Pais."

"Don't call me that." How dare he act as if they were friends. Besides, she only allowed Judah to use that nickname.

"Paisley, then." He squinted. "I can't leave you here by yourself."

"Yes, you can. I've been on my own for a long time."

His eyes brightened. "You're a tough bird. I admire that about you."

"Don't admire me." She set the chair down but clutched the wooden cross pieces. "Judah's coming back today. You should go." Just mentioning her husband's name made her feel more confident.

"I doubt he'll make it back for a few more days. No one can enter the area until the National Guard allows them to." Craig wiped his forehead with the back of his hand. "The entrance into town is badly damaged."

"He'll find a way. He promised."

"Like he got here yesterday?" He seemed to be baiting her. Why?

"Thanks to you, he couldn't." Anger replaced her previous fear.

"I came back to make sure you were safe."

What a liar. She shoved the chair forward a couple of inches, showing him she felt anything but safe around him. "As you can see, I'm fine. You can go."

"Can't leave a lady in distress alone."

"I'm not in distress!"

"I can see something's wrong. I can't leave you here." His gaze lied. As if he were a caring, thoughtful person.

She hated that. Wouldn't be deceived. "Because friends treat a pal's wife the way you treated me three years ago?"

His steely gaze didn't flinch.

She'd wasted enough time. Had to get inside the house. "For your information, I'm not alone. My dad's here. So you can get your sorry backside out of town without any fake remorse."

His eyes widened. Because of her vehemence? Or her news about Dad? "I care about your well-being. And your father's. That's why I'm still here."

"Oh, right. That's why you came here drunk last night? Because you 'care.'"

"I didn't come here drunk. I told you I found your dad's stash. I'll show you." He turned as if to leap off the porch.

Her chance! She clenched her fingers tightly around the wooden spindles and let out a growl as she plowed the rocker against his side. Craig flew off the porch, thudding against Judah's pickup. He dropped to the ground, rolled.

Paisley didn't wait to see if he was hurt. She barreled into the house, slammed the door and locked it, then ran for the fridge. She yanked on the handle. It didn't open, probably stuck because of the flooding. She pulled again, and it gave. A sour smell made her hold her breath. She shoved her hands between the lukewarm food containers and jars, searching for medicine. Her frustration mounted when she didn't find anything.

The front door rattled.

"Paisley!" Craig yelled. "Open the door. You've paid me back for my insolence three years ago. Can you let it go now?"

"No!" She moved aside butter, mustard, ketchup. There. In the door shelf was a narrow box. She held it up, shook it. Empty. "Oh, no."

Craig climbed in through the window—she'd forgotten about that access—clumsily tripping over the apple tree, sliding on the wet floor.

Ignoring him, she tried to read the label. She tensed at the sound of the man's boots sloshing through the standing water. Reaching into the fridge, she grabbed the first thing her hand touched—the glass ketchup bottle. She held up the jar threateningly like she did with the Mason jar the previous night. "Stay back! I mean it. I will throw this at you."

"Thanks a lot for shoving me off the porch." He rubbed his shoulder. Winced.

She kept the jar raised, imagining other things in the refrigerator that she could throw at him too.

"Who's the insulin for?" He nodded at the box in her other hand.

"Insulin?" Her jar-throwing hand lowered.

"Are you a diabetic?"

Diabetic? That's what was wrong with Dad? She stared at the box.

In her hesitation, Craig stepped forward and grabbed the empty container from her hand. "Who needs this, Paisley?" His voice took on a harsh tone. "Is this your dad's?" He stared at the box, squinting. "Paul Cedars." He must have read the faded prescription label.

Even though she hated him knowing anything personal about her or her family, she felt bewildered, dazed, and didn't answer. Dad was a diabetic? And she hadn't known?

"Is he acting lethargic? Sick?"

She nodded.

"Where is he?" He stood taller, his voice demanding. "He could be in grave danger without this."

"Don't you think I know that?" She didn't want Craig Masters involved in any aspect of her life. However, Dad's health was at stake. Since Craig worked as an emergency responder, if he knew something about this medicine, about this disease, she might have to swallow her pride. Her fear.

"Where's the rest of it?"

"I don't know." She turned away from him and yanked open cupboard doors, searching. "He said in the fridge." She grabbed the box from Craig, tried to read something that might give her a clue.

"We'll have to hunt everywhere." Craig opened and shut several cupboards and drawers. "These pens don't have to be refrigerated. Which means they could be stored anywhere." So he did know something about the medicine. Whatever he knew was more than she did.

She tugged open the rest of the drawers, trying to ignore the proximity of her and Craig, side by side, working together to find the insulin. Every movement where their paths crossed created horrible tension within her. She couldn't believe she was in this predicament, depending on the man she loathed. But she couldn't focus on that. Where would her dad stash extra medicine?

"Maybe it's in his bathroom." Craig's voice sounded husky.

"That would be on the second floor."

"I know."

That's right, he rescued her from that room yesterday. Was it only a day ago? It already felt like a week.

She turned to look at the gaping stairwell where the stairs exploded the night of the hurricane. Craig turned at the same time. They bumped into each other.

"Stay back."

"Sorry."

She hated being in the same room with him. Wouldn't relax around him, wouldn't let down her guard. He might be playing the nice-guy card right now, but she knew the truth. He was a scoundrel.

She remembered something else. "When I was stuck in the bathroom, I checked the shelves behind the mirror. I didn't see any medicine. That leaves Dad's bedroom."

"Come with me." He stomped across the living room and rushed out the front door.

Like she'd do anything just because he commanded her to. Glad for the reprieve of his exiting, she scrounged through the fridge again. Her hands shook from tension and the horror of knowing she couldn't find what Dad needed. Something scraped against the front of the house. A ladder?

She ran outside, jumped down from the porch.

Craig was already at the top rung, climbing into Dad's bedroom window.

She didn't want to follow him up the ladder. But shouldn't she be the one looking through Dad's stuff? Not a stranger. Not him. Especially not him. Even in an emergency, she didn't want him handling her family's belongings. She trudged to the foot of the ladder, waited.

A couple of minutes later, Craig thrust his hand out the open window, holding a box. "I found this on his closet shelf."

She nodded, bit her lip. Dad would have his insulin. Craig could go away and leave her alone. They never had to speak with each other again.

She clutched the ladder to keep it steady while he climbed onto the upper rung. Their roles were reversed. Yesterday morning, she tentatively descended the ladder while he held the metal steady. Now, he barreled down like it was a slide. Paisley stepped back so he wouldn't touch her.

"Where's your dad? I can help him."

"What? No." She'd take the insulin to her father. She held out her hand to receive the box he found.

"I know what I'm doing, Paisley." He nearly growled. "I'm an EMT with C-MER. And my mother is a diabetic. I've helped her before." He held up the box, one eyebrow raised.

She lowered her hand. Dad's life might depend on this man's expertise and knowledge about a disease that Paisley knew nothing about. Because of the evacuation, they were isolated from any outside medical help. Was Craig Dad's best option in this emergency? *Ugh.* How could she agree to let this man who she didn't trust come with her to the other house? Nowhere would be safe from him. Or far enough away from him.

"I couldn't find your dad's blood sugar testing strips or meter. But I have some in my emergency field bag." He strode to his truck, opened the door, then withdrew a dark-colored bag. He slammed the door. Faced her again. "Where is he?"

"He's at my sister Paige's." She despised having to tell him.

Craig took off, nearly sprinting in the direction of Pastor Sagle's church and the subdivision. Apparently, he knew exactly where Paige lived.

All Paisley could do was run after him and hope for the best.

Ten

"Brad!" Judah had been following the fisherman for about ten minutes, barely able to keep him in his sights. He thought the guy was heading to his car. Instead, he trudged in the direction of the river, maybe the marina. Brad, who had been a few years ahead of Judah in high school, didn't seem to hear him calling. Or else, ignored him.

At a coffee shop not far from the port area, Brad stepped inside, much to Judah's relief. His injured leg could use a much-needed rest. Another cup of steaming hot coffee appealed to him too.

The congested shop smelled of delicious coffees and pastries, and for a second Judah just wanted to inhale the scents. He gazed around the room at the varied populace—fishermen, businessmen, elderly folks, couples, groups of women, even children—lining the counter and clustered about small tables. There was Brad, sitting with his back toward the entrance. Judah strode across the room, then dropped into the opposite seat at his table.

Brad glared at him.

"I don't know if you remember me or not. I'm Judah Grant. I hope you don't mind if I sit here for a minute. The place is packed."

Brad sipped his drink that looked dark enough to be black coffee. Didn't comment. Didn't seem very friendly, either.

Back in high school, Judah knew of the Keifer brothers and their reputation for being brawlers. But their paths hadn't crossed much in the years since.

"I'm sorry to barge in on you this way." He stretched out his sore leg. "I've been following you since you left the information booth a while ago."

Still no comment from Brad.

"I overheard your conversation about needing to get back to Basalt Bay."

"What's it to you?" The man wiped his hand over his bushy mustache.

"If you don't mind my asking, what's your plan?" Judah didn't wait for small talk to ease the awkwardness between them.

"And if I do mind?" Brad's green eyes squinted at Judah as if he were a nuisance.

"I need to get back there. Today, if possible. It's urgent." Judah linked his fingers over his knee, trying to scale back his intensity, making it easier for the other man to do the same.

"Wait in line." Brad growled. He turned sideways as if terminating the discussion. Almost as an afterthought, he added, "Maybe you should call and ask your all-powerful, swindling father to bail you out."

Judah clenched his jaw. So, here sat another person with a beef toward Mayor Grant. He wouldn't be put off that easily. "This doesn't have anything to do with my dad."

"No?"

"No. I want to know how you plan on getting home." Judah leaned forward, his elbows on the table. "I'd like to go with you however you're returning to Basalt Bay."

"Not happening."

"Please. I'm desperate." Judah pinched the bridge of his nose. "I don't know what you have against my father, but I assure you, I am not him."

Brad shook his head. Squinted. Sizing Judah up, it seemed. Did he find him wanting? Weak? If it weren't for his leg—

"Why are you in such an all-fired hurry to get back to Basalt?"

Judah decided to go for the truth. "My wife is stuck there. Alone, as far as I know. Without a working cell phone. I need to get back to her. She may be in danger." He briefly described their stay in her father's house through the storm. Judah's accident. Her not going to Florence with him. Their last communication.

"Why did she stay behind?" Brad seemed more interested now. Even turned slightly toward Judah.

"That's not important. What I need is—"

"Hey, it's important to me." The other man's voice rose gruffly. "If I'm risking my life to bring another person along in an open skiff in rough waters, I want to know the whole story." His cup landed on the table with a clunk. "Especially with a guy who can't keep up. Can't fend for himself. I saw you hobbling back there."

Judah disliked that the fisherman perceived him as frail, maybe even crippled. But he stuffed his pride aside. "Okay, sure, I have this injury. I may be hobbling, but that means I'm moving forward. I'm determined to get back to my wife, with or without your help. I work on a skiff for C-MER. I know how to handle myself in rough seas."

"Why did you leave your wife behind?" Brad's question was blunt, his voice gruff, eyes glinting with judgment.

"I didn't 'leave' her." Judah sighed. "She didn't want to ride in the vehicle with the person who came for us. Refused, actually." Normally he wouldn't tell a stranger so much about their personal lives. However, Judah knew he had to give Brad the information he wanted, or he wouldn't even consider helping him.

"Family feud? Maybe she didn't want to go with *you*." Brad checked his watch. "Grants are notorious for stirring up strife."

Judah groaned. "Let's just call it an injustice caused by someone else. Not me." He didn't want to say anything about the matter between her and Craig. Small town gossip traveled far.

"Who's your wife, anyway?" Brad shuffled his hat on his head. Tapped the table. Apparently in a hurry to be on his way now.

"Paisley Grant. Was Cedars."

The man's jaw dropped. "Little fireball Paisley?" He guffawed. "I have been out of town too long. Pete's kid sister married a Grant?" He grinned and his white teeth contrasted with his reddish beard.

Judah didn't know whether to be offended or proud. "She did."

"The two were inseparable when we were kids." Brad chuckled. "High school changed that. They grew apart."

"Right. Peter left to go fishing in Alaska."

"Both of us did." Brad drained his mug. "I eventually returned to fish closer to the mainland."

A pause.

"About that boat ride?"

The fisherman's eyes gazed at something through the window. For a few moments, he seemed lost in thought. "I'm still waiting for a callback from a guy." He pulled a cell phone out of his coat pocket and thumped the screen. "Nothing yet. Give me your number and I'll call when I find out more details about renting a skiff."

"I don't have a phone right now." Judah stood and thrust out his hand to shake Brad's. "I'll stick around here until you hear something."

"Fine." The fisherman returned his handshake.

Judah shuffled across the room to the counter and ordered a latte, even though he'd had one earlier. He found an available bar stool and plopped down, hoping Brad would have good news for him soon.

Paisley didn't know that things had turned out rotten in his attempts to make it back to Basalt Bay. If there was any way to let her know, he would. He didn't forget his promise. He still wouldn't give up. Although, he had limitations. He massaged the calf muscle near his bandage, wishing it felt better.

The barista called his name. He raised his hand, waving to get her attention. She set the to-go cup on the counter in front of him. He sipped his hot drink slowly. Sighed. If only his circumstances were as pleasing. *Lord, could you—*

"Judah, that you?" Mia.

He groaned.

"I keep running into you."

"So it seems."

Did she follow him here, too?

"Any news?" She waved at someone across the room.

"Possibly. Just waiting to hear."

"Have you talked to anyone from C-MER? Oh, just a sec." She turned to the barista. "I'll have a half-caf, oat milk, extra-foam macchiato."

The frazzled, overworked twenty-something gawked at her. "Oat milk, really? We're swamped. Almost out of supplies. Definitely don't have any highfalutin—"

"Okay, okay. Fine. I'll take soy milk." Mia huffed as if it were the worst stepdown ever. "Oh, do you have stevia?"

The barista rolled her eyes. "No, we do not." Shaking her head, the young woman returned to her tasks.

"Someone isn't getting a tip." Mia scooted back to Judah, continuing the conversation like she hadn't stepped away. "I called Craig a couple of times."

"You did?" He tried not to overreact to the man's name. Still, his unsettled business with his supervisor fed his agitation. "Where was he?"

"He didn't answer." She grinned at someone. Waved. "Weird that he hasn't stayed in contact with his employees, don't you think? Seems he would have called by now."

"Maybe he's AWOL. Or his cell died." Any other reasons caused too much angst inside Judah's chest.

"Maybe." She nudged his arm. "Can you picture that? Our wonderful fearless leader without his cell phone?" She snickered. "Doesn't compute."

Judah didn't buy into her complimentary assessment of Craig. Her eyes shone too brightly. Were the two romantically involved? Or did their supervisor just happen to be another person she flirted with? He sighed. Not his concern. "When did you last speak with him?"

"Hmmm?" She leaned closer.

"Craig? When did you—"

Mia stepped back, bumping into Brad. "Oh, excuse me." She batted her eyes at the fisherman, grinning. "Why, if it isn't Brad Keifer. Funny running into you here."

Brad glanced at her with the briefest acknowledgement, then faced Judah. "Meet me at Wharf C. Two o'clock. Don't be late."

"All right, I will. Thank you." Did this mean he would be with Paisley today? A rush of joy danced through his heart. Things were looking up.

Brad strode out of the bustling café.

"What's with him?" Mia's lips creased into a pout. Apparently, she wasn't used to anyone ignoring her. "What's going on?"

"I'm catching a ride back to Basalt Bay with him." The less she knew, the better, so he added, "I don't know all the details yet."

"Two o'clock, huh?" She touched her lips with the matching red nail of her index finger.

Too bad she heard that. Nothing Judah could do about it now.

Eleven

Paisley kept ten feet between her and Craig as they rushed silently toward Paige's. If it weren't for her desperate awareness of Dad's medical problem, she would have grabbed the insulin container and ditched Craig. Did she really give him permission to treat her father?

The fact that Craig carried the medicine package like he was the one in charge bothered her. She could snatch it from his hand, but what good would that do? He seemed to know where Dad was, where Paige lived. He'd just find them. And what if he could help Dad? Would she deny her father medical treatment because of her own unease around the man?

"Your dad shouldn't be drinking alcohol, either." That was the first thing Craig said to her since they started walking.

Dad had never been a heavy drinker. But what did she know about his current lifestyle? Maybe after Mom died, he drowned his sorrows in the bottle. She wouldn't judge him. She'd found relief by running away. Temporarily, anyway.

"Alcohol can have unpredictable effects on a diabetic," Craig stated, his voice flat, monotone, like he was reciting data unemotionally. "It can mask symptoms, even those leading to a diabetic coma."

Was he trying to scare her? Did that happen to his mother? A diabetic coma sounded horrific. Paisley's heart rate accelerated, as did her worry for Dad. They were miles from a medical facility. Maybe they'd have to get him medevacked out. But surely his condition wasn't as bad as Craig made it sound.

"You should dump out all those bottles I found."

"Stop telling me what to do."

He glanced over his shoulder as if her sharp response surprised him.

Plenty more angst where that came from. She'd let him check Dad, since there didn't seem any deterrent to that happening. Then she'd tell him to hit the road, Jack. Whatever Dad needed from here on out, she was the one helping him. She wasn't an EMT like Craig, but she was his daughter. She'd make the decisions now. Her and Paige, once her sister returned.

Glancing at the ocean between the space of a couple of houses, she noticed the rough waves and charcoal clouds hovering over the bay. Was another storm coming? Would it keep Judah away longer?

Her thoughts drifted back to Dad. If he needed an airlift, how would they contact the authorities? What about Craig's cell phone? She hadn't seen him texting. Did it still have power? If it did, she could call Judah. Hadn't he called her using Mia's phone last night?

"Does your phone still have battery power?" She made herself ask, even though she didn't want to speak to him.

"No. It's dead."

"Oh." Then they were in trouble if Dad needed medical help that went beyond his need for insulin. Although, Craig's monster truck was still parked in her dad's yard. Maybe he could drive around whatever blockade the National Guard had set up and take Dad to the ER in Florence.

When they reached Paige's house, Craig strode up the driveway, past Dad's car parked sideways, and into the debris-strewn backyard. He seemed to know just where to go.

Entering the back door behind him, Paisley called out a warning. "Dad, it's me. I have someone with me."

No answer.

"Dad?" She pushed past Craig and ran into the living room. Her father was slumped over on the couch cushions. His mouth hung open wide. Was he breathing? Unconscious? Or—

"Dad!" She shook his arm.

"Mr. Cedars!" Craig rushed around her, pushed her out of the way, and dropped the insulin package and the bag he carried onto the coffee table. Kneeling on one knee, he put two fingers against the side of her dad's neck, checking for a pulse. He leaned his ear close to Dad's mouth.

"Is he—?"

"He's alive," Craig spoke tersely.

Paisley dropped to the edge of the couch beside Dad. She heard his breathing. It was shallow, barely noticeable, and had a catch to it like he was struggling to inhale oxygen. She knew what that felt like. How terrifying it was to breathe in empty-feeling air. "Dad?"

"His breath smells fruity. Dry lips. His skin isn't pale." Craig seemed to be speaking to himself.

She watched tensely, fearful they hadn't gotten back with the insulin soon enough.

Craig peeled Dad's eyelids back one at a time, peering into them. Then he yanked open his bag, withdrew a stethoscope. He pressed the circular chest piece against Dad's shirt, listening with the headset against his ears. "I don't have intravenous saline solution in my field bag."

"Okay." She didn't know why he told her that. Maybe he thought she understood more about Dad's problem than she did.

Craig checked her father's pulse again.

Dad twitched, jerked a couple of times, but didn't open his eyes.

"He did that earlier too. It scared me." She blinked rapidly, wouldn't give in to tears in front of Craig. "What's wrong with him? Can you tell?" Having to ask the man questions about her father, relying on him for wisdom and advice, was difficult for her to stomach.

"High blood sugar. Hyperglycemia, most likely." Craig dug in his bag and pulled out a small kit, probably the one he mentioned earlier. He tore open a package of wipes, filling the air with the scent of alcohol. He rubbed the cloth over the side of Dad's index finger. He withdrew other gadgets. A meter. A pen-like device. A small cannister. He inserted a narrow strip into the bottom of the meter. Twisted the top off the pen.

Even though Craig's eyes were bloodshot, and he probably had a hangover headache, his hands were steady.

Paisley didn't know what any of the paraphernalia was for, what Craig was doing as he pressed the pen against Dad's index finger that he just wiped clean. She had to trust him. Her immediate concern was for her father's health. *Lord, please touch my dad. Heal him. Give us a chance to work things out.* She wished he'd open his eyes, say something. At least, she could tell he was breathing, still alive.

Craig milked Dad's finger, drawing a droplet of blood to the surface. He picked up the meter with the test strip, touching the tip to the blood. He released Dad's finger, stared at the screen. He turned the device toward her. The display read "523."

"Is that bad?"

"Extremely high. I'll administer the insulin now."

"Okay." She didn't know what else to say, what to do. She was grateful she didn't have to face this crisis alone.

He set the meter on the coffee table, and his hand bumped the peanut butter sandwich she made earlier onto the wet rug. She'd take care of it later.

Tearing open the insulin box, he pulled out another pen-type object. He held it up; removed the cap. He opened a tiny package that had a smaller cap. He pulled a tab off that, and twisting the cap onto the pen, exposed a small needle. He worked with the insulin pen, squirting some clear liquid into the air.

"Lift his shirt at the waist."

She tugged up on Dad's flannel shirt and the stained white t-shirt beneath, exposing his belly, glad to have a task, something to do to help.

Craig held the pen like a pencil and pressed the needle into Dad's skin a couple of inches from his belly button. With his other hand, he pushed the button at the opposite end of the pen, releasing the liquid.

Paisley hated to watch, felt squeamish, but she wouldn't turn away. She might have to help Dad with this procedure. She needed to know what to do.

When Craig pulled the pen away from Dad's abdomen, Paisley tugged down on his shirt, covering him. "Will he be okay now?"

"We'll wait and see." Craig twisted the small cap onto the pen, turned counterclockwise, removing the needle. He recapped the top. Set both on the table. "As soon as he's alert, encourage him to drink water. He's probably dehydrated which is problematic with high blood sugar."

"All right." She tried to take in all the information as she watched, waiting for her dad to wake up. "How long will it take?"

"Varies. The insulin is working; give it time." Craig put some items back into his bag. The stethoscope still around his neck, he pressed the chest piece against Dad's shirt. "Sounds better."

"Good." She held her dad's hand, watching him, waiting. Praying.

A few more minutes passed. Craig stood, probably tired from the way he was squatting. He pressed his fingers against his temples, closed his eyes. It seemed she was right about the headache.

Dad's eyelids fluttered. "Craig, look. Dad!"

Craig squatted back down. "Paul?"

Dad moved slightly. His tongue wet his lips. His eyelids opened a little. He peered up at her through narrow slits. He winced. His gaze moved to Craig. Back to her. Did he recognize her?

"It's me, Dad."

"I'm Craig Masters from C-MER, remember me?"

Dad didn't respond to either of them.

"He gave you your insulin." She rubbed her father's hand, hoping he'd squeeze her fingers, say he knew who she was. He didn't. His hand was still limp.

Craig checked his eyes again. Took his pulse. Listened with the stethoscope on his chest.

Finally, Dad's gaze met hers with a foggy look, his eyebrows quirked. Was he wondering how she knew about the insulin? About his illness?

She gripped his hand tighter. "You're going to be okay. We're here to help you." She remembered what Craig said about the water. She let go of Dad's hand, then reached for the water bottle she'd given him earlier. Uncapping the top, she leaned the ridge against his lower lip. "Drink some of this, okay?"

He swallowed a little bit of water. Grumbled. Shook his head.

She glanced at Craig. He nodded as if telling her to keep trying.

"Can you drink a little more? It's good for you to drink as much as you can." She pressed the bottle to his mouth again. "I want to help you."

He took some water in, then pressed his lips closed tightly. "Don't . . . need . . . your . . . help." He turned his head away from her.

She felt his rude rejection all the way to the bottom of her heart.

Craig eyed her, but she ignored his unspoken question. "Paul, how long has it been since your last dose of insulin?"

Dad shrugged. "A week, or so."

"You should test yourself regularly, every day."

"Yeah, yeah. Leave me alone." Even though Dad hardly lifted his head off the pillow, he seemed combative.

"How long since you last ate something?" Craig asked.

Dad huffed. "Don't know. Don't care. I've been too sick. Sick and tired."

Paisley held the water bottle out to him again. "Can you drink some more?"

"No. Let me be, will you? You had no right to give me that insulin."

Why was he acting this way? As if he didn't want to get better. As if she'd done something wrong.

Craig frowned. "Do you know what day this is? Who's the president?"

"Who cares? Leave me alone . . . to die in peace." The last words were huffed out on a shaky breath, barely audible. He shut his eyelids as if closing himself away from them.

To die? "I won't leave you alone." Paisley smoothed her palm over his sleeve, fighting the urge to weep. "I love you, Dad. I want you to get well. I want us to talk and share our lives again. Things are going to be better between us. I promise." Her dad didn't even want to live? How long had he felt so hopeless? "Think about Paige. What about Piper? Don't you want to see her grow up? She needs her grandpa."

"Papa," he muttered gruffly.

"Piper calls you Papa?"

He nodded, still not opening his eyes.

"That's so sweet. See there, you need to get well so you can spend time with the little girl who calls you Papa." She sniffed, fighting her battle with tears.

Craig pointed at the water bottle, reminding her of her task.

She picked up the plastic container again. "You need to drink more water." She uncapped the lid. Held it to his stubbornly clamped lips. "Please? I want you here with me for a long time. I need you."

"You don't need anyone." His voice sounded raspy.

"Yes, I do."

Craig threw her a curious glance. "You should try to drink the water, Mr. Cedars. In a few minutes, I'd like to retest your blood sugar."

"No."

"I strongly recommend that you test yourself and take the needed doses of insulin daily." Craig squinted at Dad. "Your reading from a few minutes ago was over five hundred."

Dad opened his eyes. "That bad, huh?"

"How are you feeling now?"

"Tired." His breathing didn't sound as shallow and broken as before.

"We'll drum up some food for you, too." Craig nodded toward the water bottle.

Paisley held it out to Dad again, but he didn't open his mouth. A memory from when she was a kid came to mind. "Remember when I fell on the boulders at the peninsula and gashed my knee? I didn't want stitches. Yelled at you to use duct tape. It fixes everything, right? I told you I wasn't going to the ER. You said if I planned to run on Basalt Beach for the rest of my life, I needed my leg fixed good as new. Well, I want to hike on the beach, search for treasures, and enjoy the Pacific with *you* for a long time. Please, get well and give us a second chance." She begged him with her gaze, and her heart, if only he could see into it.

She avoided Craig's glance. Didn't want him privy to her family's pain. But he was here. Silently observing.

She knew she'd hurt Dad by leaving Basalt without telling him goodbye three years ago. And he never understood about her not attending Mom's funeral. But she longed for a real father-daughter relationship with him again, somehow.

Craig checked Dad's pulse. "Will you let me test your blood sugar again in a few minutes?"

"All right, stop pestering me, both of you." Dad glared and crossed his arms.

Maybe they'd gotten through to him. She should thank Craig for his help. What if he hadn't been here? What if she had to deal with this all by herself? But even with those thoughts, she didn't have the words to say to him.

Dad sighed and closed his eyes as if he were going to take a nap. She pulled the comforter up to his chin.

"We'll have to watch him closely." Craig picked up the used needle cap and nodded for her to follow him into the kitchen.

She grabbed the soggy sandwich off the floor, then left the room to give her father some peace and quiet. When she had internet access, she'd study up on diabetes and find out how she could help him more. She walked to the trash can and tossed in the sandwich.

"If he's drinking alcohol on top of the diabetes, that's a bad combination." Craig picked up an empty soda can, dropped the used needle cap into it, and set it in the garbage.

"You should lay off the sauce too."

His face flushed. "We all have our vices."

And he was mean under the influence of his. Although, today he seemed different. Not that she trusted him.

"It might be a week until we get electricity." He stuffed his hands into his jean's pockets. Maybe he felt awkward too. "Your dad needs to drink lots of water, eat healthy food, fresh vegetables, and get daily exercise for his recovery."

A whole week without electricity? She couldn't imagine living in the dark, cold dampness that long. And where would she find fresh vegetables and healthy food in this devastated town? Even locating fresh water might be challenging. She swallowed what felt like a wad of cotton, wishing he'd go. Leave her to think. But what if something else went wrong with Dad?

"Guess we'll have to focus on survival."

We'll? Did he imagine she still wanted his help? Needed him? He was delusional. And yet, Dad might very well need him for the next hours. Days, even?

Ugh.

"There's a barbecue grill in the backyard."

"So?" She hadn't noticed one. She'd seen the messy yard, the wrecked swing set.

"Why don't you check the freezer for usable meat?" He strode to the back door. "I'll see if there's propane to fire up the grill. Then I'll come in and check on your dad." He exited quickly.

She should have told him she didn't want him here. He was a horrible human being. A cad. That's what she still considered him, right?

She sighed.

He was correct about one thing. Their survival depended on food and water. A clattering noise came from the backyard. Probably him dragging the barbecue grill across the patio.

She tugged on the freezer handle above the standard-sized fridge. She found packages of hamburger, steak, and chicken already thawing out. She grabbed two pounds of hamburger, noticing the grass-fed stickers. That should be healthy enough for Dad, for all of them.

Craig deserved a meal too. Afterward, she'd thank him for his help, and that would be the end of this weird little interlude of dependency on a man she couldn't stand to be around.

Twelve

After they finished eating charred hamburgers and cold canned beans, Paisley noticed that Dad seemed more alert. Even talkative, mostly with Craig. She hadn't worked up the nerve to tell that man to leave yet, but she would soon if he didn't take the initiative.

Now, Dad was stretched out on the couch with his eyes closed. Craig was still doing something outside.

Dusk had settled in, making the rooms less inviting, full of shadows. After a perusal of the house, using the flashlight, she found it had two bedrooms. A queen-sized bed was the centerpiece in Paige's room. Dad had probably slept here. The second bedroom contained a child-sized bed. And a futon lined the opposite wall— the most obvious place for Paisley to rest. Either that or she'd sleep on the living room couch. Without electricity, there wouldn't be a night-light for either place; she always kept one going after dark.

So far, Judah hadn't arrived. It seemed unlikely that he would this late in the day. If he was detained due to the road closure, he must have tried everything he could to get back to her. He was injured. Probably couldn't walk far. And the conditions must be bad everywhere along the coast.

She wouldn't allow herself to imagine him hanging around Mia at the storm shelter, possibly trapped in her flirtatious web. Right.

The woman's face repeatedly popped up in her thoughts every time she wondered what Judah might be doing.

She needed a task, something to distract herself. Maybe she could find enough candles to stave off the coming darkness. This flashlight wouldn't last forever. She grabbed a cinnamon scented candle from the mantle of the electric fireplace. Too bad that wasn't a wood stove, instead of it being electricity dependent. She set the candle jar on the coffee table. After scooping up the snack wrappers and throwing them away in the kitchen garbage, she checked the cupboards for matches. She found a box, then grabbed two medium-sized candle jars from the windowsill. She smelled the pumpkin and vanilla scents before setting them on the coffee table in the living room.

One other place might have candles—Paige's room. She discovered two more. She placed them all together in a cluster. That should be enough wick power to keep the room lit for a while.

"Good job." Craig paused at the doorway. "It will be dark soon."

He didn't have to remind her of that.

Dad stirred from his catnap. "What's going on?" He squinted at Craig. "Who are you?" Apparently, his mind was still fuzzy.

"Craig Masters." The tall man thrust out his hand and shook Dad's like he was a caring neighbor, a friend.

Paisley grumbled as conflicting feelings battled within her.

"I work with Judah, remember?" Craig smiled widely. "I'm here to offer my assistance to you and Paisley in his absence, however either of you might need help."

He sounded so noble, and he didn't meet her gaze, her glare.

Dad sat up. "Got any soda?"

Paisley handed him a water bottle. "Try this."

He complained about not liking water, but he took a sip.

"How are you feeling, sir?" Craig squatted beside him.

Dad inhaled and exhaled, rubbed his palm over his stomach. "Some better, I think."

"That's good to hear." Craig stood and rocked his thumb toward the door. "I should probably get going."

Paisley was relieved he came to that conclusion himself.

"I'll head out to my place." Craig took a couple of steps. "I'll check back in the morning."

"Where do you live?" She probably shouldn't have asked that, since she didn't want him thinking she was interested in his life.

His eyebrows lifted. "I live on the south side. Not far from Judah's cabin. Oh, um, and yours, of course."

They were neighbors? Maybe he'd purchased a place since she went away. "That's a long walk." On second thought, his staying a mile away sounded perfect.

"I'll just—" He strode to the door. Stopped. His back toward her, he seemed reluctant. "You sure you'll be okay? Maybe I'll sleep in my truck. Stay closer."

"Why?" She preferred his first plan—his going somewhere far from her. Tonight she'd like a good sleep, knowing he wasn't going to barge in on her and make her fearful.

Dad's health problems kept her from making a disparaging comment. He might need Craig's help with another insulin shot. When would he require the next one?

"I feel responsible for you."

"Don't. You aren't." How could she forget how afraid she was last night, hiding in the pantry? Even if Craig acted differently today.

"Why don't you just sleep here?" Dad patted the couch. "Plenty of room."

"Dad—"

"I'll head back to the bedroom," he continued. "No reason to hike all that way in the dark."

Plenty of reasons. "Dad—" She shook her head, glared a warning.

"What? It's the Christian thing to do. Provide shelter. We're all in this disaster together." He was speaking more coherently now.

For her to state her opinion of Craig would require her to explain about their past. Something she didn't want to do with him standing right here.

"It's settled then."

Nothing is settled!

Dad pushed off the couch. Wobbled. Paisley leaped forward and grabbed his arm. Craig crossed the distance in two strides and held onto her father's other arm. Dad's voice sounded stronger, but his body was still weak. Together they led him back to Paige's room. Helped him get out of his damp clothes and into bed. How would she have done all that by herself? She grudgingly admitted to herself, again, that she appreciated Craig's assistance.

"I can leave," Craig said as soon as they entered the living room.

"Probably for the best."

"But your dad—"

She looked at him sharply, guessing what he might say. Dad might need his help in the night. Craig had EMT training. She didn't.

"Okay, fine. You can stay on the couch like Dad said. Tonight, only." She hated acquiescing. Hated giving this man permission to stay in the same house with her.

His eyes widened. Her acceptance of the situation must have surprised him too.

She blew out all but two candles, then grabbing one, stomped back to Piper's room. Her nemesis sleeping under the same roof? She slammed the bedroom door and leaned hard against it. She shined the light from the candle onto the doorknob.

No lock? She groaned. How would she ever get to sleep in this room without one?

Thirteen

At two o'clock, Judah had met Brad at Wharf C, only to discover that the boat the fisherman planned to rent from Richard was gone. Someone else offered the owner more money.

Richard attempted to placate them, promising they could rent the boat in the morning. He said he was sorry. That the other client had an emergency. What else could he do? However, if there was a serious situation—one more serious than Judah's—why would the boat owner even mention the higher payment? Could they trust that he was telling the truth about the next day's use?

Frustrated, Judah left the wharf, nearly dragging Brad along with him. The fisherman was beside himself, railing at the owner's business ethics, then threatening to steal one of the other boats tied to the dock. Although, Judah couldn't see any worth committing a crime over. Several skiffs were damaged from the storm. One upside down on the wharf. A couple half sunk. None were boats he wanted to use to travel twenty miles in unpredictable, possibly rough, waters.

Brad said he'd never rent from the guy again. But they still needed a boat, even if they couldn't get one until morning.

Judah had failed Paisley, again. That's what bothered him the most. He assured her he'd be with her today. And he tried. Man, he tried. Now, it was too late. What must she be thinking? How was she? Was she safe? Agitation gripped him in the gut until he felt physically sick. Sometimes things just all went wrong. So frustrating. Maddening. His sigh came out like a moan.

Finally, exhausted, discouraged, and with his leg needing a break, he plopped down on the low cot in the storm shelter. Closing his eyes, he sighed and reminded himself that he and Paisley were in God's hands. But what if his wife thought he deserted her? What if she was still in trouble? Or waited eagerly for his arrival, only for him to let her down, again.

He groaned. Massaged his face with his palms.

"You okay?" Mia spoke from somewhere that felt too close.

"Yeah, fine." He growled the words. Then regretted his short fuse.

"Judah?"

He leaned up on his elbow. "I'm okay. Just trying to sleep. Forget this day."

"Sorry things didn't work out for you to return home." She stared at him from her cot. "You tried. Paisley will understand."

"Thanks. I hope so."

"Tomorrow will be better."

"I know." He laid back down. A little while later, fatigue overrode his churning thoughts, and he relaxed despite the hum of noise in the crowded gym.

Hours later, he opened his eyes to light coming in through the upper windows. Did he sleep all night? He checked his watch beneath the blanket. Almost six in the morning. He stretched his calf muscles. Winced in anticipation of pain. It still hurt, but not as badly as yesterday. Good. He might have a lot of walking to do today.

He sniffed, smelled coffee, and his thoughts raced to Paisley. How did she survive another night? Was she still at her dad's? She probably didn't have any coffee to drink like he did, since the town was without electricity. She might even need food or water. A troubling thought.

Today, nothing would stop him from getting back to Basalt Bay. *Please, God, let it be so.*

But first he'd locate Brad and check on the boat arrangements. If there was a snag, maybe Dad had connections. He might know someone who would loan a skiff to two desperate guys in Florence. Not that Judah wanted to call and beg his father for a favor. Especially not after what Paisley told him about the mayor paying her off to leave town three years ago. He still struggled with that. His own dad taking such malicious steps to intrude on his and Paisley's marriage? The thought tore him up inside. Outraged him. Still, if push came to shove, he'd stuff down his frustrations, his pride, and humble himself and call Dad.

"You already aw-wake?" Mia's voice croaked.

"Yeah." He spoke quietly, not wanting to bother the people sleeping next to her.

"I can't wait to get back to my own bed. This cot is miserable." She ran her hand over her hair, smoothing it out. "What's the plan?"

"Nothing." No plan of his involved her.

He sat up. Rubbed his palm over his scruffy face. What would Paisley think of his unshaven—he sniffed himself—bad smelling condition? How many days had he gone without shaving or showering? Three? She used to say she liked it when he let his whiskers grow out on the weekends. That it made him look wild and carefree. Maybe she'd be attracted to his appearance. Although, not his odor. He chuckled.

"What's with the grin?" Mia's voice was soft.

"Nothing, really." He needed to watch what he said around her.

He slipped his feet into his shoes. Stood. Pulled on the second-hand coat. He checked the item in the pocket—the only thing that went right yesterday. Then he smoothed out the blankets on the cot. Hopefully, he was all done sleeping here.

At the table laden with coffeepots and platters of donuts, he filled a cup and picked up a maple bar. James Weston was already there. His expression looked downcast.

"Something wrong?"

James took off his glasses, wiped his hand over his eyes. "I've been standing here trying to figure out how to get back to my house. They say we can't return for a few more days, but I've got a list of things to do. I've had all I can take of sitting and waiting."

"Any solutions come to mind?" If James figured out a way to get back home, maybe Judah could catch a ride.

The older man rocked his thumb toward the gym doors. "Take a gander at that."

Judah stared through the glass on the doors. Dark gray clouds loomed overhead. Hard raindrops fell. The trees swayed in the wind. "Oh, no."

"Storm." James put his glasses back on. "Ruins my plans."

Judah's too, maybe. Why did one thing after another seem to be preventing him from getting to Paisley?

Lord, could You make a way where there doesn't seem to be a way?

He took a sip of his hot drink, contemplating the storm and how it might affect his return to Basalt Bay.

"Hi, guys." Mia's voice.

"Morning." James stepped over near Judah. "How long do you suppose this will last? I'm worried about my place. The thought of looters makes me see red."

"Me too. Maybe someone has access to the news. Let's find out how the road crew is doing. This weather will impede progress, I'm afraid." Judah leaned closer to the other man, trying to keep his voice quiet enough that Mia wouldn't hear. "Before, when you spoke of going home, what were you thinking about doing?"

"You know the old road to the lighthouse?"

"Yeah. It's nearly impassable."

"Thought I'd drive the long way around, come in farther north of where the guards are stationed." James nodded at another fellow approaching the table. "I heard a couple of guys talking of doing the same thing last night."

"That right?" Judah could walk that far, from the lighthouse to Paul's. Easier than hiking across the dunes.

"No one can keep us from protecting our property." James clenched his fist in the air. "We have rights."

The men guarding the entrance to town might take exception to that, but Judah didn't say so.

Mia stepped between them. "What are you two plotting with such serious faces?" She sipped her coffee, grimaced. "I can't wait to stop drinking this awful watered-down brew."

"No one's forcing you to drink it, young lady." James scowled.

"I just prefer my regular coffee. Don't you?" She smiled and patted the man's arm as if to smooth out his ruffled feathers.

"I suppose that's true." James nodded, his voice changing to a more pleasant tone.

"How long have you lived in our lovely town, sir?"

"I've lived in the same house my whole life. Paul Cedars and I attended grade school together." James's chest seemed to puff out with pride.

Mia grinned again. "You must be one of our town's most upstanding citizens."

James chuckled. His face hued red. "Don't know about that."

Judah couldn't believe how Mia's schmoozing changed the man's countenance. She had a way with men. Or pure manipulation. Had she treated Judah that way before?

"I was telling Judah how I plan to get back to Basalt Bay."

Uh-oh. James was rambling.

"That's fascinating." Mia leaned closer to him. "How will you do that?"

Judah stepped in before James said anything else. "I think the storm may hinder us from doing much today." He nodded toward the entryway, drawing James away from Mia. "Let's take another look."

"Nice chatting with you, miss." James lifted his cup in her direction.

"Same here." She tugged on Judah's coat sleeve. "You're staying put, right?"

"We'll see." He avoided giving her any details. He followed James back to the door. Peered outside. The weather appeared the same as before. Not good. A strong gale would make a sea journey difficult, although not impossible. And the skiff's owner might not let them use his rental in these conditions.

"Such a shame." James groaned. "Maybe I'll drive north tomorrow."

"If I don't find my own way out of here today"—Judah hated even saying that—"could I catch a ride with you?" He wanted to keep his options open. In the meantime, he'd pray for the storm to let up.

"Sure, sure. Would enjoy the company." James patted him on the shoulder. "Nice girl you work with." He nodded toward the coffee table where Mia conversed with a couple of other men. "Anything going on between you two?"

"What? No! Nothing like that." He held up his left hand, displaying his wedding ring. "Still married."

"Uh-huh." James nodded. No doubt he'd heard the gossip in Basalt Bay. "Paul and I go way back."

Oh, right, Paul. Judah drank down the rest of his lukewarm coffee in a big gulp. "I think I'll get ready for the day." He shook the man's hand. Then dropped his Styrofoam cup in the garbage on his way to the restroom.

After washing up, he was leaving the facilities when Brad Keifer entered the gym. The man tugged the front door closed with both hands, the winds fighting his hold. Judah walked toward him.

Brad shook off his hat. Brushed rainwater from his coat. "It's terrible out there."

"So I see. Any word from your friend?"

"He's not answering his phone." The fisherman rubbed the soles of his boots against the mat, then stomped toward the coffee table. "Probably doesn't want to speak to me."

Judah didn't blame the guy for being leery of Brad's temper. "Do you think he'll let us rent his skiff in this weather?"

"Who knows? I'd rather not do business with the scum."

"Have any other plans for getting back to Basalt Bay?"

"Wait for a break in the storm, I guess." Brad scooped up an apple fritter. "Although, I'm sick of waiting," he said around a mouthful.

"Me too." Judah bit his lower lip, willing away frustration. Too bad he didn't listen to himself. His thoughts rushed headlong through the things that troubled him. His inability to get back to his wife. His dad's interference in his life. Mia's constant hovering and flirtations. And where was Craig? Why had he disappeared and stayed away?

"About the boat. There is another idea." Brad gazed around the room furtively. "Not that I would stoop to such a low, you understand."

"No, of course not." Wait. What did the fisherman mean?

"How badly do you want to get to the bay?"

"Badly enough." Judah glanced over his shoulder, making sure Mia wasn't within earshot.

"I say, weather permitting, we take the skiff—borrow it. Pay Richard later." Brad bit into another donut. "I doubt anyone will go out in these winds, other than you and me. Besides, he said we could use it this morning."

He had, but— "Just take it?" That went against everything honest in Judah, even if Brad used the term "borrow." What about his integrity in the community? What if word got out that he took a skiff? Mia might spread tales. Did Judah's need to get back to Paisley justify such actions? This *was* an emergency. There were extenuating circumstances.

"What do you say?" Brad flicked donut crumbs from his beard.

Judah gulped. His moment of truth. Or temptation. The boat owner said they could use the skiff. And he did undercut their plans yesterday. "I think you should call the guy again. Leave a message. Go to his house. We should do everything in our power to contact him before we borrow any of his equipment." Even if that meant Judah wouldn't get to see Paisley today. He felt the weight of his decision all the way to his toes. The disappointment that their plans might fall through, again, felt crushing.

Brad glared at him for about twenty seconds. "Fine. But I don't know how the cheat stays in business."

"Me, either. But two wrongs don't—"

"Yeah, yeah." Brad hauled his phone out of his pocket. Stared at the screen. Held it up higher as if checking for bandwidth. "Useless phone. C'mon." Brad grabbed another donut then trudged toward the door.

Judah glanced over his shoulder. Mia lifted her hand in a wave. He nodded and scrambled after Brad, bracing for the wind and downpour just beyond the door.

Lord, please help me get back to Paisley.

Fourteen

Wind and rain beat hard against the boarded-up window in the child's bedroom where Paisley had slept, reminding her of the harrowing night she spent in Dad's bathroom during the hurricane. A bad memory still. Except for those moments when she and Judah linked pinkies beneath the door. She smiled at that remembrance. Then, it felt like not only were their pinkies touching, but their hearts too. She'd never forget that—the sweetness of his hand resting against hers all night, feeling connected with him again after those years of hurts and sorrows. And especially after the earth-shaking kiss they shared. Those mental pictures were stuck in her thoughts like super glue. If only she could print them out as photos for the mantle.

Sigh.

Noises reached her from the kitchen. Pots rattled. Cupboard doors opened and closed. Was Craig searching for breakfast food?

Groaning, she realized she had to face him again. Last night after she came into Piper's room and found the door didn't have a lock, she propped a chair under the handle the way she'd seen characters do in suspense movies. Now, she stood and ran her hands down her clothes to smooth them out. She was thankful for the sweatshirt she found in the gallery yesterday. And the leggings she unearthed in Paige's drawer were thick and comfy. She shoved her feet into a pair of hiking boots she discovered in her sister's closet.

For a moment, seeing the child's bed, the stuffed animals on a low shelf, the dolls in the corner, she imagined what Piper was like. Her photos showed a blond toddler with the cutest grin. Maybe dimples. Seeing her, Paisley wondered again if Misty Gale, the sweet infant she miscarried at six months, four years ago, would have resembled her cousin. The old ache burned in her. The longing to know her daughter, to hold her, to kiss her soft cheeks, to watch her grow up. Would that pain, that feeling of loss, ever go away?

She shoved the chair out from its tipped position beneath the doorknob. Then, opening the door, she trudged down the hall to the kitchen, her heart still tender following her recent thoughts. The rain pounded on the roof like pebbles falling overhead, a perfectly depressing start to another day. Would the downpour swamp the road into town again? At this rate, it could be days before Judah reached her. Would she be stuck in this house with Craig until then? She shivered.

No, this thing with him hanging around, acting like he and Dad were best buddies, must end. Or, if he stayed, she'd leave. Maybe go to Dad's. Um, well, the front window was still broken. Everything was soaked. A tree leaned against the roof, could crash through at any time. No place to sleep other than the pantry. No thanks. She could just order Craig to leave. Insist that he vacate the premises, despite the disaster, and stay away.

As she entered the kitchen, natural light flooded the room. Someone had removed the plywood from the window. Craig's doing? See how he was endearing himself to Dad? Paisley groaned.

Thankfully, her father, and not their guest, opened and shut cupboard doors. A tomato-based casserole, probably thawed out from the freezer, rested on the counter, billowing delicious-smelling steam. Mmm.

She went straight to Dad and wrapped her arms around him. "Good morning, Daddy." Even though he didn't return her embrace or comment on her endearment, she was determined to keep taking chances, especially considering the discouraged funk he was in yesterday. She wanted to reaffirm her gratefulness that he was alive. That she appreciated this second chance to reconnect. "Nice to see you up and about. You look ready to tackle the day."

"Craig and I decided to rustle up some grub." Dad opened a can of garbanzo beans with a hand-crank can opener. He dumped the food into a foil packet. He did the same thing with a can of mixed veggies.

"Are you going to heat this on the grill?"

"Yep." He splashed in a little olive oil, salt and pepper, then crimped the top of the foil. He set the packet on a plate. "Craig's our grill guy. Good thing he showed up, huh?"

Yeah, yeah. Lucky them. She turned away so Dad wouldn't see her grimace.

The taller man burst through the doorway, shaking raindrops from his hat. "Good news. Weather's supposed to improve by mid-afternoon." He glanced at her. "Oh. Good morning."

The muscles in her chest contracted. How could she get used to him walking in and out of the house as if he were part of the family?

"Glad to hear it." Dad handed him the plate.

Craig spun around and went back outside. The two of them sure seemed chummy. Had they even spoken before yesterday?

The C-MER employee's words about the weather report suddenly blasted through her thoughts. "Wait a second. How does he know when the storm's going to pass? He said his cell phone's out of power."

"Beats me. I don't own one."

"You never replaced your old phone?" Momentarily distracted, she remembered how Dad dropped his archaic folding phone into the ocean before she left home.

"No reason to pay the bill since *no one* calls anyway." He shot her a pointed glance.

Guilt swept through her, again.

He opened the lid of a bottle of apple juice, then poured three short glasses full, his hands shaking slightly. "Besides, landline works fine."

Not now. She thought of the dead phone line at his house.

"How did the old place weather the hurricane?" He moved the glasses away from the edge of the counter.

Was he well enough to handle bad news? "Not so well, I'm afraid. The stairs collapsed. The flooring is ruined. Some windows are broken. The big tree in back fell on the roof."

A shadow crossed his face. "Guess we'll have a lot to do to fix it, huh?"

We'll?

"Yes, we certainly will."

"When's Judah coming back?" Dad took down three turquoise plates from the shelf by the sink.

"Yesterday, I wish."

"Impatient as always." At least he remembered that much about her. He'd made some mental progress since yesterday. His eyes seemed clearer, too.

"Craig says the weather and the bad roads will keep him away another day or so." Dad set three slices of bread on the counter next to the casserole.

"What does he know?" The weather could change any second. Anyone who lived on the coast knew that.

Dad was going all out on this breakfast. She should tell him to ration the food. Who knew when they might find more supplies? But seeing him doing something so enthusiastically seemed miraculous. And she was hungry. They all had to be.

A few minutes later, Craig reentered the room carrying the steaming vegetable mix. Paisley preoccupied herself with rearranging dirty dishes in the sink, avoiding eye contact. After the men dished up their food, she fixed hers. She dropped onto a chair at the kitchen table, scooting closer to Dad, creating more space between her and Craig as she set her plate down.

"I'm glad your sister had food in her freezer." Dad scooped up a spoonful of the casserole.

"She must enjoy cooking," Craig contributed.

If so, that was news to Paisley.

Dad waved his fork with a noodle on it. "Since Piper came along, she cooks more."

"Makes sense." Paisley ate a bite of the pasta. Not bad. If Paige made this, she was a better cook than Paisley. Although, even Judah cooked better than her. She preferred opening a can or heating up packaged food in the microwave.

"Do you enjoy cooking?"

It was hard to ignore Craig's direct question with her father sitting there scrutinizing her. She chewed dramatically, stalling. Then she remembered what he said earlier. "How did you hear about the weather?"

He took a long time swallowing his food this time. "On my cell."

What? His cell phone worked? Her hackles rose like antennas protruding from her skull. "You lied to me? You said your phone didn't work." Did he say that to keep her from contacting Judah? So much for thinking she might have misjudged him. That he might be a nice guy, after all. He was a snake. As soon as this meal ended, he was out of here.

"Uh, well." His cheeks turned crimson. He squirmed in his chair. "I thought the battery died." He guzzled from his glass. Blinked fast.

If her glare could strike him with lightning, he'd be on fire.

"Next time I checked, the weather icon flashed for a second." He shrugged. "Then it died."

Hmm. She pondered his explanation, and some of her rage dissolved. The other night when she was hiding—from him, no less—she got bursts of cell power before the phone died, enough to send Judah a couple of texts. Craig's explanation might be plausible, but she had doubts about anything he said. Once a con, always a con, right?

A twist of discomfort in her chest reminded her that she too had been misjudged by others. Maggie. Miss Patty. Edward. Aunt Callie. Even Dad.

Was she judging Craig the same way? Wait a second. Didn't he come to her father's home late at night, uninvited? Saying "Peek a boo, I see you." Calling her "Little Miss Riding Hood." Not to mention the stuff that happened three years ago. No, she hadn't misjudged him.

She finished eating in silence, then stood. "We need fresh water to wash dishes. Heated would be nice." She stacked her plate and silverware. "Any ideas about where to find clean water?"

Dad shrugged. "Beats me. Saltwater is plentiful."

Craig rubbed his index finger and thumb over his overgrown chin hair. "There's a creek not too far away. Saltwater may have backed into it during the storm, so it isn't potable. Okay for dishes. Flushing the toilet. I can take a couple of buckets over and check."

"Fine." So they were still dependent on the scoundrel. When he came back, she'd tell him to leave. She and Dad could get by on their own. Even if Judah didn't show up today, they'd be okay.

"It's still raining out." Dad stood, then bent over, shuffling things around in a cupboard. He handed Craig a large metal bowl. "Why don't you put this outside to collect rainwater?"

"Good idea." Craig left through the back door.

"You don't trust him. Why not?" Dad adjusted his glasses, peering at her the way he did when she was young and backtalked.

She piled up the dishes and carried them to the sink. She couldn't explain the whole situation to her father. And nothing less would do.

"I saw it in your eyes." He followed her, then stood next to the counter, watching her.

She'd have to answer, say something, anything. "Okay, I don't like him saying Judah can't make it back today. Who's he to spread gloom and doom?" That was partly the truth.

"Are you going to give him another chance?"

"Craig?"

"Judah."

"I haven't decided." A small mistruth. And another topic she didn't wish to discuss with him.

"You could have done worse than marrying a man like him, even if he is a Grant." He wiped the counter with a paper towel.

Her dad's affirmation of Judah surprised her as much as his chatting and puttering around the kitchen did.

"It's complicated." She dried her hands on a dishtowel.

"Of course, it is." He shuffled toward the living room. "What would you expect after you left him for three years?"

She would have followed him and defended herself if Craig hadn't entered the kitchen.

He wiped rainwater from his face. "Where would I find buckets?"

Paisley yanked open a couple of cupboards. "Dad! Where's a big pot or bucket?"

"Under the sink. Might be two."

She leaned down and opened the doors beneath the sink, not liking how Craig also bent down, peering over her shoulder. She spotted two matching red buckets, grabbed them and eased away from him. She set the pails on the table instead of handing them directly to him.

"As soon as I get back from the creek, I'm heading out." He shuffled his feet. "Judah might not understand my being here."

"No kidding. I don't understand it, either." Although, he did help her father in his crisis, which meant in some small way he helped her. She hated acknowledging that, even to herself.

He tugged on his hat. "I think Judah might be on his way here." He grabbed the buckets and strode toward the door.

"Wait. How would you know that?"

He paused, didn't face her. "I may not have been entirely honest before."

"May not?" Her heart pounded hard against her ribs.

"I'm leaving. Look out for your dad's health. Make sure he does his testing, okay?" The door closed behind him.

She peered out the kitchen window, watching the tall man speed walk across the yard and turn at the corner. What couldn't he explain? What secret was he hiding?

Dad shuffled into the kitchen with his coat buttoned up to his chin, his wool cap pulled down over his ears. "Thought I'd take a look-see at the beach."

"It's still stormy out." She heard the sharpness in her tone, a leftover reaction to her conversation with Craig. She cleared her throat. "Do you feel well enough for a walk?"

He shrugged. "It's my favorite time at the seashore, you know that."

They used to walk together at the beach, hunting for treasures following storms. Once, she found a Japanese glass fishing float in perfect condition. "Want some company?"

"Sure." He stuffed his hands in his coat pockets. "Just like old times."

Something warm and powerful filled her chest. Who cared if it rained? Who cared if Craig's strange disclosure unsettled her? Right now, the most important thing was spending time with Dad.

"Let me check Paige's closet for a coat. I'll be right out." She grabbed a flashlight and hurried down the hall to her sister's bedroom. Rummaging through the closet, she found a thick sweater and a raincoat. Good thing she and Paige were similar in size. On the top shelf, a plastic tub held hats. She picked out a gray knitted one and pulled it on, tugging it over her ears.

She marched back down the hall, dropping off the flashlight on the kitchen table. Dad waited for her by the back door, shuffling his feet as if he were antsy to get going. His bright eyes and his eager smile brought joy to her heart.

Thank You that he's doing better.

Without talking, they exited into the rain. She followed him down the driveway, along the sidewalk. They crossed the street, then veered onto the trailhead which led to the beach. She heard the breakers crashing against the rocks. Smelled the salty, musty scent of the seashore. *Her ocean.* Sharing it with Dad made it even more special.

As they broke free of tree cover, the wind churned against them, pushing them back. She squinted out toward the water. The waves pounded the beach, the sea spray whirling into the air like a giant beater mixed it. White foam rushed up and down the sand. When Paisley was young, she ran barefoot through the dancing foam, feeling the spray rush up her legs. Now, she and Dad stood huddled together, both with their hands tucked into their coats, their shoulders bent slightly forward, bracing into the wind.

"Did you notice the missing boulders out on the peninsula?" She spoke loudly, trying to be heard over the roar of the pounding waves.

"Won't ever be the same." Dad shuffled his feet. "It'll need repairs. Wouldn't want tourists walking out on the point and falling in."

She couldn't wait to go out there again, even with the damage. When C-MER resumed operations, they'd probably post signs warning people to stay off the rocks until the completion of repair work. She wouldn't pay attention to such signs.

"You be careful too." Nice to hear the fatherly concern in his voice. He knew she liked to sit out on the point. He'd done the same thing when he was a boy. He'd told her so plenty of times.

Facing into the wind, she blinked against the raindrops. They walked slowly down the beach, trudging toward Paige's building.

"What was Paige's gallery like before Addy hit?"

"Her pride and joy." She heard the smile in Dad's voice. "She and your mama used to talk and talk about their art gallery ideas."

She didn't remember such discussions. Maybe that's what they spoke about when Paisley and Peter were out playing on the beach, fighting their imaginary dragons.

"Too bad Mom didn't get to see that dream come true." He scrubbed the back of his hand beneath his nose.

Emotion stuck in Paisley's throat. Her mother's last words to her crept through her thoughts. *"You are an ungrateful daughter!"* Was she? Had she ever understood her mother? Had her mom ever understood her?

"What about you? Have any dreams?"

His voice drew her from her contemplations, from her confusion. "Not so much anymore."

"And Judah?"

"What about him?"

Dad tugged on her arm. "You're still married to him, aren't you?"

"According to the law." Their last kiss flitted through her thoughts. *Maybe more than just according to the law.*

"You know Mayor Grant isn't my favorite person."

She bet a lot of townspeople felt that way, her included.

"You could have picked a better father-in-law." Dad chuckled. "But he comes with the package deal. Pastor Sagle says everyone has at least one redeeming quality. I wonder what the mayor's might be."

Her thoughts leapt to the night Edward yanked her away from Craig. How he stepped into a volatile situation and rescued her. Was that a redeeming quality? But didn't he cancel it out when he paid her to leave his son? Or did that fall on her since she followed his wishes? *Sigh.*

"Look!" Dad thrust his finger toward the sea, holding down his hat with his other hand.

"What is it?" She squinted toward the breakers, didn't see anything unusual.

"A skiff! Wait. There it is!" He shuffled to the midpoint of the rocky shoreline.

Judah? If so, Craig was right about his arrival. "Can you see who it is?" She followed Dad, stepping around a couple of large rocks.

"The sea's too rough for a beach landing here."

"Judah would know that." Oh, there. The bow of a skiff rose beyond the foaming waves. It fell, disappearing into a trough. One person manned the boat. It could be him. Still too far away to tell.

Dad leaned forward, peering through his wet glasses. "Think it's him?"

"I don't know." Whoever it was faced powerful breakers just ahead. Dangerous ones. Why was he even landing here?

Plodding to the edge of the tideline, they watched the skiff battling turbulent waves. The way the guy steered the skiff, how he tipped his head down, bracing into the wind with the top of his head, reminded her of Judah. "It might be him." If so, he was coming to her by way of the sea. A lightness she hadn't felt in days filled her. Made her grin like a teenage girl with a crush on a boy.

Unless it wasn't him. But who else would ride into town in a skiff on such a blustery day? In waves that could capsize him. It had to be Judah.

Fifteen

Judah had already dropped off Brad at what remained of the old cannery dock. Now, he was steering the skiff through heavy rain toward the beach at Basalt Bay. Not the best landing place. In fact, one of the toughest. But it was the most direct approach to town. If he could get past the breakers separating open waters from the cove, he'd pull the skiff onto shore, anchor it, then rush over to Paul's. His only goal, his one desire, was to see Paisley, to hold her in his arms and make sure she was okay.

He was soaked through, thanks to not having on his usual rain gear. With each slam of the bow against the waves, his teeth rattled. More water sprayed over him, adding to his soggy condition.

Despite his eagerness to see his wife, he needed to stay focused and get through the next battle with the sea. Strong winds and gusting rain had made traveling from Florence to Basalt Bay challenging. Judah and Brad, being experienced boatmen, didn't express doubts or any inability to navigate through the rough waters. Still, Judah recognized the clenched-teeth grimace on the other man's face, a man who'd weathered plenty of storms and rough seas. They'd taken a risk. Fortunately, they made it this far.

Judah steered into a trough, keeping the boat angled slightly west. The craft rose on the crest of the next wave, and he had a quick glimpse of the beach. He turned the bow, aiming for the smoothest section of shoreline. Not far ahead, a large boulder was hidden beneath the water; he'd seen it at low tide many times. He had to carefully veer around that rock. Sea spray splashed over the boat, sending foam splattering onto his shoulders, his face. He tasted saltwater. Spit. He scrubbed the back of his hand over his eyes. The salt burned. No time to pause.

On the next rise, for just a sec, he thought he spotted someone on the beach. The boat dropped into a dip and a wall of gray water shielded him from seeing the shore. Coming up again, he stared hard at the shoreline. Two people! Was one Paisley?

The boat plunged. The waves blocked his view. He rode it out, rose on another crest. That might be her, but who was the guy? Craig? *No way!* Judah steered crosswise into the next wave. His wife would not be anywhere near that man.

The boat dipped harshly. Water poured over the side. *Yikes.* He picked up the bucket and bailed fast. With his other hand, he steered through another wave, praying it didn't capsize him. He perused the bubbling white water of the breakers ahead. Clenched his teeth. Stared down the waves, hoping to get through them without trouble.

He held the steering mechanism tightly. The craft jerked left. Water arced over the bow, spray hitting him full in the face. He spit. Bailed. Not much farther. Down the trough; ride the wave. More water poured over the gunwales. The boat was about a third full of seawater now. With all this water rolling over the skiff, he was relieved the engine didn't stall. One big wave could sink him. He wouldn't let that happen, if he could help it.

The skiff ploughed heavily through the surf, but Judah angled shoreward. More pounding waves splashed over the back of the skiff, over the engine. He spit. Wiped his eyes. Kept bailing.

He caught another glimpse of Paisley—it had to be her. She waved at him with big movements like she was doing the motions for the "YMCA."

The boat rose then dropped, jarring his teeth. He groaned. Seawater inside the skiff reached the midpoint of his calf, soaking his wound.

Suddenly, the keel rammed into something. The engine sputtered. The skiff lurched sideways. He held on and turned the tiller to avoid a second strike. Had he miscalculated the rocks? The bottom of the engine scraped along whatever the boat crashed into before he had time to lift it.

The motor glug-glug-glugged. Died. Waves struck the side of the skiff, turning it east, hurling it west. Any second the next wave could pound over the sides, tossing him into the sea. He dropped the bailing bucket. Held onto the gunwales with both hands, riding it out. There wasn't time to try to restart the engine.

A couple of days ago, in a different location and with a different skiff, he was forced to jump into the sea to save himself and his employer's boat. If it came to that, he knew what to do. Still bobbing in the merciless thrashing of waves, he yanked the oars out of their clasps. One by one, he plunked them into the oarlocks. Fighting to regain a directional bead on the shore, he reefed on the oars, groaning with the exertion of moving the weighted skiff.

"C'mon." He groaned, pulling hard on the oars. *Pull. Pull.* His injured leg was numb to the burning sensation he experienced earlier. Because of the lack of pain, he worked harder, exacting more strength and stamina from himself.

He let up on the oars, hoping the next rush of water would propel the craft onto the wet beach like a rocket. Utter failure. Instead, a wave crashed against the port side. Judah didn't have time to react. The boat jerked upward, tipped nearly on its side, sliding him into the sea like hot butter off a chunk of crab. Ice-cold seawater rushed over him, over his head. Submerged him.

He jackknifed his boots off the bottom of the sea floor. As he came up gasping for air, he reached out for the skiff, but it was already too far away. He couldn't lose it now. Taking a long draw of air, he swam hard toward the boat bobbing with the waves.

"Judah!" Paisley's voice.

He lunged for the skiff, kicking his shoes hard in the water. He pulled against the frigid waves with his arms, swimming determinedly.

The boat was being swept toward open waters by the tidal force and the strong winds. He had to pursue it.

"Judah, come back!"

He glanced over his shoulder between breast strokes. She was in the water now, too. The waves hit her knee-high. He wanted to tell her to stay back, to stay safe. Instead, he kept swimming against the current, kicking with all his might, knowing the conditions were too cold for him to be in the water much longer.

Finally, he reached the half-sunken boat and grabbed hold of the starboard gunwale. He drew in great gulps of air, trying to catch his breath. He moved his hands along the top edge, gripping closer and closer to the bow until he reached the floating rope. With the line in his left hand, he swam on his right side, scissor kicking as hard as he could, slowly pulling the resistant boat. At times if felt like he wasn't making headway at all. The water chilled him. Made his movements stiff and clumsy.

Then Paisley was on the other side of the boat, holding on to the rope, swimming and pulling the craft, too. Even though seeing her in the rough surf made him concerned for her safety, he was thankful for her assistance, encouraged by it. Her jumping in the sea with him, unreserved, was typical of her. She wouldn't be afraid to fight the waves with him.

He swam until his shoes bumped into muddy ground. He stood on wobbly legs, spitting out water, coughing. He gripped the side of the boat, tugged on it. Paisley did the same. The wave action worked in their favor, now, pushing the skiff toward land.

"Falling into the sea is becoming a habit with you." She tossed him a cute grin, her hair dripping wet, but then she slipped. She landed on her knees in the water, flailing out her hands.

"Paisley!"

She stood quickly. "I'm okay. My b-boots s-stuck in the m-mud." Her teeth chattered as she grabbed the port side of the skiff again.

Keeping an eye on her, he shuffled to the stern, shoved hard against the weighted boat.

That's when he saw the other person on the beach was Paul. Not Craig! His father-in-law swung his arms to his right as if directing Judah where to land the skiff. Paul waded into shallow water too, helping them drag the boat in, but his movements seemed clumsy and stiff. Probably due to the cold.

Judah shoved; the other two pulled. It took all three of them to get the half-swamped boat through the mud and mostly out of the surf.

As soon as he dropped anchor, Paisley splashed through the water toward him, dove into his arms, her wet arms wrapping around his shoulders like an octopus, clinging to him. He laughed, fighting for balance, and returned her embrace—boy, did he ever. He nearly got knocked over by the next wave. She was laughing too, reminding him of how they used to play and have so much fun in the ocean when they were younger. He wanted to kiss her, but with her dad standing right here watching, he held back. Besides, they were both shaking from the cold.

"I'm s-so g-glad to see you." She slid out of his arms, stepped back, lowering her gaze. Was she uncomfortable being close to him? Because of her dad watching?

"Me too." But they were freezing. He had to secure the boat. Find dry clothes. She did too.

He lifted his hand to wave at Paul. The older man was shaking, also.

Paisley scurried over to where her dad extended the towrope as if checking its length. Judah knew the approximately twenty-foot rope wouldn't reach any boulders where it could be tied. He'd have to find longer rope. Until then, he hoped the anchor would hold the boat when the tide rolled back in.

He scooped bucket after bucket of water from the inside, dumping it on the sand.

"W-where've you b-been all this t-time?" Paul shivered and adjusted his wet glasses.

"Dad—"

"I tried to get here yesterday." Judah glanced at Paisley. She scuffed the toe of her boot against a broken crab shell. Was she avoiding his gaze? "Mia drove me north and—" He briefly explained yesterday's events while he kept bailing. He couldn't ignore the awkward silence. The tight look on Paisley's face. Because he mentioned Mia?

"C-come up to Paige's house. W-we all n-need dry clothes." Paul's teeth chattered.

"So, Paul, were you the one who showed up the other night? The one who made Paisley and me scared out of our wits?"

Paisley shook her head harshly at him. A warning? What did he say to elicit such a dark look?

Paul scratched his nose, his hand shaking. "I d-don't know w-what you're t-talking about. Haven't been h-home since the s-storm." He wrung his hands. "S-so c-cold."

"Let's go, Dad." Paisley draped her arm over her father's shoulders, shooting Judah another strained look.

He'd been out of touch with her nuances for a long time, but it seemed she expected him to know something. Or maybe his brain was too foggy after his icy swim.

Paisley and Paul shuffled down the beach. Paisley's arms encircled her father's shoulders like she was trying to shield him from the cold. Was something wrong with him, other than him being wet and chilled? Something seemed odd, out of sync. But Judah's landing had turned out weird, anyway. Not the homecoming he envisioned.

He kept bailing but watched over his shoulder. Father and daughter stopped. Paul gesticulated, seemed agitated, pointing back at Judah. Paisley shook her head, then resumed her gait across the sand.

So Paul hadn't returned to his house since the storm? How could that be?

Wind gusts pounded against Judah's wet back, chilling him. His teeth chattered as he worked, but he didn't stop until he dumped out most of the seawater.

After he checked the anchor, he tromped across the mud flat, his shoes sliding in the wet muck as he followed Paisley and Paul.

Since his gimpy leg was still numb, he was able to push it, although he might be sorry later. He veered around partially filled sandbags that had been torn up and displaced by the waves. He grabbed a collapsed lawn chair in his path and tossed it up on the rocks so it wouldn't get swept away by the tide. The metal frame clattered, but the roar of the sea overpowered the noise.

He trudged across the wet sand, making a quick perusal of the seashore like he would if he was on the job. The beach needed a major cleanup. At the peninsula, a gaping hole remained where the five-foot boulder he labeled Sample D used to sit. He recalled the night of the storm and how the geyser of water cascaded over the old breakwater. How he feared Paisley might be out there. Thank God she wasn't. Samples B and C were missing too. As was a section of the point. C-MER and the town council would have decisions to make about reconstructing the harbor's protective barrier.

Thanks to Paisley and Paul's snail-like pace, he caught up to them at the beach parking lot. She glanced up with a startled expression. The sound of the ocean waves and the wind must have muffled his footsteps.

"Hey." He dared to take her cool hand in his. "I want you to know that I couldn't wait to get back to you. I went crazy with worry. Tried everything I could think of to get back here. I'm sorry it took me so long."

She withdrew her hand from his. "Me too." Her other hand was linked in her father's arm. She seemed to be pulling him forward.

Judah sighed. "Any idea where I can find some clothes?" He doubted Paige had anything his size at her house. He gazed at the beach houses up ahead. "I might have to break in somewhere."

"Hard to believe you would consider doing such a thing." Her frown almost made him laugh. As if he said he was going to rob a bank.

"I'll leave a note. I doubt anyone will mind since it's an emergency."

"True. My dad's going to need some—"

"No, I don't," Paul interrupted her. "I have overalls at Paige's for when I work on things there."

"Why didn't you tell me that yesterday?"

Paul shrugged.

"I doubt Paige has any rope," Paisley said. "You'll have to search elsewhere for that, too."

He'd nearly forgotten about the rope. "Thanks for the reminder. I'll come over to your sister's after I get the skiff situated."

"You know where she lives, right?" She squinted at him as if asking some other question.

"Sure, I've been there before." He'd visited their niece. Was invited to her second birthday party. Piper called him *Unca Dzuda.*

"Okay. See you later."

"Pais, is something wrong?" Even though they were freezing, trudging along in the rain, he had to know.

She shook her head, shrugged, didn't meet his gaze.

He sighed. Now probably wasn't the time to push for an answer. "I would have been here for you if I could. You know that, right?"

"I want to b-believe that." Her lip trembled.

He longed to take her in his arms the way he thought of doing down on the beach. Kiss away her doubts. Tell her how their separation ate away at his patience, even his faith, a few times. All that seemed a lifetime ago now that he stood beside her. Yet, something was amiss. An invisible brick wall had risen between them.

Paul coughed.

"We have to go." Paisley walked away with her arm draped over her dad's shoulders.

Frustration pounded through the icy places in Judah's heart. They were separated for three years. Together as a couple—if he could even call them that idyllic term—for less than twenty-four hours. And in the last two days, he lived and breathed the hope of reuniting with her. Them starting where they left off after the storm. Now, this.

Chills overcame him. He needed dry clothes. A coat. Maybe a comforter to wrap up in.

Then, could he and Paisley sit down and discuss whatever had caused such a great divide between them?

Sixteen

Judah stood on the sidewalk in front of James Weston's beach-front house. Piles of shingles, kelp, and displaced items were scattered across his yard and the neighbors' yards. All the windows on the five homes facing the sea were covered with sheets of plywood. The same was true of the houses across the street, except for Paul's. At his father-in-law's, Judah would have to climb a ladder to reach the second story, and with his leg aching as it was now, he'd rather not do that if there was an alternative.

Since he'd recently been in contact with James, that man's house seemed the best option for breaking into. Surely, Paul's friend and neighbor would understand Judah's need for dry clothes and rope.

His coat and jeans dripped seawater. He was shaking almost uncontrollably. If he didn't find a change of apparel soon, he might be in danger of hypothermia. Bolstered by the adage about "desperate times calling for desperate measures," he trudged across the wet lawn toward James's back porch. As he moved, his wet, stiff pant legs made a scraping sound against each other. Every time he lifted his knee, the firm fabric tugged against his stitches where the bandage had come loose while he was swimming. Hopefully, the stitches were still okay. He'd have to search for another bandage and a first aid kit.

He hobbled up the steps, tugged on the doorknob. Locked, of course. He shoved his arm and shoulder against the door to test it.

Nothing happened, other than his leg aching and throbbing with renewed vigor. He grabbed hold of the doorknob with both hands and shook harder. Nothing gave.

He groaned.

This break-in attempt wasn't such a great idea. And James was a bit of a curmudgeon who might even be upset about Judah trying to break down his door. However, this was an emergency. Judah's health depended on getting out of these drenched clothes.

One more try. Taking a breath, he planted the foot of his injured leg as solidly as he could against the porch. Then he lifted his other foot and rammed his heel against the wood near the lock, the weakest spot on the door. Pain ricocheted up his sore leg. He groaned, held his breath, waiting for the tremors in his calf to cease.

Nothing on the door broke free, either. Time for Plan B.

He hobbled down the steps, contemplating how he could climb the ladder at Paul's and enter through the bedroom window he exited two days ago. He limped across the flooded street, noticing the large pile of shingles and garbage in the front yard. Paisley did a lot of work here. Good for her!

Where was that ladder Craig used? Judah trudged around the left side of the house, sloshing over wet muddy ground. The backyard was still swampy but mostly cleared of shingles and garbage. No ladder here. He backtracked to the front and checked the right side of the lot. Two days ago, Craig didn't take it when he rushed Judah to the ER. Since then, had he come back for it?

Judah swallowed a lump in his throat. What if it was Craig who came here the other night? The person Paisley feared. Was that why she freaked out when he questioned Paul about it, earlier?

There he was jumping to conclusions. It could have been his own father. But wouldn't Paisley have mentioned that? Someone obviously took the ladder. Looters?

Seeing his truck that was slammed against Paul's front porch during the hurricane, he remembered that he sometimes kept work-related supplies in there. Maybe even rope. Since the driver's door was jammed against the porch, he opened the passenger side, then released the front seat to see into the back compartment. He shoved a container of tools on the floorboard out of his way. Checked under the seat. There. A tangled-up wad of rope. Perfect!

What was in the black garbage bag next to the rope? He tugged on the plastic, tore it open. A pair of grubby jeans and a stained sweatshirt tumbled out. He nearly wept. He forgot all about the clothes he stored in his truck for doing messy work at C-MER. He grabbed the items and headed for the porch.

He pulled himself onto the floorboards, opened the front door—good thing it wasn't locked—and trudged inside. The apple tree didn't protrude through the gaping front window the way it did during the storm. Instead, thick plastic sheeting covered the opening. He noticed the neat line of nails. Paisley's work? Or Paul's? That's right. Paul said he wasn't here. If Paisley could put down a straight row of nails like this, she'd be a great asset when it came time to fix their beach cottage.

He hobbled into the kitchen, stripped down and checked his purplish wound—the stitches were still intact—then gently pulled on the jeans and dry sweatshirt. He'd like to ditch the wet socks and shoes. Maybe find a coat. He shuffled around the damp house, looking for any kind of outerwear. He checked inside the dryer. Scrounged through some cupboards, keeping in mind his need for a bandage, too. Came up empty. He wished he could climb into the gaping hole, up to the second story, and find what he needed. Although, he knew he wore a different shoe size than Paul.

As he shuffled past the back door, he saw several empty alcohol bottles in the garbage can. Whose were those? *Oh, no.* Was Paisley drinking again? Was that the reason for her aloofness? Thoughts of how erratic she became when she drank excessively in the past barreled through his mind. He didn't want to go down that road again. Prayed it wasn't happening. Just seeing the bottles, and contemplating what they might mean, rattled him.

Sighing, he walked across the wet floor, assessing the damage. The carpet would have to go. As would the wet, lower portion of the sheet rock. Getting heat flowing into the room was essential, the sooner, the better. Unfortunately, that couldn't happen until the electricity came back on. He trudged toward the pantry, the room he knew Paisley hated as a kid. She'd never explained why, just said she despised it. He opened the narrow door and stared into the semi-darkness. A colorful rumpled towel was spread out on the shelf. Is this where she slept? In this tiny dark room that was little more than a closet? He hated to think of her being alone in here.

Canning jars lined the top shelf. A couple of long skinny boards lay on the middle shelf. Was this where she hid when she talked to him on the phone? When she told him someone was here? He suggested she grab something to use as a weapon. Did she hold these two sticks? He tried to picture it, recalling the fear in her voice. The pounding horror he felt in his own chest. He gulped. Then thanked God for keeping her safe, for being with her. For His help in getting Judah back to town, also.

He lumbered into the living room, his leg wound cramping with each step. The bare walls had discolored rectangular shadows where pictures used to be. All the paintings were on the floor, some face down. It was disheartening to see so much ruined art that had been his mother-in-law's passion when she was alive. The whatnot shelf lay on its side. Broken glass and porcelain pieces were scattered on the rug.

Maybe he'd come back tomorrow and clean up. Remove the carpet. He and Paisley could work on this together. Might give them time to talk. Maybe she'd be more communicative away from her father. And Judah could explain why he rode in Mia's car.

He shuffled to the porch. The deep ruts and mounded ridges where a vehicle drove through the front yard were obviously a truck's. Dad's rig? When the mayor tried to get Paisley to go up to his house, did he drive across the grass? Or did he come back later? Scare her.

Judah groaned. It was hard on him, not knowing. Second guessing everything.

He lowered himself from the porch to the ground, using his truck as leverage. He opened the passenger door, then climbed into the cab and scooted across the seat to get behind the wheel.

Hopefully, the truck was in working order, even though it had been hurled around during the tidal surge. The key was still in the ignition. The engine gagged, coughed, barked. Water around the moving parts needed expulsion, no doubt.

He revved the engine several times until it sounded better. He put the truck in four-wheel drive, turned the steering wheel sharply, and gave it a little gas. The bogged-down tires inched forward in tiny jerks. He pushed harder on the gas pedal, and the vehicle lurched ahead, crunching over a couple of branches in the yard. Once the truck reached the street, Judah veered around several downed trees. Turning west, he headed toward the community church. There, he cut across the parking lot, steering slowly through the subdivision west of town. He had to drive across a few sidewalks and yards to bypass garbage, a motorcycle on its side, and a sailboat smashed into a roadside tree.

Finally, he reached Paige's single-level blue house and pulled into the driveway behind Paul's VW parked sideways. Did the storm surge do that? No plywood sheets lined the windows, here, like on the neighbors' houses. It appeared as if some post-storm cleanup progress had been made.

He tried the driver's door. It wouldn't budge, so he scooted across to the passenger door, shoved against it, then slid to the ground. He winced at the ripping sensation in his leg. Too bad he decided to ram himself against James Weston's door like a thug. All that rowing and swimming in the sea didn't help, either. Sigh. He scooped up the rope. He'd walk down to the skiff as soon as he talked with Paisley.

He plodded through the wet carport, then he saw her standing near the back of the house, her arms crossed, her eyes narrow slits. Was she warning him to keep his distance?

Not likely. "Hi." He strode right for her, forcing himself not to limp. He didn't want her feeling sorry for him, thinking of him as an invalid.

What had she gone through to put that icy look in her gaze? The caution. He smiled, trying to reassure her that he was happy to see her, to finally be here with her. Couldn't they put the past days behind them and hug again, the way she greeted him in the surf when he first arrived?

"I see you found some clothes." She raised her eyebrows. "Wasn't there anything better to steal?"

"Nope. I found these oldies in my truck." He wanted to sweep some strands of hair off her cheek, but he kept his fingers at his sides. "I tried breaking into James's. Couldn't do it. It appears I'm a failure as a thief. So I went over to your dad's."

"Oh? How did it look?"

"You've been there, right?" He pictured the plastic nailed to the front window. Would she tell him about the liquor bottles if he asked? Probably best not to discuss that right now. Not when she already seemed to have a chip on her shoulder. Or a grudge, or something.

"Not since—"

"Not since what?" He took her hand. With the fingers of his other hand, he dared to stroke back a clump of hair from her face, his fingers pausing near her ear. What wasn't she telling him?

Be patient. The two words resounded in his brain. Hard to do when he wanted things to progress faster between them. He wanted reconciliation and healing. For them to move on to the being married part. *Give it time, Grant.*

"Nothing." Her lips clamped shut. She stepped back, removing his fingers, denying them access to her cheek.

Inwardly, he groaned. Had his inability to get back to Basalt Bay caused this rift?

She took another step back. "My dad's sick. I'm distracted. That's all."

"What's wrong with him?"

"Diabetes. He had a high blood sugar incident." She lifted her shoulders. "I didn't even know he was ill. He wasn't taking his medicine. Depressed. Acting like he wanted to die."

"Wow. Sounds like he needed an intervention."

"Yeah, he was in a bad way."

Her gaze flitting anywhere other than looking him in the eye shouted something was wrong that had more to do with him than Paul's sickness. What? Maybe he shouldn't press her, but hadn't he pledged to not let things go unspoken? Didn't he plan to pursue his wife, pursue her heart? And yet, the only thing he needed to know right now was that she was okay.

"How are you doing through all of this?" He kept his tone soft. And he kept his distance, assuming that's what she wanted.

"I'm fine."

He knew, saw, she was anything but fine. And he also knew she didn't want to talk about it. Her body language spoke volumes.

"I'm heading down to the beach to secure the skiff." He held up the rope. "Care to join me?"

"I should stay with Dad. He might need my help."

"Right. Okay, sure." He watched her go inside. Disappointment raked through him. His dreams of arriving in Basalt Bay as her rescuer, as the husband who she was eager to see and be with, wilted and died.

What had happened to Paisley in his absence to cause this chill?

Seventeen

Paisley felt warmer thanks to her sister's supply of clothes. Too bad that warmth didn't quite reach her core. Instead, agitation churned in her gut as she fingered the soggy items in the freezer. Everything appeared thawed, lukewarm, and ruined. She grabbed the trash can and dragged it across the floor. Yanking out the items from the upper compartment, she hurled them into the can, enjoying each of the thudding, crashing sounds. Next, she bent over and emptied perishables from the fridge in the same grab-and-slam manner.

Where would she find more food? Dad needed sustenance for healing and getting stronger. Where was she supposed to find healthy food? No fresh vegetables in town. She hated the thought of breaking into people's houses. She did plenty of mischievous stunts in her youth, including a few break-ins that she still had to make amends for. She didn't want to add to that list of wrongs.

Dad shuffled into the kitchen in overalls. "Anything good in there?"

"No. Couldn't you sleep?"

"Nah." He ran his fingers through his gray hair. "Did I hear Judah's truck? Is Craig still around?"

Ugh. What if Judah ran into him here? Was the other man even in town? Or did he slither away the way he came?

"It was Judah."

"Where's the boy now?"

The boy? Judah was hardly a boy. That Dad thought fondly of him still surprised her.

"He's down at the skiff tying it up." She dropped a half-gallon of milk into the trash.

Why had Judah asked Dad whether he was the one who showed up the other night? If he didn't know that it was Craig, perhaps hadn't seen the text—she swallowed hard—then he probably didn't know the rest, either. All these days, she thought he knew that she told him she loved him.

Then, when she saw him flailing in the waves, thinking of his injury, she rushed into the cold water after him. Would have done anything to help him. And when they brought the skiff to shore, she jumped into his arms, thrilled to be able to do that, knowing he knew she loved him. But something was wrong. She didn't see that special gaze in his eyes that she was looking for. Instead, he seemed to be asking her questions that she couldn't answer in front of Dad.

And she had questions too.

Why did it take so long for him to get back? Sure, he was injured. But two days? She was desperate for him to return, for him to share in the struggles she experienced after the storm, and he hadn't. Instead, she had to accept another man's help. Just the thought of having to tell Judah about that made her tremble.

And what about Mia? Why did her name slide so easily off his lips? They were coworkers, but the woman was trouble. Paisley knew that from the first day she met her. Even now, thinking of the flirty blond made her slam things into the trash a little harder than necessary.

"What's going on here?" Dad stood next to the can, watching, probably thinking she was acting childish.

"Sorry." She threw in a head of rotten lettuce.

One of Dad's eyebrows quirked. "What happened between you and Judah?"

"Not much." She dropped a glass dish of moldy peaches into the trash.

"You don't have to throw the bowl away too."

"It's gross. I don't want to wash it." Cleaning this one with its gray, fuzzy peach chunks stuck to the sides, in cold water, would be awful. Dad probably thought she was being childish about this too, but she'd always hated washing dishes, especially messy ones.

He leaned over and dug out the bowl. "I'll do it." He shuffled to the sink and set the dishware on the counter next to the pile of dirty dishes. A few cups and plates already soaked in sudsy water. Craig's doing, no doubt.

She continued emptying the fridge while Dad scrubbed the bowl.

"Are you going to tell me what's going on with you two?" Dad spoke over his shoulder.

"Nothing like washing dishes in cool water, huh?" She changed the subject.

"It's a kindness that we can wash dishes at all, thanks to Craig."

Yeah, yeah. Everything good around here is Craig's doing.

Dad poured water from the red bucket into the sink to the right. Then dipped clean dishes into it. "There's a little rainwater in the bowl Craig set outside. Not enough to do anything with."

Paisley pulled out a couple of containers from the fridge. "And there's only one bottle of water left. We'll have to find more today." Where? City Hall? Maggie Thomas's inn? An unholy glee rose up in her at the thought of breaking into that woman's establishment. Maggie might even be the type to have a stockpile of food and water. Only, did Paisley want to stir up more angst with the innkeeper who had a reputation for spreading gossip? They already had a history of disagreements and accusations between them.

"I have a few bottles at my house." Dad rattled silverware in the sink.

She thought of the other kind of bottles over there, too. The ones Craig said were Dad's. "Judah and I used those water bottles during the storm."

"Oh. How about at the gallery?"

"That's a good idea." She remembered seeing juice containers when she was there yesterday. "I'll walk over and grab an armful."

"Maybe you should wait for Judah."

"Why?" She'd lived on the southside of Chicago. She wasn't about to slink around Basalt, a small coastal town, as if she were afraid of her shadow—even if she had cowered in the pantry the other night. She wasn't that scared child any longer. She was a strong woman, or wanted to be one. The only person she didn't care to run into today was Craig.

"Looters. That's my concern, Craig's too." Dad placed a couple of pans on a towel he spread out on the beige countertop in lieu of a drying rack. "They might do anything to get what they want."

So would Craig. Why did Dad act as if the man were angelic? "I can take care of myself."

"I don't doubt that." He chuckled.

At least he had some confidence in her. Whatever they needed, she would find it. They had to have water; she'd figure it out. What about the small grocery store? How difficult would it be to break in there? She could keep a tab of what she took. Write an IOU.

She and Dad worked together in silence, except for the occasional clink of dishes. She finished her task first. After she tied the knot on the garbage bag, she went in search of an outdoor trash receptacle.

The wind was calming down, finally. A gentle rain fell, unlike the downpour from earlier. She should head for the gallery. Or try to get inside City Hall or the grocery store. Both were probably bolted down. Hiking out to Maggie's would mean a half-mile walk each way, plus hauling whatever she found. She didn't want to be gone from Dad that long.

Under the carport, she found a large can and shoved the bulging bag inside. The ocean wasn't in view from Paige's house, but Paisley heard the crashing waves in the distance. They drew her, called to her like a favorite song. She wished she could go down and sit on a rock and experience the sea. For a little while, she'd like to forget about the problems that had befallen her since her return to Basalt. To focus on herself. But she could hardly do that with all the responsibility she felt for Dad's health and for finding food and water.

Judah was probably still down at the skiff. Maybe she should go by and see how he was doing.

She hustled back into the house. "Dad?" He wasn't in the kitchen.

"In here."

She strode into the living room and found him resting on the couch in the semi-darkness. "You okay?"

"Just tired." He let out a long sigh.

She hoped fatigue was his only problem, and that his getting wet at the beach hadn't made his condition worse. He was better since he took the insulin, wasn't he? Part of her wanted to stay right here with him. To watch for any changes that might signal another crisis. But if she didn't find the needed supplies, they would have another type of emergency. "I'm going to the gallery. I'll grab whatever liquids I can find."

"Good. Maybe check on Judah?" His slight smile made it hard to tell him to stop playing matchmaker.

"Get some rest. I'll be back soon."

"Okay." He closed his eyes.

She walked down the hall, grabbed a coat and a knit hat from Paige's closet. Then she marched out the door, down the driveway, and along the sidewalk toward the church. As soon as she got her first glimpse of the ocean, her footfalls increased in speed. She wanted to run straight for the peninsula, to sit on the point and lose herself in the glory of sea spray dancing over her. Although, she didn't have any desire to get soaking wet when she'd just changed, especially since there wasn't any heat source in the house.

Still, seeing the waves rolling up on the beach, hearing the roar, made her want to stand here and take it all in, even though tasks awaited.

Maybe she could take just a minute for herself.

Eighteen

Paisley closed her eyes, her hearing in tune to the sounds of the sea, the pounding rhythm of waves against rocks, the rustling of wind blowing through hollowed-out logs. Nature's melodies blended perfectly with the throbbing of her heartbeat in her ears until she could barely tell the difference between the two. She released a long sigh that felt drudged from the bottom of her lungs. In increments, her muscles relaxed from her shoulders to her ankles.

Oh, to stay in this restful feeling of being at home, at peace, next to the sea. Of life returning to normal, whatever that meant in her post-hurricane world. She had survived the ordeal of the storm. And somehow survived her enemy's presence. Surely God was watching out for her, helping her.

Breathing in the salty air, she glanced up at the sky and her thoughts turned prayerful. *Lord, thank You for keeping me and Dad, and even Judah, safe during the storm and through all that's happened since. I don't want to only pray when things go badly. I'd like to sit here on the beach and talk to You every day, the way I once did. I want to find a way back to You, too.*

She gazed toward the opposite side of the beach where Judah was in the skiff doing something at the stern. He hadn't let the rough seas keep him from getting back to her, had he? Even if his arrival wasn't as quick as she would have wanted, he had made a valiant effort to reach her.

The words she texted him the night she hid in the pantry ran through her thoughts like lyrics. *I love you. I love you.* Her heart picked up a stronger beat. Her chest filled with warmth. If only he knew what she was thinking. If only she were brave enough to walk right up to him and tell him. Dive into his arms again. She smiled at the thought of how she met him earlier, then she strode purposefully in his direction.

As she drew closer, she saw the long rope that extended from the tip of the bow all the way to a rock beneath James Weston's home. She could tell Judah was preparing for high tide.

He glanced up, his gaze tangling with hers. This time she didn't look away. He smiled warmly. Lifted his hand in welcome. At the endearing look he gave her, a chilly place in her heart melted. It wasn't a head-over-heels kind of love she felt for him. Attraction, sure. Friendship, yes. And thankfulness that he still wanted to be a part of her life, her husband. Yet she couldn't say those three words stuck in her throat.

"Hey, beautiful."

Oh. She hadn't imagined him saying that.

"Nice of you to drop by and see me." He tugged on the anchor line, probably checking its resistance, or its ability to hold during the hours of tidal shifting to come. The waves lifted the back of the boat, rocked it.

"I'm heading to the gallery to gather supplies. Find water." She nodded toward Paige's business, keeping things neutral. Non-romantic. Right. Like that could happen. "Not much edible food left at the house. Dad's hungry." She chattered, filling in the empty spaces.

"Hold up and I'll come with you."

"Oh, uh, sure."

"If you don't mind, that is." There was vulnerability in his gaze.

"I don't mind." She glanced up at the open window of the art gallery. Just then, someone darted past the gaping space. *Craig?* Had he been watching her? Her heartbeat suddenly throbbed in her temples. The muscles in her esophagus tightened. Intense pressure weighed on her chest. Shallow, raspy breathing. Sweaty palms. Apprehension. She hated the precursors of a panic attack.

"Paisley?" Judah's worried voice.

She didn't dare glance at him. Didn't appeal to him with her gaze as if she wanted him to hold her in his strong arms. She didn't want that, right? Facing the ocean, away from the gallery, away from Judah's watchful eyes, she forced herself to search for something to distract herself. Five things. *Focus. Breathe.*

A seagull swooped down over shallow waters; came up with a small fish in its mouth, maybe a minnow. Farther out, a salmon leaped. *Inhale, exhale.* A foaming wave crashed against the skiff, tipping it one way then the other. A child's red shoe danced in the surf, disappeared. A crab scuttled along the sand as if running from her.

There.

She inhaled a deep cleansing breath, blew it out slowly. Her heart still pounded rapidly beneath her ribs. Why did she respond so adversely to thoughts of Craig being near, when she'd already put up with him being in the house helping Dad? Didn't make sense. She shuddered, anyway.

Judah's hands came around her shoulders. He pulled her into his chest, into his sweatshirt that smelled warmly of him and the sea. She sighed against him. Let his arms engulf her. No one could hurt her, here. Could they stay this way forever? No talking. Just being. Resting. Together.

"Did I say something wrong?"

She shook her head. Sighed. The caring tone of his voice soothed her. No matter that he didn't come to her aid fast enough. He was here now, holding her. She needed someone to be her calm. Her true north. *Him.*

"I thought I saw, um"—she wouldn't mention Craig's name—"someone in the gallery."

Judah swiveled toward the building with her still in his arms, his blue eyes peering pensively at the window. She noticed his several-days-old beard. Had an inkling to run her fingers over the whiskers to feel their softness. But if she did—

"You sure?"

"Huh? Oh, I thought so." She pulled back a little, but he didn't let go of her.

He lifted her chin and his fingers heated up the skin on her face where he touched. "Want me to go check?"

See how sweet he was being. "No, that's okay." This time, when she stepped back, he released her. She felt bereft of his warmth, of his tender touch.

She glanced toward the open window again. Didn't see anyone. She gazed into her husband's eyes. *Her husband.* Not her "ex" like she dubbed him for three years.

"We could go together. Grab some food and water." If Craig was up there, surely he'd disappear before they reached the door.

"That would be great."

"A power line is down a little west of First Street. We should avoid that."

"Definitely." Judah took her hand as they strolled along the beach, linking their fingers together like they belonged. Always belonged. She felt his thumb stroke her bare ring finger as if he were checking to see if she put her ring on yet.

She gulped. *I wish I still had my wedding ring.*

His gaze caught hers. He smiled.

I love you.

Why couldn't she just say the words?

His blues shone like the reflection of the sun on the surface of the sea.

I love you.

The intensity in his gaze made her wonder if he was thinking about kissing her. Before she saw someone in the window, possibly watching them, she might have gone along with the idea of kissing him back. Of feeling his mouth hovering a breath over hers. Forgetting all the parts of their relationship that they still had to dissect and rehash. To form a bridge over the chasm of the last years. Could a simple kiss do that?

Might, if it was like the one they shared a few days ago. *Deep blue sea in the morning!* The remembrance of that passionate moment heated her up as if she were sitting next to a toasty fire. Glancing into Judah's eyes, seeing his warm look, made her think he might be thinking the same thoughts.

But her romantic reminiscing came to a stammering halt. If Craig was in the gallery, heaven forbid, everything was bound to come out about where he stayed last night. How he assisted Dad. Slept on the couch. Judah would hate that—but she hated it just as much.

They hurried toward the rocks near Miss Patty's rental. Judah led her up the boulders, even though she used this passageway plenty of times as a kid back when she and Peter charged down to the beach through their neighbors' yards. Still, she appreciated Judah's gentlemanly actions as he assisted her up the rocky embankment that had water flowing down from the street above. A woman could get used to such chivalry.

"It's strange not seeing anyone along Front Street." His limp was more pronounced when they reached even ground. "The town will need a huge restoration." He didn't add, "Like us," the way he did a couple of days ago.

"When will the others return?" She let go of his hand.

"Brad Keifer came back with me. I dropped him off at the cannery."

"Oh."

"The rest will return in a couple of days. There's a mudslide between Florence and Basalt Bay. Crews are working on it. And, last I knew, the entrance into town is badly damaged." He cleared his throat. "I expect someone will check on utilities soon. Have you seen anyone around?"

Other than Craig? So Judah really didn't know about the man's late-night intrusion and scare tactics?

They reached the gallery and she still didn't answer his question. He seemed distracted as he shoved open the front door that was slightly ajar.

"Looks like someone was here."

"I came by yesterday." She stepped through the foyer, peering around the room cautiously, just in case someone might still be inside. "The door was stuck open then."

"Probably from the storm surge." He shoved against the door a couple times as if his manpower could get it unstuck. "It's swollen from water damage."

"Uh-huh. Let's see what food we can scrounge up and get out of here."

Judah walked beside her to the coffee bar. The building creaked. Wind gusts coming through the gaping window made the canvas tarp on the floor rise and fall. Something clattered. She jumped. Glanced over her shoulder.

Judah opened a cupboard, dropped something. His gaze met hers. "Just me. You okay?"

"Mmhmm." She opened the cupboard where she found water bottles yesterday. She leaned down to see farther back. Six bottles of water; no juice. Several juice bottles lined the shelf before, she was sure of it. Someone must have helped himself.

"Something wrong?"

"A few juice bottles are missing."

"Looters?"

Or Craig. Maybe Brad. She shrugged.

Judah strode into the gallery, stopping at the window. His hair fluttered in the wind. His shoulders tensed. "Someone's on the beach."

"What? Who?"

"I don't know. Stay here." He marched across the gallery. "I may have discovered our thief."

"Judah, wait up!" She scooped up the water bottles, but he was already gone. She ran to the open window.

A tall, solid-looking man who resembled Craig's stature stood in the skiff. His back was to her, so she couldn't be certain. He seemed to be fiddling with the engine. *Oh, no.* Was he planning to take the skiff?

Paisley rushed back to the counter, found a plastic bag and threw in all the liquid and packaged food items she could find, praying the person in the boat was not Craig.

Nineteen

Judah alternated between running and hobbling down the sidewalk. He tried to catch a glimpse of the skiff between Sal's and the first beach house. Who was the guy? Brad? It didn't look like him from the gallery window. If someone was stealing the rented boat, Judah had to stop him.

He crept down the rocks they'd recently come up, being careful not to slip on the wet stones and the water pouring down from the street above. He didn't want to alert whoever it was of his approach, either.

Maybe Brad finished his tasks and was leaving early. But didn't he say he'd be busy for the rest of the day? That he planned to leave town early in the morning?

As soon as Judah climbed off the last rock and landed on the wet sand, he scrambled across the pebbled beach the best he could. At least, the rope was still tied to the rock where he secured it. Wait. Was the man—who was *not* Brad—pulling up the anchor?

"Hey, you!" Judah ran with adrenaline shooting through his veins. "Leave the anchor alone!"

The thief turned. *Craig?*

Judah stumbled.

Why was Craig in Basalt Bay? And what was he doing stealing a boat?

"You can't take that skiff, Masters. Get out of it, now!" Judah doubted the engine would even start since it stalled earlier, but it might.

Craig continued messing around with the outboard. He yanked on the starter cord a couple of times. The engine coughed. Sputtered. Died.

Why would Judah's supervisor take a skiff that wasn't his? That was like someone stealing a horse in a western movie, a hanging offense.

Craig pumped the gas valve. Pulled the cord again.

"What do you think you're doing?" Judah didn't stop when he reached the water. He plowed through the surf, the waves pounding against his knees, up to his thighs. *Man.* There went his dry clothes. "You can't take that boat. Brad Keifer needs it tomorrow." He reached the side of the skiff and gripped the gunwale. "Did you hear me, Masters?"

Craig stumbled to the bow of the bobbing craft. Drew something out of his front pocket. A knife? He planned to cut the skiff loose?

You've got to be kidding me.

"Put that knife away." Judah gritted his teeth.

Craig gazed at him with a dull gleam in his eyes.

Judah wouldn't fight him. But stop him from stealing the skiff? That he would do. He ran his hands along the gunwale, trudging through the waves toward the bow. "Don't you dare cut that line. This boat stays here."

"I'm not *shtealing* it. I'm 'borrowing' it." Craig guffawed.

What was with his slurring? And his emphasis on "borrowing?" It sounded like the verbiage Judah and Brad used when they spoke about Richard's skiff earlier. How would Craig know about that discussion?

Craig stumbled. "You been tempted to do that, r-right? Borrow something that isn't yours." He lunged toward the rope with the knife. A wave hit the boat and he tumbled backward.

"Leave this skiff alone. It's not mine." Judah groaned as another wave hit him. "You know better than this."

"I know *whooosh* boat it is. Richie won't mind. I know where to r-return it."

"It's staying here." A cold wave sloshed up Judah's hip. "Brad's taking it in the morning."

"In your *condish-shion*, you can't do anything to *shtop* me." Craig pulsed the knife blade toward the rope again, his arm outstretched, his hand flailing the air—Judah's chance to stop him. He lunged forward, reaching over the edge of the boat, and smacked Craig's wrist hard, knocking the knife out of his hand. The metal flew like a silver fishing lure, twirling to the bottom of the sea.

"Look what you did!" Craig bellowed. He slammed both of his palms against Judah's chest.

Judah stumbled backward, trying to regain his footing, but not before catching a pungent whiff of something on Craig's breath. Alcohol. Was Craig drunk? And planned to take the skiff? C-MER promoted the "Don't Drink and Drive" message for boating. Craig taught on it in seminars. He was being irresponsible now. Judah had to stop him, whatever it took.

He lunged back to the bobbing boat where Craig was fingering the knot Judah had tied to the bow. "Get out, Masters. I don't know why you're doing this, but just stop. Why are you even here?"

"Same as you." A glint of steel shone in Craig's eyes. "*Shpending* time with your *shweetie*."

Judah saw crimson. And clarity. Craig *was* the one who barged in on Paisley the other night and scared her. Despite his supervisor's condition, Judah sprang forward over the side of the skiff, ignoring the pain in his leg, and grabbed Craig by the front of his coat. His knuckles itched to connect with the man's jaw, but he demanded self-control of himself. "Why have you been hanging around Paisley, my wife?" Thoughts of what might have happened blurred his boundary lines of nonviolence.

"You mean, were we 'lone? Cozy?" Craig flung up both elbows, disengaging Judah's grip. "Why else would I come back?" He belched a foul-smelling breath. "She doesn't wear a wedding ring. An' she *likesh* me."

Even though Judah knew that to be a bald-faced lie, a bitter roar bellowed up from his chest. With both hands, he shoved downward with all his weight on the gunwale. The skiff tipped sharply toward him, then rocked in the opposite direction.

"Wa-a-a—" Craig stumbled backward, toppled over the edge of the boat, his hands flailing the air as he plunged into shallow water.

Judah charged around the skiff, its unanchored stern making it a deadly force in the churning waves. Craig leaped up and his fist collided with Judah's left cheek before Judah had a chance to do anything. The force landed him on his backside in the water. Craig's hands shoved against his chest, pinning him beneath the waves. Judah held his breath. Kicked at Craig. Slugged him.

Finally, he wrenched free, probably due to the other man's weakened state. He scrambled to his feet, shoving Craig away from him, gasping for air. "You weasel!" Judah wiped seawater off his face. Glared at the guy who he once thought of as his friend. Hate. Revenge. Retribution. All rose up in him. Had Craig harmed Paisley in any way? Because if he did—

Judah thought of the distance he felt between him and her. Was this why? "What have you been doing with my wife?"

"Sang her a love *shong*." Craig spit. "An' she loved it."

"You're a scum. And a liar."

"I was here when she needed a man. *Shtrong* man like me." Craig thumped his chest that already seemed puffed up with pride. Water poured down his face from his wet hair. "Where were you? Oh, yeah. Hanging out with the *workplashe* hottie."

Judah winced. "You know where I was." He jabbed his index finger at Craig's chest. "Stuck in Florence, thanks to you."

"Judah! Judah!" Paisley shouted at him from the shoreline. When did she get here? How much had she heard?

Craig must have lifted his fist to strike Judah again because Paisley screamed at him. "Craig! You moron, stop!" She plunged into the water, kicking up sea-foam, somehow wedging herself between Judah and Craig. "Don't listen to anything he says. Get out of the water. Now." She put her arm around Judah's waist, leading him toward shore, glaring at Craig. He liked that—her siding with him, casting surly looks at the other guy. She thrust out her hand toward Craig, who seemed as surprised as Judah to find her here. "Just stay back! Never come near me again, you hear?"

Craig squinted at Judah. "You're fired!"

"I quit!"

"Can't quit when I already fired you." The man stomped up the beach, swayed sideways, stumbled.

Judah never wanted to work for the sleaze again, anyway. Although, he couldn't believe that after eleven years of employment at C-MER it had come to this. Ended like this.

"Look at you." Paisley glowered. "How could you fight him?"

"But I—" Judah never even threw a punch. But he'd wanted to. Now his face hurt. His leg hurt. He was freezing. And what was she upset about? He had been defending her. Them. "Didn't you hear what he said about you two?"

"Doesn't matter." She crossed her arms over her middle. "He's a jerk. He doesn't have to open his mouth for us to know that. He's not worth fighting when you're already injured. What were you thinking?" She whimpered and the sound gripped him in his gut. "You didn't know, did you?"

"D-didn't know what?" He gazed at her, recognizing the pain emanating from her dark eyes. "What is it, Pais? What's wrong?"

"Never mind. Now isn't the time. We're soaking wet, again. Let's head back to Paige's." She took off marching across the sand, didn't wait for him.

Groaning, Judah turned and watched Craig climb up the rocks near James's house. He slipped twice. Judah feared he might topple down the boulders. Hit his head or something. But he made it up to the sidewalk, then disappeared beyond the buildings. Good riddance.

Judah's teeth chattered as he waded back into the water. He pulled the stern of the skiff in line with the rope. He grabbed hold of the anchor, dropped it into the sea again. Couldn't believe all that had just transpired.

He trudged toward land, hobbled down the beach, and finally caught up to Paisley at the parking lot. She must have paused to wait for him.

"What did you mean? I didn't know what?"

She started walking again. "That Craig was the one who scared me the other night. I thought you knew."

"How would I know?" He glanced at her as he strode beside her. "I feared it was. Prayed it wasn't."

"I texted you."

"What? When?" He clasped her arms, stopping her forward motion. Even though they were cold and wet, this conversation was too important to not be facing her. "When did you text me?"

"After you said . . . you loved me . . . on the phone." Her eyes filled with moisture.

"What did you say in your text?"

"Doesn't matter." She pulled away from him.

He dodged around her, held out his hands. "Oh, yes, it does matter." Especially now that he'd heard what Craig said.

"I was scared. I needed you, Judah." Her small, wounded-sounding voice tugged on his heart.

"I know." He'd failed her. "I'm sorry I wasn't here for you. I wanted to be. I felt crazy not knowing what was happening. Knowing you could be in danger." He wanted to take her in his arms and hug her. A kiss seemed out of the question, although not far from his thoughts.

"Come on. I'm too cold for this. You are too." She tromped around him, walking up the trail.

He didn't try to stop her. But as he turned to follow her, he glimpsed the empty parking lot between him and the peninsula where her car had been the night of the storm. "Where's your car?"

"The sea took it," she said over her shoulder. "My dad saw it during low tide."

"Oh, wow. I'm sorry."

They trekked up the narrow trail single file, crossed the street, then trudged across the church parking lot.

"Can you tell me what happened with Craig that night?" he asked as soon as he could walk beside her.

She was silent for several steps. "He banged into things. Was drunk. Then he fell asleep."

"That's it?" Relief battled his disbelief, even though he guessed she was giving him the abbreviated version of the story.

"It was a lot for me to handle."

"Of course." He didn't mean to diminish her experience. "Did he, um, sing to you?"

She looked at him sharply. "Why would you say that?"

"He bragged that he sang a love song to you, that you liked it. Drove me nuts."

"He crooned some pathetic country tune. I hated it. Hated him. I was his p-prisoner." The crack in her voice struck him, a sword hitting its target.

"I'm sorry you went through all of that." Something Craig said still gnawed at him. "He mentioned that you don't wear a wedding ring. Like it means something to him."

She huffed. "He helped with Dad's insulin. He knew medical stuff." Her voice got louder. "That's the only reason, and I repeat, the *only reason* I let him come into the house."

"Wait. He was with you at Paige's?"

"Just to help Dad." She thrust out her hands, palms up. "What was I supposed to do? Refuse the only medical help available to my father?"

"No, I suppose not."

As they walked the rest of the way in silence, a question lingered in his mind. Why was Craig making such an effort to cause trouble between Judah and Paisley?

Twenty

By the time they reached Paige's house, Paisley was shivering uncontrollably. She needed dry clothes. Maybe a couple of blankets to wrap around her shoulders until the shaking stopped.

She and Judah slipped out of their wet shoes and boots, leaving them side by side on the porch—something they used to do after beach walks at the cottage.

"Paisley. Judah. There you are." Dad shuffled into the kitchen from the living room as they came through the back door. His eyes widened. "What happened to you two? Chilly for another sea dip, isn't it?" He chuckled.

"Yes, s-sir." Judah nodded at him.

Paisley didn't comment. She waved for Judah to follow her down the hall. She didn't know what she could find for him to wear. He might have to drape blankets around himself until his clothes dried out. In this cold house, that might take days. She heard his footfall, the uneven rhythm of his steps, behind her.

They hadn't spoken in a while. His claim that Craig mentioned her not wearing her ring, as if that gave the guy permission to hang around her, was ludicrous. She'd put a ring on her finger, right now, if that alone would stop him from coming around. If she had a wedding band, that is. Unfortunately, a pawn shop in Chicago took care of that—another thing she dreaded having to explain to Judah.

In Paige's room, Paisley dug through the dresser drawers. Not finding anything big enough for Judah, she searched the closet. She nudged a cardboard box labeled "shoes" and found another one marked "fat clothes." *Fat clothes?* Paisley imagined what her sister might have looked like at nine months pregnant. She carried the box to the bed, then yanked open the top. She plunged her stiff, cold hands into the pile of garments, pulling up one after another. "This might work." She flung a pair of baggy turquoise stretch pants on the end of the bed close to where Judah stood.

He held them up, a dumbfounded expression crossing his face. "You've got to be kidding. What are these?"

"Maternity clothes." She snickered, despite her chills. He probably wouldn't appreciate her humorous take on his wearing her sister's "fat" pants.

"Just great. A p-perfect finish to this d-day." He shivered and pointed toward the box. "Find something else, please. I h-have my p-pride." He tossed the stretch pants back on the bed.

She fingered several items. Held up a flannel forest-green shirt. "This might be a man's shirt." She tossed it toward him.

"This'll w-work. Not those g-girly things." He slid his arms out of his wet coat. His shirt came off next.

Realizing she was staring at his bare chest, she averted her gaze. She rummaged through the box, distracting herself from thoughts she shouldn't be thinking—that she liked seeing him without his shirt. She picked up a pair of boxers and a navy t-shirt. "Hey, look." She tossed them on the bed, glad for something to do other than watching him undress.

"That's more like it." He picked up both items. He held the t-shirt to his chest. "Will probably fit. Anything for pants?"

"You might be stuck wearing the ones I showed you."

"No, thanks. I'll stay in my wet jeans."

"Suit yourself." Flinging the rest of the clothes from the box onto the bed, she checked a couple more items, wishing her cold fingers worked better. She saw a thick pair of black leggings. She grabbed them and read the tag. "Extra-large leggings work?"

"Seriously?"

She tossed them at him. "Good thing my sister wore big clothes at one point in her life, or you wouldn't have anything to wear. Oh, how about these?" She held up a pair of pink-floral flannel pajama bottoms. "Maybe the leggings and pj's can work together for thickness." She piled the finds on the bed. "Beggars can't be picky."

"You expect me to wear these?"

"Why not?" She glared at him, her patience wearing thin. It was time to find the things she needed. "Just be thankful for something that fits and is dry. Remember, we're in a disaster here."

His lips clamped shut.

"Come on. It's temporary. Nobody's in town to see you other than my dad and me." Unless Craig showed up, but she wouldn't mention that. "Now, I have to find some clothes for myself. I'm freezing too."

"Of course. Sorry. Thanks for, um, these." He held up the pj's and grimaced.

She scooped up the clothes, stuffing them back in the box, then rummaged through Paige's drawers. Finding a thick sweater, under-clothes, and jeans, she headed for the door.

"If you see any large bandages, I could use one."

"Sure thing." She left the room and closed the door to give him privacy.

Ten minutes later, Judah trudged down the hall with a begrudging expression. His squinty eyes warned her not to say anything. "My father would have a cow if he saw me in these." Bright pink flowers decorated his long legs. Above his bare feet, at least three inches of his ankles were exposed. She wanted to snicker; his glare kept her from doing so.

"Where shall I put these wet things?" He held out a wad of dripping clothes.

She pointed toward the bathroom. "Over the shower rod. And I found a first aid kit. It's by the bathroom sink."

"Thanks." Judah left the room.

Paisley dropped onto the couch next to Dad, wrapping an afghan from the recliner around her shoulders. The light streaming in was an improvement over the previously dark room.

"Good thing Craig was here to help take down those boards, hm?" Dad nodded toward the large window.

"Uh-huh." Too bad he mentioned Craig's name. Judah might hear and—

"Craig?" Judah strutted into the middle of the room, his hands empty. "What was he doing here?"

She shook her head at him, trying to convey that she'd explain later. He stared right back at her, demanding answers, now.

"He helped Dad, remember?"

Judah squinted at her.

"He's been doing a few things around here since he stayed over." Dad sounded pleased with that fact.

"As in, he slept here?" Judah braced his hands on his hips. "You didn't tell me he stayed here, Paisley."

Like this was her fault?

"Sorry." Not her sincerest apology. This wasn't how she would have told him about Craig's overnighter. But seeing Judah standing here in all his male bluster and pride, wearing hot-pink maternity clothes, glaring at her as if she were to blame for the whole problem, caused a snicker to rise in her throat. She covered her mouth and snorted, but his sour-grapes glare toned down her mirth. "I told you he helped us. I didn't want to be in the same room with him." Oh dear. Now she revealed information in front of Dad that she didn't want said. She could almost hear the wheels turning in his mind.

"What's the problem here?" Dad adjusted his glasses. "Craig's been nothing but helpful to me and has been fixing things up for Paige. What's wrong with him pitching in?"

"Right. Desperate times and all that." Paisley tried to appease Dad while appealing to Judah with an imploring glance. "Can we talk about this later? We have more important things to discuss."

"More important than getting to the bottom of what Craig's doing here? After all the stuff he's done?" Judah's voice rose. "You defend him now?"

"Just let it go, will you?"

"What does he mean?" Dad's voice sounded thick and scratchy. His eyes seemed foggy. His shoulders slumped. He'd tested himself and taken his insulin today, right? "What did Craig do?"

"Nothing for you to worry about." She threw another glare in Judah's direction. If he didn't take the hint this time, she'd grab his arm and march him back into Paige's room. Give him a piece of her mind. Who did he think he was stomping in here and making demands? They were in a calamity, for goodness's sake.

A scowl crossed his mouth, but he didn't say anything else.

Dad leaned forward and pointed at Judah. "That how you got the shiner? From Craig?"

Paisley didn't notice a bruise. She gazed at his cheek. Oh, my, he had a doozy. "They fought like schoolboys, that's what." She winked at Judah, hoping he'd drop his grudge and keep things light.

"That's not fair." He thrust his index finger toward her. "You didn't hear what he implied about you two."

"You and Craig?" Dad peered at her intensely.

"A misunderstanding, that's all." She glowered at Judah. "Can I speak with you privately?" She leaped from the couch, then strode outside with the afghan still draped around her. The garbage strewn across the backyard—another task to be dealt with—seemed symbolic of all the garbage she was still dealing with in her life. With Dad. Craig. Now Judah.

At the sound of him shutting the door behind her, she whirled around. "What was that? You come back, fight with Craig, and blab to my father, who I haven't explained things to yet, about stuff I don't want him asking about?"

Judah clomped down the two porch steps in bare feet. She forgot that he didn't have dry shoes to wear when she chose to come outside.

"I'm sorry, okay?" He didn't sound sorry. "Why didn't you tell me Craig was here as soon as I arrived?" He shuffled toward her, almost nose to nose.

"I thought you knew! I told you that."

"Because of the text." He sighed, rubbed his forehead with his palm. Groaned. "Well, I didn't." Moisture flooded his eyes. "I . . . I wish I had."

Seeing his tender, perhaps regretful, expression, some of her anger dissipated. Her throat clogged with emotion. "Yeah, so do I." Then he'd know what she texted him, even the part where she said she was sorry for hurting him. If he knew, would his gaze be softer? Would he pull her into his arms, kiss her like a man who loved his wife and knew she loved him back? Instead of standing here looking wounded and miserable. "If you had known, what would you have done differently?"

"I don't know. I was stuck in Florence." His hands smoothed down his wet hair. "I did my level best to get back. Couldn't walk all the way. Couldn't seem to make anything go how I wanted it to." He groaned. "I need to know what else happened those nights with Craig."

"It's over now."

"Is it?" He tapped his chest. "In here it isn't." He cast his finger toward the ocean. "A man I highly respected as a friend and colleague is now a louse and a scum to me. I can't tolerate his disregard for you or for our m-marriage."

The tremor in his voice spoke to her heart. All his ranting must really be about his deep feelings for her. His love. She could melt into that kind of caring and affection. Would, if things were different between them. But they weren't. Would they ever be again?

"This thing between us"—he rocked his thumb back and forth— "I'll do anything to protect that, even when it seems we aren't moving forward at all. I mean it, Pais."

"I know you do." A powerful wave of longing hit her. Made her want to fall into his arms, press her cheek against his chest and listen to the beat of his heart.

And yet, when he opened his arms to her, inviting her to bridge their emotional gap, she was stuck in the mud of indecision. Should she turn away from what he said about protecting what was between them? Protect her own heart by waiting until they cleared the air between them. Or should she step into his arms? Accept him for who he was. Who they were together, with their troubled past and their unknown future. To do what she told him to do. *Let it go.*

His hands lowered. Did she wait too long? Taking a gulp and a leap of faith—*God, help me make the right decision*—she stepped forward. Her arms slid easily around his waist, her hands clasping together at his back. Sighing, he pulled her shoulders in, snuggling her against his chest. His chin came to rest against her head. Her cheek caressed the soft fabric of her sister's shirt where Judah's heart beat a powerful rhythm beneath her ear. Some of the ache she'd carried ever since he rode away in Craig's truck to get medical help, and Craig's return and all the problems that followed, eased.

"I'm sorry I wasn't here for you when Craig showed up." He whispered near her ear. "I would have done anything to be with you. To protect you from him."

"I know."

"Did he . . . did he hurt you in any way?" He stroked his fingers down her back.

She shuddered. "No." Not in the way he meant.

"I'm glad." He held her without speaking. Then, "I've messed up in a million ways over the last years."

She had too. Tears flooded her eyes, and she blinked fast to combat them.

"But you have my word that I'm sincere about loving you. About wanting to be a good husband for you. About not wanting to let our marriage go. I want 'us' back. If there's any way for that to happen—and I believe God has a way—we'll find it together."

I love you, Judah. Why were the words so hard to say?

He leaned back. Stared at her, smiling. He glanced at her lips, into her eyes, back at her lips. His tender look seemed to be asking if she was ready for romance. For love. Was she?

The moment passed, and he stepped back. "I know you explained some of what happened that night. I'd like to hear the rest, if you don't mind."

"Okay."

"After you told me on the phone that someone was at your dad's, what happened?"

He deserved to hear the details, so she explained. Occasionally, he asked a question, giving her his full attention. At some point, they walked up on the porch to get out of the rain.

The only thing she kept back was the message in that second to last text. Because when she said those words, they would be her commitment to him. Her promise to keep loving him for the rest of her life. A vow that she too wanted their marriage rescued. That would be a gigantic step for her after three years of thinking they were finished as a couple.

And she had a question too. "From the second our conversation got disconnected, what happened with you?" Playing with the buttons on his shirt, she gazed into his eyes. She wanted to hear about Mia, but she wouldn't bring up the woman's name.

Judah shared about his experiences over the last two days. She heard the frustration in his tone. His worry, not only about their recent separation but his dread over not knowing how she'd fared for the last three years. He mentioned Mia's name on his own, with no prompting from her. When he explained how the C-MER receptionist admitted to thinking he was attracted to her, his cheeks reddened. He looked uncomfortable, but his honesty was important to her. Even so, a spark of jealousy twisted in Paisley's heart. Hadn't she witnessed Mia's overt flirtations? Even at the emergency town meeting before the storm, Mia flirted with several guys, Mayor Grant included.

"Finally, we were able to rent a boat and head home." He sighed. "I wish it would have been sooner, but I'm grateful that you and your dad were okay."

"Me too. And I'm thankful you're here now." She turned in his arms to better see him. Not for her lips to line up with his. Although, that's what happened. She blinked a few times, waiting for him to narrow the gap. Wishing he would; afraid he wouldn't.

He cleared his throat. "What shall we do before it gets dark? Clean the yard?"

"Sure." She glanced away, hiding her disappointment. "Better not get those clothes wet. They're the only things left in this house that fit you."

He chuckled. "Wouldn't want to have to go without."

"No, we wouldn't want that." Uh-oh. Did they just cross into husband/wife flirting? Time to go inside and check on Dad.

Judah clasped her hand as she retreated. "Sorry. I was just kidding." He gave her that endearing smile she used to love. Still loved.

She gulped. Slipped her fingers away. Hurried to the door.

He scooped up his wet shoes from the porch. "I'm going to work out here for a while."

"Okay." She stepped into the kitchen, leaned against the door, took a couple of deep breaths. Something sweet was happening between them. But the kissing, sharing intimacies like a married man and woman, she didn't think she was ready to take that step. *Ugh.* Then why was she disappointed that Judah hadn't kissed her?

In the living room, she found Dad napping on the couch. She covered him with an afghan. Then she went back to Paige's room and grabbed a coat. Judah was probably cold too. Was there anything in Paige's closet that might work for him? Something to go with the pink pj's, perchance? She snickered.

When she was about to give up on finding anything, she spotted a thick item rolled up on the far end of the shelf. She pulled it down. Unrolled it. A letterman's jacket from the Siuslaw High School in Florence? Whose old coat was this? It had a Viking mascot patch. Another patch, perhaps a name tag, had been torn off the front, leaving a bright rectangle of color.

Was this part of Paige's secret? A piece of her past?

Paisley groaned. She had enough secrets of her own without trying to figure out her sister's. She scurried back outside and handed Judah the jacket. "Look. I found this in Paige's closet."

"Thanks." He pointed at the patch. "Go, Vikings!" They shared a grin since they'd both attended the same high school. He slipped on the jacket, snapped the front closures, sighed as if instantly warmed.

They worked together for about an hour, cleaning up the back and front yards. When Judah scooped up a pile of seagrass and kelp, winking at her as he walked past her to throw his armful of stuff on the trash pile, her heart flip-flopped. On his way back, he put both his hands, one on top of the other, over his heart. He grinned at her and winked again. Swoon-worthy stuff.

Was this what working with him on rebuilding their cottage, and the town, would be like in the coming days? If so, she couldn't wait to get started.

Twenty-one

Judah rolled over onto his side on the lumpy couch where he slept last night. His shoulders ached. So did his neck. He grimaced at the discomfort. At least, he was under the same roof as Paisley. Although not as close as he'd like to be. He was here in the living room. She was sleeping in Piper's room with the door closed, probably locked.

He chuckled at that, even though he would never intrude on her space if he thought she didn't want him there. And she hadn't given him any reason to think she wanted him to be closer. Other than the way he found her watching him a few times yesterday. Her eyes wide. The way she blinked slowly in his direction. He remembered a couple of times when he winked at her, how she smiled back. Seemed slightly out of breath.

That gave him hope she wasn't completely unmoved by his romancing. And he couldn't forget the way she dove into his arms on the beach. Even if things got icy afterward, he had that sweet memory to cling to.

His stomach growled. What he wouldn't give for a hot cup of coffee and a pile of pancakes.

Today was foraging day. His prey would be packaged food, canned goods, and bottled water. Maybe some coffee grounds and an old percolator. Would that work on the grill? He'd search for supplies anywhere he could get in—Paul's, City Hall, the cottage.

Paisley mentioned Maggie's. He preferred to keep a wide berth between him and the grumpy innkeeper who chased him off her property with a broom a couple of times in the past.

He groaned as he sat up. Felt the swollen place on his cheek with his fingers. "Thanks a lot, Craig." Ice would help. But without electricity, he wouldn't find any.

He heard a rumble coming from somewhere outside. Machinery? Sounded like large motors. Perhaps the road crew would get through today. Soon, neighbors would be showing up, joining in the work of getting the town back to normal.

He stood, grumbling at the tug in his stitches along his calf. He quickly put on the shirt and jacket Paisley unearthed for him yesterday. The emblems on the letterman's jacket caught his attention. Basketball. Football. Drama. Interesting combination. Just seeing the jacket brought back memories from his high school days.

He slipped the pajamas over the leggings, and the bright pink fabric shocked him, still. Today he would find, had to find, something masculine to wear, preferably a pair of jeans.

The back door squeaked opened. Paisley entered carrying two buckets of water. He hurried into the kitchen and took one from her grasp.

"I didn't know you were awake." He set the bucket on the floor by the sink. "I would have helped you carry these."

"I don't mind hauling a few buckets." She set the other one down. "I've been to the creek twice already. The first time was for water to flush the toilet."

"Oh man." He'd shirked his duty and it wasn't even seven a.m. yet.

"My growling stomach woke me up." She smiled.

"I know the feeling." He rubbed his flat belly. "I could use a bucket of coffee."

"Don't mention that word! Just thinking about missing my morning brew makes me crazy." She pointed to three cans of food on the counter. "That's breakfast."

Judah read the labels. "Peas. Garbanzo beans. Carrots." He hid his internal reaction of blech. "Mmm."

"Not worth starting up the grill for." She opened each can, then evenly distributed the contents into three bowls.

Paul shuffled into the room. "Morning." He ran his hand over his hair that was sticking up.

"Good morning."

"Hey, Dad." Paisley smiled at her father, then frowned. "Rough sleep?"

"Uh-huh."

Judah glanced at Paul. Dark shadows lined his eyes. His whiskers were scraggly. But so were Judah's. He ran his hand over his face, feeling his chin and cheeks that he usually kept hair free.

"Here." Paisley handed each of them a bowl.

Paul muttered something about preferring biscuits and gravy.

Judah chuckled but didn't say anything that might get Paisley's hackles up.

They ate their portions of bland vegetables silently. Food was food. But this unappealing, cold meal made Judah more eager to find a decent supply of canned goods.

"What's the plan?" Paul's voice sounded gravelly, dry.

"We'll hit the places we have access to. Your house." Judah nodded at his father-in-law. "The cottage. If we can't round up enough grub between our places, we'll try some of the others like we discussed."

"The cottage is a mile away." Paisley scraped her bowl. "Is your leg up to that long of a walk?"

"Sure." Even with his injury he could make it a mile, maybe two, coming back. "We need the food. And I need real clothes." He did a pirouette, pulling the pajama fabric out to the sides.

Paisley snickered.

"I heard some motors." Paul shrugged. "Might be fixing things up at the junction."

"Yep, that's what I think too. Won't be long now." Judah set his empty bowl in the sink. "Thanks for breakfast."

He used the facilities and checked his bandage. Then he scooped up his wet shoes from the porch, dropped down on a kitchen chair, and tugged them on. The wetness bled through the thin socks Paisley gave him. Another reason to head out to the cottage.

From down the hall, he heard Paisley questioning her dad about taking his insulin. He told her he didn't need a nursemaid. She and her dad seemed to disagree a lot, not unlike Judah and his own father.

"Ready?" Paisley charged down the hall and exited the back door without waiting for him.

"Hey, wait up." He followed her out, but she trudged past several houses before he caught up with her. "I see you're in a hurry this morning."

"My dad was so sick when I got here. I'm still worried about him, but he won't talk about his testing and injections. Or let me help him. Not that I know anything about it, but I want to help." She swung her arms as if thrashing the air with her stride. "For a while I thought, well, Craig said my dad might be an alcoholic."

"Craig said that?" His anger toward that man exploded inside of him way too easily. "Why would he say such a thing?"

"He said he found Dad's stash." She slowed down her pace. "Apparently, he drank his share of it that first night."

Stash? Was she talking about the bottles in the garbage can at Paul's? Those were her father's? What a relief. But obviously not for her. He touched her arm. "Do you still think that might be a possibility? That your dad's drinking excessively?"

"I don't know. But I can tell you this, if we find liquor at his place, I'm dumping it all out!" She threw him a vehement glare.

"Maybe Craig found more of it at your dad's yesterday."

"What do you mean?"

"When he slugged me and tried to steal the skiff, I smelled the sauce on him."

She stopped walking. "He's horrible when he's wasted. That's probably why he hit you. Why he acted so stupid. You didn't say anything. Let me blame you for—"

"It doesn't matter." He may not have thrown a punch, but he'd certainly wanted to.

Paisley walked faster again, crossing the church parking lot. "Dad's first, right?"

"Yep."

"Maybe we'll find enough food there to last a couple of days." She pushed a branch out of the way with the toe of her boot. "We wouldn't have to walk out to the cottage today."

"If you don't want to hike that far, that's okay." He rolled his eyes, attempting a comical expression. "I, on the other hand, am getting into my man-clothes today."

"Oh, come on." She grinned, the previous tension fading. "Pink isn't a bad color on you."

"Right."

She pointed at his floral pajamas. "Too bad we don't have a camera."

"Yeah, too bad."

As they approached the Cedars's two-story house where he and Paisley waited out the storm, he noticed the squaring of her shoulders, the slowing down of her footfall, the frown on her lips. Was she nervous about going inside?

He laid his palm at her elbow, tugging her to a stop. "Shall I go in the house alone? I can bring stuff out on the porch for you to sort. You don't have to go inside if you don't want to."

"I'm not some frail flower."

"I would never think that." Sometimes he couldn't win. Even when he tried to be caring and loving toward her, he wound up saying the wrong thing. "You'll do just fine." He stood quietly beside her for a couple of minutes, gazing at the front yard. "You did a great job making that pile of shingles and debris."

"Thanks." Her shoulders shook. Her jaw clenched.

He put his arm lightly over her shoulder, trying to show his support. "Good work covering the front window with the plastic, too."

She jerked away from him, staring at the house. "That wasn't me. The last time I was here the apple tree protruded through the window. Must have been . . ."

Craig.

His name, even unspoken, lingered between them.

She groaned, then marched toward the porch.

He caught up to her in a few footsteps. He helped her get up onto the porch, even though he knew she didn't need his help. Where were the steps, anyway?

He climbed onto the porch floor, easing his sore leg up. Then he stood and followed Paisley into the still-damp house. In the kitchen he found her opening and slamming cupboard doors. He went straight for the freezer, tugged it open. The smell of rotten food hit his nostrils. "Phew."

"No kidding." She lined up jars and cans on the countertop.

"Know where any trash bags are?"

She pointed at a lower drawer.

He opened it and grabbed a black bag. That's when he noticed his wet clothes were still on the counter from yesterday. Not wanting Paisley to take care of them, or to go through the pockets, he grabbed the pile and strode across the living room. "I'll be right back." He stepped onto the porch, then flung the shirt, pants, and coat across the railing. They might even dry out here. He dug the small package out of the coat pocket and stuffed it into the letterman's jacket. One day he'd show her what he bought. Not until she was ready, but soon, he hoped.

He returned to the freezer. While he filled the black bag with thawed meat and warm stuff from the fridge that had to be thrown away, he listened for unusual creaks overhead. Nothing sounded threatening or made him think the house was unstable. The tree on the roof would have to be cut down soon, or else it might fall and hit power lines—or worse, injure a bystander.

He hauled the smelly bag out to the front porch and tied a knot in the top. When he returned, Paisley was filling a garbage bag of her own, her movements less jerky. Maybe she'd let off enough steam about being back here, about Craig having been here again.

"What did you find?" His stomach gurgled. "Any coffee?"

She cast him an evil eye. Oh, right. She didn't want him mentioning caffeinated drinks.

"Chili, soup, and corned beef. Probably Dad's regular fare since becoming a widower." She shrugged. "He upgraded to a coffee machine that uses K-cups. No use to us without electricity."

"The rest sounds good." He'd get the grill going as soon as they got back. "Here, let me carry that."

She squinted at him as if declaring her independence. He kept his hands outstretched, and she finally handed it over.

"I didn't find any water." She trudged across the wet floor. "Just a couple of juices."

He followed her into the living room. "Do you want to go out to the cottage with me? I still need to find clothes."

"If we could access the second floor, you'd find plenty of stuff here." She paused and pointed at the hole in the ceiling.

"The ladder's gone. I checked yesterday."

"Seriously? The one Craig used was alongside the house." She marched out the door, shoulders back, like she was on a mission.

He knew she wouldn't find the ladder, but he didn't say anything. He supported the bottom of the heavy bag as he walked out on the porch and shut the door.

In a few minutes, Paisley came around the side of the house. "You're right. It's gone."

"Craig probably took it, since it was his." Judah bent his knees and lowered himself from the porch.

"Mr. Weston! *Mrs. Thomas?*" Paisley's voice rose dramatically.

Judah glanced up. James trudged along the sidewalk, stumbling over branches and garbage, grumbling over his shoulder. Maggie Thomas wasn't far behind him, looking frazzled, her grayish hair in disarray. She scowled at James, muttering something that sounded derogatory.

"Hey, James!" Judah waved and strode across the street, joining Paisley.

James nodded at him, but his gaze fell on the disaster in his yard. His jaw dropped. He spread out his hands. "What happened here?" He stopped next to his tent trailer that was on its side in the watery grass, gaping at it.

"Hurricane Blaine happened, that's what," Maggie snarled. "Everywhere we've walked it's been the same, *Mr.* Weston."

"I can see that, *Mrs.* Thomas," James shot back at her.

The two weren't getting along, that much was obvious.

"I'm surprised to see you both here." Judah shuffled the bag in his arms. "I mean, it's good, great, to see you made it back okay. Welcome home."

"Okay? You call *this* okay?" Maggie thrust her hands toward her muddy shoes and dirt-speckled pants. "Look at my ruined pumps! I'll never be able to wear these pants again. I hardly made it back unscathed." She glared at James. "Besides making me walk through miles of debris, this man can barely see to drive. His archaic truck rumbled over so many downed limbs and trash I'm bruised from the jolting ride."

"Now, hold on." James jabbed his index finger at her. "You've yammered at me for three hours straight. I'm sick to death of it!"

"Insufferable man." Maggie harrumphed. "Won't listen to advice, even if kindly given."

"Kindly given? This, this woman"—James shuddered—"wouldn't stop yacking the whole way from Florence to here."

Maggie gasped. "You couldn't see the trash in front of you, right in front of your eyes. What were you thinking driving over that bicycle?"

"You drove over a bicycle?" Judah stared back and forth between the two.

"Yes, he did!" Maggie plopped one hand on her hip.

Judah glanced at Paisley. Her hand covered her mouth, and her shoulders shook with suppressed laughter. Seeing her reaction, it took all his self-control not to chuckle, too. He couldn't imagine how heated Maggie's and James's disagreements must have been on the drive back from Florence.

James stomped his foot. "The bike was smashed already, so what's the big deal?"

"Was that any reason to make me suffer while you crushed the whole thing? The man is unconscionable." Maggie wiped her brow with the back of her hand and whimpered.

"So, did you come down the alternative road?" Judah decided to redirect the subject.

"Alternative road?" Maggie huffed. "Is that what you call it?"

James spit. "Only way in. I abandoned my vehicle well before the lighthouse, thanks to fallen trees on the old road. Impassable, really."

"Sorry to hear that."

"Shouldn't have come that way at all." Maggie rubbed her hand over her hip. "Could have killed me. Then he forced me to walk. Without water. I'm about to die standing right here. Any emergency services? I might need oxygen."

"None yet, Mrs. Thomas." Paisley's snicker turned into a snort. She was obviously still trying to suppress her mirth and failing.

Maggie's glare froze in Judah's direction. Her mouth dropped open. She pointed at his pink-clad legs. "Why, I never. What happened, young man?"

Oh man. He forgot all about his apparel.

James coughed like he was choking on something.

Judah's face must have hued as rose colored as his clothes. "Pink's the color of the day." He tried to make a joke of it.

"Another terrible decision in a line of bad choices." Maggie squinted accusingly at Paisley.

Inwardly, he groaned.

Paisley stepped behind him; her snickering vanished.

"I think I've made some great choices." He glanced back at his wife, winked.

She gave him a panicked look.

Maggie made a disgruntled snort.

Time to change the subject again. "James, at least your place fared better than some, huh?" Judah rocked his thumb toward Paul's property. "Still, a lot of work to be done around here."

"That's for sure." The man heaved a sigh.

"I have to get back to my inn. See what terrible things have befallen me. My life's work ruined by the sea." Maggie sniffed, her face crumpling as if she were about to break down emotionally. She squinted at Judah. "Are you capable of driving me home, young man? Do you have any pity left for your fellow neighbors, or are you as hardnosed and selfish as your father?"

He felt badly for her situation, but her demanding tone and mean attitude grated on him. "Roads are littered with downed trees and mud and junk. I can drive you part way, but it will be a rough ride."

Maggie groaned. "I have to sit down." She tromped across James's yard, trudged up the steps, then dropped down on the bench. She covered her face with her hands. "I don't know if I'm going to make it. I'm so tired."

Under normal circumstances, Mrs. Thomas was a force to be reckoned with—stubbornly strong-willed and opinionated. Seeing her like this, wilted, whiny, and seemingly giving up, Judah hardly knew what to think, what to say to the woman he'd feared and avoided for most of his life.

"What's this?" Maggie lifted the corner of a blanket as if it were filthy.

"Oh, that's my—" Paisley stepped forward, stopped. "My blanket."

"Why is it on my porch?" James's voice turned harsh; his tone judgmental.

"It's a long story." Judah stepped in so Paisley wouldn't have to explain. He walked to the porch, controlling his limp, and held out his hand. Maggie passed him the blanket, a scowl on her face. She probably had her own thoughts as to why his wife's blanket might be on a neighbor's porch. He wasn't clarifying anything. "Thank you."

Hearing Maggie's long, weary-sounding sigh, he felt compassion for her. She probably needed a glass of water. A dry place to put up her feet. Maybe even to take a nap. Perhaps, there was another solution, other than her going out to the inn and facing whatever problems the hurricane had created, alone. "Maybe you should stay here for a while and rest."

"Here? Why?" Her eyes bugged.

"She can't stay here. Huh-uh." James stomped his boot, sending mud flying. "We're already in a war, her and me."

"I didn't mean that you should stay here, exactly, Mrs. Thomas." Judah adjusted his foot to ease the tension in his leg. "Without electricity or water, is it a good idea for you to be half a mile away from all of us, alone at the inn? You might need help with something, and you couldn't call anyone for assistance."

Maggie whimpered again. "What else can I do? I want to go home."

Judah glanced at Paisley. Would she mind terribly if he offered the older woman a place to stay for the night? His wife had past issues with the innkeeper, too. Could she set those aside, considering the hardships Maggie was facing?

Paisley squinted at him. Shook her head. Did she guess what he was thinking? They should be willing to provide shelter for anyone in need, right? Even Maggie Thomas. "You could . . . stay with us." He gulped.

Paisley's sharp intake of breath coincided with Maggie's.

"Judah."

"Stay at Paul's?" Mrs. Thomas put her hand on her chest. "Why, I couldn't."

"Not at Paul's. We—that is, Paisley, Paul, and I—are staying at Paisley's sister's in the subdivision." He jostled the black bag in his arm. "We have food for dinner. James, you're welcome to join us, too."

"I have my own supplies." James picked up some trash.

"Judah—" Paisley tugged on the bottom of his shirt.

He didn't dare meet her gaze. "What do you think, Mrs. Thomas?"

"I don't know. I'm so, so tired." She sighed.

"You probably need to relax for a few minutes."

Paisley gripped his arm above his elbow. "We have to talk, now."

"Oh, I do, I do." Maggie probably didn't hear Paisley's plea. "I don't know if I could take another step, truth be known."

Paisley tugged on Judah's arm again, this time more forcefully.

He met her gaze. *I'm sorry.* He cleared his throat, preparing to address the innkeeper. "I'm going to get my truck. I'll be back in a few minutes."

Maggie sagged onto the bench and seemed exhausted. Judah's heart went out to her. But he felt equally concerned about his wife's pale face. Her wide eyes. That scared-deer expression. She stared at something over his shoulder, probably fighting a granddaddy of panic attacks at the mere thought of sharing a room, a house, with the woman who accused her of stealing Maggie's heirloom pearls.

He clasped Paisley's hand, willing her to look at him. To find strength in him. But she didn't even meet his gaze.

"Every yard's a disaster. Never seen it so bad." James talked as if unaware of the emotional undercurrents. "Houses that have been in the neighborhood my whole life are ruined."

"It's sad, but we'll recover if we stick together. Help one another." Like inviting Maggie over. He remembered something else. "Oh, James, I tried getting into your house to find some clothes. I kicked the door."

"You what?" The man stared at his house like it might collapse.

"Don't worry. I was unsuccessful."

"Good. I'll take your help as repayment." James eyed him sternly.

"I didn't hurt anything, honest." Judah sighed, realizing James was serious. "What do you need help with?"

"Assistance with taking down the plywood from the windows, for starters."

"I can do that." Not that he considered it repayment.

"What about me?" Maggie yelped. "Are you leaving me stranded with this awful man?"

Having her cantankerous attitude in Paige's small house was going to be problematic. But he could hardly go back on his word, despite Paisley's tugs on his arm.

"I'll be right back after I get my truck." He waved to the other two, hoping they could be civil to each other until he returned. With his free hand, he clasped Paisley's. Her expression said it all—he should not have invited Maggie without her express permission.

Which, of course, she never would have given.

Twenty-two

Paisley strode into the backyard, her thoughts churning as she replayed Judah's excuses for inviting Maggie over. *"We have to help our neighbors through this disaster. Even if it is Maggie Thomas."* Dad would go through the roof. He and Maggie had never gotten along, even when Mom was alive. Maybe he couldn't stomach the woman's gossiping, or her snickering and whispering with Aunt Callie and Miss Patty, either.

Judah said he wanted to do the Good Samaritan thing, to do what was right. Paisley told him, as sweetly as she could, that it was okay he'd made a mistake. He could just uninvite the woman. Which he refused to do.

Now, she had to break the bad news to Dad. Judah volunteered to come in the house and explain, but she told him no. She'd take care of it, even if he was the one who caused this added turmoil in their lives. How was she going to smooth things over with Dad?

"Paisley." The gruff male voice interrupted her thoughts, stunned her, kept her from proceeding up the steps.

She swiveled around.

Craig sat on a chair on the patio. He stood slowly. Stuffed his hands in his coat pockets. His dark eyes peered at her with wariness.

"What are you doing here?" She shuffled backward. She didn't need this, his showing up here again, now.

"I've been waiting to talk with you. Can I carry that bag? Looks heavy."

"I'm fine." She readjusted the weight of the canned goods in the bag. "I don't want your help. Never did, other than with my dad." She had enough on her plate without him hanging around and causing trouble with Judah. Besides, he put her on edge. Always would, probably.

"I'm trying to help you guys get through the crisis, that's all." He took a step closer. His eyebrows formed a tight V in the middle. "I hauled more water for you. Came by and checked on Paul."

"And now you want my thanks?"

"No."

"Then, what?" She imagined herself hitting him with the bag of cans if he dared to reach a finger toward her.

"I'm doing my job. Being neighborly."

"You're off duty. C-MER is closed." She gripped the bag tighter. "Just stay away from me, will you? And my father. I'm taking care of him now." She stomped up the porch steps.

"Then why isn't he taking his insulin?"

"What?" Her heart thudded to the floor. She turned back, met his gaze. "But I thought, I was sure he did."

"He didn't." His face looked deadly serious. "He hasn't tested himself or taken any insulin since I helped him the last time."

"No way." That couldn't be true. She asked Dad about the insulin several times. Although, he argued with her about it just this morning. Told her to mind her own business.

"You'll have to push him until he sees the benefit for himself." There he was telling her what to do again, taking charge, butting his nose into her family's business. He drew the bag from her arms. For some reason, maybe because she didn't want it to burst in a tug-of-war, she let him. But she didn't need his help. His intrusion. However, it seemed Dad still did. Just wait until he heard Maggie was coming. He'd blow a gasket.

"I don't mind helping him." Craig strode into the kitchen ahead of her. "Like I said, I don't mean any harm for either of you."

"What about Judah?" She followed him, still irked. "Did you *not* mean harm when you held him under the water? When you punched him?"

"That's none of your concern."

"Excuse me, but if it involves my *husband*, it is my concern."

He set the bag on the counter. "Just watch out for your dad, okay?"

"I am!" Oh, she wanted to throw something at him.

"Can I help with anything else while I'm here?"

"No. Just . . . just go. Please." All she needed was for Judah to return and find him here. Or for Maggie to walk in and see Paisley alone with him. The rumor mill would explode with tales. Why did Judah have to invite that troublemaker here?

Paisley scooped up the bag to move it to the opposite side of the sink, felt the bottom give way as she hefted it into her arms. Cans and plastic jars thudded to the floor in a cacophony of noise. She groaned. Craig jumped right in and had most of the cans in his arms before she picked up three.

"Craig, you're still here." Dad entered the kitchen with a grin on his face. He didn't seem as fatigued as he had earlier.

After Craig set the cans on the counter, the two men shook hands like long-lost pals.

"I'm just helping Paisley." He made himself sound like her rescuer. As if she needed him, which she did not.

She picked up a juice bottle and opened it. She poured some into a glass and handed it to Dad, eyeing him. "Feeling better?"

"Fine as rain in a storm." Dad sipped the drink. He shuffled to the counter and fingered a can of chili. "From my house?"

"Yep."

"Good. I'm hungry. Let's fire up the grill, Craig."

"Of course." Craig winked at her.

She wanted to scream at him as they tromped outside, laughing and chatting about camping trips and mismanaged fire rings.

This was bad. Judah could show up with their guest at any moment, and Paisley still hadn't told Dad about her arrival. She followed him to the patio. "Dad, there's something I have to say to you."

Craig glanced at her, a shadow darkening his face.

"Yes?" Her father's smile faded.

"Maggie Thomas is coming over. She's going to spend the night here." She delivered the words quickly.

Dad's eyes bugged. "You've got to be kidding. Why on earth would *that* woman come here?" He removed his glasses. Glared.

"Judah, he, um, invited her. He felt she shouldn't be alone out at the inn." She took a breath. "Makes sense. You know, looters, whatever."

"You just uninvite that backstabber." His eyelids scrunched to small slits.

"I'm sorry, but I can't."

"I won't stay under the same roof with Maggie Thomas." Dad shuffled toward the door with jerky movements.

"Dad, it's an emergency. We're in a disaster. Isn't that what you said about him"—she jabbed her thumb toward Craig—"staying here? Let's be Good Samaritans and all that." She thought of Judah's explanation.

Craig cleared his throat loudly, then rattled something with the grill.

"I don't care if there's a Hurricane Catherine and a Cyclone Frank on their way. That Thomas woman is not welcome here." Dad scuffed his shoes on the mat in front of the door. "After what she said about your mother? About you?" He coughed a couple of times. "How could you let her darken this door?"

"I didn't. But Judah thought—" Paisley sighed. So she wasn't the only one burned over things Maggie had spread around town. "I'm sorry this is hurting you." Another apology. "But he's trying to do something good, okay? We don't have to like it. But I'm afraid, for tonight, we're going to have to put up with Maggie. For Judah's sake, if not for hers."

"I disagree."

"Well, maybe it's time to bury the hatchet." She heard the gruff sound of her own voice.

Dad's jaw dropped open.

Craig cleared his throat loudly this time. Was he pointing out her hypocrisy? If she could bury the hatchet with Basalt's biggest gossip, why not him?

"Forget the wrongs she's done against us?" Dad wagged his index finger at her. "Against you? Isn't that why you ran?"

A breath lodged in Paisley's throat. The man behind her was a huge part of why she ran.

"She was partly to blame." And Mayor Grant. Miss Patty. Aunt Callie. How could she forget the gossip and lies that tormented her for years? Yet the way Judah opened his arms, his heart, to her since she returned, and all his reminders about God's love for her, were changing her. Making her want to act differently. Kinder. "Forgiveness has to begin somewhere. Even between us, Dad."

He harrumphed, trudged into the house.

Craig clapped his hands. "Nice speech."

Infuriating man. She clenched her jaw and marched inside. In the kitchen, she found Dad standing by the sink, opening cans and dumping them into a pot. "I'm sorry about all of this."

He didn't respond.

"I knew you wouldn't want Maggie here. I didn't, don't, want her here, either." She tapped the counter with her fingernails. "What would you have me do? Yell at Judah and tell him Maggie absolutely cannot stay? Cause a gigantic stink in front of Mrs. Thomas and Mr. Weston? Make things worse between Judah and me?"

"James is back?" Dad faced her, his eyes lighting up as if he hadn't heard any of the other things she said.

"He is." A seed of mischief came to mind. "You know, your neighbor is the one who caused this problem with Maggie in the first place."

"How so?"

"He brought her back to town. If you're upset with anyone, it should be with him."

Dad harrumphed. But he might have cracked a smile as he went back to opening cans.

She felt a little reprieve from the tension.

Dad asked Craig to carry the pan of chili outside. Paisley pulled four bowls from the cupboard near the sink. Then remembering their other guest would probably be hungry, she added another. Did Maggie even like chili? She searched for the same number of spoons, feeling shaky. Her stomach cramped at the thought of food. She wasn't starving. Just hungry. And the lack of caffeine for several days was taking its toll on her nerves—as was the idea of sitting at the same table with Mrs. Thomas. Craig being here was bad enough.

Carrying the bowls outside, she wished she and Dad could eat alone and talk. She opened the conversation with that business about forgiveness. Did he even feel a need to reconnect with her or to forgive her?

Right now, he just seemed annoyed. And things were bound to get worse when Judah arrived with Maggie.

Twenty-three

Judah didn't want to leave Paisley alone to face her father with the news of Maggie's arrival. He offered to explain the situation to Paul, but she insisted that she'd do it. He drove back to James's house, praying the evening ahead wouldn't be too unbearable.

Instead of waiting for him on the porch like he imagined she would, Maggie sat in a chair in James's living room, sipping a drink, her feet propped up on a stool. Almost like a queen. She peered at him with the briefest of glances, then closed her eyes. Apparently, she wasn't in any rush to leave now.

Judah went outside to help James. The older man was already prying plywood sheets off his windows. It didn't take long for the two of them to uncover the first-story glass and the front door. Judah assisted James with carrying the plywood pieces to the garage for storage. He promised to return on another day to help with the second-story windows, too.

He called to Maggie from the front doorway, letting her know he was ready to leave. Then he climbed into his truck. Moments later, the loud rumble of another vehicle approached. Dad's black truck skidded to a stop in the watery muck still lingering on the road, splattering Judah's rig and his arm that rested on the window edge.

"Son."

"Dad."

The words were exchanged stiffly. His father looked slightly down on him, since his truck was taller.

"I heard you were back in town."

"Who told you that?"

"Doesn't matter." Dad grinned with his mayoral toothy beam. "Your mother wants you to come home. Eat a meal with us. We have plenty of space for staying over."

Mom wanted him home. Not Dad, hmm?

"You know how your mother is." Dad laughed, almost mockingly. "Always looking out for the kid in you. Foolishly, I might add."

Mom was a gem for sticking with Dad all these years. That his father dared to badmouth her upped Judah's irritation.

Maggie climbed into the passenger side of Judah's truck, slammed the door, glared at Edward.

"Mrs. Thomas, what a surprise." Dad lifted his hand in a slight wave.

"Hmph." She shuffled on the seat, turning her back to him. Maggie had made it abundantly clear in town meetings and in local gossip that she didn't approve of the mayor.

"Heading out to the inn, I presume?" Dad asked.

She didn't answer. Appeared to be giving him the cold shoulder.

Dad's cheeks hued red. His chuckle sounded forced. He glanced at Judah. "What do you say about heading home with me?" He messed with his phone. "You and, and your, and your—"

"My *wife*?"

"Oh, right." Dad wrinkled his nose as if smelling something repugnant. "I can run both of you up to my place. I have a generator. Hot water." He stared pointedly at Judah's chin. "A place to shave. Not to mention, grilled steaks and a perfect view."

He didn't include Maggie. Or Paisley's dad. Judah perused the road ahead, taking in the remnants of the recent disaster. Downed trees. Garbage spilled across wet yards. Outdoor furniture tossed here and there. Shingles speckling every yard on the block.

How could he and Paisley leave the others behind? For them to seek comfort—hot showers, real beds, coffee—while family and friends went without? How many times did he already say that to get through this crisis they had to stick together?

"Well?" Dad pushed.

"I don't think so. Thanks, anyway." Judah glanced at the back of Maggie's head. He invited her to join them at Paige's. He still meant to help smooth out whatever awkwardness that decision might cause. Besides, he doubted Paisley would consider going anywhere with Judah's dad, let alone leaving her own father behind.

"Interesting clothes you have on, Son."

Oh man. How could he have forgotten about those again?

"Not quite your color." Dad smirked.

"I got soaked in the drink. Had to borrow these." Judah's cheeks heated up.

"Another reason to come up to our house. Plenty of clothes there."

Judah pictured himself dressed in a pair of the mayor's slacks and a crisp button-up shirt. Would he be expected to wear a tie, too? "We should go. Paisley's expecting us."

"Finally," Maggie muttered.

"A lot of people for such a tiny house." Dad messed with his phone again.

How did he know how many were staying there? "Who told you I was back in town?" Judah returned to his earlier question.

"I'm connected." Dad lifted his phone. "It's my job to know what's going on in my town."

His town.

"You got yourself a nice shiner there. How'd you let that happen?"

Dad probably knew the answer to that, too. Was he communicating with Craig? Or Mia? Although, Mia didn't know about the fight. Unless Craig told her.

"All righty." Dad revved his truck engine loudly, then drove down the road in the direction of Paige's. Why was he going that way and not toward his house on the cliff? Judah didn't have a choice but to follow him.

"Is he coming to the house too?" Maggie's voice hit a high octave. "Because if he is, I won't go in! I promise you, I won't!"

"I don't think that's going to happen, Mrs. Thomas." What was the mayor up to? Was he planning to strongarm Judah into doing what he wanted?

To avoid downed trees, he had to swerve and drive over a couple of yards, causing the truck to lurch and bounce.

Maggie groaned and glared at him. "Why I never! What a horrible driver you are!"

The wheels bogged down in some of the flooded yards. Thanks to his four-wheel-drive vehicle, they kept moving forward, didn't get stuck. He sure got an earful, though.

"You're as bad of a driver as James Weston!" Maggie wailed. "I've never seen more thoughtless driving in my life than I have today."

"Sorry, ma'am." He couldn't do anything about the road conditions. However, he slowed down even more to show her he didn't intentionally cause her pain.

Just ahead of him, Dad's truck veered into the church parking lot. Why was he stopping there? Judah pulled in beside him. Lifted his hands in a questioning shrug.

"What are we doing here?" Maggie shrieked. "I thought we—"

"I know. I know. Just a sec."

Dad jabbed his index finger toward the grassy knoll at the back of the church property. The area appeared littered with debris and roofing. Judah didn't see any reason for him to be pointing. Then, Paisley trudged from around the back of the church building, a bulging black garbage bag clutched in her hands. Judah shut off the engine, ready to leap out of the truck.

"We're staying here?"

"Just for a minute." He shoved against the driver's door, hoping it opened this time so that he didn't have to ask Mrs. Thomas to move. The door rattled, budged a little. He tried again. It creaked open, making a metal against metal scraping sound. He slid from the seat, his feet landing in a couple inches of water on the pavement. He hid his wince at the tug in his calf.

"I thought we were going to a house where I could rest." Maggie glowered.

"We will. Sorry for the delay." After her harping over his driving, he was relieved to step away from the cab for a couple of minutes. "Just wait here. I'll be right back."

"What else can I do?"

He strode a few steps across the parking lot, stepping over branches and rocks. He lifted his hand to wave at Paisley, but Craig marched around the corner of the church. Judah's hand froze. Outrage lit a fire in the middle of his chest. What was Craig doing here with Paisley? Judah lowered his hand and stomped across the parking lot, a few choice words churning in his brain.

"Wait, Son."

Had Dad known what was going on here? That this cleanup crew included Craig Masters hanging out with Paisley?

Judah wanted to yell out in frustration. Instead, he purposefully made the words *"Mercy and grace, mercy and grace"* repeat through his brain. But it didn't soothe his temper this time.

Before he reached Craig, Paul sauntered from behind the church with a pile of papers in his arms. "Where do you want these, Paisley?"

"Over here." She pointed to a stack of debris. Her gaze clashed with Judah's.

He recognized the trepidation in her eyes, not the reaction he wanted to promote. *Don't do anything rash.* Oh, he wouldn't do anything too crazy. Well, maybe just—

"Masters, I want a word with you!"

"Son, wait." He heard Dad tromping across the pavement behind him.

"What's going on here?" Maggie's demanding voice sounded close, like she was following, too.

He may have made a terrible mistake in bringing her along. Whatever she witnessed in the next few minutes would probably be broadcast to all eleven hundred of Basalt Bay's returning residents.

"What do you want?" Craig squinted.

"I want to talk with you. Now."

"Judah, hold up." Dad grabbed his shoulder. "Son, it's not worth a fight."

"I'm not planning to fight." He jerked away from his father's grip. "I said I wanted to *talk*."

Craig dropped the metal chunk with a clatter. He clenched his right fist as if giving Judah a warning.

Judah would gladly finish what they started yesterday. That scuffle, the way Craig held him beneath the saltwater, still burned in his gut.

"Judah—" Paisley's voice came softly. "Can I talk to you? Explain. Please."

He didn't blame her for Craig butting in where he didn't belong. He understood what she told him before, about her father needing the guy's medical know-how. That didn't mean he had to stay around her. Judah couldn't forget Craig's words about him spending time with Judah's "sweetie," either.

"You've helped my family. Thank you for that. Now it's time for you to leave."

"Or what?" Craig's eyes narrowed.

Adrenaline shot through Judah's veins. "You have no right to be here." His family, his wife, were off-limits to this man.

Craig guffawed. "You own the church property now, too?"

"Masters!" Judah's dad barked the word.

Craig's chin rose. His nostrils flared. But he lowered his fist to his side, flexed his fingers.

What kind of influence did the mayor have on this guy that he yelled one word and Craig responded?

"We're just being good neighbors—your wife and me. And Paul." Craig nodded at the older man.

His words "wife and me" twisted triple loops in Judah's chest. "I'm Paisley's husband. She and I are together again."

"That so?" Craig glanced toward Paisley.

"Yeah, that's so." Judah didn't check his wife's expression. "Stay away from her." He lowered his voice. "I mean it."

"You Grants think you own everything." His ex-supervisor thrust his index finger at Judah's chest. "Does the need to control the world run in your veins, too?"

What ran in his veins was the impulse to slug the guy in the face and return the favor of a bruised cheek. Maybe a black eye.

"Judah, please. Can we talk?" Paisley touched his elbow.

Did she give Craig permission to hang out with her? Perhaps, gave him hope about something romantic happening. *No way!* But that's what Craig wanted, right? For him to doubt her. To drive a wedge between them. But why?

"I had it right all along." Maggie cackled gleefully. "There *was* another man. Callie Cedars denied it. Wait until I—"

"No, you're wrong!" Paisley shouted.

"You don't know anything." Paul glared at Maggie, his eyes as wide as golf balls. "I told you she shouldn't be allowed in our house. Gossiper. Liar. Talebearer."

"Dad."

Craig grinned as if he thought the whole thing was humorous. Then he strode toward the garbage pile. Did he plan to keep on working even though Judah told him to leave?

Judah stomped after him. "This is the last time I'm telling you, Masters. Stay away from my wife."

"Grant men talk tough. Fight like girls." Craig pointed at Judah's pants. "Case in point. And, what, you couldn't resist wearing that old high school relic?" He nodded toward the jacket.

Judah gritted his teeth; tried to control his temper.

"There's a better way to solve disagreements." The mayor cleared his throat.

"I know your way of fighting, Mayor. Dirty." Craig picked up the metal piece he carried earlier. He hurled the chunk onto the pile. The metal clattered. He strode over to Paul who was still holding the wad of papers.

"Well, that was something." Judah's dad unwrapped a piece of black licorice. Stuck it in his mouth. "I didn't know you had it in you to stand up to Craig, Son. How about you get your gal and let's head up to the house? Put some distance between you and Masters."

Tempting thought. For about five seconds.

He'd put off talking with Paisley long enough. "Excuse me." He nodded at his father, then walked straight to his wife and clasped her hand. He drew her toward the church steps. "Why is Craig still here?"

She jerked her hand free. "He helped Dad with his insulin. He ate with us. That's all."

"That's all?" Judah's voice leapt higher. When she flinched, he wished he'd controlled his tone better. "Look, I'm sorry. I'm just . . . upset."

"No kidding. I didn't invite him. My dad did. Like you invited Maggie!" She glared at him, her angry gaze telling him she was enraged at his actions. "He helped my father. The two of them have become friends."

"I couldn't believe he was here. With you." He thrust his fingers through his hair. Frustration pounded in him. If his leg was better, he'd go for a jog. Burn off the rage. He thought he put those emotions behind him.

"All this . . . anger . . . isn't like you."

"Today it is." He ran his knuckles over his sore cheek. "When Dad pulled into the parking lot and I saw—"

"Yeah, why is *the mayor* hanging around?" Her dark gaze locked with his.

"He invited us up to their place. Hot bath. Comfortable bed. Coffee."

Her glare intensified. "Maybe you should go and enjoy the luxuries your family can afford."

"Maybe if—"

"No! I'm taking care of my dad. I don't know how you could even suggest I go with Edward when I wouldn't go with him after the storm. Even though I was all alone and desperate for help, I refused to ride with him." Her voice lowered. "You know how I feel about him."

Some of his molten fury dissipated. "But I would be with you, Pais. That's the difference." He wanted her to admit that his presence, him being close to her, would make a difference in how she felt toward his father, toward life in Basalt Bay.

"You've changed, Judah." She kicked at a rock, shuffling it in the muddy water. "I don't even know who you are right now."

"Yes, you do know who I am."

"Fighting with Craig?"

"Hey, that's—"

"Acting as if you hate him." She thrust out her hands toward him. "What's with that? You call that being a Christian, how a man professing to know God acts?"

Judah gulped, unable to refute her words. They took him from fury to humility, maybe humiliation, in about five seconds. Hadn't he encouraged her to trust God? To believe that He had a good plan for their lives, for them being together. What did he do? Blew it earlier, and now again. He wanted revenge that went way beyond just protecting his wife. He wanted Craig to take back the things he said about Paisley. He wanted to rub the man's face in the dirt. Maybe she knew him better than he knew himself.

"How could you bring Edward here when you know how much he h-hates m-me?" Her voice trembled.

"I didn't bring him here." He wasn't accepting the blame for everything. "He is my father. And you and I are still married, making him your father-in-law." He hoped she still wanted to be married to him, but so much was messed up between them since the night of the hurricane when they kissed.

"Did you forget he paid me to l-leave you?"

How could he forget that? "I'm sorry he did that to you, to us." He gnawed on his lower lip. What else could he say? Nothing he said would make amends for the wrongs of the past.

"Maybe you should go to your parents' house. That would give you time to think things over."

"After all I did to get here? To be with you?" Was that what she wanted? For him to leave. "Nothing doing. I'm not leaving you, that's a promise. Not even for a hot cup of coffee."

She may have almost smiled at that.

"I'm here for you. Always will be. As long as you'll have me." He meant that, even if he acted stupid earlier.

She sighed. "I need to go help my dad. I'll meet you and Maggie at Paige's."

He watched her walk away, her accusation "you've changed" pounding through his thoughts. He'd have to ask the Lord to help him get over the anger still swirling in his veins, in his desire for payback. He sighed. None of those things, other than prayer, mattered as much as making things right with his wife.

"Well?" Dad demanded as soon as Judah approached him.

"We're staying here."

"But we have a generator. Comfort food. Hot water."

"I know, Dad." He shook his father's hand. "Thanks for the offer."

"What am I going to tell your mom?"

"The truth." Judah walked toward Paisley. "Tell her I love my wife. She'll understand."

"Of all the—"

Judah didn't hear the rest of what Dad muttered. He followed Paisley to where she was dumping the contents of a black bag onto the garbage pile. He grabbed hold of one side of the plastic and helped empty it. She nodded at him, a softer look in her eyes.

Craig and Paul dragged some wood chunks from behind the church. Judah couldn't believe Craig hadn't left yet. He picked up a few items, dropped them on the garbage pile, but mostly he watched the other man. How long would he have to stay on alert?

As long as it takes.

Twenty-four

Paisley scooped up more trash off the muddy church lawn, stuffing cans, plastic containers, and seaweed into another garbage bag. She'd be glad when they were finished here. Maggie had gone back to sit in Judah's pickup. Her accusation that Paisley had another man in her life soured in Paisley's gut. How would she endure the woman's sharp tongue for the rest of the evening? How would Dad? She groaned.

Judah and Craig both dropped an armload of junk onto the pile at the same time. They glared at each other as if they were about to exchange heated words. Something made a vibrating sound. A cell phone? Who still had bandwidth? Edward? No, that noise came from Craig!

"What was that?"

Craig met her gaze for a half second, then yanked his cell phone out of his back pocket. He stared at the screen. "I have to take this."

"*Take this?* Does your cell work? Did it have battery power this whole time?" With each question, her voice rose higher. "I don't believe it." He was a scum. Judah was right not to trust him. She didn't trust him.

Craig turned away, his other finger to his ear. "Hello. Yeah. Uh-huh. I can hear you." He walked toward the church building.

"Can you believe that?" She whirled around to face Judah. "I could have called you."

Understanding dawned on his face. "He must not have wanted that to happen."

"He's controlling. Manipulative. Cruel."

"What's wrong?" Paul wiped his nose.

"All this time, Craig's cell phone worked. I could have called Judah."

"Would that have made any difference?" Dad shrugged as if Craig's deception didn't bother him in the least. "The road was still unusable."

"Sure. But it would have made all the difference in the world to me." If she had talked to Judah, told him that she loved him, he'd know. Everything would be different between them.

"Doesn't seem like it matters." Dad turned away, trudged toward the church.

She groaned.

Judah touched her hand as if he understood.

"Anything else I can do to help?" Edward strode by, sounding too chipper.

Yeah, go home. If he and Craig left and took Maggie with them, everything would be simpler for Paisley. The older woman wasn't going to appreciate Paige's cold house, their limited canned goods, or sleeping on a lumpy futon—although it was the best they had to offer.

Judah ran his palm over his scruffy chin. His beard made him look roguish like a pirate. She could get used to that look. She didn't smile at him, but she must have stared at his face too long.

He gave her a sweet smile, his eyes twinkling. Brave of him to do that with his father standing here watching them—and with the way she chewed him out such a short while ago. He must have taken her words to heart. He seemed more cooperative and humbler ever since.

"There's plenty of work to be done here and around town," Judah finally answered his father's question. "Neighbors helping neighbors. You're welcome to join in."

"Oh, right, sure."

Since Edward and Bess had amenities, Paisley decided to take a chance on her idea. "Edward, why don't you take Mrs. Thomas up to your house? You have spare rooms. Food." This disaster had made her bolder. Judah's eyes widened, but he gave her a slight nod.

Edward sputtered. "That doesn't s-seem r-right. Oh, look at the time. I have to go." He stomped, nearly ran, toward his truck, apparently reneging on his offer to help.

Judah chuckled.

"I guess he didn't appreciate my suggestion."

"Guess not."

With his phone lifted in his hand, Craig charged after Edward. "Mayor! Wait up. There's been a riot at the junction."

"A riot?" The mayor pivoted toward him. "Tell me."

"Vehicles are in a logjam at the road barricade. Residents are riled up, demanding access to their homes. Sounds like chaos. They need your assistance to bring order. Say a few words."

Edward stood taller. "I'll go where duty calls. Masters, come with me." He jumped into his vehicle.

Craig motioned to Judah. "Grant, let's go."

"I don't work for you anymore."

"Well—" Craig took a step toward Paisley's dad. "Sorry I can't help any longer."

"Go, go." Dad waved. "You've done plenty."

Oh, he certainly had. He caused trouble. Lied. Insinuated things. Riled Judah. Paisley was thrilled to see him get in Edward's truck and leave. After the mayor tore out of the lot, the wheels spitting mud, silence followed. She let out a relieved sigh. The air felt easier to breathe.

"Ready to head back?" Judah asked.

"I am." She tied a knot in the bag she'd been filling. Left it next to the pile. "I'll walk over with my dad."

"I have the truck."

"And Maggie." How were they going to get along with the outspoken woman? "Dad, let's go and get something to eat. You need to rest."

"Okay."

Judah cleared his throat. "Sorry about, you know, before. You were right. I have been acting as badly as Craig."

"Not *as* badly. I may have exaggerated. I'm sorry for what I said too."

"Don't be." He swallowed. "I do wonder why he seems to think there's hope for you and him."

"He's delusional and a troublemaker, that's why."

"Ready?" Dad's cheeks were ruddy and his eyes bright. He seemed to have enjoyed the outdoor labor.

She hoped he hadn't overtaxed himself. She'd keep an eye on him. Make sure he ate and drank plenty of water.

As she trudged along beside him toward Paige's, she glanced over her shoulder and watched Judah climb into his pickup. Why were constant roadblocks keeping them from finding their way back to each other? Would it ever get easier?

Twenty-five

From where she slept on the couch last night, Paisley awoke to find Judah leaning over her, grinning.

"W-what is it?" Her voice cracked as she peered up at his smiling, bearded face. "Is something wrong?"

"Nothing's wrong." His fingers brushed hair off her forehead. "Good morning, beautiful. I couldn't resist saying that for another second."

She must look a disaster, hadn't showered in five days. Still, his manly smile did wild things to her heart. Thinking of her morning breath, she pulled the blanket over the lower part of her face. "Why are you waking me up?" The room didn't seem light enough for this intrusion. He'd set up an outdoor lounge chair in the kitchen to sleep on. Maybe he hadn't rested well.

He tugged the blanket down to her chin, exposing her mouth. "I thought we could get an early start."

"For—?"

"For the cottage. To gather food. Clothes. The wind died down. It's low tide. We can walk along the beach." His eyes were wide. He seemed fully awake.

She, on the other hand, was zonked. Wanted to keep sleeping. Without coffee to start her day, staying burrowed beneath the comforter was her only wish. She yawned. "What about Dad and Maggie? I can hardly leave them alone." She thought of the squabbling duo she contended with during dinner and afterward last night. How Maggie complained about everything—the bland chili, the cold house, the dark bathroom, the lumpy futon in a child's bedroom, the company. How Dad alternated between throwing critical comments at her and giving her the silent treatment. Leaving a livid cat and an irritable dog by themselves would be safer. "Why not take your pickup?"

"Downed trees and power lines. Besides, I know how much you love beach walking." He winked at her.

"I'd love a beach walk." However, there was the matter of Dad and Maggie. And Paisley's need to stick close to her father. She sat up, brushing her fingers through her messy long hair that needed a shampoo.

"Maggie already left."

"What? When?" Paisley slipped her feet into the boots she'd borrowed from her sister's room.

"I heard her getting around this morning, creeping past me in the kitchen. She left about an hour ago, mumbling about 'getting out of the enemy's camp.'"

"I wonder where she went."

"Her inn, most likely."

"That's a long walk for her in those shoes." Paisley smoothed her hands down her rumpled shirt sleeves.

"Yep. So, what do you say?"

She wouldn't have to worry about Maggie and Dad being at each other's throats, now. "Okay, I'll hike out to the cottage with you." She stood. "First, I'll use the bathroom. Then check on my dad." She scurried down the hall, knowing she'd have to haul water later.

Without eating breakfast, they were out the door in a few minutes. She'd found Dad reading in bed. He grinned when she told him that Maggie left. He joked about them bringing back eggs and bacon for a celebration.

She and Judah walked toward the church in silence. They didn't hold hands, but she felt an emotional rope tugging them closer. Her hands moved back and forth in time with her stride, and she bumped into his arm a couple of times. She recognized a familiar longing in his eyes, like he wanted to bridge the gap between them. Maybe link their fingers together. Or their pinkies.

A low fog hung in the air above the bay, making it seem earlier than it was.

Did Maggie make it out to her inn okay? The woman was spunky, despite her plethora of grievances. Last night, besides mourning every aching joint and the "awful" food, she expressed anxiety about her property. That looters might have broken in and stolen things like "someone" did to her precious jewelry a few years back—something she still blamed that "someone" for doing. She glared at Paisley with open hostility, but Paisley didn't rise to the bait.

When she and Judah reached the parking lot near the beach, they paused.

"Skiff's gone. Brad, most likely." Was he worried that Craig might have taken it? He held up his hand to his ear. "Listen."

She heard something too. A loud truck or a machine engine. "What is it?"

"Let's go find out." He took her hand and she liked how comfortably her fingers fit with his.

Instead of heading for the beach, they strode toward downtown along the sidewalk. They had to walk through a couple of inches of muddy water, stepping over or around debris. His limp didn't seem as bad today, which must mean he wasn't in as much pain.

They passed by James Weston's, Dad's, the Anderson's. She stopped and pointed at the downed power line across the street that she'd been avoiding.

"Oh man. That looks bad." Judah tugged her hand, leading her closer to the oceanside buildings, making a wide berth around the danger zone.

When they reached Miss Patty's rental, kitty-corner from City Hall, he pulled her around the building. Then he peered around the corner like a spy.

"What are you doing?" She snickered.

Before he could answer, two utility vehicles veered out of the company's parking lot. The trucks didn't go far. They stopped next door, just outside City Hall.

"That's where they're working first? Instead of in the neighborhoods?" That didn't make sense to her.

"The mayor." Judah groaned. "Takes care of himself. He'll say it's business. City Hall needs to be open for meetings." His voice took on a deeper tone like his father's. "I'm a man of the people. Go where I'm needed." He snorted. "Hogwash."

"Yep."

Judah nodded toward the ocean like he was ready to get going, then they climbed down the rocks. On the beach, Paisley kept her gaze on the wet soil and the tidal pools in case something amazing had washed up that she could collect.

"How do you think the cottage survived the high winds?" She marched around a pile of seaweed, leapt over a small stream.

Judah splashed through the water. Too bad he didn't have boots on. "Similar to your dad's place, I imagine. I didn't put plywood on the windows, either."

"I hope your stuff is okay."

"Our stuff." He gazed at her intently.

She sighed. They still had a lot to talk about—why she left, why she stayed away—before she considered the cottage and the things inside partly hers.

The sound of ocean waves lapping against the craggy beach below them was invigorating and inviting. She wished she had time to sit down on a boulder, close her eyes, and listen for an hour. To forget the chaos of the hurricane, Judah's absence, and anything having to do with Craig. The tidal rhythm might even bring her peace the way it did the day she drove into town and rushed out to the peninsula.

Too bad the sea couldn't wash away the past the same way it did sand on the seashore. She thought of how the waves scooped up dead, dried stuff from the beach, and hauled it out to sea, leaving behind a layer of smooth, unblemished sand. If God made the ocean capable of doing such a magnificent renewal process, He must be able to do that to a human heart. To her heart.

Sigh.

She stopped walking, closed her eyes, listening to the sound of the roaring surf. She didn't have an hour, even a half hour, to spend here. Maybe thirty seconds. Just a few heartbeats, really. But she'd take what she could get. She heard the rush of water, the abatement, the churning waves that created a wonderful blend of music.

"Something wrong?" Even Judah's voice sounded melodic. He touched her hand.

She didn't open her eyes, didn't pull her hand away. Maybe they could experience this magical moment together. Would he understand her need to pause? To absorb this love she had for the sea.

He linked their pinkies. Ah, he did understand.

She didn't know if his eyes were closed or not. She didn't peek. She inhaled the musty, tangy, salty odor she associated with joy. A funny scent for happiness. But perfect to her.

Judah didn't rush her. Even though they were in a hurry to get out to the cottage, find food, and get back to Dad. She needed this. Maybe he did too. She breathed in deeply. Sighed.

Then, opening one eye, she found his eyes closed. He wore a slight smile of pleasure, or peace? She felt so relaxed with him. Like they were good friends who understood each other. And they did, didn't they? She noticed his scruffy cheeks. Entertained a passing notion of running her palms over the soft bristles. How would it feel to do that again?

"Are you watching me, Pais?"

She was caught. "Maybe." She dragged out the word.

He opened his eyes fully. So did she.

Despite the weird way he acted last night, he was such a good guy. Craig could make them both act crazy and irrational. So could Judah's dad. But she didn't want to think of either of those two.

She was thankful for how Judah had closed his eyes, listening to the sound of the waves with her. He didn't tell her they needed to hurry up and get going. Didn't let out longsuffering sighs. He simply waited with her, enjoying what she was enjoying.

She met his gaze. Swallowed. His eyes spoke a volume of poetry to her heart, all in the span of about fifteen seconds. In her mind's eye, she pictured him the way he looked standing over her this morning. Calling her "beautiful." Their gazes blending, dancing.

"We should probably get going, huh?"

"Oh, sure, okay." She walked ahead of him, lest he see the confusion, the foggy unsurety, in her gaze. What was wrong with her? Why couldn't she just tell him how she felt?

"You okay?"

"I'm fine." Would be, if she could get beyond the unsaid words clogging her throat.

They trudged past the dunes on the far side of the old cannery, the powerful winds gusting off the surface of the tide tossing her hair every which way. A few strands got stuck in her mouth and she brushed them away.

They passed the sandy beach near the Beachside Inn where they ate takeout from Bert's Fish Shack a few days ago. Paisley perused Maggie's inn. She couldn't see any visible damage to the buildings. Had the innkeeper made it home all right? Hopefully, no one broke in and caused problems the way the woman feared. Paisley said a simple prayer for Maggie's safety and well-being. *New beginnings.*

They kept following the beach along the seashore, dodging tidal pools and rocks. When they finally reached the narrow beach in front of their cottage, more driftwood had been thrust onto the top edge of the sand. Seaweed was peppered over the usually tidy beach as if manually scattered—more results of the hurricane.

"That's awesome." Judah pointed at the house, chuckling.

"What is it?"

"I forgot that the front windows were still boarded up from Addy." He sounded relieved, but then he moaned. "Oh, no."

She followed his gaze. The roof above the porch had collapsed. The splintered narrow columns lay like a pile of toothpicks in the grass. Shingles and wood chunks were mounded on the porch floor and all around the front of the house.

"What a mess." He rushed ahead of her. "Stay back."

"Why?" Like she wouldn't help him after they came all this way? She immediately scooped up boards and threw them into a pile. He didn't protest, but she noticed him watching her—not romantically, more as a protector. He didn't need to act that way. She was tough. Could take care of herself. However, she didn't mind finding his shiny gaze intertwining with hers occasionally as they hurled wood chunks and shingles. A woman could be flattered over such attention. Even if the guy doing the flirting was her husband. Or maybe, especially then.

"Uh-oh. Key's gone." Judah leaned over the place where the crab shell with the key in it used to be.

"What now?"

He rammed his shoulder against the door. The damaged entry didn't give. "I'll be right back." He strode around the corner.

She kept working, grabbing tree branches out of the driveway and hurling them to the side.

In a few minutes, she heard Judah doing something at the back door. It sounded like it was stuck, too. Kicking sounds. A few groans. A couple of minutes later, the front door scraped open. He leaned against the doorframe, his face red as if he used a lot of exertion to break in. "Welcome home, Pais."

Home. She gulped.

His goofy grin, like he offered her the world—and maybe he did—as he swept his hand into their beach house the way a maître d at a fine restaurant might, made her smile. She wasn't ready to fall into his arms yet—right?—but his sincere words, his reassuring touch on her elbow as she passed him, made her feel welcome and safe as she entered their house.

Wet papers, household gadgets, pillows, and pictures lay scattered across the floor. Mostly ruined by the looks of it.

"Wow, this place took a beating." She trudged around the soaked flooring.

Water puddled in some places. The kitchen window was busted. Water must have come in through the living room window, even though it was covered with plywood from the previous storm.

"Could be worse."

"Like?"

"I don't know. The roof gone?" Judah strolled around the room as if taking inventory. His shoulders drooped. "This will take a lot of work for us to fix."

"Sorry."

"It'll be okay." He sighed. "It's still our castle."

Or ruins, maybe?

She trudged across the wet floor and entered the guest room. Her private space. How long would it be until Judah might expect more than them just being roommates? He seemed patient, amazingly so. And for that she was thankful. She had to know her own heart before she agreed to share a room, a bed, with him. She remembered not too many days ago when she yelled at him, saying she'd never share his bed again. Now, she was having second thoughts. In the last few days, her emotions, her spirit, had undergone a transformation, it seemed.

Thinking again of Judah's sparkling gaze down at the beach when he opened his eyes made her heart somersault. Maybe love, the great heart changer, was in the sea air today.

The carpet felt squishy beneath her boots. A few things lay on the floor in the wetness, blown off the dresser or walls during the storm. The soft comforter on the bed looked inviting. She was tired of sleeping on the futon. The couch wasn't comfortable, either. And she felt sleepy after the hike. Did she dare stretch out, relax, even for a few minutes?

Without taking off her boots, she flopped down on the twin bed. Rumbled a sigh. Closed her eyes.

A moment later, Judah's footfall gave him away. She peeked through lowered eyelids. He stood in the doorway, leaning his shoulder against the frame. A smile lined his way-too-handsome scruffy face. "Kind of a small bed for two, don't you think?"

For two? "Don't even think of it." Her voice came out in a
hoarse whisper.

"What do you mean?"

"Whatever it is you might be thinking about doing, don't." She
should stand up. Put distance between them. But she didn't move
fast enough. Or maybe she didn't want to.

"Oh, you mean—" He strode to the side of the bed. Leaning over
her, one hand landed on each side of her arms. His thumbs brushed
her elbows. He stared down at her, grinning his maddening grin that
turned her insides to mush. Made her not think straight. "Or did you
mean I might be thinking of something like this?" He lowered his
face, his lips within two inches of hers. She felt his breath on her
skin. What was he doing? What was she allowing him to do?

His blue eyes were amazing pools of sky and sea. She remembered
how his kisses used to taste of cinnamon from his chewing gum.

She tried not to invite him closer with her gaze that might look
sleepy, or softly compelling. But his sapphire eyes drew her to him,
begging her to let him kiss her, despite her reluctance to cross that
line. They were husband and wife. But not really, right? Not until
the words were said. Not until they made promises that would last a
lifetime, this time.

"Or this?" His mouth brushed her cheek whisper soft in three
places, his beard tickling her skin.

Oh, my. She caught a whiff of something spicy. He must have
found some deodorant to put on. The manly mix of spice and Judah
was intoxicating. Soft lips she knew, had known, so well lingered
near hers, not coming any closer. Seemingly waiting for her permission.
But her breath was caught, trapped behind her stubborn lips that
refused to move any closer to him.

"Judah," she dragged out. She shook her head slightly.

He exhaled a breath. The foggy haze of desire in his eyes lifted.
He backed away. Glanced at her. One look of longing. Then he
scrambled out the doorway, shutting the door behind him.

She let out her breath. Stared at the ceiling. Disappointment
mixed with relief. If she gave into a moment of affection with him,

what then? One toe-curling romantic kiss. Nothing would have been wrong with that. But one kiss might lead to other things she wasn't ready for.

Until she was sure beyond any doubt that she wanted everything marriage with Judah offered, passion had to be put on hold. Would her heart and her head agree the next time she felt his lips so near hers?

Twenty-six

Judah leaned his palms against the edge of the kitchen sink. *Oh man.* Did he come on too strong and push Paisley before she was ready to start kissing him again? He thought she was warming up to him, but maybe he read her wrong. What now? Did his actions just throw them back to the starting line? Back to where she kept him at arm's length.

He thrust his fingers through his hair that felt a little shaggy, unkept.

He needed to be patient. To wait for Paisley's heart to blossom into love with him. That could take time.

He opened the cupboards and pulled down canned goods and packaged food. He tugged on the fridge handle. A bad smell hit him. It worked as a distraction.

He heard Paisley enter the room. Sensed her watching him.

"Before we go, I'll have to dump everything from the fridge and freezer. It stinks."

"I can help with that." She stepped into view beside him. Gave him a timid smile. "Have any cookies around like you used to?"

"Of course. Even your favorite." He reached his hands to an upper shelf.

"Chocolate chips?"

"Are there any others?" He winked, trying to get back to the light mood they enjoyed before he noticed her on the bed. He pulled down the treat package he put on a shelf before the storm. He ripped open the container with pictures of chocolate chip cookies displayed on the top and sides.

He held out the package to her. Their fingers touched. No denying the attraction between them. Paisley picked up two cookies, her dark eyes glimmering at him. It took all the restraint he possessed not to pull her into his arms. He stuffed a whole cookie into his mouth, watching her.

She downed her cookies too.

He popped the top off a bottle of sweet tea. He offered her the container first. She guzzled half of it.

"Mmm. That was good."

He drank the rest. Wiped the back of his hand over his mouth, still watching her.

She gazed at him and cleared her throat. "I, um, I'm going to go grab my clothes."

"Me too." He rocked his thumb toward the master bedroom. His room. Which used to be theirs. The one he hoped would be theirs again someday.

"Thanks for the cookies."

"You're welcome."

Their gazes were still locked. Time seemed to stand still.

She moved away first, walked back into the guest room, closed the door.

He exhaled, hobbled into his room and changed every item of clothing, including the pink pj's. When he was dressed in a gray sweater, jeans, and hiking boots he stood outside the closed guest room door, feeling like a new man.

"You need anything?" he called to her. "How about another bag?"

"No. I have my backpack. Thanks." She opened the door, wearing different clothes too. He liked her soft-looking bulky blue sweater that hung down over dark leggings.

"I'll get started on the fridge." He nodded toward the kitchen. "Then we can go."

"Need help?"

"Sure."

It seemed she was okay with being around him. Maybe he wasn't all wrong about his thoughts of them kissing, taking their relationship to another level.

She set her pack down. "Those clothes feel better?" He heard the laughter in her voice.

"Much. I'm all done wearing hot pink."

"You may never live that down now that Maggie, Craig, and the mayor saw you in them." She snickered. "However, I thought you looked kind of cute."

"Right." Thinking he might push the flirting envelope just a little, he added, "What, you don't think I'm cute now?"

She laughed. "What can I say? I'm fond of pink."

He groaned, then dove into emptying the fridge. Paisley pulled out the items in the upper freezer compartment. They accomplished the task quickly then hauled the trash outdoors. When they returned to grab their coats, extra clothes, and the food stuff he already accumulated, she reached for the cookie bag. "One more."

He chuckled, grabbed one also, then headed for the door.

They trudged back along the beach the way they came. Kept up a steady pace, heading northwest, without saying much. As they rounded Baker's Point, her moan coincided with his.

"Tide's coming in." Judah stopped walking. The beach ahead of them was nearly submerged and would soon be impassible. He should have paid better attention. Kept track of the time.

"Guess we took too long." She sighed.

"Do you mind hiking over the dunes?" Judah gazed toward the mountain of sand to their right. The front side of the hill had a steeper than usual slope where the storm surge had eroded the dune. That might be tough climbing. He gazed toward the ocean. "Wish we had a skiff."

"Maggie does. Maybe she'd let us borrow it."

"You think since we gave her a place to stay for one night that she considers us friends now?" Judah shuffled the weight of the bag he carried from one arm to the other.

"Um, no, I'm pretty sure I'm still on her Ten Most Despised People list."

"Then the dunes it is."

They trekked across loose sand on the way up the dune, their boots sliding in the steep parts. Harder walking than crossing the beach. Tougher on his injured leg, but he didn't mention it.

Paisley was quiet, seemed to be thinking. Out of the blue, she spoke quickly. "One time I borrowed a skiff from Maggie's inn. Me and Peter."

"Borrowed?" He tried to keep pace with her, but his boots slid a few more times, causing him to fall behind.

"We called it borrowing. She called it stealing." She made a wry face at him over her shoulder. "Maggie and I disagree on a lot of things."

He could imagine that, but he was intrigued by her story. "What mischief were you and Peter up to that you needed Mrs. Thomas's skiff?"

"The good kind of mischief." She stopped walking, let him pass by her as they approached the top of the dune.

"Is there such a thing as good mischief?"

A handful of sand pelted his back. He whirled around. Jaw dropped. "You didn't just do that."

"I sure did." She cackled, dusting off her hands. She scrambled past him, leaping, her boots sliding in the sand as if it were snow and she were wearing skis.

Her sudden frolicking reminded him of the young woman he fell in love with. The one who ran and laughed and played with him many times on these dunes. He tried to pursue her now, but he had a disadvantage with his gimpy leg. And he carried the heavy bag that could fall apart at any second if he wasn't careful. Still, he couldn't resist chasing her.

He scooped up a handful of sand, thinking of some mischief of his own. When he got close enough, he took aim and hurled the grit at her backside—not hard, but he hit his target.

"Judah Grant!" She whirled around, hands on her hips. But she was laughing too. He thought she might scoop up more sand to toss back at him. Instead, she seemed to be breathing hard, staring out over the panoramic view of the ocean.

He caught up to her, laughing. Enjoying the playful interaction they had.

While she seemed entranced with the seascape, he watched her. Took in her shining, gorgeous dark eyes, fringed by equally dark lashes outlining them. Seeing her, loving her, made him want to pull her into his arms, maybe kiss her breathless. But she'd already rejected his romantic advances once today. And he was carrying this plastic bag full of canned goods. They should probably get going, check on Paul.

"We were just kids"—she spoke as if the sand throwing didn't happen at all—"determined to set crabs free from a crab pot. Neither Peter nor I could stand to see crabs awaiting their death sentence in those cages."

"So, you're a softy at heart."

She nudged him in the gut with her elbow.

"Hey."

"Can't eat crab to this day."

"Really?" He'd just learned something new about his wife. "Here I thought you didn't like the way I cooked them."

"I can't stand the whole cook-them-alive thing."

"You do have a tender heart." He expected another elbow jab. When it didn't happen, he decided to come clean too. "I was recently tempted to steal a boat."

"No way."

He laughed. "Yep."

"Tell me about it."

As they hiked across the top of the dune, their boots sliding in the sand, he shared about Richard denying them the use of his skiff. How they knocked on the door of his house the next morning, instead of taking it without asking. He liked the way her gaze kept dancing in his direction. Made him wish this time with her, trudging across the sand, could last long enough for their hearts to connect and be healed.

After they descended the dune on the opposite side, and finally reached South Road, they paused. He dug out a peach-mango juice bottle from the bag, and they both took long drinks.

Paisley's hair flew about her face in the wind. Reaching out, he stroked a few strands away from her cheek, enjoying the soft feel of her skin beneath his fingers. He recognized that sweet look in her gaze, just like earlier in the guest room, and he was tempted to lean forward and touch his lips to hers. But he didn't want to seem pushy about the whole romance thing and make her nervous, wary of him. He lowered his hand to his side.

"We should get going. Dad. I, um, have to check on him." She huffed. "We've taken enough time here."

"Of course." Despite his resolve not to push her for more than she was comfortable with, her abrupt dismissal hurt. And, maybe, thanks to his disgruntled feelings, he had a momentary lapse in judgment about his next question. "Do you know anything about the missing necklace Maggie mentioned last night?" He had been curious about that ever since the woman showed up at his workplace demanding repayment for her stolen jewels three years ago.

Paisley's jaw dropped. She glared at him. "You think I stole that too?"

"No, uh, I didn't." He pointed toward the Beachside Inn. "It's just, you said you stole the boat."

"Borrowed," she said through gritted teeth.

"Right." How could he backpedal? "I'm sorry. I shouldn't have brought up a sensitive topic. You mentioned taking the boat, so—"

"So you figured I stole other things from her too? I can understand why you wouldn't trust me." Her voice was devoid of emotion. "No one else does." She turned away, expelled a breath.

"Wait." He touched her shoulder. "I'm not judging you, Paisley. Honestly." When she glanced at him, he hated seeing the raw pain, the acceptance of his doubt, in her gaze.

"For the record, I did not take Maggie's jewels."

Moments ago, they were having fun together, laughing and being playful. How did things shift so abruptly?

He sighed. "I told her you didn't."

"You did?" Her shocked tone pierced him.

"Of course, I stood up for you. I will always stand up for you. You're my wife."

Her face puckered like she might be about to cry. "Well, thank you for that." She wiped her cheek beneath her eye. "Few ever have."

He was going to respond, but a truck engine rumbled up behind them. The mayor's rig.

"Get in the back." Judah's dad rocked his thumb toward the rear of the vehicle. "I'll give you a lift. Don't want all that sand in my truck."

Craig peered at them from the passenger side.

Judah glanced at Paisley. "What do you think?" Even though his leg hurt, and he knew she needed to get back to check on Paul, if she didn't want to ride in the mayor's vehicle, he'd politely decline. Seeing to her needs, what she felt comfortable with, was more important to him than his own ease, or going along with what his father wanted.

She glanced inside the truck, blinked a few times, then met Judah's gaze. "I'll ride in the back with you."

He nodded toward Dad. "Thanks." He strode to the tailgate, pulled it down, then climbed in and set down his bag. He held out his hand to Paisley. She could do it herself, they both knew that; however, she didn't reject his offer, probably due to Dad and Craig watching them through the back window.

Judah closed the tailgate. They dropped down on the floor. Paisley drew up her knees and wrapped her arms around them. She may have inched a little closer to him. He slid his arm over her shoulder. If they were jostled, he wanted to be holding her.

As the truck took off, she asked, "Did you find anything good for dinner?"

"Sure, we can mix stuff together. Add ketchup. Best glop in Basalt Bay." He winked.

"Ketchup was your solution to all my bad cooking."

"Hey, I happen to like ketchup."

When the truck leaped over something on the roadway, she was nearly thrown onto his lap.

"Oops. Sorry." She chuckled, sounding embarrassed.

Judah didn't mind their closeness. He wrapped his arms about her more snugly. Heard her sigh.

"We may have to offer them dinner," he whispered near her ear.

She gawked at him. Perhaps questioning his sanity. "Well, then, you're in charge of the meal."

"Just like old times." He snickered. "Dad will have news about what happened at the junction. Should be interesting."

Whether or not that warranted inviting the two in the cab to a meal, he wasn't sure. Especially when he still wanted to keep a safe distance between Craig and Paisley.

Twenty-seven

Side by side, Judah and Paisley worked on meal prep, opening and dumping canned goods—chili, stew, green beans, boiled potatoes, pumpkin—into a stew pot. While he felt confident the mix would be palatable, she stared skeptically at his concoction. He had to admit, the mixture was a shocking orange, thanks to the pumpkin base.

"Want to taste it?" He held out a tablespoon of the glop to her.

"No, thanks."

"Ketchup will fix it. I promise."

She raised one eyebrow. "You think ketchup fixes everything."

If only. He set the spoon on the counter and sighed.

A few minutes ago, when Craig announced that they ran out of propane, Paul suggested they dig a hole in the backyard and cook over a campfire the old-fashioned way. Even Judah's dad seemed gung-ho at the prospect of helping with the firepit. When had his father ever been interested in outdoor activities? At least, it kept the three men busy, working together.

His dad said he wouldn't stay long. That Mom probably had a meal fit for a king planned for him up at their house. Yet he kept hanging around. Judah noticed Paisley's stiff shoulders, her set lips, whenever the mayor or Craig stepped through the doorway. So far, his father hadn't explained what happened at the junction, a topic Judah was still eager to hear about.

Through the window, he watched Paul heading back from the neighbor's yard with an armload of wood—more borrowing. Craig dug a hole for the campfire. Dad stacked rocks in a circle around the pit. The three of them seemed to be working companionably, but Judah had detected unspoken tension between Dad and Craig ever since they arrived at Paige's house.

Paisley set mugs and spoons on a tray while Judah added a little more pepper and garlic salt to his mix. They'd barely spoken since their return, other than his ketchup jokes. He may have invited trouble when he asked his father and Craig to eat with them, especially after his invitation to Maggie just last night.

He glanced out the window again. The campfire sputtered and danced about the logs that were probably soaking wet like everything else around the bay. He grabbed the handles of the stew pot and was heading toward the back door when someone knocked loudly at the front door. He jerked, nearly let loose of the handles. A splash of orange landed on the floor, on his boots. *Just great.*

Behind him, carrying the tray of mugs and spoons, Paisley inhaled a sharp breath. "Who could that be?"

"James? Or Maggie." He set the pot on the kitchen table. "Can you get one of the guys to put this on the fire?"

"Okay."

Had James changed his mind about coming over? Judah strode to the front door. Pulled on the doorknob.

Deputy Brian stood on the porch, tapping his mud-speckled black boot, a clipboard in hand. A grizzled frown made him look older than Judah knew him to be. "Judah."

"Deputy." Judah's heart rate increased. "Can I help you? When did you get back into town?"

"I could ask you the same question." The lawman thumped the clipboard with his pen. "How many people are here illegally?"

"Illegally?"

The deputy threw a glare. "Really? You, a C-MER employee who knows how our town evacuation works, need ask that question?"

Judah gulped. Technically, he wasn't employed by C-MER now.

"How many people are present who aren't supposed to be in town, per evacuation orders?"

Judah didn't answer.

Brian thumped his pen on the clipboard. "I asked you a question, Mr. Grant."

"Okay, five. But they're not all staying here." He swallowed. "Is there a problem, Officer?"

"Other than your ignoring the evacuation notice that you issued? Is the mayor present?" The deputy's voice deepened.

"He is."

"May I come in?" His question sounded like a command.

"Sure." Judah stepped back. "The others are in the backyard." How much trouble was he in for venturing back into town before the evacuation notice lifted? Did Deputy Brian know that Paisley and Paul had been in Basalt Bay all along?

The deputy strode through the living room, then paused in the middle of the kitchen as if analyzing the space. "Is this where you weathered the storm?" So he knew about that.

"No. I, we, that is, my wife and I were at my father-in-law's house."

"Your wife? She's back in town?" Brian scribbled something. Acted even more agitated. "And your father?"

"Is this way." Judah tried walking normally as he headed for the back door.

"How did you hurt yourself?"

He cleared his throat. "Flying glass during the hurricane."

"Exactly why you weren't supposed to be in the area during Blaine's assault."

Judah would have evacuated with everyone else, but he stayed for the best of reasons, even if Deputy Brian might not agree.

"I'd offer you some coffee if we had any." He opened the back door. "If you're hungry, we have an odd-colored stew."

"I'm here on official business. Not a social call."

As the deputy stepped onto the back porch, Judah observed the reactions of the four gathered around the campfire. Paisley averted her gaze, took a step behind Paul. The mayor's jaw dropped. Craig set his fists on his hips, glared.

Paul waved enthusiastically. "Deputy Brian, welcome! Want some dinner?" He pointed to the pot hovering over the fire, propped up by rocks.

"No, thanks." A pause, then, "Mayor? A word."

Dad and Craig exchanged a tight look.

"Now!"

That anyone, including a policeman, would speak to his father in such a forceful manner and not get a tongue-lashing shocked Judah.

The mayor grumbled about the abuse of power—like he had room to talk—then shuffled toward the uniformed man. "What can I do for you, Officer?"

"Inside." Brian jerked his head toward the door.

Dad shrugged toward Judah like he didn't have a clue what this was about. He and Brian went inside. Judah remained on the porch where he might hear their conversation.

"What do you mean, arrest me?" Dad shouted from inside the kitchen.

Arrest him? Judah inched closer to the door.

"You incited a riot, didn't you?"

A riot? His father? No way.

"There's a penalty for that." Deputy Brian's voice rose too. "You know that, *Mayor* Grant."

"I was not inciting a riot!" Dad thundered. "I was calming folks down. Helping the citizens of my town get through what many deemed an unfair situation. That's my job!"

"And is it your job to stir the mob into a frenzy?" The deputy huffed.

"That's not the way it happened, not at all."

"Then you tell me, Mayor."

Judah heard a tapping like Deputy Brian was hitting his pen against his clipboard again. Footsteps, Dad's probably, tread back and forth across the kitchen laminate.

"I stopped people from acting foolishly, from doing things they'd regret. I told them to wait for the road to be fixed." Dad's voice got louder. "Sure, I listened to their complaints. Basalt Bay is my town! A man looks after what's his own."

Judah rolled his eyes at his dad's mayoral creed that didn't extend to his own family.

Paisley stepped up onto the porch beside him. "Hear anything?"

"Dad's getting busted."

"Going to jail?"

"I hope not."

She leaned closer to the crack near the doorframe. Her forehead touched his cheek as they listened.

"What are you doing?" Dad's voice. "You're not fining me, are you?"

"I'm issuing you a citation. And, yes, a possible fine."

"Who do you think you are?"

"You may think you own the town, Mayor Grant, but you are not above the law." The officer's voice deepened to a near-growl. "None of you are supposed to be in Basalt Bay."

"You have no control over—"

"I have more control than you can imagine!" the deputy shouted.

Ten seconds of silence passed.

"Maybe I should go in there." Judah grabbed hold of the door-knob. "Try to diffuse the situation."

Paisley didn't comment, but her fingers stroked his hand in passing as if showing her support.

"Uh, Dad, could I speak with you?"

"Not now." The mayor leaned against the counter, an obstinate glare lining his face.

Brian stood in front of him, scribbling on a pad of paper.

"Dad, what's going on? What did you do?" Judah walked tentatively toward the men.

"This young authoritarian"—his father thrust his index finger toward the policeman's chest—"thinks he's the king, and we should bow to his wishes." Dad cleared his throat. "As the mayor, I tried to calm people down last night. Not incite them like this . . . this minion believes."

"Minion?" Brian cast Dad a sour look. "Getting them to chant 'Open the gates to our town' your idea of calming folks? What about throwing rocks? Is that your idea of helping, too?"

His father threw rocks at the Guardsmen? Unbelievable.

"I didn't start any of that. Or encourage it." Dad scowled, yet he seemed nervous.

"Eyewitnesses might say otherwise in a court of law." Brian flipped over a page on his clipboard. "Did you say"—he squinted at the paper—"'Pick up arms. Show them we mean business'? Did you and Masters grab rocks? Threaten our personnel in uniform?"

"Dad!" That sounded like an insurrection.

His father's face hued redder than Judah had ever seen it.

"I did not throw stones. I took rocks out of the hands of those who would have done damage." He shook his head, his lips bunched together. "Maybe I need my lawyer present."

"Maybe you do." Brian tore a form-like sheet of paper from the pad, held it out to the mayor.

Dad stared out the window, not taking the citation. "You're issuing that to the wrong person. There's your culprit." Dad pointed toward someone outside.

Was he referring to Craig standing out by the firepit? Certainly not Paul.

Brian set the paper on the counter. "Last I checked, the mayor should lead the residents in obeying the law. In following an honorable code of conduct." He stuffed the pad in his coat pocket. He met Judah's gaze with accusation. "What about you?"

"Huh?" Judah swallowed.

Brian stared at something, or someone, beyond Judah. "Paisley Cedars." By his scornful tone, he could have spit after saying her name.

"Grant." Judah glanced over his shoulder. Paisley stood in the doorway, a strained look on her face.

"I should have known. Trouble follows her wherever she goes."

He lifted his chin, stared intensely at Judah. "Were you at the junction last night?"

"No, sir." Although, he felt nervous despite his lack of involvement. What did the officer mean about trouble following Paisley? How did he know her?

"Did you join in the rock throwing?" Brian's voice rose tightly.

"I said I wasn't there."

"He wasn't," Paisley spoke up. "He was . . . with me."

Brian scowled.

Judah heard her shuffle back outside, close the door.

"You've done your duty. You should leave." Dad nodded toward the front of the house. "My lawyer will be contacting you."

The deputy bristled. "You are in direct violation of public safety laws. All of you need to leave town. No one has permission to be within the city limits."

"Since we're here, why go?" Judah wasn't trying to be troublesome, but how could they even travel out of the city when the road connecting them to Highway 101 wasn't accessible? "Won't the other residents be returning soon, anyway?"

"Until utilities are fixed, and the road is cleared, this town is under evacuation." The deputy thumped his finger in a rhythmic beat against the clipboard.

"Isn't the road almost repaired? Utility workers were here today."

"Working on City Hall only." The deputy glared at the mayor.

"My offices will be open tomorrow." It seemed Dad threw down a gauntlet.

"Not unless prerequisites are met." Brian bit out each word. "I can arrest you. All of you. Plenty of room in the jail."

"A building you happen to share with me!" Dad tossed up his hands. "What do you want, Deputy? Are you just here to cause trouble?"

"I am the law in Basalt Bay!" Brian closed the gap between him and Dad, his index finger stabbing the air. "You might get away with stirring up a crowd intent on pushing their way into town. But if either of those two men who were guarding the road suffer irreparable damages, I will hold you personally responsible." He stomped across the living room, slamming the door on his exit.

Dad's chuckle sounded forced. He massaged his forehead. "Can you believe that young spitfire?"

Twenty-eight

Judah took Deputy Brian's place in front of the mayor, although not as brazenly. "Was someone hurt when you and Craig drove out to the road closure? Did you incite the crowd?"

"What? No, of course not. Son, listen. I went there intending to help. Thought I did. But"—Dad blew out a breath—"I don't know."

"Was Craig involved?"

The mayor crossed his arms, didn't answer.

"Did he start the problem?" If Craig incited the riot, that might be grounds for his dismissal from C-MER.

"I should go." Dad shuffled his shoes against the floor. "Your mother's waiting."

Avoidance—Judah recognized the trait. Grant men took evasion tactics to the level of an artform.

"Why don't you have a bite to eat before you go?" Paisley would be shocked to hear him give the invitation for a second time in the same day. "About Craig?"

"He was there, same as me. That's all I will say about it." A grimace on his face, Dad clamped his lips shut.

Judah understood Deputy Brian's frustrations. Still, they had food. He was hungry. Maybe Dad would come outside and talk. "Come on, if you want to eat something. It's up to you." He headed out the door.

"How did it go?" Paisley asked as soon as he stepped on the porch.

"Not good." He strode to the firepit. He held his hands over the warmth. Paul and Craig were still standing by the fire, eating the food from their mugs. Paisley followed him, then dished up two more cups. She handed one to him, one to his father when he approached.

Before Judah tasted his, he grabbed the ketchup bottle off the ground where someone had set it and doused his food. He took a big bite of orangish-red glop, chewed. Not bad. "Brian wants us to leave town," he said as soon as his mouth was empty.

"Not me. I'm not leaving." Paul huffed. "I told you that before the weather went to the devil."

"So you did." The mental video clip of Judah knocking on Paul's door to give his pre-storm warning and his father-in-law stubbornly declaring that he wouldn't leave town played through his thoughts.

"If Dad stays, I'm staying." Paisley lifted her chin as if she expected Judah to argue.

"And I'm staying with you, so that's settled." He smiled at her despite the tension with his father, and with Craig standing right here. He wouldn't leave her again. Come high water, or a jail sentence, they were sticking together. "If we get arrested, maybe the deputy will put us in the same cell together." He rocked his eyebrows.

Her cheeks turned rosy.

Craig cleared his throat. Rolled his eyes.

"You can all come up to my place. I doubt Deputy I'm-King-Of-The-World will drive that far to haul anyone to jail." Dad stuffed a spoonful in his mouth, gagged. "Our food will taste better than this—"

"Watch it." Judah lifted his mug. "I'm thankful for our glop."

"Hear! Hear!" Paul grinned.

"Plenty of hot water at my house, too, thanks to a new state-of-the-art generator." The mayor was still pushing his agenda. "Take it or leave it."

"Thanks, anyway." Judah took another bite of his food.

"I should go." Craig adjusted his knit cap.

"Where?" That came out before Judah remembered they weren't friends any longer. He didn't need to be concerned about his ex-supervisor's well-being, right? However, he was curious about his involvement in last night's debacle. "What's your take on what happened at the junction?"

Craig squinted. "Nothing."

The mayor set down his full mug on a chunk of wood. "It was a fiasco that shouldn't have happened, that's what. We did our best to help."

Craig snorted. Then, grumbling something indistinguishable, he strode around the corner of the house.

"I'm leaving too." Dad trudged toward the carport. "Last call for a warm place to stay with modern conveniences." When no one took him up on his offer, he said, "Give me a call if you get thrown in the pokey." Then he left.

"Guess we should let this fire die down." Paul rubbed his hands over the low flames.

Paisley sighed. "What a day, huh?"

"What's with you and Deputy Brian?"

Her jaw dropped.

Maybe Judah shouldn't have fired that question at her quite so fast.

"The deputy was her prom date. Didn't you know?" Paul's eyes sparkled in the remnant of the fire's glow.

"I guess I didn't." Was that why Brian acted so weird toward her? "Prom date, huh?"

"A really, really bad one." She glared at her father like he shouldn't have said anything.

Paul dumped a bucket of water over the hot ashes. A pillar of spitting steam rose.

A chill hit Judah. "He seemed annoyed to see you."

"He doesn't like that I know what he did on graduation night." She kicked at a rock beside the firepit. "What I got blamed for. Now that he's 'the law'"—she made air quotation marks—"it might be embarrassing if word gets out exactly who did what." Her eyes glimmered toward Judah. "Leverage for another time, hmm?"

Judah chuckled at his wife's leap to mischief, which reminded him of their sand throwing on the dunes.

"Paisley Rose, what secret do you know about Deputy Brian?" Paul squinted at his daughter.

"Things better left unsaid, for now."

"Guess we should try to get some rest." Judah used a stick to spread out the wet ashes. "And hope the law doesn't come after us in the middle of the night."

He and Paisley exchanged a look. Was she thinking of what he said about them sharing the same cell, like he was?

Twenty-nine

Paisley stretched and yawned, then remembering Judah was asleep in the room with her, she sat up and wiped her dry lips, smoothed her hands over her hair. Now why did she do those things? Judah had seen her with messed-up hair and no makeup plenty of times. Yet, his being in the same room with her overnight, after three years apart, made things seem more intimate between them than they were, even if he was sleeping on the floor several feet away from where she rested on the futon.

Last night, he made a convincing argument. If Deputy Brian showed up, Judah said he wanted to be near her, to protect her, to portray a unified front to the lawman. She agreed. But then, she woke up in the middle of the night and heard him snoring. She'd forgotten about that habit of his. She laid there quietly, listening to his breathing, thinking how nice it was to have someone else in the room, in the dark with her, even if that someone snored.

Now, tired of the uncomfortable futon, she stood and tiptoed around his sleeping form. After making her way to the bathroom, she freshened up by the dim glow of the flashlight that kept flickering. She flushed the toilet with the last of the water in the bucket, realizing her first chore of the day would have to be walking to the creek and refilling buckets. She couldn't wait until the electricity and water were restored.

They had made it to morning without the deputy pounding on the door and serving them arrest warrants. Maybe he had second thoughts. Perhaps, he realized allowances needed to be made during a disaster. And, fortunately, Judah didn't press for answers about what trouble the two of them got into at the end of high school.

Back then, they acted on dares she was sure they'd both rather forget. Brian deserved his second chance as much as she did, right? Whoa. Did she just think that about herself? That *she* deserved another chance? Well, glory be. Hope lit a tiny flame that shone brightly in her heart for about ten seconds. Then poof, her thoughts turned dark. What about her leaving Judah and not telling him where she was? What about the hurts between her and Dad? The trouble she caused in town. The uncertainties that still lingered between her and Judah. *Ugh.*

Several shallow breaths and the feeling of a hundred-pound pressure on her chest reminded her that she'd better think of something else quickly. No reason to panic. She was going to take one day at a time. Make amends with those she could, including Judah and Dad. And Judah, being the wonderful man he was, said he still loved her. So did Jesus, it seemed. And she was working on having trust and faith in both again.

When she pulled open the bathroom door, there was Judah, leaning against the wall in the hallway. A grin lined his lips, and he exuded way too much masculine charm. How did he do that without saying a word? He ran his hand through his messy hair. Smoothed it over his scraggly beard.

Her thoughts leapt to imagining her palms smoothing over his whiskers. Her lips touching his. But, no, she wasn't ready for that. Hadn't she already made that decision? She gulped. "Oh, um, good morning." They had lots of work to do today. Water buckets to fill. Drinking water to find. No time for standing here gawking at the man like he was eye candy.

"Morning." His gravelly voice flip-flopped her heart.

His eyes were shimmering pools of light a woman could swim in. Paisley figured she could stand here all day staring into his blues and never tire of it.

"My turn?" He pointed toward the bathroom.

"Mmm-hmmm." She heard the dreamy sound in her voice, cleared her throat to hide it. "Let me get out of your way."

He winked as he passed by her. Leaned in as if he might be thinking of kissing her good morning, too. Would, if she let him. *Deep blue sea in the morning!* Why didn't she just nod? Or lean in herself? But didn't they have too much rubble between them to just start kissing again? Too much past to dive into a future with him without weighing the cost.

A few blinks later, he shuffled into the bathroom and closed the door. She hurried down the hallway, bucket in hand. Chores awaited. Even if her thoughts were whipping up a delightful interlude with the man. *Settle down, my heart.*

"If you hold up a sec, I'll go with you to the creek and help haul water."

She whirled around. He stood in the kitchen doorway, still looking sleepy and handsome.

"Sure. Okay." If she kept standing here gawking at him, she might do something foolish. Telling herself she was one love-starved puppy, she hunted for the other bucket. That's right, they used it outside last night. She'd scoop it up on the way to the creek. She perused the food items Judah brought from the cottage. Finding another peach-mango juice, she removed the lid and took a long guzzle.

He walked straight toward her. She tensed, anticipating something might happen between them—her primal reaction to the way she felt toward him, not because of anything he did. Silly girlish heart. But it was a strong beating womanly heart. Not a dead one like she thought she had for so many years. Maybe she was more ready to kiss him than she even imagined. *Maybe?*

He held out his hand for the juice container. That twinkle in his eyes shone brightly. Like he knew how she felt. Recognized her longings. She wasn't that transparent, was she?

She handed him the partially filled bottle. He took several swallows. Intrigued, she watched his lips moisten. When he handed the container back, she fumbled it in her hands.

"Thanks." She took another drink, distracting herself from his probing blues.

"We have to find more drinking liquid, hopefully clean water, today." He moved away. He grabbed a knit hat from the table and pulled it onto his head, covering his soft, messy hair. Hair she wouldn't mind strumming her fingers through. Taming it a little.

She cleared her throat. Stared at a black spot on the flooring. Glanced at the ceiling, looking anywhere but at him.

"Water's a priority for survival."

"Uh-huh." So was kissing. Linking pinkies. Telling him she loved him.

"After we secure that, we can tackle the next thing on the list."

"Which is?" What were they talking about?

He thrust his arms into his coat. Arms she wished would wrap around her. Forget water.

"I thought we should work on your dad's house. Or the cottage. We'll need our own place to stay once Paige and Piper return." He rocked his thumb toward the bedroom. "A decent bed is another priority."

Right. Beds. Her cheeks felt hot. He didn't say anything wrong or suggestive. Yet her mind leapfrogged to married life with him, perhaps sharing a bedroom.

"Ready?"

She gazed into his eyes. "For what?"

"For . . . hauling water." He stared back at her, his eyebrows making a V. "You okay?"

"Of course, water. Yep, I'm ready." She picked up the bucket and hustled out the door. Time to get going and stop daydreaming about married love. Wow, her heart was changing so fast it was hard to keep up.

"What did you think I meant?" His voice had a funny twinge to it.

She glanced over her shoulder. He was grinning. He knew, didn't he? Or thought he knew. She groaned, then walked to the firepit and grabbed the other bucket.

"Even though we'll be busy today, we should do something fun, too." He pulled one of the buckets from her grasp.

Their fingers touched. She may have held his hand for just a second in the exchange.

"Like?"

"Something lighthearted. Just you and me." His inviting grin was followed by a wink. "We could walk down to *Peter's Land*. With all the damage, we can't hike out on the peninsula, but we could take a look."

That he used her nickname for the rocky outcropping pleased her. "I'd like that."

He swung the bucket back and forth, making her think of them being like Jack and Jill going to get their pail of water.

"Me? I'd rather do something more adventurous."

"Such as?" She stepped over a cluster of branches on the sidewalk.

He gazed toward the ocean as if he were looking at it, even though they couldn't see the water yet. "Mmm. Go for a boat ride with you."

"And where would you get a boat?"

His face sobered. "I don't know. Now that I'm not working—"

"Maybe Craig wasn't serious about firing you." She swallowed, knowing this might be a touchy subject for him.

"Yeah, he was." As they approached a downed tree, he gently touched her elbow, leading her around it. "I tried to quit. He jumped in and fired me. Just as well, though."

"I'm sorry. I know how much you love your job." She turned at the corner and walked up the street toward the creek. "What about Mike Linfield?" She thought of the company manager who told her at a Christmas party how much he appreciated Judah's work ethic. "Couldn't he veto Craig's decision?"

"I doubt it."

They reached the creek that was overflowing its narrow bank from the flooding and the heavy rains during and after the storm. Bending over, they each submerged their buckets into the cold water.

"Got mine." Judah stood, hefting his full load.

"Same here." She groaned as she stood, lifting the weight of the bucket. "How many times will we do this before the crisis is over?"

Judah smiled again. "I'd walk here with you to get water for the rest of my life if it meant we could spend time talking like this. Sharing our hearts."

She knew what he meant, but she thought she would keep things light. "When did you become such a romantic?"

He grabbed his chest with his free hand. "You wound me. I've got plenty of romance for you, sweetheart." He stroked her cheek with the back of his fingers.

So much for keeping things light.

"Where is all this dreamy talk coming from?" Was he trying to say the right things, to be more romantic, in order to get her to move in with him as his wife?

He set down his bucket. Took hers from her hand and set it down next to his. He gazed into her eyes with such a depth of caring, or love, it made her feel breathless, but in a good way.

"You need to know this, Paisley Rose Grant." He stroked a strand of her hair back, his fingers lingering near her left ear. "With every fiber of who I am, with every beat of my heart, I love you."

She swallowed down a lump in her throat as dry as swallowing cotton.

His eyes, gazing into hers, shone like the brilliance of the sea on a summer day with a burst of sunlight on it. "I know you aren't ready to say those words to me yet. And that's okay. But I'm going to keep loving you and romancing you and showing you how much I want us to be a real couple for as long as it takes. That's a promise you can count on."

I love you too, Judah. The words danced in her spirit. In her throat. Why couldn't she tell him? Her pride? Was she holding onto grudges? Their past?

"You've been through a lot." His palms stroked her upper arms. "So have I. But I believe God is doing a work in both of us. He'll help us with the whole restoration thing. There's no rush. We can take our time." He leaned in and his mouth brushed her cheek. She felt his whiskers touch her skin briefly.

Just tell him.

"Until you're ready for more, I'll wait. But if you think I'm being a phony in the way I feel about you, you're wrong." His gentle smile took any sting out of his words. He picked up both buckets of water, then limped down the sidewalk toward Paige's house.

When did he become so vulnerable and willing to talk about stuff that he would have clammed up and run for the hills over in the past? And talk about romantic. She was about to melt at his feet after listening to his sweet declarations.

"Wait up." She ran after him. "I'm perfectly capable of carrying one of those."

"I know. Let me be the tough guy this once."

"Okay, fine."

The tangy scent of the sea wafting on the wind tempted her to forget the day's work. She looked forward to whenever they could take a break and go down to the peninsula. She pictured the waves bursting against the rocks, sea spray billowing into the air. She imagined her and Judah searching the beach for treasures like she did hundreds of times as a kid. Her idea of fun. That Judah understood that about her was part of their history together. Part of their love story.

She pondered what he said about his willingness to wait for her to be ready for their marriage to be restored. Did he mean that he would wait for her no matter how long it took?

Thirty

Judah was removing items from Paul's living room, relocating salvageable furniture into the kitchen, throwing others outdoors, and discarding ruined knickknacks and memorabilia into the trash, in preparation for pulling up the soaking wet carpet. Suddenly he heard a series of loud rumbles. "Listen to that."

"What is it?" Paisley held several of her mother's flood-ruined paintings in her arms.

"Heavy equipment trucks, I think." He moved to stand near the couch. "Not long until the road opens."

"Good. Maybe Deputy Brian won't haul us to jail."

"Unless he does so out of spite, or mere legalities. I think he's met his match if he tries dragging you down to lockup." He teased her as he lifted one side of the couch, testing its weight.

"Yeah, just let him try." She grinned one of those smiles that had a way of wrapping around his heart.

Ever since he told her that he'd wait for her however long it took, it seemed she was gazing into his eyes differently. More intensely. Like now.

"How about helping me haul this couch outside?" He pointed at the last large piece of furniture left on the soggy carpet.

"Sure." She set down the paintings on the wooden coffee table he'd already moved.

Paul entered the living room from the kitchen. "What's this doing in the pantry?" He held up a beach towel—the same one Judah saw on the shelf the other day.

"Oh, uh." Paisley's face flushed. "It's what I used for bedding the night I stayed here."

Just like Judah thought.

"You slept in the pantry?" Paul's eyebrows knit together above his glasses. "Why would you do that?"

It seemed a serious message passed between father and daughter. Paul shuffled his feet and averted his gaze. Was he feeling awkward about the topic or about her pointed glare?

"That was the only dry place I could find." Her voice rose. "I hated it. Have always hated the pantry. But you know that."

Should Judah step in? His and Paisley's relationship needed healing, but so did Paul's and hers. They required their own time to work things out between them without his interference. Still, he'd stay close in case she needed him. He trudged to the other side of the living room, gazing through the plastic-covered window, giving them a few moments to talk. He prayed for them too.

Paul mumbled something about women and things men would never understand about them, then stomped into the kitchen. Judah turned and witnessed the towel his father-in-law had been holding sail through the air and land on the washing machine.

Paisley's boots thudded as she followed Paul into the other room. "Why didn't you ever c-come for m-me?" Her voice broke, sounding small and childlike.

Paul shuffled boards that fell from the stairway during the storm.

"Dad?"

Paul kept working. Evading conflict? Judah empathized with that emotional cop-out. Although, he learned the hard way that it never solved a thing.

Lord, help them see that they still have each other. Touch Paisley. Heal her heart. Heal all of us.

"I w-wanted, n-needed, you to rescue m-me." Her voice broke. "To save me from the d-darkness. From Mom's unjustified wrath."

She expelled a breath, like the telling was wrenched from her soul. "You never came. Not once. Never got involved. Why not?" Her voice rose with a demanding tone, then fell. "D-didn't you l-love me enough?"

Oh, Paisley. Save her from what darkness? Judah knew about her fear of the dark. That she preferred to keep a night-light on. She used to lay close to him after he turned out the light, as if she couldn't bear to be alone in the dark. He swallowed hard. All those nights by herself in Chicago, two-thousand miles from him, how did she cope?

Knowing she was never out of God's sight had comforted him during their years apart. He prayed for so long for her to come back. And here she was. Full of hurts. All of them were. But Judah knew who to turn to. Was Paisley aware of her heavenly Father opening His arms of love to her, even if her earthly father seemed uncaring, even cold, now?

"Aren't you going to answer me?"

"Nothing to say." Paul picked up a couple of handrails, tossed them on the pile.

"Nothing?" Paisley's face blanched.

Judah wished Paul would step up and be honest, even if that meant admitting to his own hurts, failures, disappointments, whatever.

"After all we've been through? The storm. Your illness. Me putting up with Craig so that you could have the medical intervention you needed?" She nearly yelled that last part.

A knot twisted in Judah's gut. He shouldn't have questioned her interactions with Craig. Her words dissolved any doubt. She had put aside her animosity toward that man so she could care for her ailing father. A sacrificial act of love in her daughter's heart.

"We need to clean this up," Paul said sternly. "That's all that matters now."

"No, that's not all that matters!"

"We have to get the house livable." Paul shuffled into the living room, scooped up the pile of paintings Paisley collected earlier. "I'll spread these outside to dry. Might save a few."

"Please, don't walk away." She followed him, a crushed look on her face.

"Why not?" Paul paused by the door they'd propped open. "That's what you did. What you're good at." His words were like a judge's gavel striking a sound block. He shuffled the canvases in his hands, then trudged onto the porch.

Paisley blew out a harsh-sounding breath. "Fine. If that's the way you want it." She covered her face with her hands.

Judah strode to her, intent on wrapping his arms around her, comforting her. "I'm so sorry, Pais."

She thrust up her hands, blocking his embrace, or his coming any closer. Her face was red. Her mouth drawn into a tight line. "We have work to do. Survival. He's right about that." A gritty look replaced her previous vulnerability.

Judah kept his hands at his sides. She needed space; he'd give her that. "Is he still angry that you left?"

"And that I missed my mom's funeral." She gnawed on her lower lip. "Can't change the past."

"He'll come around. He loves you. Always has."

She eyed him skeptically.

"Anything I can do?"

"Let's move the couch. Get this over with."

"Okay." He strode to the other end of the water-logged piece of furniture. "Might be heavy. We'll lift, then shove."

"I got it." She raised her end quickly. She undoubtedly had a load of adrenaline pulsing through her. A crash was inevitable.

He lifted his end slowly, wishing he bore the greater weight. He cringed at the tug in his leg but hid his reaction by tucking his head down. Backing up, he led the way toward the front door. When he reached the opening, he set his side down. It took some maneuvering to get the old relic on its end, then shuffled out the door. They heaved it off the porch and onto the soggy grass near the recliner Judah already threw out.

"Guess I'll need new furniture." Paul's mouth drooped into a deep frown. He rubbed his forehead with the back of his palm like he was tired. Maybe emotionally exhausted.

Judah felt badly for him too. He patted the man's shoulder.

"You and half the town." He nodded toward Paisley. "Let's pull that rug, then take a break."

The atmosphere tense, the three of them worked at yanking up the carpeting, then they tore out the foam underlayment. Throughout the process, Paisley and Paul didn't speak to each other. They hauled the wet mess outdoors and made a giant pile. Paul found the tools they needed to pry up the tack strips. Once that was done, he went outside. Paisley disappeared around the corner, into the kitchen.

Relieved the job was finished, Judah checked over the floor that was still soaked. Some of the wood was warped and would have to be replaced.

He heard voices coming from outside. James and Paul chatted back and forth across the street. Judah watched through the doorway as Paul trudged over to his friend's property. The two men shook hands.

Maybe he could get Paisley away from here for a while. She stood at the kitchen sink, staring out the window as he approached.

"I'm curious about the engine sounds. Want to take a walk and check?"

"Sure. Why not?" She spoke in a monotone.

"Would be great to get some fresh air. Stretch our legs."

"I said, 'sure,'" she said sharply.

"Okay."

She shot out the door faster than he could get out and climb from the porch. Finding the old steps, or making new ones, was high on his list of things to be done. It took effort for him to wade down the flooded street, and Paisley had gone half a block before he caught up to her. By then, she was walking on the sidewalk on the opposite side of the street. Without talking about it, they made a wide berth around the downed power line.

When he held out his hand toward her, she raised an eyebrow as if asking him "*really?*" He dropped his outstretched hand.

Two steps backward.

He couldn't even walk beside her for some of the way, since they had to step over so many branches and piles of shingles. The place reminded him of a war zone, like an explosion went off. It was astounding what catastrophic damage high winds and tempestuous waves could do. He hoped they never had another hurricane on the west coast again. Although, if it did happen, he wanted to be one of the people warning folks as he did with Blaine. That's the main reason he loved his job. The company's mission to help neighbors in a disaster or crisis meant a lot to him. Too bad things had gone south between him and Craig.

He sighed as they walked past the art gallery.

"Something wrong?"

"Just thinking about the storm and all the damage."

"Me too. What a mess, huh?" She kicked a rusty can out of her way. Flexed her shoulders. Sighed.

He shifted a little closer to her. "It'll take the whole town working together to fix it up. All of us helping each other."

"We'll need a leader too."

"You mean other than the mayor?"

"Yes. Other than him." She lifted her chin, a sparkle returning to her gaze. "You could use your C-MER experience to help as a regular citizen, Good Samaritan, whatever."

It was nice of her to think of him as a leader in the community.

They passed by Miss Patty's hardware store, the floral shop that was closed after Hurricane Addy hit, and Bert's Fish Shack. He couldn't believe how wrecked the front of Bert's was with that boat smashed into the front. He imagined the owner, who had called him "Sonny" since he was a kid, being overwhelmed, possibly discouraged, by the reconstruction ahead of him.

Paisley had gone quiet, and he remembered the words spoken between her and Paul. Hurtful words that probably replayed in her mind, eating at her.

He draped his arm across her shoulder. Taking a risk. "You okay?"

She tensed. "Why wouldn't I be?" Her glare was a forcefield telling him to get his arm off her shoulder.

He stuffed his hands into his coat pockets. Okay, she still needed space. But he wanted them to be able to talk, share their hearts, get past the walls. Which meant he had to keep pushing a little.

"Can you tell me what's going on with you and your dad?"

She stopped in front of the old cannery and thrust out her hands. "Isn't it obvious? I've failed everyone. Dad. You. My mom. Paige. Aunt Callie. I'm a walking, breathing, stinking *failure*." She reminded him of a teapot boiling over with steam and unspent energy. "How did I ever imagine I could come back to Basalt and make things right? Miss Humpty Dumpty is not only busted up, she's shattered b-beyond r-recognition." Her voice broke. "N-nothing c-can fix that."

Was she speaking of herself? Their marriage? Her relationship with Paul? He didn't know what to say. Which part to address. He was afraid to say or do anything for fear it would be the incorrect thing, again. He stood there, watching her, wishing he knew how to make everything better.

"You're not going to talk to me, either?" She squinted at him.

He felt the pain in her gaze pierce his chest, rush through his lungs. "It's not that at all. Of course, I'm going to talk with you. I'm just so sorry. Stymied, really." He reached out. Pulled his hands back. "I'm not sure what to say. Or do. I don't want to say the wrong thing."

She kept glaring, so he kept talking. "You and I have plenty of stuff to talk about, believe me, I know that. But I think, right now, you're more upset about your dad and your past with him, than with me."

"I'm such a mess." She covered her face like she did earlier. "Oh, help. Why did I even come back to Basalt? How did I ever think this would work?"

Surely that outcry was his cue. Taking another chance, he stepped forward and slid his palms around her elbows, drew her against his chest. When she didn't pull away, he wrapped his arms completely around her, held her to him as closely as she allowed. "It's going to be okay, Pais," he whispered near her ear. "You're going to get through this. We both are." He kept murmuring reassurances, feeling her relax. "I'm so thankful you came back. That you're here with me now. Everything's going to get better, even if it happens in tiny increments. We're going to stick together and face everything as a couple, okay?"

He was determined to let her know, again, that he was here for her, for as long as it took for her to feel comfortable with him. He leaned his cheek against her head, thankful for the chance to be holding her. "I love you, sweetheart. Will always love you, no matter what."

She sagged against him. Stayed almost limp in his arms for several minutes. He didn't hear her crying. He listened to her breathing, checking for any irregularities. That part of her seemed okay. She let out a deep sigh. And an anguished whisper. "Where were you with your strong arms and kind words when I needed them?"

Which time frame was she referring to? "You mean when you were in Chicago?" They still needed to talk about that time in both of their lives.

"When I was locked up in the pantry." She spoke in that small girl's voice again.

Something gripped him in his chest. "You were locked in the pantry?" That's why she was so angry with her dad? He leaned back enough to see into her gaze. Swept a few strands of hair from her cheeks. A couple of teardrops. "In the dark?"

She nodded slowly.

That explained her nighttime fears. Some of her other insecurities too.

"My punishment. To this day I hate the dark."

"I'm so sorry." He pulled her to him again. Rubbed her back. Wanted to protect her from anything bad ever happening to her again.

"He never came to my rescue." She sniffed. "But you did."

"When did I do that?" He'd wanted to rescue her when she was stuck in Basalt Bay and he was in Florence. Thought he failed epically.

"You rescued me on the peninsula when I came back."

Oh. The day she fell on the rocks and he feared she might slip into the sea before he reached her. So much had happened since then.

"And you rescued me when you landed the skiff on the beach three days ago."

"I finally made it back to you."

"Yes, you did." She touched his cheek, stroking her palm down his whiskered chin. She was initiating contact between them. His heart pounded like heavy rain on a tin roof in his ears. "And now," she whispered.

"Now?"

"Your strong arms around me. Your faithful love. Gentle words. You've rescued me all over again, Judah. How did I ever live those years without you?" She glanced up at him with tears in her eyes, looking at him so sweetly.

"Oh, Pais." He felt humbled. And when her hand stilled on his cheek, her gaze mingling with his, an unexpected bucket of hope poured through him. It took everything within him not to bridge the narrow gap between them and kiss her the way he wanted to for days. Not to push for more than she was ready for. But what if she was ready? What if her shining eyes gazing up at him were proclaiming that she wanted him to kiss her? He leaned his forehead against hers, waiting.

He made the mistake of thinking she was ready before. He didn't want to make the same error again.

When she slipped her arms around his neck, leaned in closer, he thought his heart might stop. Her fingers played softly with his ears and fireworks exploded in his chest. He rested his hands lightly at her waist. Snuggled her closer. He lifted her chin with his finger, still taking this slowly. Watching for any sign that she wanted him to step back, to not kiss her.

"Sometimes a girl needs a hero."

"Yeah?" He heard the husky sound of his voice.

He watched as she glanced at his lips. Into his gaze. Back at his lips. A breath hitched in his throat as she smiled at him the way she

did on their wedding day. Like the world was theirs, just the two of
them in their own perfect bubble, and her gaze invited him to dance
with her.

Just like now.

Oh, Pais. It seemed the earth trembled beneath his, their, feet.

Her lips drew closer to his, maybe an inch away. "Judah?" Her
breath on his mouth was warm, inviting.

"Yes?"

"I've been wanting to tell you something."

"Okay."

"That night when I texted you about Craig—"

Wait. Why was she bringing up that man's name?

Thirty-one

Paisley saw the way Judah squinted at her when she mentioned Craig's name. She hoped she wasn't completely ruining their romantic moment. But she had to revisit the incident, five days ago, when she desperately tried to send Judah a message. "I'm sorry to even say his name, right now, but that night there was something important I wanted you to know."

"Okay." He leaned back slightly.

She smiled up at him. Did he see the love in her heart? That she wanted his kiss, needed it like she needed air, but she felt compelled to say this first.

"What was it, Pais?" His knuckles smoothed down the side of her cheek.

"Before I texted you that it was Craig"—ugh, she mentioned his name again—"I told you something else. A very important secret from my heart to yours."

"What did you tell me?" His words were whisper soft.

She leaned her cheek against his jacket, listening for his heartbeat. There. Strong and steady. She pulled back and gazed into his beautiful blues again. "I texted you . . . that I love you."

"Really?" A wide smile broke across his lips.

"Really."

"All those days ago, you told me you loved me?"

She nodded slowly.

His mouth opened, then closed. He chuckled. His mild-sounding mirth turned into full-on laughter. Then she was laughing too. "Oh, Paisley." He cleared his throat like he was trying to suppress his amusement. "I was so worried that I ruined everything between us by not getting back to you. Why didn't you just tell me when I got here?"

"I thought you knew. When I realized you didn't, I was afraid to tell you. To expose my feelings."

"Ah, c'mere, sweetheart." He pulled her into his arms again. "And now?"

His gaze drew her closer, said she could trust him with her heart.

"Now? I love you, Judah. More than ever."

She heard his small inhalation of breath. Moisture flooded his eyes. The tender look he bestowed on her was so sweet, so magical, she wanted to weep.

Finally, their lips met softly, tentatively, almost like a cautious first kiss. Then, everything she remembered about kissing this man came flooding back to her. Their kiss deepened, becoming more demanding and consuming as each of them expressed the love that was lost to them, then found, incredibly found. Who knew who made the first move? His lips claimed hers with fiery passion, or hers claimed his with wild *deep-blue-sea-in-the-morning* abandon. Either way, her lips were caressing Judah's with all the love in her heart. She was claiming her man, her husband. A kiss of a lifetime. One she'd never forget. One she hoped he'd never forget.

He broke away first, his lips trailing her cheek, her neck. Then he stepped back, his warm gaze dancing with hers, their hands clasped. With a soft groan, he pulled her to him again, his head resting against hers. "Pais, my sweet."

She heard the happiness in his voice, in the way he sighed. She smiled, too ecstatic to do anything else.

They were standing at the edge of town. Basalt was still desolate. Destruction everywhere. But love was taking possession of places in her heart that she once thought dead.

"I love you." His breath still had a little catch in it. "I've waited so long for this. For us. God has answered my prayers."

"Mine too."

She heard quiet whisperings, like he was praying, thanking God for this miracle. She closed her eyes and did the same.

After a while, he spoke. "I know there are still things we need to talk about."

"Like Chicago?"

He nodded. "I need to tell you about the day I went there."

She pulled back. "You went to Chicago?"

"I did." He sighed, seemed slightly troubled.

"I thought you said you bought a ticket but didn't go there."

"I'm sure we both have things we need to say to each other." He blinked slowly, his moist eyes staring back at her.

"True." A few thoughts came to mind. Her reasons for leaving him. Their losses. Her not calling him for three years.

"But first, there's something else I want to say to you." He looked so serious.

"Is there any way it could wait?" She wanted to hold onto this goodness, this loving feeling, a while longer. "I hate throwing cold water on what we just experienced by talking about the past."

"I agree. That's why—" He dug into his coat pocket. With his other hand he clasped her right hand. Slowly, he knelt on one knee on the muddy sidewalk in front of her.

"Judah?" What was he—

"Paisley Rose Grant, will you do me the honor of marrying me again?" He grinned up at her, his blue eyes shining.

She'd imagined them saying vows to each other privately. But this—

"Oh, Judah." She dropped down on both knees in front of him, in the mud. His eyes widened as she closed the gap between them and initiated a deep kiss. There would be no mistake about who started this one. "Judah Edward Grant"—she whispered against his mouth—"yes"—she touched her lips to his one more time—"yes, I will marry you again."

He slipped a ring onto her finger. She held up her hand, amazed by how easily he did that. "Why, it looks just like—"

"I tried to match your other one."

Sadness over the lost ring and intense joy over this gift meshed together, making tears flood her eyes. "I love it. When did you get it?"

"In Florence, before I left." He grimaced, his leg probably aching. They held hands and helped each other stand.

Her knees were mucky and wet, but she didn't care.

"What does this mean?" She stared at the topaz jewel surrounded by clusters of exquisite tiny diamonds. "Do you want to have a real wedding this time?" She thought of their previous elopement. Of her vow to him: *"I promise to love you 'til the end of time."*

"I do. Whenever you're ready."

He was being so sweet. She hated to say anything that might disappoint him. And yet— "I'm sorry to have to mention this, but I sold my wedding set. For rent and food money."

He nodded. Didn't seem upset or saddened. "I figured that might be the case. I got a wedding band for you, too. Your set will still match mine."

She threw her arms around his shoulders. "You're the best husband a girl could wish for."

He chuckled. "A guy could get used to hearing that. I do have one other request."

"What is it?" She gazed into his sparkling eyes.

"I don't want to rush you, but can we have a short engagement?"

She chuckled. His smile was too tempting to ignore. She leaned into his mouth, kissed him again. "Yes, please."

Thirty-two

Pinkies linked, Paisley and Judah walked back toward the center of town, following the hum of engines that sounded like ten motors were going at once. A logging truck rumbled down Front Street with eight or nine trees piled on the flatbed. The giant truck stopped in the middle of the road, and Paisley watched as a long metal arm swung out. The boom crane scooped up the last of the downed trees on the street, dropping them one by one onto the pile.

"Look!" Judah pointed up at a couple of utility poles.

She glanced up. Two linemen stood inside waist-high, cage-like platforms that were extended high into the air from utilities trucks. Two other men had climbed up the poles using spurred climbing boots. Other workers assisted from the ground, hoisting up new wire with the help of long ropes. At the pole they'd been avoiding, a backhoe nudged it upright, while several utilities employees labored to stabilize it.

"They're making progress. Maybe we'll get that coffee before the day's over." Judah pushed a branch out of their way with the toe of his boot.

"Just think, if we can have coffee, then we'll be able to take hot showers, wash our clothes, and eat a cooked meal that doesn't have pumpkin in it." She chuckled.

"Miracles can happen."

"Oh, yes, they can."

They gazed into each other's eyes, and for a moment, she felt lost in his blues, lost in his love. Or maybe at home, finally, here in Basalt with him.

She still needed to face some things. Getting back together with Judah hadn't erased that. But something compelled her to focus on the man beside her. To make amends here. With him.

She glanced at the shining ring on her finger that represented a new beginning for them. A glorious start.

"Listen." Judah tugged on her hand, walked faster in the direction of City Hall.

"What is it? Where are you going?" She matched her speed to his but didn't like where they were headed.

"I heard a horn honk that didn't sound like one of the big rigs." He lifted his free hand, waving at someone. "See! Over there."

Paisley glanced toward the government building across the street. Mayor Grant stood in the parking lot. Was Judah going to tell his father that he proposed to her? Was she ready for that leap back into the Grant family?

A dark gray sedan pulled into the parking lot in front of City Hall. That must have been the car Judah heard honking.

"The road's open!" His voice rose. "Do you know who that is?"

"No." Should she?

Edward walked straight to the car, opened the driver's door. A woman with dark hair stepped out. She leaned into the back doorway, then drew out a young girl with blond hair and held her in her arms.

"Paige?"

"Yep." Judah lifted Paisley's hand with the ring on it. "Can't wait to tell her about this."

Paisley laughed despite her trepidation. This would be the first time she saw her sister in over three years. The last time they spoke they exchanged harsh words. How would Paige feel about seeing her now?

This would also be Paisley's chance to meet Piper. Her heart spasmed with internal thoughts of her own daughter who she missed terribly. Yet, joy flooded her too. She was an auntie. She wanted to meet her niece. Hold her. Play on that swing set with her.

"Paige!" Judah hollered. Waved.

Paige lifted her hand and smiled. Then, as if realizing it was Paisley with him, a troubled look crossed her face. Her hand lowered.

Paisley slowed down. Felt Judah's tug on her hand.

"Wait." She stopped.

Someone else stepped from the shadows of City Hall. A tall man with broad shoulders.

Craig?

She heard Judah's groan.

Craig lumbered forward, a wide smile on his face. He embraced Paige and Piper in a group hug, the way a family would.

Paisley's breath caught in her throat, choking her.

Craig leaned in and kissed Paige, whether on the mouth or her cheek Paisley couldn't tell from here.

She felt Judah squeeze her hand. He didn't know about this, did he?

Craig took up the child in his arms, bouncing her. The little girl who looked like a cute dolly giggled, patted both his cheeks as if that were the most natural thing for her to do.

A horrible glug settled in the middle of Paisley's stomach. Her jaw seemed to hit the ground. She glanced at Judah. He had the same disbelief on his face.

Was Craig Piper's father?

If you enjoyed *Sea of Rescue*, or mostly enjoyed it, please take a minute and write a review wherever you purchased this book. They say reviews are the lifeblood for authors. Even one line telling what you liked or thought about the book is so helpful. Thank you!

About Basalt Bay:

I took many creative liberties with Basalt Bay, my imaginary town on the Oregon Coast. To all those who live nearby, please forgive my embellishments. I enjoy the Pacific Ocean and the Oregon Coast so much that I wanted to create my own little world there.

If you would like to be one of the first to hear about Mary's new releases and upcoming projects, sign up for her newsletter—and receive the free pdf "Rekindle Your Romance! 50+ Date Night Ideas for Married Couples" at www.maryehanks.com/gift

I want to say a heartfelt *"Thank you!"* to everyone who helped with this story.

Paula McGrew . . . Thank you for your editorial critique and for helping me deepen the characters and the plot. I appreciate your comments and encouragement so much.

Suzanne Williams . . . Thank you for taking on my cover ideas, and for being willing to tell me when something doesn't work. By doing that, you made this design more beautiful than I imagined.

Jason Hanks . . .Thanks for being my sounding board and for helping with mechanical questions. And thanks for encouraging me to follow my dreams.

Kathy Vancil, Kellie Wanke, Mary Acuff, Beth McDonald, Joanna Brown, and Jason Hanks . . . Thank you for being A+ beta readers. You each found different things to encourage, challenge, and critique with this story. I love that! Thank you for saying "Yes" to being beta readers for me.

Hanna Hanks . . . Thank you for critiquing and offering advice about the medical intervention in this tale. I know you were busy, yet you took the time to help me out. Thank you!

(This story is a work of fiction. Any mistakes are my very own! ~meh)

Daniel, Philip, Deborah, & Shem . . . For all the days of my life, you are my dreams come true. Traci, my first daughter-in-law, thanks for being a part of our tribe and putting up with our shenanigans.

www.maryehanks.com

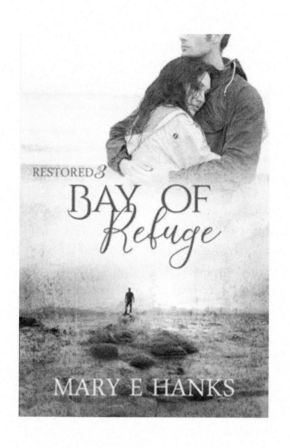

Bay of Refuge

Restored 3

Mary E. Hanks

Suzanne D. Williams Cover Design

www.feelgoodromance.com/

Cover photos: micromonkey @ iStock; vernonwiley @ iStock

Visit Mary's website:

www.maryehanks.com

You can write Mary at

maryhanks@maryehanks.com.

For Charles,

aka Dad or Lanny,

Thank you for accepting my brothers and me as your own and
loving us.

For Jason,

You are still the one.

God is our refuge and strength, an ever-present help in trouble.

Psalm 94:19

One

Paisley Grant clutched Judah's hand as she watched her sister, Paige, and Craig Masters standing across the street acting like a happy couple, or a family for that matter, until she couldn't bear to watch them anymore. She'd rather have saltwater poured into her eyes or be imprisoned in the pantry staring at her mother's ghastly abstract paintings than to see Paige with *that* man.

But what if they were married? What if Craig was the father of Paige's two-year-old daughter, Piper?

A bitter taste filled Paisley's mouth. She pivoted away from the scene in front of City Hall and glanced at Judah, her previously estranged husband with whom she was reconciling. Could he comprehend the horror she felt at the thought of Craig being her brother-in-law? How could she cope with the cad showing up at family gatherings? Christmas dinners? Ugh. Of course, Judah had his own grievances with the guy.

She glanced back as Craig tossed Piper into the air, then caught her. Piper squealed. Paige smiled up at Craig with such a sweet, loving expression that Paisley wanted to gag.

Even though it wasn't hot, her forehead dripped with sweat. Her lungs seemed to shrink into themselves, starving her of air. Why did her respiratory system rebel against her? Why couldn't she breathe while under duress the way normal people did?

Maybe she should leave Basalt instead of staying here. Why torment herself? If she kept living in this small town like she originally planned, how could she avoid Paige and Craig? How could she ignore the gossip that would circulate about them? Everyone knew everyone's business.

Exactly. Didn't her sister hear the rumors about Craig and Paisley running away together, three years ago? Hadn't the town's gossipmongers prattled about it within Paige's hearing? The tales were lies, but her sister should have recognized Craig as a man not to be trusted. Someone to avoid in the co-parenting department.

Although, anyone could be blindsided by kindness, right? Even Paisley had been taken off guard when Craig jumped in and helped with Dad's high blood sugar incident four days ago. He may have even saved Dad's life and, in doing so, almost convinced her of his sincerity. *Almost.*

Just thinking of how she had to coexist with Craig during that dreadful time caused tension to strangle her airway. Her inhalation became raspy. A burning sensation crawled up her breastbone. A familiar weight of anxiety pressed down on her chest. She snagged Judah's gaze. *"Help!"* she tried to communicate.

"You okay?" He slid his arm over her shoulder and pulled her to his side.

His closeness, his caring attitude, should have reassured her that everything would be okay. That they could face whatever life threw their way together. Instead, she gritted her teeth and fought the urge to call for a Lyft to transport her away from Basalt. Maybe go to Florence or Coos Bay. But turning her back on him a second time? Hurting him when they just reconnected, when only today she promised to marry him again? He didn't deserve that. She wasn't heartless, either, no matter what her dad said about her being good at running.

In fact, his accusation from earlier made her want to stay and prove him wrong. That's right! New resolve coursed through her. No way was she leaving. She'd stand her ground and show Dad,

Judah, and everyone else in this small-minded town that she came back to make things right.

Inhale. Exhale.

As if he sensed her panic, Judah wrapped both of his arms around her and pulled her against his chest. She pressed her cheek next to his sweatshirt, closing her eyes to the scene she was appalled and mesmerized by. She breathed in his warmth and pleasant male scent. He held her to him, not saying anything, just stroking her back. Mumbling something, maybe praying.

Was it only an hour ago when he dropped to his knee in the mud and asked her to marry him again? And she joined him on the sidewalk, kissing him like a woman wildly in love. Her world felt righted. God smiled on her. She and Judah were better together than they ever would be apart—that's what he told her, right?

But then *this* happened. Paige and Craig and Piper. But wouldn't there always be a *this*? Life was a sea of turbulence with trials, problems, and regrets hitting her like waves crashing into the rocks. While she succumbed to fear and panic, how did everyone else cope? She took a deep breath, trying to rein in her focus and her crazy, mixed-up emotions.

She leaned back and noticed a troubled expression on Judah's face. Was he avoiding her gaze? Why? He didn't know about Paige and Craig before today, did he? What if he knew all along and didn't tell her? No, surely not. But what if—?

She staggered backward. Her skin felt on fire. She set her palm on her chest, unable to draw in a full breath.

"Paisley?" His face contorted. "What is it? What can I do?" He tugged on her arms as if to draw her closer to him again. Like that would solve everything. *If only.*

She shook her head, holding out her free hand for him to stay back.

"Paisley? Do you hear me?" His words sounded tinny and far away.

She glanced toward City Hall again. Paige took the little girl from Craig's arms and pointed in their direction.

478 Mary E. Hanks

"Unca Dzuda!" Piper pulsed her hand, lunging her body up and down while somehow managing to remain in her mother's arms.

Judah waved and smiled. He seemed so accepting and nonjudgmental. Far from how she felt.

The engagement ring slid down her finger, and she twisted it back and forth. She fell for Judah again so quickly during the chaos of the hurricane and Dad's illness. Was she too hasty? She swallowed hard. No, she wasn't having second thoughts. She wanted to marry him. Loved him.

It was just …

A tightness in her stomach raced headlong into her chest, strangling her throat, pinching her esophagus like seaweed caught around the prop of an outboard. She sucked in dry, useless air, needing more oxygen. Maybe if she went to the beach, got away from Craig and Paige—Judah, too, if only for a few minutes—and breathed in the sea air, she'd feel better.

"I'm sorry. I just—" She turned away and rushed down the muddy sidewalk, dodging debris left over from Hurricane Blaine, hoping Judah didn't hate her for running from him. Her boots slipped in the few inches of dirty water lingering on the street from the storm surge. She didn't acknowledge any of the utility workers who were laboring over electrical wires and mending telephone poles.

"Paisley!"

Judah wouldn't be able to keep up with her with his bum leg. Although, even she couldn't run as fast as normal with her struggling oxygen intake. She nearly tripped going down the boulders to the beach below street level.

Once she reached the sand, she trudged along at a steady pace. To her left, the waves pounded the beach, crashing against the rocks. Beyond the cove, a fishing boat chugged past. On the peninsula, sea-foam exploded in pulsating repetitions and, as if they had a homing instinct, her boots turned in that direction.

"Paisley! Wait up."

She pushed herself to stay ahead of him, leaping over and around the surf dancing up and down the seashore. The closer she got to *Peter's Land*, the rocky point she dubbed in honor of her brother as a kid, the easier she breathed. Her lungs expanded naturally. The sea air was healthy for her. Another reason to stay in Basalt, right?

A few hours ago, Judah suggested that they come down to the peninsula and check on it. Although he said they wouldn't walk on it, nothing was stopping her from reaching her destination now. Not Judah's voice. Not even her own inner warning system telling her that it might be dangerous.

Sitting on the tip of the peninsula with seawater bursting over her might be exactly what she needed. Maybe then she could figure out how to live around her sister and Craig without going mad.

The idyllic beauty of the ocean usually filled her with peace. Would that happen today?

Two

Judah stomped down the beach after Paisley, but he couldn't keep up, thanks to his limp. Not that his reaching her any sooner would stop her from doing what she seemed determined to do. But he wanted to be with her in case something bad happened. Like her fainting, again, or slipping on the wet rocks.

In her haste to reach the point of the peninsula, she probably wasn't considering that the long, narrow land mass was unstable after Hurricane Blaine. No one should charge past the gaping holes left by the storm six days ago. Yet, he witnessed her panic. He knew she'd seek sanctuary on the unsafe boulders. And even if he yelled her name until his face turned as gray as a sea lion's, she wouldn't listen to him.

How they went from kissing, talking about a vow renewal ceremony, to her running from him as if he were at fault for the situation back there with Craig and Paige, he didn't get. *Women.* He tromped around a tidal pool, chewing on his agitation.

If only she ran to him instead of away from him. If only she could find refuge in their love. What husband didn't want to be an anchor for his wife to depend on? Sure, being her North Star, her everything, would feed his ego. Might make him feel better about himself after their three-year separation, and all that may or may not have happened in Chicago that they still hadn't discussed.

He groaned.

But she needed far more than his inflated male ego and his desire for her to want him. She needed healing and restoration and a peace only God could give. She needed a Savior. Something Judah could never be. Never wanted to be. But that didn't stop him from wishing he was the one she leaned on, the one she desired as a husband, and not the one she ran from.

He stepped over a chunk of driftwood, not breaking his stride, and watched his wife scurrying down the beach. Maybe his father-in-law was correct about his daughter being good at running. At the time, he sounded heartless. Now Judah wondered. Thinking of Paisley being a runaway bride was torture. Would she keep doing this? His footfall stumbled. Should he keep chasing after her?

Ugh.

Of course, he would. He was her husband, legally and at heart. He loved her. Hadn't he asked her to marry him again? He'd follow her to the ends of the earth or Chicago or wherever she might run until she sprinted back into his arms. But how long would it be until she embraced him as her husband?

A pain burned in his chest that had more to do with his emotions than the way he pushed himself to trudge through the sand on his sore leg. He stepped wide to avoid crushing a crab scuttling for shelter. Running from him too? Did he have that effect on everyone? He groaned again.

Not far ahead, Paisley reached the cluster of boulders extending into the cove and climbed upward. If something happened, it would take him precious minutes to get out to the point.

She'd tell him he was being silly for worrying. That after living here for twenty-five years, she knew her way around the coastal rocks. Still, the boulders were slick from saltwater pouring over them. Although, not any slicker than last time. *Last time?* A breath caught in his throat. That day she fainted, and he barely got to her in time. He pushed himself to go faster.

There, she reached the top and seemed steady. A surge of waves barreled against the peninsula, bursting water and froth into the air.

For the slightest second, she glanced back, a hint of a smile on her lips. He held his breath as she skirted the gaping places where large boulders that he labeled Samples C and D for his reports had been before the hurricane. Just as she reached the farthest point, where narrow rocks extended into the sea, white spray erupted into the air and fell over her like a waterfall. The scene looked magical, but he knew the dangers.

He reached the pile of boulders and clambered up. Since he'd been climbing these rocks for a couple of decades, he instinctively knew where to place the soles of his boots.

Out on the point, Paisley dropped down onto what he knew to be her favorite perch on a chunk of basalt. Even from here, he saw the waves rolling up, splashing onto her lap.

He braced himself as he climbed, battling wind gusts that nearly knocked him backwards. He stretched his hands out, balancing himself. Once he reached the top of the peninsula, he headed toward the point. "Paisley!" He yelled so she'd hear him over the sound of the surf.

She glanced back, met his gaze for a half-second. A foaming, powerful wave crashed against the rock she sat on. Water splashed over her, arcing and cascading downward. She lifted both hands into the spray of saltwater, laughing. A dazzling array of droplets shimmered in the sunlight around her. The beautiful, mesmerizing sight made him pause.

With her hands uplifted, water pouring over her, he felt drawn to her like steel to a magnet. She was the woman he wanted to be with for the rest of his life. He'd do anything to bridge the gap between them, to make her feel safe, and to help her life be better. Starting with staying by her side. Mentally, he fortified himself for getting soaking wet and freezing cold in the next few steps.

"I'm going to sit by you now." He warned her so she didn't get startled when he dropped down beside her on the narrow place.

Another blast of water showered over her as Judah came closer, soaking him too. He gasped, even though he told himself to be ready for it. He lowered himself next to her as another icy spray cascaded over them. He inhaled sharply.

Paisley swiped seawater off her face. "Isn't this amazing?"

"Uh-huh." Judah blinked hard to rid his eyeballs of the sting of saltwater. He shuffled closer to her, making sure he didn't slip and pull her into the drink with him. "How are you?" he asked when the waves receded.

"Better now."

"Glad to hear it." He took a risk and draped his arm over her shoulder. He wanted to keep her safe, but he also needed ballast for his precarious position. They sat for a few minutes with the sea dancing about them. Each rush of water felt a little less frigid and invasive. Either he was adapting to the chill of waves splashing over him, or his body had become numb to the jarring cold.

Paisley leaned against him as if drawing warmth from him and into herself. Water droplets running down her face, she met his gaze. Her deep dark eyes sparkling in his direction made him want to lean in and kiss her. He didn't, but he wanted to.

"I'm sorry for running from you."

Her words soothed the ache in his chest. "You're with me now. That's all that matters." Even if it meant getting drenched and shivering with ridiculous tremors. He clenched his teeth to stop them from chattering. Hardly effective.

"Did you know about Paige and Craig? Before, I mean."

It was difficult to hear her over the sounds of the surf.

"What? No. Of course not. Paisley, I couldn't believe they were together."

She stared at him for several heartbeats. He held her gaze, hoping she knew she could trust him. Another wave hit them. They both gasped and sputtered.

"I thought maybe you knew and kept it from me."

"Why would I do that? I thought Craig and Mia might be together."

"Why?"

"The way she giggles when she talks about him." Although, the receptionist for Coastal Management and Emergency Responders— called C-MER—acted flirtatious toward Judah, too. Good thing he already told Paisley about that.

"I couldn't stand it." She gazed toward open waters. "Seeing my sister with the man who—" She coughed then buried her face in his sweatshirt. She trembled in his arms. He held her but, due to his soaked condition, couldn't offer her much warmth.

Another spray arched over them and he closed his eyes. Lifting his face, droplets fell on his cheeks. When he opened his eyelids and brushed the moisture away, Paisley watched him.

"Thank you."

"For what?"

"For following me. Even when I thought I didn't want you to. Even when I pushed you away."

At least she realized she did that. If only she grasped how much he wanted them to be together, sharing their lives. Yet, her propensity to run was disconcerting. Something for him to pray about in the coming days.

Three

After another saltwater shower, Paisley shook her head to clear her ears and face of water. She met Judah's gaze, feeling calmer now. Drenched, but calmer. "Thanks for staying with me. For not pummeling me with advice. I get enough of that from Aunt Callie."

"And Maggie Thomas." He wiped his left hand over his wet dripping hair. "What advice would I have? I don't know what you're going through."

"Exactly."

"But—"

"No, don't ruin it!" But her curiosity got the better of her. "Okay. But what?"

He gave her one of his sweet smiles. The kind that curled her toes in her boots. He stroked his cool palm down her wet cheek, his gaze holding hers captive. She didn't move.

"I wish—" Water dripped from Judah's hair, rolling down his face and landing in his six-day-old beard. His pale cheeks looked concave from the cold. He licked his bluish lips, which made her think back to when they kissed such a short time ago. "Okay."

"Okay?" Did she miss something?

"I wish ... when you felt the urge to run ... you'd find strength and courage in me, your husband. The man who loves you more than any person in the world." He swallowed like doing so hurt. "I'm here for you, Pais. Honest, I am. But I'm no superhero. I'll make

Mary E. Hanks

mistakes." More water crashed over them. "But I promise you …
I'm going to be by your side, doing the best I can for you as long as
we both shall live." His words sounded like vows.

A spray of water hit them, splashing into their faces. They both
spat and sputtered.

His words replayed in her mind. Wait. Did he think she expected
him to mend their past? To fix them. Of course, he couldn't. Even
she couldn't do that. Hadn't she tried? At least, he was being honest
and real about their flaws. About her need for more than he could
offer.

He said he wanted her to run to him, but was he strong enough
to hear her heart? Her struggles? What if the doubts and failings she
wrestled with drove them further apart? Maybe she could show him
that she was trying to reach out to him, too, by sharing something
honest and being vulnerable. That's what he wanted, right?

She cleared her throat. "When I saw Paige with Craig, I wanted
to get away from them, away from my thoughts and anxieties. I'm
sorry, but part of me still wants to run."

He let out a long sigh. Perhaps, an accepting sigh.

"I thought of heading south and going somewhere on the coast."
She wiped seawater off her face. "I never want to be far from the
Pacific again. Maybe Coos Bay."

"Paisley." He groaned.

She clenched her jaw. How could she be honest with him if she
couldn't talk about the deepest parts of her soul? Her fears, grief,
and even her urge to run.

She imagined a set in a movie with a closet so crammed full of
junk that when the actor opened it, the items exploded into the
room. Just like what her hidden emotions might do if they were ever
exposed. Maybe that's why she ran three years ago and why she
wanted to run now—to escape the truths and lies she stuffed away
for so long.

Could she remarry Judah and jump back into the same existence
she ran from? She found such joy in falling in love with him again.
In reveling in his kisses. Imagining their honeymoon. But in her

honest-to-goodness life, could a Cedars and a Grant have a forever kind of happiness? It didn't work before. Were they making a terrible mistake again? Anxiety twisted knots in her stomach. She had to move, or run, or—

"I have to go." She jumped up.

"Paisley?" Her name sounded wrenched from his lips. Raw pain zagged across his face. "You're not ... not going to leave me again, are you?"

She told herself she wouldn't. "I was a horrible wife to you before." She shuddered at the picture of her midnight escape. "You don't deserve the same fate." She yanked off the diamond ring and held it out between her trembling thumb and index finger. The shock and agony on his face made her ashamed. "I'm so sorry." Why did she agree to his proposal? She could have saved him this misery. Her too. "You're a good man. I'm the one who's messed up. I can't drag you through another marriage. Through another possible failed r-romance."

"You are n-not a horrible w-wife. Never." He clasped her free hand. "W-we went through a crisis. We both lost our footing. I want you back. You!"

His humility, his not blaming her, his still wanting her, was tender and beautiful. Yet her fingers continued to extend the engagement ring.

He wobbled to a standing position on the rocks beside her. "I want you as you are, Paisley. We still love each other." He laid his palms on her cheeks, staring into her eyes.

Oh, Judah. Love wasn't the issue. How to live as husband and wife, talking heart to heart, exposing the deepest parts of themselves without judgment or rejection, that's what they failed at.

He dropped his hands, closing them around her fingers clutching the ring. He probably feared it might fall into the ocean. She didn't want that, either.

"Please, keep it. Give us time. Everything's going to work out, you'll see." His facial expression relaxed.

She almost agreed, but then another round of waves burst over

Mary E. Hanks

them. She slid the ring back onto her finger. Better safe than falling into Davy Jones's Locker.

"Don't make a hasty decision and break up with me because you're upset with Paige." He shouted over the noise of the wind and waves.

His words felt like a slap. He assumed she was ending their engagement because of her sister's stupid decisions? Her core heated up. Inner fumes raced to her temples.

She jerked backwards. Too late she realized what she did.

Four

Judah watched in horror as Paisley tripped over a rock and fell backwards into the sea. "Paisley!" He lunged for her flailing hands but missed her fingers. In seconds she disappeared beneath the churning waves.

He screamed her name again and fought to remove his boots. His frozen hands made his movements clumsy. Where was she? When she didn't bob to the surface, he took a deep breath and executed a shallow dive into the waves. Frigid water encapsulated him like an icy tomb, leeching the warmth from his body. He froze, rebelling against the cold. But he forced himself to swim, begging his limbs to obey, and fought the current. He surfaced and gasped, drawing in gulps of air. Not seeing her, he plunged into the darkness again.

He couldn't recognize anything beneath the surface. Only blurry, nonhuman shadows. How far did the undertow take her? He kicked and flailed his arms, thrusting his hands outward, desperate to touch her hair or clothing. He didn't feel anything but churning water rushing past him. In desperate need of air, he lunged for the surface again. Gasping in great gulps of air, he bobbed in circles, searching the troughs of waves where a person might be hidden. He floated on a crest, then got thrown backward by the powerful tug of the surf.

He ignored the freezing, gnawing cold and kept thrashing about in the sea, constantly moving as he hunted for her. "Paisley!" A mouthful of saltwater gagged him. He coughed and nearly choked. He shouted again. Just about to dive beneath the roiling waves, he heard a sound. A voice.

"J-u-u-d-d-a-ah."

He turned around 180 degrees, following the direction where he thought he heard her. A swell crashed over him, submerging him, blinding him. Was that his one chance to find her? No! He couldn't lose her. He kicked frantically, begging God in silent pleas. *Save her. Help me find her.*

Some twenty feet away, her hand bobbed into the air. But then, the bubbling sea swallowed her. He swam the breaststroke harder than he ever had, his breathing raspy as his arms and legs sliced through the water. With each arm rotation he combatted the waves, the frigid cold, and his fears. *I will find her. She will be safe. God, help us!* He repeated the phrases in time to the throbbing of his heart. As he swam, his weighted clothes pulled him downward as if dragging him to the ocean floor. He wouldn't succumb. Would battle to reach his wife and save her.

Was that—? Yes, blue fabric. Her sweatshirt. It disappeared. A mirage? An optical trick? No, he saw something. "Paisley! Hold on!"

Despite his exhaustion, he swam toward her, hammering the surface with his arms and kicking his legs until his limbs felt numb. Useless.

He raised his head and took a breath. There she was! Not far away, she floated on her back, her arms crossed over her chest. Hallelujah! It was a good thing she knew the basics of survival in the sea. That it didn't take extreme cold to get hypothermia—just colder than normal body temperature. If Judah felt the sluggish weight in his limbs, she had to feel it worse since she had been underwater longer than him.

The next time he glanced up, she jerked, her hands flailing, then she vanished into a wretched whirlpool like a monster yanked her feet straight down beneath her.

"Paaaaaaisssssleeeey!"

With the peninsula jutting into the bay, opposing currents sometimes created a dangerous powerhouse of swirling water capable of dragging a victim into its vortex. How would he pull her out? He didn't have lifesaving gear. No one lined the beach to help with forming a human chain.

Paisley's life depended on his quick action. And God's intervention. *Please.*

He swam straight into the churning waters. At the outer boundary of the bubbling cylindrical shape, the downward pull nearly tore off his pants. The swirling whirlpool jerked him, yanking and twisting him, a prisoner in its clutches. Terror pressed in on him, squeezing him, as the sea yanked him downward. Could he even survive? Was he too late to rescue Paisley?

Fighting the crushing forces, he flung his hands outward, searching for her. But the monstrous ocean hurled him in circles, trouncing him like a broken toy. Down he went, deeper into the dregs of the whirlpool, a mountain of water almost overpowering him. Soon he wouldn't be able to hold the breath in his mouth. His air gone. *Lord Jesus.*

Then thud. He rammed into something. Someone. Before he could grab hold of hair or limbs, she was snatched away—it had to be her. *Paisley! My love.* He flailed his hands and kicked his feet. There. Hair. Face. Fingers. He wanted to sob but couldn't. He grabbed hold of her body, none too gently, clenching his limbs around her limp form like an octopus.

He tried to feel her neck for a pulse. An impossibility. He must get her to the surface. But going straight up into the whirlpool would be deadly. They had to go even deeper, which could also be fatal. He let go of her with one hand, then shoved his palm upward against the sea, repeating the motion, pressing against the waters, forcing them lower into the ocean.

His head felt like it might explode from the pressure. Then, sensing a reprieve from the whirling oppressive monster, he lurched sideways, still holding Paisley and kicking with all his might. He prayed he wouldn't let go of her, begging God to save them and for his air to last.

Once they were far enough out from the whirlpool's grasp, he kicked hard to the surface. *Hold on. We're almost there.* He broke free of the water, coughing and gasping, drawing in ragged breaths. Air never tasted so sweet.

"Paisley!" Still limp. He pressed his fingers against her neck, kicking to keep them afloat. There, a pulse, maybe. He had to get her to shore. The waves were too rough to perform lifesaving procedures. He rolled onto his back, drawing her with him, as water splashed over them. He swam as hard as he could with one hand and held onto her with the other. His energy failing, he let his body ride the waves toward the peninsula.

Suddenly, she jerked and gasped, shoving against his chest. *Thank God!* She was alive! She coughed and vomited, but he held her and kept swimming toward shore. When she swung her elbows, fighting him as if he were the enemy dragging her to her death, he called out to her. "It's m-me, P-Paisley. I've got you."

"I c-can swim on my own. Let go." She glared back at him. "Let go of me."

She looked so pale. Every protective fiber within him balked at the idea of releasing her. If she swam on her own, she might get dragged back into the whirlpool.

"L-let g-go, Judah!" She kicked him, her legs getting tangled with his.

"Okay. But I'm staying right beside you." She went unconscious before. It might happen again. Did she have hypothermia? He'd watch her closely. "If you feel too weak, hold onto me."

She gave him a slight nod.

Together, side by side, they swam toward the northwest side of the peninsula. The pounding waves propelled them forward, almost too fast. At the last second, he wrapped his arms around her to shield her from getting dashed against the rocks. She crawled onto the shore on her hands and knees, the water pounding over her. She collapsed on the rocks, panting. Her dark eyes stared at him dully as he climbed up beside her.

"You okay?" His legs shook. So did his shoulders and arms. He collapsed beside her, gasping and spitting and breathing hard.

She closed her eyes.

"Paisley, stay awake!" He smoothed his hand over her face, feeling her cold clammy skin against his fingers. "Paisley, stay with me, please." His insides felt ragged, his lungs burning from the physical strain he endured, and his heart aching from the emotional turmoil of nearly losing her. "Pais?" He rubbed her shoulder gently.

"I'm okay."

"Thank God. I'm so glad you're okay."

"M-me t-too."

Now to get her warm and dry. Where were his boots? He needed his boots. He checked around the rocks. Didn't see them. The waves must have dragged them out to sea. Great. Now he had to walk to Paige's, carrying Paisley, in his drenched socks. Or barefooted. He was exhausted too. But he'd do whatever was necessary to get her to warmth and safety.

She still lay on the rocks, her body shivering. Placing his hand on her back, he felt it rise and fall slowly. Even with shallow breaths, hearing her inhaling and exhaling comforted him. "Pais? Can you hear me?"

She didn't answer.

He ran through the list of hypothermia markers. Shivering. Slurred speech. She had stuttered. Shallow breathing. Yep. Weak pulse. He touched two fingers to her neck. Slow. She was drowsy and energy-less. Lost consciousness in the water. Confusion? Maybe. To be on the safe side, he'd move her gently so as not to trigger irregular heartbeats that could bring on cardiac arrest.

"Paisley, we have to find warmth. You need to get dry."

She squinted like the sun was too bright, instead of seeing the gray overcast sky above them.

"D-did you f-fall in?" She pointed at his socks leaving a trail of wetness.

Didn't she remember? Confusion. Memory loss. Check. Check. He needed to get her to Paige's fast. Maybe take her to the ER. "C'mon, Pais, stand up. No sudden movements."

She lifted her head in increments. As her torso came off the rock, he wrapped his arms around her, pulling her against his chest.

"You're cold and w-wet." She shivered.

"Both of us are." He gritted his teeth to stop them from chattering. A wind gust hit them, and he held onto her.

"*Thatssss fuuunny.*"

"What is?"

"The air *blowwwing upmynossse.*" She slurred the words together.

"Can you walk?" If not, how would he carry her across the rocky peninsula without tripping in his socks? Hefting her over his shoulder might endanger her more. "If you can't walk, I'll carry you. But you should try walking on your own."

"I can w-walk, *silllly.*" She snorted.

"You're wet and freezing. You might have—" No use alarming her. Taking her right hand with his right hand, he led her forward while he kept his left arm braced across her back.

Fortunately, he took a proactive stance. She stumbled a couple of times. Once, she would have landed back in the water if he wasn't guiding her. They trudged slowly across the rocks. He shook so hard he couldn't walk straight, but she trembled even worse. Something fierce gripped him inside his chest. He had to protect her, keep her safe.

Just as they reached the parking lot, she went limp, almost sinking to the ground. He caught her and scooped her up. His footfall somewhat unsteady, he kept his stride aimed toward the subdivision where blankets and dry clothes awaited.

"W-where you t-taking m-me?" She squinted at him.

"Paige's."

"No." She swayed in his arms, fighting his hold. "*Pleeeeassssse,* no."

"We have to get to Paige's. Our stuff is there."

"I *donnntwanna* go there." She made a moaning sound. She slid from his arms, pushing her palms against him. She wobbled, nearly falling over, but he held onto her. "That way to m-my d-dad's." She pointed a shaking finger toward town.

"We have to change our clothes at your sister's." He tugged on her hand, leading her with him. He felt the stitches in his leg pinch. His limbs must be getting more sensation into them now.

"I w-want t-to go to my dad's." Teeth chattering, she clutched the fabric of his sweatshirt. "Please, Judah?"

How could he refuse her anything after what they'd just experienced? "Fine. But it will be a longer walk." During the storm, the stairs exploded at Paul's. How would he get up to the second story to get clothes and blankets?

He scooped her up again.

"Judah—"

"Just stay quiet." He heard the gruff tone of his voice, but it couldn't be helped. He was fatigued and worried. Carrying her was the safest way to get her to Paul's.

His wet pant legs rubbed against each other as he passed the community church. His dripping socks hung off his toes by a couple of inches. In his arms, Paisley's frame shook. She hadn't spoken in a while. "Paisley." He jostled her in his arms. "You awake?"

She groaned. At least she was conscious enough to respond.

Tonight, he'd monitor her breathing and make sure she warmed up slowly. The old method of using a naked body to warm up a victim with low body temperature crept through his mind. From his C-MER training, he knew a patient with mild hypothermia should warm up with passive rewarming, not with direct heat. He would search for thick blankets. Borrow some from James Weston, Paul's neighbor, if he had to.

If her condition worsened, he'd drive her to the ER in Florence. Or, now that the road was accessible, he could call for an emergency vehicle. Since they still didn't have electricity, he'd plug his cell phone into the truck's lighter ASAP.

When they reached the house, he would have to do something Paisley might not like—might even be mad about. His first task was getting her out of her wet clothes.

Then he'd start warming her up.

Five

Paisley was stuck in a horrible dream. The ocean kept grabbing her, twisting her, sucking her down into a dark whirling tunnel. Then it hurled her body along the waves like a bouncing ball. The nightmare played over and over until she awoke with a start. Breathing heavily, she thrashed her arms, fighting whatever held her down. She clawed at the fabric around her body but couldn't free herself. Where was she? She stared wide-eyed at the ceiling. Dad's?

What pinned her arms? Did the sea mummify her? She glanced downward at what appeared to be swaddling blankets. Even her head was wrapped in a cocoon of some sort. The only exposed part was her face. The blanket brushed against her bare skin on her legs and stomach. She drew in a breath. Bare skin? Where were her clothes? Who took them off?

Inside the blankets, she skimmed her palms down her torso. Warm skin. Damp underwear. Whew. At least she still wore her panties and bra. She rotated her shoulders in the cramped space. Just barely able to wiggle her fingers and toes, it appeared everything worked. Why was she in her dad's living room? She couldn't remember anything after—

Oh. She fell into the sea. Was drowning. Swallowing water. Judah rescued her. Brought her here because she didn't want to go to Paige's. Then what?

The mattress rocked beneath her like a rowboat adrift on the ocean. Must be an air mattress. She turned her head to the left and found Judah's blue eyes staring back at her. All but his face was covered up, too.

"How are you?" His voice sounded scratchy.

Why were they sharing the same bed? "Are we married?" Did they have their vow renewal ceremony and she forgot? They planned to wait—she knew that much.

"Of course, we're married." He smiled in a lazy way. "I married you seven years ago, remember? You're still my wife."

"But, um, not again? We didn't—"

"Not yet." His grin infuriated her.

She huffed. "Then why are you in bed with me?"

"Would you have me sleep on the floor?"

"Maybe."

He snickered. The air mattress swayed up and down as he rotated onto his side. "How are you this morning, other than inquisitive?"

"Grumpy. Tired." And, yes, curious. She eased her hands upward until they reached beyond the blankets. "I feel like a mummy."

"Me too." His cheek rested on his pillow. The way his gaze danced, she half expected him to lean in and kiss her good morning. "Do you remember anything about yesterday?" He stared at her intently. Maybe checking her pupils.

"Um, you asked me to marry you."

"Yes, I did." His smile grew wider.

"I ... I kissed you." The words caught in her throat. If their kissing only happened in her dreams, she'd be so embarrassed for mentioning it.

"Yes"—the word came out breathy—"you did. And?"

"Paige and Craig ..." The thoughts she tried to escape yesterday flooded back. "I ran from them. From you." She scrunched up her shoulders. "I had a bad dream about the ocean trying to kill me." She attempted to sit up, but the blankets pinned her down. Then she remembered her lack of clothing. "Did you undress me?"

"I had to." He explained about the rescue and his borrowing the air mattress from James. "Can you wiggle your toes?"

"Yes, I tested them."

"Fingers?" He wiggled his.

"Yep."

"Good. We survived another crisis." He sighed. "The Lord rescued you again."

"Apparently, He used you."

Judah's face hued red.

"I don't remember you taking off my things. What about your clothes?"

"Came off too."

So they were lying side by side, both nearly naked, and she hadn't even known?

"I was a complete gentleman."

"Hmm. Any plans for getting our dry stuff?"

"James will bring over a ladder." Judah nodded toward the ceiling. "Then I'll go up and dig around for some warm things."

"Good." She tried sitting up again but fell back on the mattress. "Can you help me?" This was ridiculous not being able to move on her own steam.

"Sure." He bobbed to a sitting position, wiggling the whole mattress as he freed himself. The blankets fell away from his bare chest.

She stared at the dark hair on his upper torso before tearing her gaze away. Goodness. She saw him without a shirt before. However, by her sudden heart palpitations, she might be more ready for their vow renewal ceremony than she realized. Or maybe that dip in the sea and Judah's rescue made her a little lovesick.

Sliding his hand beneath her back, he lifted her upper body with his arm. She folded in half like a taco. "Ugh."

He unwound some of the blankets, stopping before she became too exposed. She weakly clutched the blue fabric about herself, lacking energy. Lying back down seemed the smartest thing to do.

"You okay?"

His concerned expression brought back a memory. Real or a dream? She glanced at her hand, relieved to see the engagement ring. Why did she think it might be gone?

"I wondered if I lost your ring." She thought of it as his ring. Not necessarily hers. She gave up her ring a few years ago to pay the rent in Chicago. He was a sweetheart to give her another one.

"I asked you to put it back on." He stared at the wall across from them.

"Back on?"

He wrapped a blanket around his shoulders, covering his chest. "You wanted to give it back. End things between us."

"No way. Why would I do that?"

"You panicked again." His eyebrows dipped. "You thought we wouldn't work a second time when things ended badly the first time."

"Oh, Judah." Some hazy part of her memory lined up with his rendition of yesterday's troubles.

He scooted to the edge of the mattress with the blanket wrapped around him. "You asked why I'm beside you in bed. I watched and made sure you breathed okay through the night."

"You watched over me all night?" Her face flushed.

"Off and on. I checked your pulse. Made sure the blankets were snug." He stretched his eyes, squinting, then blinking. "Around four, I dozed off." He yawned.

And she planned to break things off with this man who dove into the water to save her? The same one who risked his life to find her. What if he hadn't been willing to do that? She could be dead. Might be if not for the guy sitting in her bed with blankets draped about him.

"You are something, Judah Grant." Heaven forgive her selfishness. Ever since she came back to Basalt, this man had loved her, shown her grace and goodness. How could she consider walking away? Return his ring? What a crazy notion. "I'm sorry for trying to give you back the ring."

His eyes filled with moisture. "I just want us." His hand left his blanket and found hers. He drew the ring on her finger toward his mouth and kissed it. "Forever." His vow?

Whatever she contemplated about breaking up with him was petty and stupid and far from how she felt now. "I want that too."

He didn't cross the small distance between them to kiss her. His shining gaze said he wanted to. Was he waiting for a signal from her? Permission? Or was he still acting like the perfect gentleman?

Fatigue and confusion made her thoughts fuzzy. She laid back down, wrapping herself up in the comforter. He snuggled one of his blankets over her. She closed her eyes. Must have dozed.

The last thought on her mind was of herself sashaying down an aisle dressed in a pretty white gown. Maybe that dream could still come true.

Six

When Judah reached the back door to Paige's, he didn't bother wringing out his socks. Earlier, when he got James's ladder and climbed up into his father-in-law's bedroom, he found a flannel shirt and a pair of pants that were too short. He still wore them, and left Paisley jeans and a shirt too. Since she was asleep, he hustled over here to grab their things and get back before she woke up.

He knocked, then entered. "Hello? Judah, here."

"I'm in the living room."

He followed Paul's voice. The older man sat in the recliner with his feet propped up. "Where's Paisley?" Paul adjusted his glasses, squinting. "Where did you two stay last night?"

An unexpected rush of guilt hit Judah. Was his father-in-law accusing him of doing something wrong? He and Paisley were married even though they had been separated. Besides, they only slept on the same air mattress. Even when he took off her clothes, he did it with the utmost care and in fear for her life. The same way he would have performed a cold-water emergency rescue for anyone. Well, maybe not *the same* as for anyone. He took extreme care of her. His Paisley. His wife.

Lying next to her this morning, he disciplined himself not to kiss her. Not to scoot close. Not to want more. Yet, he couldn't deny his eagerness for them to exchange vows and renew their commitment to their marriage. Then loving her completely would be the greatest gift imaginable.

For now, he'd be patient. Wooing her. Waiting for her to want to be with him as much as he wanted to be with her. However, that day couldn't come fast enough.

Paul stared at him with a stern expression, apparently still awaiting his answer.

"Oh, um, er, we stayed at your house. James lent us an air mattress. I set it up in the living room."

"Oh?" Another frown.

"Paisley may have had a mild case of hypothermia."

Paul shoved himself off the chair. "Is she okay?"

"She's sleeping now. If she shows any signs of distress, I'll take her to the ER."

"What happened? How did she get so cold?" Paul ran his palms over both his arms as if he felt a sudden chill, too.

"We went out on the peninsula." Judah shrugged. It wasn't his place to tell Paul about the anger Paisley felt over Paige being with Craig. However, there wasn't any harm in explaining about the accident. "We were talking. She stepped backwards. Lost her balance and fell in the water. She got sucked into one of those whirlpools."

"No." Paul wiped his nose. "I never would have expected such a thing. She's been near the sea for most of her life. Knows the current. Swims good." He shook his head.

"It happened fast."

"You saved her?"

Judah nodded, shrugged, downplaying his part. "The good news is she's doing better. I warmed her up with plenty of blankets."

"Good, good." Paul rocked his thumb toward the hall. "You here for your bags? They're by the bathroom."

"Thanks." Judah took several steps, then paused. "I asked her to marry me again."

"You did?" A wide smile crinkled Paul's face. "Why, Son, that's the best news I've heard in years." He lumbered toward Judah, then embraced him and patted his back. "How did my daughter take your proposal?"

"She said yes." Judah's face stretched into a huge grin. No reason to mention that she almost gave him back the ring.

"Maybe I'll get more grandchildren now, hmm?"

Um, well, did Paisley even want kids? After a couple of first trimester miscarriages, then losing Misty Gale at six months into the pregnancy, would she be brave enough to try again? Would he? A knot formed in his stomach.

He excused himself to locate his and Paisley's bags. Right next to their stuff, someone had placed his shoes. Perfect. He dug through his belongings for a pair of dry socks, then slipped into the footwear. What a relief after trudging around in soaking wet, filthy socks.

He grabbed the wet clothes they threw over the shower rod during their stay. Then he returned to the kitchen with his arms full of damp things and their luggage. Paul stood by the back door in his coat and rainhat.

"Going somewhere?"

"Thought I'd go back to my own house."

"Oh, okay." Was Paisley ready for that? Paul's and her last conversation ended badly. Judah didn't want her getting upset in her condition.

"Besides, you two might need a chaperone."

His cheeks heated up. "We are married, sir."

"Oh, right." Paul nodded but didn't step away from the door. "Paige and the little one will be awake soon. They must be beat. Sleeping in this late."

"I can imagine." Judah took a couple more steps. "I have my truck. You want to ride along?"

"I'll drive my car."

"There's a lot of mud and debris in the streets. Might be hard for a low-riding vehicle." He readjusted his load.

"Maybe I should ride with you, then."

"Yep. Maybe we can start fixing up your place."

"My thoughts exactly. Let me help." Paul clasped Paisley's pack.

Judah trudged out to his truck and tossed the wet items in the back, followed by both bags. He remembered his father-in-law's medical situation. "Did you grab your insulin?"

"I'll get it later. Don't worry about it."

"Where is it? I'll run back and grab it." His hand on the passenger door, Judah waited for the man's answer.

Paul huffed. "I don't need anyone bossing me around, playing nursemaid."

"Uh-huh. And I don't want Paisley running back over to gather things you could take care of now."

Paul harrumphed and crossed his arms.

A car pulled into the driveway next door. Evacuees returning home by the looks of their dazed faces as they exited the vehicle. Judah waved. The older neighbor shook his head as if he couldn't believe how bad things were. A lot of citizens probably felt that way about Basalt Bay.

"Where did you say it was?" Judah persisted.

"On the end table in the living room." Paul grumbled. "In a black grooming bag."

"Be right back." Judah shut the truck door. He hustled into the house, trying to be quiet.

Paige entered from the hallway. Her messy hair looked like she just woke up. "Oh, I didn't expect to see you here."

"Hey, Paige." He felt awkward after what happened yesterday when Paisley saw Paige and Craig together. "Welcome home."

"Thanks." She wiped her hands over her face. "Did you get all your stuff?"

"I did. I need to grab something of your dad's." He continued toward the end table. Was she aware of her father's illness? Should he mention something? As Paisley's husband, he was a member of this family. But he should stay out of it. Let the two sisters figure out their father's medical needs.

"Where is he?" She squinted toward the kitchen.

"He's going back to his house where Paisley and I are staying." He picked up the black bag.

"Oh, right." Her eyes widened. "I saw you two holding hands. That surprised me."

No more than the shock he and Paisley experienced about her

and Craig. "Yeah, it's kind of a miracle. I asked her to marry me again."

"You did?" Her voice rose high.

"She said yes."

"That's amazing." Paige smiled. "Welcome to the family, again, Judah." She gave him a quick hug, rubbing her hand over his shoulder.

"Thanks." If only he could explain about Paisley's reaction yesterday. "I should go. Paul's waiting."

"Right. Go ahead."

He strode outside and jogged down the steps. His leg didn't feel too badly after yesterday's difficult swim and all the weight he put on it carrying Paisley.

"Judah?"

He paused.

"I wish—" Paige stood on the porch, glancing up at the sky. "Just tell Paisley hi for me, okay?" She met his gaze with a teary smile.

"Will do." Part of him wanted to close the distance and give her a brotherly hug. Maybe tell her everything would be all right. Sisters unable to talk to each other had to be one of the saddest things. But how could he judge when he barely spoke to his father? The Cedars and Grant families both needed interpersonal healing. Something else for him to pray about in the coming days.

As he slid behind the steering wheel, dropping the bag between them, Paul grumbled like he was upset about Judah interfering and bringing the insulin. No one could force him to take the required dosage. But if Judah didn't bring it along, Paisley would stomp over here and grab the meds herself, whether she was physically up to it or not. He couldn't let that happen.

He put the truck in reverse, contemplating how she might react to her dad after their previous argument. Heaven help them all.

Seven

Paisley blinked several times, gazing around the room. Still at Dad's. Still wrapped in toasty blankets. She moved and felt the hard floor beneath her back. The mattress must have lost some of its air. She wiggled her toes and fingers. Her muscles felt stiff. She rocked back and forth, trying to sit up on the sagging air mattress. After several attempts, she freed herself of the blanket straitjacket.

"Judah?"

No response.

A red checkered flannel shirt and a pair of men's jeans lay folded at the foot of the mattress. Her dad's? Judah must have gathered them. She slid her feet onto the damp floor and stood slowly. At least, the room didn't sway. She picked up the jeans. She barely got into the men's clothing when she heard a thump-thump on the porch. A loud knock.

"Judah?" Why would he knock?

"Paisley?"

That voice. Why was *he* here?

She buttoned the shirt fast, but her fingers fumbled with the task.

Another round of banging came at the door. Should she pretend she wasn't home? Last time that didn't work well. Craig just found a way to barge in.

She heard footsteps again. He peered through the plastic covering the living room window. She gulped. Her heart pounded rapidly. If he tried breaking in, the thin sheet wouldn't hold. What would she do then? He waved, but she didn't reciprocate.

Her mind still felt fuzzy from sleep, and maybe from being so cold and going unconscious yesterday.

Judah, where are you?

"I just want to talk to you." Craig's muffled voice came through the plastic. "Please, open up." He pointed toward the door.

Did he know she was alone? That Judah wasn't here to oppose him. What choice did she have other than to see what he wanted? She unlocked the door and held it open about four inches. "What do you want?" Her voice sounded low and scratchy. She cleared her throat and glared at him through the narrow space.

"What's wrong? Are you sick?"

"Never mind." She started shutting the door. Opening it was a mistake.

He thrust his shoe into the gap. "Wait. We need to talk."

"No, we don't. Not when you were peeking in my window. You should leave." She clutched her father's baggy shirt tighter at the neckline while leaning against the door. Craig's clodhopper remained stuck.

"You wouldn't answer the door." He gritted his teeth. "I'll leave as soon as I get something off my chest—if you'll let me have my shoe back." He glanced downward.

She was tempted to shove harder on the door. But remembering the way he helped her dad, convincing him to take his insulin, she eased back. "Haven't you caused enough trouble?" A snapshot of him and Paige flashed through her thoughts.

"You saw me with Paige." He exhaled. "You were probably shocked to see—"

"So what? You and Paige. Big deal." She pretended it didn't matter.

"Would you mind stepping out onto the porch so we can talk? Or shall I come inside?" He lifted his hands, palms out. "I don't mean you any harm. I promise."

She heard that before. "Why should I believe anything you say?"

"I helped with your father, didn't I?"

Yes, he was kind to her dad, but that didn't mean she trusted him. Even villains had moments of compassion and humanity.

She stared into his dark eyes, loathing the fear he caused her in the past. But then, a wave of fatigue and weariness came over her. "I have to sit down." She swayed. Hated appearing weak.

"Something is wrong."

She held out her hand. "Don't touch me." She shuffled toward one of the decrepit rockers that had been on the porch for as long as she could remember.

"Do you have the flu?"

"No." She dropped onto the chair, bracing herself lest it give suddenly. One of these days it would have to be replaced. Craig sat down on the other rocker, even though she didn't invite him to do so. She remained tense, wary, ready to jump up and go inside at the slightest provocation. She didn't forget the night he stomped through this house, yelling out her name, petrifying her. How she clutched a Mason jar in her hand, ready to strike him.

"If you're too sick—"

"Whatever you came here to say, say it. Then go." She sighed. Even talking was exhausting. "Just stay out of my life, would you?" She took a couple of breaths. "Judah will be back any second." *Hopefully.*

"I can't do that." His mouth formed a grim line.

"Because of Paige?" A rock of bitterness thudded in her gut. "Are you two married?" She clutched the wooden handrails of the rocker, her fingernails digging into the soft wood.

"Married?" He chortled. "Why would you think that?"

Relief shot through her. "You're not married?"

"Definitely not."

Oh, good. "Are you ... romantically involved with my sister?"

"That's for her to say." He stared back at her with a scowl.

At least they weren't married!

"Okay. So, what did you want to say? Just say it, then go."

Judah's mantra about grace and mercy skipped through her

muddled thoughts, but she stuffed them away. Even he would be angry if he saw Craig sitting on her father's porch talking to her.

"You still consider me the enemy after all I did to help you and your dad?" Craig thrust his fingers through his dark unkempt hair.

"You're still here when I told you to leave. Is that helping me?" She gritted her teeth to keep from saying something mean. Didn't work. "Why come around me at all when you know I can't stand you?"

He winced. "I came by to explain something. Although, I can't tell you everything." He ran his palm over his face. Then sighed like whatever was on his mind weighed too much. Guilty thoughts, perhaps.

"How about just being honest?"

"Look, there's more at stake here than you know."

"What do you mean?"

He leaned over the broken railing and spat. "Starting with the mayor."

"What about him?" Her heart rate skipped a beat.

"He knows about us." He clenched his lips together. "He'll use the information for his own purposes."

"Us?" She snorted. "There's no us. Never has been."

"Not according to Mayor Grant. He orchestrated the fiasco between—"

"Between whom?"

"The night that I—the night you and I—" He huffed. "I shouldn't say anything. It's just, I care about—"

Judah's truck roared across the lawn, coming to a brake-squealing stop below the porch.

Craig shot to his feet. "He's not going to like my being here."

"No kidding. Neither do I." Although, now, she wanted to hear his explanation. What did her father-in-law orchestrate that night?

Judah leapt out of his truck, his face red. "What are *you* doing here?" He charged up onto the porch and stood in front of Craig.

"Judah. Don't—" She leaned forward then sank back into the chair.

The two men stood like enemies in a battle, glaring at each other.

Another door opened. Dad slid out of the vehicle and stared at the trio with wide eyes.

"I said, what are you doing here?" Judah's voice rose.

"Talking with Paisley. That a crime?"

"Possibly. What were you discussing?"

Craig's chin lifted. His look haughty. He thrust back his shoulders.

Judah took another step forward, fists clenched.

Two hotheads in a faceoff.

"Let's all calm down, huh?" Paisley tugged on one of the belt loops of Judah's jeans that appeared too short. Dad's probably.

He glanced at her. "You okay?"

"Been better. Just tired."

"What happened to you?" Craig squinted at her.

"It's not your concern." Judah spoke gruffly. "You shouldn't be here."

Craig smirked. "Lord of the castle throwing out usurpers, huh?"

"At least you admit that you're a usurper."

"Guys, hey, stop." She shoved herself off the rocker, swaying, and stepped between them.

Judah grabbed her arms. She almost toppled backward and he helped her sit down again. "Just rest, will you? You're still weak."

"Then don't start a fight I have to referee."

"I'm not." He nodded toward Craig. "I didn't invite him here."

"Neither did I." She wiped her forehead. "I'm so tired."

"You okay?" Dad strode across the wet grass, staring up at her.

She was warmed by his concern, even though the last thing he said to her wasn't very nice. "I stumbled into the water. No biggie."

Craig's shoulders sagged. "Something did happen. Paisley?"

"Hypothermia," Dad supplied.

"What?"

"Possibly," Judah corrected.

Craig dropped on his haunches beside her and took her wrist to check her pulse.

She jerked away from his touch. "Like Judah said, it's not your concern."

He stared at her, then stood. "Are you taking her to the doctor?"

"Yes."

"No."

Judah and Paisley both spoke at once.

"I'm fine. Stop worrying."

"You don't look fine," Craig muttered.

"Thanks a lot."

"I should go." He stepped off the edge of the porch, landing on the grass. Then paused. "Just take care of her." He marched down the sidewalk, heading toward Paige's.

"Good riddance." Judah winced. "What did he want?"

She sighed. "Can we just let it go?" She was too fatigued. And with her father standing here listening, she didn't want to get into a conversation over the cryptic things Craig mentioned.

Judah's eyebrows raised. "So, you feel any better?" He scuffed his shoe against the warped porch.

"Sleeping helped."

"You're both wearing my clothes, I see." Dad chuckled.

"Yeah. Thanks." What he said about her being good at running replayed in her thoughts. Something else for her to forgive and get over.

"I brought our bags." Judah nodded toward the truck.

"It'll be nice to have my own things."

"Me too." He lifted his leg, exposing his bare ankle between the edge of the pants and his shoes.

"You took a dunk in the bay, huh?" Dad spoke. "Not like you to be so careless."

She stiffened.

"She tripped. Just an accident." Judah defended her.

"Maybe she was upset. Not thinking straight." Dad squinted at Judah like he might be to blame.

"I saw Paige and Craig together, okay?" She glared at her father. "So, yeah, I was upset."

He shrugged. "Paige and Piper came home, but I didn't see Craig until just now." He nodded at Judah. "Ready to get started on the house?" He trudged inside.

She groaned, annoyed by his lack of understanding.

"I'll be in shortly." Judah leaned closer to her. "You sure you don't want to go to the doctor?"

"I'm just going to rest." She rocked the chair, listening to the creaking sounds.

"I told your dad I asked you to marry me." He rocked his eyebrows.

"What did he say?"

"That it's the best news he's heard."

"Doesn't surprise me." She ran her hands over the worn arms of the rocking chair. "He may like you more than me." A strange melancholy filled her.

"Even if I'm a Grant?"

"Even then."

"Judah!" Dad called from inside.

"Guess I should help him get started on the renovations." He stroked his fingers over her hand. "If you change your mind about going to Florence—"

"I won't. But thanks."

He brushed his lips against her cheek, making her heart rate pick up, then he strolled into the house.

She sighed and closed her eyes, wishing she could shut out the frustrations she'd dealt with since waking up.

A few minutes later, she heard loud thuds—wood chunks being thrown or piled up. Then hammering. No luck shutting out the racket.

She rocked the chair, letting herself melt against the frayed backing. But despite her determination to relax and possibly fall asleep, Craig's visit replayed in her thoughts. What did he mean about Mayor Grant knowing about him and her? As if they were a couple? Ridiculous!

Was Edward somehow involved in her attack three years ago? If so, how could she discover the truth?

Eight

Before they started working on the stairway, Judah took pictures of the flood-damaged house with his newly charged cell phone. Later, he'd send them to Paul's insurance adjuster. He would do the same thing at the cottage when he got the chance to drive out there.

He pounded a hammer against the wall in the stairwell, listening for a dull thud to confirm the location of the next stud. He and Paul were building temporary, interior stairs resembling a ship's ladder, so they wouldn't have to climb in through the second-story windows. The materials were a hodgepodge of remnants left over from when the previous stairs exploded.

They'd asked James for any large pieces of wood he might have. At first, he said he needed all his spare materials. Who knew when the next disaster might hit? But after they pleaded and cajoled, he showed them two long planks—leftovers from a decking project— that were a perfect size for bracing the stairway at a shallow angle. The stairs would be a far cry from passing inspection but would be stable and usable.

Judah heard something. Was someone shouting? Paisley? He stopped pounding nails. More yelling. He dropped his hammer and sprinted for the front door.

"I did not!" Paisley coughed as if she struggled to catch her breath. "You're small-minded and mean and just plain wrong about this."

Judah reached the porch and saw her standing on the muddy sidewalk in front of the house, wagging her finger at Patty Lawton, the hardware store owner. The older woman's face was a burgundy hue, and her clenched teeth made her look rabid. His first instinct was to sprint to his wife and protect her. He leaped from the porch, wincing, then charged across the lawn.

He knew Miss Patty was part of a group of businessowners who accused Paisley of breaking into their stores and stealing, or doing damage, on the night of her graduation. Although years had passed, some still held it against her.

"Who else would kick in my door and steal lumber and nails?" Miss Patty planted her fists on her hips and scowled.

"Someone steals and you automatically think it's me?" Paisley tossed up her hands. "How bizarre is that?"

"As soon as I heard you were in town, I knew there'd be trouble!" Miss Patty shouted.

Judah dodged between the two women, facing the store owner. "What's going on here?"

"She thinks I stole something." Paisley grabbed his arm and nudged him out of the way. "It wasn't me!" She glowered at the other woman, seeming capable of fending for herself.

Still, Judah stepped to her side, ready to intervene if necessary.

"All that hammering." Miss Patty jabbed her finger toward Paul's house. "I know where those nails and boards came from. You can't fool me."

"No, you don't know where they came from." Judah didn't appreciate being accused of thievery, either. "We didn't take anything from your store!"

"This doesn't concern you." Miss Patty scowled at him.

"You're accusing us of deeds we didn't commit." He wouldn't touch her, but he took a nonthreatening step forward. "That concerns me plenty."

She avoided his gaze and glared at Paisley. "Are you going to be honest now?"

"I have been honest." Paisley crossed her arms. "Since returning to Basalt, I haven't entered your store. Miss Patty, I couldn't break down your door if I tried."

"I remember your wily ways, Paisley Cedars."

"Grant"—Paisley and Judah spoke at once, correcting her on Paisley's last name.

Judah had heard enough. Maybe he should escort the woman back to her business establishment. But first, "What's this about? Why are you accusing my family?"

"Now she's your *family* after being gone for years?" Miss Patty cackled.

A fire burned in his throat. About to tell the woman off, he felt Paisley's hand link softly into the crook of his elbow. Was she telling him to calm down? *Lord, help me.*

He took a breath and redirected his thoughts. "Think about it. Our neighbors are in a crisis. Someone may have needed emergency supplies."

"Someone like you?" She gave him an icy stare. Her intensity could elicit a confession from an innocent bystander.

"Not me, and not Paisley. Now, if your store carried food, things might be different." He glanced down the street. "I might do anything to provide for my family."

Miss Patty gasped.

"But your store doesn't have food. However, everyone in Basalt Bay needs supplies. Some don't have money." He kept his tone calm. "I'm not saying it's right, but you can't blame folks for trying to get their lives back."

Miss Patty jabbed her finger toward him. "I'm telling Mayor Grant what you said. Bad communications do corrupt good manners." She glared at Paisley before whirling around and trudging down the sidewalk.

Paisley tugged on his arm. "Let it go."

But he couldn't. "Miss Patty, hold up." He jogged after her. "A little compassion would go a long way toward being neighborly."

She spun around so fast she nearly slapped him. "How dare you lecture me. All I need is another Grant giving me orders!"

Her vehemence surprised him, and yet he pushed on. "You call yourself a Christian, right?"

"Do *you?* Last I checked, Grants weren't notorious for having a high morality rating."

What did she mean? Was she referring to the mayor's public opinion polls? "My father doesn't have anything to do with this situation, or how we should be treating each other."

"Okay, fine. But I'm not swinging wide my doors for people like you and Paisley to take what they want." Her glare insinuated he did just that.

"For goodness' sake, we didn't break into your business."

"I say it was *her*"—she jabbed her finger beyond him—"and you're covering for her."

Paisley stepped next to him. "Then you'd be wrong." She faced her accuser with a calmer manner than Judah had. "I would never steal from you or anyone else."

"With your past misdeeds, how can I trust you? How can anyone?"

"Because I've changed." Her voice went soft.

Judah was so proud of her. She *had* changed. They both had. That's what would make their marriage stronger this time around.

"And because I'm sorry."

Her humble words seemed to take the starch out of Miss Patty. "You admit to doing the wrong?"

"I'm not admitting to this break-in." Paisley wiped the back of her hand across her forehead. She looked pale. Had she overexerted herself?

Judah wanted to scoop her up and carry her back to the porch where she should have stayed. To demand that she rest for the remainder of the day. He doubted she'd approve of such an action, especially in front of Miss Patty, one of the town's formidable gossips.

"Then what are you saying?" The older woman's tone ratcheted higher.

"That I'm sorry for my past mistakes." Paisley gulped. "I apologize for throwing mud at your windows when I was a teenager."

Miss Patty's jaw dropped open.

"For stealing ... batteries ... gum ... and trinkets. That was wrong."

Judah put his hand at the small of her back, amazed by her honesty and contriteness.

"I knew it!" Miss Patty hooted. "You're a thief and a reprobate! How could you not be with a mother—"

"Don't you say a word about my mother!" Paisley thrust her index finger toward the store owner. "This has nothing to do with her. I take responsibility for *my* actions." She sighed. "And, just so you know, I wasn't the only one who stole from you on graduation night. But what I did was wrong, and I'm sorry."

One of Miss Patty's eyebrows rose. "Is this a trick to get me to remember past mischief, instead of focusing on what you did this week?"

"I didn't break into your store recently." Paisley groaned. "But if it would help ... I'm willing to do some ... community service hours ... for the mistakes I made in the past."

Judah's admiration for her jumped a few notches.

"I came back to Basalt to make amends." She shrugged. "That's what I plan to do."

"It's about time." Miss Patty thrust her shoulders back. "Meet me at the hardware store in the morning. You can wash windows and clean up the flood damage."

"I'll be there first thing."

"Good." The woman eyed her for a good thirty seconds before shuffling down the street. "I'll lock up anything of value too."

Judah gritted his teeth.

"That went well." Paisley must not have heard Miss Patty's parting jab.

"You were fabulous." He squeezed her hand. "You okay?"

"Tired. But, yeah. Thanks for standing up for me."

"Of course." He linked his fingers with hers as they headed back toward Paul's.

"What's next on your agenda?"

The soft way her dark eyes stared into his gaze made his footsteps lighter. What did she ask? "Oh, right. Removing the tree from the roof. Getting the bathroom door unstuck."

"Wish I could help."

"You're going to rest and only rest for the remainder of the day."

"Yes, sir." She gave him a mock salute.

He chuckled, doubting she'd do what he said.

Nine

Five hours of work had never seemed so long. Between Miss Patty's snippy attitude over everything Paisley did, and how tired she was, she had to keep reminding herself that making amends was worth it. For each task she completed, the woman gave her another. How many more chores would the store owner expect her to do?

"Have you finished cleaning the windows?"

"Yes."

Miss Patty squinted toward the front of the store. "You call that clean?"

"I tried."

"Try again."

"Yes, ma'am." Feeling like a teenager working off a grounding, she grabbed the glass cleaner. Her shoulders ached from all the reaching. Plus, her crisis in the sea made her especially tired. Even so, she was determined to give this her best effort.

"Have you swept the floors?"

"Uh-huh."

Miss Patty peered at the linoleum. She bent over at the waist, adjusting her glasses. "Aha!" She stabbed her finger toward something. "Sweep that again!"

"Okay." An hour later, Paisley felt wilted. Still, she asked, "Anything else you need me to do before I go?"

"Before you go?" Miss Patty gaped at her. "Grab the duster off the counter and dust all the shelves."

"All?" The woman was a tyrant!

"Are you here to work, or not?"

"Yes, but—" Paisley groaned. "Fine. I'll take care of it." She gave Miss Patty a halfhearted smile. How did Dad put up with the woman's demanding attitude for all those years while he worked for her?

"Well? We don't have all day."

"Right." She grabbed the brown feather dusting tool and whisked it across shelf after shelf. Needing a distraction, something to keep herself from bolting for the door, she let her mind wander to thoughts about Paige and Craig. Not a healthy diversion, but effective. How long were they dating? How did they meet? What would Paige say if Paisley told her that she thought she was dating a creep?

Inhaling dust, she coughed and waved her hand through the air filled with floating particles.

"What's wrong? Are you lollygagging again?" Miss Patty harped as if Paisley took a ten-minute break instead of spending ten seconds coughing.

"The dust irritates my lungs." She swallowed back another urge to cough. "Would you mind if I left? I'm so tired and still recovering." That probably sounded like a lame excuse.

"Look at all the work we still have to do." Miss Patty swayed her hands toward a pile of items they removed from the shelves earlier.

"Couldn't we finish tomorrow?" No, wait. She didn't want to return tomorrow. She wasn't under any obligation to work for Miss Patty. She did volunteer hours out of the goodness of her heart, in hopes that the woman might forgive past mistakes. So far, that didn't happen. The store owner seemed as grouchy and vindictive as ever.

"If the electricity comes back on, the store will be open tomorrow." Miss Patty adjusted the edge of her baggy shirt. "I had hoped you would accomplish more. I should have known better about a Cedars."

Paisley gritted her teeth and dusted faster, stirring up more dirt, using the motions to work off her annoyance. See if she ever came into this store again.

Someone entered the front door, causing the little bell to chime.

"I'm not open," Miss Patty hollered.

"Paisley here?"

Judah! Hearing his voice thrilled her. Did he come here to take her home? Beautiful man.

"She's busy. Come back later," Miss Patty barked.

"Paisley?" Judah called out.

Good. He didn't follow the woman's command.

"Over here." She dropped the duster on a shelf, then met him half-way up the aisle. She charged into his arms, hugging him. Her lifesaver.

"Hey, sweetheart. What's wrong?"

She shook her head, not trusting herself to speak within Miss Patty's hearing. She smelled the scent of wood on his clothes and clung to him a little longer.

"You okay?" He pulled back.

She tried to communicate *"I need to get out of here!"* with her gaze.

"We've got a serious problem at your dad's."

"We do? Is something wrong with him?" Was Judah going along with her wanting to leave, or was he serious about there being a problem? "Is Dad okay?"

"Can you step outside so we can talk?"

"Oh, sure." Good idea. Get her outside, then make a run for it. She made the mistake of glancing at the stern-faced shop owner.

Miss Patty tapped her wristwatch. "Time's wasting."

"I'll, um, be back in a second." Now, why did she say that?

Judah clasped her hand and led her out the door.

"What's happened? Or was that a fake warning to get me out of there? If so, good going." She sighed, relieved to breathe fresh air.

"It's Callie. She's back in town and mad as a hornet."

"At whom?" Paisley pictured her aunt's angry face. Red blotchy skin. Double chin jutting out. Her scowl could make spiders flip over and die.

"She's mad at the world. You. Paige. Your dad. He's the one who sent me to get you." He nodded toward the street. "Ready to leave? Paul and Callie already exchanged heated words."

"Did she demand that he make her sweet tea?"

"How'd you guess?"

"It's her MO. She plops down on the rocker and expects instant service."

"Yep. Sounds right. Paul ordered her to go home and make her own tea." Judah held his palms together in a pleading gesture. "Can you come back and pacify her? It's World War III over there."

She snickered at the familiar ritual between Aunt Callie and Dad. "If I go, Miss Patty will be irate." She glanced back toward the windows she cleaned earlier. "But I've done enough here."

"Excellent." His arms came around her in a squeeze. "How are you doing?"

"Exhausted."

His eyes widened. Before he could comment on how she shouldn't be overdoing, she tapped his chest with her finger. "Wait here." Taking a fortifying breath, she trudged back into the store. "I'm sorry but I have to return to my dad's."

"But you aren't finished. You promised—"

"I know, but"—Paisley swallowed—"I could ... come back later." Ugh.

"Why can't you follow through on what you promised?" Miss Patty harrumphed. "Maybe your word isn't—"

"My wife's word is gold." Judah followed her. "If you can't see that, you're blind."

His sticking up for her was sweet.

"Aunt Callie needs me. She's at Dad's."

"Callie's back?" The older woman peered around the room, probably seeing all the work left to be done. "She'll have plenty to say about her rebellious niece disappearing for three years."

Judah groaned.

Paisley tugged on his arm. "Don't worry. I talked with her before the storm. Sorry to leave you in a lurch."

"Promise to come back later?" Miss Patty called as they exited the door.

When Paisley and Judah arrived at Dad's, Aunt Callie sat on one of the dilapidated rocking chairs on the porch. The chair's lower rails thudded unevenly against the water-damaged floorboards.

"Hi, Aunt Callie," Paisley called as she crossed the still soggy yard.

Her aunt's brow furrowed. "Paisley Rose, where have you been? I've been sitting here forever waiting to talk to you. No one would bring me tea, either." She glared at Judah.

"Sorry. I didn't know you were back. I've been helping at Miss Patty's store." She trudged up the wooden porch steps that someone, probably Judah, built today. No wonder he smelled of wood. One step was longer than the other two, but they felt sturdy beneath her shoes.

"Last I knew you and Patty Lawton didn't get along." Aunt Callie sniffed.

"We don't."

"Yet, you're helping her when you haven't offered your aunt any help."

Aunt Callie sure could be a pill sometimes.

"Do you need something, Auntie? Are you having trouble?"

"I could hardly get up those stairs." She jabbed her chubby index finger toward the new construction. "Why make such irregular steps? A body could fall off the side and no one would care." She was in fine form today. Full of complaints. She made a gurgling sound as she glared at Judah.

"The stairs are fine and functional. You should have seen us before, hopping up and down off the porch." Paisley glanced back and winked at Judah. Then she stepped closer to her aunt and patted her hand. "What's the problem, Auntie?"

"Ask my hardheaded brother." She muttered something about stubborn men.

Apparently, siblings never outgrew some squabbling.

"What has he done now?" Paisley peered through the plastic covering the front window. Where was Dad hiding? What did he say that got Aunt Callie all riled this time?

"He wouldn't listen to me. Never listens to me!" Aunt Callie pelted another squinty-eyed glare at Judah. "This is a private matter, young man. Cedars family only."

"He's family too, Auntie."

"He's a Grant."

"So am I." Paisley sighed, tired of the interaction. "What's this about?"

"Maybe I should go inside." Judah trudged up the steps, met her gaze for a second, then disappeared into the house.

"Tell my brother I'm still waiting for refreshments!" Aunt Callie rocked the chair more fervently. "Paige is back. There are rumors, again."

Again? From when Paisley left town? Or from her teenage years?

"There are always rumors. Besides, aren't you one of the instigators of some of Basalt's finest tales?" She said it jokingly but knew it was true.

Aunt Callie gasped and sputtered. "H-how dare you s-say s-such a thing? Accuse me of being a gossip? Why, I never."

Paisley played along. "So this is real news? What have you heard?"

"She's together with *him*."

"Him?"

"Her love interest—that Masters fellow. Everyone's talking about it." Aunt Callie yanked a tissue from her baggy shirt's wristband, then dabbed at her nose.

"What's the problem?" Paisley had her own beef with Craig. Judah did too. Why was her aunt concerned?

"Have you spoken to her?" Aunt Callie stared at her.

"No."

"Why not? Isn't it about time you two buried the hatchet?"

"Why don't you and my dad bury the hatchet?" She was being bold, but turnabout was fair play.

Aunt Callie snorted. "Why, Paisley Rose, your father and I get along fine until he gets his stubborn streak all in a dither. Then he hides like a five-year-old kid. Won't talk. Same as when he married your mother." She clapped her hand over her mouth. Her face turned red and splotchy. "Forget I said that."

"What about when Dad married Mom?"

Her aunt wiped her hanky beneath her eyes. "We don't speak about it, so don't ask."

That made Paisley even more curious.

"Your sister having a child outside of marriage"—Aunt Callie rushed her words as if trying to change the subject—"and hanging around that man. It's not right. Something needs to be done."

"What Paige does is her own business." Paisley wouldn't contribute to the local gossip wheel.

"Fiddlesticks." Aunt Callie harrumphed. "What she does affects the whole family, especially in a small town like ours. Your father should do something. Say something. I told him so!"

Oh. No wonder he was hiding. "I'm tired. Do you mind if we finish this conversation another time? About the tea ... we don't have any to offer you until the electricity resumes."

Aunt Callie moaned. "Whose fool idea was it to say we could return to town when the power wasn't back on?"

"Mayor Grant's."

"Figures."

"Everything takes more time than planned." At her aunt's glare, Paisley tried to appease her. "Miss Patty says the lights will come back on any second. Then you can go by and visit her."

"Hmph."

Sinking onto the porch floor, too tired to stand for another minute, Paisley leaned against the bare wall where shingles were torn off by fierce winds during the hurricane. She closed her eyes and sighed.

"Something wrong with you, child?" Aunt Callie's rocking stopped.

"Just tired." Dead tired.

"Pauly said you had an accident. Didn't tell me what kind."

"I fell into the sea."

"Didn't your mother tell you to stay off that treacherous peninsula?"

"About fifty times." But Mom had been afraid of even wading in the ocean.

"What are we going to do about Paige?" The rocking resumed.

"Nothing."

"Nothing?" the woman yelped. "I'll have you know—"

Paisley blocked out her aunt's rambling. The last thing she heard was something about another person ruining the Cedars name.

Someone else besides Paisley.

Ten

Judah laid down on the air mattress next to Paisley, staying so close to the edge he nearly rolled off. Earlier he found the slow leak and put duct tape over the hole. Best case scenario—come morning they wouldn't be lying on the hard floor.

Exhausted, yet wide awake, he tried not to move. He didn't want to awaken his wife who had to be as beat as he was, since she went back to work for another hour at Miss Patty's. He was proud of her for trying to do the right thing for others, but he wished she'd take it easy for a few days.

Trying to fall asleep, he counted imaginary orcas leaping in the sound. Quoted Psalm twenty-three. Yawned a couple times.

His mind wandered over the day's events. They finished the crude interior stairs. Then, while he worked on the outdoor steps, a front-end loader came by and scooped up debris from the street and dropped it into a dump truck. Not a perfect fix, as some trash still littered the road, but most of the garbage piles on the block were cleared away.

Later, a logging truck stopped in front of the house, and one of the workers said they were doing salvage logging. The guy volunteered to bring down the tree leaning against the roof in exchange for the wood. A great trade as far as Judah was concerned. Using a crane called a cherry picker, attached to the rig, they safely brought the tree to the ground. Another guy used a chainsaw to cut it in half, and they loaded the pieces onto the logging truck—all without Judah and Paul having to do anything.

The lights flashed on and off in the kitchen. Yes! Judah sat up, trying to stop the air mattress from rocking.

Outside, a cheer rang out. Clapping and whistling sounds followed. Folks were celebrating the return of electricity. Lights, heat, and power for tools would be a huge step in getting their lives back to normal after the hurricane.

Paisley moaned. "What's the ruckus?"

"Electricity's on. We survived!" He felt lighthearted just saying it. They ought to kiss like on New Year's, or hug, or something.

Her eyelids closed. A peaceful expression crossed her face. He listened to her steady breathing and thanked God for His goodness in keeping her alive.

After ten minutes of sitting on the edge of the mattress, and still not feeling sleepy, he stood and shuffled to the front window. He gazed through the plastic—another thing in need of repair—and saw lights shining from the houses across the street. Throughout the day, voices and hammers rang out in the neighborhood. Now, with the return of power, the noises might keep going through the night.

He shuffled back to the mattress and grabbed the blanket he'd been using. He wrapped himself in it, making sure Paisley was covered in her blanket, then he sat on the floor near the window. He'd stay here until he got good and sleepy. He had plenty to think about. Pray about too.

At some point things quieted down. Hammers were put to rest. Without even realizing it, he dozed off leaning against the wall. Hours later, he awoke to noises coming from the kitchen. Eggs cracking? Who had eggs? What a delicious smell! Dare he hope for coffee?

He stood and shoved the blanket off. A kink in his neck made him cringe. Sleeping while sitting on the floor was a bad idea. As he ambled toward the kitchen, he stretched the tightness out of his shoulder muscles. He sniffed some wonderful scents and grinned at the domestic scene of Paisley standing in the kitchen, cooking breakfast.

"Mornin'."

"Good morning." She raised her mug. "Coffee?"

"You bet."

With her back to him, she worked with the coffee machine. He strolled closer and peeked over her shoulder. Scrambled eggs steamed in a large frying pan. "Where'd you find eggs? Everything smells great, by the way." He sniffed her neck. "Mmm. You too."

"I have mysterious ways for getting what I want."

"I don't doubt that." He chuckled, happy to hear a cheerful tone back in her voice. "It's hard to imagine anyone having fresh eggs in Basalt Bay."

"Who said anything about fresh?" She winked.

Kissing her sassy mouth splashed through his thoughts. "You must have slept well."

"Yep. I feel more rested." She handed him a cup of black steaming coffee.

Their fingers touched in the exchange. He felt a little zing. Did she feel it too?

"No creamer. Sorry. Can't have everything."

No, he guessed he couldn't. "That's okay." He sipped the drink. The heat nearly burned his throat, but it hit the spot. He sighed in pleasure. "I've been waiting for this."

"Me too. I'm on my second cup."

Paul thudded down the steps in his boots. "Something smells good."

"Coffee and eggs, if you want them." Paisley even smiled at her father.

"I'll have both." He moved stiffly, finally reaching the main floor. "You two sleep okay on the camping mattress?"

"I did." She messed with the coffee machine and gave Judah a pointed glance.

Did she wonder why he slept on the floor? Might she assume he slept away from her for some reason other than insomnia? Avoiding temptation, perhaps?

He almost laughed. What red-blooded male didn't have *that* on his mind when he slept next to the woman he loved? But with all the work, his injury, her falling into the sea and nearly drowning, then having potential hypothermia, he was dealing with a lot of things other than contemplating their next step. And as far as he knew, they were waiting to share a bedroom until they exchanged vows.

Still, he would take flirting with her as far as he could. He stepped behind her while she scooped eggs onto three plates. He leaned in to plant a kiss on her neck. Instead, he got an elbow in his gut. He groaned.

She made a wry face at him and nodded once toward her dad.

"What? I was just going to kiss you."

"Mmhmm." She passed him a blue lunch-sized plate piled with eggs.

What got into her this morning? Yesterday, she was lethargic, and worked for Miss Patty when she shouldn't have. Of course, he was just as preoccupied with getting this house livable. Now she seemed feisty. Happy, even.

He liked it. Loved her. And he'd watch for his chance to kiss her good morning. Maybe talk about whatever she thought was the reason for him not sleeping in the same bed as her. Might be an interesting conversation. For now, let her think what she wanted.

Paisley handed her dad a cup of coffee and a plate like Judah's. "Compliments of your neighbor, James."

"James?" Paul's eyes widened. He guzzled about half the cup in one swallow.

"Says he has connections to the outside world."

"Well, glory be." Paul set his cup on the counter, then stuffed eggs in his mouth. "I'll go by later and tell him thanks."

"Want to sit on the porch?" Judah snagged Paisley's gaze and nodded toward the front of the house.

"Sure."

They carried their plates and coffee cups outside and dropped into the old rockers. The silence was comfortable while they ate. Life felt good.

"Thanks for fixing this."

"I heard some bad news this morning." She sipped her coffee. "James says there's a community meeting at eleven." She rolled her eyes. "What do you suppose that's about?"

"Maybe the mayor has a restoration plan for the city. About time, nine days after the storm." He took the last couple bites of his eggs. With his mouth cleared, he spoke again. "Might be a good idea to pool resources. Think the grocery store will open today?"

She shrugged. "If so, there'll be a rush on it. Same as Miss Patty's. Yesterday, she expressed concern about that."

"Nice of you to help her, even when she didn't exhibit the kindest nature."

"She never warmed up to me." Paisley chuckled. "That woman doesn't have a chip on her shoulder. She has a massive chunk of basalt."

"She needs the Lord's grace in her life, like we all do." He sipped his coffee. "Did you want to go to the town meeting?"

"Hardly. I hate City Hall."

"I figured." He took her empty plate and piled it on top of his. "Plenty of stuff to be done here. Not that you should do anything. I mean, you can rest while your dad and I work."

She wrinkled her nose at him. "I'm not afraid of hard work."

"I meant, after your near miss, you should take it easy. You worked too hard yesterday."

"So did you." Her gaze scolded him. "You have an injury too. And you got as wet and cold as I did in the ocean."

"There's so much to do." The responsibilities and tasks weighed on him. He still had repairs to do at the cottage, and he needed to find a job to provide for them and pay the mortgage.

"That's why you need my help." She gave him another sassy grin.

He could get used to these flirty expressions. Her mischievous side had always been alluring to him.

Now probably wasn't the time to talk about the air mattress, what she thought of their sleeping arrangements, and when they'd say their vows. The diamond ring sparkled on her left hand in the morning sunlight. At least she still wore it. *Focus on that, Grant.*

"So, did you want to go together?"

"Where?" He was distracted by her dark eyes shining back at him. The way she licked her lips.

"To the community meeting." One of her eyebrows arched. "Maybe you didn't get enough sleep last night, huh?"

Aha. She *was* thinking about that. He hid his grin. Then he stood, bent over with the plates in his hands, and kissed her cheek. His bearded chin nuzzled her face an extra second before he stood back up. "You still smell nice."

She snickered.

"We can go to the meeting together, if you want." His turn to wink. "If we dare."

"Dare?" A wide smile crossed her mouth and her eyes twinkled. "I have a dare for you, Mister Grant."

Mister? "Oh, yeah?"

Her impish grin made him a little nervous.

She jumped up, giggling. The plates rattled in the space between them. At her intense gaze, his breath caught. He'd go along with anything she said to keep a warm glow in her gaze and a sweet smile on her lips.

"So, here's the deal." She tipped her head, still grinning. "If I leave City Hall before the meeting is over, I'll do one thing you want me to do."

He gripped the plates tightly. "One thing, huh?"

"And if you leave the meeting before it's over, for any reason, you have to do one thing that I want you to do." Her wink and grin made his heart flip-flop.

His thoughts leapt to kissing her. "I'm game."

"Good." She skipped around him and reentered the house.

He blew out his breath. *Tone down your thoughts, Romeo.* He shook his head and chuckled. Not a chance.

One thing was for certain. He would not leave the town meeting before she did for any reason.

Eleven

Paisley dropped into a chair a few rows from the back of the community room in the basement of City Hall. Judah sat beside her. Challenging him to a dare was fun and exciting to consider, even if she might not be able to force herself to sit through Mayor Grant's speech.

Judah's gaze met hers. Was he thinking about the dare, too? If she left the meeting first, what might he ask her to do? Move out to the cottage with him? Yikes. She may have opened a can of worms. But if she won ...

He still hadn't shaved his beard, which made him look rugged and sexy. She grinned at him as her thoughts leapt back to when he kissed her face on the porch. How he stayed close, their cheeks touching, a few extra seconds. His beard felt ticklish, and she was tempted to shuffle and turn his brief kiss into a real toe-curling one.

Regrettably, she didn't. They agreed to focus on getting the remodeling work accomplished before they moved forward with their vow renewal. Yet, when they were being flirty and romantic, she had a hard time remembering why they made such an agreement.

This morning, when she woke up and discovered he didn't sleep beside her, she was a tad disappointed. Even though they were wrapped in separate bedding the night before, she liked sleeping next to him. Waking up beside him. Not being alone. Sigh.

Mayor Grant entered the room and paused by their row. Decked out in a three-piece suit, his designer attire seemed like overkill, insulting even. Most attendees were dressed in work clothes, jeans and sweatshirts. Dirty clothes at that, since there had been little time for catching up on laundry. Was this another case of the mayor not being empathetic to the people in his jurisdiction?

He reached out and shook Judah's hand, ignoring her. "Son, glad you could join us." His voice boomed as if including the rest of the group. "I'm pleased to hear you didn't end up in the pokey." He guffawed.

Yeah, real funny. He referred to their fear of Deputy Brian throwing them in jail for staying in town against the evacuation order. Fortunately, that didn't happen.

"Thanks, Dad." Judah slid his arm over the back of her chair. Was he trying to include her?

Edward grimaced in her direction, then walked on, greeting people loudly as he strode toward the podium.

The interaction made her stomach turn. Heat rose up her neck. Her throat tightened. She tugged on her neckband. If she needed air, she'd go outside. Forget the dare. But she didn't want to forget about it. She'd rather tune out Mayor Grant and imagine what one thing she might ask of Judah.

Just then, Craig and Paige strolled down the aisle. Paige carried Piper. Craig grinned like he owned the world. Wasn't this what Paisley feared? That nowhere in Basalt would there be a safe place not to see them.

Paige glanced at her and smiled. Paisley returned a nod but pivoted away when she found Craig's gaze on her. She fiddled with a hangnail on her thumb to preoccupy herself.

A white-haired woman scooted past Judah's knees, past Paisley's, and dropped into the next seat. "Why hello there, dear."

"Oh, Kathleen, I didn't recognize you. It's great to see you!" Paisley smiled at the woman who gave her a jar of peppermint oil to sniff during her panic attack on the night of the hurricane. "How are you?" She settled back in her chair.

"I survived the evacuation." The older woman chuckled. "My house is okay. A little damaged. Others fared far worse, so I can't complain."

Paisley nudged Judah. "Judah, this is Kathleen. Sorry, I don't remember your last name."

"Baker." She extended her hand.

"Hello." He lowered his arm from behind Paisley and shook the woman's hand. "It's nice to meet you."

"My pleasure."

"Kathleen's new to Basalt. I met her during the storm of all storms that none of us will ever forget."

"Isn't that the truth?" Kathleen chuckled.

Judah leaned forward. "Where did you stay during the evacuation?"

"Inland with friends." The woman shuddered. "What a terrible drive in the storm. Oh, my, I was thankful to reach safety. You two?"

"I stayed here." Paisley rocked her thumb between them. "We both did for part of it."

"Here in town?"

"We did. Foolishly, perhaps."

"I'm so glad you're safe." Kathleen smiled. "Maybe we can get back to normal living, huh?"

"Definitely." Paisley glanced at Judah, and he winked. What did he think "normal living" meant to them? Sharing the cottage. Waking up together. Gulp.

"Uh-oh. Don't look now. Trouble's coming." The white-haired woman nodded toward the back of the room.

Maggie Thomas, the innkeeper of the Beachside Inn and one of Paisley's most difficult people to get along with, marched up the aisle, head held high.

What did Kathleen know about Maggie Thomas's brand of trouble? Did she already have dealings with the sharp-tongued woman?

Maggie dropped into a chair in the front row with her shoulders thrust back and her chin lifted. She nodded at someone as if communicating something. What did she have up her sleeve?

"I'd like to call our post-Blaine community meeting to order. Welcome, everyone." Mayor Grant's sparkly-white grin would have made his hygienist proud. "If you can take your seats, we'll get this chat over with so we can all go home."

A few attendees agreed. Others laughed. Some shuffled to empty chairs.

"I'm glad all of you made it safely through the evacuation and your stay in various host cities." The mayor leaned one elbow on the podium. "We appreciate the shelters whose doors were open to us. Let's give it up for our safe havens." He led the group in a round of applause.

Before the clapping ended, Maggie jumped up. "Mayor, why didn't you go to a shelter like the rest of us were required to do?"

His chuckle sounded odd. "Now, Maggie, you know my house is on the highest location in Basalt Bay. No need to leave my fortress. The missus and I were safe. Thank you for your concern."

"I thought you had to leave town, too." Her voice rose as she faced the crowd. "The town ordinance is for *all* citizens, right?"

"That's what I thought too!" Sounded like Aunt Callie.

Paisley scooted lower in her seat. She didn't mind the mayor getting put on the spot and publicly humiliated, but even Maggie Thomas returned to Basalt before the evacuation order lifted. She glanced over Judah's shoulder. A couple rows back, her aunt sat on the far left. Miss Patty sat next to her. One woman whispered in the other's ear. Both were gesticulating. What had them all worked up?

"Are you excluded from following the laws of our town?" Maggie persisted. "Maybe the mayor can do anything he wants, huh?"

"Now, Maggie, why don't you take your seat? Let's get on with our city business."

The innkeeper harrumphed but sat down.

Mayor Grant cleared his throat. "Is everyone's power back on?"

"Yes!" "Finally." "About time." People called out responses.

"Rest assured I've been urging the utility company to get your electricity back on since day one."

Leave it to Edward to pat himself on the back. Even in a post-disaster meeting, he made himself out to be the hero.

"It's true." He took a sip from a water bottle on the podium. "If not for my diligence, many of you would still be out at the entrance of town, twiddling your thumbs, waiting for the all clear."

Maggie leapt to her feet again. "I have good reason to believe—"

"Are you leading this meeting, Maggie?" The mayor grimaced. "I'm sure we all have plenty to complain about. Big messes to fix." He lifted one boot. "My favorite cowboy boots nearly got ruined in the mud. I'm upset about that."

Some laughed at his attempt at humor.

Paisley rolled her eyes.

Maggie sat down stiffly.

"How about we dust off our grateful attitudes, hmm?" Edward grinned again. "We're back in our homes. Back in our city. Electricity's on. We're safe and alive."

"Here, here." Craig? Why would he speak up for the mayor? The two hardly got along.

Mayor Grant droned on for a while about the town's disaster and clean-up protocols, calling on the citizenry to jump in and help their neighbors. He even encouraged folks to go the extra mile and be Good Samaritans whenever possible.

Paisley nearly choked on his hypocritical words. Just four days ago, when she suggested that he take Maggie to his safe, warm home on the hill in the aftermath of the hurricane, he refused. So no one could blame her for tuning him out now. When she glanced at Judah, his attention was focused on someone other than his father. Craig?

That man stood. "I agree with you, Mayor Grant. Those who remained after the emergency evacuation caused unnecessary safety risks to themselves and to those on the rescue team. It cost valuable man hours. Fortunately, no lives were lost." Craig's voice deepened. "Those people who took risks for themselves and others should be fined or required to do community service hours as a penalty for not following the town's security protocol."

What? She gripped Judah's arm. His muscles tensed beneath her hand.

"That's right!" "Yeah." "I agree." A cacophony of voices rose.

She and Judah exchanged glances. She wanted to slink even lower on her chair, maybe melt to the floor and crawl out the door.

"People!" Mayor Grant palmed the air to quiet the group. "Mr. Masters—"

Craig was "Mr. Masters" now? What was going on with these two? Didn't Craig try to warn her about Edward?

"Can you give examples of these infractions?" The mayor crossed his arms.

"Of course." Craig turned and stared at her.

The rat. She squinted right back at him, warning him to shut up with her gaze.

"For one, Paul Cedars refused to leave town."

How dare he talk about her father!

"Even when prompted to leave by a C-MER employee, he refused."

Paisley gritted her teeth. Gnashed them together, more like.

"The man had a serious medical condition." Craig's voice rose. "He needed immediate attention. Might have even died without intervention."

Paige, sitting next to Craig, glanced up sharply.

Paisley's glare sent a hundred fire darts hurtling in his direction. If only one of them would strike him dumb.

"He should have been transported to the emergency room," Craig continued in an authoritative voice. "I did what I could to help him. Otherwise, things wouldn't have ended so well for Mr. Cedars."

He sounded so noble. Paisley wanted to leap out of the row, sock him in the nose, and run from the building. Dare or no dare, she had enough of this community nonsense.

A rumbling of voices grew louder.

"Then what happened?" Mayor Grant hollered over the clamor as if he wasn't apprised of the situation. He probably coerced Craig into talking. Or paid him off.

Paisley's fury toward both men quadrupled.

"I stayed in town and risked my life to help him."

Judah gripped the top of the chair in front of him with both hands. She touched the crease of his arm. No reason to come unglued over a parasite like Craig. Besides, maybe that's what he and the mayor wanted. To get the town's suspicions off themselves.

Paisley wished her sister would glance back so she could read her expression. Did she experience any of the irritation and betrayal Paisley felt? She appeared to be entertaining Piper by pointing out pictures in a book. Maybe not listening now.

"Mr. Cedars wasn't the only one who stayed behind, right?" Edward asked. Why would he publicly embarrass his son and daughter-in-law like this?

Craig coughed as if something was stuck in his throat. Guilt, probably. "That's correct, Mayor Grant."

What about the riot these two may have incited near the entrance to town? Someone should mention that. Let embarrassment fall on those most deserving.

"Paisley Cedars Grant remained in Basalt Bay also."

The louse. Her insides quaked. And not with fear.

Judah clasped her hand and held it firmly. Keeping her, or himself, from jumping up and saying something in their defense?

Kathleen patted her other hand, trying to comfort her. It didn't help. Paisley's heart pounded erratically beneath her ribcage. A fire burned in her soul.

"The woman in question has disobeyed orders before." The mayor adjusted his tie, giving the audience another toothy grin. "She's got a record a mile long for causing trouble, we all know that." Another rowdy laugh.

She wanted to jump up and call him a dirty liar. A scoundrel.

Judah leapt to his feet, beating her to it, although not the liar or scoundrel part. "Now, hold on, *Mayor.* Leave my wife out of this! I stayed here too. I'm as much to blame for *Mr. Masters* being inconvenienced and risking his personal safety as anyone."

"Here, here." Deputy Brian's voice sounded snide behind them. "I'll take them into custody, now, Mayor."

Custody?

Judah spun around. "You had your chance."

Uh-oh. Maybe he shouldn't have said that. The deputy already had conflicts with him and her.

"Any time works for me." Deputy Brian took a step forward.

A rumble of voices rang through the crowd. Might be another riot right here.

"What's this? A family feud?" Brad Keifer, the fisherman who helped Judah get back to town in a skiff, stood up behind Craig. "I thought this meeting concerned getting the town up and running. Making smooth transitions. This bickering garbage is a waste of our time."

"Yeah!" "That's right." "Get on with it." Residents shouted.

The mayor pounded a gavel. "Be quiet! Mr. Masters has the floor."

Paisley clenched her jaw. While she was tempted to get up and flee from the absurdity of this meeting, she also felt compelled to stay and hear whatever might be said. Especially with Judah standing as if he wasn't finished talking.

"I say Mr. Masters is done giving his biased account, anyway." Judah's voice grounded out. "No one wants to hear about him being such a humble *Good* Samaritan."

Paisley almost laughed at the shocked reaction on Craig's face.

"That's for sure!" Maggie called out.

"If it wasn't for me, pal"—Craig punched his finger toward Judah—"you could have gotten gangrene. Or worse."

Judah lunged into the aisle.

Oh, no. Oh, no.

"If it wasn't for you, my wife wouldn't have been scared out of her mind."

"You don't know what you're talking about." Craig scrambled past people, making his way into the aisle.

"I know about you sneaking around my father-in-law's—"

"Let's take this outside!" Craig thumped his finger against Judah's chest. "Now!"

"You'd like that wouldn't you?" Judah's hands clenched at his sides. "To fight. Cause more trouble."

Some in the crowd stood, pummeling the air with their fists, yelling out for one or the other to take the first punch.

Paisley's heart pounded fast. She remembered the last time these two fought in the ocean. She stopped them, then. Would she have to do that now?

Mayor Grant pounded his gavel. No one seemed to be listening.

Judah and Craig stood opposite each other, looking like gunslingers in an Old West duel.

Brad Keifer jumped into the middle of the possible fray, his hands extended in both directions. Deputy Brian grabbed Judah's shoulders and yanked him backwards.

"Hey!" He shouted, fighting the deputy's hold.

Brad pointed at Craig, telling him something, probably to stay put.

"Order! Order!" Mayor Grant's voice rose as he pounded his gavel.

When Paisley spun around to check on Judah, he and Deputy Brian were already gone.

Twelve

Judah sat on the edge of the cot in the jail cell, his elbows on his knees, staring at the wall an arm's length away. His first time behind bars. Hopefully, his last. The deputy told him lunch would be delivered soon—not much comfort in that. Irritation churned and gnawed in his gut. He needed to get out of here and find Paisley. To somehow forget the last hour had happened.

Why did he stand up in that meeting? And charging at Craig? He was normally a peaceable man. But he had to defend his wife. Would do the same, if given another chance.

He stared at the gray walls, feeling them closing in on him. How long would he have to stay here? Locked up. Incarcerated. Such disturbing words.

Did his father set him up with that stunt of Craig's, knowing Judah would defend Paisley? Did he prompt the police officer to be ready then laugh as Judah was dragged from City Hall?

Too farfetched even for the mayor, right? Edward Grant was a prideful man with faults, but turning on his own son? Judah groaned.

Back in the meeting, he thought they'd discuss efforts to coordinate resources, figuring out the best ways to help folks and get the town put back together. What a mockery. Instead, Mayor Grant and his puppet, Craig, pointed fingers at Paul, Paisley, and

Judah. Hearing his previous coworker lambaste his wife and father-in-law had been too much.

Lord, why did it come to this? Me sitting in a cell stewing for who knows how long? Would he have to spend the night? "Why" bounced around in his brain, in his mouth, until the bitter taste made him want to gag.

What would they write in his file? Did he have a file? Would Deputy Brian note that Judah "almost" got into a fight, sticking up for his wife? Or the other thing they accused him of—remaining in Basalt contrary to evacuation orders. A record would make finding another job difficult.

He groaned and covered his face with his hands. He'd just wanted to reconnect with Paisley, help Paul fix his house, and get the cottage ready for his bride to come home. Now, this.

He should never have attended that lousy meeting. He learned his lesson—stay away from his father, and Craig. Why wasn't that man thrown in jail? He instigated the near fight.

Another thought hit him. What if Craig followed Paisley home? Continued harassing her? Especially now that he knew Judah was detained in the jail.

He moaned, hating this feeling of confinement. Had to get out! He jumped off the cot and banged his palms against the bars. "Hey, Corbin!" He yelled the deputy's last name several times. No response. Maybe Brian could check on Paisley for him. That was his job, right? To ensure citizens' safety. Not just to do the mayor's bidding.

If only Judah could wake up and discover this whole ordeal was a nightmare. He paced the six feet of floor space in front of the bars. Then retraced his steps.

He was supposed to be helping Paul fix the jammed bathroom door today. Not standing idle in this shoebox, wishing he punched Craig in the face. Why did he hesitate?

He blew out a long breath.

I'm sorry, Lord. I'm angry. Still wanting revenge. I should be contemplating what I'm thankful for, how all things work together for good. That there's something to be learned here. Maybe humility. Sigh.

He dropped back onto the cot. After a few minutes, he stretched out on his back, staring at the stark white ceiling. It seemed to get lower and lower. An optical illusion? He shuffled on the stiff mattress. What a miserable, uncomfortable bed. How long would he have to sleep on this? How could he sleep on it? How could anyone?

He tried to pray. To accept and make sense of what happened. *Our Father…* Ugh. He couldn't stir up the humbleness he should have. He felt lacking and irritated.

His thoughts traveled back over the last couple of days, and he recalled some of the good parts. Paisley and him reconnecting—an answer to prayer. A miracle, really. Asking her to marry him and her saying yes. Such a beautiful moment full of God's goodness. He almost smiled at the memory of Paisley's response to his proposal. How she dropped on her knees in front of him and initiated a sweet kiss. Thoughts of his wife would keep him sane in this box. As was relying on the Father who he knew loved him.

I need Your peace, God. He closed his eyes. This time when he prayed the Lord's Prayer, he meant it.

A while later, he heard voices. He sat up. A woman yelled. Paisley? She said something about knowing a secret. That she'd tell everyone if he didn't— The deputy interrupted her gruffly. Was he denying her the right to talk to Judah?

"Let me in. I demand to see my husband!"

Yes! Paisley was insisting that she wanted to see him. He couldn't interpret Brian's low-toned reply. Did he tell her no? Did he inform her that Judah was in solitary confinement? He stood and banged his open palms against the bars like he did before. "Paisley!"

"Juuudaaaah!"

Sounded like a scuffle. Deputy Brian restraining her? He'd better not touch her! A fresh fire burned in Judah's gut. He hit the bars again. "Paisley!"

"Let me go!" she yelled.

"Corbin, leave her alone!" He crossed his arms against the bars, pressing his forehead against his wrist. He felt so helpless. Useless.

A phone rang.

Then a strange silence.

He hated the not knowing. Had Paisley been kicked out of the building? Did she give up and go home? He groaned. How did his life come to this? One problem after another. Now jail? He never would have imagined himself here. And yet, he wouldn't allow himself to get swallowed up in doubt and despair, or in vengeful thoughts, either. But wasn't that how he'd been thinking? Wanting to fight Craig. Enraged at his father.

Ugh.

God, I overreacted with Craig. I felt justified in standing up for my wife, but I let pride take over. I need You. I don't like being locked up. I hate it. Please get me out. And be with Paisley. Give her peace and assurance. I said I'd be there for her. I feel so—

An overwhelming sense of being stuck in the claustrophobic room, behind bars, pressed in on him, like the walls seemed to do a few minutes ago, until he wanted to weep. But then, he shook himself, barely averting panic. Wasn't God in control of his life? Even of this situation? Wasn't he still trusting the Lord? God had a good plan for him and Paisley getting back together and becoming a family again. For that he was thankful. *Focus on that, Grant.*

He dropped back onto the cot and closed his eyes. A long afternoon and night lay ahead. He quoted a few verses and prayed silently.

Some time passed. The door rattled. Who—?

He sat up, expecting lunch. Instead, Deputy Brian shuffled toward the bars, keys outstretched, his cold expression unreadable. The lock clunked as the keys engaged. "You're free to go."

"What?" Judah leapt to his feet. "Really?"

Brian shrugged, gazing at the floor, whether embarrassed or disappointed Judah couldn't tell.

"Well, okay, thanks!" He strode past the deputy and scrambled into the empty office.

"Must be nice having friends in high places."

"Must be. Is Paisley here?"

"Was." Brian dropped onto the chair behind the wooden desk covered in paperwork and plopped his shoes on top. "She made such a fuss, I told her to leave, or I'd make you stay twice as long. Would have, too, if not for—" He shrugged, glanced away.

Her standing up for him made Judah proud.

The deputy withdrew a plastic bag from the desk drawer. "Your belongings."

Judah grabbed his cell phone and stuffed his wallet in his back pocket. "Will this be on my record?"

"Charges are dropped if you keep your nose clean."

If? Why were the charges dropped? Did his father intervene? Or was it something Paisley said? "Glad to hear it." He just wanted to get out of here.

As soon as he hit the sidewalk, he ran. Had to find Paisley. A half block ahead, she stepped out from behind a bush. She dashed toward him and they met in the middle, hugging and clinging to each other.

"Oh, Judah." She sounded near tears.

"I'm okay. Everything's going to be all right now." He was out of jail. Holding the woman he loved. Thank God!

"Brian wouldn't let me see you. He's such a jerk. Always has been."

Judah couldn't argue with that. He stepped back and clasped her hand. "Let's hurry back to your dad's. I want to get the upstairs fixed."

"Wait a sec." She chuckled. "You get thrown in jail and the first thing you want to do when you're released is work on my father's house?"

"Yep. The sooner I finish up there, the sooner I can get the cottage done. Maybe, then, you'll want to come home with me, hmm?"

He heard her soft gasp. Her eyes moistened.

He smoothed the back of his knuckles along her cheek. He pictured himself sitting in the jail cell, missing her. "Actually, the only thing I want to do is this." He leaned in and kissed her, breathing her in, tugging her closer. "Or maybe this." Loving that he had the freedom to touch her, to hold her, he deepened the kiss like she was food, or air, and he couldn't get enough of her. Then, remembering they were in a public place, he pulled back, clearing his throat. "I needed this. You and me being together." Forget working on the houses. Maybe they could talk to Pastor Sagle today.

"Me too." She sighed and smiled up at him with such happiness or contentment that his heart melted. Then her expression changed. "Why did Brian let you out? He said he'd detain you for as long as the law allowed. He threatened to make you stay longer, even when I told him I'd tell everyone what he did on graduation night."

"So that's what the yelling was about." Nice of her to stick up for him like that. He led her up Front Street, moving farther away from City Hall and the jail.

"Yeah. Although, he acted like he didn't care."

"He mentioned something about me having friends in high places."

"The mayor?"

"Probably, but I won't question it. I'm just glad to be out." He glanced over his shoulder, making sure no one followed them. "Good thing I didn't get into a fight with Craig again. I sort of went crazy."

"Sort of?" She snickered and stopped walking. "Yesterday, when you saw him talking to me on the porch, he was telling me something about the mayor. That there were things about him I should know."

"Like what?" Not that he trusted anything Craig said.

"Something about the night—" She shook her head. "I don't know. Did you catch how he and Craig directed the meeting away from their involvement with the riot?"

"I did. Instead, they threw blame on us staying in Basalt Bay."

"Seems fishy."

"Yep."

They continued strolling down the sidewalk, holding hands.

"I'm sorry for getting you into trouble by staying here through the storm." She slowed down the pace. "If I didn't stay in Basalt— if I didn't come back—"

"Hold on. Please, don't say that. Come here." He wrapped his arms around her and kissed the side of her head. Her hair smelled good. Like freshly picked berries in the summer.

She laid her cheek against his sweatshirt. He sighed. This was how he wanted them to face all of life's difficulties—together, his arms around her, her leaning into him.

Too soon, she pulled away and strode forward again, tugging on his hand. "What do we do now?"

"Fix up your dad's. Then our place. Help our neighbors." Get married again. Have babies. Live happily ever after. But he didn't say those things out loud.

Almost to Paul's, she chuckled. "Hey, I just thought of something. You lost."

"Lost?"

"The dare. You left the meeting first!"

He forgot about the dare. Didn't give it a second thought. "That's not fair. The deputy removed me from the building."

"Still, I won." She winked and seemed way too pleased with herself.

Playing along might not be such a bad idea. "Okay. Let's say, hypothetically, you won. What one thing would you want me to do for you?" He had a few ideas of his own.

"When you least expect it, I'll tell you what I want." She chortled, and the musical sound filled the air around them.

Thirteen

With a lighter feeling than she experienced in days, Paisley skipped across Dad's still-mucky yard. She didn't care about her muddy boots. Or how the town meeting turned sour. Gladness oozed through her, warmed her. Judah was released from jail! Thank God. Yes, thank God. *He* answered a prayer she didn't even think to pray.

As she and Judah reached the front stairs, they both came to a halt. Aunt Callie and Maggie Thomas sat in the rocking chairs on her father's battered porch, staring at them with matching scowls.

Paisley gulped. "H-hello."

"Paisley." Aunt Callie's eyebrows twitched. "Judah." Her voice deepened.

"Callie, it's nice to see you." He sounded polite. "Maggie."

The innkeeper didn't respond, but by the look of her grumpy expression she was upset about something.

Paisley and Judah shuffled up the three steps like criminals about to face judgment.

"What's going on?" Her dad must be hiding somewhere the way he did whenever his sister or Maggie came around.

"That debacle at the meeting was unbecoming of a Cedars, or a Grant." Aunt Callie puffed up like a helium balloon. "This town needs to pull together, not be jerked apart. And Mayor Grant ridiculing you two?" She huffed. "If my brother knew folks were talking publicly about him, he'd stew in humiliation for a month! Best not to tell him." Her glare turned on Judah. "What were you thinking, young man?"

"That wasn't Judah's fault!" Paisley defended him. "The mess in City Hall was Craig's doing. The mayor's fault. Not his."

He clasped her wrist. "However, I'm sorry if my remarks offended you."

"Hmph." Aunt Callie exchanged a disgruntled glance with Maggie. The innkeeper's nose rose higher.

These two gossipmongers took their haughty attitudes too far.

"Aunt Callie, Judah stood up for me and Dad. I wouldn't call that a debacle. I call it heroic." She would take on both harpies if they said another word against him.

His fingers clutched hers. She returned an answering squeeze.

Maggie's gaze zeroed in on their clasped hands and her scowl deepened. What? She didn't approve of a couple giving each other a second chance? Maybe Paisley wouldn't invite her, or any of her family, Aunt Callie included, to the vow ceremony. Eloping worked fine the first time. Might be fine again.

Her aunt rocked furiously in the old chair. "Who does Mayor Grant think he is?"

With each back and forth motion, the rocker clunked against the wooden floor. Should Paisley warn her that the porch furniture was archaic and weakened by flood waters?

"Bringing his own son to task during a community meeting?" Aunt Callie harrumphed. "And my niece too! I'm appalled a leader of our city would behave in such a despicable manner."

"He's a disgrace to Basalt Bay." Maggie kept her chair's rhythm going too.

How was Judah taking this? He rolled his eyes, giving her his silent answer.

Aunt Callie shuffled her backside deeper into her chair as if settling in for a long stay. "It's about time the mayor came down a notch. I have an inkling of just how to achieve that."

"Me too." A sinister expression crossed Maggie's face.

"Maggie, Patty, and I say he should be replaced. Impeached!" Aunt Callie nodded her double chin. "I don't care if he is your father-in-law, Paisley Rose, I'm going to stand up for my town, my family, and do something."

By the way she plopped her palms on the chair's handrails, it looked like she might stand up and do something right then. Instead, she stared hard at Judah. He cleared his throat and shuffled his shoes as if he felt awkward. No wonder. How could Paisley get these two gadabouts onto a different tangent? While she supported the idea of ousting the mayor, she cared about Judah's feelings, too.

"We'll start a citywide recall petition." Maggie's gray hair fluttered in the wind. She brought the rocker to a stop. "Would you sign such a document?" She cast a squinty-eyed glare at Paisley.

"Oh, well, I—"

"Brilliant idea, Maggie." Aunt Callie clapped. "We'll get everyone in Basalt Bay to sign. Cheer on the agreeable. Pressure the reluctant. Who doesn't have a beef against Mayor Grant?"

Who, indeed?

Judah cleared his throat and stared at the ground.

Maggie stomped her foot. "Even Deputy Brian disagrees with the mayor's storm protocol. The way he stayed in town when everyone else left was wrong. Does the mayor picture himself the king? And what about the business with the riot? I witnessed him and Masters leaving for the barricade. I'll testify against both."

"But you don't know for sure what happened, right?" Judah spoke softly. "You weren't at the entrance of town that night."

"W-well, I-I"—Maggie stammered—"I h-had a right to speak up at today's session. To state my opinion. That's why I went to the meeting, but Mayor Grant shut me down."

"The man had an agenda, that's for sure." Aunt Callie pounded the air with her index finger. "I smelled a rat as soon as Masters opened his mouth. His sitting next to my niece made me itch." She scratched both armpits as if to prove her point.

"The rumors are flying too." Maggie huffed.

Aunt Callie whirled around and faced Paisley and Judah so fast it was a wonder she didn't get whiplash. "What do you two know about it?"

Judah shuffled closer to Paisley.

She grasped for a distraction. "Did you ask Dad for some sweet tea, Auntie?"

Her aunt's eyes widened. "Haven't seen Pauly. I bet he's hiding. But when I first climbed those rickety stairs"—she glared at Judah—"I heard something inside. You got tea?"

"There's no ice." Paisley grinned at her success in redirecting the topic. "However, since the electricity is on, I can whip up some hot tea."

"That would be nice."

"I'll be right back." Paisley nodded at Judah to follow her inside.

"Ladies." His footsteps clomped across the floorboards behind her.

She put the teakettle on the front burner and Judah leaned against the sink with his arms crossed. She grabbed teacups and enough tea bags for the ladies and herself. "What do you think about what they said?"

"Kind of a sensitive subject. Not for you. You can ask me anything." He gave her a reassuring smile, although the lines around his eyes still looked tight.

"Okay. So, how do you feel about it?" Maybe she shouldn't push, but they were trying to be more honest with each other.

"I hate the thought of an uprising in Basalt Bay. We're just getting over a gigantic storm and its destruction. The town ought to be pulling together." He sighed. "Kind of like us, you know?"

She did.

"Then there's my dad. What would he be, if not the mayor?" His shoulders rose then fell. "I'm not defending him. Just saying."

"I understand. He's your father."

She took a couple of steps to where he stood. Wrapping her arms around his waist, her cheek came to rest against the soft fabric covering his chest, her favorite way to be close to him. No matter what trouble the women on the porch might be instigating, she was thankful that Judah was here with her and not in jail. His head leaned against hers as they stood silently, hearts connecting, until she heard the teapot's whistle.

"Would you check on my dad?" She made a couple of furtive nods toward the stairs, giving him an alternative to going back outside.

"Thank you." His voice rose in volume. "I should check on Paul. We need to get the bathroom door unstuck." He winked at her before taking the stairs two at a time.

She grinned and added plenty of honey to the cups. She scooped up the tray with the three teacups rattling against each other, then hurried to the porch.

"Finally," Maggie grumbled.

"Sorry for the wait."

Both ladies sipped their tea in silence. A blessed silence. Leaning against the porch column, Paisley drank her hot beverage, wishing she made herself coffee instead.

"Now, for answers!" Aunt Callie sent her one of those spider-killing scowls.

What else could she use as a distraction? "Everything okay at the inn, Mrs. Thomas?"

"No. Someone stole a boat from my property." She squinted at Paisley like it might have been her.

She took a long swallow of tea. Once, a long time ago, she borrowed Maggie's boat.

"I made a full report with the deputy." The innkeeper managed to rock the chair on its uneven rails and sip her tea without spilling. "Someone broke into one of my rental units, too."

Aunt Callie stomped her foot. "Paisley Rose, tell me about your sister and that man!"

"That hunk, you mean?" Maggie spoke without cracking a smile.

Paisley nearly choked on her tea.

"You think he's handsome?" Aunt Callie coughed. "He's a menace, that's what. Now, tell me what you've heard about this romance. Is your sister involved with the brute?"

"I haven't spoken with Paige yet."

"What?" Her aunt's jaw dropped.

"Craig told me they're not married. Otherwise, I don't know what's going on." Other than the cozy way they acted when she first saw them together.

"Of course, they're not married." Aunt Callie scoffed. "I would have heard about that. What they're doing together at all is what I'm determined to find out. And I will find out."

Me too. Paisley waited until the last slurps signaled the two women finished their tea. She held out the tray for them to set their teacups down.

Maggie shoved off the chair. "See you tomorrow, Callie."

"I'll call folks. Stir the pot." Aunt Callie remained in her chair.

Maggie descended the stairs, glancing back as if to say something. Then she must have tripped. Her hands flailed in the air and she thudded onto her backside. She groaned and whimpered, sitting on the last step and her legs on the wet grass.

Paisley dropped the tray on the railing then rushed to her. "Are you okay?" She squatted beside Maggie, laying her hand on her shoulder.

"No, I'm not okay," the woman snapped. "Terrible steps."

"I told you those stairs were unacceptable." Aunt Callie harrumphed.

They felt sturdy to Paisley. This was just an unfortunate accident.

"You okay, Maggie?" Aunt Callie sounded worried.

"I will be." Maggie ran her right hand down her hip, squinting at Paisley. "Nothing's broken, good thing. Bruised though."

"I'm so sorry." What else could she say? Hopefully, Maggie wouldn't sue Dad for her misstep.

Judah ran out of the house. "What happened? I heard—" He drew in a sharp breath. "Mrs. Thomas, what happened?" He rushed to her.

"She fell on the steps." Paisley met his gaze and cringed.

"Can you stand?"

"Probably." Maggie whimpered.

Together, Judah and Paisley helped her to a standing position, their arms supporting her back.

"How do you feel?"

"How do you think I feel? I hurt! I want to go home. You should have warned me about those uneven steps." Maggie nailed Paisley with a biting glare. "Your negligence wreaks havoc again."

"I'm sorry you got hurt. Really, I am."

"How about if I drive you home?" Judah seemed to know how to deal with the irritable woman better than she did.

"I wouldn't say no." The innkeeper drew in a sharp breath. "Ooh. That hurts." She limped a couple of steps.

"Do you need to see a doctor?" Judah helped her get into his truck. Over his shoulder, he shrugged at Paisley as she followed behind them.

"Just a sprain, probably." Maggie moaned.

Judah ran around and hopped into the cab.

"Sorry," Paisley said again and shut the door.

Hopefully, Maggie wouldn't cause them legal trouble. Blaming Paisley for her woes? That seemed inevitable.

Fourteen

For the next two days, Judah worked on Paul's house, hefting the greater workload since his father-in-law wasn't quite strong enough. Paisley worked alongside him too, but her well-being concerned him, also. Their trio of carpenters made an unlikely group. Paul with his insulin deficiency. Paisley with her hypothermia scare. And him recuperating from his leg injury.

But they accomplished plenty, even scraping out some time to help their neighbors. And with assistance from James and Brad Keifer, who showed up after the town meeting to check on Judah, they repaired the damaged roof. Eventually, it would require a massive re-shingling. For now, it was mended.

After Judah watched a few YouTube videos, they tackled the damaged bathroom ceiling and doorframe. They stabilized the walls and beams in a way that Chip Gaines might even be proud of.

While Brad held up a board, he razzed Judah. "So what's with the public family feud, Grant?"

"Beats me."

"Never saw anyone so red faced as you when the deputy hauled you off to the slammer." He guffawed.

"Yeah, yeah. I'd rather forget about it."

"No wonder. Can't imagine sitting down to Sunday dinners with the mayor." He hooted. "Pass the peas, but first you have to vote on whether they should have been sautéed or steamed."

Judah put up with the teasing, since he appreciated Brad's help. But he was glad when the conversation moved on to other topics.

Now, he and Paisley were teamed up, tackling the removal of damaged sheetrock from the lower portion of the walls. A fine white dust filled the air. They'd scrounged up dust masks, one from Paul's toolbox, and one borrowed from James. As Judah pried boards off the walls, his thoughts wandered.

Earlier today, he tried convincing Paul to leave the house while they attacked the boards and the ensuing dust that could potentially harbor mold. The older man balked, arguing that he could handle any task they could. But when James stopped by and invited him to a salmon bake—he'd gone fishing at the lighthouse and caught a couple of silver salmon—it was too much for Paul to resist.

Judah knew that today would be his last day of working here, and he was hoping for a few minutes to talk with Paisley. Oh, he'd pop back over if they needed him to do something. But it was time for him to tackle the repairs at the cottage. Although, he hated leaving his wife here.

Soon they'd share the same house and bedroom, he kept reminding himself. Some days that seemed like an impossible dream. Other times, when he caught her gazing at him, or she slipped her palm against his and linked their fingers, or even stole a quick kiss, then the impossible seemed possible. Those blessed moments gave him renewed hope. And hope was a beautiful thing that made the sunset more brilliant, the sunshine brighter, and lightened a man's spirit. Truly.

They were on a journey, the two of them. Having her come home to him, to want him with her whole heart, for her not to run anymore, was worth every second he waited for her. And he would continue to wait, however long it took. So help him God.

Paisley stepped next to him, blinking, the dirty mask covering her nose and mouth. She nodded toward the door. Her dark eyes gazed at him through the plastic safety glasses, a question in her expression. An invitation, it seemed.

He could use some clean air to breathe and some time alone with her. He followed her outside. About ten feet from the house, he dusted off his clothes before he pulled off his mask and safety glasses. He inhaled deeply.

She did the same, dusting herself off. "What a mess, huh?" A white layer covered her hair, making her look like a fairy princess.

"Yep." He whisked white dust from her upper lip. He let his fingers dawdle near the right corner of her mouth. Gulp.

Their gazes held. Her warm expression thrilled him, made him want to forget about working and kiss her. His heart rate hit hyperdrive fast. *Take this slowly, Romeo.* He didn't want to scare her off. Didn't want her assuming romance was the only thing on his mind. Not the *only* thing. He chuckled to himself.

They were staring into each other's eyes more since his jail release. Smiling. Flirting. He considered those moments treasures. Each one made him want more. He hoped they kept acting romantic long after they renewed their vows. He'd make sure they did, this time.

"I'm beat. How about you?" She wiped her forehead.

"Take a break. You should catch up on some rest."

She laughed. "As long as you're working, buddy, so am I. Can't get rid of me."

"Never." A little dust caught in his throat. Or emotion. He coughed. "I've been meaning to talk with you about something."

"Oh?" Her eyes darkened.

"Nothing bad. Just stuff about the cottage. So much work to be done out there also."

"Oh, right. You're probably in a hurry to get started. With all this"—she swayed her hand toward Paul's house—"I've kind of forgotten about the cottage. Not to mention working off past bad behavior with a certain neighbor."

He toyed with a strand of her hair. "You've done a good job with trying to make amends. Building bridges. About the beach house? Would you mind if we went out and took inventory?"

Her white-dusted eyebrows furrowed. "I want to help. Really, I do."

He lowered his hand and brushed off his jeans.

"Dad still needs me here." Her cheeks hued the rosiest pink. "Also, we haven't discussed our vow ceremony. When it will be. What expectations there might be."

Expectations? Did she think—? "I didn't mean for us to stay out there together, yet."

"You didn't? Oh, well ... things are so hectic." She looked flustered. "The ruined sheetrock. Mudding. I still haven't talked with Paige."

He recognized her nervousness by the way she chattered.

"I understand." Although disappointment clogged his arteries. He stared down the block at people hauling garbage to both sides of the street, tidying up, making their properties look better. Like he should be doing at the cottage.

Paisley's hedging about coming with him stung. Just a setback, though. They were separated for three years. Adjustments needed to be made. He was the one in an all-fired hurry. But didn't he ask for a quick engagement? Didn't she agree?

Inwardly, he groaned. Maybe it was busyness and chores that kept them from moving forward. Nothing more. Nothing else he should read into it. And, she was right, they hadn't talked much about the future. Did he avoid discussing certain things with her, afraid those topics might set them back further? Was she, perhaps, avoiding things too?

She gazed down at her shoes. Gnawed on her lip. Was she feeling shy around him, now? Had they already gone backwards in their relationship?

"Hey." He caressed her shoulder. "If you want to hang out here with your dad for a while longer, you should. No worries on my account."

"Really?" She blew out a breath. "Thanks for understanding."

"Of course." He nodded, making sure he smiled, even if it didn't quite reach his heart. He'd continue being patient, but he couldn't deny feeling a tad disappointed by the delays.

"When this is over"—he rocked his thumb toward her father's house—"will you go on a date with me? A real, get dressed-up sort of date?"

A smile crossed her lips—lips he refrained from meeting with his own. "Yes, of course, I would love to go on a date with you."

"And after we go on a date together …"

"Mmhmm."

"And after we do some talking …"

"Yes?"

"Then will you marry me again?" His heart lay exposed on his sleeve. What if she thought she made too hasty of a decision about them getting back together? What if she changed her mind again?

She stared into his eyes, making knots twist and tangle in his chest. He didn't sever the invisible cord. Wouldn't. Could barely breathe as he kept his gaze glued on hers.

"After we have a date, or two or three"—she spoke almost musically—"and after we do some serious heart-to-heart talking, I will marry you, Judah Grant. I promise."

The air whooshed out of his lungs. "Sounds great." Perfect. Magical. He wanted to scoop her up in his arms and kiss her breathless. But they were covered in dust. And she said a date or two or three. More delays. "Guess we should get back to work."

"Guess we should."

He linked his fingers with hers. Dust or no dust, he needed to feel that bond between them. Then it hit him. Three dates? Shoot. Three dates could happen in twenty-four hours. Breakfast. Lunch. Dinner. No problem.

However, Bert's—the local diner with the best burgers on the West Coast—was closed. As were most businesses in town and even in some of the nearby coastal cities. He'd have to drum up some creative ideas about where and when to date her.

First, sheetrock removal at Paul's. Fixing things up at the cottage. Then focusing on the most important thing—winning back the love of his life.

Fifteen

Having electricity and hot running water made a huge difference in the ease of life after their disaster existence of the last twelve days. Following two cups of coffee, showering with lots of hot water, and eating real food, Paisley felt more human, even if she slept in her childhood bedroom that conjured up too many thoughts of the past. Three days had passed since the fateful town meeting when Judah went to jail. One day since he returned to the cottage.

She already missed him. She was used to his being around, winking at her, sneaking kisses, touching hands. The little flirtations— she missed those.

She could have gone to the cottage with him, so she had no one to blame but herself. But she chose to stay with Dad. He needed her, she kept telling herself. Yesterday, James came over and the three of them cut and hammered sheetrock into place. Today, mudding and taping loomed. She'd never done either.

She stared out the kitchen window into the backyard. No more debris or tree limbs were scattered about. The swampy water remaining on the grass for days finally evaporated or was absorbed into the ground. The sun shone. A great start to this fall day.

Yesterday, the grocery store opened. As did Miss Patty's hardware store. The shop owner still hadn't thanked Paisley for her help. Might never acknowledge it.

Dad entered the kitchen dressed in his usual flannel shirt and stained jeans. A dust mask hung around his neck. "Ready to get started?"

"Sure. The sooner we get done the better." She stayed to help him but, today, her heart was elsewhere.

For a few moments, she got lost in thoughts of Judah working alone at the cottage. Probably fixing the roof—that's what he told her. What if he slipped and fell? Or injured himself with a power tool? As quickly as the dire thoughts came, she felt silly for thinking them.

Judah was smart. A strong worker. He had a cell phone. If he encountered a problem, he'd call someone, even if it wasn't her. As soon as she got her first paycheck—whenever she found a job—she'd buy a cell phone. Priority number one.

Speaking of work, what kind of job did she want to pursue? Serving at the diner? An image of the sailboat thrust through the front window of Bert's Fish Shack dampened the notion. The local restaurant would probably be closed for a while. Although, it wouldn't hurt for her to walk by and inquire.

"Paisley?" Dad called from the living room.

"Coming." She tromped into the front part of the house. Hours of smoothing mud over sheetrock tape lay ahead of her. Would her efforts pass her father's inspection?

Much later, her knees ached as if she walked a mile on them. Her shoulders were stiff. Mud was caked around her fingernails. She mentally griped at the inventors of tape and joint compound, and Hurricane Blaine. Dad hinted that she redo several of her first mudding attempts. Sigh. After two hours of intense labor, she got the hang of smoothing out the mayonnaise-like mixture. However, she wouldn't choose to do this type of work again.

Someone clomped up the front steps. Judah? Paisley stood and scowled at the dried mud on her jeans. Did she have joint compound on her hair and face, too? She licked her lips. Tasted mud. Blech.

"Are we expecting someone?" Dad smoothed the trowel across the mesh he installed over a hole.

"Not me." Unless it was Judah.

The door swung open. Paige stepped into the room, then stopped and stared at Paisley. Her gaze swung toward Dad. "I need h-help." Her voice broke.

"What's wrong?" Dad dropped his tool. Mud flecks splattered the wall where he worked. He wiped his hands on a cloth and shuffled over to his youngest daughter.

Paisley didn't move.

"Where's Piper?" He patted Paige's shoulder, getting mud on her too. "Is she okay?"

"She's playing at the neighbor's house." Paige squinted toward Paisley.

Did she want to talk to their father alone?

"I can go upstairs. I could use a break anyway. Wash up." She moved toward the first step.

"No. Wait." Paige moaned. "I need you to hear this too."

If she was in trouble, family came before Paisley's grudge about the kind of company her sister kept. "What is it? What's wrong?"

"Mayor Grant—" Paige's face puckered up.

"Is he sick? Having a heart attack?" She could imagine that with his high stress level.

"No. He ... he ..." Paige covered her face and sobbed.

Dad wrapped his arms around her. "There. There. It can't be that bad."

"But it *is*." Paige wailed. "He bought my *building* from the bank." She pressed her hand to her mouth. "I d-don't know w-what to d-do."

Paisley tried to catch up with her sister's problem. "Bought it as in ... you must get out, today, or what?"

"He says I can either rent from him or get out." She hiccupped. "He's doubling the cost. I'm still waiting for the flood insurance money. And there's all the artists to reimburse." She sniffled. "I don't know how I'll survive. I have to provide for Piper."

"Of course, you do," Dad said.

"Why would the mayor even want your old dilapidated building?" Paisley glanced at her sharply.

"Oh, um." She didn't mean to sound disparaging. "Why would he invest in the gallery when it's so damaged?"

"He's scarfing up buildings all over town." Paige swayed out her hands. "He even tried to get Bert to sell to him."

"No way. Burt would *never* sell his place to Mayor Grant." She would bet big money on that, but just the idea of the mayor taking over the town, being even more in control, riled her.

"That's what I thought." Paige wiped her nose with a tissue she took from her coat pocket. "I didn't have a choice in the matter since I'm leasing. But I planned to buy it someday."

"What can we do to help?" Dad shuffled his glasses up his nose.

"I thought Judah might be here. Might know what to do." Paige rubbed her hands over her coat sleeves.

"Like what?"

"Maybe stop his dad from taking over the town." Paige stared back at her.

"Not likely." Paisley almost laughed, but her sister's glare stopped her.

"He's good with this kind of stuff. Standing up for a cause. I thought he might jump in and help me."

Sure, Judah might offer her advice. But go against his dad? Paisley doubted that. Especially after his stint in jail and the mayor possibly influencing his release.

"Mayor Grant's taking advantage of folks who are already in a bad way." Dad pulled a multi-colored hanky out of his pants pocket and blew his nose. "Such a shame."

Taking advantage of others sounded just like Edward. But why would he bother with the ruined gallery? Was he stockpiling real estate? Was the building even worth his investment?

"Where is Judah?" Paige glanced around the room.

"At the cottage working." Paisley toed a bump on the floor where the linoleum bulged. "The same as everybody and their brother's doing in Basalt today."

"Oh, right. I should have known. Sorry to have bothered you guys." Paige whirled around and stomped toward the door.

Dad glared at Paisley.

"What?"

"You could have been nicer."

This wasn't her fault. Just because Edward happened to be her father-in-law didn't mean she had access to his evil brain. Besides, what could Judah do?

Still, she needed to work things out with her sister. "Hold up." She followed Paige to the porch. "I didn't mean to sound insincere. I'm sorry about your building getting into the mayor's greedy paws. I can't imagine that tyrant as a landlord."

Paige nodded. "Thanks."

Dad's footfall landed just behind hers. "If you want to talk to Judah, call him."

"That's right. His cell phone should be charged now." Although Paisley still doubted that he could do anything to change the situation with the art gallery.

Paige's lower lip trembled. She sighed a long, weary-sounding sigh.

"What do you need us to do, Sis?" Dad clasped Paige's hand, surprising Paisley with his show of affection. Even his voice sounded gentler when he spoke to his youngest.

A dig of jealousy from long ago twisted in her heart. Silly childish feelings.

"Um, would you"—Paige nodded toward Paisley—"be willing to come with me to talk to the mayor?"

What? "Where?" Not to his house. Please, not to his house.

"To his office. Or maybe his house. I don't know." Her voice rose. "You're still his daughter-in-law, aren't you? I mean, you can talk to him, right?"

Paisley snorted. "Technically, yes. However, we don't get along." Understatement.

Dark brown eyes mirroring hers shimmered back. Some said she and Paige could be mistaken for twins. She never bought into the assessment. They were too unalike.

"Aren't you and Judah back together?"

The question riled her a little. She had her own questions to ask Paige. *Are you dating Craig? Is he Piper's daddy?* Instead, she took a breath and answered truthfully. "We're working on it."

"Judah asked her to marry him again." Dad pumped the air once with his fist.

She expected Paige to frown or roll her eyes. Instead, she wrapped her arms around her. "I'm happy for you." She backed up, folding her hands in front of her waist. "By now you've probably heard I have a little girl. Piper."

Paisley nodded. "She's perfect."

Paige's face creased into a beautiful smile. "She's the best thing I ever did. The most holy version of life I will ever experience."

An image came to mind of Paisley holding her premature stillborn daughter in the hospital. Touching her tiny fingers. Her sweet little face. Had anyone tended the miniature grave where she put flowers before she left Basalt three years ago? Did the storm surge do any damage to the gravesite? Terrible thought. She'd check as soon as possible. Fortunately, the cemetery was at a higher elevation than most of the town.

"I look forward to meeting Piper." She forced the words past the lump in her throat.

"She'll love you." Paige gazed at her. "About the mayor? Will you come with me? Maybe if I can explain how important the gallery is to me and other artists in the area, he'll listen."

Tension seeped through Paisley's pores like a fever, spreading fast. She inhaled, then exhaled, controlling her breathing. "I guess I could."

Dad walked back to the door. "How did you get the news about the buyout?"

"Certified letter." Paige stuffed her hands in her coat pockets. "They warned me. The bank gave me ten days to drum up the cash. But when the second hurricane hit, how could I?"

"Edward knows that. He's a reasonable businessman." Dad shrugged. "Go talk to him."

Reasonable? Paisley coughed hard.

Dad frowned. "Even if we don't see eye to eye, he didn't get voted into office for being a sleaze. The people of this town trust him."

She had a much different view but bit her tongue.

"Before Blaine, Mayor Grant came to the gallery and helped me. I thought he was a decent guy, being neighborly." Paige scowled. "I was naïve. Should have known he was interested in my troubles for his own gain."

"A shark in kitten's fur," Paisley muttered then strode to the rocking chair. She pushed it back and forth, listening to it clunk against the aged wood beneath.

"The art gallery is my livelihood. I have to do what I can to save it." Paige lifted her shoulders as if to make herself taller or braver. "I can do this. Mayor Grant isn't the monster some make him out to be."

Right.

Even though Paisley's legs quaked, and her heart beat double time at the thought of facing her father-in-law, if her sister needed moral support, she'd go with her. Maybe the mayor wouldn't be at his office or his house. Was that too much to hope for?

Sixteen

Paisley lifted her fist in front of the mahogany door of the mayor's house, then froze. Three years had passed since her last visit here. Anxiety ratcheted up her ribs. Shivers crawled across her neck, chilling her. If she didn't faint, this would be her lucky day. What would the mayor say when he saw her? Accuse her of being unfit to marry his son, again?

Paige stood next to her, their arms touching. If only her sister knew of Paisley's great fear. How her knees knocked. How much she wanted to run away from this property.

"Did you bring a cell phone?"

Paige nodded.

"If anything happens to me—"

Judah's mom opened the door. Not the mayor—what a relief. She must have heard the car drive up because Paisley's knuckles didn't connect with the door. Her mother-in-law's eyes and mouth widened. "Oh, my. Paisley! You're here. I've wanted to talk to you." Bess's arms surrounded her in a warm embrace. "I'm so glad you came home, honey. So glad for Judah. For all of us."

The woman's kindness soothed some of her nerves, acting as a balm to an inner wound she couldn't quite identify.

Bess glanced at Paige. "Oh, hello, dear. Welcome. I'm Bess Grant."

"Thanks. I'm Paige, Paisley's sister."

"I remember you."

The two shook hands.

Heavy footsteps thudded toward them. Bess cringed and mouthed, *"Sorry."*

"What's going on here?" the mayor thundered as soon as he came into view. He yanked Bess roughly away from Paisley. When he released his grip, Bess stumbled backwards. She clutched her arm and massaged the area where the ogre manhandled her. Paisley wanted to go to her and see if she was okay. But crossing the threshold? Edging past him? No, thanks. However, she would if he dared to touch Bess again.

Paige linked arms with Paisley. Fear and dread bound them together.

Could a woman marry a man and not claim his father as a relative? She would do that in a heartbeat. She tightened the crook of her arm snugly around her sister's.

"What do you two want?" Edward growled, crossing his arms over his dark gray sports coat. A red stain marred his light gray tie. Jam? Wine? It would serve him right to wear a dirty tie all day and no one mention the stain. Then, later, for him to see it in the mirror. "I'm just about to leave. Say what you came to say, then go."

Paige cleared her throat but didn't speak. She gnawed on her lip and stared at the ground.

Paisley squinted up at Edward, despite his domineering stance that was surely meant to intimidate them. Where did Bess go? Hiding in the shadows? Poor woman married to such a man.

"My sister needs to talk to you about the certified letter she received in the mail today." She nudged Paige's arm.

"Go on." Edward's voice deepened.

Paige lifted her chin. "Mr. Grant"—her voice came out quietly— "I want to keep my business. It's important to the artists in our community. I've put a lot of money and work into it. Please, let me keep my lease."

"What business?" He scoffed. "Your little enterprise is washed up. You and half the town. You should thank me for rescuing you from your financial mistakes and ruin."

"Rescuing me?" Her voice rose. "Are you crazy?"

Edward's nostrils flared. The pores on his nose expanded. His hands clenched at his sides. One of the soles of his leather boots tapped the cement landing. He reminded Paisley of a bull preparing to attack the matador. She let go of her sister's arm and shuffled slightly in front of her.

"You may view me as someone who needs 'rescuing.'" Paige pulsed her index finger. "But if you think I'll let you take control of what I've worked hard for, dreamed about for so long, you are mistaken! I'll fight you with every breath in my body."

Go, Paige! Paisley was bursting with pride that her docile sister would stand up to the mayor like that.

"Do you imagine a wisp of a woman like you can rail against the mayor of Basalt Bay and get away with it unscathed?" He guffawed. "Just try it. You'll fail."

Was that a threat? Paisley squeezed her fists. Bopping the man on the nose passed through her thoughts. As did bragging about it to Aunt Callie and Maggie, ladies who'd consider it a badge of honor to spread such a story all over Basalt.

Paige glared at Edward. "How you purchased my building, and other buildings in town, and whatever little insider tricks you're playing while businessowners are down on their luck, is indefensible. Inhumane."

"You have no idea what you're saying. You should leave. Go!" Edward thrust his hand toward Paige's car.

A fifteen-second standoff of grimaces ensued.

"I plan to report your unethical acts to ... to Deputy Brian."

What? Paisley swiveled toward her sister. Why did she bring up Brian Corbin? Wasn't he one of the mayor's pawns?

Edward guffawed. Then he lunged forward, his finger jabbing the air. Paisley and Paige jumped backward. "Don't you dare accuse me of unethical behavior. You Cedars girls—" He spat. "Your precious deputy is nothing. A wart on a toad. If I want him fired, he'll be fired within the hour."

Precious deputy? What was he talking about? And how he rushed at them, yelling, threatening, made Paisley's blood boil. Wait until Judah heard about this.

"You're disillusioned to think people respect and admire you." Paige glowered at him, not giving up her fight. "They let you have your way because you're the mayor and you're rich. Not me. You can't take what's mine." She stomped her foot.

"Just watch me." He snorted. "You left the gallery ransacked. Abandoned. You broke your contract."

"I did not abandon it!" she yelled, surprising Paisley. "Everyone left their homes and businesses during the hurricane. It was the law. Didn't you prove that by having your own son thrown in jail?"

A tic twitched in Edward's jaw. "Get off my property! And don't come back."

"Edward!" Bess rushed forward from wherever she'd gone. "He doesn't mean it. You're both welcome here."

"No, they're not. Stay out of this." Edward lifted his hand as if to subdue her, then he squinted at Paisley and stuffed his hands in his pockets.

The cad. Anger burned through her. She clenched her fists until her nails dug into her palms.

He stepped toward her with a menacing gleam, but she didn't back away.

"Come on. He's crazy," Paige whispered then ran for her car.

Paisley didn't move.

"You're always welcome here," Bess said in a soft tone.

"No, she isn't." Edward thrust his finger toward his wife. "Stay out of my business!"

Bess and Paisley exchanged a meaningful glance. Something was wrong here.

"Paisley, let's go," Paige called from the driver's seat.

Just then, a loud engine roared up the hill. Judah's white pickup swerved around the corner, coming to a screeching stop next to

Paige's car. He thrust open the door and leapt out. He strode across the gravel and came straight to Paisley. "You okay?"

She nodded. How did he know she was here? Did her dad tell him?

"What's going on?" Judah crossed his arms and stood opposite his father.

"Hello, Son." Bess rushed forward and hugged him. "Thank you for coming."

Oh. Did she call him?

"Mom."

"Why are you here?" Edward's voice didn't sound as mean, now.

"Because my wife is here." He reached back and clasped her hand.

She squeezed his fingers. She owed him big time for this.

Paige scurried back over, apparently bolstered by Judah's arrival.

"Is something going on that we should discuss as a family?" His voice had a hard edge to it. "Paige is my sister-in-law."

"Just business. A misunderstanding." Edward huffed. "Nothing to concern yourself with."

"Paisley and her sister are my concerns."

The mayor shrugged. "Want to come in for coffee? Your mother made scones."

Seriously? After threatening Paige and ordering them off his property, he wanted them to come in for snacks?

"That's right." Bess wrung her hands. "We can sit down and have a pleasant conversation."

How could they ever have a pleasant conversation?

An awkward silence followed.

Judah glanced at Paisley. She shook her head discreetly. Even if half the house belonged to Bess, she refused to tiptoe through Edward's half.

"Not this time. But thanks." He gave his parents a tight smile. "When I finish fixing the beach house, we'll have you over for a barbecue."

Paisley would make sure to have a job by then so as not to be home. Maybe even request the late shift.

"Dad." Nodding at his father, Judah drew Paisley toward the vehicles.

Paige slipped behind the steering wheel of her car and started the engine.

"Paisley, wait!" Bess hurried over to them, patted Judah's arm, then faced Paisley. "I wanted to say, again, how happy I am that you came home. I hope we can be friends."

"I'd like that too." She clutched her mother-in-law's hand.

Judah must have gotten his sweeter side from her. Not from his dad.

Bess hugged Judah. "Don't stay away too long."

"Love you, Mom."

"Bess, let them go," Edward yelled.

Bess glanced toward Judah, then Paisley, with an agonized glint in her eyes.

"Is she going to be okay?" Paisley whispered as he opened the passenger door of the car for her.

"What do you mean?"

"Your mom. I'm worried about her."

"She's up here on the mountain by herself way too much."

Bess being up here *alone* wasn't what had her worried.

Seventeen

Two days later, Paisley and her dad were almost finished painting the living room walls with a cream-colored paint that resembled sage more than tan when it dried. The taping and mudding had turned out okay. Not professional, by any means. But she wouldn't have to hide her section of work behind a couch or deny her part in the project, either. Dad touched up some of her earlier efforts, but she didn't mind. With practice she got better at smoothing out the joint compound.

The next task was tackling the kitchen. Fortunately, it had fewer walls.

She wished Judah could help them still, but he had his own property to fix. Their property. She sighed. A few days had passed since they last spoke about their vow ceremony. Was she just imagining an emotional gap widening between them? Yesterday, he followed her back to her dad's house after they left his parent's place. But then he waved and drove off. Presumably to the cottage, but she'd wanted to talk to him about his mom.

She rolled more paint. This slow, tedious work gave her too much time to think. Did Judah even remember about the date nights they were supposed to be having? Spending time together alone, talking and planning, should be a priority, right?

Suddenly, Dad groaned and slumped to the floor next to his paint can.

"Dad, are you okay?" She dropped her roller and rushed over to him. "Can you hear me?"

"I ... hear ... you." His eyes opened. "Just tired. Weak." He leaned his forehead against the back of his paint-splotched hands resting against his knees. He exhaled a loud, throaty sigh.

"You're working too hard, Dad. You need to rest." She rubbed his shoulder. "Why don't you take a breather? Go upstairs and lie down for a while."

"Still too much to do."

"There's no rush." She gulped. She'd been pushing herself to get tasks finished, too. She didn't want her dad overdoing it. Better for her to step up and accomplish more. "Your health is important. Take it easy, okay?" She should take him to the doctor since he hadn't been checked since his low blood sugar collapse.

"You're one to talk." His tired gaze washed over her. A paint smudge decorated each cheek and the tip of his nose.

"I feel better now." She grabbed the paint cloth dangling from his back pocket and wiped some of the paint off his face. The rest dried already. He was right that she didn't rest as much as she should have after her near-death experience. But what about his diabetes? Was he testing himself? "Dad—"

"Don't start harping again."

"I'm worried about all the work you're doing." She took the risk of inciting his anger. "See how tired you got. Are you testing yourself daily like Craig told you to do?"

By his answering growl, the question frustrated him.

"Are you?"

"No! I didn't test today. Or yesterday." He scooted away from her on the floor. "Happy?"

"Are you kidding me? Of course, I'm not happy." Irritated? Yes. "So"—she tried speaking calmly—"you've been testing all the other days, right?"

"Mostly." He wiped the back of his hand over his chin which caused another smudge.

They weren't getting anywhere. "Let's take a break, huh?" She stood and held out her hand to him. "Then you can test yourself and we can both rest. Deal?"

Dad wobbled to a standing position.

He didn't want to be mothered. She got that. But she cared about him and wanted him to be around for a long time. Why was he so stubborn about his health? After the storm, she took up the mantle of pushing him toward taking better care of himself. But sometimes it seemed as if she wasn't making any progress.

After she washed the paint off her hands, she fixed them both a salad. Fortunately, the grocery store had fresh vegetables in stock. She took Dad's portion up to his room where she found him sitting on his bed with his back against a pile of pillows, reading.

She trudged back through the house, picked up her salad topped with balsamic vinaigrette and headed for the front door. Outside, she dropped onto the rocker and plopped her work shoes on the railing. Sighed. She stuffed a couple of forkfuls of spinach into her mouth. Then closed her eyes and chewed, savoring the food and relaxation.

"Paisley!"

She peeked an eye open. Maggie Thomas barreled across the street toward her. The woman's injury from her fall must be a lot better. What did she want?

Paisley chewed quickly. Heaven help her if she smiled with broccoli stuck between her teeth.

"Didn't you hear me?" Maggie's cranky-sounding voice climbed an octave. "I've been yelling your name."

"Hello, Mrs. Thomas." Paisley swallowed, then swished her tongue over her front teeth. "Did you need something?"

"I do." Maggie stood at the bottom of the stairs, huffing, glaring at her. "Pardon me if I don't climb those awful stairs again."

"Right. Um. How can I help you?" She dropped her shoes to the porch floor and stood, holding her plate.

"I heard from Patty Lawton that you're making the rounds. Sign me up!" Maggie's squinty eyes glowed. Her gaze darted from the stairs to Paisley and back to the stairs. Was she trying to make Paisley feel guilty about her fall?

The woman's words registered. "What rounds?"

"You know"—the innkeeper twirled her purse like a policeman's nightstick—"making amends. Community service to pay for your past misdeeds. Where do I sign up for the free labor?"

Paisley bit off a groan. "I offered to help Miss Patty, that's all." Working for Maggie Thomas? No deal.

"You wronged me too. If you're volunteering to make amends, I accept."

Paisley coughed. Goodness. Work for the crabbiest woman in Basalt? The same woman who accused her of stealing some gawdy heirloom jewelry?

"Well?"

"What, um"—she could hardly form the words—"what did you have in mind?" Alternative responses blared in her thoughts. *I will never work for you! I didn't steal your crummy jewels.*

"Can you start immediately?"

"No!" She had a lot of work to finish here. A lot. "I'm helping my dad. He needs me."

"I'm sure he does. But 24-7? Pshaw." Maggie tapped her foot. "Meet me at the inn tomorrow at nine. I have repairs lined up for you."

"But I'm not ... I can't—"

"Patty says you're a tolerable laborer. Nothing to brag about. I'm tickled to be on your indebtedness list." The woman nearly frolicked down the sidewalk. "Too-da-loo. Until tomorrow."

Paisley groaned. Of all the sinister twists. Of all the people she didn't get along with, Maggie Thomas was at the top of the list. Right next to Craig and Mayor Grant. Her appetite gone, she dropped onto the rocking chair. She should have defended herself. Or told Maggie she'd rather clean barnacles off the rocks with her teeth than to work for her.

But she had promised herself she'd do whatever was necessary to make amends. But working for the innkeeper?

She took a bite of salad as a past wrong flitted through her mind. Regret flipped over like a pancake in her gut. As a teenager, she had pelted Maggie's inn with mud balls and took her skiff without asking. Did Maggie find out about that?

She stuffed a cherry tomato into her mouth. Perhaps she could volunteer for one hour. Two, at the most. Then any past misdeeds would be paid in full. Sigh. Even if she worked twenty hours, Maggie probably wouldn't let her live down whatever it was she held against her.

She carried her plate into the kitchen. The house was quiet. Did Dad fall asleep? If so, she'd let him keep sleeping.

She picked up the paint roller and resumed her position by the living room wall. More painting meant more time to ponder stuff. More time to wish she hadn't started this making amends business. Then there was the way Edward treated Bess. Paisley couldn't let another day go by without telling Judah about that.

And she still hadn't collected on her dare. Maybe it was time to ask him for that one thing.

Eighteen

Judah took a long guzzle of ice-cold sweet tea. Ahhh. It hit the spot. For the last half hour, sweat trickled down his neck and dripped between his shoulder blades as he hauled rolls of tar paper up the ladder for the cottage's roofing job. An hour ago, he yanked off his shirt and hurled the soaking wet fabric over the side. A couple of boats passed by in the bay, and one enthusiastic female boater even wolf whistled at him. He'd snickered.

He took another long swig of tea before resuming his work.

Ever since Mom called two days ago, telling him to come and save his wife from Dad's wrath, he'd been mulling over what she said about his father buying up businesses, including Paige's. On the day Blaine hit, Judah had gone by the gallery to help his sister-in-law. Even then, he felt suspicious of his dad's interest in the art establishment. Perhaps the mayor wasn't as altruistic as he tried to make people believe he was.

Judah unrolled another row of roofing paper, hoping this one didn't blow off the side like the last one did thanks to strong gusts coming off the ocean. He still needed to go down and retrieve it and haul it back up here. Using the battery-powered stapler, he zapped the thick black paper a bunch of times as he moved down the line paralleling the roof's ridge.

He heard a car engine. A door closing.

"Judah?" Mia Till's voice.

Oh man. Why was she here?

If he remained quiet, would she think he wasn't home and leave? Not a nice way to treat someone. But Mia put him on edge. She flirted too much with him, along with every guy she met, it seemed. And here he was not wearing a shirt. Just great.

"Judah, you up here somewhere?"

The ladder swayed. Was she coming up in her high heels? If so, she could seriously injure herself.

"I'm on the roof. Stay where you are. Be right down." He leaned over the edge, waved. "Hey, Mia."

"Well, *helllooo*." She put her hand over her eyes, shielding them from the sunlight. She smiled brightly. Her gaze pulsed to his chest. "My, my, don't you look yummy!"

His cheeks burned. Why did he throw his shirt to the ground? He'd never felt more uncomfortable being bare chested than he did right now.

Mia fanned her face with her hand. "Judah Grant, you do impress a girl."

"Just get off the ladder, okay? And be careful." He wasn't in any mood to tolerate her flippant, flirty behavior.

"Hurry and join me. I have news!" Her voice almost got lost in the wind gust. "Oops."

"Everything okay?" He peered over the side. She held down her skirt. And, yep, she wore spiked heels.

"I'm okay." She waved and giggled. She backed down the rungs and stepped off the ladder.

Relieved, he sighed and made quick work of descending. As soon as he reached the sand, she hugged him. Hugged him! Sweaty torso and all.

"Excuse me." He disengaged himself. Then he jogged around the cottage to grab his t-shirt. He yanked it over his head, smoothing the damp fabric over his chest. Dirt smudges clung to the material, but he ignored the sweat and grit. "How are you?" he asked when he saw she followed him.

582   Mary E. Hanks

"Fan-tas-tic," she said in three exaggerated syllables. She pointed toward the roof. "How's the maintenance going?"

"Should be less leaks this winter." He tried keeping things light, still waiting to hear why she drove to the south side of town.

She ogled his t-shirt for so long he squirmed. She smoothed her hands down a pink short skirt with a hot-pink belt over a tucked-in white shirt. A dangly necklace swayed in front of her. Those heels sure were tall.

"What brings you out this way on a workday?" He needed to resume his roof repair. Lots to do before nightfall.

"I'm here to see you, of course. I miss you at work." She stepped toward him, placing both palms lightly on his arm.

He stepped back, freeing himself from her touch. Awkward.

"Mr. Linfield sent me here on official business." She giggled like she was here for anything but professionalism.

"What's up?"

"Other than this amazingly beautiful blue sky?" She gazed up at the heavens and squealed. "Wouldn't you just love to be out on the water on such a gorgeous October day?"

"Sure."

"C-MER's in business again, you know, and we need our right-hand people at the helm." She winked. "Good looking ones, if you know what I mean."

"Mia." He growled. How many times did he have to remind her that he was married? That he didn't want her flirting with him.

"Okay, okay. Can't a girl have a little fun?" She huffed. "I'm here waving a white flag, if you didn't notice."

"White flag? How so?" While working on the roof, he contemplated his job loss. He figured it turned out okay since he had the time that he needed to fix things up at Paul's and here at the cottage.

"Mr. Linfield sent me. Surprise! He wants you back." She clapped her hands.

"But Craig—"

"Has been demoted."

"What?"

She bobbed her head. "Mike sent me to extend an offer to you, Judah Grant, to take Craig's supervisory position. You'll have an office and everything."

"No way." He wiped his hands down his jeans. "What's this really about?"

"I'm serious. He's offering you the position."

"Craig's position?" He couldn't wrap his brain around it. "What about him?"

"Don't worry about him." She chuckled in a tinkly tone. "Good thing I'm not taking an employee photo. You are one big mess. One hot mess, Jude."

"Judah. And don't talk to me like that, please." He walked toward her sports car, hoping she followed. He needed some time to think about the job offer.

"Don't get your feathers all in a knot. What do you say? I'm supposed to bring back an answer." She fell into step beside him. "Interested?" She quirked her eyebrows.

"You're serious that Mike sent you?" He wouldn't put it past her to fib. He opened the driver's door and waited for her.

"I'm serious about the job, your good looks, everything." She winked.

"Stop with the flattery."

"Some guys wouldn't mind."

"I do. I'm married." He held up his hand with his ring to validate his point.

"Right." She gazed toward the ocean, still not getting into the car. "Lovely view you have here."

"Mmhmm. Why did Craig get demoted?"

"For firing you." She grinned. "And he was a naughty boy. Rumor has it, he did something that got him in heaps of trouble with the bigwigs." She clasped her hands in front of her hot-pink belt. "So, are you in or not?"

"I should, um, talk with Paisley first."

"Good grief. The woman left you. Why ask her anything?"

He scuffed his shoe in the sand. "She's my wife. Of course, I'll talk to her. Then I'll come by and talk to Mike myself." He wouldn't take anything Mia said at face value.

"Fine." She put one foot into her low-slung vehicle. Her short skirt flipped about in the wind. She grinned like she knew her power over men.

Judah averted his gaze. Wouldn't fall for her tricks. Would be on guard if he went back to C-MER.

"Did your dad mention I'm the chairperson for the town's reconstruction committee? I can't wait to work with him. He's such a great guy." She dropped into her car. "See you later, Jude." She backed up fast, her sports car spitting sand, and zoomed off.

"Judah." But he knew she didn't hear him.

Did Mike Linfield really want him back? It seemed the winds of change might be blowing.

Nineteen

Paisley stood near the door and perused their accomplishments. The living room walls were dry and looked nice. The flooring was a different story. She and Dad still needed to talk some more about that. He wanted linoleum, and she hoped to convince him to go with laminate or vinyl planking. Something easy to install.

He strolled into the room carrying a pile of Mom's old canvases. Uh-oh. He must have been scrounging through the pantry.

She cringed at the thought of the paintings she abhorred as a kid displayed on the walls again. Weren't those canvases ruined with the other flood-damaged items? "Are you going to put those up?" She heard the cranky tone of her voice. Couldn't help it. Those paintings brought out the worst in her. "I mean ... they're really ... ugly." Her voice dropped off.

His black glasses slipped down the bridge of his nose. He huffed. "It's my house. I can decorate how I want."

"That's true."

However, if he hung the one of the giant eyeball, or the one with black lips and a bleeding nose, she'd avoid this space like the plague. She never understood Mom's obsession with abstract-impressionistic art.

"Your mom loved her paintings." His voice sounded wistful.

"Doesn't mean she was good at it."

He glared at her.

"Sorry." If only she could explain and get some things off her chest. Yet something held her back. Maybe the grief in his eyes. The sadness as he gazed down at a painting of a child—or a dog?—hanging upside down from a tree. Were they comforting for him to look at? A hard leap for her to imagine.

She trudged into the kitchen. They replaced the sheetrock. Now it was time for more taping and mudding. Thankfully, the room was small. However, if people kept stopping by asking for help, she might never get Dad's house finished.

"Someone's here," Dad called from the other room.

See, people kept stopping by.

The front door creaked open.

"Hey, Paul."

"Judah!"

Judah? She peered around the dividing wall between the kitchen and living room. The two men shook hands.

"Good to see you."

He waved at her. "Hi, Pais."

"Hey." She smiled back. He looked good. Probably smelled good. With his damp hair, he must have just gotten out of the shower. He shaved his beard too. His smooth reddish face appeared sore after his two weeks of not shaving. He wore crisp jeans and a button-up shirt. He wasn't picking her up for a date, was he? She glanced at his black, steel-toed work boots. Nope. No date.

"Looks like you two have gotten a lot done. Good job."

"We sure have." Dad led him to a corner of the room and showed him something, maybe one of the flawed sections she worked on that he fixed.

Judah patted Dad's shoulder, then walked toward her. "Hey, beautiful."

"Hi." She smoothed her hands self-consciously down her paint-stained, mud-flecked t-shirt and jeans.

He kissed her cheek. Yep, he smelled spicy and good. He stroked his finger down her cheek. Held her gaze for several breathtaking moments.

"What's going on? You're dressed up. I thought maybe you came by to pay up on your date debt." She pointed at his shoes. "Until I saw those."

"Date debt? Oh." His cheeks flushed. "I'm here to talk with you."

"You dressed up to talk with me? Sounds ominous."

He glanced at her dad. "Can we talk privately?" He nodded toward the pantry.

Like she'd step foot in that room for a casual talk. "How about the front porch?"

"Or upstairs?"

Yeah, her dad would hear them on the porch.

"Sure." She led the way up the stairway. In front of her old bedroom, she paused and faced him.

"Mia visited me today."

That little troublemaker. "Why would she come out to your house?" Mia probably knew he was home alone and took advantage of the opportunity. "How long did she stay?"

"Not long." He blinked a couple of times and stared at her as if assessing her emotional state. "She was flirty like usual. Or more than usual. I just wanted to tell you. Keep things honest."

"Okay." She trusted him. Mia? Not a chance. "So, why did she go out there?"

"Mike Linfield sent her to offer me a job."

He said it so matter-of-factly she had to mentally replay his words. "She offered you a job with C-MER?"

"Yep. Craig got in some trouble, and they're offering me his position."

"You're kidding. A supervisor's job. That's great! Congratulations." She hugged him. When she stepped back, his expression sobered. "It is great, right?"

"Sure. I'm puzzled too."

"About why he sent Mia? Why didn't Mike just call?"

"Right." He spread out his hands. "So, what do you think? Should I take the job?"

"Why ask me?"

He groaned. "Pais, I want us to share in everything." His voice became almost stern. "I don't want us to keep living separate lives. Haven't we done that long enough?"

His pointed words hit hard. She gulped.

He raked his fingers through his damp hair. "Man, I'm sorry. I didn't mean to sound so abrasive." He looked contrite. "I'm nervous. Feeling trepidation about taking Craig's position."

"I understand." Although, his uneasiness set her on edge. He loved his job, so working at C-MER would probably make him happy. Him being around Mia again? That would cause her sleepless nights. And Craig? How would he and Judah get over past differences?

He took her hand. "What's your honest opinion about my taking another stab at a job with C-MER? Your opinion matters to me." His shoulders lifted. "Being on call all the time. Taking risks on the sea. All those played into our struggles before. Maybe that's why I feel apprehensive." His voice went soft. "Sorry about getting all tense before. I want more for us now, talking about stuff, you know?"

"I know. Thanks for including me in your decision." Even if it seemed by the way he was dressed that he made up his mind back at the cottage. Still, it was nice of him to stop and ask her.

"So—?" His blue gaze danced.

"This is your career. Your hopes and dreams. What do you want?"

He leaned in and brushed his smooth, beard-free face against her cheek. For a second, she wished he hadn't shaved it off. "What do I want? You by my side. Us, together. Forever."

A shiver rustled down her spine.

"I don't want to work somewhere if it's going to keep me from you, or our family if we choose to have one, any longer than necessary."

She inhaled slowly. They hadn't talked about kids in a long time. She disengaged her fingers from his. "You should do what's in your heart. I trust you to make good choices. If something doesn't sit right"—like with Mia, she wanted to say—"you'll figure out what to do."

"Thank you." He sighed. "Pais, what do you want? I mean, what do you really want?"

Why did things get so serious? But maybe this was her chance to take a leap toward honesty. "When I'm with you, I want this." She leaned her cheek against his dress shirt. Smelled his spicy deodorant. Heard the thudding of his heart. "Other times, I'm not as sure."

He nodded. His hands smoothed over her shoulders, her back. "I've missed you."

"Me too."

If he worked at C-MER again, she'd have to accept the receptionist as part of his world. Could she do that without stressing? He smelled way too good and was far too handsome to be in Mia's territory every day.

"Any chance you could fire Mia?"

He snickered. "You have nothing to worry about in that corner. I want to be with only you."

"You say the sweetest things."

"I'm just getting started." He tilted up her chin. His glassy gaze looked like he was going to kiss her. Maybe one of those deep kisses that bonded them together so beautifully. He drew closer, his minty breath on her mouth.

Footsteps clunked up the stairs. She jumped back as if she'd been caught kissing a boy back in high school.

"Excuse me," Dad said gruffly as he trudged past them and entered the bathroom.

As soon as the door closed, they both snickered and scurried down to the first floor.

"So, we're agreed I should take the job?"

She shrugged. "You need a job. So do I. Taking an old friend's position? How do you feel about that?"

"Not good. I plan to talk about it with Mike."

"Is that why you're all duded up?"

"Yes. And to see you." He kissed her chastely on the lips. Not what she anticipated upstairs. But his palms slowly moving down her arms made her want to spring back into his embrace.

She followed him out to his truck. Remembering about Maggie, she told him of the innkeeper's demands.

"Want me to have a chat with her?"

"Nah."

He opened the driver's door of his pickup. "She can't make you work for free. Amends are what you choose to do. Not what someone else dictates. Don't let her bully you."

Too late.

As he drove off, she wondered if Mia had anything to do with his rehire. Was the receptionist out to get something for herself? Namely Judah?

Paisley sighed and tromped back inside her dad's house. En route to the kitchen, her gaze collided with the evil eyeball of Mom's painting. A shudder coursed through her. She promised to finish the tasks here, but after that she was moving back to the cottage.

Or else she had to convince Dad to get new artwork.

Twenty

Later that day, Judah stopped by and handed Paisley an unmarked bag. "For you." He grinned. "Actually, it's a gift for both of us."

She opened the package. Inside she found a new cell phone. "Oh, thank you." She hugged him. "It's a wonderful gift."

"Even though we're both busy, I want us to stay connected." He tapped the box with his finger. "Unlimited minutes. We can talk every night the way we did when we were dating."

Hmm. Sounded promising.

He rocked his eyebrows. "I'll whisper sweet nothings in your ear. Say *goodnight* before we go to sleep."

Bridging the gap between them, planting a kiss on his lips, was tempting. But she remembered his job offer. "How did things go with your meeting at C-MER?"

"Better than expected."

"Really?" She should be glad for him. Not focused on Mia and her possible trap to ensnare him.

He made a slight bow. "You're looking at the new supervisor of coastal responders."

"Wow. Congrats." She stroked his arm, letting her palm rest against his elbow. "You deserve it, Judah."

"I'm glad to have a job. A pay raise too." He sighed. "I didn't run into Craig. Mia said he hasn't been back since the conflict."

Would Paisley's stomach clench every time he mentioned the woman's name?

"What is it?"

"Nothing. Silly worries."

"We're still working on 'us.'" He stared at her intensely. Maybe saw her doubts. "Nothing's changing that."

Surely, even he realized the reprieve following the storm was a holiday compared to his hectic lifestyle with C-MER. Since Basalt sat next to the Pacific Ocean, the agency he worked for was on an alert of one kind or another almost all of the time.

She felt him watching her. She stared at the swollen plywood flooring. Avoided his gaze. "What do you think about this wood? Should we pull it up?"

He crossed the empty room, scuffing his shoes over several of the swollen spots on the floor. "Best to replace it." He stopped in front of a picture of a potato-shaped face with a giant eyeball in the center. He squinted at it. "Interesting concept."

She glanced over her shoulder, hoping Dad didn't come down the stairs. "My dad and I disagree about the artwork."

"I can imagine. It could make a kid cry."

"Oh, it did. Believe me."

"I still need to get some work done on the cottage tonight, so I should go." He strode toward the door. Then he rocked on the soles of his black shoes. "Would you be interested in coming out to the house tomorrow? I want to show you what I've accomplished."

"I have that gig with Maggie."

"Oh, right." He stared at the floor. Not leaving but not saying anything.

Why did their relationship feel tentative? A couple of days ago, she felt so close to him. Living separately wasn't helping. Both of them being preoccupied with house repairs at two locations wasn't helping, either. Maybe the cell phone would make a difference.

She sighed. "I could come out for dinner after I finish at Maggie's."

He glanced up, a boyish smile on his lips. "That would be perfect." He took her in his arms, crushing her against him. "Oh, Pais, I miss being together. I want you to come home with me so much."

So he felt the distance too. Here in his arms she felt safe. Her refuge, if only for a few minutes. But he wanted her to take the giant leap. To meet him halfway, perhaps.

"There's so much to be done here. It's hard to just leave." That was true. Not an excuse. "But I am moving forward, trying to wrap things up."

"That's good." He released her. His baby blues hued almost navy. She detected a sadness in them. Loneliness?

Right now, they couldn't resolve the issues that would bring them completely back together. But she had determined to mention something the next time she saw him. "I'm worried about your mom."

He tipped his head. "Why?"

"Was your dad ever abusive?"

"No." His face paled. "Do you mean with my mom?"

She nodded. "You should ask her about it—soon."

He drew in a long breath. "Did something happen that I should know about?"

She adjusted her weight from shoe to shoe, uncertain how to explain. Would he think her view of his dad's rough treatment was due to her bias against him? Even so, she couldn't let it stop her from sharing what she observed. "Your dad grabbed your mom's arm like this." She clutched Judah's wrist. His eyes widened. "Then he yanked her backwards." She tried to demonstrate but couldn't move him.

"You're sure?"

"Absolutely. When you ask her, just be sensitive, okay?"

He stared at her so long she wondered if he even believed her.

Twenty-one

"When you're done sweeping up the broken glass, come straight to my office," Maggie barked. "I need you to haul boxes, lots of boxes, to the storage room. Then—"

Paisley blocked out the woman's third to-do list of the day. At some point, she'd just say she was done and leave. Maybe sprint away during a break, if she got a break. Four hours should be more than enough community service time to pacify the innkeeper. But would anything absolve the woman's grudge?

After Maggie left the room ranting about Paisley not accomplishing expected tasks, not listening to instructions, Paisley grumbled and swept up the broken glass. Earlier, Maggie told her to cover the broken window with plastic sheeting until a glass installer could get here. Since Paisley knew the waiting list for professional assistance in the hurricane and flood-stricken town was lengthy, she tried to do a thorough job.

After she finished stapling the plastic on the outside window, Maggie stomped over to her. "You're not doing it right!" Her voice screeched.

Paisley gritted her teeth. Free labor shouldn't be ridiculed. "How else do you want it done?"

"Stapled from the top, of course. You left too much plastic hanging over the sides. That part is puckered. Rain will get in!" Her snarky tone made Paisley's stomach churn. "You should have noticed your mistake and corrected it."

Or not done it at all. Or walked away three hours ago.

"I'll try to do it your way, Mrs. Thomas." Why did she agree to this exasperating work? All for the hope of reconciliation? Sigh. Yes, for such a hope. Although, the idea of working off her past mistakes seemed to be epically failing.

She stood on a short step ladder, and Maggie remained right next to her, watching her intensely, as she plucked staples from the wood—not an easy task.

The older woman made annoying tsk-tsk sounds. "Why, I never imagined you doing it like that."

"I've never covered a window in plastic before."

"Get out of the way." Maggie grabbed her arm and pulled her off the step ladder, then climbed up herself. "If you want something done properly, do it yourself."

If Maggie required perfection, then she ought to do it herself.

"What else do you want me to do before I leave?"

"Before you leave?" Maggie whirled around, nearly toppling off the ladder.

"This is such a waste of—" She bit back the words she wanted to say. *My time. My life!* "I have things to do. Helping my dad." And she was having dinner with Judah at the cottage—the highlight of her day.

"You haven't done half the chores on the list." If Maggie's glare could kill, Paisley would be limp on the ground. "I didn't know you were such a slow worker."

Her words stung. "A free worker, Mrs. Thomas."

"Not free." The woman stepped down from the ladder. "Your wrongs have piled up over the years like a canker sore eating away at my soul!"

Whoa. Paisley didn't have to put up with this. "I should go."

"No, you should not." Maggie's chest heaved. "I said I needed your help moving boxes. You have not fulfilled your obligation to me!" Her voice hit a screeching tone again.

"I've done enough." Anger pulsed through her. "More than enough."

"Cleaning up a little broken glass? Washing the bathrooms. Pshaw. You think that constitutes making amends for thievery?"

Paisley wanted to walk away, run away. To not put up with Maggie's antagonistic attitude for one more second. But she forced herself to speak humbly. "I admit I did some foolish things as a kid. But I never stole jewelry from you. *Never.*" It was time she stood up for herself.

"I don't believe you. Will never—"

"Too bad." Paisley cut her off. "I'll help with the boxes, but then I'm done."

When she finally got back to her dad's, although worn out, she jumped in with prying out the old floorboards alongside him. If nothing else, the physical labor helped get rid of some of her angst toward Maggie. *Some.*

Later in the afternoon, she and Dad walked over to the hardware store and arranged for the next day's plywood delivery. Miss Patty agreed to let them add the costs to Dad's account until his flood-insurance money came through for repairs. During the transaction, the two hardly spoke. He stood tightlipped and grumpy acting. Miss Patty kept her gaze on the computer screen. Their "cold shoulder" attitude toward each other was puzzling.

Finally, a little before five p.m., Paisley put on her boots and hiked out to the cottage. She could have driven dad's VW, but a beach walk sounded perfect. It gave her time to unwind and breathe in the salty air she loved. Time to put aside the unpleasant parts of this day. At the front door, she left her boots beside the entrance. She knocked once to let Judah know she arrived. "Hey. I'm here."

A spicy smell of barbecued meat reached her as she stepped into the living room. "Mmm. Smells great in here."

Judah entered from the kitchen, a giant spatula in his hand. "Hey, Pais. You made it."

"Finally." She heaved a sigh.

"Rough day?"

"Yep."

He strolled straight for her and kissed her cheek. Nice to come home to that every day for the rest of her life. Her thoughts skipped ahead to a simple wedding dress. Some new lingerie. Romantic thoughts danced in her head like sugar plums. Too bad it wasn't Christmas. Sigh. Other things needed to be done first. Things for them to discuss. Their hearts mended. Maybe tired as she was, she felt ready to skip some steps she previously deemed important.

"What made your day difficult?"

"Oh, you know, Maggie."

"Ahhh."

"The work at Dad's was strenuous too."

He nodded like he understood. Then he pointed toward the patio. "Join me on the veranda?"

"Okay." She noticed some of the improvements. "Hey, you already pulled the carpet and removed the damaged sheetrock."

"Yep. Roof's fixed too."

"Amazing." She stepped onto the pavers they installed a few years back. Memories hit her. Judah grilling and them eating meals in front of the sea. Dancing in the moonlight. Holding hands and walking on their beach. She thought of the last time they shared a meal together, here. So much transpired since their breakfast before Blaine hit.

"Excuse the sorry table arrangement." He pointed at a large cardboard box with a square of plywood lying across the top. "I lost our patio set during the storm surge."

"Oh, too bad. This is nice, though. Simple."

Chuckling, he pulled out her chair. "Have a seat. I'll grab the meat."

"If I sit down, I may never want to leave." She dropped into the chair and sighed. Her words hit her. *I may never want to leave.* She glanced up.

Their gazes met. "Sounds perfect to me, Pais."

She gulped.

He set a plate of barbecued chicken between them on the board and her attention homed in on the delicacy. She was hungry after her day's work and then walking out here. Two bowls of food already graced the table. Baked beans and potato salad. Deli specials from Lewis's Super. She recognized those from meals and picnics they shared in the past.

"Looks great."

He sat opposite her. Held her hands and prayed, his gaze facing the sky. When he finished, he asked, "So, really, how are you?"

"I'm okay."

She loved this, his attentiveness, his awareness of her, the way he gazed into her eyes. If only it could last. She recalled how cold things were between them before she left three years ago. Even though she agreed to a second chance with him, and wanted one too, she didn't forget what she hoped to avoid. Would this loving feeling survive another time around?

"I'm not perfect."

What? "What do you mean?" She disengaged her fingers from his. "I don't expect you to be perfect."

His eyebrows raised.

"I don't." Goodness, she knew better than that. She let out a little huff. But his gaze probed hers. She swallowed. Okay, maybe, in some small way even she didn't want to admit, he might be right. Perhaps she expected a smidge of perfection from him. Or for him to be her knight in shining armor like in the princess stories, or something. No flaws. No human weaknesses. But that wasn't fair. She wasn't perfect. Far from it.

"Good. Because at some point I'm bound to fail you." A somber expression shadowed his handsome face. His blue eyes glistened. But his honesty, and his truth, tugged on her heart.

That's what she wanted, right? For him to talk openly with her. For them to be able to discuss the hard parts of life and marriage. It made her want to be honest also. "I'm sure I will fail you too."

"Okay, good." He wiped his hand across his forehead as if wiping away sweat. "We got that out of the way."

She chuckled, feeling disarmed. Is that why he started the meal with the line about failing her?

He passed her the food plates. They ate and chatted about the house projects, his job, and her helping Maggie. Just normal husband and wife stuff. Something felt so right about being here with him with the sea breeze blowing over them. Not comfy like an old pair of slippers. Comfy like she fit. Belonged. The ocean waves pounding the shore, a lovely man in front of her, a bit of honesty exchanged between two wounded hearts. The realization and the hope that their lives were better together made her feel at home, at rest, with him.

It was tempting to stay tonight. To talk under the stars. To dance with him in the moonlight. To let whatever might happen between them happen. They were still married, after all.

"I'm enjoying this." Judah wiped his mouth with his napkin. "Talking like we've been together forever."

"I was thinking almost the same thing."

Did he hear the wispy sound of longing in her words? By the way he gazed into her eyes for a long time, maybe he did.

He shuffled his chair to the side of the table facing the ocean. He motioned for her to do the same. She inched the kitchen chair closer to his but kept some space between them. Maybe she didn't trust herself. Her emotions.

His raised eyebrows hinted that he knew how she felt. Yet his soft smile assured her he'd wait however long it took. Didn't he tell her that once before?

He linked the fingers of his left hand with her right. They sat for a few minutes, staring at the bay. A fishing boat chugged past. An orange-colored buoy bobbed on the distant waves.

"This is nice. The view. Being with you." She nodded toward the table. "Great meal. Thank you."

"You're welcome. And you can come over, or stay over, any time you want." He cleared his throat. "Not trying to push you. Just saying."

If he only knew.

"We can go on a real date, too, as soon as Bert's opens. Or we could drive to a nicer restaurant up the coast."

"That would be great. When do you start working at C-MER?"

"Monday." He made a wry face. "I want to get as much done here as I can, so it will be ready for you to come home." He lifted her hand to his warm lips and kissed her knuckles.

"You're so sweet." She placed her other hand over the top of his. "About the workload, I know you're super busy, but—" She hated to add more to his plate.

"Yes?"

"Would it be possible—and feel free to say no—for you to come over tomorrow and help lay the floorboards? James will be there. Dad and me. A motley crew. If you can't, I understand."

"For you? I'll do anything."

Their gazes tangled. Oh, boy. She couldn't look away. Didn't want to. He stroked his fingers down the side of her cheek, down the side of her neck. The stirrings of love, or desire, warmed her. Kissing him seemed the most obvious thing to do. But, considering her own thoughts about staying, how would she stop the fire once it started?

"Did you, um, talk to your mom?" Maybe they needed a shift in topics. A subject to cool their ardor.

He sat up straighter. His gaze darkened. "Uh, not yet." He cleared his throat. "Have you thought any more about when you might be ready for our vow renewal?"

"When do you want to get remarried?"

"Tomorrow?" He kissed her mouth. One brief kiss with a truckload of promise.

Heart pounding, she took a long breath. "Tomorrow. Is that even possible? There's so much to do." Even though it would only be a small gathering for a ceremony, even that took some planning.

He chuckled. "Wishful thinking, I guess." His face grew serious. "The reconstruction of the town, your dad's house, our cottage, will all take time. Rebuilding is a slow process. Takes time to mend."

Their gazes met and held. Goosebumps raced over her skin.

He broke the rope-like connection. "Is there anything you want us to do before we exchange vows?" He released her fingers and folded his hands in his lap.

"I'll have to think—" She held her breath an extra second. "Oh, I know."

"What?"

"Misty Gale." She pushed the word past the lump in her throat. "Her gravesite. How would you feel about us taking flowers over there together?"

"Of course. I should have thought of it myself."

"You don't mind?"

"No." He leaned back. "Wait. Did you think I might not want to go to my daughter's grave?"

"Oh, I didn't know." She swallowed. "Since we didn't, um, share much in the grieving process before, I'm not sure how that part of our lives will work now. Being at her grave after three years will be tough for me." A tender emotion overcame her, but she subdued it. Wouldn't give in to tears tonight.

He tugged his arm around her, drawing her closer. "For me too, Pais."

Sighing, she leaned her face into his neck. His understanding and sharing in the heartache were good signs. Steps in their healing process. *God, please, let it be so.*

Twenty-two

Judah finished yanking up the last of the ruined carpet from the bedrooms. He already threw out a giant pile of carpet chunks and foam underlayment, mounding it at the end of the short driveway. The city garbage trucks would hit this side of town by Monday or Tuesday, scooping up trash and ruined building materials left over after Hurricane Blaine.

He stomped around the empty living space, inspecting the flooring. Mushy. Not what he hoped to find. He'd have to rip out all the plywood like they were doing over at Paul's. Oh, right. He checked his watch. Paisley asked him to stop by at one o'clock. Almost time.

He heard a car door slam. He strolled to the door, swinging it wide.

His mom stood on the porch with her fist raised as if to knock. "Mom?"

"Oh, Judah." Her face crumpled and she burst into tears. Covering her face with her hands, her words came out stilted. "I didn't know ... I didn't know where to go. What to ... to do."

"What's happened? Come in. You're always welcome here." He laid his arm over her shoulder and led her into the bare living room. He'd never seen her so broken up. "What's wrong? Did something happen to Dad? Is he sick?"

"No, no." She wept and muttered something about not knowing how to explain.

He didn't have any furniture to offer her a seat. Other than— "Let me grab a chair from outside." He scrambled out to the patio where he and Paisley dined last night. Grabbing two chairs, he hauled them back to the empty living room. He set them in the middle of the space, facing each other.

Mom dropped into one, her gaze downcast. She wrung a tissue between her hands.

He should be heading over to help Paisley, but this crisis was more urgent. "What's going on? Please tell me." He sat in the other seat and leaned forward, elbows on his knees, facing her, giving her his full attention.

When she lifted her chin, her eyes were red rimmed with tears puddling in them and dripping down her face. That's when he saw an ugly, fist-sized greenish-purple bruise covered most of her left cheek.

"Mmmoooom?" His voice came out strangled. "What happened?"

"I left your father."

"Did he ... did he do this?" Anger ignited his core. His chest felt on fire. His fists clenched and unclenched. What kind of a coward would do this to a woman? To his mother?

"I don't want to talk about it." She wiped a tissue beneath her eyes. "He's your father." She sniffed a few times. "Even if I never wish to be in the same room with the man again, he's your dad. Always will be."

Judah didn't want to think of his paternal bond with Edward Grant right now. His gaze intent on the bruise, he forced himself to ask, "Did he do this to you on purpose?"

"When h-hasn't he h-hurt me on p-purpose?"

"Oh, Mom." He jumped to his feet. Couldn't sit still. He had to talk to his dad. Get to the bottom of such a horrible act. His father, the mayor of Basalt Bay, struck Mom? Unbelievable.

He rubbed his temples as he paced between his mother to where the kitchen began and back again. He reached out to rest his palms on her shoulders, but she jumped as if his touch hurt her. He pulled his hands back and dropped onto his chair again, trying to appear calm. But he couldn't pull it off.

"Has Dad done this to you before … hurt you?" His heart pounded hard. How could this be happening in his family? His father was a dignified, somewhat respected, leader in the community.

Mom glanced furtively around the room. "Can I stay here? I see you don't have furniture, but I can sleep on the floor. I won't take much room."

"Of course, you can stay. I have some furniture that didn't get ruined." He took her hand, trying to be gentle. "You want some coffee? Tea?"

"In a while, tea would be nice." She waved her other hand toward the back of the house. "Is Paisley here?"

"No, we aren't living together yet." He released her hand and scooted back in his chair. "We're waiting until we exchange vows again."

"That's wise. I'm proud of you, Judah. And Paisley." She patted his knee. "I'm thrilled you're getting back together. There are things—" She broke down crying again.

How could he comfort or reassure her? If his dad were standing here, he'd have plenty to say to him. *Rat fink coward. Hypocritical cad. Horrible husband and father.* But those thoughts stirred up his anger and weren't anywhere close to the love he should feel toward his parent. He'd ponder that later. Right now, he needed to be comforting and helpful to his mom.

Eventually, she let out a long sigh. "My leaving him will take some getting used to for all of us. I'm sorry to disappoint you. I held it together for as long as I could."

"Don't worry about me." He stared at her bruise again and still couldn't believe this happened. Mom had been the cream in the Oreo between Judah and Dad's relationship for a long time. He avoided his family home for years due to his father's antagonistic attitude toward Paisley. Even when she mentioned her unease about Mom, Judah didn't drive up and inquire. Now, he felt like a heel for not acting on her concerns. "Can you tell me what led to this?" He swayed his hand toward Mom's face, not even knowing how to address the issue.

"Does it matter?" She stared hard at him. Was she offended?

He gulped. "What did I say? Mom, I'm proud of you for staying with Dad. For trying to make it work. You've been a jewel. If he isn't aware of that, if he doesn't know you're the one whose held our family together, he's a fool."

"Thank you." She sighed again. "He'd never admit that. I've prayed for him for years. Hard to give up, even now. But I've endured too much, hoping he'd change." She shuddered and wrapped her arms around herself. "I won't take any more 'accidents' at his hands."

"Accidents?"

"His so-called accidents. Mistakes made during angry outbursts." She coughed, then cleared her throat. "I shouldn't say anymore. You need to have a relationship with your dad that isn't tarnished by my problems with him."

"Too late."

"Oh, Judah."

"No, Mom. I mean, I've had issues with him for years. You know that."

She stared at the wall for a long while. "So, where can I start?" She scooted to the edge of her seat.

"Start what?"

"Helping you. Painting, whatever. How can I assist you in getting things fixed up?"

"Mom, you should rest."

"That's the last thing I need. I prefer busy work. I've been stuck up in the house—" She shook her head. "What's the next thing? Floorboards coming up?" She stood and rolled up her sweater sleeves.

Judah groaned. He could hardly tell her no.

His cell phone vibrated. Paisley, no doubt.

"Um, Mom, I promised to help Paisley with the flooring over at her dad's." He slid his phone out of his pocket and held it up. "I'll tell her there's been a delay."

"No, you won't." She moved her chair to the far side of the room. "Tell me what to do. I'll get started while you help her. Keep your word to your wife." She stared intensely at him.

"Okay. But I'm not leaving you alone." Wouldn't this be the first place his dad came looking for her?

"I doubt he'll show his face here."

"He might." Judah wouldn't put it past him to try dragging her home like a caveman—even in a three-piece suit.

"Fine. I'll come with you and help Paul and Paisley."

He saw sincerity and determination in her gaze. And a brokenness he recognized from the way his own eyes looked in the mirror during the years Paisley was gone.

"As long as you don't overdo."

"Yes, Judah." She rolled her eyes.

Her sarcastic tone and eye rolling surprised him. She always seemed content with her life. Passive, even. Did she hide her personality, subdue her true self, because of Dad's dominance? Inwardly, Judah groaned. How well did he even know her?

He tapped out a text to Paisley. *Running late. Be there soon. Mom too.*

"Do you mind if I bring my suitcase in?" She headed toward the door.

"Not at all. Let me help." He ran ahead of her and opened the back of her rig. Only one suitcase rested on the carpeting. Thirty-four years of marriage and she left the house with one piece of luggage?

She set her hand on the hood of the SUV as if she needed the support. "It's been packed and hidden for a long time. I left quickly."

He clutched the suitcase handle with one hand and laid his other arm over her shoulder. "It's going to be okay. You're going to be okay." He'd make sure of that.

But what would happen to their family if she divorced Dad?

Twenty-three

Paisley heard a truck engine pull up. Judah's? She tiptoed across the exposed two-by-eight floor joists to reach the porch. A short while ago, she got a text from him saying he was running late. And that his mother was coming over too. What was going on?

She trudged down the uneven stairs, then scurried across the lawn.

Judah and his mom were just exiting his pickup. Bess reached her first and hugged her. Leaning back, Paisley stared into her mother-in-law's sad-looking eyes. Then she bit back a gasp when she saw a nasty bruise on her cheek. Edward's doing? Her gaze flew to Judah's. He shook his head.

"It's so good to see you." Bess's smile didn't reach her eyes. "Just tell me what to do. I want to help."

"You sure?" She laid her palm on her mother-in-law's shoulder. "Are you okay?"

"I will be." Bess linked Paisley's arm with hers and sighed. "How's Paul? Judah told me about his health scare on the drive over. How terrifying for that to happen while the town was deserted. I can't imagine what you went through."

"He's better. Stubborn, but better."

"I've met a few men like that." Bess winked at Judah.

Other than some awkwardness as each person glanced at Bess, they had a productive work session. Besides Judah and his mom,

James, Kathleen, and even Paige, came by to help. Paige and Paisley worked amicably, hauling boards and hammering nails, even though they hadn't discussed their personal issues yet. No one brought up any controversial topics. Even Dad didn't mention Bess's shiner.

At one point, she noticed Kathleen and Bess talking by themselves. The two women were huddled near the stairway, speaking quietly. Paisley knew Kathleen to be a kind and sympathetic soul. Hopefully, she had some encouraging words for Bess.

She was just about to take a coffee break when someone pounded on the door. His shoulders tense, Judah crossed the newly laid plywood floor and pulled open the door.

Edward stood there glowering. "Judah."

"Dad."

All work came to a halt. Paisley shuffled in front of Bess. Kathleen, with her small frame and slightly bent shoulders, did the same, the two of them forming a barricade. Paige trudged into the kitchen, obviously putting space between her and the mayor.

"Is your mother here?" Edward stepped across the threshold.

"I think it's better if you leave."

"Too bad."

Judah's stiff position, with his arms crossed and legs braced, kept his father from coming any farther.

"Hello, Mayor." Paisley's dad waved as if he didn't sense the tension in the room.

Edward lifted his chin, his pinched gaze traversing the group. He reminded Paisley of the bad guy in a Western about to face off with the sheriff and his posse.

"Where is she?" He stared hard at Judah. "You can't keep me from seeing my wife."

"I can keep you from hurting my mother!"

Edward wiped his knuckles beneath his nostrils. "So, she cried on your shoulder and fed you her lies, did she?"

Judah's muscles flexed beneath his work t-shirt. He opened and closed his right fist. "What lies would she tell me?"

"Some whiny drivel. How she doesn't want me to be the mayor. Doesn't want me cavorting with female constituents. How she tripped and—"

"Liar!" Bess pushed forward between Paisley and Kathleen. "Leave now or I'm calling the police!"

Paisley grabbed her arm, stopping her advance.

"Don't tell me what to do." Edward huffed. "Bess, you've carried on this foolishness long enough." He pointed toward the open doorway. "Come on. I'm bringing you home where you belong. I saw your car at Judah's."

"She's not going anywhere with you," Judah said sternly.

"Stay out of this, *boy*."

Bess lunged ahead like she was ready to do battle herself, but Paisley's linked arm stopped her from reaching Edward. Paige rushed over and clasped the woman's other arm.

"I haven't been a 'boy' in a lot of years." Judah stood almost nose to nose with his father. "You should go. When Mom's ready to talk, she'll call. Leave her alone until then."

"You think you can tell me what to do?"

"I guess I do, *sir*."

Edward thumped his index finger against Judah's chest. "I call the shots in this family."

"Not this time. You need to leave." Judah's tone sounded gritty as he stepped forward.

Paisley couldn't tell if he shoved his dad onto the porch, or if Edward backed up on his own.

"Every marriage has a few problems." The mayor spoke contemptuously. "You know that more than anyone. You and that whor—"

Judah gripped the mayor's coat and propelled him down the steps. Edward flailed his arms and yelled several profanities.

Paisley's heart pounded in her ears. Her mouth went dry.

Kathleen marched over and slammed the door.

Bess gasped and shuddered, almost falling backward. Paisley supported her arm and back in case she collapsed, even though her own heart rate hadn't returned to normal.

Kathleen brushed her hands together. "That's that. Back to work, ladies and gentlemen. We have things to do." She smoothed her hand over wayward strands of white hair.

"You okay?" Paisley slid her arm over her mother-in-law's shoulders.

Bess shivered like she had a high fever. "I will be. Thank you for your kindness. I didn't mean to drag my son into this. Or you. What must he think?" Her blue eyes, so like Judah's, peered back at Paisley.

"That he loves you. Will protect you, no matter what."

"That's not a son's job." Bess's lips trembled. "Should I go out there and talk to Edward?"

"No!" Paisley, Paige, and Kathleen said at once.

"I'm going to make coffee. Want some?" Paige patted Bess's arm.

"Tea?"

"Absolutely." In passing, Paige squeezed Paisley's free hand. They had things of their own to work out. Big things. But they were sisters. Family. They stood together against Edward twice now—that counted for something.

Male voices rose outside. More yelling.

"Oh, dear," Bess muttered.

"It'll be okay. Would you care to sit down?"

Bess shook her head but kept staring toward the front window. "Edward wouldn't dare hit Judah. He never hit him, even as a boy. I made sure of it."

That made Paisley want to weep. Bess had put up with Edward's manhandling since Judah's childhood? Despicable man.

Paisley's dad and James started hammering again, covering over the voices outside.

After Paige handed teacups to Bess and Kathleen, the two older women trudged upstairs. Maybe Kathleen would show Bess where the bathroom was. Or listen to her plight.

Paisley carefully stepped across the partially nailed flooring to get to the front window. Out by Edward's truck, Judah stood by the driver's door rocking his thumb toward the south end of town as if ordering his dad off Cedars' land. Edward said something that caused his mouth to snarl up. Cussing, probably. Then, the engine revving, the truck zoomed up the street in the opposite direction from where Judah had pointed.

When he strode toward the house, Paisley let out a sigh. "You okay?" she asked as soon as he entered the living room.

"Uh-huh. Where's my mom?"

"Upstairs with Kathleen."

"I'll have to watch her. Be on alert. Who knows what he'll do next?" A tight expression on his face, he trotted up the stairs.

Tension whirled back up into Paisley's throat.

"Crying shame," James spoke.

"What?" Dad fingered his glasses.

"My pop used to treat my mom the same way." He pounded the floor with the hammer aggressively. "Rough. Mean. Especially when he was drinking."

"The mayor's been drinking?" Dad's jaw dropped. "I doubt he's the sort to get drunk during the day."

"It's best if we don't talk about it right now." Meeting his gaze, Paisley nodded toward the stairway.

"Oh, sure. These things usually work themselves out."

They did? When did things ever work out without effort? Three weeks ago, when she returned from her stint in Chicago, Dad hardly spoke to her. If she didn't push and pry to keep the lines of communication open, they still might not be talking.

She glanced at Paige. When would they get their chance to talk? That her sister reached out to her about the banking issue, assisted with the flooring, and her kindness toward Bess gave Paisley hope that they could put the past behind them. Maybe embrace a sisterly closeness in the future.

Especially if Craig wasn't a part of her life.

Twenty-four

Judah leaned his backside against the porch railing and sighed. Tired from the day's work and disheartened by his family problems, he watched as Paisley rocked in the chair and spooned soup into her mouth. A simple act, yet he became mesmerized with the drops of moisture on her lips. Luscious lips he'd enjoy taking possession of, finding comfort in. Blame it on fatigue. Not thinking rationally. He didn't even want dinner. Maybe that was the problem. Too tired. Numb. Needy. "I should go." Before he did something Paisley might interpret as him being too pushy.

"Are you okay with your mom staying with us?" She gazed up at him.

Her tender look tugged on his spirit. Drowned him in another wave of yearning. "Probably." Not really. He wanted Mom to stay at the cottage where he could keep an eye on her. Protect her from his dad, if he dared come around. "Too bad my beds are all torn apart." He didn't think that through when he cleared the floors of all his worldly goods.

"She can stay in Peter's old room. My dad doesn't mind." Paisley scooped another bite of food into her mouth. "You can stay here too, if you want." She whispered the last part.

"With you?"

Her eyes widened. "Oh, w-well, I uh ..."

The altercation with his father still strummed in his gut, blurred his thoughts, made him act unlike his usual level-headed self. The idea of the man laying a finger on his mother— "Sorry. That comment ... I'm just tired."

"It's okay."

He sighed, again. "I appreciate your taking care of my mom. The cottage is a disaster. I need more hours in the day." He ran his hands through his hair, wishing he were home and curled up on a mattress. Or punching a boxing bag. More time in the day? He wanted this day to be over.

Mom shuffled onto the porch. "Shall I head back with you, Judah?"

"It's up to you."

"It felt good to lie down for a few minutes." She pointed at the night sky. "What a beautiful display of stars."

He glanced up. Sighed. How many times did he sigh in the last fifteen minutes? "What do you want to do, Mom?"

"I enjoyed visiting with Kathleen. A new friend. Do you realize how long it's been since I had a friend?"

A more peaceful expression graced her face than he'd seen in a long time. Why hadn't he noticed her strained expression before? Of course, he stayed clear of his parents' house for years to avoid Dad's callous remarks. And he was never good at calling his mom to check in. He clenched his jaw to stop himself from sighing again.

"Kathleen's great." Paisley stood and yawned. "She comforted me during the town meeting before the storm. Maybe we could have her over for dinner or something."

"Sounds wonderful."

The two women hugged, and such loving expressions rested on their faces that Judah felt the first inkling of peace since his mom showed up at the cottage. During Paisley's three years away, Mom used to call and tell him she was praying for her return. Her faithful reminders were an encouragement during his time of struggle. Maybe he could do that for her also.

"You don't mind if I go out to the house with Judah, do you?" Mom asked.

"Not at all." Paisley shrugged. "Just take care of yourself."

Mom brushed her fingers beneath her eyes. "I will. Things are going to be different now. I'll grab my jacket, then I'll be ready." She strolled inside, leaving him and Paisley alone.

"You knew something was wrong."

She nodded. "I hoped not. But I thought so."

"I'm sorry I didn't do something." He groaned. "If I went up there, if I called and asked her, it might have stopped this latest thing from happening."

"Might have." She clasped his wrist and stroked her thumb across the back of his hand. "Don't blame yourself. Your mom may have denied it. Made excuses for Edward. Or called it an accident."

"Maybe." He shifted his hand to link their pinkies. Being this close to her, sensing her empathy and understanding, was comforting. He sighed again, couldn't help himself. "Thank you for being so supportive."

"Of course. We're family."

Family. He touched his lips to her cheek. It wouldn't take much to deepen it into a more satisfying kiss, a more needy one, but he refrained. Things were too emotional. Too unsettled.

Mom returned to the porch, zipping up her jacket.

Paisley took a couple of steps toward the door. "Goodnight, you two."

"Night." He faced Mom. "Ready to go?"

"Mmhmm. I'll sleep good tonight."

"Me too." Unless his brain kicked in with more frustrating thoughts and questions.

During the truck ride home, he broached the subject he avoided all afternoon. "Do you mind telling me how you got the bruise? What did Dad do?" He didn't have to know, but he hoped to better understand the situation.

Her lengthy pause either meant she didn't want to talk about it, or she was pondering her answer. She let out a breathy sigh. "He yelled and threw a couple of hardback books at me. One contacted my face."

"Books? On purpose?"

Her glare, even in the darkness of the cab, reached him.

"I'm sorry. I didn't mean to sound like I disbelieve you. It's just … a book?"

"He's been acting more aggressive. Enraged about everything." Almost to the beach cottage, she spoke again. "He forces me to stay at the house."

"What do you mean?"

"He doesn't want me to talk to anyone. No phone calls. No coffee visits. Not even with you."

"Why would he treat you like that?"

"I might say something that'll embarrass him. Tell someone he's a selfish hypocrite."

"I'm so sorry for what he's put you through." He groaned. "And I'm sorry for not seeing it."

She shivered like she was freezing even though he turned the heat up as high as it would go.

"When he came to Paul's house demanding that I go home with him, he meant it. He'll come after me again. You can count on it."

"You're a grown woman. He can't make you do his bidding. You can do what you want."

Her sarcastic laugh didn't even sound like her. "I haven't done what I wanted in years. Until today." She sank back into the seat. "For now, I'm free."

For now? "You can stay with me as long as you want."

She patted his hand where it rested on the steering wheel. "You've been so hospitable, welcoming me into your home. Thank you for that. But you and Paisley have your own lives. I'm looking forward to your vow renewal. Wouldn't miss it for anything. And I won't get in the way by hanging around your cottage too long."

"We've got a lot to do before then." He swallowed the dryness in his throat. "I confess to being impatient. I want to get on with being married."

"Of course, you do."

"I've waited a long time to get my wife and my life back."

"Yes, you have. I'm so proud of you for waiting. For accepting her back."

"I love her. She is a part of me."

"She's a lucky woman." After a pause, Mom continued. "Your dad and I used to love each other too. There are things—" She shook her head.

"What were you going to say?" He pulled into his driveway and shut off the engine.

"Some things are better left unsaid." She opened the door.

Judah opened his. "Even though Dad's being a jerk, I'm sure he loves you."

"Loves me? You must not have heard a word I said. Edward Grant loves Edward Grant. He's no longer the man I married."

"Why didn't you leave him before?"

"Because of you, our wedding vows, and my lack of courage." She sighed. "I held onto hope that things would improve. That he'd change. Like you've wished about Paisley for the last three years."

He and Mom had more in common than he realized. "And now?"

"I'm all done living in fear." She trudged around the other side of the truck, meeting him near the engine. "I am sorry for disappointing you." She clasped his hand, her fingers icy.

"I'm the one who's sorry for not recognizing what Paisley did. For not believing what she told me."

"She's a lovely girl."

"I know." His words came out hoarsely.

At the front door, she spoke, "Paisley recognized what you couldn't because of her own past with abuse."

A cold nausea rushed through his middle. "I never abused her. Would never—"

"Not you. Of course not." She patted his coat sleeve. "You're a good man. A loving husband."

Nice to hear. But how did she know about Paisley? And what had she heard about his wife's past?

Twenty-five

Someone pounded on the front door. Judah groaned and grabbed his cell phone. Six a.m. Still dark out. He pushed himself off the mattress he placed on the floor last night and pulled on his jeans. The banging continued. "Okay. Okay."

"Judah?" His mom's voice sounded faint, weak. Scared? "Do you think it's—?"

"Uh-huh."

"I can get up and speak with him."

"No. I'm dressed. I'll take care of this." He shoved his feet into his slip-on shoes. "Stay put." He rushed by the guest room where he set up the twin bed for her.

Striding past the kitchen, he flipped on the light switch. He'd go out on the porch. No way was his father coming inside. But as soon as he cracked open the door, Dad shoved past him and barreled into the empty room.

"Dad. Wait." Was that alcohol on his breath at this time of morning? "Hold on. You can't just—"

"Where is she?"

"This is a safe place for her. Lower your voice. Stay calm." What if Judah couldn't contain him? He'd call Deputy Brian if he had to.

"Bess! Bess, get out here!"

"Stop yelling." Judah grabbed his arm.

"No one tells me what to do!" Dad yanked free of his grip then stomped around the room. His hands chopped back and forth, his eyes bugging, tension rippling along his shoulders. "Bess! Get out here before I come get you."

"Dad, stop. Quiet down or leave."

"Don't tell me—"

"This is my house. You're an intruder. I *will* tell you what to do." He braced out his hands toward the older man, prepared to do what he had to do to stop him.

"Get your mother before I—"

"She's not going anywhere with you."

His dad nearly butted noses against his. That's when Judah got a strong whiff of the man's horrendous breath. Smelled like a distillery.

"This is a squabble between her and me. Butt out of my affairs."

Affairs? Judah winced.

"Bess, come out here right now." Dad clambered toward the bedrooms.

Judah stomped after him, grabbing his arms.

His father yanked away, punching the air in front of him. "Don't do that again."

"Don't do what you did to Mom ever again." His temper ignited. "Don't manhandle her. Don't hurt her. Treat women with respect, isn't that what you taught me?"

"Get your mother, *now*, or you'll be sorry."

"I won't." He stiffened himself to resist a punch or whatever Edward—he didn't even want to think of him as "Dad"—intended. In the past, he experienced a plethora of angst-filled moments with this man. None compared to how he felt now.

The guest room door creaked open. "Judah?"

"Mom, stay back." He glanced over his shoulder as she stepped into the short hallway.

Edward's gaze homed in on her. He didn't smile, but he sighed, perhaps relaxing a little.

Mom wore a sweatshirt and a pair of pajama bottoms. Her arms were crossed over her middle. "I'll talk to him for a minute."

"Not here in the hall. Not like this."

"Fine." Edward stomped into the living room. "Get in here, Bess." His commanding tone left no doubt he expected obedience.

"You don't have to do this," Judah spoke to her. "He's been drinking. Might be volatile."

"He'll just keep coming back if I don't talk to him." Her shoulders sagged. "Don't worry. I'm not going with him."

Judah set his arm over her shoulder and felt her tremble. If she had a teaspoon of the adrenaline rushing through his veins, she'd possess the courage to face Edward with her chin held high and boots ready to kick him in the rump.

"Grab your stuff!" Edward yelled. "We're leaving."

Take a hike—Judah wanted to say. But as much as he wanted to interfere, he wouldn't except to defend his mother.

"I'm not going with you," Mom said quietly.

"Judah, give us some privacy." Edward rocked his thumb toward the front door. "This is none of your concern."

"I'm not moving." He crossed his arms. "And use a nicer tone when you address Mom."

"So, what's your plan, Bess?" Edward's voice came out snarly.

"I said use a nicer tone!" Judah took a step toward the man he wanted to kick out of his house.

Mom squinted at him as if she was surprised by *his* tone. "I'm staying here until Judah and Paisley's ceremony."

"That could take months." Edward thrust out his hands.

Not quite.

"Then what?"

"I'll find another place to stay. Rent a room." She shrugged. "Maybe buy a condo."

"A condo?" Edward roared. "With what?"

"Savings." She squinted at him. "How about with alimony?"

Edward inhaled like he had a fish bone stuck in his throat and couldn't cough it up. "Not this side of the Pacific, you won't." His voice rose a couple of decibels. "Taking a break from our marriage is one thing. Present company did that." He sent Judah a piercing glare. "Getting divorced is out of the question."

Judah gritted his teeth, fighting the urge to respond.

"See this bruise?" Mom's voice rose. "You did this."

Edward jerked, then huffed.

"You will never hurt me again. Just so you know"—she tapped her cheek—"I took photos of it."

Edward shuffled his shoe against the raw board. "Ah, Bessie"— he whined, sounding much different than moments ago—"I didn't mean to hurt you. I love you. You know that, right?"

She made a strangled cry. "You didn't mean to sprain my wrist a month ago, either. You didn't mean to leave bruises on my shin before that." With each indictment, her voice got louder. "You didn't mean to throw the pottery plate at my head and cause the scar I've kept hidden beneath my hair. Need I say more?"

Judah's stomach roiled. "Dad?" His voice sounded just as strangled as Mom's.

His father didn't answer. Didn't refute her statements, either. His shoulders slouched. He appeared a decade older than yesterday. He swiped the back of his hand beneath his nose. "Come home with me, please. I'll make it up to you. I promise to never do those things again."

"You said the same thing last time." Mom exhaled a loud breath. "And the time before. Just go ... leave me alone."

"I agree. You should go." Judah pointed toward the door, his hand shaking. "Before I do something I'll regret."

Edward didn't budge.

Judah stepped closer. "Don't make me force you to leave, because I will. Do what's right."

Edward glared at him like he was going to refuse, but then he trudged toward the door. With his hand on the doorknob, he paused. "What am I supposed to tell people? What do I say?"

Leave it to him to worry what others thought instead of being concerned about losing his family. His marriage. His wife.

"Figure it out yourself," Mom said. "I'm done caring what other people think."

Edward opened the door and trudged outside. As the cool air hit Judah, something sharp twisted in his gut. He had been guilty of indifference in his marriage. He contributed to Paisley's feelings of being lonely, sad, and unloved. But how did Mom put up with her husband's violent actions? How did she survive? Had she ever confided in anyone?

"I'll be back tomorrow." Edward stomped across the porch.

"No!" Mom yelled after him. "Don't come back. If you talk with a counselor, or a pastor, I might speak to you. Otherwise, I never want to see you again."

Edward pivoted on the steps, his eyebrows raising to his hairline. "What do you mean? Expose my failings to a stranger?"

"Pastor Sagle is hardly a stranger."

"To me he is!" Edward shouted then marched through the sand to his rig.

Judah had one more question to ask him. "Mom, I'll be right back."

"Don't try to intervene. This is our business. Your dad's right on that point."

Even so, he closed the door then jogged out to the truck.

The window rolled down. Glaring eyes peered back at him. "What? Haven't you caused enough grief?"

"Are you ... are you having an affair with Mia Till?"

Edward slapped the steering wheel. Swore. "What kind of a question is that for a son to ask his father?" Smoke seemed to spew from his ears. "I'm not telling a traitor like you anything."

Judah ignored his lashing out. "Are you?"

Edward grabbed the gearstick. The engine revved. "I'm the mayor of Basalt Bay. That blond, while gorgeous and flirtatious as all get-out, is young enough to be my daughter."

Judah couldn't forget her implications. "An emotional affair, perhaps?"

Edward hawked and spat, just missing Judah's face, then gave the truck too much gas, spinning the tires, pelting sand in the driveway. Once the vehicle reached the road, its tires squealed. The rig flew down the road.

He shouldn't even be driving. And he didn't answer Judah's question.

What kind of trouble might he cause next?

Twenty-six

Paisley strode across the empty living room to answer the door. She'd had her morning coffee. Had a mental list of things she needed to accomplish. Text Judah. Check on Bess. Finish the mudding and taping in the kitchen. Gut the pantry—could she just burn down the dreadful room? She opened the front door.

Paige stood on the porch holding Piper. "Good morning."

"Hi." Paisley's gut reaction was to shut the door. A ridiculous response. She wasn't a child to run from trouble. These two were family. Her sister and her niece. Still, their appearance made her feel unsettled. "Come in." She backed up. "Dad hasn't come downstairs yet."

Paige stepped inside. "Piper wants to see him." She smiled at her daughter. "Don't you, Piper? You want to visit with Grandpa?"

The girl nodded, then hid her face against her mother's sweater. "She's shy."

Paisley shut the door and followed Paige into the kitchen, wading through awkwardness a foot deep.

"Is he awake yet?"

"I haven't heard any noises from upstairs."

Paige set the toddler down and squatted beside her. "Piper, this is your Auntie Paisley."

Auntie. Gulp.

Paige and Piper gazed up at her. Seeing the sparkly-eyed child filled her with yearnings for motherhood. Or aunthood. Was this her sister's olive branch?

She squatted beside them. "Hi there, Piper. I'm glad to meet you." She held out her hand.

The girl hid her face against her mother's clothes, keeping her hands tucked between them.

"She's not good at shaking hands with people." Paige stood.

Paisley stood also. "I hope we can be friends." She patted Piper's shoulder.

"Auntie Paisley is married to Uncle Judah."

"Unca Dzuda! Unca Dzuda!" Piper danced around and ran for the front window.

"She loves Judah." Chuckling, Paige strolled to the bottom of the stairs. "Dad! I brought Piper over. Can you come down and say hi?"

"Be down in a minute," his rough morning voice called.

Paige lifted her shoulders. "It's our routine."

"You come over every morning?" Dad didn't say anything about it. Were they staying away because of her?

"Most days. Not every day."

"So, did you know about his illness?" Maybe she had it wrong. Perhaps Paige worked with him, trying to get him to take his insulin, taking part in his care.

A shadow crossed her sister's face. "I'm sorry to say I didn't. He's been slowing down. Aging. Normal stuff, I thought." She sighed. "I wish I recognized his decline sooner. I guess I've been preoccupied with being a single mom while you were gone."

While she was gone. The sting.

Paisley lifted her chin, pride filling her empty chest cavity. But then her angst melted. She didn't want to cling to grudges anymore. "When I came back, I saw a difference in him. Aloof and disinterested, but not sick, you know?"

Paige nodded. Perhaps relieved for them not to fight about their father's health. Paisley did, after all, leave town without warning. Stayed away for three years. Things for her to remember when she talked with her sister about reconciliation. Although, there was still the matter of Craig.

Dad shuffled down the stairs, his hair sticking up, and his unbuttoned flannel shirt revealing a stained t-shirt beneath. "There are my girls."

His girls. Was he including Paisley? Or just referring to Paige and her daughter? Who wouldn't love a dolly like Piper? Misty Gale may have even looked similar with darker hair. Where did the two-year-old get the blond hair? Most of the family had dark hair. Even Craig's was dark brown.

"Hi, Dad." Paige hugged him when he reached the main floor.

Piper squealed and charged at her grandfather. He scooped her up and bounced her. She asked him to take her to the window so she could show him something.

"Care for some coffee?" Paisley strode to the coffee machine, needing a task.

"No, thanks. I drank plenty already." Paige pointed toward the lower walls of the kitchen. "Looks like you have lots of work to do."

"Never-ending tasks." Paisley watched the coffee maker drip brown liquid into her cup, searching for small talk. Maybe something about the ocean. Or her time in Chicago. Or Paige's art. What did sisters talk about after three years of no communication?

"When are you and Judah going to have your c-ceremony?" Why the catch in her voice? Paige gazed out the kitchen window as if her thoughts traveled a million miles away.

"We haven't set a date. Still catching up on house repairs after the storm."

"Oh, right." A pause. "I hope I'm invited." Her tentative expression reminded Paisley of the young sister who used to sit at their mom's side doing art, painting, sketching, trying to appease the difficult woman by doing everything right. Such a burden.

She, on the other hand, had never been able to please or appease Mom. But why regurgitate that subject when she was trying to let it go? "Of course, you're invited."

"Good. Thanks."

When they were growing up, she and Paige were never close the way she and Peter were. Nor was there a horrible clash. Not until she didn't attend Mom's funeral. Then the two hurled insults spanning twenty-some years of sisterhood. Did Paige remember that awful day?

"You're selfish and unkind"—Paige's words. *"You only think of yourself. She wanted to talk to you, make things right before she died. But you couldn't set aside your blame. Your hate!"*

Paisley stared out the window, putting emotional distance between them. From then, and now.

"I should go." Paige shuffled a few steps away. Maybe she felt the gap too.

Paisley poured creamer into her coffee, stirring, contemplating what the future might be like if everything were different. If she went to the funeral. Never met Craig. Never left Judah. Didn't go to Chicago. Mind boggling what-ifs. Irreversible decisions that affected more than her. Maybe she should just jump in and ask Paige about Craig. Get the conversation over with. Wasn't he the elephant in the room?

Instead of walking away, Paige retraced her steps. "I wanted to tell you that I plan to speak with someone at the bank today. And maybe a lawyer." She nodded toward the living room. "I can't let Mayor Grant control my business affairs, threaten me and others in town, without putting up a fight."

"Sounds good." Paisley grabbed her mug. "It's about time someone put the mayor in his place."

"You don't care?" Paige looked uncertain. "Even though he's your father-in-law? Judah's dad?"

"With the obnoxious way he acts? Hardly."

"Good to know. I'll talk to you later." Paige lifted her hand.

Childish squeals came from the other room. Laughter. Goodbyes. Sweet sounds.

Paisley sipped her coffee and stared out the plastic-covered window, imagining what Misty Gale would have been like as a four-year-old.

Her phone vibrated. She focused on the screen.

Had a visit from Edward. Judah's text.

How did it go? She tapped in, noticing he didn't say "my dad."

Not good. Demanding as ever. Typical Mayor Grant.

How's your mom? She cared about Bess. Edward could take a long walk off a short dock.

Mom wants to stay here. She told him to get counseling.

Good for her! She inserted a happy-face emoji.

I'm going to work here today. Start the job on Monday.

Two days. Not much time for them to talk about sensitive issues they still needed to face, or to go on one of those dates.

Sorry I can't be in two places at once.

No worries. Look after your mom. Make sure she's okay. Same as me with my dad.

What a pair we make, huh?

She thought of his warm kisses. Of the way his arms surrounded her and made her feel at home with him. Of the spicy scent of his deodorant and aftershave lingering on her after she hugged him. Yes, they made quite the pair. Even though the tone of his texts was serious, she decided to send him a flirty one. He could use something lighthearted. So could she.

Tell me one thing you like about me. She sent an emoji of a girl shrugging.

He sent four emojis. A heart. A rose. A kissing face. Two hearts.

Tell me one thing, she persisted.

I love the way you gaze into my eyes like you really see me.

Her breath caught in her throat.

I love your smile.

The way your heart beats in time to mine.

That was three things. His responses stirred up deep emotions in her.

She tapped the screen. *You're a sweet man. I love that you love me.* She held her breath, waiting.

I do.

She exhaled. Soon they'd exchange those two words in a ceremony. When would that happen? Her thoughts skittered in a different direction.

I'm still waiting to cash in on our dare. She couldn't let him forget about that.

Bring it on!

She laughed and ended the texting session.

She and her dad worked for a couple of hours in the kitchen. Yesterday, when Judah and James came by, they cleared out the fridge and stove, leaving easy access to the walls.

"I hope we never experience a hurricane again." Dad moaned. "My father would be outraged to see his house flooded. Walls torn apart. The tree he used to climb chopped up and gone."

"It's been rough. But, other than the tree, things are nearly as good as new, right?" She spread some mud with the trowel.

"Never the same."

"No. But what if it's better the second time around?" For her, speaking up took a step of faith, a chance to look for something positive in the middle of the hardships. "If we never had the storm, we wouldn't have had all this time to work together. Time to talk."

Unexpected tears flooded her eyes. What if he had died after the hurricane? What if she never got the chance to make things right with him? A grief she didn't realize she still carried twisted in her chest, followed by a sorrowful moan. She set down the trowel and pressed her fist against her mouth to subdue it. She bent her head so her dad wouldn't see her tears. Silly tears.

"What's wrong?" He tipped his head down, staring at her.

He wouldn't understand. Goodness, she barely understood.

His arms came around her. "What happened, Paisley Bug?"

Paisley Bug? His pet name for her was her undoing. She leaned into his flannel shirt and cried.

"Did I say something wrong?" He sounded baffled.

"I'm just so sorry for leaving the way I did."

His arms stiffened. He pulled back. He probably didn't want to dig up old memories. Neither did she. Yet, the moment seemed to be glaring her in the face.

"I know I hurt you." She gripped his wrist, preventing him from moving farther away. "I regret that."

"We talked about this the day of the storm. What's done is done."

She leaned back with her legs folded beneath her and faced him. "But you didn't accept my apology. We still ... need to talk ... until we can make things right."

"Don't see why." He slapped some mud on the wall. A few splatters hit the floor.

"I disappointed you when I didn't attend the ... Mom's ... funeral."

A tic throbbed in his jaw. His bluish gray eyes squinted at her. "Why discuss what can't be changed? Are you sorry you didn't attend your mother's funeral?"

"Yes."

He jerked like the word startled him.

If she could go back and fix that part of her life, of course, she would. "I'm sorry for the bad decisions I made. For hurting you. Mom. Paige."

He gazed at her with a softer look, nodding like he understood. Finally.

Another issue came to mind. Should she say something? Would there ever be a better time? She took a deep breath, knowing he probably wouldn't appreciate her question. "Why didn't you ever rescue me from the pantry?" The words tore from her lips, from her heart. A weight pressed down on her chest.

Dad released a slow breath. "She"—he cleared his throat—"called it a quiet place. Somewhere for you to mull over your actions. I didn't see any harm in it at first."

His words nearly sent her heart into palpitations. She grabbed a wet cloth and wiped mud off her trembling fingers. "Did you question that a dark locked room wasn't a healthy place for a child?" She kept her voice as calm as possible. "Did you?"

"I—" He bit his lip. "I can't speak ill of your mother."

Powerful emotions surged through her. "Please. I've waited a long time to hear your explanation."

He stared into the mud bucket. Lost in thought, perhaps. "I questioned her. Told her to let you out."

"You did?" The tension squeezing the air out of her throat eased. One by one, chains unlinked. Air flowed more freely into her lungs. Easier to breathe. "And—?"

"I said you were small. You shouldn't be left alone." He stared at the wall as if watching a scene in the past. "You weren't a bad child. Adventurous. Sometimes mischievous. Not bad."

He stuck up for her? Defended her! Oh, goodness. This changed everything. Everything! She linked her arm with his and leaned her cheek against his shoulder. "Then what?" She felt like a little girl and her father, the man she trusted, was telling her a story with great meaning. A story about her and him.

"We fought. Terrible arguments. She said I was gone from the house too much to pass judgment on her parenting." He picked up the mudding tool and spread some goo on the wall as if Paisley's arm wasn't still linked with his.

She lowered her hands to her lap, shuffled back a little. "Didn't you argue for your right to have a say in your daughter's upbringing?"

"Yep. Slept on the couch for a week." He gulped. Staring at her, he sniffed. Was he fighting his emotions? "I told myself you'd be okay. You had a fiery personality. You were okay, right?"

Such a travesty. Such a loss. "No, Dad, I wasn't. I'm still not okay."

His lips trembled. So did his hands. His eyes filled with moisture. "I'm s-sorry t-too." His face crumpled into a grimace that tugged on her heart. "I n-never would have p-put you in there. Never. I hated it more than I hated anything in the world." His shoulders shook.

She leaned forward and wrapped her arms around him, pressing her face against his shirt. In her heart of hearts she knew her loving father could never have approved of that treatment. Yet she blamed him, too. Her heart ached for the parent who saw injustice and didn't do anything to stop it.

So many times she begged God to send Dad or Superman or Jesus to free her from the pantry. The remembered walls closed in on her now, reminding her of their power. How could she cross the bridge to peace? Toward healing? Judah would probably say it started with love and ended with grace. Was it that easy?

If so, why did it feel so difficult?

Twenty-seven

Judah received an email that a community meeting was scheduled for five o'clock tonight. He deleted the notification. After what happened last time, he wasn't attending anything at City Hall. He'd rather keep his distance from the mayor. And Mom wouldn't want to attend, so he'd stay home with her.

Any chance you're coming to the town meeting? Paisley texted him later in the day.

Not planning on it.

I could use a shoulder to cry on.

What? His stomach lurched. *What's going on?*

Stuff with my dad. Paige.

There must have been a conflict for her to say she needed a shoulder to cry on. Did she mean it literally? Did she need him to go to her?

You want me to come over now?

Nah. I'll be alright. She sent a sad-faced emoji. *Just wanted some sympathy. A great big shoulder like yours.*

You got it. Going to the meeting? Even though he didn't want to attend, he could stop by for a few minutes to see her.

Dad wants to. Thought I would. But I hate to run into certain people.

I know what you mean. I'll meet you there.

Really? Have I told you lately that you're a nice man?

Not enough, he thought, then sighed. Did he dare leave Mom alone?

An hour later, after she assured him of her well-being and shooed him out the door, he slid into the seat next to Paisley in the community room at City Hall. She clasped his right hand with both of hers and squeezed.

"You okay?"

She nodded, shrugged. Not much to go on. When she shuffled closer to him and leaned her head against his shoulder, his heart hammered. He slid his arm around her, and she nestled her cheek against his chest. Did she hear his heart's reaction? How many more days until she came home? Until they could start their lives together?

He glanced toward the front of the room. Wait a second. Why was Mia Till behind the podium? Where was the mayor? He perused the crowded room but didn't see Edward anywhere.

Oh, no. Did he make a terrible mistake by leaving Mom alone? He couldn't stay with her all the time, but he had felt conflicted about whether he should remain at the cottage with her or come here to be with his wife. What if Edward showed up at the beach house? Hurt Mom or coerced her into going back to their place. He groaned.

"What is it?" Paisley whispered.

He shook his head. He should go now, but he hated to leave when he just got here.

"Hey, everyone!" Mia tapped the microphone and laughed. "I'm the chairperson for the town's reconstruction committee." She pulsed her arms in the air like she was doing a dance move.

A few people clapped. Mia bowed, hamming it up.

Judah lowered his arm from Paisley's shoulder, about to explain why he had to go.

"Why do we need a chairperson?" Maggie Thomas called out. "Who's paying for the luxury? Better not be me."

"Me, neither." A female voice in the back sounded like Paisley's aunt.

Judah edged forward in his seat, but Paisley tugged on his hand. What made her feel so vulnerable tonight? She didn't care for these meetings or City Hall. Maybe that's what troubled her.

At the podium, Mia rocked on her heels. "I get paid ten times what the last volunteer received. Get it?" She laughed and waved at some people—probably men—in an unprofessional manner. Judah recognized her way of smoothing over uncomfortable topics with a flirty grin.

"Where's the mayor?" Brian Corbin leaned against the back wall, not in his deputy uniform. A few coworkers and neighbors stood at the back also.

"Hey, Deputy." Mia waved. "Mayor Grant will be here shortly. He's been detained."

The man was never late for official functions. Judah's dread deepened.

"Why summon us to a meeting he doesn't value enough to attend himself?" Maggie Thomas stood quickly. "What a waste. I'm leaving."

A rustling followed. Others stood as if leaving too.

"Hold on! Wait, please." Mia waved her hands. "Come on, you guys, I have important news. Even if the mayor doesn't make it back tonight, you've got to hear this."

Why wouldn't Edward make it back? Where was he? Judah clenched his jaw.

"Sorry I dragged you to this fake meeting," Paisley whispered.

"It's okay. Just worried about my mom." He nodded toward the back of the room. He'd explain later.

"Go." She nudged his arm. "I shouldn't have sent such a desperate text."

"I want you to reach out to me." He whispered goodbye and waited for his chance to exit without much notice.

"We're starting a brigade of neighbors helping neighbors," Mia spoke. "The group you'll be assigned to depends on where you live." She clicked a remote and a PowerPoint slide of a map of the city flashed on the wall behind her.

Some of the people who stood up before sat down, mumbling. A ruckus of some sort happened at the back of the room.

"Let me by. Get out of the way." The mayor stomped up the aisle, strumming his fingers through his messy hair, then straightening his jacket and dusting himself off.

Where had he been? And what detained him? Since he was here, Judah might as well stay a while longer. Wait. Did the mayor have on mismatched cowboy boots? One, tan. One, brown. Good grief. He was going to be embarrassed about that.

"Let's give it up for Mayor Edward Grant—father, husband, friend, and town hero!" Mia clapped her hands high over her head like she was welcoming a celebrity.

Judah's gut clenched as he pictured Mom's bruise. Some hero.

A few loyalists joined Mia's enthusiastic welcome. The mayor bowed his head as if he were a humble leader.

Paisley clutched Judah's hand again. Then it hit him like a two-by-four across the head. Had Mia been warming up the crowd? Filling in time until the mayor arrived?

Edward cleared his throat. "I apologize for my tardiness."

"Something wrong with your eyes, Mayor?" Maggie Thomas cackled. "Got stars twinkling in those orbs so bright you can't tell the difference between brown and tan?"

"Whatever do you mean, Maggie?"

She pointed ostentatiously at his boots, garnering laughs.

The mayor glanced downward. His face paled. "Oops. Happens to the best of them." He shrugged like he didn't mind, but Judah knew better. "Tonight, I want you to hear a message from my heart."

This ought to be good.

Regret burned in Judah's gut for how badly he felt toward Edward. But it dueled with his anger over the unconscionable way the man had treated Mom. Deep in his heart, he knew that whatever deplorable ways the mayor acted, he was still his father. And the love of God constrained him to love everyone, including Edward Grant. *Mercy and grace.* However, he didn't feel either of those kindnesses right now.

Hopefully, Edward didn't go by the cottage. Didn't harass Mom. Judah sat on the edge of his seat. Should he head back to the house and check on her, or stay with Paisley?

"Some of you have questioned my loyalty, my involvement in what happened at the barricade the last night of the evacuation." Edward swayed his hand toward the back of the room. "The deputy and I have come to an agreement about that."

"Hold on, Mayor." Deputy Brian cleared his throat. "No discussing an ongoing investigation."

"Right. I only meant to say, all the citizens of Basalt Bay have an obligation to help our neighbors, to come alongside each other and do what needs doing for the good of our town." His voice rose and sounded more refined than usual. Was someone coaching him? Mia, perhaps?

"Here. Here." Another male voice. Craig's? Was he still schmoozing the mayor?

"What Miss Till shared with you about the way we've split up the town into brigade's—her brainchild, by the way—will benefit all of us." The mayor clapped in Mia's direction, saying something indistinguishable to her. Judah imagined him grinning like a fool.

Mia laughed and winked.

Gag.

Paisley leaned forward, her elbows on her knees, closing her eyes as if she couldn't stand to watch the proceedings any longer. That's how Judah felt too.

"I have served as mayor of this fine town with a dedication few could fault." Edward clutched his lapels and rocked on his boots like he was giving a stump speech.

Few could fault? Right.

Whispers and snickers reached Judah. He glanced back. Callie and Miss Patty chattered a couple of rows behind him. Callie tugged on Miss Patty's arm. The store owner shook her head. Then more whispers. Were the gossipers getting ready for some mudslinging?

He tuned into his father's words. "I beseech you to listen to Miss Till's presentation with an open mind and a loving heart toward your neighbors. Then we'll split up into groups and make plans for our town's ongoing reconstruction."

Good ideas. Excellent ideas, even. Didn't Judah and Paisley talk about doing something similar in the aftermath of the hurricane? However, he didn't understand the change in Edward's demeanor. *A loving heart toward your neighbor?* Not his MO. Was he over-compensating because his marriage was on the rocks? Trying to act more compassionate so, when people found out about him and Mom, they wouldn't be quick to blame him?

Or was the sprucing-up-the-mayor campaign Mia's doing? If so, even she wouldn't condone his faux pas in the shoe department. What would she say, what would the townspeople think, if they discovered the extent of the mayor's cruelty and lack of honor toward his wife?

Wasn't a public servant supposed to be held to a higher standard?

Twenty-eight

Before church started the next day, whispers passed from one pew to another about a mayoral-recall signature drive. Murmurs reached Paisley, sitting between Judah and her dad. By Judah's tense posture and the way he leaned forward with his eyes closed, he probably heard too.

Bess, seated on his left side, appeared relaxed. She waved at a couple of people and smiled. Would she condemn her husband, if given the chance? She might be glad if he lost his leadership position in Basalt. Might even vote against him.

As delighted as Paisley would be if Edward Grant got kicked off his high horse, she cared more about the two Grants sitting next to her. It was unlikely that the three troublemakers—Miss Patty, Aunt Callie, and Maggie Thomas—would drum up enough signatures to impeach him, anyway.

The plan Mia introduced last night for the town's renovation came to mind. Paisley still wanted to talk with Judah about that, since he left to check on Bess before attendees split into neighborhood groups. She didn't know why Mia insisted that Paisley and Judah participate separately. Something was strange about her rise to leadership with the whole reconstruction thing, too.

After they sang a few worship songs, Pastor Sagle stepped behind the pulpit and read a familiar verse about love not failing.

She and Judah used to have a plaque with that quote on their living room wall. The idea that love might not fail was intriguing. But with the shortcomings of mankind, how could it not break apart the way everything else did? It would take a powerful love to be so resilient that it never caved.

Pondering how Judah kept saying he loved her, watched out for her, and risked his life to save hers, a tender feeling rushed through her. She linked her fingers with his. She didn't want to interrupt him from hearing the pastor's words, but she needed to feel connected with him.

He leaned back against the seat, met her gaze, gave her a small smile. His eyes looked so tired. She wished she could encourage him the way he did with her so many times.

The silver-haired pastor who gave her a ride to Dad's the night of the horrible storm perused the congregation with a thoughtful expression. He glanced in Judah and Bess's direction, then sighed. "Friends. Neighbors. Flawed humans. Broken, all."

What a strange way to address them. Paisley sank against the wooden seat and scooted down a little. Quite a few years had passed since she darkened a church door on a Sunday morning. Today, since her dad asked her to attend, and she didn't want to tell him no, she came along. Also, Judah texted her that he was bringing his mom. Did she want to join them? Of course, she said yes.

But coming to the old church where she attended growing up? Entering the place where she remembered how some of the meanest people could act spiritual, then later say horrible things to her, made her shudder. Running out the door was tempting.

Pastor Sagle remained silent for a good thirty seconds. He perused the congregation so intently that she wanted to slink down lower and hide, lest his gaze cross hers.

A restlessness prevailed in the room. The sound of shuffling and rustling of fabric on wooden seats grew louder. A few coughs. Whispers.

"Love is a beautiful thing."

All rustling stopped.

For ten minutes, Pastor Sagle spoke in a quiet voice about a tender love that transcended all human loves. A perfect love that went beyond failings or duty or pride. Far above wealth or a name or a person's bank balance. Beyond hurts. Beyond the cares of this world. Beyond disappointments and loss.

Some of his points felt like the pastor had been reading her mind. She knew he spoke of God's love. Of sacrificial, selfless love like Judah sometimes talked about. But several times it seemed like he was referring to intimate love between a husband and a wife, too. Then Judah held her hand a little tighter. Sending her a message? Reminding her that he was eager to restart their marriage? Sigh.

Pastor Sagle ended his talk with, "The purest love any person can know, the most satisfying and eternal, is the precious love of God." He closed in prayer.

After the benediction, the congregation dispersed. Paisley and Judah strode down the center aisle. He seemed in a hurry to get outside. Bess and Kathleen walked slowly behind them. At the foot of the outdoor steps, Paisley's dad stopped and chatted with James.

When she and Judah reached the parking lot, she slowed down their pace. "Pastor Sagle's brevity surprised me."

"He doesn't preach long but says a lot." His gaze met hers. "What did you think of what he said?"

"I, well, I think there are lots of forms of love." Her grin felt a little impish. "I love coffee. I love walking out on the peninsula."

"I love your eyes." He leaned toward her as if he might kiss her.

She batted his arm. "We're in the church parking lot, silly."

"So?"

"So let's not give people something else to talk about."

He groaned and slapped his hand to his chest.

"Not that I wouldn't enjoy ..."

"Yes?" He tilted his head.

"You know. Us. Kissing."

"Uh-huh." He grinned.

Heat rose in her cheeks. "But people ogling us? Gossiping about us. No, thanks."

"All right. I get that."

They strode the rest of the way to the truck. She leaned against the driver's door. "What about the whole Father's love business? He meant God, right? It's hard to grasp unconditional love."

"We've both had challenges with our parents."

"Exactly." The things he was dealing with about Edward and Bess came to mind. "I'm sorry. Maybe I shouldn't have said anything."

"Nothing to apologize for. You can talk to me about anything. I mean it. Anything, anytime."

"Okay. Thanks."

Both stood quietly for a few minutes.

He started up the conversation again. "I believe God's love is greater than anything you or I have experienced in our families. For me, my mom's love comes closest. But she's human. Fails like we all do." He slid his arm over her shoulder. "Just like we talked about before, I'm bound to mess up and fail too." He leaned his chin against her head. "But God's love, Pais, it's amazing. He's always there for us. He's a good Father who loves us. The songs say that, but I've found it to be true in my life."

She met his gaze. "You're different now. More peaceful. Kind. I mean, you were always a nice guy. Not perfect by any means."

He chuckled.

"But since I've been back, you've shown me such grace and love, it's remarkable."

He linked their pinkies. "I want you to know that I love you. But I also want you to know God's love. For all the times I can't be with you, can't make things better—even though I want to—He will be there. Loving you. Forgiving you. Holding you up."

See, he was being so sweet.

She was talking to God more. But this thing about accepting His love ... believing that He cared for *her* ... might take a leap of faith she wasn't ready for.

"I finally talked with my dad." She changed the subject.

"The text about needing my shoulder?" He moved and leaned against the door beside her. "How did it go? The talk, I mean?"

"Hard. Good. We cried." She groaned. "I asked him about my lockups. Why he didn't do something. He said he was sorry."

"I'm glad it went okay." He gave her a sympathetic hug.

Just then, while his arms were around her, three older women approached the car parked next to his truck. They stared at them until Paisley pulled away and trudged to the back of the pickup.

"Ladies." Judah followed her and they both leaned against the tailgate. "Did you reach some closure with your dad?"

"Kind of. I wish—"

"What?"

"I wish forgiveness and getting over things was easier."

"Yeah, me too. That petition stuff was embarrassing. I almost walked out. Too much to handle after the last few days I've had with my parents."

"I'm sorry. Must be hard."

"Yeah, but I'm glad I stayed. People will talk regardless." He leaned in and briefly touched their lips together, maybe making a point. People would talk about them no matter what, also.

The car with the three ladies in it backed up with the driver squinting at them like they were doing something wrong.

"You and I still have some things to talk about." He swept a strand of her hair back as if he didn't notice they had an audience.

Paisley sighed in relief when the car moved away. "Yeah. I'm nervous about that discussion." She didn't want to talk about it now, either.

"Maybe, after we chat, you'll feel more comfortable about setting a date." His statement sounded like a question.

"Maybe. Oh, look, it's my dad." Was she too obvious that she wanted to change the subject? "Ready to go?"

"I'm ready for lunch." Dad jiggled his car keys, heading toward the burnt sienna Volkswagen in the next row. "Leftover potpie calls."

"Too bad Bert's isn't open." She glanced at Judah. "Maybe I should try to get a job there."

"If that's what you want to do." He frowned like he was puzzled by the switch in topics.

"I need to do something. Work somewhere. I can't just"—she blew out a breath—"mooch off my dad. Or you. Or do a big fat nothing."

"Paisley, you've worked ever since the hurricane." He stuffed his hands into his pockets. "There's still a lot to do at the cottage. And in town."

"But that doesn't help us or my dad financially."

"No. But—" He shuffled his shoes against the broken pavement making a scratching noise. He moved a little farther away from her. It seemed a coolness settled between them. "I should go." He rocked his thumb toward the church. "I'm picking up my mom in front. We'll talk later, okay?"

"Yeah. Sure."

He hopped in the truck and started the engine. What bothered him more? Her talking about getting a job, or that they still had things they needed to discuss? For her, it was the latter. Why, she didn't have figured out.

Twenty-nine

On Monday morning, nineteen days after Hurricane Blaine hit, Judah strolled into C-MER as a supervisor, not just an employee. That awareness, and the sense of greater responsibility, settled over his shoulders. Was this God's plan for his life? Being a leader in this company? If so, why wasn't he more enthusiastic? What happened to his peace? Maybe he had a bad case of nerves, that's all.

He needed a job for provision for him and Paisley, maybe even for Mom. But something about the way he got this position, or the way Mia sprang the news on him, smacked of underhandedness. He despised that.

Four of his previous cubicle buddies waved. Then each one dropped out of sight behind their divider walls. Avoiding interactions with him? Were the guys feeling loyal to their previous supervisor? Perhaps, they judged it unfair that Judah got promoted. He sighed and glanced around without finding Craig. The receptionist's desk had been empty when he walked in, too.

He trudged into Craig's, er, his, small office. As soon as he crossed the threshold, a bad smell hit him. Something rotten. Just great. Papers were scattered across the desk. A dirty coffee cup and empty pastry packages littered the space between the laptop and the papers. The garbage can spilled over with scrunched up papers, empty soda cans, candy wrappers, and store-bought sandwich packaging. Was that the cause of the stench?

Judah removed his jacket, draped it over the back of the black office furniture, then gathered up the garbage from the floor. He could barely tie a knot in the heaping, bulging trash bag before setting it in the doorway. He stacked loose-leaf papers, files, and mail into a single pile on the desk. He'd sort through it later.

Two coworkers scurried past the open door, muttering. Were they also disgruntled about the change in command? Craig did great work for C-MER, even Judah admitted that. Too bad the guy acted so erratic lately and got himself into trouble. Something soured in Judah's stomach. Perhaps he took the supervisory job without enough forethought.

He dropped into the swivel chair and pinched the bridge of his nose. *Lord, did I make the right choice in coming back here?*

He pictured his mom at the cottage. When he left this morning, he told her to bolt the locks and stay inside. She rolled her eyes like she didn't take his warning seriously.

But if Edward heard through the grapevine that Judah returned to work, he might make another unannounced visit. Mom said he had shown up at the beach house the night of the community meeting. That he apologized and asked her to go to City Hall with him, for appearance's sake. She declined—good thing.

Judah talked with her about the possibility of getting an emergency restraining order against Edward. Beneath her makeup, she still had the bruise to prove the domestic abuse. But she said she didn't want to create more hardship for him. Go figure. Didn't he give up that right?

Judah gripped a paper cup and squeezed until it was flat before throwing it away. Then sighed.

Lord, I've been caught up in a lot of frustration about my family, and now with this job. Could you watch over Mom? Give her peace. And me too.

"You're already here!" Mia rushed through the doorway, side-stepping the garbage bag. She dashed around the small space, scooping up the stack of papers, grabbing Craig's coat and a few other items. "Too many things going down. Sorry for the mess."

"No problem."

She scurried out the door, grabbing the trash bag on her way, nearly running on her high heels. About thirty seconds later, she reentered the room. Scuttling from one side of the small office to the other, she filled her arms with loose items. She tossed Judah a smile. "I would have cleaned this up for you. Sorry it's such a disaster."

"It's okay." Craig should have done it himself, but he probably left the building upset. Or was escorted out. "You said stuff's going down. What stuff? Can I help?"

Her movements came to a halt, and he caught a whiff of her overpowering floral perfume. She touched his arm. "You're so thoughtful. We're going to get along just fine."

He moved out of her reach. She stepped closer. He backed up against the file cabinet in his attempt to keep his distance.

"If there's ever anything—*anything*—I can do for you, just push 'one' on the phone." She lifted her index finger. "I like being Number One, if you know what I mean." She winked then whirled around, her dress flouncing as she sauntered away.

Good grief. He'd hit "one" on the phone only as a last resort.

"There you are." Mike Linfield stopped in the doorway, still wearing his jacket.

"Mike. Good to see you."

The older man with silvery slicked-back hair swayed his thumb toward the east side of the building. "Meet me in my office in five?"

"Sure thing."

The manager took furtive glances over his shoulder, acting jumpy, then dodged away. What was up with that?

Ten seconds later, Mia popped back into the office. "Just wanted to warn you. Craig's here. I'd avoid him if I were you."

Did she expect thanks for the warning? If anything, her popping in and out telling him things annoyed him. He yanked open a couple of drawers to inspect the contents. Oh, nasty. Something had rotted. *Peeuuw.* An apple? Yep. And more empty candy wrappers. Even a moldy sandwich.

Mia rushed forward. "Let me do that. You have a meeting to prepare for." She extended the drawer with the disgusting items as far as it would open. "Craig, what were you doing?" She grabbed the trash can and dumped in the offending wrappers and packages.

"That wasn't necessary. But thanks."

"You're welcome." Her blond multi-hued waves bobbed as she exited. At the last second, she whirled around. "We're still friends, right?"

"Uh, I guess." Some things she did in the aftermath of the storm flitted through his thoughts. Still bugged him. Her touching his cot at the storm shelter. The way she stroked his hand, implying more than simple friendship was going on between them. How she kept minimizing his relationship with Paisley.

"I'm so glad you're back"—her lips spread in a wide red grin— "I could just hug you."

"Please, don't."

She held up her hands as if in surrender. "Don't worry. I've learned my lesson."

"Good."

She palmed the doorjamb, glancing back at him and grinning, then scurried around the corner. She said she learned her lesson, but he'd be on guard. Why hadn't anyone taken her to task about her flirtatious behavior on the job? Had she and Craig been involved? Her and Edward? Better not go there.

He dropped into the swivel chair and pressed the power button on the computer. An oceanic scene appeared on the screen. What was the password? Each of the company's devices had individualized passwords that were changed monthly. He opened the desk drawers searching for a scrap of paper with a series of numbers or a code. Nothing. Maybe he'd have to call "one" after all.

He felt someone's gaze on him. He glanced toward the door.

Craig leaned against the doorjamb, a deep scowl creasing his face. His dark eyebrows almost touched his nose.

"Morning." Judah took the initiative, even though their last interactions didn't go so well. He pointed at the screen. "The password is—?"

"A mystery, apparently." Craig stomped away.

Just great.

By mid-afternoon, Judah had sat through three meetings, avoided calling Mia, and missed lunch. One long planning session was with Mike. Two others were with different department heads. He'd never been in a supervisory position before, so he spent most of the time listening. Mike told him about a dispute among some employees concerning Craig's demotion. That accounted for his coworkers' aloofness. Craig had filed a complaint with the parent company, and Mike was expecting a call from the leadership before day's end. Judah's job might be in question—not a great thing to hear on his first day back.

When he returned to his office, he plopped down in front of the computer—which he still didn't know the password to—and bemoaned his situation. How could he work here, if they allowed him to continue in this role, and regain the trust of his coworkers? What they weren't aware of was that Craig was drunk when he fired him. That Judah tried stopping him from stealing a skiff, or possibly getting killed or injured in a boating accident. What if the higher ups sided with Craig?

A long sigh rumbled out of him.

Mia popped in with a note from an outside agency inquiring about access to the harbor. Judah took the opportunity to ask her about the password. She promised to hunt it down.

When the end of his workday arrived, he drove away from the C-MER building thankful it was over. Hungry and exhausted, he stopped to pick up groceries at Lewis's Super. Grilled steaks sounded fantastic. As did relaxing in front of his ocean view and forgetting about the office problems he encountered today.

"Judah!"

Mom? What was she doing here? She strode toward him wearing a green Lewis's Super apron and carrying two loaves of bread.

"What's going on? What's with the apron?"

"I got a job. Isn't it great?" She grinned and set the loaves on the shelf next to the other bread.

"You took a job here? Does Dad know?"

She shot him a disparaging glare.

"Oh, uh …" Mentioning his father wasn't the best thing to say. And he reverted to thinking of him as "Dad."

"Why should your father care where I work?"

"I, well, um, because he is, well, he will—"

"What?"

"Never mind. It doesn't matter what he says, right?"

"No, it doesn't." She lifted her chin.

But wait until he hears.

"I had to do something." She shrugged. "I can't sit around your place painting my toenails all day."

No, she couldn't do that, not after she'd been a prisoner in her house on the cliff. His telling her to lock the doors and stay in the house probably didn't help, either. "I'm proud of you, Mom."

"Really?" Her wide grin made her appear younger.

"Of course. This is a brave thing you're doing, working at Lewis's." He didn't mention that if the mayor walked in, every customer, perhaps everyone on the block, would hear him yelling. No doubt, he'd holler at Lewis, too, demanding to know why the store owner dared to hire the *mayor's wife*. He pushed those thoughts aside. "How do you like the job?"

"Love it. I enjoy all the people. Chatting now and then. It's therapeutic." She smiled at a customer walking past and seemed a natural at interacting with people.

How long had it been since he saw her so happy? He nodded toward the groceries he collected in his cart. "Thought I'd fix steaks for us."

"Sounds heavenly. I'll be done at six."

"Bess Grant." A male voice announced over the intercom. "Clean up needed in aisle four."

"That's me." She rushed down the aisle, calling over her shoulder, "Duty calls!"

He didn't know what to make of this new development. If her working here surprised him, he hated to think what his father's reaction might be.

Thirty

Judah and his mom sat down on the kitchen chairs he returned to the patio. A well-done steak rested on each of their plates along with a dollop of potato salad and a small pile of green veggies. This was his favorite type of meal: grilled food, a fabulous view, and the wind moving through his hair. Maybe that wind would blow away his work-related angst.

"What a treat. These look fabulous." Mom picked up her fork and steak knife, her eyes gleaming.

Before Judah took a bite of his steak, a loud engine and a blasting horn alerted him to someone's arrival. He groaned. He'd been afraid of this since finding Mom working at the local grocery. His gaze collided with hers.

"He's here." Her steak knife clattered to her plate.

"Yep." A knot tightened in his middle. He stood and shoved his chair from the makeshift table. Before he reached the sliding glass door, his father barreled through the living room and stomped outside onto the pavers.

"Dad."

The mayor didn't pause or address him. He strode to the table, parking himself across from Mom with his hands fisted at his hips, wheezing like he ran to get here. "What's the meaning of this?" He huffed and leaned forward, eyes bulging. "I heard you took a job at Lewis's."

"Hello, to you too, Edward," Mom said crisply.

"Care for some steak?" Judah would split his if it would soothe the tension between his parents. He remained standing in case he had to intervene somehow.

"No, I don't want your food." Dad's chin jutted out. Beneath his reddened eyes, dark baggy skin revealed he wasn't sleeping well, or else was drinking too much.

"What has you worked up this time?" Mom picked up her knife and cut her meat. Apparently, she was used to dining in the middle of stress.

Not Judah. He couldn't sit down and eat as if his father wasn't standing here, glaring and huffing. All the anticipation of a fine meal was thwarted.

"Worked up, you say?" Dad snorted. "How could you humiliate me by taking that kind of a job? My wife working as a grocery bagger. You've got to be kidding me!"

"Humiliate you?" Mom pulsed her knife in the air. "I'll have you know I put in a hard day's work. I'm pleased with my labor. So is Lewis, I think. And I'll work anywhere an honest person who isn't intimidated by you will hire me." She stuffed a chunk of meat into her mouth and chewed. "Mmm. Good steak, Judah."

He almost snickered.

"No wife of mine is going to work!"

Mom groaned.

"Come on, Dad. It's the twenty-first century."

"Doesn't matter." His father pounded the unsecured tabletop with his hand. The cardboard swayed and dishes rattled.

Judah grabbed hold of his plate to protect his steak.

"I'm the leader in this family. What I say goes!"

Mom laughed outright.

"Stop howling, woman." Dad leaned his fists on the table which made everything sway to that side.

"Don't ever speak to me like that, or tell me what to do, again." Mom stood, glaring at him. "Watch out, or I'll tell people the whole story about you. What do you say to that, *Mayor* Grant?"

He sucked in great gulps of air as if hyperventilating. Would Judah have to make his father leave? Take him to the ER?

"*If* you must work, where you work matters." He shot Judah a glare before resuming his intense stare toward Mom. "The type of job this family has matters to my constituents."

"Hogwash!" She grabbed her glass and gulped some water.

What did he mean by "the type of job?" Did he speak to Mike Linfield? Pressure him to—? "What did you do?"

"Nothing." The older man's eyes twitched. "I'm here to tell your mother I don't want her working in Lewis's Super, that's all." His gaze fastened on Mom's. "Do you understand me?"

Still standing, her fingers gripped the glass so tightly her knuckles turned white. "Do I understand that my estranged husband is commanding me not to work in a place he deems unfit?" She harrumphed. "Want to know what I think about that?" She jerked the glass toward Dad, and water splattered his face. Liquid ran down his jacket and dripped onto the table.

He sputtered and yowled, swiping his sleeve across his mouth and cheeks.

Judah couldn't believe what he just saw. What should he do? He wanted to stay close to his mom in case she needed him, but he forced himself to dash into the kitchen and grab a dish towel off the oven door. He scrambled back outside and tossed the fabric to his father.

Mom scooped up plates and food like an agitated busser in a busy restaurant. With her arms full, she stomped into the house.

"I can't believe she did that." Dad wiped his face with the towel and sniffed a couple of times like water went up his nose.

The water drowning Judah's steak and salad, and the emotional outbursts, had ruined his dinner. There was one thing he had to know. "Did you talk with Mike Linfield about my job?"

Dad wiped his face again.

"Did you?"

He dropped the towel on the table. "If I did, be thankful I used my influence to help you out of an unfair situation."

"I'm not thankful! I've been doing fine on my own for a long time."

"Could have fooled me."

Judah gritted his teeth. "Stay out of my business."

"And you stay out of mine." Dad thrust his finger at him. "Harboring my wife. Accusing me of having an affair!"

"Get off your throne." Judah hurled the towel across the patio. "You hurt Mom! How could you? She's the nicest, gentlest woman in Basalt Bay. And you abused her."

The mayor's blustering pride seemed to wither. He shrank before Judah's eyes, sinking onto the chair Mom vacated. "An unfortunate mistake. I never meant for—"

"You need help. Serious help."

"I have it under control. I promise it won't happen again."

"And tonight's display? Another example of you being under control?" He pointed in the direction of the driveway he couldn't see from the patio. "You probably drove like a maniac to get here. Stomped through my house. Barreled outside as if you intended harm. Yelled at Mom. She's a woman. Your partner in life. Maybe ... maybe you should start respecting her."

"How am I going to get her to come home?" His voice sounded small and weak.

"She might not be willing to go with you, ever."

Dad glanced up. "That's odd coming from a man whose wife left him for four or five years."

"Three." Judah gritted his teeth. His father knew how to push his buttons. He sighed and sat down. Maybe he could say something meaningful that might get through to his dad. Worth a shot. "I didn't know if or when Paisley would come home, but every day I prayed for her. I loved her with all of my heart, even when she hadn't returned yet."

Dad stared at him with a dull expression like he couldn't comprehend his words.

"I had to change. Me." He pointed at himself. "A little humility in your heart might go a long way toward reconciling, too."

"I can act humble." The mayor's chest puffed up—with hot air, no doubt. "Didn't you see me stroll into the community meeting? Affable, congenial, a regular guy next door. People love me."

Judah groaned. "I didn't say *act* humble. Humility is the opposite of pride. The opposite of how you behaved tonight."

"So, things still working out between you and—"

"Paisley. Yes." He paused. Should he say anything else? Was his dad even listening? "You know, you could pray too. Ask God to help you to be a better husband."

Dad laughed harshly. Then he marched across the sand and rounded the corner, out of sight. The Grant men's way of dealing with uncomfortable things—walking away, not talking, not being vulnerable. A good reminder for Judah of how he never wanted to act again.

He listened to the sound of the truck engine, the vehicle's revving, and the acceleration as the rig rumbled out of the yard. If his father were willing to sacrifice his pride and self-righteous attitude for his wife's happiness, he might salvage his marriage.

But it seemed he was too stubborn for that.

Thirty-one

Paisley swept the kitchen floor and admired the finished walls, glad that her dad didn't display any of Mom's paintings in here. She inhaled, smelling the scent of paint even though the walls were dry.

This morning Dad and James went to Eugene to hunt for second-hand appliances and furniture. They probably wouldn't find many used items with so many residents along the coast searching for similar pieces. Her dad's Plan B included visiting a furniture store and applying for a payment plan to tide him over until the insurance money arrived. Fortunately, a lot of businesses were offering discounts to hurricane victims.

For the last ten days, Paisley's focus had been on assisting her dad with his remodel, but now she needed to expend some good faith on the cottage. Soon, it would be her home again. Since Judah went back to work, he wouldn't have as much time for completing the renovations. Or talking or dating. A little dig gnawed at her middle. His mom still lived with him, which Paisley understood and supported. But it meant they didn't have many opportunities to hang out or share their hearts the way they did after the storm. If she spent more time at the cottage, maybe they could go on some beach walks and talk when he got home.

She finished a few more chores, then threw on a sweatshirt before heading outside. She planned to drop by Bert's and have that chat about getting her old job back.

As she strode past Miss Patty's rental, Kathleen rocked in a chair on the front porch. "Why, hello! Are you renting this house?"

"Paisley, good afternoon." The older woman smiled and waved. "Yes, I am renting it. I hope to get into something bigger soon, but it's been great for just me." She gestured toward the one-story beach house. "How about a cup of tea?"

"Oh, no, thank you. Another time, perhaps."

"You sure?"

"I'm on a mission. Soon, though, okay?"

"Very well." Kathleen rocked in the chair. "I'll keep enjoying this beautiful fall day."

"Me too." Paisley waved and continued walking. Next door, she saw Sal in the souvenir shop knee deep in debris. Poor man. His merchandise and building were ruined. The roof had partially fallen off and landed on the ground. She sent the storekeeper a sympathetic smile. He could use two of the volunteer brigades to help him.

She strode past Paige's art gallery. Loud voices reached her through the open plywood door, and she paused. A man and a woman were arguing. Who was in there with her sister? Edward?

Craig barreled out the door, muttering to himself. Paisley stepped back against the wall. He stomped past her as if he didn't see her, grumbling and biting off words. He marched down the block, almost colliding with Miss Patty who carried an armload of bags in front of the hardware store. Heated words were exchanged between the two.

In the shadowy doorway, Paige started to close the door of the gallery. Her gaze met Paisley's. "Oh, hello." Her eyes were red. Her face blotchy like she'd been crying.

"Are you okay?"

Paige's expression crumpled. "Not so great. Did you want to come in?"

"Oh, um, sure." Paisley trudged into the dark room. The empty space appeared the same as it did the last time she was here, except for the swept floors. "I'm on my way to talk to Bert. Ask for my old job." She chattered, filling in the awkward silence.

Paige walked to the center of her destroyed studio. "Here's my dream. My storybook ending. Until Addy and Blaine destroyed everything." She covered her face and groaned.

"I'm sorry for your loss. This has to be a harrowing experience." Paisley remained in her place, not breaching the distance between them, between their hearts.

Paige shuddered, lowering her hands. She shook her head like she was clearing her thoughts. "How are things at Dad's?"

"We're almost finished with the interior. He and James went to search for appliance bargains."

"Good luck with that."

"I know, right?"

Paisley wanted to ask her about Craig. But how could she without sounding like a snoop or being insensitive? She trudged to the open window and stared out over the sea. A gust of wind billowed against her. Turbulent waves pounded the rocky beach below. Seawater exploded into the air like foaming fireworks. If she reached out far enough, it seemed she could touch the sea spray.

Had Paige and Craig fought? Broken up? She took a deep breath and faced her sister. "So, what's with you and Craig?"

"Nothing." Paige's shoulders buckled. "Everything." A pitiful cry wrenched from her.

This time Paisley didn't hesitate to go to her. She wrapped her arms around her sister, and Paige cried into her shoulder for a few minutes.

"It'll be okay." Paisley tried to reassure her, even though she didn't know what was wrong.

"Sorry." Paige sniffled, wiping her shirt sleeve over her face. "So many things are hitting me at once." She took a few steps away.

"Want to talk about it?"

"Not really." Paige shook her head but kept talking. "The mayor's playing dirty. Telling me what I can and can't do with a building I thought I'd own. Threatening if I don't do what he says—exactly what he says—he'll evict me. Craig's his henchman."

"Really?" Hadn't he warned Paisley about the mayor? He didn't seem sympathetic to him then. However, he did stick up for Edward at the community meeting.

"He says if I don't comply with Mayor Grant's wishes, the powerful man will cause me more trouble than it's worth. That I should get out. Yield to Edward's plans like every person on this street will do."

Not Bert. He would never go along with the mayor's intimidation tactics. "Edward has big schemes, huh?" If it came to a takeover, would the town council stand up to him? Did anyone ever go against Edward Grant's wishes? Other than Maggie Thomas.

"He's amassing properties. Taking over Sal's. Bought Casey's. Rumor has it he's pressuring Bert too."

"No way." Paisley paced to the window and back. "Bert and the mayor don't get along. I can't imagine him doing anything just because Edward says to."

"If he goes under financially like the rest of the business owners, he might not have a choice." Paige wiped her fingers beneath her eyes, then stooped over and picked up a shell. She flung it out the broken window. "The strangest things made their way inside during the storm surge." She picked up something else. Tossed it.

"I wonder what the mayor's endgame is."

"To possess the whole town." Paige sighed. "Probably rename it Grant Bay."

"Or Edwardsville."

At least she and Paige were talking. Maybe this was how reconciliation would work between them, by fighting the powers that be together. She nodded toward the damaged door. "Judah and I could help you fix that."

"I'd appreciate the help."

"I should go and talk to Bert." Paisley took a couple of steps toward the door. "I'll find out if the mayor's strong-arming him."

"If I could offer you a job, I would." Paige followed her and clasped her hand. "We're sisters above all else, right?"

"Right." She'd have to remind herself of that the next time Craig came between them. She released her hand, started to turn away.

"I broke up with him before the second storm."

Paisley glanced back. "You did? So, you're not with him?"

"No."

"Not dating or anything?"

"No. Just friends."

What a relief. Yet they had been arguing. Craig left angry. Paige cried. "What about Piper?"

"What about her?"

"Isn't he—" She swallowed back the question. "She seems to like Craig."

"She does."

"Is he … is he her father?"

Paige's mouth dropped open. "That's none of your concern." She grabbed a box from off the counter and stomped into the coffee shop area. "Ancient history."

"I'm sorry. I just—" She shouldn't have said anything. Must be a sensitive subject.

"Craig told me you two had a fling." Paige eyed her from behind the counter.

"That's a lie." Even so, her heart skipped a beat.

"He said you flirted with him before you left Judah. That you were … passionate toward him." A dark look crossed her face.

"He'd say anything to make himself look better."

"He told me he loved you."

"That's not true!"

Paige gnawed on her lower lip. "He says you may have loved him, also."

"He's just making up stuff." She gulped. "Okay, he's right about my flirting three years ago. I was seeking relief from grief. In alcohol.

In male company." She drew in a breath. "I wish it didn't happen. And I've explained it to Judah."

"Did he believe you?"

"Yes. He forgave me."

"So, when you and Craig stayed together after the storm"— Paige's words sounded rushed—"did you push for more to happen between you?"

"What? No! Why would you think that?"

A familiar emotional wall rose between them.

"He said you're to blame that he succumbed."

"Succumbed to what?" This conversation was getting worse by the second.

"Kissing. Emotional entanglement." Hurt blared from Paige's gaze. "You and him."

"There's no him and me." Paisley would have laughed at the idea if her sister didn't look so anguished. "There's no entanglement. You have to believe me, Paige."

"Oh? I should believe the one who couldn't be bothered to visit our dying mother?"

An old wound twisted in Paisley's chest.

"The one too absorbed in her own life to attend Mom's funeral or care that others were hurting, too."

Her words were arrows hurtling into Paisley's heart.

"What I'll never understand"—Paige's voice rose—"is how you could kiss another man while you were married to an amazing guy like Judah. A man who's waited for you like a lovesick puppy. Even when women have thrown themselves at him, he remained faithful. And you—" She shook her head like she was disgusted. "If you'll excuse me, I have work to accomplish."

So much for reconnecting, or sisterhood. Paige could fix her own door. With a heavy heart and leaden feet, Paisley trudged across the room. She paused in the doorway. "This is what he wants."

"Who?"

"Craig." She drew in a long breath. "I never kissed him during the storm. He terrified me. Still terrifies me." Another breath. "I love Judah. I never loved Craig."

"Not even three years ago?"

"Not even then. He was a diversion, nothing more." Should she tell her the rest? "Just so you know, he tried forcing me to go against my vows to Judah. Ask Mayor Grant if you want proof."

She strode out of the gallery. She had enough of sisterly bonding.

Thirty-two

Mia Till buzzed into Judah's office and plopped down in the chair on the opposite side of the desk from him. She crossed her legs and swung her high-heeled foot, grinning with an I've-got-something-up-my-sleeve look.

"Can I help you?"

"I'm sure you can." She batted her thick black, fake eyelashes. It didn't take long for her to reestablish her flirtatious ways with him.

If he ignored her, maybe she'd grow weary of rejection and leave. "I'm busy." He pointed at his laptop. For the last hour, he'd labored over a report to headquarters about their evacuation procedures during Hurricane Blaine. What worked. What failed. He made a list of suggestions for future evacuations. Even if he couldn't keep this job, he wanted something to prove that he had the experience and the smarts to fulfill it.

"I have a big favor to ask. Any chance you could escort me to an event?" A confident smile stretched across her mouth.

"Escort you? Are you kidding me?" He stood, hands on the desk, leaning forward. "You know better than to ask me that kind of question. I'm married."

"Don't overreact." She frowned. "I never realized how much you're like your father."

That stole some of his thunder. His dad's recent behavior came to mind. He sat back down. "So, explain yourself."

"I'm in a jam. I need an escort to a function at City Hall tomorrow. Please, pretty please, would you come with me?" She clasped her hands together and puckered her lips in a begging pose. "Paisley won't mind."

He doubted that.

"You two staying in the same house yet?" She tipped her head one way, then the other. "Last I heard the mayor's missus crashed at your place. How's that affecting your love life?"

"Watch what you say." A second more of this and he'd order her out of his office.

"Fine." She sighed as if weary of the conversation. "Your father suggested that I ask you to escort me, so I thought I'd give it a shot."

His dad? That was even more suspect. "Why would he do that?" Other than to cause trouble between him and Paisley. Or to get back at him for inquiring about an affair.

"You'll have to ask him yourself."

"What's the event?" He kept his tone aloof. He knew better than to sound curious.

"It's an appreciation dinner for the leaders of the brigades." She grinned. "You're the best leader material we have in Basalt, Jude."

"Judah." He chose to ignore her flattery. "Thank you, but I decline." He pointed toward the door. "Let's get back to work, huh?"

"Calling the shots, now, *Mr.* Grant?"

He couldn't tell if she was being flirtatious, kidding, or insubordinate. "Yes, I am. You know the chain of command?"

She stood, gave him a mocking salute, then clicked her heels across the room. At the doorway, she paused, her hand on the doorjamb. "Come to the dinner, Jude. Tomorrow night at six. No escort required." She scurried out the door.

"Don't call me Jude!" He groaned. Why would his father encourage Mia to coax Judah into attending a dinner with her? Dirty manipulator, trying to control everything. He still hadn't broached the topic of how he might have gotten the job with Mike Linfield. Did his father coerce the manager into giving him the position?

If he influenced that, what about other suspicious things? Like Mia being at the same storm shelter with Judah. Her cot next to his. Her offering to drive him to Basalt when no one else would help him. Was that too farfetched to think his father could manipulate those things?

He pulled out his cell phone even though company policy restricted employees from texting during work hours.

Had the strangest visit from Mia. He punched in the letters and sent a text to Paisley. *She invited me to dinner at City Hall.*

???

As her escort.

As in DATE?

Maybe.

His phone vibrated.

"Hey."

"Mia Till asked you out on a date?" Paisley's tight voice. "The little snake!"

"She said 'escort.' I labeled it a date."

Craig strolled by the doorway, glared at Judah, then continued toward Mike's office.

"I have to go."

"Sorry. I had to call."

"That's okay." He got an idea. He swiveled the chair so his back faced the doorway. "What would you say to us crashing the dinner Mia just invited me to?"

Paisley snickered. "Are you kidding?"

"Nope. Will you be my date?"

"You bet!"

"Then I'll pick you up tomorrow evening."

Judah arrived to pick her up just before six the next day. Seeing her in a sexy, sleeveless royal blue dress, he whistled. She blushed and giggled. An excellent beginning to their evening.

On the front porch, he clasped her hand and kissed her cheek, wishing he brought a bouquet of flowers to celebrate their night out. "You look amazing."

"Thank you." She smiled, a little wide-eyed, like no one had complimented her in a long time. "You look pretty nice yourself." She touched a button on his pale blue shirt.

"Oh, yeah?" He nuzzled her ear with his nose, eliciting another chuckle. If he had more time, he'd kiss her with some sizzle she'd remember. Maybe later. He escorted her to his truck.

"How is this going to work? You didn't tell Mia you planned to attend, or about me coming with you, right?"

"No. If I did, we couldn't crash the party." He gave her what he hoped was a reassuring smile. "Don't worry. It'll be fun." He closed her door and dashed around to his side of the truck.

"Why are we doing this, again?" she asked when he was seated.

He started the engine. "Getting to the bottom of some things." He drove down Front Street and recalled what Mia said about him being a leader. It was silly to be pleased about that since she was only flattering him. Still, it stuck in his mind. "What neighborhood brigade are we in?"

"I'm with my dad, James, and others on their block."

"What about me?"

"Mia put you with the southern group." Her voice got quieter. "Same as Craig."

Judah groaned. "You and I are married. We should be in the same volunteer group."

"I know." She made a huffing sound. "I tried, but the mayor's Girl Friday wouldn't listen."

Hearing Mia called his dad's *Girl Friday* had the power to sour his evening. Something he couldn't let happen. Even if he and Paisley were assigned to different committees, he planned to enjoy his date with her. "I'll just sit in on your group."

"You will?"

"Of course. You and I are sticking together." He winked at her. Their gazes held for a moment. When he pulled into a parking space next to the art gallery, Paisley turned toward her sister's building and let out a long sigh. Was something wrong?

"Ready?"

"Sure."

Inside the community hall, rectangular tables were spread with navy tablecloths. Mia and a couple of ladies bustled about setting out dinnerware.

A woman with long red hair—he couldn't place her name—wearing a white apron rushed up to them. "More Grants? Do you have reservations with the committee?"

Why the tone? Paisley's hand tensed in his, but she didn't say a word to the other woman.

"I have a place reserved." He released her hand and put his palm on her back. "My wife is attending with me. You remember Paisley?"

"How could I forget?" The redhead deadpanned. "Paisley."

"Lucy."

Ah. Lucy Carmichael. The two of them had some high school feud, if he remembered right.

"Can you make room for two?" He smiled at the server, hoping to dispel some of the tension.

"Mia won't like it." Lucy rolled her eyes. "Mia's in charge of *everything*! But since you're the mayor's son ..." She shrugged. "Whatever. Wait here." She rushed toward the far-left side of the room.

He rubbed his palm over Paisley's tight shoulders. What were the weird vibes between her and Lucy?

The redhead switched a couple of name tags and shuffled plates and glasses at one of the tables. She waved them over. He kept his hand at Paisley's back as they walked between the seated guests. He nodded at a couple of people.

"Lucy"—Mia skidded to a stop beside the woman rearranging chairs at the table—"what are you doing?" She spoke through clenched teeth.

"Making room for her." Lucy jerked her head toward Paisley.

Mia squinted at Paisley with a snobbish gleam that spiked Judah's irritation. "We didn't plan on *your* attendance. But, since you're here, protocol be tossed in the sea, right? Paisley, so nice of you to join us." Her tone turned sugary and fake sounding. She readjusted the name tags Lucy had switched. "This will never do." She grabbed one and thrust it into the redhead's hand. "Find another place for him."

Lucy strode down the center aisle and dodged around a few tables.

"Thanks for understanding, Mia."

"I understand. But will your father?" Head held high, she traipsed after Lucy.

He pulled out a chair for Paisley. "Sorry about that."

"It's okay."

Plates of food were soon placed in front of attendees. Roast beef and rice with a creamy gravy on top looked delicious. Smelled great too. One chair remained empty at their table.

Speeches commenced as brigade leaders introduced themselves and told success stories about people working together in the neighborhoods. They shared how tasks were getting accomplished as people pooled resources and assisted each other—all thanks to the mayor's and Mia's initiative, yada yada.

Judah recognized some of the points from the C-MER training manual. Their mission as a company included taking care of neighbors during storms and disasters. Did Mia take ideas from the workplace and bring them to life in the community? For the welfare of others? Or was there a more selfish reason behind her charitable actions?

Craig entered the community hall and strode toward their side of the room. Oh, no. The empty chair. Who planned this? Mia didn't know about Paisley attending. But she asked Judah. Did she place Craig across from him on purpose?

As soon as his coworker dropped into the chair, Paisley's troubled gaze flew to Judah's. *Don't panic*—he tried to convey. With her hand shaking, she lifted her fork of beef to her mouth. He might have to make their excuses and rush her out of the building. Take a beach walk to calm her.

Craig squinted toward them. Judah tried not to replicate his negative facial expressions.

Brad Keifer took the podium. "I'm sure some of you are surprised to find me here. I hate these meetings."

Folks laughed.

Judah nodded, surprised at the fisherman partaking in any civic duty.

"The thing is the beach is a mess all along the coast. We need volunteers to befriend our sea animals and help with cleaning up the plastic and debris-strewn beaches after the hurricanes."

He had Judah's interest.

A minute later, Paisley's brusque tone distracted him from Brad's speech.

"You're despicable," she stage whispered.

"What have I done now that displeases you?" Craig smirked.

At the front of the building, Brad appealed to locals to join forces and combat the trash plague. Judah focused on Paisley. Other than Craig being at their table, why was she so upset?

"You're a troublemaker and a dirty liar!" She wrenched her body and kicked Craig under the table.

What in the world?

Craig jerked and clenched his teeth. "Tame your wife, Judah."

"Paisley." He leaned toward her. "What's wrong?"

She clutched the edge of the table, her livid gaze aimed at Craig. "Why are you telling Paige falsehoods? Trying to hurt her? Or me?"

"What are you talking about?"

"What you told her. What you invented. It's all lies!"

Judah smoothed his hand over her shoulder. "Sweetheart, this isn't the time."

"No?" She shot to her feet, glaring at Craig as if he'd done the vilest thing imaginable. "Stay away from my sister! Stay away from me!" Her voice rose. "And keep your stinking lies to yourself."

Brad stopped speaking. Silence filled the room.

"Is there a problem here?" The mayor's voice bellowed over Judah's shoulder.

He stood slowly. His plan to crash the party was over. "Let's go," he whispered to Paisley, putting his hand at her elbow.

"What's going on?" someone asked.

"It's that crazy Cedars girl." A feminine voice guffawed. Lucy?

"Get her out of here," the mayor ordered.

His father's command tempted him to sit back down. Let Paisley kick the snot out of Craig. But if he did, he'd regret it later. So would she. He led her away from Craig, away from the mayor, away from the whisperings traveling from table to table.

"This is a nightmare." She jerked from his grasp, ran from the room, from the building.

He followed her into the night air. Laughter came from the assembly behind him.

Why did he think it would be a good idea for them to attend this meeting? "I'm so sorry." He unlocked the truck door and helped her climb inside.

She pulled away from him like she didn't want him touching her.

Just great. He ran around the rig, then climbed in behind the wheel. "What did Craig say to you?"

"He's a dirty, filthy, lying scum."

"Yes, but what did he say to you?"

She pounded her fists on top of the dashboard, groaning. "If only I were a man—"

Judah didn't put the key in the ignition. "What happened? Tell me."

She gave him an anguished look. "He told Paige that I ... that I kissed him. Loved him." She stared forward again, her hands buffing her arms. "Things were starting to get better between Paige and me. Now, this. When he sat with us, I couldn't stay silent. Couldn't do nothing."

"Of course, you couldn't. Come here." He scooted across the seat and pulled her into his arms. "Pais, I'm sorry. I wouldn't have wanted any of this to happen."

She leaned into his chest, shivering.

A thunderclap of adrenaline raced through him as he pondered her words. "Did he mean three years ago?"

"No. After the storm." She swallowed. "Paige is so mad at me. But I did not, would never, kiss that scumbag."

"I know." He sighed. Anything he said could be the wrong thing, but he had to try to comfort her. "I understand why you got upset. You and Paige will work this out. It'll be okay."

"How can it ever be okay again?" She drew in a raspy-sounding breath. "I'm getting blamed for things I didn't do. Paige ... she doesn't understand."

He had the urge to retrace his steps, grab Craig by the collar, and haul him outside to answer for his words. That would make him feel better. Wouldn't help Paisley. He needed to focus on her. "Do you want to come out to the cottage?"

"Why?"

"To talk things through." He smiled, trying to lighten the mood. "Drink coffee. Eat chocolate. Sit on the veranda and listen to the ocean."

"I have a better idea." Her eyes suddenly sparkled. "Do you know where Craig lives?"

"Uh, no. Why?"

"I want to cash in on that dare now. Remember, you owe me one thing."

"I do, but—"

With that mischievous gleam in her eyes, he wasn't going to like her idea.

Thirty-three

"What does the dare have to do with Craig's house?" Judah shuffled his hands over the steering wheel.

"We're going to bombard his house with mud!" She made a squealing sound.

"Wait a sec. Paisley, no way."

"Come on. I need your help." She reached out and clutched his right hand. "Please, help me do this. It'll be fun. You and me and mud ..."

For a fraction of a second, he got lost in her coaxing tones. Lost in the idea of doing something so radically bizarre ... with her. But taking revenge on a coworker's house with mud? That could get them into a lot of trouble. It wouldn't be very Christlike, either. "Sweetheart, throwing mud balls at someone's house isn't going to make the problem with that person go away."

"Of course, it won't. But it will make me feel better. Us, right?" She gripped his hand tighter. "You owe me for the dare." She challenged him with her gaze.

Of all the mischievous things she ever concocted, this one took the cake. How would he talk her down without making her angry with him?

"Couldn't you contact someone?"

"What do you mean? Contact who?" He slipped his hand away

from hers. Started the engine. Giving himself time to figure out what to do next. What to say. Stalling. Someone had to be rational here.

"How about Mia? Call her and ask for Craig's address."

He couldn't believe she would suggest that he call Mia. "I will not." That's all he needed was for the receptionist to tell people—his father, or Deputy Brian—that he called and inquired about Craig.

Paisley clicked her fingernails against the dashboard, then pulled something out of her handbag. She held up the cell phone he purchased. "I'll check online for an address."

Groaning, he put the truck in gear and made a U-turn in the middle of the street.

"Where are you going? Judah, you're heading the wrong way." Her voice went higher. "He lives on the south side."

"I know. I'm taking you back to your dad's." He clenched his jaw. He'd rarely gone against something she wanted to do. But this idea of hers could get them both into a lot of trouble. Neither of them was spending the night in jail, if he could help it.

She lowered the phone. "So you're not going to help me?" She scowled, her mouth tugging downward into a pout.

"You told me you weren't doing these kinds of things anymore. That you changed." While true, that might be a sore subject for him to bring up.

"But Judah—"

"No, you came back here to make amends."

"Yes, but not with Craig." She groaned. "He caused me all kinds of trouble. He's lying and getting away with it."

"I know." He clutched the steering wheel. While he was aware of the evil things the guy had done, he couldn't give in. Wouldn't.

"Paige might not even talk to me." She slammed her phone down on the seat. "I can't find anything on him. Seems to be invisible."

"Let's go back to your dad's and talk. Maybe sit on the porch, okay?"

No answer.

"Paisley, I'm sorry. I just can't throw mud at someone's house."

"Because you're the mayor's son," she said in a snarky voice.

"No, not because I'm the mayor's son." He gritted his teeth at his own sharp response. "Because it's not right. And I'm trying to act like a Christian. A caring person in our community."

With jerky movements, she scooted to the far side of the seat, her back facing him.

"You shouldn't be doing those things, either. You're an adult."

"No kidding." She mumbled something about him not understanding her.

Terrific. Their first argument since getting back together was about Craig. "Paisley?" He kept his voice soft.

She didn't respond. He almost snickered at her slumped over, pouting position. He didn't. Of course, he didn't.

He parked next to Paul's house and shut off the engine. "Pais?"

While she didn't answer, she didn't leap out of the truck, either.

"I'm sorry Craig hurt you and Paige again. That makes me mad too." Frustration simmered in his chest, close to reaching the boiling point. Didn't he nearly go back into City Hall and take the jerk to task? But hurling mud at his house? Not happening.

She sniffled and cleared her throat as if suppressing her emotions. That twisted more angst inside him. What could he do to make peace between them? This night had turned out all wrong.

Then an idea came to mind. Something that might help to soothe her hurt feelings. Might make things better between them.

"I'm sorry for the lousy first date." He touched her back with the tips of his fingers. "I have an idea. Want to hear it?"

"No."

"It's a good one."

"I don't want to go out to the cottage with you."

"I know."

"Then what?" Her tone still sounded sharp.

"How about if we change into some grubby clothes, then we can talk about it?" He opened his door. "Meet me on the porch in ten minutes."

She whirled around. "You changed your mind?"

"Maybe." He hoped she wouldn't be too upset with his fudging.

She leapt out of the truck and sprinted up to her dad's porch. Her agility in her fancy dress and heels surprised him.

Inside the house, he talked to Paul and asked if he could borrow a change of clothes that might get messy. Paul agreed and told him where he could find a flashlight, too.

Ten minutes later, dressed in holey jeans and a thick flannel shirt with rips in the elbows, he scrounged in the shed for an old bucket. He also located two gardening spades. With Paul's flashlight in hand, he waited for Paisley on the porch.

She exited the door dressed in leggings and a long baggy sweat-shirt. At least, she had her own clothes here. "Did you find out where Craig lives?" Her wide eyes sparkled like a kid on Christmas Day.

"Not quite." He hated to disappoint her. He placed the handle of the bucket over his right arm, still gripping the flashlight. Then he reached out his left hand toward her.

"What?" She frowned, not taking his hand. "We're not going to Craig's?"

"No, we're not." He nodded toward the beach. "Come on. This'll be fun too."

She groaned. "Where are you taking me?"

"I owe you for that dare and for the bad date."

"And?" She trudged warily beside him.

"It's low tide. Great mud on the flats."

"Really?" Her eyes widened. She may have cracked a smile. She walked faster.

He had to hurry to keep stride with her.

"What are we going to throw mud at?"

"We'll figure that out."

He kept the flashlight aimed toward the rocks as they descended to the beach below. The surf roared in the distance, but low tide would be perfect for gathering moist mud.

Once they reached the beach, she took off running toward the ocean. He ran too, glad his leg was improving, and relieved that she seemed distracted from her previous plans for retribution.

Just ahead, she squealed and laughed, sliding in a section of wet sand. "This will be perfect." She dashed back and grabbed one of the spades from him. Her eyes glowed in the light. "Come on." She took his hand this time.

She dropped to her knees next to a large muddy section. He set the flashlight on top of a two-foot rock, aiming it toward them. He shivered in the chilly air as he dropped beside her and set down the bucket.

For the next fifteen minutes, they dug up mud with their spades and formed balls—like snowballs without being frozen—with their hands. They laughed and joked, tossing around ideas about where they might hurl their collection, and he was relieved their previous tension seemed to be gone. He mentioned City Hall. She suggested Maggie's. Then she admitted she never wanted to do community service hours for that woman again.

Eventually, their bucket overflowed with globs of pressed mud. A pile rested on the beach too.

Judah stood with dirt-caked hands outstretched. Paisley stood also and showed him her muddy hands. Then, unexpectedly, she brushed her fingers against his cheeks, laughing.

"Hey!" He swiped his shirt sleeve over his face.

She cackled and ran in a wide circle, still within the light's glow. He chased after her, feeling like a teenager flirting with the cutest girl in school. He laughed and the wind chafed his cheeks, but the exercise kept him warm. He caught up to her and grabbed her hands. In the flashlight's beam, and beneath the brilliance of the moonglow, he kissed her. He didn't care if he still had mud on his face—and if he did, she was getting some of it. He might have even rested his palms against her cheeks.

She snuggled against his borrowed shirt. He wrapped his arms around her, holding her, being careful not to get any more mud on her.

"That was fun." She giggled. "But it's not over."

"No, it's not."

She pulled away. "Come on. Let's find our target!" She scooped up the pile of mud balls from the ground. "Where shall we throw them? Other than where I want to throw them?" She still had a mischievous gleam in her eyes.

He grabbed the flashlight, the small shovels, and the overflowing bucket. "How about at one of the boulders on the peninsula?"

"Okay, but I'm going to pretend it's Craig's house."

"All right." He chuckled.

Their arms were full as they crossed the flats to the peninsula. The chilly wind pounded against them, but it didn't hamper their enthusiasm. When they got within throwing distance of some big rocks, Judah set down the items he held. He propped the flashlight so that it faced a boulder he hadn't classified with a letter of the alphabet before Blaine hit. "How about that one?"

"Looks good." She dropped her mud balls in the wet sand. "Are you game for a contest?"

"Uh, sure. What does the winner get?"

"Um." She gazed at the dark sky. "To set the date?"

His heart skipped a beat. "Our vow renewal ceremony date?"

"Mmhmm. Just remember, I'm good at this."

Living with this woman would never be boring. "You're on." He scooped up three mud balls the size of tangerines. One immediately disintegrated in his grip. "Oops."

Paisley snickered and compacted a wad of mud, working it between her hands. "My hands are freezing. How about yours?"

"Yep." He pressed one of the balls in his hands, following her lead. "Ready?"

"Ladies first." She hurled a mud ball straight at the boulder. Thud. It slammed hard against the rock and mud chunks flew outward. She cheered.

"One point for you." He threw the next mud ball. Thud. "Yes!"

"One to one." She hurled two in a row. Thud. Thud. "Take that, Craig Masters!"

Judah chuckled at how she was still getting her feeling of revenge but using a safer route. Since she threw two, so did he. Only one hit. Man. One point behind her, he had to focus.

"Three to two." She chortled.

"So it seems."

They used up their pile of mud balls faster than he could have imagined. Too bad they didn't make more of the muddy spheres. It was a blast throwing them. The score was eighteen to sixteen. Paisley missed once. He missed three times. Once because his mud ball fell apart before it reached its destination. He called for a mulligan, but she disagreed. Said they had to take what life gave them. Maybe she was trying to tell him something. But he remained intent on catching up and winning this contest, then he could set the date for their ceremony.

Four mud balls remained in the pile.

Paisley threw one. Missed! She groaned.

He didn't comment, but he was back in the game. He hurled the next one as hard as he could. Splat.

"Eighteen to seventeen!" She pulsed her fist in the air. "One more each."

"We could m-make some m-more." His teeth chattered. She must be cold too.

"Nah. Winner takes all." Easy for her to say. She wound up and flung the mud ball overhand. Smack. She whooped and hollered, leaving no doubt she hit her target.

No way to even the score now. He threw his last hardened clump of mud. At least it hit.

Paisley cheered. "I won!"

"You sure you don't want to make some more? Best of two rounds?"

"I'm ready to wash up and get warm."

"Yeah, me too."

She scooped up the pail and dropped the spades in. He grabbed the flashlight.

"So, you get to decide on the date." If it was up to him, he'd pick tomorrow, no doubt about it. But she won. He'd be a good sport about it.

"Yeah." She sighed. "That was fun. Safer than pelting Craig's house."

"Sure was." He took a chance. "Feel better?"

"Uh-huh. Sorry for getting so grouchy."

"Fifteen years ago, I would have gone along with you to Craig's." She nudged his arm. "I didn't think you were that kind of teenager. Edward Grant's son. The perfect kid."

He balked. "Not perfect. I keep telling you that."

"Right. Right."

They climbed the rocks beneath the beach houses. Once they reached Paul's, they used the outside spigot to wash off the grit.

"Brrrr. That water's freezing." She splashed liquid on her face, removing dirt smudges.

"I'll grab my clothes, then I should go." He rocked his thumb toward the street. "I have lots to do tomorrow."

"Okay." She tugged on his shirt sleeve, then leaned up and kissed his cheek. "Thank you."

He smiled, wanting to ask what she had in mind about a date for their vow renewal. But he'd be patient for a while longer.

Thirty-four

At first light, Paisley buttoned up her jacket and headed outside. Low tide made the air tangy, almost pungent, but even with the slightly abrasive scent, the roar of the waves in the distance drew her. Called to her.

As she trudged toward the seashore, making her way down the slippery rocks, she mentally rehashed yesterday's events. The trouble between her and Paige. The things Craig said. That kick she gave him was a stupid move. Childish, as Aunt Callie would say. But Judah's solution of making and throwing mud balls on the beach, even going along with a contest, turned out wonderful, and helped ease her frustration and embarrassment.

Now she had to decide how soon she wanted the vow renewal ceremony to be. Surely, Judah would ask her about it when she saw him today.

She kicked an empty white seashell and sent it tumbling into the water. Why did she feel reluctant? She loved him, so what was the problem? Was it her fear of them wandering into the same problems as before? Or of Judah getting so caught up in his career that he forgot about her. Or, maybe, of her dropping into a black hole of despair again.

Inhale. Exhale.

"Trust" skidded through her thoughts and burned a path right to her heart. Could she trust Judah to do what he said? That this time things would be different? Better, even?

She nudged a wad of seaweed with her boot and a crab scuttled down the beach. The waves rolled up the shoreline, crashing against boulders and driftwood, creating a cacophony of sound. A couple of times, she dashed up the beach to avoid getting splashed by the incoming tide. At the peninsula, white water billowed and crashed in such majestic beauty it tempted her to go out there. But she promised Judah she'd head out to the cottage and help him with the remodeling. No time for getting soaking wet today.

Not far ahead, a boulder she climbed on many times as a kid glistened in the morning sunshine. Eagerly, she strode toward it. Almost to the tide line, she climbed up, using her hands and knees for leverage, and centered herself on top of the rock. She shuffled her backside until her back faced town and the full panoramic view— the old cannery to her left, the bay straight ahead, the peninsula to her right—spread out before her in a spectacular display.

She could sit here all day, if she hadn't made plans, watching the waves roll in and pound the shoreline. Bursts of sea-foam exploded into the air near her. Her gaze followed the surf as it rushed out to sea, then rolled back in, the process repeating itself over and over. Like life's rhythms. A storm. The calm. A storm. Then peace.

Was that like her and Judah? What if another storm hit their marriage? What if she got pregnant and lost their child again? She couldn't bear to think of that. Her eyelids clamped shut as she felt the pain of loss, the agony of grief, pressing in on her. Losing a baby had felt like it almost killed her. She couldn't risk that again. But to never have children because of her fear didn't make sense, either. So where did that leave her?

She opened her eyes, staring at the waves. Judah probably wanted kids. Was that one of the reasons she put off setting a date?

She sat on the boulder long enough for the waves to hit the rock beneath her. Water splattered onto her pants. She pulled her feet higher. If she didn't get off this chunk of basalt, she'd be forced to wade into the sea to reach dry land. And yet, she stayed.

A few minutes later, she heard something. What—? Strong arms wrapped around her. Craig? She twisted, wrenching her upper body, and attempted to free her striking elbow—just in case.

"Whoa. Pais, it's me."

Judah? She exhaled a breath. "What are you doing? Why didn't you say something?" She faced him as he dragged her off the rocky perch.

He grinned, holding her in his arms. "Sorry. I wanted to surprise you."

"Oh, you did."

He waded through knee-deep water. "What are you doing out here? Planning to swim back?"

"Maybe." He smelled good and spicy. Might be nice to snuggle her nose into his neck. Press her cheek against his skin.

He tripped, or else faked tripping, so she had to cling to him tighter. When he reached dry ground, he set her down. "Good thing I came along to rescue a lady in distress, huh?"

She smacked his arm. "Do you see anyone in distress?"

"Not anymore."

"I suppose if I needed rescuing, which I'm not admitting I did, you are the cutest rescuer in Basalt." She kissed his cheek.

"Nice to hear. Want to beach walk with me?"

"Sure." That sounded more inviting than remodeling work.

They strolled across the city beach in comfortable silence. How did he know where to find her? Was he here to ask about the date for their ceremony?

They crossed to the other side of the peninsula, following the rocky shoreline on the west side of town. Noticing the C-MER building up ahead, nestled between some sand dunes, she asked, "How's the job going?"

"Not great." He pointed toward his workplace. "The mayor is taking credit for my rehire."

"What? You're kidding."

"He's meddling and interfering."

"And Craig?"

Judah's eyebrows rose.

"I mean, you have his position. How's he handling that?"

"What you witnessed last night shows how he feels about it."
Judah drew her around a large piece of driftwood.

"Is that why—"

"Can we not talk about Craig?"

His abrupt tone surprised her. "Okay." Didn't he say they could
discuss anything?

"I'm sorry." Stopping, he rubbed his hand over his forehead.
"When your dad said you went for a hike, I panicked, thinking you
might be out on the peninsula."

"So that's why you came to my supposed rescue."

He didn't smile this time. He heaved a sigh.

"What's wrong?"

"I'm just … sorry … for how things came down last night. Sorry
that I put you in such an awkward situation at that dinner."

"It's okay. Craig's the jerk."

"We can agree on that. So, we're okay?"

"We're okay." She smiled and linked their fingers. "I enjoyed
our target practice."

He nodded toward the roiling sea. "For the last two weeks,
everything has been in chaos. But when I'm with you the uncertainty
goes away. I just want to be with you."

"You're that for me too." She stepped closer, hoping he could
handle her honesty. "But I also have doubts. How things turned out
before plays over in my mind."

He nodded, sighed. "Would you mind if we hiked farther? I
wanted to show you something down the beach."

"Sure. Are we going out to the lighthouse?"

"Not that far."

"C-MER?"

"Nope. It's a secret." He smiled like some of his tension eased.
The problems with his dad and mom must be bothering him. And

her saying she still had doubts probably wasn't encouraging for him, either.

The wind picked up and gusted harder against them, but they trudged forward. The waves pounded up the shoreline in a constant roar, rolling closer with the incoming tide. When they headed back, they'd have to climb on the rocks and hike near the trees since the beach would soon be under water.

A couple of raindrops hit her nose. "Uh-oh." She pulled up the hood on her jacket.

Judah zipped his coat. "We better hurry." He pointed toward the western sky where dark gray clouds piled up over the Pacific.

Ever since Blaine, she didn't care to see an approaching storm. "Maybe we should head back."

"We're almost there. Come on."

It was difficult to resist his grin. "Okay."

"Unless the weather report is wrong, the squall will head out to sea quickly."

"That's good to hear."

He knew this beach as well as she did, maybe better since he worked the coastline for eleven years. He knew where to hunker down to wait out a storm, if it came to that.

He led her past the clump of rocks where she and Peter built a fort when they were kids. Past a pile of driftwood they called their pirate ship. How many times did she walk the gangplank there? They trudged over the C-MER dock where part of it sat on dry ground. With Judah's workplace so close, she wanted to mention his employment again, but she refrained since it seemed like he didn't want to discuss it.

Farther down the beach, the lighthouse, a broken-down relic of yesteryear, sat as a testament to the town's history with water safety. Many times, her parents had warned her and Peter to stay away from the crumbling monument. Only once did they dare to hike that far. Their secret.

"Here it is." Judah turned to the right, guiding her up the rocks that made a natural barrier between the ocean and the land.

She noticed some giant boulders where cracks between the rocks made cool hiding places. She remembered that from childhood excursions with Peter. Judah stopped in front of a large rock that was as tall as him and had branches leaning against it. He grabbed several limbs and tossed them aside.

"My coworkers found this after Blaine." He yanked a few more branches away, exposing a cave-like opening within the formation.

She bent over and saw all the way through the rock to the other side. "Oh. That's awesome."

"The waves during Addy and Blaine must have crashed against the weakened stone. Then chunks washed away under the pressure of the storm surge. Only the outer layer remained." Judah rested his hand on the stone roof. "Should be stable. My guys checked it out."

The rain suddenly fell hard as if the clouds were wringing themselves out overhead. They laughed and lifted their faces into the moisture. She opened her mouth, catching some drops. He did too. It reminded her of other times they played on the beach in the rain when they were dating, then later in the early days of their marriage. Happy memories.

If they didn't take shelter, they'd soon be soaked. She ducked down and settled into the hollow place in the rock. On her bottom, with knees bent, she wrapped her arms around her legs. Judah squeezed in beside her, snuggling his right arm around her shoulders. His closeness, his warmth, made it easy to relax despite the rain and wind just beyond their hiding place.

"The rain can't reach us here."

She wiggled her shoes. "Maybe just our feet."

He gave her a wry grin. "My shoes are already soaked."

"The price of hero-hood." She snickered as she thought of him wading into the surf and scooping her off the boulder.

"I don't feel very heroic." He sighed, staring toward the ocean with a troubled look.

"Why do you say that?"

Raindrops dripped from his hair down his cheek. Reaching up

and snagging them with her fingers was tempting. But she didn't want to disrupt his thoughts or whatever he was about to tell her.

"The job. How I got it." He gulped. "It bothers me that my coworkers blame me for getting promoted and Craig getting demoted. Although, they don't know the whole story. I'm not going to explain it to them, either."

"Is he causing trouble?"

"According to Mia."

Paisley grumbled at hearing the woman's name. "What will you do?"

"I haven't decided. Still praying about it."

He wiped a wet strand of hair off her cheek, their gazes getting lost in each other's. His cool fingers skidded over her facial skin. She caught her breath, surprised by the strong reaction every time he touched her.

He drew in a sharp breath too. Did he feel the same way? But then he glanced away, sighing. "Mind if I ask you something?"

"Go ahead."

"Have you thought any more about us saying our vows?"

"Thought about it?"

He nodded. "Other than the renovation of your dad's house and the cottage, is there something hindering us from moving forward?" His expression was vulnerable yet cautious.

She gulped. "When we're together, like this, there's nothing I want more than to be with you. Married. Life partners. Crazy in love."

"Me too." He grinned.

"But when I think about the wifely stuff, I get a thick lump in my throat. Sort of emotional heartburn."

"Wifely stuff, huh?"

"Not the intimate stuff," she clarified, and her cheeks burned.

"Oh?" He tipped his head, staring at her.

"It's the what-if-I-fail-as-a-wife stuff."

"Pais." The sweetest smile crossed his lips.

She'd better glance away. Because if she didn't—

His cool mouth fell across hers with the most delicate, delicious caress. Heavens. How could he do that, make her feel like the 4th of July fireworks exploded around her, in the middle of a fall storm? Especially when she felt windblown and frumpy.

He touched the tips of their noses together, Eskimo kissing her. She opened her eyelids that she didn't even mean to close and stared into his blue eyes. Her heart pounded out a vigorous beat.

"Our love is going to get us through everything. Wifely stuff. Husbandly stuff." He pointed at the massive rock structure above them. "Just like this shelter covers us from bad conditions. Protects us. That's what our love will do, too, if we'll let it. What God's love will be for us. The best refuge imaginable."

If only she grasped what seemed to come so easily, so naturally, for him. Grace. Trust. Belief. Even love. "I failed before."

"So did I." His knuckles smoothed over her cheeks. "All I want is to be with you. To be there for you in good times and in bad. In hurricanes and in balmy seas. For us to love each other for the rest of our lives—warts and all."

"You think I have warts?" She snorted.

"I have some." He snickered. "But your warts are cuter."

"Right."

His lips caressed hers again, feather soft. Sweeter than before. Longer than before. His kisses deepened, becoming more passionate. She didn't pull away. Wouldn't have stopped. But he did. He pulled back a couple of inches, his dazed gaze dancing with hers. *Deep blue sea in the morning!* The deep emotion she felt for those few moments sent shockwaves through her system. She gazed into his eyes, trying to convey that she wanted more of what they just experienced. Apparently, he was choosing to exercise restraint. Still being a gentleman. She sighed.

"I will fail you, at some point, I'm sorry to say."

His words cooled her right down.

"And you will fail me."

His admission, while unsettling, touched her heart. Moisture filled her eyes. Was rain getting into her face again?

"We're both human and flawed. But this life—"

She took his hand in hers, listening, wanting to hear every word.

He swallowed. "This life can be hard. We found that out before. But, together"—he gripped her hands—"you and me together, we're stronger, better, more vibrant, more alive, and we'll make it. Not just barely, either. Our love is going to thrive." His voice rose. "Grow stronger. I can't wait to get started on our forever."

"Me, either."

A calm she hadn't felt in years filled her soul. But would it last?

Thirty-five

For three years, Paisley dreaded this day. Her limbs shook. Her heart thudded in her temples. Her hands clutched two clusters of flowers she bought at the grocery store tight enough to break the stems.

Judah trudged beside her across the expanse of grass that had been cleaned of debris since the hurricane, probably by one of the brigade groups. He told her he came to the cemetery a few times over the last couple of years. A comforting thought. Still, the ache that had been building within her throbbed with each beat of her heart, with each footstep bringing her closer to her baby's gravesite.

I can do this.

If she hyperventilated and fainted, at least the grass would soften her fall.

Judah led them beyond the tall headstones, past the rows of inground grave markers of previous residents, past the crematorium. With each step, she felt herself slowing down. Taking more breaths. Compensating for her anxiety.

At the far side of the lawn, a white picket fence that encircled a cluster of tiny grave markers came into view. One step through the gate, she froze. Several days had passed since her last full-on panic attack. *God, help me,* she prayed even though she still hated desperate prayers.

"Paisley? You okay?"

"I n-need a m-minute."

He took one of the clusters of flowers. "Here, sweetheart. Hold my hand. Lean on me."

She inhaled, then exhaled, and gripped his hand. Should she search for five things to distract herself? After a couple of deep cleansing breaths, she breathed easier and was able to move forward again.

Judah stopped and knelt beside a tiny marker. She dropped to her knees beside him. Leaning into him, she let him be the strength she lacked. She laid the yellow and orange cluster of flowers next to the words forever ingrained in her heart.

Misty Gale, daughter of Paisley and Judah Grant

Trembling, she laid her hand on the damp grass. "I love you, Misty Gale. Will always love you. I've never forgotten you. Never will." She sniffed, fighting tears.

"Me too," Judah added. "Daddy loves you."

Daddy. Hearing that tender endearment unraveled her emotionally. It seemed her soul cracked open and wretched tears cascaded down her face. She collapsed into Judah's arms, crumpling onto his lap. He held her and rocked her. He sniffled then whispered something about God's love pouring over them. He didn't rush her. They kept their arms wrapped around each other for a few minutes, sharing in their grief.

After a while, he stood and assisted her to her feet. "Can you handle seeing the other one?" His understanding and kindness meant a lot to her.

"I'm going to try." She scrubbed away the last vestiges of tears and what little makeup she put on this morning.

As they strolled through the gate, she glanced back. She'd return another day. Maybe then she wouldn't feel so broken. Or maybe that gripping emotion never went away.

They walked between the rows of inground markers. Judah stopped at another grave but didn't kneel. She stood beside him and read the engraving.

Penny Cedars, beloved wife and mom

Due to her previous emotional outburst, Paisley felt weepy again. She dropped to her knees and Judah didn't miss a beat. He knelt beside her, supporting her. She set the flowers next to a cluster that was wilted. Who had been here recently? Dad?

"I'm a terrible daughter. I'm sorry that I missed her funeral." She drew in a tattered breath. "My dad might never forgive me."

"I'm sure he will. And you have a beautiful heart, Pais." Judah held her, leaning his head against hers. "God's grace heals things. He's got this too."

"I told my dad I'm sorry."

"I'm sure he understands."

"I hope so." She stood, staring at her mom's name. Then, as they strode down the grassy slope toward the truck, she sighed in relief. "That was tough."

"It'll get easier."

"You're saying I should come back to Mom's grave?"

He gave her a sad smile. "It's up to you."

"Then I won't."

He chuckled lightly.

"Why are you laughing?"

"I'm sorry. You are just so stubborn sometimes."

"What? That's not nice." But, at least, his comment made her feel more combatant, instead of emotional.

"Don't get me wrong. I love your stubbornness."

She stopped walking. "*My* stubbornness?"

He linked their pinkies. "It's your Cedars' stubbornness that will help you remember that you want to marry me again. And it's your stubbornness that will prove to you and me and this whole town that you love me with all your heart."

"My stubbornness is going to do all that?"

"Yep. Just watch and see."

Hmm. She'd have to think about that.

Thirty-six

On Monday afternoon, Paisley tackled the walls of the cottage while Judah was at work. Being here gave her a sense of what it might be like to live in this house again. It already felt homey, so she didn't have to worry about feeling like a stranger.

When Judah got home, they tossed frozen prepackaged meals into the microwave the way they used to do, ate quickly, then kept pounding away on the renovation. He explained C-MER's plans to restore the peninsula and how signs were posted for people to stay off the dangerous rocks.

"That means you too." He squinted at her.

"You know me. I always obey signs on the beach."

He guffawed. "I don't want to drag you out of the drink again."

"But you would, right?"

He stared at her a good thirty seconds. "But I would." He stood close enough that his breath touched her cheek. Clearing his throat, he stepped back. "We should talk."

His abrupt change in tone sent up a mental alarm. "About?"

"Just stuff. Want to walk down to the beach?"

"I always want to walk to the beach, but we have all this work to do." She lifted her mud spreading tool.

He held out his hand toward her. "Please, come with me?"

"Of course." She set down the tool then clasped his hand.

Isn't this what she hoped for, that they would walk on the beach and talk when he came home from work? Why would she even delay exchanging vows with this man, living with him—eating with him, watching the stars together, and sharing a bedroom—when being this close to him stirred her heart to such a frenzy?

They stopped by the outside spigot to wash their hands, then trudged over the slight rise in the sand toward the seashore. When they reached the place where the waves rolled up to the highest point on the sand, they stopped and faced the water. The ocean's rhythmic melody soared in her mind like a symphony reaching a powerful crescendo.

"I was thinking—"

"You need to—"

They spoke at the same time.

"You first."

"I'd rather kiss you than talk." He brushed loose strands of hair from her face yet didn't bridge the gap between them. "Before you set the date for our vow renewal, there are things we promised we'd talk about."

"Oh, um, don't forget about going on some dates." She grasped for something to keep things light.

"More mud flinging?" He grinned.

"Might be nice to get dressed up and go somewhere fancy."

"I agree."

They stood silently for several minutes.

Then Judah sighed. "The day I came to Chicago, based on the detective's information about you, I waited outside your apartment in a rental car, watching your door."

Her body reacted to his words before her mind did. Her heart hammered faster. Her skin became clammy. He went to her apartment and sat in a car watching her door? Why?

He covered his face with both palms and groaned.

That freaked her out. "What is it, Judah?"

He lowered his hands. "What's in the past is in the past. Whatever happened, I already forgave you." He met her gaze with a tortured look. "I want a future with you, no matter what we talk about today. Is there even any reason to rehash our old stuff?"

Was he letting her opt out of a difficult discussion? "Only if it still hurts you."

His face crumpled as if her words stabbed him.

"Tell me."

"You were with another man." Tension strained his voice. "I waited forty-five minutes. A guy went into your apartment. Didn't come out. So I waited."

She swallowed with difficulty. During her three years away, she went on a couple of outings with coworkers. Two dates. Times when she wanted to forget Basalt. Bury her past. But this—

"Why come all the way to Chicago and not talk to me?" She stuffed down her apprehension and fear and went for gut honesty. "I was lonely. Grieving. Felt abandoned. By you. My dad. God. Even Misty Gale. I-I would have wanted to see you." Even in her darkest time, she would have wanted to know he came looking for her.

He groaned again. "When you came outside dressed up, your arm linked with some guy's, I froze." He stared hard at her. "He kissed you. Maybe on your cheek, I don't know, but I saw red. You giggled and touched his arm the way you used to do with me. I'd heard rumors. Tried not to listen. Even when my dad—" He bit his lower lip. "But there you were. There he was."

Her heart pounded frantically. She inhaled and exhaled, controlling her breathing. "Was it in December?"

"Yes."

"Must have been Glen, a guy I met at the diner."

What were the chances of Judah crossing two-thirds of the country on the same day she had a date? And waiting forty-five minutes? Did he assume they were doing something that would make reconciling even more difficult? Oh, Judah. That agonized look in his eyes hurt her heart.

"Why didn't you just get out of the car and say something?" Thinking of how he must have felt angry and betrayed gnawed on her emotions.

"The kiss. The laughter. I hated to imagine how far you may have strayed from our marriage." He lifted his hands in a helpless gesture. "For my own mental health, I had to get out of there. Even your note spoke of someone else."

Her note. A Dear John letter tucked under his pillow. What a terrible way to have told him she was leaving.

"I wanted to belt the guy in the face, so I left." He stared at the sand.

"We went out around Christmastime." She rubbed her forehead. "Judah"—she made herself say his name softly—"is this a deal breaker?"

"What? No. Absolutely not." He huffed. "I thought we should talk about it, that's all. Be honest with each other."

"Okay." She didn't want to drive another wedge between them, but he brought this up. "What if I did more in that forty-five minutes?" She felt raw and vulnerable even asking.

He made a moaning sound. Gazed up at the sky.

"We were separated." She took a step back, her boots settling in the sand. "Minus the divorce papers, our marriage had ended. I'm sorry, but if I did cross that line, would you still want to renew our vows?"

"Yes, of course!"

If eyes were windows to the soul, she searched his for truth. What if she did the worst thing imaginable? She'd thought of doing it. Of forgetting every promise she ever made.

She was thankful that she hadn't. Judah was hurt enough by her actions and the lies swirling around town about her. But she needed to know where his heart was in this matter. He talked about grace, said he forgave her, but how far did that grace stretch?

"Judah?"

He drew in a long breath. "I didn't want to bring up this stuff. I've avoided it. But I want us to talk about everything—even the difficult things. I want a clean slate when we make new promises to each other." He stared out toward the bay, then faced her again. "Even a messy chalkboard can be wiped clean. That's what I'm hoping for us, no matter what happened in the past."

She kicked at a mound of sand. "All this time that we've been getting closer, talking about renewing our wedding vows, you thought I may have been intimate with someone else. How could you do that?" She couldn't fathom what struggles he went through. Even though he thought she might have been unfaithful, beyond the unfaithfulness of leaving him, he didn't condemn her. Instead, he wooed her, kept saying he loved her, showed her such beautiful grace. What kind of man did that? She didn't deserve such a man. Such love.

"Don't get me wrong." He blew out a breath. "I prayed it hadn't come to that."

She nodded, holding her tears and emotions in check.

For several heartbeats they stared at each other. Then he spread out his hands toward her, a tender, inviting expression on his face. She didn't hesitate to step into his embrace. She wrapped her arms around him, clinging to him. He held her, his chin resting against her head. His heart beat strong beneath her ear. She sighed.

Needing to say one more thing, she leaned back. "I told you before that I'm sorry for hurting you."

"You did."

"I'm sorry about this too. For the way I hurt you when you saw me with someone else." She imagined Mia flirting with him and how that drove her crazy. "Nothing else happened with Glen. I want you to know that."

His eyelids closed for a moment. Then he smiled at her. "That's good to hear. Thank you for telling me." He stroked his thumb down her cheek. "I can't wait to marry you."

She watched his gaze land on her lips, the question in his eyes. She didn't close the gap. Didn't flirt with him—yet.

"Is there anything else about my leaving that you want to ask me?" They talked about it when she was locked in the bathroom during the hurricane. But she wanted a clean slate, too.

"Maybe just one thing." He led her back along the beach. By his silence, he still wrestled with something. Then, "How did you and Craig meet?"

* * * *

Maybe Judah should have left well enough alone. Paisley's question about whether he'd still want to get back together if she had been with someone else momentarily stunned him. But he came to terms with that a couple of years ago. Forgiveness was forgiveness. Still, he felt relieved by what she told him. And he was curious about—

"Mia introduced us."

"Mia?"

"At Hardy's Gill and Grill, she joked about us being a C-MER family. Then she disappeared, leaving Craig and me alone."

A kick in his gut.

"I've resented her for three years. Hated that you work with such a flirt. Then, the other day, Craig started to tell me something about your dad's involvement in what happened that night." She grimaced like she was afraid of what his reaction might be. "I shouldn't have mentioned it. Sorry. I just—" She groaned and took off walking fast.

"Wait!" He jogged to catch up with her, his shoes sliding in the sand. "I want to hear what you have to say. Please, tell me."

"I don't want it to cause more trouble between us. More hurt."

"It won't. I promise." He clasped her hands.

A seagull squawked overhead. The sea roared alongside them, but he zeroed in on his wife's voice and her lovely dark eyes staring into his gaze.

"Craig didn't get the chance to finish explaining." She adjusted their hands so their pinkies linked. "But I must find out if Edward was involved in that fiasco, even if it means talking to Craig again. Even if it means unearthing something hurtful in the past."

Was his father embroiled in that incident? Or was Craig just trying to make himself sound less offensive?

"How about if we find out together?" Judah wanted answers too.

"That would be great." She smiled, looking relieved. "Thank you."

She stepped closer to him and smoothed her palms over the upper part of his jacket the way she did sometimes when they were about to kiss. He slid his arms around her, his hands coming to rest against her back. He liked this—holding her in his arms and her gazing up warmly at him.

"You know how you asked me to marry you?"

The atmosphere shifted and felt charged with electrical currents.

"Yes?" His heart did triple beats.

"And I won the dare, so I get to choose a date ..."

"I remember." He was thankful they faced some difficult things and were still clinging to each other. "If it were up to me, I'd marry you right now."

"That might be a little tricky to arrange."

A surge of hope rushed through him. "Want to go over to City Hall and check?"

Her jaw dropped. "You want *the mayor* to marry us?"

"Not really. We can ask Pastor Sagle." Their elopement pulsed through his thoughts. "Although, he turned us down last time."

"True. He may want to offer us marital counseling first." She lifted an eyebrow. "We might need it, too."

He groaned. "That could take weeks. City Hall it is."

"Didn't you say I'm worth the wait?" She winked at him.

"I did. And you are."

She tipped her head and gave him a flirty grin, even licking her lips as if anticipating a kiss. *Ah, Pais.* She was reeling him in with her soft gaze, her moist lips, her smile. He chuckled and succumbed, kissing her like a starving man. A man who loved his wife with all of his heart and wanted her to come home with him.

"How about one week?" She spoke softly against his mouth. "Then you and I will be Mr. and Mrs. Judah Grant again."

"One day?"

She giggled and leaned her cheek against his chest. Did she hear his heart galloping? With each beat he said her name, said he would always love her. And he thanked God for bringing them back together.

"Judah?" Her lilting voice was music to his soul. "I wish I never left you."

His heart nearly stopped. What could he even say to that? "I'm so glad you're with me now."

"Me too."

Holding her in his arms for the rest of his life would be a dream come true. One week? What was seven days compared to waiting three years? It would give them time to finish the cottage. Time to pass out invitations. Have that marriage counseling session.

Then let the romancing of a lifetime begin.

Nothing was going to stop them from being together.

Thank you for reading the Restored series! I hope you've enjoyed the first three books and are rooting for Judah and Paisley's journey together. Please take a minute and write a review wherever you purchased this collection. Even one line telling what you liked or thought about the story is helpful. Thank you! ~Mary

I took many creative liberties with Basalt Bay, my imaginary town on the Oregon Coast. To all those who live nearby, please forgive my embellishments. I enjoy the Pacific Ocean and the Oregon Coast so much that I wanted to create my own little world there.

If you would like to be one of the first to hear about Mary's new releases and upcoming projects, sign up for her newsletter—and receive the free pdf "Rekindle Your Romance! 50+ Date Night Ideas for Married Couples." Check it out here:

www.maryehanks.com/gift

Check out *Tide of Resolve* (Part 4) in the Restored series:

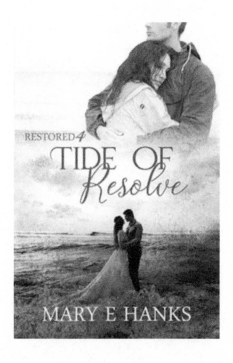

Paisley and Judah promised each other they'd renew their vows in seven days. What a whirlwind, dilemma-packed, suspenseful week it will be.

Thank you to everyone who helped make this story a reality!

Paula McGrew . . . You are a gem for walking this journey with me. Thank you for fine-tuning my words and ideas. I appreciate you so much!

Suzanne Williams . . . I love your creative designs. Thanks for bringing these covers to life!

Jason Hanks . . . Thanks for always supporting me and reminding me that I am a writer. I love your encouraging texts!

Kathy Vancil, Kellie Wanke, Mary Acuff, Beth McDonald, Joanna Brown, and Jason Hanks . . . Thank you so much for being willing to read this installment, even though it was during the holidays, and being excited to do so. That cheered my heart! I appreciate all of you giving your time to this project. Thanks for finding things I overlooked and helping me dig deeper into Judah's and Paisley's hearts.

(This story is a work of fiction. Any mistakes are my very own! ~meh)

Daniel, Philip, Deborah, & Shem . . . You always and forever have this mama's love.

Readers ... I'm humbled and thrilled that you are reading my work and following this series. Thanks so much for your kindness and support!

www.maryehanks.com

Books by Mary Hanks

Restored Series

Ocean of Regret (Part 1)

Sea of Rescue (Part 2)

Bay of Refuge (Part 3)

Tide of Resolve (Part 4)

Waves of Reason (Part 5 coming in 2021)

Second Chance Series

Winter's Past

April's Storm

Summer's Dream

Autumn's Break

Season's Flame

Marriage Encouragement

Thoughts of You (A Marriage Journal)

About Mary E Hanks

Mary loves stories about marriage restoration. She believes there's something inspiring about couples clinging to each other, working through their problems, and depending on God for a beautiful rest of their lives together—and those are the types of stories she likes to write. Mary and Jason have been married for forty-plus years. They know firsthand what it means to get a second chance with each other, and with God. That has been her inspiration in writing the Second Chance series, and now in the Restored series.

Besides writing, Mary likes to read, do artsy stuff, go on adventures with Jason, and meet her four adult kids for coffee or breakfast.

Connect with Mary by signing up for her newsletter:

www.maryehanks/gift

"Like" her Facebook Author page:

www.facebook.com/MaryEHanksAuthor

Thank you so much for reading the Restored series!

www.maryehanks.com

Made in the USA
Coppell, TX
06 March 2022

74556129R00412